MATTER

In a world renowned even within a galaxy full of wonders, a crime within a war. For one man it means a desperate flight, and a search for the one – maybe two – people who could clear his name. For his brother it means a life lived under constant threat of treachery and murder. And for their sister, even without knowing the full truth, it means returning to a place she'd thought abandoned forever.

Only the sister is not what she once was; Djan Serity Anaplian has changed almost beyond recognition to become an agent of the Culture's Special Circumstances section, charged with high-level interference in civilisations throughout the greater galaxy.

Concealing her new se... ...set of abilities – might be a c... ...d to which Anaplian ret... ...determining the appropriate level of interference in someone else's war is never a simple matter.

By Iain M. Banks

CONSIDER PHLEBAS
THE PLAYER OF GAMES
USE OF WEAPONS
THE STATE OF THE ART
AGAINST A DARK BACKGROUND
FEERSUM ENDJINN
EXCESSION
INVERSIONS
LOOK TO WINDWARD
THE ALGEBRAIST
MATTER
SURFACE DETAIL
THE HYDROGEN SONATA

By Iain Banks

THE WASP FACTORY
WALKING ON GLASS
THE BRIDGE
ESPEDAIR STREET
CANAL DREAMS
THE CROW ROAD
COMPLICITY
WHIT
A SONG OF STONE
THE BUSINESS
DEAD AIR
THE STEEP APPROACH TO GARBADALE
TRANSITION
STONEMOUTH
THE QUARRY

IAIN M.
BANKS

MATTER

orbit

www.orbitbooks.net

ORBIT

First published in the Great Britain in 2008 by Orbit
This paperback edition published in 2009 by Orbit

12

Copyright © 2008 Iain M. Banks

Extract from *Consider Phlebas*
Copyright © 1987 Iain M. Banks

The moral right of the author has been asserted.

A CIP catalogue record for this book
is available from the British Library.

ISBN 978-1-84149-419-7

Typeset in Stemple Garamond by
Palimpsest Book Production Limited, Grangemouth, Stirlingshire
Printed and bound in Great Britain by
Clays Ltd, St Ives plc

Papers used by Orbit are from well-managed forests
and other responsible sources.

MIX
Paper from
responsible sources
FSC
www.fsc.org   FSC® C104740

Orbit
An imprint of
Little, Brown Book Group
100 Victoria Embankment
London EC4Y 0DY

An Hachette UK Company
www.hachette.co.uk

www.orbitbooks.net

For Adèle

With thanks to everybody who helped:
Adèle, Les, Mic, Simon, Tim, Roger,
Gary, Lara and Dave le Taxi

Contents

Prologue   1

The Expeditionary

1   Factory   11
2   Palace   24
3   Folly   41
4   In Transit   55
5   Platform   72
6   Scholastery   98
7   Reception   115
8   Tower   132
9   One-finger Man   156

Depth of Field

10   A Certain Lack   163
11   Bare, Night   182
12   Cumuloform   204
13   Don't Try This At Home   223
14   Game   243
15   The Hundredth Idiot   258
16   Seed Drill   283
17   Departures   299
18   The Current Emergency   319
19   Dispatches   350

The Integrity of Objects

20   Inspiral, Coalescence, Ringdown   363
21   Many Worlds   385
22   The Falls   400
23   Liveware Problem   424
24   Steam, Water, Ice, Fire   435
25   The Levels   459
26   The Sarcophagus   491
27   The Core   532

Appendix   569

Epilogue   589

Contents

Preface

The Opera Gallery

1   Prologue
2   Palace
3   Death
4   Theatre
5   Relatives
6   Children
    Reception
8   Exits
9   (Open Door) Inner Music

Origin of Field

10   A German Tragedy
11   Bare Life
12   Continuous
13   Lower B - The Whole Planet
     the Game
14   The Unreadable
     Knowledge
     Descartes
15   The Continuous Experience
     The Active

The Intensity of Origin

20   Inquiry: Understood Happiness
     Jonathan Webb
22   The Fall
23   Unwritten Relation
24   Going West, To There
25   The Seven
26   In the Singular
27   The Tree

Appendices

Bibliography

Prologue

A light breeze produced a dry rattling sound from some nearby bushes. It lifted delicate little veils of dust from a few sandy patches nearby and shifted a lock of dark hair across the forehead of the woman sitting on the wood and canvas camp chair which was perched, not quite level, on a patch of bare rock near the edge of a low ridge looking out over the scrub and sand of the desert. In the distance, trembling through the heat haze, was the straight line of the road. Some scrawny trees, few taller than one man standing on another's shoulders, marked the course of the dusty highway. Further away, tens of kilometres beyond the road, a line of dark, jagged mountains shimmered in the baking air.

By most human standards the woman was tall, slim and well muscled. Her hair was short and straight and dark and her skin was the colour of pale agate. There was nobody of her specific kind within several thousand light years of where she sat, though if there had been they might have said that she was somewhere between being a young woman and one at the very start of middle age. They would, however, have thought she looked somewhat short and bulky. She was dressed in a pair of wide, loose-fitting pants and a thin, cool-looking jacket, both the same shade as the sand. She wore a wide black hat to shade her from the late morning sun, which showed as a harsh white point high in the cloudless, pale green sky. She raised a pair of very old and worn-looking binoculars to her night-dark eyes and looked out towards the point where the desert road met the horizon to the west. There was a folding table to her right holding a glass and a bottle of chilled water. A small backpack lay underneath. She reached out with her free hand and lifted the glass from the table, sipping at the water while still looking through the ancient field glasses.

"They're about an hour away," said the machine floating to her left. The machine looked like a scruffy metal suitcase. It moved a little in the air, rotating and tipping as though looking up at the seated woman. "And anyway," it continued, "you won't see much at all with those museum pieces."

She put the glass down on the table again and lowered the binoculars. "They were my father's," she said.

"Really." The drone made a sound that might have been a sigh.

A screen flicked into existence a couple of metres in front of the woman, filling half her field of view. It showed, from a point a hundred metres above and in front of its leading edge, an army of men – some mounted, most on foot – marching along another section of the desert highway, all raising dust which piled into the air and drifted slowly away to the south-east. Sunlight glittered off the edges of raised spears and pikes. Banners, flags and pennants swayed above. The army filled the road for a couple of kilometres behind the mounted men at its head. Bringing up the rear were baggage carts, covered and open wagons, wheeled catapults and trebuchets and a variety of lumbering wooden siege engines, all pulled by dark, powerful-looking animals whose sweating shoulders towered over the men walking at their sides.

The woman tutted. "Put that away."

"Yes, ma'am," the machine said. The screen vanished.

The woman looked through the binoculars again, using both hands this time. "I can see their dust," she announced. "And another couple of scouts, I think."

"Astounding," the drone said.

She placed the field glasses on the table, pulled the brim of her hat down over her eyes and settled back in the camp seat, folding her arms and stretching her booted feet out, crossed at the ankle. "Having a snooze," she told the drone from beneath the hat. "Wake me when it's time."

"Just you make yourself comfortable there," the drone told her.

"Mm-hmm."

Turminder Xuss (drone, offensive) watched the woman Djan Seriy Anaplian for a few minutes, monitoring her slowing breathing and her gradually relaxing muscle-state until it knew she was genuinely asleep.

"Sweet dreams, princess," it said quietly. Reviewing its words immediately, the drone was completely unable to determine whether a disinterested observer would have detected any trace of sarcasm or not.

It checked round its half-dozen previously deployed scout and secondary knife missiles, using their sensors to watch the still distant approaching army draw slowly closer and to monitor the various small patrols and individual scouts the army had sent out ahead of it.

For a while, it watched the army move. From a certain perspective it looked like a single great organism inching darkly across the tawny sweep of desert; something segmented, hesitant – bits of it would come to a stop for no obvious reason for long moments, before starting off again, so that it seemed to shuffle rather than flow en masse – but determined, unarguably fixed in its onward purpose. And all on their way to war, the drone thought sourly, to take and burn and loot and rape and raze. What sullen application these humans devoted to destruction.

About half an hour later, when the front of the army was

hazily visible on the desert highway a couple of kilometres to the west, a single mounted scout came riding along the top of the ridge, straight towards where the drone kept vigil and the woman slept. The man showed no sign of having seen through the camouflage field surrounding their little encampment, but unless he changed course he was going to ride right into them.

The drone made a tutting noise very similar to the one the woman had made earlier and told its nearest knife missile to spook the mount. The pencil-thin shape came darting in, effectively invisible, and jabbed the beast in one flank so that it screamed and jerked, nearly unseating its rider as it veered away down the shallow slope of ridge towards the road.

The scout shouted and swore at his animal, reining it in and turning its broad snout back towards the ridge, some distance beyond the woman and the drone. They galloped away, leaving a thin trail of dust hanging in the near-still air.

Djan Seriy Anaplian stirred, sat up a little and looked out from under her hat. "What was all that?" she asked drowsily.

"Nothing. Go back to sleep."

"Hmm." She relaxed again and a minute later was quietly snoring.

The drone woke her when the head of the army was almost level with them. It bobbed its front at the body of men and animals a kilometre distant while Anaplian was still yawning and stretching. "The boys are all here," it told her.

"Indeed they are." She lifted the binoculars and focused on the very front of the army, where a group of men rode mounted on especially tall, colourfully caparisoned animals. These men wore high plumed helmets and their polished armour glittered brightly in the glare. "They're all very parade ground," Anaplian said. "It's like they're expecting to bump into somebody out here they need to impress."

"God?" the drone suggested.

The woman was silent for a moment. "Hmm," she said eventually. She put the field glasses down and looked at the drone. "Shall we?"

"Merely say the word."

Anaplian looked back at the army, took a deep breath and said, "Very well. Let us do this."

The drone made a little dipping motion like a nod. A small hatch opened in its side. A cylinder perhaps four centimetres wide and twenty-five long, shaped like a sort of conical knife, rolled lazily into the air then darted away, keeping close to the ground and accelerating quickly towards the rear of the column of men, animals and machines. It left a trail of dust for a moment before it adjusted its altitude. Anaplian lost sight of its camouflaged shape almost immediately.

The drone's aura field, invisible until now, glowed rosily for a moment or two. "This," it said, "should be fun."

The woman looked at it dubiously. "There aren't going to be any mistakes this time, are there?"

"Certainly not," the machine said crisply. "Want to watch?" it asked her. "I mean properly, not through those antique opera glasses."

Anaplian looked at the machine through narrowed eyes for a little, then said, slowly, "All right."

The screen blinked into existence just to one side of them this time, so that Anaplian could still see the army in the distance with the naked eye. The screen view was from some distance behind the great column now, and much lower than before. Dust drifted across the view. "That's from the trailing scout missile," Turminder Xuss said. Another screen flickered next to the first. "This is from the knife missile itself." The camera in the knife missile registered the tiny machine scudding past the army in a blur of men, uniforms and weapons, then showed the tall shapes of the wagons, war machines and siege engines before banking sharply after the tail end of the army was passed. The rushing missile stooped, taking up a position a kilometre behind the rear of the army and a metre or so above the road surface. Its speed had dropped from near-supersonic to something close to that of a swiftly flying bird. It was closing rapidly with the rear of the column.

"I'll synch the scout to the knife, follow it in behind," the drone said. In moments, the flat circular base of the knife missile appeared as a dot in the centre of the scout missile's view, then expanded until it looked like the smaller machine was only a metre behind the larger one. "There go the warps!" Xuss said, sounding excited. "See?"

Two arrowhead shapes, one on either side, detached from the knife missile's body, swung out and disappeared. The mono-filament wires which still attached each of the little warps to the knife missile were invisible. The view changed as the scout missile pulled back and up, showing almost the whole of the army ahead.

"I'll get the knife to buzz the wires," the drone said.

"What does that mean?"

"Vibrates them, so that whatever the monofils go through, it'll be like getting sliced by an implausibly sharp battleaxe rather than the world's keenest razor," the drone said helpfully.

The screen displaying what the scout missile could see showed a tree a hundred metres behind the last, trundling wagon. The tree jerked and the top three-quarters slid at a steep angle down the sloped stump that was the bottom quarter before toppling to the dust. "That took a flick," the drone said, glowing briefly rosy again and sounding amused. The wagons and siege engines filled the view coming from the knife missile. "The first bit's actually the trickiest . . ."

The fabric roofs of the covered wagons rose into the air like released birds; tensed hoops of wood – cut – sprang apart. The giant, solid wheels of the catapults, trebuchets and siege engines shed their top sections on the next revolution and the great wooden structures thudded to a halt, the top halves of some of them, also cut through, jumping forward with the shock. Arm-thick lengths of rope, wound rock-tight a moment earlier, burst like released springs then flopped like string. The scout missile swung between the felled and wrecked machines as the men in and around the wagons and siege engines started to react. The knife missile powered onwards, towards the foot soldiers immediately ahead. It plunged into the mass of spears, pikes, pennant poles, banners and flags, scything through them in a welter of sliced wood, falling blades and flapping fabric.

Anaplian caught glimpses of a couple of men slashed or skewered by falling pikeheads.

"Bound to be a few casualties," the drone muttered.

"Bound to be," the woman said.

The knife missile was catching glimpses of confused faces as men heard the shouts of those behind them and turned to look. The missile was a half-second away from the rear of the mass of mounted men and roughly level with their necks when the drone sent,

– Are you sure we can't . . . ?

– Positive, Anaplian replied, inserting a sigh into what was an entirely non-verbal exchange. – Just stick to the plan.

The tiny machine nudged up a half-metre or so and tore above the mounted men, catching their plumed helmets and chopping the gaudy decorations off like a harvest of motley stalks. It leapt over the head of the column, leaving consternation and fluttering plumage in its wake. Then it zoomed, heading skywards. The following scout missile registered the monofil warps clicking back into place in the knife missile's body before it swivelled, rose and slowed, to look back at the whole army again.

It was, Anaplian thought, a scene of entirely satisfactory chaos, outrage and confusion. She smiled. This was an event of such rarity that Turminder Xuss recorded the moment.

The screens hanging in the air disappeared. The knife missile reappeared and swung into the offered hatchway in the side of the drone.

Anaplian looked out over the plain to the road and the halted army. "Many casualties?" she asked, smile disappearing.

"Sixteen or so," the drone told her. "About half will likely prove fatal, in time."

She nodded, still watching the distant column of men and machines. "Oh well."

"Indeed," Turminder Xuss agreed. The scout missile floated up to the drone and also entered via a side panel. "Still," the drone said, sounding weary, "we should have done more."

"Should we."

"Yes. You ought to have let me do a proper decapitation."

"No," Anaplian said.

"Just the nobles," the drone said. "The guys right at the front. The ones who came up with their spiffing war plans in the first place."

"No," the woman said again, rising from her seat and, turning, folding it. She held it in one hand. With the other she lifted the old pair of binoculars from the table. "Module coming?"

"Overhead," the drone told her. It moved round her and picked up the camp table, placing the glass and water bottle inside the backpack beneath. "Just the two nasty dukes? And the King?"

Anaplian held on to her hat as she looked straight up, squinting briefly in the sunlight until her eyes adjusted. "No."

"This is not, I trust, some kind of transferred familial sentimentality," the drone said with half-pretended distaste.

"No," the woman said, watching the shape of the module ripple in the air a few metres away.

Turminder Xuss moved towards the module as its rear door hinged open. "And are you going to stop saying 'no' to me all the time?"

Anaplian looked at it, expressionless.

"Never mind," the drone said, sighing. It bob-nodded towards the open module door. "After you."

The Expeditionary

1. Factory

The place had to be some sort of old factory or workshop or something. There were big toothed metal wheels half buried in the wooden floors or hanging by giant spindles from the network of iron beams overhead. Canvas belts were strung all over the dark spaces connecting smaller, smooth wheels and a host of long, complicated machines he thought might be something to do with weaving or knitting. It was all very dusty and grimy-looking. And yet this had been that modern thing; a factory! How quickly things decayed and became useless.

Normally he would never have considered going anywhere near some place so filthy. It might not even be safe, he thought, even with all the machinery stilled; one gable wall was partially collapsed, bricks tumbled, planks splintered, rafters hanging disjointed from above. He didn't know if this was old damage from deterioration and lack of repair, or something that had happened today, during the battle. In the end, though, he hadn't cared what the place was or had been; it was somewhere to escape to, a place to hide.

Well, to regroup, to recover and collect himself. That put a better gloss on it. Not running away, he told himself; just staging a strategical retreat, or whatever you called it.

Outside, the Rollstar Pentrl having passed over the horizon a few minutes earlier, it was slowly getting dark. Through the breach in the wall he could see sporadic flashes and hear the thunder of artillery, the crump and bellowing report of shells landing uncomfortably close by and the sharp, busy rattle of small arms fire. He wondered how the battle was going. They were supposed to be winning, but it was all so confusing. For all he knew they were on the brink of complete victory or utter defeat.

He didn't understand warfare, and having now experienced its practice first hand, had no idea how people kept their wits about them in a battle. A big explosion nearby made the whole building tremble; he whimpered as he crouched down, pressing himself still further into the dark corner he had found on the first floor, drawing his thick cloak over his head. He heard himself make that pathetic, weak little sound and hated himself for it. Breathing under the cloak, he caught a faint odour of dried blood and faeces, and hated that too.

He was Ferbin otz Aelsh-Hausk'r, a prince of the House of Hausk, son of King Hausk the Conqueror. And while he was his father's son, he had not been raised to be like him. His father gloried in war and battle and dispute, had spent his entire life aggressively expanding the influence of his throne and his people, always in the name of the WorldGod and with half an eye on history. The King had raised his eldest son to be like him, but that son had been killed by the very people they were fighting, perhaps for the last time, today. His second son, Ferbin, had been schooled in the arts not of war but of diplomacy; his natural place was supposed to be in the court, not the parade ground, fencing stage or firing range, still less the battlefield.

His father had known this and, even if he had never been as proud of Ferbin as he had of Elime, his murdered first son, he had accepted that Ferbin's skill – you might even term it his calling, Ferbin had thought more than once – lay in the arts of politicking, not soldiering. It was, anyway, what his father had wanted. The King had been looking forward to a time when the martial heroics he had had to undertake to bring this new age about would be seen for the rude necessities they had been; he had wanted at least one of his sons to fit easily into a coming era of peace, prosperity and contentment, where the turning of a pretty phrase would have more telling effect than the twisting of a sword.

It was not his fault, Ferbin told himself, that he was not cut out for war. It was certainly not his fault that, realising he might be about to die at any moment, he had felt so terrified earlier. And even less to his discredit that he had lost control of his bowels when that Yilim chap – he had been a major or a general or something – had been obliterated by the cannon shot. Dear God, the man had been talking to him when he was just ... gone! Cut in half!

Their small group had ridden up to a low rise for a better look at the battle. This was a modestly insane thing to do in the first place, Ferbin had thought at the time, exposing them to enemy spotters and hence to still greater risk than that from a random artillery shell. For one thing, he'd chosen a particularly outstanding mersicor charger as his mount that morning from the abroad-tents of the royal stables; a pure white beast with a high and proud aspect which he thought he would look well on. Only to discover that General-Major Yilim's choice of mount obviously pitched in the same direction, for he rode a similar charger. Now he thought about it – and, oh! the number of times he'd had cause to use that phrase or one of its cousins at the start of some explanation in the aftermath of yet another embarrassment – Ferbin wondered at the wisdom of riding on to an exposed ridge with two such conspicuous beasts.

He had wanted to say this, but then decided he didn't know enough about the procedures to be followed in such matters actually to speak his mind, and anyway he hadn't wanted to sound like a coward. Perhaps Major-General or General-Major Yilim had felt insulted that he'd been left out of the front-line forces and asked instead to look after Ferbin, keeping him close enough to the action so that he'd later be able to claim that he'd been there at the battle, but not so close that he risked actually getting involved with any fighting.

From the rise, when they achieved it, they could see the whole sweep of the battleground, from the great Tower ahead in the distance, over the downland spreading out from the kilometres-wide cylinder and up towards their position on the first fold of the low hills that carried the road to Pourl itself. The Sarl capital city lay behind them, barely visible in the misty haze, a short-day's ride away.

This was the ancient county of Xilisk and these were the old playgrounds of Ferbin and his siblings, long depopulated lands turned into royal parks and hunting grounds, filled with over-grown villages and thick forests. Now, all about, their crum-pled, riven geography sparkled with the fire of uncounted thousands of guns, the land itself seemed to move and flow where troop concentrations and fleets of war craft manoeu-vred, and great sloped stems of steam and smoke lifted into the air above it all, casting massive wedged shadows across the ground.

Here and there, beneath the spread of risen mists and lowering cloud, dots and small winged shapes moved above the great battle as caude and lyge – the great venerable warbeasts of the sky – spotted for artillery and carried intel-ligence and signals from place to place. None seemed mobbed by clouds of lesser avians, so most likely they were all friendly. Poor fare compared to the days of old, though, when flocks, squadrons, whole clouds of the great beasts had contended in the battles of the ancients. Well, if the old stories and ancient paintings were to be believed. Ferbin suspected they were exaggerated, and his younger half-brother, Oramen, who claimed to study such matters, had said well of *course* they were exaggerated, though, being Oramen, only after shaking his head at Ferbin's ignorance.

Choubris Holse, his servant, had been to his left on the ridge, digging into a saddle bag and muttering about requiring some fresh supplies from the nearest village behind them. Major – or General – Yilim had been on his right, holding forth about the coming campaign on the next level down, taking the fight to their enemies in their own domain. Ferbin had ignored his servant and turned to Yilim out of politeness. Then, mid-word, with a sort of tearing rush of sound, the elderly officer – portly, a little flushed of face and inclined to wheeze when laughing – was gone, just gone. His legs and lower torso still sat in the saddle, but the rest of him was all ripped about and scattered; half of him seemed to have thrown itself over Ferbin, covering him in blood and greasily unknowable bits of body parts. Ferbin had stared at the remains still sitting in the saddle as he wiped some of the gore off his face, gagging with the stink and the warm, steaming feel of it. His lunch had left his belly and mouth like something was pursuing it. He'd coughed, then wiped his face with a gore-slicked hand.

"Fucking hell," he'd heard Choubris Holse say, voice breaking.

Yilim's mount – the tall, pale mersicor charger which Yilim had spoken to more kindly than to any of his men – as though suddenly realising what had just happened, screamed, reared and fled, dumping what was left of the man's body on to the torn-up ground. Another shell or ball or whatever these ghastly things were landed nearby, felling another two of their group in a shrieking tangle of men and animals. His servant had gone too, now, Ferbin realised; mount toppled, falling on top of him. Choubris Holse yelled with fright and pain, pinned beneath the animal.

"Sir!" one of the junior officers shouted at him, suddenly in front of him, pulling his own mount round. "Ride! Away from here!"

He was still wiping blood from his face.

He'd filled his britches, he realised. He whipped his mount and followed the younger man, until the young officer and his mount disappeared in a sudden thick spray of dark earth. The air seemed to be full of screeches and fire; deafening, blinding. Ferbin heard himself whimper. He pressed himself against his mount, wrapping his arms round its neck and closing his eyes, letting the pounding animal find its own way over and around whatever obstacles were in its path, not daring to raise his head and look where they were going. The jarring, rattling, terrifying ride had seemed to last for ever. He heard himself whimpering again.

The panting, heaving mersicor slowed eventually.

Ferbin opened his eyes to see they were on a dark wooded track by the side of a small river; booms and flashes came from every side but sounded a little further away than they had. Something burned further up the stream, as though overhanging trees were on fire. A tall building, half ruined, loomed in the late afternoon light as the labouring, panting mount slowed still further. He pulled it to a stop outside the place, and dismounted. He'd let go of the reins. The animal startled at another loud explosion, then went wailing off down the track at a canter. He might have given chase if his pants hadn't been full of his own excrement.

Instead he waddled into the building through a door wedged open by sagging hinges, looking for water and somewhere to clean himself. His servant would have known just what to do. Choubris Holse would have cleaned him up quick as you like, with much muttering and many grumblings, but efficiently, and without a sly sneer. And now, Ferbin realised, he was unarmed. The mersicor had made off with his rifle and ceremonial sword. Plus, the pistol he'd been given by his father, and which he had sworn would never leave his side while the war was waged, was no longer in its holster.

He found some water and ancient rags and cleaned himself as best he could. He still had his wine flask, though it was empty. He filled the flask from a long trough of deep, flowing water cut into the floor and rinsed his mouth, then drank. He tried to catch his reflection in the dark length of water but failed. He dipped his hands in the trough and pushed his fingers through his long fair hair, then washed his face. Appearances had to be maintained, after all. Of King Hausk's three sons he had always been the one who most resembled their father; tall, fair and handsome, with a proud, manly bearing (so people said, apparently – he did not really trouble himself with such matters).

The battle raged on beyond the dark, abandoned building as the light of Pentrl faded from the sky. He found that he could not stop shaking. He still smelled of blood and shit. It was unthinkable that anyone should find him like this. And the noise! He'd been told the battle would be quick and they would win easily, but it was still going on. Maybe they were losing. If they were, it might be better that he hid. If his father had been killed in the fighting he would, he supposed, be the new king. That was too great a responsibility; he couldn't risk showing himself until he knew they had won. He found a place on the floor above to lie down and tried to sleep, but could not; all he could see was General Yilim, bursting right in front of him, gobbets of flesh flying towards him. He retched once more, then drank from the flask.

Just lying there, then sitting, his cloak pulled tight around him, made him feel a little better. It would all be all right, he told himself. He'd take a little while away from things, just a moment or two, to collect his wits and calm down. Then he'd see how things were. They would have won, and his father would still be alive. He wasn't ready to be king. He enjoyed being a prince. Being a prince was fun; being a king looked like hard work. Besides, his father had always entirely given everybody who'd ever met him the strong impression that he would most assuredly live for ever.

Ferbin must have nodded off. There was noise down below; clamour, voices. In his jangled, still half-drowsy state, he thought he recognised some of them. He was instantly terrified that he would be discovered, captured by the enemy or shamed in front of his father's own troops. How low he had fallen in so short a time! To be as mortally afraid of his own side as of the enemy! Steel-shod feet clattered on the steps. He was going to be discovered!

"Nobody in the floors above," a voice said.

"Good. There. Lay him there. Doctor . . ." (There was some speech that Ferbin didn't catch. He was still working out that he'd escaped detection while he'd been asleep.) "Well, you must do whatever you can. Bleye! Tohonlo! Ride for help, as I've asked."

"Sir."

"At once."

"Priest; attend."

"The Exaltine, sir—"

"Will be with us in due course, I'm sure. For now the duty's yours."

"Of course, sir."

"The rest of you, out. Give us some air to breathe here."

He did know that voice. He was sure he did. The man giving the orders sounded like – in fact must be – tyl Loesp.

Mertis tyl Loesp was his father's closest friend and most trusted adviser. What was going on? There was much movement. Lanterns cast shadows from below on to the dark ceiling above him. He shifted towards a chink of light coming from the floor nearby where a broad canvas belt, descending from a giant wheel above, disappeared through the planking to some machinery on the ground floor. Shifting, he could peer through the slit in the floor to see what was happening beneath.

Dear God of the World, it was his father!

King Hausk lay, face slack, eyes closed, on a broad wooden door resting on makeshift trestles immediately beneath. His armour was pierced and buckled over the left side of his chest, and blood was seeping through some flag or banner wrapped around him. He looked dead, or close to death.

Ferbin felt his eyes go wide.

Dr Gillews, the Royal Physician, was quickly opening bags and small portable cabinets. An assistant fussed beside him. A priest Ferbin recognised but did not know the name of stood by his father's head, his white robes soiled with blood or mud. He was reading from some holy work. Mertis tyl Loesp – tall and partially stooped, still dressed in armour, his helmet held in one hand, his white hair matted – paced to and fro, armour glinting in the lanternlight. The only others present that he could see were a couple of knights, standing, rifles held ready, by the door. The angle was wrong to see further up than the chest of the tall knight on the right side of the door but Ferbin recognised the one whose face he could see; Bower or Brower or something.

He should reveal himself, he thought. He should let them know he was here. He might be about to become king, after all. It would be aberrant, perverse not to make himself known.

He would wait just a moment longer, all the same. He felt this like an instinct, he told himself, and his instinct had been right about not riding up on to the ridge, earlier.

His father's eyes flickered open. He grimaced with pain, one arm moving towards his injured side. The doctor looked at his assistant, who went to hold the King's hand, perhaps to comfort him, but certainly preventing him from probing his injury. The doctor joined his assistant, holding scissors and pliers. He cut cloth, pulled at armour.

"Mertis," the King said weakly, ignoring the doctor and holding his other hand out. His voice, usually so stern and strong, sounded like a child's.

"Here," tyl Loesp said, coming to the King's side. He took his hand.

"Do we prevail, Mertis?"

The other man looked round at the others present. Then he said, "We prevail, sir. The battle is won. The Deldeyn have surrendered and ask our terms. They conditioned only that their massacre cease and they be treated honourably. Which we have allowed, so far. The Ninth and all that it holds lies open to us."

The King smiled. Ferbin felt relieved. It sounded like things had gone well. He supposed he really ought to make his entrance now. He took a breath to speak, let them know he was there.

"And Ferbin?" the King asked. Ferbin froze. What about him?

"Dead," tyl Loesp said. It was said, Ferbin thought, with somewhat insufficient grief or pity. Almost, a chap less charitable than himself might have thought, with relish.

"Dead?" his father wailed, and Ferbin felt his eyes moisten. Now. Now he needed to let his father know that his eldest surviving son still lived, whether he smelled of shit or not.

"Yes," tyl Loesp said, leaning over the King. "The vain, silly, spoiled little brat was blown to bits on Cherien ridge, some time after midday. A sad loss to his tailors, jewellers and creditors, I dare say. As to anyone of consequence, well . . ."

The King made a spluttering noise, then said, "Loesp? What are you—?"

"We are all of one mind here, are we not?" tyl Loesp said smoothly, ignoring the King – ignoring the King! – and looking round everybody present.

A chorus of low, muttered voices gave what must have been assent. "Not you, priest, but no matter," tyl Loesp told the holy man. "Continue with the reading, if you would." The priest did as he was instructed, eyes now wide. The doctor's assistant stared at the King, then glanced at the doctor, who was looking back at him.

"Loesp!" the King cried, something of his old authority back in his voice. "What do you mean by this insult? And to my dead child? What monstrosity of—"

"Oh, do be quiet." Tyl Loesp laid his helmet at his feet and leaned further forward, putting his knuckles to his cheeks and resting his mailed elbows on the King's armoured chest; an act of such unprecedented disrespect that Ferbin found it almost more shocking than anything he'd heard. The King winced, breath wheezing out of him. Ferbin thought he heard something bubbling. The doctor had finished exposing the wound in the King's side.

"I mean the cowardly little cunt is dead, you old cretin," tyl Loesp said, addressing his only lord and master as though he was a beggar. "And if by some miracle he's not, he soon will be. The younger boy I think I'll keep alive for now, in my capacity as regent. Though – I'm afraid – poor, quiet, studious little Oramen may not live to the point of accession. They say the boy's interested in mathematics. I am not – save, like yourself, for its trajectorial role in the fall of shot – however I'd compute his chances of seeing his next birthday and hence majority grow less substantial the closer the event creeps."

"What?" the King gasped, labouring. "Loesp! Loesp, for all pity—"

"No," tyl Loesp said, leaning more heavily on the blood-bright curve of armour, causing the King to moan. "No pity, my dear, dim old warrior. You've done your bit, you've won your war. That's monument and epitaph enough and your time is past. But no pity, sir, no. I shall order all the prisoners of today killed with the utmost dispatch and the Ninth invaded with every possible severity, so that gutters, rivers – heavens, water wheels too, for all I care – run with blood, and the shrieking will, I dare say, be terrible to hear. All in your name, brave prince. For vengeance. For your idiot sons too, if you like." Tyl Loesp put his face very close to that of the King and shouted at him, "The game is over, my old stump! It was always greater than you knew!" He pushed himself back off the King's chest, making the prone man cry out again. Tyl Loesp nodded at the doctor, who, visibly gulping, reached out with some metal instrument, plunging it into the wound in the King's side, making him shudder and scream.

"You traitors, you treacherous bastards!" the King wept, as

the doctor took a step back, instrument dripping blood, face grey. "Will no one help me? Bastards all! You murder your king!"

Tyl Loesp shook his head, staring first at the writhing King, then at the doctor. "You ply your given trade too well, medic." He moved round to the other side of the King, who flailed weakly at him. As tyl Loesp passed, the priest stuck out a hand, clutching at the nobleman's sleeve. Tyl Loesp looked calmly down at the hand on his forearm. The priest said hoarsely, "Sir, this is too much, it's – it's wrong."

Tyl Loesp looked at his eyes, then back at his clutching hand, until the priest released him. "You stray your brief, mumbler," tyl Loesp told him. "Get back to your words." The priest swallowed, then lowered his gaze to the book again. His lips began to move once more, though no sound issued from his mouth.

Tyl Loesp moved round the broken door, shoving the doctor back, until he stood by the King's other flank. He crouched a little, inspecting. "A mortal wound indeed, my lord," he said, shaking his head. "You should have accepted the magic potions our friend Hyrlis offered. I would have." He plunged one hand into the King's side, arm disappearing almost to the elbow. The King shrieked.

"Why," tyl Loesp said, "here's the very heart of it." He grunted, twisting and pulling inside the man's chest. The King gave one final scream, arched his back and then collapsed. The body jerked a few more times, and some sound came from his lips, but nothing intelligible, and soon they too were still.

Ferbin stared down. He felt frozen, immobilised, like something trapped in ice or baked to solidity. Nothing he had seen or heard or ever known had prepared him for this. Nothing.

There was a sharp crack. The priest fell like a sack of rocks. Tyl Loesp lowered his pistol. The hand holding it dripped blood.

The doctor cleared his throat, stepped away from his assistant. "Ah, the boy, too," he told tyl Loesp, looking away from the lad. He shook his head and shrugged. "He worked for the King's people as well as us, I'm sure."

"Master! I— !" the youth had time to say, before tyl Loesp shot him as well; in the belly first, folding him, then in the head. The doctor looked quite convinced that tyl Loesp was about to shoot him, too, but tyl Loesp merely smiled at him and then at the two knights at the door. He stooped, took a towel from the waistband of the murdered assistant, wiped his pistol and his hand with it, then dabbed a little blood from his arm and sleeve.

He looked round the others. "This had to be done, as we all know," he told them. He looked distastefully at the body of the King, as a surgeon might at a patient who has had the temerity to die on him. "Kings are usually the first to talk, and at some length, of overarching destiny and the necessity of fulfilling greater purposes," he said, still wiping and dabbing. "So let's take all that billowy rhetoric as heard, shall we? We are left with this: the King died of his wounds, most honourably incurred, but not before swearing bloody vengeance on his enemies. The prancing prince is dead and the younger one is in my charge. These two here fell prey to a sniper. And we'll burn down this old place, just for good measure. Now, come; all our fine prizes await."

He threw the bloodied towel down on to the face of the felled assistant and then said, with an encouraging smile, "I believe we are concluded here."

2. Palace

O ramen was in a round room in the shade wing of the royal palace in Pourl when they came to tell him that his father and his elder brother were dead and he would, in time, be king. He had always liked this room because its walls described an almost perfect circle and, if you stood at its very centre, you could hear your own voice reflected back at you from the chamber's circumference in a most singular and interesting fashion.

He looked up from his papers at the breathless earl who'd burst into the room and broken the news. The earl's name was Droffo, from Shilda, if Oramen was not mistaken. Meanwhile a couple of the palace servants piled into the room behind the nobleman, also breathing hard and looking flushed. Oramen sat back in his seat. He noticed it was dark outside. A servant must have lit the room's lamps.

"Dead?" he said. "Both of them? Are you sure?"

"If all reports are to be believed, sir. From the army command and from tyl Loesp himself. The King is – the King's body is returning on a gun carriage, sir," Droffo told him. "Sir, I'm sorry. It's said poor Ferbin was cut in half by a shell. I am so sorry, sir, sorry beyond words. They are gone."

Oramen nodded thoughtfully. "But I am not king?"

The earl, who to Oramen looked dressed half for court and half for war, looked confused for a moment. "No, sir. Not until your next birthday. Tyl Loesp will rule in your name. As I understand it."

"I see."

Oramen took a couple of deep breaths. Well, now. He had not prepared himself for this eventuality. He wasn't sure what to think. He looked at Droffo. "What am I supposed to do? What is my duty?"

This, too, seemed to flummox the good earl, just for an instant. "Sir," he said, "you might ride out to meet the King's bier."

Oramen nodded. "I might indeed."

"It is safe, sir; the battle is won."

"Yes," Oramen said, "of course." He rose, and looked beyond Droffo to one of the servants. "Puisil. The steam car, if you would."

"Take a little while to get steam up," Puisil said. "Sir."

"Then don't delay," Oramen told him reasonably. The servant turned to go just as Fanthile, the palace secretary appeared. "A moment," Fanthile told the servant, causing Puisil to hesitate, his gaze flicking between the young prince and the elderly palace secretary.

"A charger might be the better choice, sir," Fanthile told Oramen. He smiled and bowed to Droffo, who nodded back at the older man. Fanthile was balding and his face was heavily lined, but he was still tall and carried his thin frame proudly.

"You think?" Oramen said. "The car will be quicker, surely."

"The mount would be more immediate, sir," Fanthile said.

"And more fitting. One is more public on a mount. The people will need to see you."

One can stand up in the back of my father's steam car, Oramen considered saying. But he saw the sense in what was being proposed.

"Also," Fanthile continued, seeing the prince hesitate and deciding to press, "the road may be crowded. A mount will slip through spaces—"

"Yes, of course," Oramen said. "Very well. Puisil, if you would."

"Sir." The servant left.

Oramen sighed and boxed his papers. His day had largely been taken up with working on a novel form of musical notation. He had been kept, with the rest of the household, in the cellars of the palace during the early morning, when the Deldeyn had first been expected to break out from the nearby Tower, in case things went badly and they had to flee through subterranean tunnels to a fleet of steam vehicles waiting ready in the city's lower reaches, but then they had been allowed out when, as expected, the enemy had been met with such prepared force they had soon ceased to be a threat to the city and their attention became focused instead on their own survival.

Mid-morning, he'd been persuaded to climb to a balustraded roof with Shir Rocasse, his tutor, to look out over the stepped palace grounds and the higher reaches of the hilltop city towards the Xiliskine Tower and the battleground that – telegraph reports now stated – stretched almost all around it.

But there had been little to see. Even the sky had appeared entirely devoid of action. The great battle-flocks of caude and lyge that had filled the ancient airs and made the battles of yesteryear seem so romantic were largely gone now; consigned – reduced – to scout patrols, messengering, artillery spotting, and raids that were little better than brigandry. Here on the Eighth such flying warbeasts were widely held to have no significant part to play in modern ground battles, largely due to the machinery and accompanying tactics King Hausk himself had introduced.

There had been rumours that the Deldeyn had steam-powered flying machines, but if these had been present today they must have been in small numbers or had little obvious effect. Oramen had been mildly disappointed, though he thought the better of saying so to his old tutor, who was as patriotic, race-conscious and WorldGodly as any might wish. They came down from the roof, for what were supposed to be lessons.

Shir Rocasse was nearing retirement but had anyway realised during the last short-year that he had little to teach Oramen now, unless it was by rote straight out of a book. These days, the prince preferred to use the palace library unmediated, though he still listened to the old scholar's advice, not entirely out of sentimentality. He had left Rocasse in the library, wrapt by some dusty set of scrolls, and made his way here, to the round room, where he was even less likely to be disturbed. Well, until now.

"Oramen!" Renneque ran in, darting past Droffo and Fanthile and flinging herself at his feet in a derangement of torn clothing. "I just heard! It can't be true!" Renneque, the lady Silbe, hooked her arms round his feet, hugging tight. She looked up, her young face livid with tears and grief, brown hair spilling. "Say it's not? Please? Not both. Not the King and Ferbin too! Not both. Not both. For anything, not both!"

Oramen leant down gently and pulled her up until she knelt before him, her eyes wide, her brows pulled in, her jaw working. He had always thought her rather attractive, and been envious of his elder brother, but now he thought she looked almost ugly in this surfeit of grief. Her hands, having been deprived of the patent reassurance of his feet, now clutched at a plump little World symbol on a thin chain round her neck, twisting it round and round in her fingers, the filigree of smaller shells inside the spherical outer casing all revolving, sliding back and forth, continually adjusting.

Oramen felt quite mature, even old, all of a sudden. "Now, Renneque," he said, taking her hands and patting them. "We all have to die."

The girl wailed, throwing herself to the floor again.

"Madam," Fanthile said, sounding kindly but embarrassed and reaching down to her, then turning to see Mallarh, one of the ladies of court – also looking tearful and distracted – appear in the doorway. Mallarh, perhaps twice Renneque's age, face pitted with the tiny scars of a childhood infection, bit her lip when she saw the younger woman weeping on the wooden floor. "Please," Fanthile said to Mallarh, indicating Renneque.

Mallarh persuaded Renneque to rise, then to exit.

"Now, sir . . ." Fanthile said, before turning to see Harne, the lady Aelsh, the King's present consort and mother to Ferbin, standing in the doorway, her eyes red, fair hair straggled and unkempt but clothing untorn, her face set and stance steady. Fanthile sighed. "Madam—" he began.

"Just confirm it, Fanthile," the lady said. "Is it true? The two? Both of mine?"

Fanthile looked at the floor for a moment. "Yes, my lady. Both gone. The King most certainly, the prince by all accounts."

The lady Aelsh seemed to sag, then slowly drew herself up. She nodded, then made as though to turn away, before stopping to look at Oramen. He looked straight back at her. He rose from his seat, still held by that gaze.

Though they had both sought to conceal it, their mutual dislike was no secret in the palace. His was based on his own mother having been banished in Harne's favour, while hers was generally assumed to be caused by Oramen's mere existence. Still, he wanted to say that he was sorry; he wanted to say (at least when he thought more clearly and logically about it later), that he felt for her double loss, that this was an unlooked-for and an unwanted promotion of his status, and that she would suffer no diminution of her own rank by any action or inaction of his either during the coming regency or following his own ascension. But her expression seemed to forbid him from speech, and perhaps even dared him to find anything that might be said that she would not find in some way objectionable.

He struggled against this feeling for some moments, thinking that it was better to say something rather than seem to insult her with silence, but then gave up. There was a saying: Wisdom is Silence. In the end, he simply bowed his head to the lady, saying nothing. He sensed as much as saw her turn and leave.

Oramen looked up again. Well, at least that was over.

"Come, sir," Fanthile said, holding out one arm. "I'll ride with you."

"Will I be all right like this?" Oramen asked. He was dressed most informally, in pants and shirt.

"Throw on a good cloak, sir," Fanthile suggested. He looked steadily at the younger man as he hesitated, patting the papers he had been working on as though not sure whether to take them with him or not. "You must be distraught, sir," the palace secretary said levelly.

Oramen nodded. "Yes," he said, tapping the papers. The topmost sheet was nothing to do with musical notation. As a prince, Oramen had of course been educated in the ways of the aliens who existed beyond his home level and outwith Sursamen itself and, idling earlier, he'd been doodling his name and then attempting to express it as those aliens might:

Oramen lin Blisk-Hausk'r yun Pourl, yun Dich.

Oramen-man, Prince (3/2), Pourlinebrac, 8/Su.

Human Oramen, prince of Pourl, house of Hausk, domain of Sarl, of the Eighth, Sursamen.

Meseriphine-Sursamen/8sa Oramen lin Blisk-Hausk'r dam Pourl.

He reordered the pages, picked up a paperweight and placed it on the pile. "Yes, I must, mustn't I?"

Just hoisting oneself aboard a mersicor, it appeared, had become rather more complicated than it had ever been before. Oramen had hardly tarried since hearing the news, but even so a considerable fuss had already accrued in the lantern-lit mounting yard by the time he got there.

Accompanied – harried might have been as fit a term – by

Fanthile, Oramen had visited his apartments to grab a voluminous riding cloak, suffered Fanthile pulling a comb through his auburn hair and then been rushed down the steps towards the yard, taking care to nod at the various grave faces and sets of wringing hands en route. He had only been held up once, by the Oct ambassador.

The ambassador looked like some sort of giant crab. Its upright, ovoid body – about the size of a child's torso – was coloured deep blue and covered with tiny bright green growths that were either thin spikes or thick hairs. Its thrice-segmented limbs – four hanging like legs, four seemingly taking the part of arms – were an almost incandescent red, and each terminated in small double claws which were the same blue as the main body. The limbs protruded, not quite symmetrically, in broken-looking Z-shapes from four black stubs which for some reason always reminded Oramen of fleshy cannon mouths.

The creature was supported from the rear and sides by a frame of mirror-finished metal, with bulkier additions behind it which apparently housed the means it used to hover soundlessly in mid-air, occasionally leaking small amounts of strangely scented liquid. A set of tubes led from another cylinder to what was assumed to be its face, set in the middle of its main body and covered with a sort of mask through which tiny bubbles could occasionally be seen to move. Its whole body glistened, and when you looked very closely – and Oramen had – you could see that a very thin membrane of liquid seemed to enclose every part of it, with the possible exception of its little green hairs and the blue claws. The Oct diplomatic mission was housed in an old ballroom in the palace's sun wing, and was, apparently, completely full of water.

The ambassador and two escorting Oct, one slightly smaller and one a little larger than it, floated over the corridor tiles towards Oramen and Fanthile as they reached the final turn in the stairs. Fanthile stopped when he saw the creatures. Oramen thought better of not doing likewise. He heard the palace secretary sigh.

"Oramen-man, Prince," Ambassador Kiu-to-Pourl said. Its

voice was that of dry leaves rustling, or a small fire starting in tinder. "That who gave that you might be given unto life is no more, as our ancestors, the blessed Involucra, who are no more, to us are. Grief is to be experienced, thereto related emotions, and much. I am unable to share, being. Nevertheless. And forbearance I commend unto you. One assumes. Likely, too, assumption takes place. Fruitions. Energy transfers, like inheritance, and so we share. You; we. As though in the way of pressure, in subtle conduits we do not map well."

Oramen stared at the thing, wondering what he was supposed to make of this apparent nonsense. In his experience the ambassador's tangential utterances could be made to represent some sort of twisted sense if you thought about them long enough – preferably after writing them down – but he didn't really have the time just now.

"Thank you for your kind words," he blurted, nodding and backing towards the stairs.

The ambassador drew back a fraction, leaving a tiny pool of moisture glistening on the tiles. "Keep you. Go to that which you go to. Take that which I would give you. Knowing of alikeness. Oct – Inheritors – descend from Veil, inherit. You, inherit. Also, is pity."

"With your leave, sir," Fanthile said to the ambassador, then he and Oramen bowed, turned and went clattering down the last flight of stairs towards ground level.

The fuss in the mounting yard mostly involved a whole blaring coven of dukes, earls and knights disputing loudly over who ought to ride with the Prince Regent on the short journey he was about to make to meet the body of the returning king.

Oramen hung back in the shadows, arms folded, waiting for his mount to be brought before him. He stepped backwards into a pile of dung near the yard's tall rear wall and tutted, shaking some of the shit from his boot and attempting to scrape off the rest on the wall. The dung pile was still steaming. He wondered if you could tell what sort of animal had left the turd from its appearance and consistency. Probably, he imagined.

He looked straight up at the sky. There, still visible over the lanterns illuminating the mounting yard from the ensquaring walls, a dull red line marked the cooling course incised by the Rollstar Pentrl, many hours set and many days away from returning. He looked to the nearpole, where Domity would rise next, but this was a relatively long night, and even the Rollstar's forelight was still some hours away. He thought he could see just a suggestion of the Keande-yiine Tower, stretching into the darkness above – the lower extent of the Xiliskine, though nearer, was hidden by a tall tower of the palace – but he was not sure. Xiliskine. Or 213tower52. That was the name their mentors, the Oct, would give it. He supposed he ought to prefer Xiliskine.

He returned his attention to the yard. So many nobles. He'd assumed they'd all be out fighting the Deldeyn. But then, his father had long since drawn a firm distinction between those nobles who brought grace and emollience to a court and those who were capable of successfully fighting a modern war. The levied troops, magnificently motley, led by their lords, still had their place, but the New Army was part full-time professional and part well-trained people's militias, all of it commanded by captains, majors, colonels and generals, not knights, lords, earls and dukes. He spotted some senior priests and a few parliamentarians in the mixture too, pressing their suit for inclusion. He had fondly imagined riding out alone, or with one or two attendants. Instead it looked like he would be leading out a small army of his own.

Oramen had been advised not to have anything to do with the battle taking place out over the plains that day, and anyway had no real interest in it, given that they had all been most severely assured it was quite certain to go their way by Werreber, one of his father's most forbidding generals, just the night before. It was a pity, in a way. Only a couple of years ago he'd have been fascinated with the machinery of war and all the careful dispositioning of forces involved. The intense numericality of its planning and the extreme functionality of its cruel workings would have consumed him.

Somehow, though, since then he'd lost interest in things martial. They seemed, even as they were in the process of securing it, profoundly inimical to the modern age they'd help usher in. War itself was becoming old-fashioned and outmoded. Inefficient, wasteful, fundamentally destructive, it would have no part in the glitteringly pragmatic future the greatest minds of the kingdom foresaw.

Only people like his father would mourn such a passing. He would celebrate it.

"My prince," murmured a voice beside him.

Oramen turned. "Tove!" he said, clapping the other young man on the back. Tove Lomma had been his best friend almost since nursery. He was an army officer nowadays and wore the uniform of the old Flying Corps. "You're here! I thought you'd be fighting! How good to see you!"

"They've had me in one of the lyge towers the last few days, with a squadron of the beasts. Light guns. In case there was an aerial attack. Listen." He put one hand on Oramen's arm. "This is so bad about your father and Ferbin. The stars would weep, Oramen. I can't tell you. All the men of the flight . . . Well, we want you to know we're at your command."

"Rather, at Loesp's."

"He is your champion in this, Oramen. He'll serve you well, I'm sure."

"As am I."

"Your father, though; our dear king, our every—" Tove's voice broke. He shook his head and looked away, biting his lip and sniffing hard.

Oramen felt he had to comfort his old friend. "Well, he died happy, I imagine," he said. "In battle, and victorious, as he'd have wished. As we'd all have wished. Anyway." He took a quick look round the mêlée in the yard. The contesting nobles seemed to be gathering themselves into some sort of order but there was still no sign of his charger. He'd have been quicker in the steam car after all. "It is a shock," he continued. Tove was still looking away. "I shall miss him. Miss him . . . well, terribly. Obviously." Tove looked back at him. Oramen smiled broadly and blinked quickly. "Truth be told, I think I'm like a half-stunned beast, still walking around, but eyes crossed as wits. I fully expect to wake up at any moment. I'd do so now, if it was in my power."

When Tove looked back, his eyes were bright. "I've heard that when the troops learned their beloved king was dead, they fell upon their captives and killed every one."

"I hope not," Oramen said. "That was not my father's policy."

"They killed him, Oramen! Those beasts! I wish I'd been there too, to take my own revenge."

"Well, neither of us were. We must hope what's been done in our name brings only honour."

Tove nodded slowly, clutching Oramen's arm once more. "You must be strong, Oramen," he said.

Oramen gazed at his old friend. Strong, indeed. This was quite the most vapid thing Tove had ever said to him. Death obviously had an odd effect on people.

"So," Tove said, with a sly, tentative smile, "do we call you sire or majesty or something yet?"

"Not yet . . ." Oramen began, then was led away by an earl and assisted to his mount by dukes.

On the Xilisk road, near the small town of Evingreath, the cortège bearing the body of King Nerieth Hausk back to his capital met with the barely smaller procession led by the prince Oramen. Immediately he saw the Prince Regent, lit by hissing travel lanterns and the slow-increasing forelight of the Rollstar Domity, still some hours from its dawn, Mertis tyl Loesp, who all the world knew had been like a third hand to the King for almost all his life, dismounted and, pulling himself with heavy steps to the prince's charger, went down on one knee on the muddied road, head bowed, so that his silvery hair – spiked and wild from the tearings of grief – and his distraught face – still

dark with powder smoke and streaked by hot, unceasing tears
– were level with the stirruped foot of the prince. Then he raised
his head and said these words:

"Sir, our beloved master, the King, who was your father and
my friend, and was friend and father to all his people, comes
back to his throne in triumph, but also in death. Our victory
has been great, and complete, and our gain and new advantage
immeasurable. Only our loss exceeds such vast accomplishment,
but it does so by a ratio beyond calculation. Beside that hateful
cost, for all its furious glory, our triumph these last hours now
looks like nothing. Your father was full occasion for both; one
would not have been but for his matchless leadership and steady
purpose, the other was invoked by his untimely, unwanted,
undeserved death.

"And so, it is fallen to me, and is my great, if ever-unlooked-
for privilege, to rule for the short interval between this most
loathsome day and the glorious one of your accession. I beseech
you, sir; believe me that whatever I do in your name, my lord,
will be for you and the people of Sarl, and always in the name
of the WorldGod. Your father would expect no less, and in this
cause, so great to us, I might begin to start some small repay-
ment of the honour he did me. I honour you as I honoured
him, sir – utterly, with all my being, with my every thought
and every action, now and for as long as it is my duty so to do.

"I have today lost the best friend a man ever had, sir; a true
light, a constant star whose fixity outshone, outstared any mere
celestial lamp. The Sarl have lost the greatest commander they
have ever known, a name fit to be clamoured down the aeons
till time's end and echo loud as that of any hero of the distant
ancients amongst the unseen stars. We can never hope to be a
tenth as great as he, but I take respite in only this: the truly
great are strong beyond death itself, my lord, and, like the fading
streak of light and heat a great star leaves behind it once its own
true brilliance has been obscured, a legacy of power and wisdom
remains from which we may draw strength, by its focus magnifying our own small allotment of fortitude and will.

"Sir, if I seem to express myself inelegantly, or without the due respect I would give your station and your self, forgive me. My eyes are blinded, my ears stopped and my mouth made numb by all that's taken place today. To gain more than we thought possible, then lose an infinity more than even that, would have shattered any man, save only the one unmatched soul it is our sad, abhorrent duty to bring before you here."

Tyl Loesp fell silent. Oramen knew he was expected to say something in return. He'd been doing his best to ignore the prattling dukes around him for the last half-hour, after Fanthile had briefly made it through the press of bodies, animal and human, surrounding him, to warn him he might need to give a speech. The palace secretary had barely had time to impart even this morsel of advice before he and his mount were nudged and jostled out of the way, back to what the more splendid nobles obviously regarded as his proper place amongst the minor nobility, the dutifully wailing priests and dour-looking parliamentarians. Since then Oramen had been trying to come up with something suitable. But what was he supposed to say, or do?

He glanced at the various resplendent nobles around him, all of whom, from their grave, almost exaggerated nods and mutterings, seemed to approve quite mightily of Mertis tyl Loesp's speech. Oramen twisted briefly in his saddle to glimpse Fanthile – now still further back in the crush of junior nobles, priests and representatives – signalling, with jerks of his head and jagged flaps of his hand that he ought to dismount.

He did so. Already a small crowd of dismounted men and people presumably from the nearby town and countryside had gathered around them, filling the broad way and jostling for position on the roadside banks. The growing forelight, pre-dawn under a sky of scattered clouds, silhouetted some folk climbing nearby trees for a better view. He still had no idea what to say in return, though he suddenly thought what a fine subject for a painting such a scene might make. Oramen took tyl Loesp by one hand and got him to stand before him.

"Thank you for all you've said and done, dear tyl Loesp," he told the older man. He was very aware of the contrast between the two of them; he the slight prince, barely out of childish clothes and dressed beneath his thrown-back cloak as though preparing for bed, the other the all-powerful conquering warrior, still in his battle armour – flecked here and there with all the marks of war – three times his age and barely any younger or less impressive than the lately killed king.

Harsh-breathing, stern-faced, still stinking of blood and smoke, bearing all the signs of mortal combat and unbearable grief, tyl Loesp towered over him. The drama of the scene was not lost on Oramen. This *would* make a good painting, he thought, especially by one of the old masters – say Dilucherre, or Sordic. Perhaps even Omoulldeo. And almost at the same moment, he knew what to do; he'd steal.

Not from a painting, of course, but from a play. There were enough old tragedies with like scenes and suitable speeches for him to welcome back a dozen dead dads and doughty combateers; the choice was more daunting than the task it might relieve. He'd recall, pick, edit, join and extemporise his way through the moment.

"This is indeed our saddest day," Oramen said, raising his voice, and his head. "If any energies of yours could bring our father back, I know you'd devote them to that cause without stint. That vigour instead will be turned to the good interest of all our people. You bring us sorrow and joy at once, my good tyl Loesp, but for all the misery we feel now, and for all the time we must rightly hence devote to the mourning of our incomparable fallen, the satisfaction of this great victory will still shine brightly when that rite has been most fully observed, and my father would surely want it so.

"The sum of his most glorious life was cause for fervent celebration well before the great triumph of this day, and the weight of that result has grown only more majestic with the exploits of all who fought for him before the Xiliskine Tower." Oramen looked round the gathered people for a moment at this point, and attempted to raise his voice still further. "My father took one son to war today, and left one, myself, at home. I have lost both a father and a brother, as well as my king and his loved and rightful heir. They outshine me in death as they did in life, and Mertis tyl Loesp, though having no lack of other responsibilities, must stand in place of both for me. I tell you, I can think of no one more fitted to the task." Oramen nodded towards the grim-faced warrior in front of him, then he took a breath, and, still addressing the assembled mass, said, "I know I have no share of this day's glory – I think my boyish shoulders would fail beneath the smallest part of such a load – but I am proud to stand with all the Sarl people, to celebrate and to honour the great deeds done and pay the fullest respect to one who taught us celebration, encouraged us to honour and exemplified respect."

This fetched a cheer, which rose raggedly then with increasing strength from the congregation of people gathered around them. Oramen heard shields being struck by swords, mailed fists beating on armoured chests and, like a modern comment on such flowery antiquity, the loud crack of small arms fire, rounds spent into the air like some inverted hail.

Mertis tyl Loesp, who had kept a stony face during Oramen's reply, looked very briefly surprised – even alarmed – at its end, but that briefest of impressions – which might so easily have been the result of the uncertain light cast by the carried travel lanterns and the wan glow of a still unrisen minor star – was close to uncapturably short-lived, and easily dismissible.

"May I see my father, sir?" Oramen asked. He found that his heart was beating hard and his breath was quick; still he did his best to maintain a calm and dignified demeanour, as he gathered was expected. Nevertheless, if he was expected to wail and scream and tear out his hair when he saw the body, this impromptu audience was going to be disappointed.

"He is here, sir," tyl Loesp said, indicating the long carriage pulled by hefters behind him.

They walked to the carriage, the crowd of men, mostly armed, many with all the appearance of great distress, parting for them. Oramen saw the tall, spare frame of General Werreber, who'd briefed them at the palace about the battle just the night before, and the Exaltine Chasque, the chief of priests. Both nodded to him. Werreber looked old and tired and somehow – despite his height – shrunken inside his crumpled uniform. He nodded, then cast his gaze downwards. Chasque, resplendent in rich vestments over gleaming armour, formed the sort of clenched, encouraging half-smile people sometimes did when they wanted to tell you to be brave or strong.

They climbed on to the platform where Oramen's father lay. The body was attended by a couple of priests in appropriately torn vestments and lit from above by a single hissing, sputtering travel lamp casting a white, caustic light over the bier. His father's face looked grey and still and drawn-down somehow, as though he was pondering – eyes shut, jaws set – some overwhelmingly demanding problem. A silvery sheet embroidered with gold covered his body from the neck down.

Oramen stood looking at him for a while. In time he said, "In life, by choice, his deeds spoke for him. In death, I must be as mute as all his undone undertakings." He clapped tyl Loesp on the arm. "I'll sit with him while we return to the city." He looked behind the gun carriage. A mersicor, a great charger, dis-armoured though in full regalia, was tied to its rear, saddle empty. "Is that . . . ?" he began, then made a show of clearing his throat. "That's my father's mount," he said.

"It is," tyl Loesp confirmed.

"And my brother's?"

"Unfound, sir."

"Let my mount be tied to the end of the carriage too, behind my father's."

He went to sit at his father's head, then, imagining Fanthile's face, thought that might be held inappropriate, and repositioned himself at the foot of the bier.

He sat there at the trailing edge of the carriage, cross-legged, looking down, while the two mersicors loped along just behind, breath steaming in the increasingly misty air. The whole aggregated column of men, animals and wagons made the rest of the journey to the city in a silence broken only by the creak of wheel and axle, the snap of whip and the snort and clop of beast. The morning mists obscured the rising star of the new day almost until the walls of Pourl itself, then lifted slowly to become a layer of overcast that hid the higher city and the palace.

On the approaches to the Nearpole Gate, where a conglomeration of small factories and what was effectively a new town had sprung up within Oramen's lifetime, the temporary sun shone only for a little while, then was gone again behind the clouds.

3.   Folly

Choubris Holse found his master in the eighth of the distinct places where he thought he might actually be, which was, of course, a significant and most propitious location to discover somebody or something a person was looking for. It was also the last place he knew of to look with any purpose beyond simply wandering randomly; indeed, with this in mind, he had left it to the afternoon of his second day of searching specifically with the hope that this might finally be where Ferbin had fetched up.

The folly looked like a small castle poised on a low cliff overlooking a turn in the river Feyrla. It was just a hollow round of walls, really, with crenellations, and had been built, pre-ruined, as it were, to improve the view from a hunting lodge a little further down the valley. It had been a place, Choubris Holse knew, where the King's children had played while their father – on one of his infrequent spells at home from his various Wars of Unity – went hunting.

Choubris tethered his rowel by the single low door to the ruin and left it noisily cropping moss from the wall. The mersicor trailing behind the rowel, brought in case he found his master mountless, nibbled daintily at some flowers. Holse preferred rowels to mersicors – they were less skittish and harder working. He might have taken a flying beast, he supposed, but he trusted those even less. Royal servants above a certain rank were expected to be able to fly, and he had suffered the instruction – and the instructors, who had not spared him their opinion that such honour was wasted upon one so coarse – but had not enjoyed the learning.

A proper searching, like so many things, was best done on foot, from the ground. Hurling oneself grandly across the sky was all very well and certainly gave the impression of lordly oversight and superiority, but what it really did was give you the opportunity to miss all details at once, rather than one at a time, which was the ration for decent folk. Plus, as a rule – a most fixed and strict rule, it had long struck Choubris – it was the people who had to make things work on the ground who ended up paying for such sweepingly overgeneralised judgementing. This principle seemed to apply to high-ups of all distinctions, whether their height was literal or metaphorical.

"Sir?" he called into the hollow round of stones. His voice echoed. The masonry was ill-dressed, worse within than without. The lower tier of piercings – much too wide for any real fortification – gave out on to pleasant views of hill and forest. The Xiliskine Tower rose pale and vast in the distance, disappearing beyond the clouds into the heavens. Plumes of smoke and wisps of steam were scattered across the landscape like missed stalks after a harvest, all leaning away from the backing wind.

He limped further into the folly. His left leg still hurt from where that seed-brained mersicor had fallen on him the day before. He was getting too old for such shenanigans; he was in his middle years now and starting to fill out nicely and become distinguished (or develop a paunch and become grey and grizzled, by his wife's less forgiving measure). His whole side, every rib, pained him when he took a deep breath, or tried to laugh. Not that there'd been much laughing.

Choubris had seen many signs of battle while he'd been riding round the area: whole wastelands of torn-up fields and shattered forests, the land raddled with a pox of craters; entire woods and brush forests still on fire, smoke walling the sky, other fires only just exhausted or extinguished, leaving vast black tracts of razed ground, seeping wispy fumes; the wrecks of smashed war machines lying crippled like enormous broken insects with tracks unrolled behind them, a few still leaking steam; some great dead battle beasts, spread crumpled and forlorn – uoxantch, chunsels and ossesyi, plus a couple of types he didn't recognise.

He'd seen bands of wounded troops, walking in lines or borne on carts and wagons, groups of soldiers dashing about importantly on mersicors, a few airborne men on caude, slowly crisscrossing, dipping and wheeling when searching for any still surviving enemy or stray fallen, or making straight and fast if bearing messages. He'd passed engineers rigging or repairing telegraph lines, and thrice he'd pulled off roads and tracks to let hissing, spitting, smoke-belching steam vehicles past. He'd patted and comforted the old rowel, even though she'd seemed unbothered.

He'd come, too, upon numerous details digging charnel pits for the enemy dead, of which there seemed a great many. The Deldeyn, Holse thought, looked much like normal folk. Perhaps a little darker, though that might have been the effect of death itself.

He'd stopped and talked to anybody willing to spare the time, pretty much regardless of rank, partly to enquire about missing nobles on white chargers, mostly because, as he would freely admit, he enjoyed flapping his jaw. He took a little crile root with the captain of one company, shared a pipe of unge with a sergeant from another and was grateful to a quartermaster-lieutenant for a bottle of strong wine. Most of the soldiers were more than happy to talk about their part in the battle, though not all. The mass-burial men, in particular, tended to the taciturn, even surly. He heard a few interesting things, as any fellow open to easy discourse was bound to.

"Prince?" he yelled, louder, voice echoing off the rough stones inside the folly. "Sir? Are you here?" He frowned and shook his head beneath the open crown of the empty tower. "Ferbin?" he shouted.

He ought not to call his master by his name like that, but then it looked like the prince wasn't here after all, and there was a thrill to be had from such address. Roundly insulting one's superiors behind their backs was one of the perks of being inferior, Choubris held. Besides, he'd been told often enough that he could use the familiar term, though such licence was only ever offered when Ferbin was very drunk. The offer was never renewed in sobriety so Choubris had thought the better of acting on the privilege.

He wasn't here. Maybe he wasn't anywhere, alive. Maybe the gaudy dope had accorded himself war hero status by mistake, riding neck-clutch like a terrified child wherever his idiot mount had taken him, to be shot by one side or other or fall off a cliff. Knowing Ferbin, he'd probably thought to raise his head again just as he went charging under an overhanging bough.

Choubris sighed. That was it, then. There was nowhere obvious left to look. He could wander the great battlefield pretending to search for his lost master, skipping through triage pens, inhabiting field hospitals and haunting morgue piles all he liked, but, unless the WorldGod took a most unlikely personal interest in his quest, he'd never find the blighter. At this rate he'd be forced to return to his wife and children, in the littler though hardly less savage battlefield that was their apartment in the palace barracks.

And *now* who'd have him? He'd lost a prince (if you wanted to take an uncharitable view of the matter, and he knew plenty that would); what were the chances he'd get to serve any other quality again, with that recorded against him? The King was dead and tyl Loesp was in charge, at least until the boy prince came of age. Choubris had a feeling in his gut that a lot of things – things that had seemed settled and comfortable and pleasantly just-so for honest, respectable, hard-working people – would change from here onwards. And the chances of a proven prince-misplacer bettering himself under any regime were unlikely to be good. He shook his head, sighed to himself. "What a sorry mess," he muttered. He turned to go.

"Choubris? Is it you?"

He turned back. "Hello?" he said, unable to see where the voice had come from. A sudden feeling inside his belly informed him, somewhat to his surprise, that he must have a degree of genuine human fondness for Prince Ferbin after all. Or perhaps he was just glad not, in fact, to be a prince-loser.

There was movement up on one wall, at the base of one of the impractically wide windows on the second tier; a man, crawling out of a fissure in the rough stonework that was mostly hidden by a rustling tangle of wallcreep. Choubris hadn't even noticed the hidey-hole. Ferbin completed his emergence, crawled to the edge of the window ledge, rubbed his eyes and looked down at his servant.

"Choubris!" he said, in a sort of loud whisper. He glanced around, as though afraid. "It is you! Thank God!"

"I already have, sir. And you might thank *me*, for such diligence in the looking."

"Is there anybody with you?" the prince hissed.

"Only the aforesaid deity, sir, if the more insistent priests are to be believed."

Ferbin looked most unkempt, and unslept, too. He glanced about the place again. "Nobody else?"

"An old though dependable rowel, sir. And for yourself—"

"Choubris! I am in the most terrible danger!"

Choubris scratched behind one ear. "Ah. With respect, sir, you might not be aware; we did win the battle."

"I know that, Choubris! I'm not an idiot!"

Choubris frowned, but remained silent.

"You're absolutely sure there's nobody else about?"

Choubris looked back to the small door, then up at the sky. "Well, there are lots of people *about*, sir; half the Greater Army is tidying up or licking its wounds after our famous victory." It was beginning to dawn on Choubris that he might have the ticklish job of telling the prince that his father was dead. This ought to mean, of course, that Ferbin was effectively king, but Choubris knew people could be funny regarding that whole good news/bad news business. "I am alone, sir," he told Ferbin. "I don't know what else to tell you. Perhaps you'd best get down from there."

"Yes! I can't stay here for ever." The drop was easily jumpable, but Ferbin made to turn round and lower himself half way to the earthen floor of the folly. Choubris sighed and stood by the wall to help. "Choubris, have you anything to drink or eat?" Ferbin asked. "I'm parched and famished!"

"Wine, water, bread and saltmeat, sir," Choubris said, forming a stirrup with his hands, back against the wall. "My saddle bags are like a travelling victualler's."

Ferbin lowered one boot to his servant's hands, narrowly avoiding scarring him with his spur. "Wine? What sort?"

"Fortified, sir. Better so than this place." Choubris took the prince's weight in his cupped hands and grunted in pain as he lowered him.

"Are you all right?" Ferbin asked when he was on the ground. He looked frightened, grey with worry or shock or something or other. His clothes were filthy and his long fair hair all tangled and matted. Also, he smelled of smoke. Choubris had never seen him look so distressed. He was crouched, too; Choubris was used to looking up to his prince, but they were of a level now.

"No, sir, I'm not all right. I had a beast fall on me in the confusion yesterday."

"Of course! Yes, I saw. Quick, let's crouch down here."

Ferbin pulled Choubris to one side, by a tall bush. "No, wait; fetch me something to eat and drink. If you see anybody, don't tell them I'm here!"

"Sir," Choubris said, deciding to humour the fellow for now. Probably all he needed was something in his belly.

As the traitors and regicides set to burn the old building, having taken themselves and the bodies of the murdered outside, Ferbin had started looking for a way out.

He felt dazed, stunned, half dead himself. His vision seemed to have shrunk, or his eyes would not move properly in their orbits, because he seemed only able to see straight ahead. His ears appeared to think he was near a great waterfall or in a high tower in a storm, for he could hear a terrible roaring noise all about him that he knew was not really there, as if the WorldGod, even the World itself, was shrieking in horror at the foulness of what had been done in that awful ruin.

He'd waited for people loyal to the King to come rushing in when they heard the shots that killed the priest and the young medic, but nobody did. Others had appeared, but they seemed calm and unconcerned and merely helped move the bodies and bring some kindling and lampstone to start the fire. They were all traitors here, he thought; to reveal himself now would be to die like the others.

He'd crept away, sick and weak with the shock of it, barely able to stand. He climbed to the next highest floor by steps set against the building's rear wall, as they lit the fires below. Smoke came up quickly, initially grey then turning black, filling the already shadowy spaces of the antique factory with still greater darkness and making him choke. At first most of the fumes made for the great hole in the gable wall, but then they thickened around him, stinging in his nose and throat. Had the sound of crackling and roaring below not been so loud, he'd have feared being heard outside as he hacked and coughed. He looked for windows on the side of the building where he'd crawled and climbed, but could see nothing.

He found more steps, leading him still further up, into what must be the building's loft and felt along the wall with his fingers, coughing now with every breath, until he found what appeared to be a window. He pulled at a shutter, pushed at some already broken glass, and it gave. Smoke surged out around him. He stuck his head forward, gulping in cool clear air.

But he was too high up! Even if there was nobody on this side to see him, he'd never survive the fall uninjured. He looked out, dipping his head beneath the current of smoke and heat exiting around and above him. He expected to see a track or yard, four storeys below. Instead he stung himself on a rain-sticky brattle bush. He felt down and his hand closed on damp earth. In the vague red afterlight of a long-set sun, he saw that he was, incredibly, somehow back to ground level. The building was situated on a river bank so steep that one side was fully four floors high while the other, pressed against the valley's steep side, was barely one.

He pulled himself out, still coughing, and crawled away across rain-wet, glutinously muddy ground to wait beneath some nearby bushes while the abandoned building burned.

"All due respect and such, sir, but have you gone mad?"

"Choubris, I swear on the WorldGod, on my dead father's body, it's just as I've said."

Choubris Holse had noticed earlier, while his master was swallowing wine from the upended bottle and tearing off lumps of bread with his teeth – it seemed that take away the table and you took away the accompanying manners – that Prince Ferbin was unarmed while he, of course, still had his trusty short-knife on his belt, not to mention an army pistol issued a couple of days ago he seemed to have forgotten to return and which was tucked into his waistband by the small of his back. Not to mention – and he rarely did – a small but exceedingly sharp emergency knife reassuringly scabbarded down one boot. These facts had, he judged, just gone from being of barely passing interest to moderately important, given that it now appeared he was dealing with a bizarrely deluded madman.

Ferbin put the bottle down and let the end of the bread drop to his lap, setting his head back against the wall of the ruin, as though looking up through the foliage of the bush he'd insisted they hide beneath before he'd been prepared to break his fast. "Even you don't believe me!" he cried, despairing. He put his head in his hands and wept.

Choubris was taken aback. He'd never seen the prince weep like this, not sober (everybody knew that to drink was to increase the hydrographical pressure within a body, thus expressing the relevant fluids from all available bodily orifices, so that didn't count).

He ought to try to comfort him somehow. Perhaps he'd misunderstood. He'd try to get the matter clear.

"Sir, are you really saying that," he began, then he too looked round as though afraid of being overheard, "that tyl Loesp, your father's best friend; the glove to his hand, the very edge of his sword and all that, *murdered* your father?" He spoke the word in a whisper.

Ferbin looked at him with a face of such desperate fury and despair that Choubris felt himself flinch at the sight of it. "Plunged his filthy fist into my father's chest and wrung the living force out of his beating heart!" Ferbin said, his voice sounding like it never had; all gasped and rough and wild. He sucked in a terrible, faltering breath, as though each atom of air hesitated in his mouth before being hauled howling to his lungs. "I saw it clear as I see you now, Choubris." He shook his head, his eyes filling with tears and his lips curling back. "And if trying to think it away, if trying to persuade myself I was in any way mistaken, or drugged, or hallucinating, or dreaming could make it so, then by God I'd jump at that, I'd welcome that with both arms, both legs and a kiss. A million times over

I'd rather be safely mad having imagined what I saw than know my only derangement is the grief of having seen what *did take place*!" That last phrase he roared into his servant's face, one hand grasping the collar at Choubris' throat.

Choubris put one hand behind his back, partly to steady himself so that he did not fall over backwards and partly to bring the army pistol within quick reach. Then his master's face went slack and he seemed to crumple in on himself. He put one hand on each of Choubris' shoulders and let his head fall to his servant's chest, wailing, "Oh, Choubris! If you don't believe me, who will?"

Choubris felt the heat of the other man's face upon his breast, and a dampness spread across his shirt. He lifted his hand to pat the prince's head, but that seemed too much like the action one would take with a woman or a child, and he let his hand fall back again. He felt shaken. Even at his most raucously or self-pityingly drunken, the prince had never seemed so moved, so affected, so distressed, by anything; not the death of his elder brother, not losing a beloved mount to a wager, not realising his father thought him a dolt and a wastrel – nothing.

"Sir," Choubris said, taking the prince by his shoulders and setting him upright again. "This is too much for me to absorb at the single sitting. I too would rather think my own dear master mad than entertain the possibility that what he says is true, for if it's so then – by God – we are all halfway to madness and the heavens themselves might fall upon us now and cause no increase in disaster or disbelief." Ferbin was biting both his quivering lips together, like a child trying not to cry. Choubris reached out and patted one of his hands. "Let me tell you what I've heard, various but consistent from a mixture of guileless strapping military types, and seen on an army news sheet, too; what is the official and authorised version, as you might say. Perhaps hearing this will make a compromise in your poor head with the fever possessing you."

Ferbin laughed bitterly, putting his head back again and sobbing even while he seemed to smile. He raised the wine bottle to his lips, then let it fall aside, dropping it to the bare ground. "Pass me the water; I'll pray some dead cur upstream polluted it, so I may poison myself by mouth as you pour it in at my ear. A job worth doing!"

Choubris cleared his throat to hide his astonishment. This was unprecedented; Ferbin putting aside a bottle unfinished. He was mad with something all right. "Well, sir. They say the King died of his wound – a small-cannon shot to his right side."

"So much half accurate. The wound was to his right."

"His death was easy, if solemn, and witnessed, not an hour's ride from here, in an old manufactury, since burned."

"By them. They burned it." Ferbin sniffed at one sleeve. "And nearly me." He shook his head. "I almost would they had," he finished, though this collided with:

"His death was witnessed by tyl Loesp, the Exaltine Chasque, the General—"

"What?" Ferbin protested angrily. "Chasque wasn't there! A lowly road-priest was all he had – and even he tyl Loesp killed! Blew his brains out!"

"And also by the doctors Gillews and Tareah and—"

"Gillews," Ferbin broke in. "Gillews alone, save for his assistant – another casualty of tyl Loesp's pistol."

"Also the General – begging your pardon, now the Field Marshal – Werreber and several of his sta—"

"Lies! Lies upon lies! They weren't there!"

"It's said they were, sir. And that the King ordered the killing of all the Deldeyn captured. Though, to admit the difference, others say the troops themselves embarked upon this sorry course on hearing of your father's death, in a fury of deadly vengeance. I grant this does not seem settled yet."

"And when it is, it will be to the advantage of tyl Loesp and his filthy accomplices." Ferbin shook his head. "My father ordered no such crime. This does him no honour. This is made to sap his reputation before he's even laid to rest. Lies, Choubris. Lies." He shook his head again. "All lies."

"The whole army believes it true, sir. As does the palace, I'd guess, and all who can read or hear, in Pourl and in the full throughoutness of the land, as fast as wire or beast or whatever other inferiority of messaging can carry the news."

"Still," Ferbin said bitterly, "even if I were alone in knowing what happened, I know it still."

Choubris scratched behind one ear. "If the whole world thinks differently, sir, is that even wise?"

Ferbin looked at his servant with an unsettling straightness. "And you'd have me do what, Choubris?"

"Eh? Why – well – sir, come back with me to the palace, and be the King!"

"And not be shot as an imposter?"

"An imposter, sir?"

"Enlighten me; what is my status according to this established version of how things are?"

"Well, yes, you're correct in that you have been ascribed dead, but – surely – on sight of your good self . . ."

"I'd not be killed on the instant of being seen?"

"Why killed at all?"

"Because I don't know the all of who is and who is not part of this treachery! Those I saw at the death, yes; guilty beyond guilt. The others? Chasque? Werreber? Did they know? Did they just claim to be present at this fictitious, easy death, to help support whatever circumstance they were presented with by those who'd wrought the crime? Do they suspect nothing? Something? All? Were they part of it from the beginning, every one? Tyl Loesp is culprit, and no one was closer to my father. Who else might not be guilty? Tell me: have you not heard warnings against spies, snipers, saboteurs and guerrillas?"

"Some, sir."

"Were there any orders of particular strictness you heard of regarding those who suddenly appeared, within the greater battlefield, resembling authority?"

"Well, just latterly, yes, sir, but—"

"Which means that I'll be held, then shot. In the back, I don't doubt, so they can say I was trying to escape. Or d'you think such things never happen, in army or militia?"

"They—"

"And if I did get as far as the palace, the same applies. How long might I survive? Long enough to tell the truth in front of a quorate sufficient to carry the day? I think not. Long enough to challenge tyl Loesp, or confront the wretch? Beyond doubt? Beyond the grave, I'd say." He shook his head. "No, I have thought long about this over the last day, and can see quite clearly the merits of the contending courses, but also I know my instincts, and they have proved unfailingly trustworthy in the past." This was true; Ferbin's instincts had always told him to flee trouble or potential conflict – rowdies, creditors, angry fathers of shamed daughters – and, whether escaping to the shelter of an obscure bawdy house, a congenially distant hunting lodge or indeed the palace itself, this intuition had invariably proved itself sound.

"Either way, sir, you can't hide here for ever."

"I know that. And I am besides not the one to enter into any such contention with the tyl Loesps of this world. I know they have the guile on me, and the easy turn to brute."

"Well, God knows, I'm not such a one either, sir."

"I must escape, Choubris."

"Escape, sir?"

"Oh, indeed; escape. Escape far, far away, and seek sanctuary with or find a champion in one of two people I never imagined I'd have to trouble for so demeaning a favour. I suppose I ought to be thankful I have any sort of choice, or just two chances."

"And they would be, sir?"

"First we must get ourselves to a Tower fitted out for travel – I have an idea for obtaining the necessary documents," Ferbin said, almost as though talking to himself. "Then we shall have ourselves transported to the Surface and take ship away across the stars, to Xide Hyrlis, who generals for the Nariscene now and who may take up our cause for the love of my dead father, and if he is unable to do so, then at least he might signpost the route ... To Djan," Ferbin told Holse with what sounded like sudden weariness. "Anaplia's daughter. Who was raised to be fit to marry a prince and then found herself dowried to the mongrel alien empire that calls itself the Culture."

4. In Transit

U taltifuhl, the Grand Zamerin of Sursamen-Nariscene, in charge of all Nariscene interests on the planet and its accompanying solar system and therefore – by the terms of the mandate the Nariscene held under the auspices of the Galactic General Council – as close as one might get to overall ruler of both, was just beginning the long journey to the 3044th Great Spawning of the Everlasting Queen on the far-distant home planet of his kind when he met the director general of the Morthanveld Strategic Mission to the Tertiary Hulian Spine – paying a courtesy call to the modest but of course influential Morthanveld embassy on Sursamen – in the Third Equatorial Transit Facility high above Sursamen's dark, green-blue pocked Surface.

The Nariscene were insectile; the Zamerin was six-limbed and keratin-covered. His dark, quintuply segmented body, a little under a metre and a half long (excluding stalks, mandibles retracted), was studded with implanted jewels, inlaid veins of precious metals, additional sensory apparatus, numerous tiny holo-projectors displaying the many medals, honours, distinctions and decorations that had come his way over the years and a smattering of light weaponry, mostly ceremonial.

The Grand Zamerin was accompanied by a bevy of his kind, all rather less impressively dressed and slightly smaller than he. They were, additionally, if that was the right word, neuters. They tended to move through the cavernous, web-filled spaces of the transit facility in an arrowhead formation, with the Grand Zamerin forming its tip.

The Morthanveld were spiniform waterworlders. The director general was a milky-looking sphere a metre or so in diameter surrounded by hundreds of spiny protrusions of varying thicknesses and in a broad spectrum of pastel colours. Her spines were mostly either curled up or gathered back at the moment, giving her a compact, streamlined appearance. She carried her environment around with her in a glistening wrap of silvery blue, membranes and fields containing her own little sample of oceanic fluids. She wore a few small spine torques, bracelets and rings. She was accompanied by a trio of more stoutly built assistants toting so much equipment they looked armoured.

The transit facility was a micro-gravity environment and lightly pressured with a gently warmed gaseous nitrogen-oxygen mix; the web of life-support strands that infested it were coded by colour, scent, texture and various other markers to make them obvious to those who might need to use them. One identified the right strand in the web and hooked into it to receive that which one needed to survive; oxygen, chlorine, salty water or whatever. The system couldn't accommodate every known life form without requiring them to protect themselves in a suit or mask, but it represented the best compromise its Nariscene builders had been prepared to come up with.

"DG Shoum! My good friend! I am glad it was possible for

our paths to cross!" The Grand Zamerin's language consisted of mandible clicks and, occasionally, directed pheromones; the director general understood Nariscene reasonably well without artificial aids, but still relied on a neurologically hard-wired translator ring to be sure of what was being said. The Grand Zamerin, on the other hand, like most Nariscene, eschewed alien languages as a matter of both principle and convenience, and so would depend entirely on his own translation units to understand the director general's reply.

"Grand Zamerin, always a pleasure."

Formal squirts of scent and packeted water molecules were exchanged; members of their respective entourages carefully gathered the greeting messages, as much out of politeness as for archival purposes. "Utli," Director General Shoum said, reverting to the familiar and floating up to the Nariscene. She extended a maniple spine.

The Grand Zamerin clicked his mandibles in delight and took the offered limb in his foreleg. He twisted his head and told his assistants, "Amuse yourselves, children." He sprayed a little cloud of his scent towards them, mixed to indicate reassurance and affection. A flush of colour across Shoum's spines gave a similar instruction to her escorts. She set her communications torque to privacy, though with a medium-level interrupt.

The two officials floated slowly away through the web of environmental support strands, heading for a massive circular window which looked out to the planet's Surface.

"I find you well?" Shoum asked.

"Extraordinarily!" the Grand Zamerin replied. "We are filled with delight to be called to attend the Great Spawning of our dear Everlasting Queen."

"How wonderful. Do you contend for mating rights?"

"Us? Me? Contend for mating rights?" The Grand Zamerin's mandibles clicked so fast they nearly hummed, signalling hilarity. "Gracious! No! The preferred specification ..." (glitch/sorry! signalled the translator, then hurried to catch up), "the preferred genotype-spread called for by the Imperial

Procreational College was far outside our bias. I don't believe our family even submitted a tender. And anyway, on this occasion there was generous lead-time; if we had been in the running we'd have bred some braw and brawny hunk especially for our dear Queen. No, no; the honour is in the witnessing."

"And the lucky father dies, I understand."

"Of course! Now *that* is a distinction." They were drifting closer to a great porthole on the underside of the facility, showing Sursamen in all its dark glory. The Grand Zamerin bristled his antennae as though lost in wonder at the view, which he wasn't. "We had such prominence once," he said, and the translator, if not Shoum's own processes, picked up a note of sadness in amongst the pride. Utli waved at one of his little holo-baubles. "This, you see? Indicates that our family contributed a species-Father sometime in the last thirty-six birth-generations. However, that was thirty-six birth-generations ago and, sadly, short of a miracle, I shall lose this decoration in less than a standard year from now, when the next generation is hatched."

"You might still hope."

"Hope is all. The tenor of the times drifts from my family's mode of being. We are downwinded. Other scents outsmell ours." The translator signalled an imperfect image.

"And you are compelled to attend?"

Utli's head made a shrugging gesture. "Technically. We fail to accept the invitation on pain of death, but that is for form's sake, really." He paused. "Not that it is never carried out; it is. But on such occasions it is generally used as an excuse. Court politics; quite hideous." The Grand Zamerin laughed.

"You will be gone long?" Shoum asked as they arrived at the great window. They were still politely holding limbs.

"Standard year or so. Better hang around the court for a while, lest they forget who we are. Let the family scent sink in, you know? Also, taking some consecutive leave to visit the old family warrens. Some boundaries needing redrawn; maybe an upstart toiler or two to fight and eat."

"It sounds eventful."

"Horribly boring! Only the Spawning thing dragging us back."

"I suppose it is a once-in-a-lifetime experience."

"*End*-of-a-lifetime experience for the father! Ha ha!"

"Well, you will be missed, I'm sure."

"So am I. Some dully competent relations of mine will be in charge during our absence; the clan Girgetioni. I say dully competent; that may flatter them. My family has always been firmly of the opinion that if it is absolutely necessary to take leave of one's responsibilities for a while, always be sure to leave surrogates in charge who will ensure your welcome on return will be both genuine and enthusiastic. Ha ha." Utli's eye stalks waggled as though in a strong wind, indicating humour. "But this is to jest. The Girgetioni clan are a credit to the Nariscene species. I have personally placed my least incompetent nephew in the position of acting Zamerin. I have the highest possible confidence in him and them."

"And how are things?" Shoum asked. "Within Sursamen, I mean."

"Quiet."

"Just 'quiet'?" Shoum asked, amused.

"Generally. Not a peep, not a molecule from the God-beast in the basement, for centuries."

"Always reassuring."

"Always reassuring," Utli agreed. "Oh, the awful saga of the Third Level, Future Use Committee proceedings rumbles on like cosmic background, though at least *that* might be swept away in some future cataclysm or Big Concluding Event, whereas said committee might plausibly go on far, far beyond that and redefine the meaning of the term In Perpetuity for any entities having the ghastly misfortune still to be around at the time." The Grand Zamerin's body shape and scents signalled exasperation. "The Baskers still wish it to be theirs, the Cumuloforms still claim it as already long promised to them. Each side has come heartily to despise the other, though not, we'd life-stake, a sixth as much as we have come to despise both of them.

"The L12 Swimmers, perhaps inspired by the japes the Cumuloforms and Baskers are having with their dispute, have waved a scent-trace to the wide winds regarding the vague possibility of one day, perhaps, if we wouldn't mind, if nobody else would object, taking over Fourteen.

"The Vesiculars of . . ." Utli paused as he checked elsewhere, "Eleven announced some time ago that they wished to migrate, en masse, to Jiluence, which is somewhere in the Kuertile Pinch and, they allege, an ancestral homeworld of theirs. That was some gross of days ago, though, and we've heard nothing since. A passing fancy, probably. Or art. They confuse such terms. They confuse us, too. It may be deliberate. Possibly too long an association with the Oct, who are most adept at lateral thinking but seemingly incapable of anything but lateral expression, too; were there a prize for least-translatable galactic species, the Oct would win every cycle, though of course their acceptance speeches would be pure gibberish. What else?" Utli's demeanour indicated resignation and amusement, then went back to exasperation again, mixed with annoyance.

"Oh yes, talking of the Oct, who call themselves the Inheritors; they have managed to antagonise the Aultridia – of ill repute, et cetera – through some inebriate machination or other. We listened to their petitions before leaving, but it all sounds lamentably trivial. Tribal wars amongst the natives of some cuspid wastelevels. The Oct may well have been interfering; it has been my curse to command the one world where the local Oct seem unable to leave well, ill or indeed indifferent alone. However, as they don't appear actually to have transferred any technology to the protégé barbarians concerned, we are without immediate excuse to step in. Ineffably tiresome. They – meaning the Oct and the ghastly squirmiforms – wouldn't listen to our initial attempts to mediate and frankly we were too taken up with our leaving preparations to have the patience to persist. Storm in an egg sac. If you'd like to take a sniff at the problem, do feel free. They might listen to you. Emphasis 'might', though. Be prepared fully to deploy your masochistic tendencies."

The director general allowed a flush of amusement to spread across her body. "So, then; you will miss Sursamen?"

"Like a lost limb," the Grand Zamerin agreed. He pointed his eye stalks at the porthole. They both looked down at the planet for some moments, then he said, "And you? You and your family, group, whatever – are they well?"

"All well."

"And are you staying long here?"

"As long as I can without unduly upsetting our embassy here," the director general replied. "I keep telling them I just enjoy visiting Sursamen but I believe they think I have an ulterior motive, and their preferred candidate is a determination on my part to find something wrong in their conduct." She indicated amusement, then formality. "This is a courtesy call, no more, Utli. However, I shall certainly seek whatever excuses I can to stay longer than the polite minimum, simply to enjoy being in this wonderful place."

"It has its own sort of blotchy, deeply buried beauty, we might be persuaded to concede," Utli said grudgingly, with a small cloud of scent that indicated guarded affection.

Director General Morthanveld Shoum, free-child of Meast, nest of Zuevelous, domain of T'leish, of Gavantille Prime, Pliyr, looked out over the mighty, mostly dark, still slightly mysterious world filling the view beneath the transit facility.

Sursamen was a Shellworld.

Shellworld. It was a name that even now brought a thrill to the very core of her being.

"Sursamen – an Arithmetic Shellworld orbiting the star Meseriphine in the Tertiary Hulian Spine." She could still see the glyphs rippling across the surface of her school teaching mat.

She had worked hard to be here, dedicated her life – through study, application, diligence and no small amount of applied psychology – to one day making Sursamen an important part of her existence. In a sense, any Shellworld would have done, but this was the place that had initiated her enchantment, and so for her it had a significance beyond itself. Ironically, the very force of that drive somehow to make herself part of Sursamen's fate had caused her to overshoot her mark; her ambition had carried her too far, so that now she had oversight of Morthanveld interests within the whole long river-system of stars called the Tertiary Hulian Spine, rather than just the Meseriphine system containing the enigmatic wonder that was Sursamen, with the result that she spent less time here than she would have considered ideal.

The dim green glow of the Gazan-g'ya Crater lit up her body and that of the Grand Zamerin, the gentle light slowly increasing as Sursamen turned and presented more of the vast pockmark of the crater to the rays of the star Meseriphine.

Sursamen collected adjectives the way ordinary planets collected moons. It was Arithmetic, it was Mottled, it was Disputed, it was Multiply Inhabited, it was Multi-million-year Safe, and it was Godded.

Shellworlds themselves had accreted alternative names over the aeons: Shield Worlds, Hollow Worlds, Machine Worlds, Veil Worlds. Slaughter Worlds.

The Shellworlds had been built by a species called the Involucra, or Veil, the best part of a billion years earlier. All were in orbits around stable main-series suns, at varying distances from their star according to the disposition of the system's naturally formed planets, though usually lying between two and five hundred million kilometres out. Long disused and fallen into disrepair, they had, with their stars, drifted out of their long-ago allotted positions. There had been about four thousand Shellworlds originally; 4096 was the commonly assumed exact number as it was a power of two and therefore – by general though not universal assent – as round a figure as figures ever got. No one really knew for sure, though. You couldn't ask the builders, the Involucra, as they had disappeared less than a million years after they'd completed the last of the Shellworlds.

The colossal artificial planets had been spaced regularly about the outskirts of the galaxy, forming a dotted net round the great whirlpool of stars. Almost a billion years of gravitational swirling had scattered them seemingly randomly across and through the skies ever since: some had been ejected from the galaxy altogether while others had swung into the centre, some to stay there, some to be flung back out again and some to be swallowed by black holes, but using a decent dynamic star chart, you could feed in the current positions of those which were still extant, backtrack eight hundred million years and see where they had all started out.

That four-thousand-plus figure had been reduced to a little over twelve hundred now, mostly because a species called the Iln had spent several million years destroying the Shellworlds wherever they could find them and nobody had been willing or able to prevent them. Exactly why, nobody was entirely sure and, again, the Iln were not around to ask; they too had vanished from the galactic stage, their only lasting monument a set of vast, slowly expanding debris clouds scattered throughout the galaxy and – where their devastation had been less than complete – Shellworlds that had been shattered and collapsed into barbed and fractured wrecks, shrunken compressed husks of what they had once been.

The Shellworlds were mostly hollow. Each had a solid metallic core fourteen hundred kilometres in diameter. Beyond that, a concentric succession of spherical shells, supported by over a million massive, gently tapering towers never less than fourteen hundred metres in diameter, layered out to the final Surface. Even the material they were made from had remained an enigma – to many of the galaxy's Involved civilisations at least – for over half a billion years, before its properties were fully worked out. From the start, though, it had been obvious that it was immensely strong and completely opaque to all radiation.

In an Arithmetic Shellworld, the levels were regularly spaced at fourteen-hundred-kilometre intervals. Exponential or Incremental Shellworlds had more levels close to the core and fewer further out as the distance between each successive shell increased according to one of a handful of logarithm-based ratios. Arithmetic Shellworlds invariably held fifteen interior surfaces and were forty-five thousand kilometres in external diameter. Incremental Shellworlds, forming about twelve per cent of the surviving population, varied. The largest class was nearly eighty thousand kilometres across.

They had been machines. In fact, they had all been part of the same vast mechanism. Their hollowness had been filled, or perhaps had been going to be filled (again, nobody could be certain this had actually been done), with some sort of exotic superfluid, turning each of them into a colossal field projector, with the aim, when they were all working in concert, of throwing a force field or shield round the entire galaxy.

Precisely why this had been thought necessary or even desirable was also unknown, though speculation on the matter had preoccupied scholars and experts over the aeons.

With their original builders gone, the people who had attacked the worlds seemingly also permanently missing and the fabled superfluid equally absent, leaving those vast internal spaces linked by the supporting Towers – themselves mostly hollow, though containing twisted webs of structurally reinforcing material, and punctured with portals of various sizes giving access to each of the levels – it had taken almost no time at all for a variety of enterprising species to work out that a derelict Shellworld would make a vast, ready-made and near-invulnerable habitat, after just a few relatively minor modifications.

Gases, fluids – especially water – and solids could be pumped or carried in to fill all or some of the spaces between the levels, and artificial interior "stars" might be fashioned to hang from the ceilings of each level like gigantic lamps. The various venturesome species set about exploring the Shellworlds closest to them, and almost immediately encountered the problem that would bedevil, frustrate and delay the development of the worlds profoundly for the next few million years and, intermittently, beyond; the Shellworlds could be deadly.

It remained unclear to this day whether the defence mechanisms that kept killing the explorers and destroying their ships had been left behind by the worlds' original builders or those who appeared to have dedicated their entire existence to the task of destroying the great artefacts, but whether it had been the Veil or the Iln – or, as it was now generally agreed, both – who had left this lethal legacy behind, the principal factor limiting the use of the Shellworlds as living spaces was simply the difficulty of making them safe.

Many people died developing the techniques by which a Shellworld might be so secured, and the same lessons generally had to be learned afresh by each competing civilisation, because the power and influence which accrued to a grouping capable of successful Shellworld exploitation meant that such techniques remained fiercely guarded secrets. It had taken an Altruist civilisation – exasperated and appalled at such a selfish waste of life – to come along, develop some of the techniques, steal others and then broadcast the whole to everybody else.

They had, of course, been roundly vilified for such unsporting behaviour. Nevertheless, their actions and stance had, in time, been ratified and even rewarded by various galactic bodies, and the Culture, although far remote in time from these now long-Sublimed people, had always claimed a sort of kinship by example with them.

The civilisations which specialised in making Shellworlds safe and who effectively took part-ownership of their interiors became known as Conducers. Sursamen was unusual in that two species – the Oct (who claimed direct descent from the long-departed Involucra and so also called themselves the Inheritors) and the Aultridia (a species with what might be termed a poorly perceived provenance) – had arrived at the same time and begun their work. It had also been unusual in that neither species ever got a decisive upper hand in the ensuing conflict which, in the only positive aspect of the dispute, at least remained localised to Sursamen. In time the situation within the world had been formalised when the two species were awarded joint protective custody of Sursamen's access Towers by the then newly formed Galactic General Council, though, importantly, without any stipulation that the two could not contend for increased influence in the future.

The Nariscene were granted full inhabitory rights to the planet's Surface and overall control of the world, formalising their long-held claim to it, though even they had to defer ultimately to the Morthanveld, in whose volume of influence the system and the world lay.

So Sursamen had been colonised, making it Inhabited, and by a variety of species, hence the Multiply- prefix. The holes in the supporting Towers that might have let gases or liquids vent to lower levels were sealed; some effectively permanently, others with lock complexes that permitted safe entry and exit, while transport mechanisms were installed inside the great hollow Towers to allow movement between the various levels and to and from the Surface. Material in gaseous, liquid and solid form had been moved in over the many millions of years of the planet's occupation, and beings, peoples, species, species groups and whole ecosystems had been imported by the Oct and the Aultridia, usually for a consideration of some sort or another, sometimes at the behest of the peoples concerned, more often at the request of others.

Interior stars had been emplaced; these were thermonuclear power sources like tiny suns, but with the useful distinction of being anti-gravitative, so that they pressed upwards against the ceiling above any given level. They subdivided into Fixstars and Rollstars, the former stationary, the latter moving across the skies on predetermined routes and on regular, if sometimes – when there were many, of different periodicities – complicated schedules.

The deaths continued, too; long after a given Shellworld had been apparently de-weaponed and made safe, hidden defence systems could wake up centuries, millennia and decieons later, resulting in gigadeaths, teradeaths, effective civicides and near-extinctions as interior stars fell, levels were flooded from above or drained – often with the result that oceans met interior stars, resulting in clouds of plasma and superheated steam – atmospheres were infested by unknown wide-species-spectra pathogens or were turned inexorably into poisonous environments by unseen mechanisms nobody could stop, or intense bursts of gamma radiation emanating from the floor/ceiling structure itself flooded either individual levels or the whole world.

These were the events that gave them the name Slaughter Worlds. At the point that Director General Shoum gazed down upon the dark, colour-spotted face of Sursamen, no mass deaths had been caused by the Shellworlds themselves for nearly four million years, so the term Slaughter World had long since slipped into disuse, save amongst those cultures with exceptionally long memories.

Nevertheless, on a grand enough scale the morbidity of any habitat type could be roughly judged by the proportion that had become Dra'Azon Planets of the Dead over time. Planets of the Dead were preserved, forbidden monuments to globe-encompassing carnage and destruction which were overseen – and usually kept in a pristine, just post-catastrophe state – by the Dra'Azon, one of the galactic community's more reclusive semi-Sublimed Elder civilisations with attributes and powers sufficiently close to god-like for the distinction to be irrelevant. Out of the four-thousand-plus Shellworlds originally existing and the 1332 unequivocally remaining – 110 in a collapsed state – fully eighty-six were Planets of the Dead. This was generally agreed to be an alarmingly high proportion, all things considered.

Even some of the Shellworlds lacking the morbid interest of the Dra'Azon had a kind of semi-divine investment. There was a species called the Xinthian Tensile Aeronathaurs, an Airworld people of enormous antiquity and – according to fable – once of enormous power. They were the second or third largest airborne species in the galaxy and, for reasons known solely to themselves, sometimes one of them would take up solitary residence in the machine core of a Shellworld. Though once widespread and common, the Xinthia had become a rare species and were regarded as Developmentally Inherently, Pervasively and Permanently Senile – in the unforgiving language of Galactic taxonomy – by those who bothered to concern themselves with such anachronisms at all.

For as long as anybody could remember, almost all the Xinthia had been gathered together in one place; a necklace of Airworlds ringing the star Chone in the Lesser Yattlian Spray. Only a dozen or so were known to exist anywhere else, and seemingly they were all at the cores of individual Shellworlds. These Xinthians were presumed to have been exiled for some transgression, or to be solitude-craving hermits. Presumption was all anybody had to go on here too, as even though the Xinthia, unlike the long-departed Veil or Iln, were still around to ask, they were, even by the standards of the galaxy's Taciturn cultures, quite determinedly uncommunicative.

Hence the Godded part of Sursamen's full description; there was a Xinthian Tensile Aeronathaur at its core, called by some of the world's inhabitants the WorldGod.

Invariably inside the great worlds and sometimes on their exteriors, the shells were adorned with massive vanes, whorls, ridges, bulges and bowls of the same material that made up both the levels themselves and the supporting Towers. Where such structures appeared on the Surface of a Shellworld, the bowl-shaped features had usually been filled with mixtures of atmospheres, oceans and/or terrain suitable for one or more of the many Involved species; the shallower examples of these – somewhat perversely called Craters – were roofed, the deeper usually not.

Sursamen was one such example of a Mottled Shellworld. Most of its Surface was smooth, dark grey and dusty – all the result of being lightly covered with nearly an aeon's worth of impact debris after systemic and galactic bodies of various compositions, sizes and relative velocities had impacted with that unforgiving, adamantine skin. About fifteen per cent of its external shell was pocked with the covered and open bowls people called Craters and it was the greeny-blue reflected light of one of those, the Gazan-g'ya Crater, that shone through the porthole in the transit facility and gently lit up the bodies of the Grand Zamerin and the director general.

"You are always glad to arrive, to see Sursamen, or any Shellworld, are you not?" Utli asked Shoum.

"Of course," she said, turning to him a little.

"Whereas, personally," the Grand Zamerin said, swivelling away from the view, "it's only duty keeps me here; I'm always relieved to see the back of the place." There was a tiny warble and one of his eye stalks flicked briefly over to look at what appeared to be a jewel embedded in his thorax. "Which we're informed occurs very shortly; our ship is ready."

Shoum's comms torque woke to tell her the same thing, then went back to its privacy setting.

"Relieved? Really?" the director general asked as they floated back through the web towards their respective entourages and the docking chutes that gave access to the ships.

"We shall never understand why you are not, Shoum. These are still dangerous places."

"It's been a very long time since any Shellworld turned on its inhabitants, Utli."

"Ah, but still; the intervals, dear DG."

The Grand Zamerin was referring to the distribution of Shellworld-induced mass die-offs through time. Plotted out, they implied only a slow dying away of such titanic murderousness, not yet a final end. The graphed shape of attacks approached zero, but did so along a curve that implied there might be one or two more yet to come, probably some time in the next few thousand years. If, of course, that was really the way these things worked. The implied threat of future cataclysms might be the result of coincidence, nothing more.

"Well then," Shoum said, "to be blunt, we would have to hope it does not happen during our tenure, or if does, it does not happen in Sursamen."

"It's just a matter of time," the Grand Zamerin told her gloomily. "These things turn killer, or disappear. And nobody knows why."

"Yet, Utli," the director general said, signalling mischievousness, "do you not find it in any sense romantic somehow – even in a sense reassuring – that there are still such mysteries and imponderables in our polished, cultivated times?"

"No," the Grand Zamerin said emphatically, expelling an emission named *Doubting the sanity of one's companion*, with barely a trace of humour.

"Not even in the abstract?"

"Not even in the abstract."

"Oh, well. Still, I wouldn't worry, if I were you," Shoum told Utaltifuhl as they approached their attendants. "I suspect Sursamen will still be here when you get back."

"You think its disappearance is unlikely?" Utli said, now expressing mock seriousness.

"Vanishingly," Shoum said, but the joke didn't translate.

"Indeed. And of course. However, it has struck us that so wonderful and enjoyable is the life we lead that a disaster of equal but opposite proportions must always be a threat. The higher you build your Tower, the more tempting a target for fate it becomes."

"Well, at least you are vacating your Tower for the next year. I trust the trip home is rewarding and I shall look forward with pleasure to seeing you again, Grand Zamerin."

"And I you, Director General," Utaltifuhl told her, and performed the most respectful and delicate of formal mandible-nips on her outstretched maniple spine. Shoum blushed appropriately.

They had reached their respective entourages and a giant window that looked out the other side of the transit facility, to a small fleet of docked ships. Utaltifuhl looked out at the star craft and emoted dubiety. "Hmm," he said. "And interstellar travel is also not without its risks."

MATTER

with my seely dabbing a blurh, he said. And inspect with early yun odlount inness.

5. Platform

Djan Seriy Anaplian, who had been born a princess of the house of Hausk, a dynasty from a wide-spectrum pan-human species lately from a median level of the Shellworld Sursamen and whose middle name basically meant fit-to-be-married-to-a-prince, stood alone on a tall cliff looking out over a rust desert deep within the continent of Lalance on the planet Prasadal. A strong wind lashed at her long coat and tore at her clothes. She still wore her dark, wide-brimmed hat and its stiff material was caught and tugged at by the gusting wind as though it was trying to tear it off her head. The hat, secured by well-tied ribbons, was unlikely to come off, but it meant that the wind made her head shake and nod and jerk as though with palsy. The wind carried dust and sand in small dry flurries that came beating up from the desert floor beneath and curling over the serrated edge of the cliff, stinging her cheeks where they were exposed between the scarf that covered her mouth and nose and the goggles that protected her eyes.

She put one gloved hand to the goggles, pulling them away from her face a fraction to let a little moisture out from the base of the frames. The sparse liquid ran down her cheeks, leaving streaks, but soon dried in the dusty force of air. She took a deep breath through the protecting scarf as the clouds of dust parted like a dry mist, allowing her an uninterrupted view of the distant city and the forces that had been besieging it.

The city was burning. Siege engines taller than its own towers buttressed its walls like gigantic calipers. The desert around it, until recently dark with the besieging army, was clearing as they poured into the stricken city, exposing sand the colour of drying blood. Smoke tried to rise from the wreckage of the shattered buildings in great curling bundles of darkness but was struck down by the force of the gale, flattened and whirled away from the various conflagrations, dipping down and back towards the desert to come rearing up again as it met the cliff so that it went billowing over Anaplian's head in a ragged, fast-moving overcast.

The wind increased in strength. Out over the plain, a wall of dust was forming between her and the city as half the desert seemed to lift into the air, gradually dimming and wiping away the view, silhouetting a series of rocky outcrops for a few moments until they too were swept under the hem of the advancing dust storm. She turned and walked a little way back to where a contraption like a cross between a skeleton and a sculpture sat poised on all fours on the exposed rock. She gathered the coat about her and stepped backwards on to the feet of the strange machine. The seatrider came alive instantly, swinging up fluidly and fitting itself about her, clasps closing round ankles, thighs, waist, neck and upper arms, nestling its thin form around her like a lover. She took the offered control grip as it swung out to her hand and pulled it upwards, sending the machine and her flying into the sky, then pushed forward so that she went racing through the storm of dust and smoke to the beleaguered city.

She rose through the haze into clearer air as she built up speed, leaving the fields down at first and letting the slipstream buffet her, the wind making her coat tails snap like whips and forcing the hat's brim to fold itself away, then she clicked the streamline field on and rode in a delta-shaped bubble of quiet air towards the city.

She dropped and slowed as she crossed over the walls and turned the streamline field off again. She flew between wind-twisted columns of smoke, watching the besieging forces as they swept into the spaces of the city, saw defenders falling back and inhabitants fleeing, observed arrows fly and a last few rocks and fire barrels land in the city's upper reaches. She smelled the smoke and heard the clash of blades and the crack and rattle of burning and the rumble of falling masonry and the ululating battle cries and war trumpets of the victorious invaders and the wails and screams of the defeated. She saw a few tiny figures pointing at her, and a couple of arrows arced towards her then fell away again. She was knocked to one side and almost thought herself hit with the violence of the action as the seatrider dodged a fire barrel; it went past with a great roar and a stench of burning oil, looping downwards to crash into the roof of a temple in the upper city, splashing flame.

She turned the full panoply of fields back on, hiding her and the machine and enclosing herself in the still bubble of protected air again. She had been heading for the centre of the city, for what she assumed would be the citadel and the palace, but then changed her mind and flew around one side of the city, level with its middle reaches, watching the general influx of invaders and the chaotic retreat of defenders and civilians while also trying to observe the slighter struggles of small groups and individuals.

Eventually she alighted on the flat, low-walled roof of a modest building where a rape was in progress and a small child cowered in a corner. The four soldiers waiting their turn gazed at her with annoyance when she appeared seemingly from thin air, stepping off the seatrider. Their frowns were beginning to turn into appreciative if unpleasant smiles when she drew a sleek chunk of a gun from a shoulder holster and, smiling thinly back, set about punching head-sized holes in each of their torsos. The first three men went flying backwards off the roof to the street below in frothy detonations of blood and tissue. The fourth man had time to react and – as he ducked and started to dive away – a tiny part of Anaplian's combat wiring kicked in, flicking the gun more quickly than her conscious mind could have ordered the action and simultaneously communicating with the weapon itself to adjust its emission pattern and beam-spread. The fourth soldier erupted across the roof in a long slithering torrent of guts. A sort of bubbling gasp escaped his lips as he died.

The man raping the woman was looking up at Anaplian, mouth open. She walked round a few paces to get a clear shot at him without endangering the woman, then blew his head off. She glanced at the child, who was staring at the dead soldier and the form lying underneath the spasming, blood-spouting body. She made what she hoped was a calming motion with her hand. "Just wait," she said in what ought to be the child's own language. She kicked the soldier's body off the woman, but she was already dead. They'd stuffed a rag into her mouth, perhaps to stop her screams, and she had choked on it.

Djan Seriy Anaplian let her head down for a moment, and cursed quickly in a selection of languages, at least one of which had its home many thousands of light years away, then turned back to the child. It was a boy. His eyes were wide and his dirty face was streaked with tears. He was naked except for a cloth and she wondered if he had been due to be next, or just marked to be thrown from the roof. Maybe they'd have left him. Maybe they hadn't meant to kill the woman.

She felt she ought to be shaking. Doubtless without the combat wiring she would be. She glanded *quickcalm* to take the edge off the internal shock.

She put the gun away – though even now the boy probably

didn't understand it was a weapon – and walked over to him, crouching down and hunkering as she got up close to him. She tried to look friendly and encouraging, but did not know what to say. The sound of running footsteps rang from the open stairwell on the opposite corner of the roof.

She lifted the boy by both armpits. He didn't struggle, though he tried to keep his legs up and his arms round his knees, retaining the ball shape she'd first seen him in. He was very light and smelled of sweat and urine. She turned him round and held him to her chest as she stepped into the seatrider. It closed around her again, offering the control grip as its sliding, clicking components fastened her and it together.

A soldier wielding a crossbow arrived clattering at the top of the steps. She took the gun out and pointed it at him as he took aim at her, but then shook her head, breathed, "Oh, just fuck off," flicked the controls and zoomed into the air, still holding the child. The bolt made a thunking noise as it skittered off the machine's lower field enclosure.

"And what exactly do you intend to do with it?" the drone Turminder Xuss asked. They were on a tall stump of rock at least as far downwind from Anaplian's earlier clifftop vantage point as that had been from the city. The child – he was called Toark – had been told not to go near the edge of the great rock column, but was anyway being watched by a scout missile. Turminder Xuss had, in addition, given the boy its oldest and least capable knife missile to play with because the weapon was articulated; its stubby sections snicked and turned in the child's hands. He was making delighted, cooing noises. So far, the knife missile had suffered this treatment without complaint.

"I have no idea," Anaplian admitted.

"Release him into the wild?" the drone suggested. "Send him back to the city?"

"No," Anaplian said, sighing. "He keeps asking when Mummy's going to wake up," she added, voice barely above a whisper.

"You have introduced a Special Circumstances apprentice-ship scheme on your own initiative," the drone suggested.

Anaplian ignored this. "We'll look for somewhere safe to leave him, find a family that can raise him," she told the machine. She was sitting on her haunches, her coat spread around her.

"You should have left him where he was," the drone said above the still strong wind, lowering the tone of its voice and slowing its delivery as it tried to sound reasonable rather than sarcastic.

"I know. That didn't feel like an option at the time."

"Your seatrider tells me you – how shall I put this? – *appeared* to the attackers and defenders of the city like some demented if largely ineffectual angel before you swooped in and carried little Toark away."

Anaplian glared at the seatrider, not that the obedient but utterly unintelligent machine would have had any choice but to surrender its memories to the drone when it had been asked.

"What are you doing here, anyway?" she asked Xuss.

She'd asked to be left alone for the day to watch the fall of the city. It had been her fault, after all; it had come about due to actions she had taken and indeed helped plan, and though it was by no means what had been desired, its sacking represented a risk that she, amongst others, had judged worth taking. It was demonstrably not the worst that might have happened, but it was still an abomination, an atrocity, and she had had a hand in it. That had been enough for her to feel that she could not just ignore it, that she needed to bear witness to such horror. The next time – if there was a next time, if she wasn't thrown out for her irrational, overly senti-mental actions – she would weigh the potential for massacre a deal more heavily.

"We have been summoned," the machine said. "We need to

get to the *Quonber*; Jerle Batra awaits." Its fields flashed a frosty blue. "I brought the module."

Anaplian looked confused. "That was quick."

"Not to slap your wrist for disturbing the war or rescuing adorable waifs. The summons pre-dates such eccentricities."

"Batra wants to see me personally?" Anaplian frowned.

"I know. Not like him." It dipped left-right in its equivalent of a shrug. "It."

Anaplian rose, dusting her hands. "Let's go then." She called to the boy, who was still trying to twist the uncomplaining knife missile apart. The module shimmered into view at the cliff edge.

"Do you know what his name means?" the drone asked as the child came walking shyly towards them.

"No," the woman said. She lifted her head a little. She thought she'd caught a hint of the smell of distant burning.

"'Toark'," the drone said as the boy came up to them, politely handing back the knife missile. "In what they call the Old Tongue—"

"Lady, when does my mother wake?" the boy asked.

Anaplian gave what she was sure was a not particularly convincing smile. "I can't tell you," she admitted. She held out one hand to guide the child into the module's softly gleaming interior.

"It means 'Lucky'," the drone finished.

The module trajectoried itself from the warm winds of the desert through thinning gases into space, then fell back into the atmosphere half a world away before Toark had finished marvelling at how clean he had become, and how quickly. Anaplian had told him to stand still, close his eyes and ignore any tickling sensation, then plonked a blob of cleaner gel on his head. It torused down over him, unrolling like liquid and making him squirm when a couple of smaller circles formed round his fingers and rolled back up to his armpits and back down. She'd cleaned his little loincloth with another blob but he wanted that gone and chose a sort of baggy shirt from a holo-display instead. He was most impressed when this immediately popped out of a drawer.

Meanwhile the woman and the drone argued about the degree of eye-averting that ought to be applied to her rule-breaking flight over the city. She was not quite yet at the level where the Minds that oversaw this sort of mission just gave her an objective and let her get on with it. She was still in the last stages of training and so her behaviour was more managed, her strategy and tactics more circumscribed and her initiative given less free rein than that of the most experienced and skilled practitioners of that ultimately dark art of always well-meaning, sometimes risky and just occasionally catastrophic interference in the affairs of other civilisations.

They agreed the drone wouldn't volunteer any information or opinion. It would all come out in the end – everything came out in the end – but by then, hopefully, it wouldn't seem so important. Part of the training of a Special Circumstances agent was learning a) that the rules were supposed to be broken sometimes, b) just how to go about breaking the rules, and c) how to get away with it, whether the rule-breaking had led to a successful outcome or not.

They landed on the platform *Quonber*, a flat slab of hangar space and accommodation units that looked like a small, squashed cruise liner, albeit one perfectly disguised by a camoufield. It floated smoothly in the warm air just over the altitude where a few puffy clouds drifted, their shadows spotting the surface of the pale green ocean a couple of thousand metres below. Directly beneath the platform lay the salt lagoons of an uninhabited island near the planet's equator.

The platform was home to another eleven SC human staff, all charged with attempting to alter the development of the various species on Prasadal. The planet was unusual in having five quite different sentient expansionist/aggressive species all hitting their civilisational stride at the same time. In all recorded history, every other time this had happened without some outside influence taking a hand in matters, at least three and usually four of the contending species were simply destroyed by the victorious grouping. The Culture's notoriously highly detailed and allegedly extremely reliable simulations confirmed that this was just the way things worked out for your average aggressive species, unless you interfered.

When the module arrived everybody else was either on the ground or busy, so they saw nobody else as one of the *Quonber*'s own slaved drones escorted them along the open side-deck towards the rear of the platform. Toark stared goggle-eyed through the drop of air towards the salt lagoons far below.

"Shouldn't you at least hide the boy?" the drone suggested.

"What would be the point?" Anaplian asked it.

The slave-drone showed them into the presence of Anaplian's control and mentor, Jerle Batra, who was taking the air on the wide balcony that curved round the rear portion of the module's third deck.

Jerle Batra had been born male. He had, as was common in the Culture, changed sex a while, and had borne a child. Later, for his own reasons, he had spent some time in Storage, passing a dreamless millennium and more in the closest thing the Culture knew to death from which it was still possible to wake.

And when he had awoken, and still felt the pain of being a human in human form, he had had his brain and central nervous system transferred sequentially into a variety of different forms, ending, for now at least, with the body type he now inhabited and which he had retained for the last hundred years or so – certainly for the decade or more that Anaplian had known him, that of an Aciculate; his shape was bush-like.

His still human brain, plus its accompanying biological but non-human support systems, was housed in a small central pod from which sixteen thick limbs protruded; these quickly branched and rebranched to form smaller and smaller limblets, maniples and sensor stalks, the most delicate of which were hair-thin. In his normal, everyday state he looked just like a small, rootless, spherical bush made from tubes and wires. Compressed, he was little larger than the helmet of an old-fashioned human spacesuit. Fully extended, he could stretch for twenty metres in any given direction, which gave him what he liked to term a high contortionality factor. He had, in all his forms, always worshipped order, efficiency and fitness, and in the Aciculate form felt he had found something that epitomised such values.

Aciculacy was not the furthest one could stray from what the Culture regarded as human basic. Other ex-humans who looked superficially a lot like Jerle Batra had had their entire consciousness transcribed from the biological substrate that was their brain into a purely non-biological form, so that, usually, an Aciculate of that type would have its intelligence and being distributed throughout its physical structure rather than having a central hub. Their contortionality factor could be off the scale compared to Batra's.

Other people had assumed the shapes of almost anything mobile imaginable, from the relatively ordinary (fish, birds, other oxygen-breathing animals) to the more exotic, via alien life-forms – again, including those which were not normally in the habit of supporting a conscious mind – all the way to the truly unusual, such as taking the form of the cooling and circu-latory fluid within a Tueriellian Maieutic seed-sail, or the spore-wisp of a stellar field-liner. These last two, though, were both extreme and one-way; there was a whole category of Amendations that were hard to do and impossible to undo. Nothing sanely transcribable had ever been shifted back from something resembling a stellar field-liner into a human brain.

A few genuine eccentrics had even taken the form of drones and knife missiles, though this was generally considered to be somewhat insulting to both machine- and human-kind.

"Djan Seriy Anaplian," Batra said in a very human-sounding voice. "Good day. Oh. Do I congratulate?"

"This is Toark," Anaplian said. "He is not mine."

"Indeed. I thought I might have heard."

Anaplian glanced at the drone. "I'm sure you would have."

"And Handrataler Turminder Xuss. Good day to you too."

"Delightful as ever," muttered the drone.

"Turminder, this does not involve you initially. Would you excuse Djan Seriy and me? You might entertain our young friend."

"I am becoming an accomplished child-minder. My skills grow with every passing hour. I shall hone them."

The drone escorted the boy from the balcony. Anaplian glanced up at the overhanging bulk of the accommodation deck and took her hat off, throwing it into one suspended seat and herself into another. A drinks tray floated up.

Batra drifted nearer, a greyly skeletal bush about head-height. "You are at home here," he stated.

Anaplian suspected she was being gently rebuked. Had she been overcasual in her hat-throwing and her seat-collapsing-into? Perhaps Batra was chiding her for not showing him sufficient deference. He was her superior, to the extent that this wilfully unhierarchic civilisation understood the idea of superiors and inferiors. He could have her thrown out of SC if he wanted to – or at the very least, make her restart the whole process – however, he wasn't usually so sensitive regarding matters of etiquette.

"It serves," she said.

Batra floated across the deck and settled into another of the seats hanging from the ceiling, resting in it like a sort of fuzzy, vaguely metallic ball. He had formed part of the side facing Anaplian into a kind of simulated face, so that his visual sensors were where the eyes should be and his voice came from where a human mouth would have been. It was disconcerting. Just having a fuzzy ball talking to you would have been much less alarming, Anaplian thought.

"I understand that events have not ended as well as they might with the Zeloy/Nuersotise situation."

"A year ago we disabled and turned back an army on its way to sack a city," Anaplian said wearily. "Today the would-be attackers became the attacked. The more progressive tendency, as we would put it, ought now to prevail. Though at a cost." She pursed her lips briefly. "Part of which I have just witnessed."

"I have seen some of this." The image of the face suggested by Batra's mass of steely-looking tendrils expressed a frown, then closed its eyes, politely indicating that he was reviewing data from elsewhere. Anaplian wondered if he was watching general views of the siege and sacking of the city, or something that included her unwarranted excursion on the seatrider.

Batra's eyes opened again. "The knowledge that so much worse happens where we do nothing, and always has, long before we came along – and that so much worse might happen here were we to do nothing – seems of very little significance when one is confronted with the grisly reality of aggression we have failed to prevent. All the more so when we had a hand in allowing or even enabling it." He sounded genuinely affected. Anaplian, who was innately suspicious of perfectly one hundred per cent natural, utterly unamended human-basic humans, wondered whether Batra – this bizarre, many-times-alien, two-thousand-year-old creature that still thought of itself as "he" – was expressing sincere emotion, or simply acting. She wondered this very briefly, having realised long ago the exercise was pointless.

"Well," she said, "it is done."

"And much more remains to be done," Batra said.

"That'll get done too," Anaplian said, beginning to lose patience. She was short on patience. She had been told this was a fault. "I imagine," she added.

The metallic bush rolled back a little, and the face on its surface seemed to nod. "Djan Seriy, I have news," Batra said.

Something about the way the creature said this made her quail. "Really?" she said, feeling herself battening down, shrinking inward.

"Djan Seriy, I have to tell you that your father is dead and your brother Ferbin may also be deceased. I am sorry. Both for the news itself and to be the one who bears it."

She sat back. She drew her feet up so that she was quite enclosed in the gently swinging egg of the suspended seat. She took a deep breath and then unfolded herself deliberately. "Well," she said. "Well." She looked away.

It was, of course, something she had tried to prepare herself for. Her father was a warrior. He had lived with war and battle all his adult life and he usually led from the front. He was also a politician, though that was a trade he'd had to train himself to do well rather than one that he had taken to entirely naturally and excelled at. She had always known he was likely to die before old age took him. Throughout the first year when she had come to live amongst these strange people that called themselves the Culture she had half expected to hear he was dead and she was required to return for his funeral.

Gradually, as the years had passed, she had stopped worrying about this. And, also gradually, she had started to believe that even when she did hear he was dead it would mean relatively little to her.

You had to study a lot of history before you could become part of Contact, and even more before you were allowed to join Special Circumstances. The more she'd learned of the ways that societies and civilisations tended to develop, and the more examples of other great leaders were presented to her, the less, in many ways, she had thought of her father.

She had realised that he was just another strong man, in one of those societies, at one of those stages, in which it was easier to be the strong man than it was to be truly courageous. Might, fury, decisive force, the willingness to smite; how her father had loved such terms and ideas, and how shallow they began to look when you saw them played out time and time again over the centuries and millennia by a thousand different species.

This is how power works, how force and authority assert themselves, this is how people are persuaded to behave in ways that are not objectively in their best interests, this is the kind of thing you need to make people believe in, this is how the unequal distribution of scarcity comes into play, at this moment and this, and this . . .

These were lessons anybody born into the Culture grew up with and accepted as being as natural and obvious as the progression of a star along the Main Sequence, or evolution itself. For somebody like her, coming in from outside, with a set of assumptions built up in a society that was both profoundly different and frankly inferior, such understanding arrived in a more compressed time frame, and with the impact of a blow.

And Ferbin dead too, perhaps. That she had not expected. They had joked before she'd left that he might die before his father, in a knife fight over a gambling game or at the hand of a cuckolded husband, but that had been the sort of thing one said superstitiously, inoculating the future with a weakened strain of afflictive fate.

Poor Ferbin, who had never wanted to be king.

"Do you need time to grieve?" Batra asked.

"No," she said, shaking her head fiercely.

"Are you sure?"

"Positive," she said. "My father. Did he die in battle?"

"Apparently so. Not on the battlefield, but of his wounds, shortly after, before he could receive full medical attention."

"He'd rather have died on the field itself," she told Batra. "He must have hated having to settle for second best." She found that she was both crying a little, and smiling. "When did it happen?" she asked.

"Eleven days ago." Batra made a bristling motion. "Even news of such importance travels slowly out of a Shellworld."

"I suppose," Anaplian said, her expression thoughtful. "And Ferbin?"

"Missing, on the same battlefield."

Anaplian knew what that meant. The vast majority of those labelled missing in battles either never reappeared at all, or turned up dead. And what had Ferbin being doing anywhere near a battle in the first place? "Do you know where?" she asked. "Exactly how far-flung a province was it?"

"Near the Xiliskine Tower."

She stared at him. "What?"

"Near the Xiliskine Tower," Batra repeated. "Within sight of Pourl – that is the capital, isn't it?"

"Yes," Anaplian said. Her mouth was suddenly quite dry. Dear God, it had all fallen away, then. It had all crumbled and gone. She felt a sorrow she barely understood.

"So was this some ... Excuse me." She cleared her throat. "Was this a final stand, in that case?"

And why hadn't she heard? Why had no one told her things had reached a point of such awful desperation? Were they afraid she'd try to return and use her new-found skills and powers to intercede? Were they worried she'd try to join the fray, was that it? How *could* they?

"Now, Djan Seriy," Batra said, "while I have been briefed in this, I cannot claim to have immediate access to an expert database. However, I understand that it was the result of what was expected to be a surprise attack by the Deldeyn."

"What? From where?" Anaplian said, not even trying to hide her alarm.

"From this Xiliskine Tower."

"But there's no way out of ..." she began, then put one hand to her mouth, pursing her lips and frowning as she stared at the floor. "They must have opened a new ..." she said, more to herself than to Batra. She looked up again. "So, is the Xiliskine controlled by the Aultridia now, or ... ?"

"First, let me assure you that as I understand it, Pourl and your father's people are not under threat. The Deldeyn are the ones facing disaster."

Anaplian's frown deepened, even as the rest of her body showed signs of relaxing. "How so?"

"Your father had effectively completed his Wars of Unity, as he termed them."

"Really?" She felt a surge of relief and a perverse urge to laugh. "He did keep busy."

"The Deldeyn would appear to have assumed that they'd be his next target. They therefore staged what they hoped would be a decisive, pre-emptive surprise attack on your father's capital city, having been convinced by the – Oct? Inheritors?"

"Synonyms." Anaplian flapped one hand again. "Either."

"That they, the Oct, would deliver the Deldeyn forces in secret to where a new portal would be opened in the Xiliskine Tower through which they might effect such an attack, taking the city. This was a ruse, and one which the Sarl were party to. Your father's forces were waiting for the Deldeyn and destroyed them."

Anaplian looked confused. "Why were the Oct deceiving the Deldeyn?"

"This is still a matter for conjecture, apparently."

"And the Aultridia?"

"The other Conducer species. They have backed the Deldeyn in the past. They are believed to be considering military and diplomatic action against the Oct."

"Hmm. So why . . . ?" Anaplian shook her head once more. "What is going on back there?" she asked. Again, Jerle Batra suspected this question was not really directed at him. He let her continue. "So, Ferbin's in charge – no, of course, he's probably dead too. Oramen, then?" she asked, looking worried and sceptical at once.

"No; your younger brother is deemed too young to inherit all your father's power immediately. A man called Mertis tyl Loesp is regent until your brother's next birthday."

"Tyl Loesp," Anaplian said thoughtfully. She nodded. "At least he's still around. He should be all right."

"Your younger brother won't be in any danger, will he?"

"Danger?"

Batra's impersonated face configured a weak smile. "It has been my understanding that, like wicked stepmothers, ambitious regents do not usually come out well from such contexts. Perhaps that is only in tales."

"No," Anaplian said with what sounded like relief. She wiped her eyes. "Tyl Loesp's been my father's best friend since they were children. He's always been loyal, fastened his ambitions to my father's. God knows, they were grand enough for two. Grand enough for a host.' Anaplian looked away to one side, where the bright, tropic air of this place that she had almost come to think of as home over the last two years now seemed as far away as it had when she'd first arrived. "Though what do I know? It's been fifteen years."

She wondered how much Ferbin had changed in that time, and Oramen. Her father, she strongly suspected, would hardly have changed at all – he had been the same forbidding, occasionally sentimental, rarely tender, utterly focused individual for as long as she'd known him. Utterly focused, yet with one eye always on history, on his legacy.

Had she ever known him? Most of the time he wasn't there to be known in the first place, always away fighting his distant wars. But even when he had returned to Pourl, his palace, concubines and children, he had been more interested in the three boys, especially Elime, the eldest and by far the most like him in character. Second in age, her gender and the circumstances of her birth had fixed the King's only daughter firmly last in his affections.

"Should I leave you, Djan Seriy?" Batra asked.

"Hmm?" She looked back at him.

"I thought you may need time alone. Or do you need to talk? Either is—"

"I need you to talk to me," she told him. "What is the situation now?"

"On what is called the Eighth? Stable. The King is mourned with all due—"

"Has he been buried?"

"He was due to be, seven days ago. My information is eight or nine days old."

"I see. Sorry. Go on."

"The great victory is celebrated. Preparations for the invasion of the Deldeyn continue apace. The invasion is widely expected to take place between ten and twenty days from now. The Oct have been censured by their Nariscene mentors, though they have blamed everybody else for what has happened, including elements within their own people. The Aultridia have, as I have said, threatened retaliation. The Nariscene are trying to keep the peace. The Morthanveld are so far not involved, though they have been kept informed."

She pinched her lower lip with her fingers. She took a breath and said, "How long would it take for me to get back to Sursamen?"

"A moment, please," Batra said, falling silent for a moment while, she imagined, he consulted the course schedules of whole networks of distant ships. She had time to wonder why he hadn't already memorised or at least accessed this information, and whether this possibly deliberate hesitation implied a criticism of her for even thinking of abandoning her post here.

"Between one hundred and thirty and one hundred and sixty days," Batra told her. "The uncertainty comes from the changeover to Morthanveld space."

Morthanveld space. The Morthanveld were the highest-level Involved species around Sursamen. As part of her training Anaplian had studied, and been suitably stunned by, the full three-dimensional map of all the various species that inhabited the galaxy and had spread sufficiently far from their homes to discover that they were profoundly Not Alone.

The standard star chart detailing the influence of the better-travelled players was fabulously complex and even it only showed major civilisations; those with just a few solar systems to their name didn't really show up, even with the holo-map filling one's entire field of vision. Generally overlapping, often deeply interconnected, slowly shifting, subject to continual gradual and very occasionally quite sudden change, the result looked like something committed by a madman let loose in a paint factory.

The Morthanveld held sway over vast regions of space, one tiny pocket of which happened to include the star around which her home planet orbited. They had been there, or spreading slowly out in that direction, for longer than the Culture had existed, and the two civilisations had long since settled into a comfortable and peaceful co-existence, though the Morthanveld did expect all but the most pressing business crossing their sphere of influence to be conducted using their own spacecraft.

Having immersed herself in the politics, geography, technology and mythology of Prasadal for over two intense, demanding years, and having almost ignored outside events for the same amount of time, Anaplian realised she had half forgotten that the Culture was not somehow the totality of the galactic community – that it was, indeed, a relatively small part, even if it was a powerful and almost defiantly widespread one.

"Would I be excused here?" she asked Batra.

"Djan Seriy," the metallic bush said, and for the first time something other than its pretended face moved, its sides expanding in a gesture that looked a lot like a human spreading their arms, "you are a free agent. Nothing keeps you here but you. You may go at any time."

"But would I be welcome back? Would I still have a place in SC if I did return home? Could I come back here, to Prasadal?"

"None of that is for me finally to decide."

The creature was being evasive. It would have a say, even if the final decision might be made by some tiny clique of ship Minds spread throughout the Culture and across the galaxy.

Anaplian arched one eyebrow. "Take a guess."

"SC, I'd imagine, yes. Here? I can only imagine. How long would you be going for, do you think?"

"I don't know," Anaplian admitted.

"And neither would we. It is unlikely you would start any return journey within a few days of arriving. You might be gone a standard year, all told. Perhaps longer; who can say? We would have to replace you here."

There was a degree of margin in the system here, of course. Her colleagues could fill in for her, for a while at least. Leeb Scoperin especially knew what Anaplian had been doing in her part of the planet and seemed to have the sort of natural understanding of her aims and techniques that would let him take over her role with as little turbulence as possible, plus he was one of those training an assistant, so the overall burden wouldn't be too great. But that sort of arrangement would not do for ever. A little slack was one thing, but leaving people feeling useless for extended amounts of time was pointless and wasteful, so the platform was not overstaffed for the task in hand. Batra was right; they'd have to replace her.

"You could give me a ship," Anaplian said. That would get her there and back quicker.

"Ah," Batra said. "That is problematical." This was one of his several ways of saying no.

The Culture was being especially careful not to offend the Morthanveld at the moment. The reason was officially moot, though there had been some interesting suggestions and one in particular that had become the default explanation.

Anaplian sighed. "I see."

Or she could just stay here, she supposed. What good, after all, could she do back home? Avenge her father? That was not a daughter's duty, the way the Sarl saw things, and anyway it sounded like the Deldeyn were about to have more than sufficient vengeance visited upon them long before she would be able to get there. Her father would have been the aggressor in all this, anyway; she had no doubt that the pre-emptive attack the Deldeyn had launched was anything other than just that – an attempt to stop the Sarl under King Hausk invading them.

Perhaps she would just make a bad situation worse if she

went back; things would be in turmoil enough without her suddenly reappearing. She had been away too long, she thought. People would have forgotten about her, and everything would have changed. Anyway, she was female. After fifteen years living in the Culture, it was sometimes hard to recall just how misogynist her birth-society had been. She might go back and try to affect things only to be laughed at, scorned, ignored. Oramen was clever if still young. He'd be all right, wouldn't he? Tyl Loesp would take care of him.

Her duty, arguably, lay here. This was what she had taken on, this was what she had to do, what she was expected to finish. She knew that could affect the course of history on Prasadal. It might not always go as she'd wish, and it could be bloody, but her influence was in no doubt and she knew that she was good at what she did. On the Eighth – and the Ninth, given that the Deldeyn had been forced into the matter – she might effect nothing, or only harm.

That was not what she was being trained to do.

Her father had sent her to the Culture as payment, if you wished to be brutal about it. She was here as the result of a debt of honour. She had not been banked far away from Sursamen as some sort of insurance, neither was it assumed she would be educated further and returned an even more fit bride for some foreign prince, to cement an alliance or tie-in a far away conquerance. Her duty, in perpetuity, was to serve the Culture to repay it for the help – through the man called Xide Hyrlis – it had given her father and the Sarl people. King Hausk had made it perfectly clear that he did not expect ever to see his only daughter again.

Well, he had been right about that.

When this bargain had first been suggested, she had struggled with the competing emotions of pride at being asked to play such an important role, and anguish at experiencing a rejection even more final and complete than all the other rejections her father had made her suffer. At the same time there had been a kind of triumph coursing through her that had been stronger still than either feeling.

At last! At last she would be free of this idiot backwater, at last she could develop as she wished, not as her father and this female-fearing, woman-demeaning society demanded. She was accepting an obligation she might spend the rest of her life fulfilling, but it was one that would take her away from the Eighth, away from the Sarl and the constrictions of the life she had gradually realised – with increasing dismay through her girlhood – she would otherwise have been expected to lead. She would still be going into service, but it was service in faraway exotic places, service in a greater cause and perhaps even one that actually involved action, not simply the requirement to please a man and produce a litter of petty royals.

Her father had thought the Culture representatives effeminate fools for being more interested in her than in her brothers when he'd insisted on sending one of his children into their employ. Even his respect for Xide Hyrlis had suffered, when he too had suggested little Djan should be the one to go, and Anaplian didn't know of anyone, save perhaps tyl Loesp, that her father had thought as highly of as Hyrlis.

Her father had barely pretended to be sorry that they had chosen his troublesome, discontented, discounted daughter rather than one of his precious sons. If, of course, she wished to go; the Culture's representatives made it very clear that they had no desire to coerce her into their employ. Naturally, as soon as they'd asked she'd had no choice – her father had been convinced he'd been presented with an absolute bargain, and hurried her departure before the Culture could see sense and change its mind – but it was precisely what she would have chosen anyway.

She had pretended. She had pretended – to her father and the rest of the court – to be reluctant to go to the Culture, in just the way that a girl chosen to be a bride was expected to pretend to be reluctant to go to her new home and husband, and she had trusted that the Culture people would see that this was an act, for appearances' sake, to observe the niceties. They had, and she'd duly gone with them when the time came. She had never regretted it for a moment.

There had been times, many of them, when she'd missed her home and her brothers and even her father, times when she'd cried herself to sleep for many nights at a time, but not once, not even for an instant, had she thought that she might have made the wrong choice.

Her duty was here, then. Her father had said so. The Culture – Special Circumstances, no less – assumed so, and was relying on her to remain here. No one on the Eighth would expect her to return. And if she did, there was probably nothing useful she could do.

Yet what was duty? What was obligation?

She had to go, and knew it in her bones.

She had been silent just a few moments. She did something she only ever did with reluctance, and clicked into her neural lace and through it into the vast, bludgeoningly vivid meta-existence that was the SC version of the Culture's dataverse.

A clamorous, phantasmagoric scape opened instantly in front of her and flicked all around. Confronting, pervading Anaplian in this mind-dazzling, seemingly frozen blink of time was a collection of inputs using every amended-range sense available; this barely graspable riot of sensory overload presented itself initially as a sort of implied surrounding sphere, along with the bizarre but perfectly convincing sensation that you could see every part of it at once, and in more colours than even the augmented eye possessed. The immediately appreciable surface of this vast enclosing globe was less than tissue thin, yet seemed to connect with senses deep inside her as the colossal but intricate simulation suffused into what felt like every fragment of her being. You thought through to an apparent infinitude of further membranes, each with its own sensory harmonics, like a lens adjusting to bring different depths within its field of vision into focus.

It was a given that this perceptual frenzy was as close as a human, or anything like a human, could get to knowing what it was like to be a Mind. Only politeness prevented most Minds pointing out that this was the drastically coarsened, savagely cut-down, vastly inferior, well-below-nursery-level version of what they themselves were immersed within throughout every moment of their existence.

Even without consciously thinking about it, she was there with a diagrammatic and data-ended representation of this section of the galaxy. The stars were shown as exaggerated points of their true colour, their solar systems implied in log-scaled plunge-foci and their civilisational flavour defined by musical note-groups (the influence of the Culture was signalled by a chord sequence constructed from mathematically pure whole-tone scales reaching forever down and up). An overlay showed the course schedules of all relevant ships and a choice of routes was already laid out for her, colour-coded in order of speed, strand thickness standing for ship size and schedule certainty shown by hue intensity, with comfort and general amenability characterised as sets of smells. Patterns on the strands – making them look braided, like rope – indicated to whom the ships belonged.

Circles and ellipses, mostly, confronted her. A few supplementally more complicated shapes squiggled through the view where ships anticipated describing more eccentric courses between the stars over the next few tens and hundreds of standard days.

Seemingly unbidden, another line formed in the overlay, almost perfectly straight, showing her how quickly the nearest available unit of the Culture's fleet of Very Fast Pickets could get her there. Crude flight time was a little over a dozen days, though it would take almost as long for the ship to get to Prasadal to pick her up in the first place. Other ships could have made the journey in even less time, though they were too far away. There was a degree of favourable uncertainty in the projection; it applied only to Culture vessels that were currently making their whereabouts known. It was entirely possible that another ship of the Rapid Asset fleet not currently bothering

to circulate its location was even closer and would respond positively to a broadcast request.

But that wasn't going to happen – Batra had made that clear.
She wiped the offending overlay from the view. She would have
to take the prescribed route, and be passed like a baton from
ship to ship. It looked complicated.

A lot of very clever processing had already gone on in her
neural lace to predict what she'd want to look at effectively
before she knew herself, and – fabulously convenient and
highly technically impressive though this might be – it was
this aspect of lace-use that most disturbed Anaplian and
caused her to keep its application to a minimum. In the end,
she didn't even need to pull out any data-ends to check the
raw figures; there was one fairly obvious route through this
tangled scribble from Prasadal to Sursamen, and it would
indeed take at least one hundred and twenty-nine and a bit
days if she left any time within the next two days, assuming
that the Morthanveld end of things went as fortuitously as it
might. A lot seemed to depend on whether the Morthanveld
Great Ship *Inspiral, Coalescence, Ringdown* decided to take
in the Nestworld Syaung-un on its way from one globular
cluster to another.

She was about to click out when a barely formed thought
regarding exactly what a Morthanveld Great Ship and a
Nestworld actually were started to blossom into a whole hierarchy of increasingly complicated explanations as the lace raced
to retrieve and present the relevant information with all the
desperate enthusiasm of an overenthusiastic child asked to
perform a party piece. She shut it down with a sort of inward
slam and clicked out again with the usual sense of relief and
vague guilt. The last vestige of the lace's presence informed her
that her heart was still completing the beat it had been beginning when she'd first clicked in.

It was like waking up, though from a dream world where
everything was more detailed, vivid, splendid and even plausible than reality, not less. That was another reason she didn't

like using the lace. She wondered briefly how Jerle Batra's normality compared to hers.

"I'm sorry. I think I have to go," she told him.

"Think, Djan Seriy?" Batra asked, sounding sad.

"I am going," she said. "I must."

"I see." Now the man who looked like a fuzzy little bush sounded apologetic. "There will be a cost, Djan Seriy."

"I know."

6. Scholastery

Ferbin otz Aelsh-Hausk'r and his servant Choubris Holse were riding along an ill-kept road through a forest of cloud trees towards the Xiliskine-Anjrinh Scholastery. They had chosen to travel through the long half-night of the Rollstar Guime, which showed as a sullen red glow spread like a rosy bruise across the farpole horizon. They had pulled off the road only twice so far, once to avoid a troop of mounted Ichteuen and once when a steam truck had appeared in the far distance. The prince no longer looked like himself; Holse had close-cut his scalp, his facial hair was growing quickly (darker than his head hair; nearly brown, which peeved him disproportionately), he had removed all his rings and other regal jewellery and he was dressed in clothes Holse had obtained from the battlefield.

"From a *corpse*?" Ferbin had spluttered, staring down at

himself wide-eyed. Holse had thought to inform the prince of the provenance of his new-to-him civvies only after he'd put them on.

"One with no obvious wounds, sir," Holse had assured him reasonably. "Just a little bleeding from the ears and nose. Dead a good two or three days, too, so any fleas would assuredly have caught cold and jumped ship. And he was a gentleman, too, I might add. An army private provisioner, unless I'm mistaken."

"That's not a gentleman," Ferbin had told his servant patiently. "That's a merchant." He'd pulled at his sleeves, held out his hands and shaken his head.

If there had been any aerial activity – unlikely in the near darkness – they didn't see it. At any rate, nobody came swooping down to inspect them as they trudged on, Holse on his rowel and Ferbin on the mersicor his servant had brought to the folly overlooking the river four days earlier. Holse had dug a couple of wads of crile root from a saddle bag to help keep them awake as they rode, and they chewed on this while they talked. It gave their conversation what Holse felt was a rather comical, munchy sort of quality, though he thought better of mentioning this to Ferbin.

"Choubris Holse, it is your duty to accompany me to wherever I might choose to go."

"I'd beg to differ, sir."

"There's no differing involved. Duty is duty. Yours is to me."

"Within the kingdom, and within the rule of the king's law, I'd not argue with you, sir. It is my duty beyond that reach I might think to question."

"Holse! You are a servant! I am a prince! You'd be best advised to do as you're damn well told even were I some lowly gent with no more than a tumbledown fort, a flea-bitten nag and too many children to his name. As servant to a prince – the senior prince, I might add – of the royal house of Hausk . . ." Ferbin broke off, choking on his own amazement and disgust at encountering such obduracy in a servant. "My father would have you *thrashed* for this, Holse, I tell you! Or worse! Damn it, man, I am the rightful *king*!"

"Sir, I am with you now, and intend to stay with you until the varsity and thence to whatever conveyance you might find beyond that which they are able to recommend you to. To that very point I shall be at your side, as faithful as ever."

"And there you damn well have to stay! Wherever I go!"

"Sir, pleasing your pardon, my allegiance – at the bottom of the pot, after all reduction, as it were – is to the throne rather than to your good self. Once you remove yourself from the furthest extent of your father's conquests, it is my understanding that I am bound to return to the seat of authority – which I would take to be the royal palace in Pourl, all other matters being in normal balance – there to take fresh instruction from, well, whomsoever—"

"Holse! Are you a lawyer?"

"Dear God forbid, sir!"

"Then shut up. Your duty is to stay with me. That's the all and end of it."

"My duty, begging your pardon, sir, is to the king."

"But I *am* the king! Haven't you been telling me for the last four days that I'm the rightful heir to the throne?"

"Sir, excuse my bluntness, but you are an uncrowned king who is riding most determinedly away from his throne."

"Yes! Yes, to save my life! To seek help so that I may return to claim that throne, if the WorldGod lets. And, I would point out, in doing so I am following the highest precedents; does not the WorldGod find its own sanctuary from cares here at the core of our blessed world? Did not the Sarl people themselves flee persecution on their homeworld, escaping here to our own dear Sursamen?"

"Still, sir. Being a king has its expectations. One is letting people know you're alive."

"Is it *really*? Well, *well*," Ferbin said, deciding to be witheringly sarcastic. "Do you tell me that now? And what else, might one ask?"

"Well, sir, acting in a kingly manner regarding the taking up of the reins of power, by dispute if needs be, rather than leaving them to fall to—"

"Choubris Holse, you will *not* lecture me in the art of kingcraft or my regal obligations and responsibilities!"

"Indeed not, sir. I agree most completely. Lecturing is the province of the scholastic monk types towards which we make our way. No argument there from me, sir."

Holse's rowel snored as though in agreement. Their animals were bred to night-walk and could literally walk in their sleep, though they needed the odd prod to keep them on the road.

"I decide my duty, Holse, not you! And my duty is not to let myself be murdered by those who have already killed one king and would not flinch from adding another – that is, me – to their score!"

Holse looked up at the near-unGodly vastness of the Hicturean Tower, rising to their left like fate. The sky-supporting stem was skirted with grassed and forested slopes, their steepness increasing as they approached the topmost edge where, piled up against the smooth, uncanny surface of the Tower, the ground and foliage broke like a dark green wave against the trunk's vast pale roundness, glowing in the low red light like the bone of some long-dead god.

Holse cleared his throat. "These documents we go in search of, sir. They don't work the other way, do they?"

"The other way? What *do* you mean, Holse?"

"Well, would they let you travel downwards, to the Core, to see the WorldGod, sir?" Holse had no idea how these things worked; he had never really bothered with religion, though he had always paid lip-service to the church for the sake of an easy life. He had long suspected that the WorldGod was just another convenient semi-fiction supporting the whole structure that sustained the rich and powerful in their privilege. "To see if its Divineness might help you?" He shrugged. "It would save all the bother of travelling to the Surface and then to the external stars, sir."

"That is impossible, Holse," Ferbin said patiently, trying not to lose his temper at such childish drivel. "The Oct and – thank God – the Aultridia are forbidden from interfering with the WorldGod; they may not descend to the Core. Therefore neither may we." He might have replied at greater length, but – following an inopportune partial inhaling of a well-chewed wad of crile root – he was struck by an attack of coughing, and spent much of the next few minutes wheezing and spluttering and refusing Holse's repeated offers to administer a forceful slap on the back.

The Hicturean-Anjrinh Scholastery sat on a low hill a day's ride from the Hicturean Tower in the direction of nearpole, so that the great column was almost directly between it and Pourl. Like most Scholasteries, the place was forbidding-looking, even if technically it was unfortified. It looked like a long, low castle with its curtain wall removed. It had two turrets, but they housed telescopes rather than guns. The visible walls actually looked quite jolly, painted in all sorts of different colours, but it still appeared somehow grim to Ferbin. He had always been rather in awe of such places and the people who inhabited them. To give yourself up to a life of study, thought and contemplation seemed like, well, such a waste. He tipped continually between contempt for anyone who could cut themselves off from so much that made life fun just to pursue this abstraction they called learning, and something close to reverence, deeply impressed that seriously clever people would willingly choose such an abstemious existence.

It was to one of these places that he knew Djan Seriy would have wanted to go, had she been free to choose. She hadn't been, of course, and anyway the Culture had made off with her. Some of her letters home to her family after she had gone with them had spoken of places of learning that sounded a lot like Scholasteries. Ferbin had formed the impression that she'd learned a great deal. (Far too much, in the snorting estimation of their father.) Later letters seemed to hint that she had become some sort of warrior, almost a champion. They had worried about her sanity at first, but woman warriors were not unknown. Everybody had thought they belonged firmly in the past, but – well – who knew? The ways of the aliens – the superior, mentor and Optimae races, and who could say what others – were beyond knowing. So much of life went in great circles, in wheels of good and ill fortune; maybe woman warriors were part of some utterly strange and incomprehensible future.

Ferbin hoped she was a warrior. If he could get to her, or at least get word to her, Djan Seriy might be able to help him.

The Rollstar Obor was spreading a slow, reluctant dawn to their right as they approached. They passed apprentice scholars leaving the Scholastery compound to work in the fields, orchards and streams around the jumble of gaily painted buildings. They nodded, helloed, waved hats. Ferbin thought they looked almost happy.

An increasing number of the cities of the Sarl were becoming host to something like a Scholastery, though these urban institutions offered more practical instruction than the ancient, usually remote and rural Scholasteries. Many merchants and even some nobles were starting to send their sons to such modern varsities, and Ferbin had heard of one in Reshigue that accepted only girls. (Though that was Reshigue, and everybody knew the people of that thankfully distant city were mad.)

"No telegraph connection that I can see," Holse pointed out, casting his gaze about the jumble of buildings. "That may be to the good. We'll see."

"Hmm?" Ferbin said.

Ferbin rarely prayed. It was a failing, he knew, but then a noble one, he'd always told himself. Even Gods, he felt sure, must have limited patience and even attention. By not praying he was leaving the floor of the divine court that little bit less crowded and so free for more deserving, less fortunate people whose own prayers would therefore stand by that same increment more likely to be heard above whatever hubbub must surely fill said assembly. In fact, he took comfort in the fact that, being a prince, his entreaties would of course have been given priority in the WorldGod's petitionary court – he would have had a naturally louder voice, as it were – and so by his modest, self-effacing absence, he did far more good than a fellow of more limited importance would have done by such an act of self-sacrifice.

Still, the WorldGod was there, and – while going to see it, as Holse had suggested, was patently ridiculous – prayers were assuredly listened to. Sometimes, indeed, the WorldGod was said to intervene in the affairs of people, taking up the cause of the good and just and punishing those who had sinned. It would, therefore, positively be dereliction of princely duty not to entreat the deity. Even if it did – as it surely would – already know of the terrible events that had befallen Ferbin and which might be about to befall the Sarl people as a whole with a usurper in their midst and indeed in charge, the WorldGod might not feel able to act until it had received a sort of formal request from him, the rightful king. He wasn't sure exactly how these things worked, never having paid attention in Divinity classes, but he had a feeling it might be something like that.

"Dear God, God of the World. Support me in my cause, let me escape my pursuers, if, ah, assuming there are pursuers. If not, then let there continue not to be any. Aid my getting out of the World and finding Xide Hyrlis and my dear sister Djan, that she may succour me. Let her be not turned away from her brother by the luxuries and, umm, luxuriances of the Culture people. Please, God, visit the most terrible and disgusting tribulations and humiliations upon the filthy usurper tyl Loesp, who killed my father. There is a foul fiend indeed, God! There is a monster in the form of man! You must have seen what happened, God, and if not, look into my memory and see it seared in there like a brand, burned and fixed for ever – what more awful crime has there ever been? What ghastliness committed between your skies can outdo that atrocity?"

Ferbin found he was growing breathless, and had to stop to collect himself. "God, if you punish him most severely, I shall rejoice. If not, then I shall take it as a sure and certain sign that you grant him not even the honour of divine retribution but leave his punishment for human hand. That hand may not be my own – I am, as your good self knows, more of a man of peace than of action – but it will be at my instigation, I swear, and it will be a sorry tower of anguish and despair that bastard suffers beneath. And the others, all who helped him; all them too. I do swear this, on the violated body of my own dearly loved father!" Ferbin swallowed, coughed. "You know I ask this for my people, not for myself, God; I never wanted to be king, though I will accept this burden when it falls to me. Elime; he should have been the king. Or Oramen might make a good king one day. I . . . I'm not sure I'd be very good at it. I never have been sure. But, sir, duty is duty."

Ferbin wiped some tears away from his tightly closed eyes. "Thank you for this, my God. Oh; also, I would ask you to make my idiot servant see where his true duty lies and get him to stay with me. I have no skill negotiating the base vulgarities of life, whereas he has and, argumentative wretch though he may be, he makes progress the smoother for me. I've hardly dared let him out of my sight since I began to worry he might run off and I cannot think how daunting my way would be without him. Please also let the Head Scholar here, one Seltis, be well disposed to me and not remember that it was I who put the tack on his seat that time, or the maggot into his pie on that other occasion. Actually, twice, come to think of it. Anyway, let him have a Tower travel warrant thing that he doesn't mind letting me have so that I can get away from here. Grant me all of this, WorldGod, and on my father's life I swear I shall build a temple to your greatness, mercy and wisdom that will challenge the Towers themselves! Umm . . . Right. With all my –

ah, well, that's all." Ferbin sat back, opening his eyes, then closed them and went on one knee again. "Oh, and ah, thank you."

He had been given a small cell in the Scholastery after they'd arrived and announced themselves as a gentleman traveller and his assistant (a title – a promotion, even – that Holse had insisted upon) who had need of an audience with the Head Scholar. Ferbin found it strange to be treated like an ordinary person. In a way it was almost fun, but it was also a little shaming and even annoying, despite the fact it was this disguise of ordinariness that might well be all that was keeping him alive. Being asked to wait while anybody other than his father found time to see him was a novel experience, too. Well, not that novel, perhaps; certain ladies of his knowledge were prone to such tactics too. But that was a delicious sort of waiting, even if, at the time, seemingly intolerable. This was not delicious at all, this was frustrating.

He sat on the small sleeping platform in the little room, looked round the bare, sparsely furnished space and briefly took in the view towards the Hicturean Tower – most Scholastery windows looked towards Towers if they could. He looked down at his clothes, stolen from a dead man. He shivered, and was hugging himself when the door was struck loudly and almost before he could say, "Enter," Choubris Holse had swung into the room, looking unsteady, his face flushed.

"Sir!" Holse said, then seemed to collect himself, drawing himself up and producing a nod that might have been the remnants of a bow. He smelled of smoke. "The Head Scholar will see you now, sir."

"I shall be there directly, Holse," Ferbin said, then, recalling that the WorldGod allegedly helped those most given to helping themselves – a treatise Holse himself most obviously lived by – he added, "Thank you."

Holse frowned and looked confused.

"Seltis! My dear old friend! It is I!" Ferbin entered the office of the Head Scholar of Hicturean-Anjrinh Scholastery and held his arms open. The elderly man in slightly worn-looking scholastic robes sat on the far side of a broad, paper-littered desk, blinking behind small round glasses.

"That you are you, sir, is one of life's great undeniables," he replied. "Do you apply for position by stating such truisms and claiming them profound?"

Ferbin looked round to make sure the door had been closed from outside by the serving scholar who had let him in. He smiled and approached the Head Scholar's desk, arms still outspread. "No, Seltis, I mean, it is *I*!" He lowered his voice. "Ferbin. Who once was your most exasperating yet still I hope most loved pupil. You must pardon my disguise, and I am glad that it is so effective, but it is most assuredly me. Hello, old friend and most wise tutor!"

Seltis rose, an expression of some wonder and uncertainty on his withered face. He made a small bow. "By God, I do believe it might be, too." His gaze searched Ferbin's face. "How are you, boy?"

"No longer a boy, Seltis," Ferbin said, taking a comfortable seat to one side of the desk, in a small bay window. Seltis remained at his desk, looking over a small cart full of books at his former pupil. Ferbin let a serious, even tormented expression take over his features. "Rather a young man, old friend, and a happy, carefree one at that, until a few days ago. Dear Seltis, I saw my own father murdered in the most obscene circumstance—"

Seltis looked alarmed and held up one hand. He turned away from Ferbin and said, "Munhreo, leave us, please."

"Yes, Head Scholar," said another voice, and, somewhat to Ferbin's horror, a young man dressed in the robes of a junior scholar rose from a small, paper-piled desk set in one alcove of the room and – with a fascinated glance at Ferbin – went to leave the room.

"Munhreo," the Head Scholar said to the youth as he was

opening the door. The young scholar turned round. "You heard nothing, do you understand?"

The young scholar made a small bow. "Indeed, sir."

"Ah. He must study the art of hiding, that one, eh?" Ferbin said awkwardly after the door had closed.

"He is trustworthy, I believe," Seltis said. He drew his own seat over and sat by Ferbin, still studying his face. "Remind me; my assistant at the palace – who would that have been?"

Ferbin frowned, blew out his cheeks. "Oh. I don't know. Youngish chap. Can't recall his name." He grinned. "Sorry."

"And did I ever implant the name of the capital of Voette sufficiently well for it to take root?"

"Ah. Voette. Knew an ambassador's daughter from there once. Lovely girl. She was from ... Nottle? Gottle? Dottle? Something like that. That right?"

"The capital of Voette is Wiriniti, Ferbin," Seltis said wearily. "And I truly do believe you are who you say."

"Excellent!"

"Welcome, sir. I have to say, though, we had been informed that you were killed, prince."

"And if the wishes of that murderous, scheming turd tyl Loesp made such things so, I would be, old friend."

Seltis looked alarmed. "The new regent? What's the cause of this hatred?"

Ferbin related the fundamentals of his story since the moment he and his party had crested the Cherien ridge and looked out over the great battlefield. Seltis sighed, polished his glasses twice, sat back, sat forward again, stood up at one point, walked round his seat, looked out through the window and sat back down again. He shook his head a few times.

"And so myself and my unreliable servant are here to ask for your help, dear Seltis, firstly in getting a message to Oramen and also in getting me away from the Eighth and from the great World itself. I have to warn my brother and seek my sister. I am that reduced. My sister has been with these Optimae the Culture for many years and has, by her own account, learned such things that even you might find impressive. She may even have become a sort of female warrior, as I understand it. In any event, she might have – or can call upon – powers and influences that I myself cannot. Help me make my way to her, Seltis, and help me warn my brother, and my gratitude, I swear, will be great. I am the rightful king even if I am not the anointed monarch; my formal ascension lies in the future, as must your reward. Even so, one as wise and learned as yourself no doubt understands even better than I the duty a subject owes to their sovereign. I trust you see that I ask for no more than I have every right to expect."

"Well, Ferbin," the old scholar said, sitting back in his seat and taking his glasses off again to inspect them, "I don't know which would be the more confounding; that all you say is true, or that your skills in fictive composition have suddenly improved a million-fold." He placed his glasses back on his nose. "Truthfully, I would rather that what you say is not so. I would rather believe that you did not have to witness what you did, that your father was not murdered, and our regent is not a monster, but I think I have to believe that all you claim is true. I am sorry for your loss, Ferbin, beyond words. But in any case, I hope you see that it is as well I attempt to restrict your stay here to a minimum. I will certainly do all I can to assist you on your way and I shall depute one of my senior tutors to take a message to your brother."

"Thank you, old friend," Ferbin said, relieved.

"However. You should know that there are rumours against you, Ferbin. They say that you deserted the battlefield shortly before your death, and that many other crimes, large and small, domestic and social, are being piled against you, now that you are thought safely dead."

"*What?*" Ferbin shouted.

"As I say," Seltis said. "They seek, by the sound of it, to make you ill-missed and, perhaps – if they suspect you are not dead – to make it the more likely that you will be betrayed by anyone you reveal yourself to. Take all care, young man that was boy, and prince that hopes to be king."

"Inequity upon infamy," Ferbin breathed, his mouth drying as he spoke. "Injustice piled upon outrage. Intolerable. Intolerable." A terrible anger built within him, causing his hands to shake. He stared at his trembling fingers, marvelling at such a physical effect. He swallowed, looking at his old tutor with tears in his eyes. "I tell you, Seltis, at every point at which I feel my rage cannot conceivably grow any further, having reached the outermost extremity of that possible for a man to bear, I am propelled further into indecent fury by the next action of that unspeakable puddle of excrement tyl Loesp."

"Taking account of all you say," Seltis said, rising, "that is hardly to be wondered at." He went to a sash hanging by the wall behind his desk. "Will you have something to drink?"

"Some respectable wine would not go amiss," Ferbin said, brightening. "My servant favours stuff you'd hesitate to rinse a rowel's arse with."

Seltis pulled on the sash. A gong rang distantly. He came and sat down with the prince again.

"I take it you wish me to recommend you to the Oct, for enTowerment, for transportation to the Surface."

"Whatever you call it," Ferbin said eagerly, sitting forward. "Yes. Naturally there are, in theory, royal prerogatives I might use, but that would amount to suicide. With a pass from you, I might hope to evade tyl Loesp's spies and informants."

"Rather more than just spies and informants; in potential, at least, the whole of the army, and even all of the people," Seltis said. "Everyone, thinking themselves loyal, will be turned against the one they ought to be loyal to."

"Indeed," Ferbin said. "I must trust to my own wits and those of my irritating but wily servant."

Seltis looked concerned, Ferbin thought.

A servant came to the door and wine was ordered. When the door was closed again, Ferbin leant forward and said solemnly, "I have prayed to the WorldGod, good Seltis."

"That can do no harm," the Head Scholar said, looking no less concerned.

Someone rapped loudly on the door. "Enter!" Seltis called. "The kitchens are not usually so—"

Choubris Holse lunged into the room, nodded briefly at the Head Scholar and to Ferbin said, "Sir; I fear we are discovered."

Ferbin leapt to his feet. "What? How?"

Holse looked uncertainly at Seltis. "Little scholar fellow on the roof, sir; heliographed a passing patrol. Three knights on caude just coming in to land."

"Munhreo," the Head Scholar said, also standing.

"Maybe they're just . . . visiting?" Ferbin suggested.

"In the circumstances, assume the worst," Seltis told him, moving to his desk. "You'd best get going. I'll try to detain them as long as I can."

"We'll never outrun them on mounts!" Ferbin protested. "Seltis, do you have any flying beasts?"

"No, Ferbin. We do not." He took a small key from a drawer, kicked a rug behind his desk against the wall and, grunting, knelt on the boards, opening a small hatch in the floor and taking out two thick, heavy grey envelopes stoutly secured with thin metal bands. He opened a flap in each package and quickly wrote their names, then stamped the Scholastery seal on them. "Here," he said, handing the envelopes to Ferbin. "The D'neng-oal Tower. The Towermaster is one Aiaik."

"Ake," Ferbin said.

Seltis tutted and spelled the name for him.

"Aiaik," Ferbin said. "Thank you, Seltis." He turned to his servant. "Holse, what are we going to do?"

Holse looked pained. "I have, reluctantly, had an idea, sir."

The three caude were tied to a hitching ring on the flat roof of the Scholastery's main building. A small crowd of mostly young scholars and servants had gathered to gape at the great air beasts, which had settled on their haunches on the roof and were munching on whatever was in their nose bags, giving every impression of ignoring the crowd around them with a degree of disdain. A warm, gusting wind ruffled their crests and made the gaudy coverings under their saddles flap. Ferbin and Holse hurried up the steps and crossed the roof.

"Make way!" Holse shouted, striding through the crowd. Ferbin drew himself up to his full height and strode manfully too, affecting an expression of hauteur.

"Yes! Out of my way!" he yelled.

Holse moved a couple of youthful scholars aside with the flat of his hand and then pointed at another. "You! Untie the beasts. Just two. Now!"

"I was told to guard them, by their riders," the youth protested.

"And I'm telling you to untie them," Holse said drawing his short-sword.

What a sheltered life they must lead here, Ferbin thought as the youngster's eyes went wide and he started fumbling with the reins of one of the beasts. Amazed at the sight of caude and impressed by a drawn sword!

"You!" Holse shouted at another youth. "Help him."

Ferbin felt rather proud of Holse, if a little envious too. Even resentful, he admitted to himself. He wished he could do something dynamic, or at least useful. He looked at the twenty or so faces confronting him, trying to remember what the scholar called Munhreo had looked like.

"Is Munhreo here?" he said loudly, cutting through a dozen muttered conversations.

"Sir, he went with the knights," said one voice. The various conversations resumed. Ferbin glanced back at the stairs that led to the roof. "Who's most senior here?" he barked.

Looks were exchanged. In a moment, one tall scholar stepped forward. "I am."

"You are aware what these are?" Ferbin asked, pulling the two fat envelopes from his jacket. More wide eyes, and some nodding. "If you are loyal to your Head Scholar and your rightful king, guard that stairway with your life. Make sure nobody else comes up it, and stop anybody from leaving the roof too, until we've gone."

"Sir." The tall scholar looked initially doubtful, but he took a couple of his peers and went to stand by the steps.

"The rest of you, kindly stand over there," Ferbin said, indicating the far corner of the roof. There was some muttering, but the scholars complied. He turned back. Holse was removing the nose bag from one of the caude. He emptied the bag with a flick while the creature was mewling in protest, turned the caude round to face towards the nearest edge of the roof and then quickly threw the emptied bag over the beast's head. "Do the same with the other one, would you, sir?" he asked Ferbin, and moved to the caude which was still tied up. "Make sure it points the same way as that one."

Ferbin did as he'd been asked, starting to understand why. He felt sick. The two caude with the nose bags over their heads laid their heads obediently on the surface of the roof and might already have been asleep.

Holse gentled the third caude, patting its nose and murmuring to it even as he brought the short-sword to its long neck. He slashed its throat, deep and hard, and the creature jerked back, snapped its tied reins and fell over backwards, wings half extending then folding back again, long legs kicking, then – to the shocked cries of several of the scholars – it went still, dark blood pooling on the roof's dusty paving.

Holse flicked blood from his sword, sheathed it and strode past Ferbin. He whipped the nose bags off the two surviving caude; their heads rose and deep grumbling noises issued from their wide mouths. "Jump on, sir," he said. "Try and keep it from seeing the dead one."

Ferbin mounted the nearest caude, fitting himself into the deep saddle and drawing its belt over while Holse was doing the same. Ferbin was buttoning his jacket tight when his caude bent its long leathery neck back and looked at him with what might have been a puzzled expression, possibly registering the fact that it had a rider different from the one it was used to.

Caude were fabulously stupid animals; the intelligence had been bred out of them as obedience and stamina had been bred in. Ferbin had never heard of one being trained to accept just one rider. He patted the beast's face and sorted its reins, then kicked its sides and got it to rise on its great long legs and half open its wings with a dry, rustling sound. Suddenly he was towering over the collection of startled, shocked-looking scholars.

"Ready?" Holse shouted.

"Ready!" Ferbin yelled.

They kicked the caude forward to the edge of the roof; the animals jumped on to the parapet and in the same heart-stopping movement launched themselves into the air just as shouts from the stairway end of the roof rang out. Ferbin whooped, half in fear and half in excitement, as the great wings opened with a snap and he and the caude started to fall towards a flagstoned court-yard half a dozen storeys below, the air roaring in his ears. The caude began pulling out of its dive, heavying him into the saddle; the wind screamed about him and he caught a glimpse of Holse to his side, grim-faced, hands clenched round the reins as they levelled out and the giant beasts took their first flap at the air. Distant popping noises behind them might have been gunfire. Something whizzed past between his caude and Holse's, but then they were beating out away from the Scholastery over the fields and streams.

7. Reception

A reception was held in a grand drawing room of the palace after the state funeral of the late king and his internment in the Hausk family mausoleum, which lay some distance outside the farpole edge of the city walls. It had rained since morning and the day was still dark beyond the tall windows of the great room. Hundreds of candles burned by mirrored walls; the King had recently had installed lights which consumed lampstone, and others which arced electricity to make light, but both had proved problematic in operation and Oramen was glad to see the candles. They gave a softer light and the room didn't stink of the noxious gases the other types of lamp gave off.

"Fanthile!" Oramen said, seeing the palace secretary.

"Sir." Fanthile, in his most formal court clothes, all trimmed with mourning red, bowed deeply to the prince. "This is the sorriest of days, sir. We must hope it marks the end of the very sorriest of times."

"My father would have wanted it no other way." Oramen saw a couple of Fanthile's assistants waiting behind him, as good as hopping from foot to foot like children in need of the toilet. He smiled. "I believe you're needed, Fanthile."

"With your leave, sir."

"Of course," Oramen said, and let Fanthile go to arrange whatever needed to be arranged. He supposed it was a busy time for the fellow. Personally he was quite content to stand and watch.

The atmosphere in the echoing great space, it seemed to Oramen, was one almost of relief. He had only recently developed a feeling for things like the atmosphere of a room. Amazingly, this was something Ferbin had purposefully taught him. Before, Oramen had tended to dismiss talk of such abstracts as "atmosphere" as somehow unimportant; stuff adults talked about for want of anything actually worth discussing. Now he knew better and, by measuring his own submerged mood, he could attempt to gauge the emotional tenor of a gathering like this.

Over the years, Oramen had learned much from his older brother – mostly things like how to behave so as to avoid beatings, tutors tearing their hair out, scandalised lenders petitioning one's father for funds to pay gambling debts, outraged fathers and husbands demanding satisfaction, that sort of thing – but this was an instance when Ferbin had had a proper lesson he could actually teach his younger brother, rather than simply exemplifying the bad example.

Ferbin had taught Oramen to listen to his own feelings in such situations. This had not been so easy; Oramen often felt overwhelmed in complicated social environments and had come to believe that he felt every emotion there was to feel at such times (so that they all cancelled each other out), or none at all. Eitherly, the result was that he would just stand there, or sit there, or at rate just be there, at whatever ceremony or gathering he was present at, seemingly near catatonic, feeling thoroughly detached and declutched, a waste to himself and an embarrassment to others. He had never suffered especially as a result of this mild social disability – one could get away with almost anything being the son of the King, as Ferbin seemed to have spent most of his life attempting to prove – however, such incidents had come to annoy him, and he'd known that they would only increase as he grew older and – even as the younger prince – he'd be expected to start taking a fuller part in the ceremonial and social workings of the court.

Gradually, under Ferbin's admittedly casual tutelage, he had learned to seek a sort of calmness in himself and then amplify what feeling was still there, and use that as his marker. So that if, after a little immersion in a social grouping, he still felt tense when he had no particular reason to, then the shared feeling amongst that group must be something similar. If he felt at ease, then that meant the general atmosphere was also placid.

There was, here, he thought – standing looking out over the people collecting in the great drawing room – genuine sadness as well as an undercurrent of apprehension regarding what would happen now with the great king gone (his father's stature had risen all the higher with his death, as if he was already passing into legend), but there was too a kind of excitement; everyone knew that the preparations for the attack on what was thought to be the now near-defenceless Deldeyn were being stepped up and the war – perhaps, as the late king had believed, the last ever war – was therefore approaching its conclusion.

The Sarl would achieve a goal they had been pursuing for almost all the life of their departed king, the Deldeyn would be defeated, the loathsome and hated Aultridia would be confounded, the WorldGod would be protected – who knew? even saved – and the Oct, the long-term allies of the Sarl, would be grateful, one might even say beholden. The New Age of peace, contentment and progress that King Hausk had talked so much about would finally come to pass. The Sarl would have proved themselves as a people and would, as they grew in power and influence within the greater World and eventually within the alien-inhabited skies beyond, take their rightful place as one of the In-Play, as an Involved species and civilisation, a people fit – perhaps, one day, no doubt still some long way in the future – to treat even the Optimae of the galaxy (the Morthanvelds, the Cultures, and who knew what alien others) as their equals.

That had always been his father's ultimate aim, Oramen knew, though Hausk had known that he'd never see that day – neither would Oramen, or any children he would ever have – but it was enough to know that one had done one's bit to further that albeit distant goal, that one's efforts had formed some sturdy part of the foundations for that great tower of ambition and achievement.

The stage is small but the audience is great, had been one of King Hausk's favourite sayings. To some degree he meant that the WorldGod watched and hopefully somehow appreciated what they were doing on its behalf, but there was also the implication that although the Sarl were primitive and their civilisation almost comically undeveloped by the standards of, say, the Oct (never mind the Nariscene, still less the Morthanveld and the other Optimae), nevertheless, greatness lay in doing the best you could with what you were given, and that greatness, that fixity of purpose, strength of resolve and decisiveness of action would be watched and noted by those far more powerful peoples and judged not on an absolute scale (on which it would barely register) but on one relative to the comparatively primitive resources the Sarl had available to them.

In a sense, his father had told him once – his contemplative moods were rare, so memorable – the Sarl and people like them had more power than the ungraspably supreme Optimae peoples with their millions of artificial worlds circling in the sky, their thinking machines that put mere mortals to shame and their billions of starships that sailed the spaces between the stars the way an iron warship cruised the waves. Oramen had found this claim remarkable, to put it kindly.

His father had explained that the very sophistication the Optimae and their like enjoyed acted as binds upon them. For all the legendary size of the great island of stars that existed beyond their own world of Sursamen, the galaxy was a crowded, settled, much-lived-in place. The Optimae – the Morthanveld, the Culture and so on – were self-consciously well-behaved and civilised peoples, and existed hip-by-hip with their fellow inhabitants of the great lens. Their realms and fields of influence – and to a degree their histories, cultures and achievements – tended to intermingle and overlap, reducing their cohesiveness as societies and making a defensive war difficult.

Similarly, there was little or nothing they ever needed to compete for and so might come to arms over. Instead, they were bound by numerous treaties, agreements, accords, conventions and even never fully articulated understandings, all designed to keep the peace, to avoid friction between those who were entirely alien in form to one another, but entirely alike in having reached the plateau of civilisational development where further progress could only take one away from the real life of the galaxy altogether.

The result was that while their individuals had what appeared to be complete freedom within their societies, the societies themselves had very little freedom of movement at all, certainly not that seemingly implied by their colossal martial potential. There was simply not much left for them to do on any grand scale. There were no – or at least very few – great wars at this level, no vast tusslings for position and power except by the slowest and most subtle of manoeuvrings. The last great, or at least fairly substantial conflict had been a millennium of Eighth short-years ago, when the Culture had fought the Idirans, and that had been, bizarrely, over principle, at least on the Culture side. (Oramen suspected that if it had not been Xide Hyrlis himself who had confirmed the truth of this, his father would never have believed anything that seemed to him so decadently preposterous.)

The Optimae had no kings to move a whole people to a single

purpose at once, they had no real enemies they felt they had no choice but to fight, and they had nothing they valued that they could not somehow produce, seemingly at will, cheaply and in whatever quantities they chose, so there were no resources to fight over either.

But they, the Sarl, the people of the Eighth, this little race of men, they and their like were free to pander to their natures and indulge in their disputes untrammelled. They could do, in effect, and within the limits of their technologies, as they liked! Was that not a fine feeling? Some of the treaties the Optimae indulged in amongst themselves were framed so as to *allow* people like the Sarl to behave like this, unfettered, in the name of non-interference and resisting cultural imperialism. Was this not rich? Their licence to fight and lie and cheat their way to power and influence was guaranteed by space-alien statute!

The King had found this thoroughly amusing. The stage is small but the audience is great, he had repeated. But never forget, he had told Oramen, that you might be in more of a theatre than you thought. The abilities of the Optimae easily encompassed watching all that was going on amongst people as defenceless to such technologies as the Sarl. It was one of the ways that the Optimae refreshed their jaded palates and reminded themselves what a more barbarous life was like; they watched, for all the world like gods, and while various agreements and treaties were supposed to control and restrict such spying, they were not always observed.

Decadent it might be, but it was the price a people like the Sarl had to pay, perhaps, for their sanction to behave in ways that the Optimae might otherwise find too distasteful to allow. But never mind; maybe one day the descendants of the Sarl would spend *their* time flying between the stars and watching their own mentored primitives dispute! Happily, by then, his father had informed the youthful Oramen, they would both be long and safely dead.

Who knew to what extent the Sarl were observed? Oramen looked about the great room and wondered. Maybe alien eyes were watching this great mass of people all dressed in their deep red clothes. Maybe they were watching him, right now.

"Oramen, my sweet young prince," the lady Renneque said, suddenly at his side. "You must not just stand there! People will think you a statue! Come, be my escort to the grieving widow, we'll pay what respects are due together. What do you say?"

Oramen smiled and took the lady's offered hand. Renneque was radiantly beautiful in her crimson gown. Her night-dark hair was not quite perfectly contained in a scarlet mourning cap; ringlets and curls had sprung out here and there, framing her perfectly smooth and flawless face.

"You are right," Oramen said. "I should go to see that lady, and say the right things."

They walked together through the crowd, which had greatly increased in size since Oramen had last paid proper attention to it as more mourners had been delivered by their carriages. There were hundreds of people here now, all dressed in a hundred shades of red. Only the Urletine mercenaries' emissary and the knight commander of the Ichteuen Godwarriors seemed to have been excused, and even they had made an effort; the emissary had removed almost all the dried enemy body-parts from his clothing and donned a brown cap that no doubt appeared red to him, while the knight commander had concealed his most shocking facial scars with a crimson veil. And not just humanity was represented; he could smell the presence of the Oct ambassador, Kiu.

In amongst this, the animals of the court: ynt, like ankle-high furry waves slinking sinuously across the floor, always sniffing, happily trailing vermilion ribbons; ryre, tiptoeing decorously, usually by walls, thinly knee-high, ever-charmed by their own reflection, watchful, barely tolerating crimson collars; choups, bouncing and skittering on the polished-to-a-gleam wood tiles, bumping into people's thighs and waists, alarmed at any alienness, proudly sporting little saddles for children, flanks tied-over with red to indicate mourning like full-size mounts throughout the kingdom on this day, all caparisoned in scarlet.

Moving through the crowd in Renneque's rustlingly red wake, Oramen gave many small smiles to many slightly anxious faces trying to hit on the right combination of regretful grief and encouraging friendliness. Renneque kept her face modestly down, yet seemed to appreciate every glance cast her way and to be energised by the attention. "You have grown, Oramen," she told him, slipping back to his side. "It seems that only yesterday I could look down on you, but no more. You're taller than me now, practically a man."

"I trust I grow rather than you shrink."

"What? Oh!" Renneque said, and squeezed his hand with every appearance of bashfulness. She glanced up. "So many people, Oramen! All would be your friends now."

"I did not think I lacked for friends before, but I suppose I must accept I was wrong."

"Will you go with the army, Oramen, down into the Ninth, to fight the dreadful Deldeyn?"

"I don't know. It's not really for me to decide."

Renneque looked down at her fine red gown being kicked out ahead of her with every step. "Perhaps it should be."

"Perhaps."

"I hope the victory is quick! I want to see the great Falls at Hyeng-zhar and the Nameless City."

"I have heard they are most spectacular."

"My friend Xidia – she's older than me, of course, but still – she saw them once, in more peaceful times. Her father was ambassador to the Deldeyn. He took her. She says they are like nothing else. A whole city! Imagine that! I should like to see them."

"I'm sure you shall."

They arrived at where Harne, the lady Aelsh, was seated, surrounded by her own ladies, many clutching handkerchiefs and still dabbing at their eyes. Harne herself looked dry-eyed, though grim.

Oramen's late father had never taken any lady to be his queen, thinking it best to leave that position free in case he needed to use it as a method of securing a troublesome or much-required territory. It was said that King Hausk had come close to marrying several times; certainly the subject had been raised amongst the ambassadors and diplomats of the court often enough, and if you believed every rumour he had been nearly married to almost every eligible princess of the Eighth and at least one from the Ninth. In the event his feats of arms had done all the securing required without recourse to a diplomatic or strategic marriage and instead he had chosen to make a series of more tactical alliances within the nobility of his own kingdom through a judicious choice of honoured concubines.

Oramen's own mother, Aclyn, the lady Blisk – who had also birthed his elder brother, the late and still sorely lamented Elime – had been banished shortly after Oramen had been born, allegedly at the insistence of Harne, who, being older, it was said had felt threatened. Or perhaps there had been a falling-out between the two women – versions varied according to whom within the palace you listened to. Oramen had no memories of his mother, only of nurses and servants and an occasionally visiting father who somehow contrived to seem more remote than his utterly absent mother. She had been banished to a place called Kheretesuhr, an archipelagic province in the Vilamian Ocean, towards the far side of the world from Pourl. One of Oramen's goals, now that he was at least approaching the true seat of power, was to secure her return to the court. He had never expressed this desire to anyone, yet he had always felt that somehow Harne must know this.

The final link in this unhappily expansive family had been Vaime, the lady Anaplia. Always frail, she had collapsed when heavily pregnant. The doctors had told the King he could save the mother or the child, but not both. He chose to save the child, expecting a boy. Instead he was presented with a tiny premature dot of a girl. He was so appalled at this disaster that the infant wasn't even named for a month. Eventually she was called Djan. Over the years, the King had made no secret, least of all towards Djan herself, that had he known her gender before birth, she would have been sacrificed for the good of her mother. His only solace had been that he might marry the girl off one day for diplomatic profit.

The King had lately taken another couple of junior concubines, though these were kept in a smaller palace in another part of the city – again, at the insistence of Harne, according to palace gossip – however, it was Harne that was recognised as his widow in all but name. The two younger concubines had not even been present at the service or internment, nor had they been invited here.

"Madam, good lady," Oramen said, bowing deeply to Harne. "It is only in you that I feel my sense of loss is matched, even outweighed. I beg you accept my most sincere condolences. If we may take one ray of light from this dark time, let it be that you and I grow closer than we have been; my father's death, and that of your son, giving birth to a more affectionate relationship between us than that which has existed in the past. The King always sought harmony, even if through initial conflict, and Ferbin was the very soul of sociability. We might honour both their memories by seeking our own concord."

He'd had this little speech, this careful formed set of words, prepared for some days now. He had meant to say "the King's death", but it had come out otherwise; he had no idea why. He felt annoyed at himself.

The lady Aelsh kept her strict expression, but made a small inclination of her head. "Thank you for your words, prince. I'm sure they would both be pleased if all could be in agreement within the court. We might all take pains to celebrate them so."

And that, Oramen thought – as Renneque fell to Harne's side and took the older woman's hands in hers and shook them as she told her how awful was her own grief – will just have to do. It was not outright rejection, but neither was it quite what

he'd been hoping for. He caught Harne's gaze briefly while
Renneque talked on. He bowed and turned away.

"How go our preparations, Field Marshal?" Oramen asked the
gauntly forbidding form of the army's newly promoted chief.
Werreber was standing, drink in hand, gazing out at the rain
falling over the city. He turned and looked down at Oramen.

"Satisfactorily, sir," he said gravely.

"The rumours say we attack within ten days."

"I have heard as much myself, sir."

Oramen smiled. "My father would have loved to have been
at the head of our forces."

"He would indeed, sir."

"We will not suffer by his lack? I mean, sufficiently for there
to be any doubting the outcome."

"He is a great loss, sir," Werreber said. "However, he left the
army in its best deportment. And there is, of course, an urge
amongst the men to avenge his death."

"Hmm," Oramen said, frowning. "I heard that the Deldeyn
prisoners were slaughtered after his death."

"There was killing, sir. It was a battle."

"After the battle, though. When by every other standard and
practice of my father, prisoners are meant to be treated as we
would want any of our own taken."

"There was killing then too, sir. It is to be regretted. Doubtless
the men were blinded by grief."

"I have heard it said that my father ordered the slaughter."

"I am sorry you have heard that, sir."

"You were there with him when he died, dear Werreber. Do
you remember such an order?"

The field marshal drew back and up a little, and appeared
positively discomfited. "Prince," he said, looking down his great
long nose at him, "it is sad, but there are times when the less
that is said about certain matters the better it is for all. A clean

wound's best left. Only pain comes from poking and prodding at it."

"Oh, Werreber, I could not be there at my father's death. I have a need – natural to any son – to know quite how it was. Can you not help fix it in my mind so that, secured, it's easier to leave it finally alone? Otherwise I must imagine the scene, the words, the actions, and all these things shift because they are not established for me. So it becomes a wound I cannot help but return to."

The field marshal looked as uncomfortable as Oramen had ever seen him. "I was not present throughout the incident of your father's dying," he said. "I was with the Exaltine, on our way having been summoned, or for some long time outside the building, not wishing to make a crowd while efforts to save the King's life continued. I heard no such order given by your father regarding the prisoners, but that does not mean it was not given. It hardly matters, sir. Done to order or in an excess of grief, the enemy concerned remain dead."

"So I'd not dispute," Oramen said. "It was more the reputation of my father I was thinking of."

"He must have been in great pain and distress, sir. A fever can afflict men in such circumstances. They become other than themselves and say things they would never say otherwise. Even the bravest. It is often not an edifying spectacle. I repeat, sir; it is all best left alone."

"Are you saying that at the very end he did not die as he had lived? He would think that a severe charge."

"No, sir, I am not. In any event, I did not see the very end." Werreber paused, as if unsure quite how to express himself. "Your father was the bravest man I ever knew. I cannot imagine he met death with anything other than the fierce composure with which he faced its threat so many times during life. Also, though, he was never one to dwell excessively on the past. Even having made a mistake, he took what he might learn from it and then dismissed it. We must do as he would have done, and turn our attention to the future. Now, sir, might I be excused?

I believe I am needed at Headquarters. There is much still to be planned."

"Of course, Werreber," Oramen said, sipping his drink. "I did not mean to detain you, or unduly press on any wound."

"Sir." The field marshal bowed and departed.

Oramen counted himself privileged to have got so much from Werreber, who was known as a man of few words. This was a description unsuited to the Exaltine Chasque, the next figure he approached seeking detail of his father's death. The Exaltine was rotund in body and face and his dark red robes bulked him out still further. He blustered over his own part in the deathbed scene, claiming his eyes had been too full of tears and his ears brimming with the lamentations of all around to recall much clearly.

"And so, do your studies progress, young prince?" the Exaltine asked, as though returning to the more important subject. "Eh? Do you continue to sup at the well of learning? Hmm?"

Oramen smiled. He was used to adults asking about favourite school subjects when they could think of nothing else to talk of or wished to get off an awkward subject, so he replied perfunctorily and made his escape.

"They say the dead look back at us from mirrors, don't they, Gillews?"

The royal physician turned round with a startled expression on his face, and then staggered and nearly fell over. "Your – that is, Prince Oramen."

The doctor was a small, tense, nervous-looking man at the best of times. He seemed now positively abuzz with energy. Also, from his continued swaying and the glassy look about his eyes, quite drunk too. He had been staring at his reflection in one of the mirrors that covered half the walls of the drawing room. Oramen had been looking for him, moving amongst the throng, accepting sympathies, dispensing solemn pleasantries and trying to look – and be – grieving, brave, calm and dignified all at once.

"Did you see my father, Gillews?" Oramen asked, nodding to the mirror. "Was he in there, looking down on us?"

"What's that?" the doctor asked. His breath smelled of wine and some unsluiced foodstuff. Then he seemed to catch up with what was going on and turned, swaying again, to look into the tall mirror. "What? The dead? No, I see no one, saw nobody. Indeed not, prince, no."

"My father's death must have affected you deeply, good doctor."

"How could it not?" the little fellow asked. He wore a doctor's skullcap, but it had slipped to one side and come forward, too, so that it was starting to droop over his right eye. Wispy white hairs protruded. He looked down into his near-empty glass and said, "How could it not?" again.

"I'm glad I found you, Gillews," Oramen told him. "I have wanted to talk to you since my father was killed."

The doctor closed one eye and squinted at him. "Uh?" he said.

Oramen had grown up with adults getting drunk around him. He didn't really enjoy drinking – the sensation of being dizzy, as though you were about to be sick, seemed an odd state to pursue with such determination – but he quite liked being with drunk people, having learned that they often gave away the true natures they otherwise contrived to hide, or just let slip some item of information or gossip they would not have parted with so casually when sober. He already suspected he had got to Dr Gillews too late, but he'd give it a try anyway. "You were with my father when he died, obviously."

"It was a most obvious death, sir, true," the doctor said, and, strangely, attempted a smile. This dissolved quickly into an expression of some despair, then he dropped his head so that his expression was unreadable and started muttering what sounded like, "Well, not obvious, why obvious? Gillews, you idiot . . ."

"Doctor. I'd know how my father was in those last minutes. This is a matter of some importance to me. I feel I can't put him fully to rest in my mind until I know. Please – can you recall?"

"To rest?" Gillews said. "What rest? What rest is there? Rest is . . . rest is beneficial. Renews the frame, redefines the nerves, resupplies the muscles and allows the mechanical stresses on the greater bodily organs to abate. Yes, that is rest, and crave it we might. Death is not rest, no; death is the end of rest. Death is decay and rotting down, not building up! Don't talk to me of rest! What rest is there? Tell me that! What rest? Where, when our king lies heavy in his grave? For whom? Eh? I thought not!"

Oramen had taken a step back as the doctor raved at him. He could only wonder at the depths of emotion the poor man must be feeling. How he must have loved his king, and how devastating it must have been for him to lose him, to be unable to save him. The doctor's two principal assistants moved in on either side to take Gillews' arms, supporting him. One took his glass and pushed it into a pocket. The other looked at Oramen, smiled nervously and shrugged. He mumbled something apologetic-sounding that ended in "sir".

"What?" Gillews said, head tipping from side to side as though his neck was half broken, eyes rolling as he tried to focus on the two young men. "My pall-bearers, already? Is it to a council of my peers? An arraignment before the shades of physicians past? Throw me in the mirror. Let me reflect . . ." He pitched his head back and wailed, "Oh, my king, my king!" then slumped in the grip of the two men, weeping.

The assistants took Gillews stumbling away.

"Dear Oramen," tyl Loesp said, appearing at Oramen's side. He looked after the departing figures of Gillews and his two helpers. "The doctor may have enjoyed his drink too much."

"He enjoys nothing else," Oramen said. "I feel outdone in unkiltered grief."

"There is appropriate grief, and inappropriate grief, don't you think?" tyl Loesp said, standing close to Oramen, towering over him, white hair shining in the candlelight. His dark red trous and long jacket contrived to make him look no less massive than he'd looked in full armour, the evening he'd brought the King's body back from the battlefield. Oramen was growing tired of being polite.

"Did my father die well, in the end, tyl Loesp?" he asked. "Tell me. Please."

Tyl Loesp had been bending over Oramen a little. Now he drew himself back and up. "Like a king should, sir. I was never more proud of him, nor held him in greater esteem, as at that moment."

Oramen put his hand on the tall warrior's arm. "Thank you, Loesp."

"It is my pleasure and my duty, young prince. I am but the stake to support a sapling."

"You have supported me well in this, and I am in your debt."

"Never so, sir. Never so." Tyl Loesp smiled at Oramen for a moment or two, then his gaze flicked to somewhere behind the prince and he said, "Here, sir. Look; a more welcome face."

"My prince," said a voice behind Oramen.

He turned to find his old friend Tove Lomma standing there, smiling.

"Tove!" Oramen said.

"Equerry Tove, if you'll have me, Prince Regent."

"Equerry?" Oramen asked. "To me? Of mine?"

"I'd hope! Nobody else would have me."

"In fact, a most able young man," tyl Loesp said, clapping both Lomma and Oramen on the shoulders. "Remember merely that he is meant to keep you out of mischief, not lay a course towards it." Tyl Loesp smiled at Oramen. "I'll leave you two to plot much good behaviour." He bowed shortly and left.

Tove looked rueful. "Not a day for mischief, prince. Not this one. But we must hope there will be many in the future."

"We'll share none if you don't call me by my name, Tove."

"Tyl Loesp instructed me most strictly that you were the Prince Regent, nothing more familiar," Tove said, and pretended to frown.

"Consider that order rescinded, by me."

"Duly agreed, Oramen. Let's have a drink."

8. Tower

"Fate, I tell you, if not the hand of the WorldGod itself . . . or whatever manipulatory appendage WorldGods possess. Anyway, the hand, metaphorically, of the WorldGod. Possibly."

"I think you underguess the workings of blind chance, sir."

"Blind chance that took me to that dreadful place?"

"Unarguably, sir: your startled mount ran cross-country until it found a track; naturally it then took the levelled road rather than the coarse ground and of course it took the easier, downhill route. Then that old mill appeared, on the first place where the road widens and levels out. Natural place for it to stop."

Ferbin looked across at the prone form of his servant, lying on the ground a couple of strides away across the leaf-littered ground with a large blue leaf poised over his head. Choubris Holse looked calmly back.

⊕

They had flown straight out from the Scholastery until hidden from it by a line of low hills, then set down on a sloped heath above the limit of cultivated land.

"I think I've heard of the D'neng-oal Tower," Ferbin said, while they inspected the two grumbling, huffing caude, "but I'm damned if I know which way it is."

"Same here, sir," said Holse. He opened up one of the saddle bags on his beast. "Though with any luck there'll be a map in here. Let me just have a quick furtle." He dug his hand elbow-deep into the bag.

The saddle bags yielded maps, some food, a little water, a telescope, a heliograph, two hefty pocket chronometers, one barometer/altimeter, some rifle and pistol ammunition but no weapons, four small bomblets like smooth hand grenades with cruciform flights, padded jackets, gauntlets, one small blanket each and the usual paraphernalia of tack associated with caude, including a good supply of the krisk nuts they found so stimulating. Holse popped one in the mouth of each animal; they mewed and whinnied appreciatively. "Ever tried these things, sir?" Holse asked, holding up the bag of krisk.

"No," Ferbin lied. "Of course not."

"Bloody horrible. Bitter as a scold's piss." He put the bag away, fastened the saddle bags and adjusted his saddle. "And these bastard knights that came to the Scholastery must be ascetics or something, for there's no sign of any of the little niceties that make life bearable for the common man, sir. Like wine, or unge, or crile. Bloody fliers." Holse shook his head at such lack of consideration.

"No goggles or masks either," Ferbin pointed out.

"Must have carried them with them."

Holse was checking one of the pistol rounds they'd discovered in the saddle bags against one from his own gun. "Let's have a quick look, and then be off, eh, sir?" he said, then shook his head and dumped all the ammunition on the heath.

They consulted the maps, one of which was of sufficient scale to show the land for nearly ten days' flying around Pourl, depicting hundreds upon hundreds of the great Towers as well as the shade limits and periods of the various Rollstars.

"There it is," Ferbin said, tapping on the map.

"What would you say, sir? Four short-days' flying?"

"More like three," Ferbin said, glad to have found a practical subject he knew so much more of than his servant. "Five Towers along and one down, four times over, then three and one. Away from Pourl, which is to the good." He glanced up at Obor. Its red-tinged bulk was still barely above the horizon as it rose upon its slow and settled course. "It's a long-day today. We shall have to let the beasts day-sleep, but we should achieve the tower before dusk."

"Could do with a snooze myself," Holse yawned. He looked disparagingly at his mount, which had tucked its long neck under its massive body to lick its genitals. "Rather hoped I'd seen the last of these things this close, I do confess, sir." Holse's caude removed its head from between its legs, though only long enough for it to fart long and loud, as though to confirm its new rider's poor opinion.

"You are not enamoured of the beasts of the air, Holse?"

"Indeed not, sir. If the gods had meant us to fly they'd have given us the wings and the caude the pox."

"If they hadn't meant us to fly, gravity would be stronger," Ferbin replied.

"I wasn't aware it was adjustable, sir."

Ferbin smiled tolerantly. He realised that his servant might not be versed in the kind of alien lore that would insist that what he and Holse had known all their lives as normal gravity was about half Standard, whatever that really meant.

"However," Holse said. "Let's get moving, eh?" They both went to saddle up.

"Best put these jackets on," Ferbin said. "It'll be cold up there." He gestured upwards. "Clouds are clearing so we'll be able to go high."

Holse sighed. "If we must, sir."

"I'll work the clock, shall I?" Ferbin held up the chronometer. "That necessary, sir?"

Ferbin, who had got lost while flying too many times, mistakenly thinking that you could never miscount things as big as Towers – or fall asleep in the saddle, for that matter – said, "I think it advisable."

They had flown without incident at the altitude best for caude cruising stamina. They had seen other fliers far in the distance, but had not been approached. The landscape moved slowly beneath them, changing from tiny fields to stretches of waste and heath that were low hills, then back to fields, small towns, and great glaring areas of bright green that marked the roasoaril plantations whose fruits went to feed the refineries which produced the fuel to power the steam engines of the modern age.

Slowly over the horizon appeared a handful of long fingers of shining water that were the Quoluk Lakes. Ferbin recognised the island that held the Hausk family estate of Moiliou. The river Quoline gathered water from all the lakes and then wound away towards the distant equator, vanishing in the haze. Canals blinked, reflecting sunlight like thin threads of silver, spearing straight over level areas and describing curving contours about raised ground.

Even in the jacket, Ferbin shivered. His knees, covered only in hose and trous, were especially cold. Not having goggles or a mask meant his eyes were watering all the time. He'd wrapped his collar scarf round his lower face, but it was all still most uncomfortable. He kept an eye on the chronometer clipped to the tall front edge of his saddle and used a waterproof pad and wax crayon also attached to the saddle to mark down the passing of each great Tower as it loomed and then slid slowly past to their right.

The Towers, as ever, were a source of a kind of odd comfort.

From this height more of them were visible than one saw from the ground and one was able to form a proper impression of their numbers and regular spacing. Only from this sort of altitude, Ferbin thought, did one fully appreciate that one lived within a greater world, a world of levels, of regularly spaced floors and ceilings, with the Towers holding one above the other. They rose like vast spars of pale luminescence, masts of a celestial ship of infinite grace and absolute, inconceivable power. High above, just visible, the laciness of Filigree showed where the Towers' splayed summits – still fourteen hundred kilometres over his and Holse's heads, for all their chilly altitude – fluted out like an impossibly fine network of branches from a succession of vast trees.

A million Towers held the world up. The collapse of just one might destroy everything, not just on this level, their own dear Eighth, but on and in all the others too; the WorldGod itself might not be beyond harm. But then it was said that the Towers were near invulnerable, and Sursamen had been here for a thousand times a million years. Whether this meant their own short-years or long-years or so-called Standard years, he didn't know – with such a number it hardly mattered.

Ferbin wiped his eyes free of tears and looked carefully around, taking time to let his gaze rest on a succession of distant points the better to catch any movement. He wondered how long it would take for word to get back to Pourl of what had happened at the Scholastery. Riding there would take five days or so, but – using the heliograph – perhaps another patrol would be attracted, and in reality the knights who'd lost their mounts only needed to get to the nearest telegraph station. Plus, the patrol would be missed when it didn't return; search parties would be sent out and would no doubt be signalled from the Scholastery. Seltis would surely be questioned; would they stoop to torture? What if he told them about the documents and the D'neng-oal Tower?

Well, he and Holse had little choice. They would make the best time they could. The rest was up to luck and the WorldGod.

Their beasts started to show signs of fatigue. Ferbin checked the chronometer. They had been in the air nearly ten hours and must have flown over six hundred thousand strides – six hundred kilometres. They had passed twelve Towers to their right, and flown left by one tower every five. Obor, a slow, orange Rollstar, was just approaching its noon. They were about halfway.

They descended, found an island at the edge of a vast Bowlsea with a rich crop of fat bald-head fruit, and landed in a small clearing. The caude swallowed fruit until they looked fit to burst. They started farting again, then promptly fell asleep in the nearest shade, still expelling gas. Ferbin and Holse tethered the beasts, also had something to eat, then found another patch of deep shade and cut down a giant leaf each to shield their eyes still further from the light while they slept. This was where Ferbin chose to share his thoughts with his servant on the course of events recently, and why ideas like predestination, destiny and fate had been much on his mind during the long, cold and painful hours in the saddle.

"Oh. I see," Ferbin said. "You are familiar with the disposition of that ancient manufactury?"

"All I'm saying, sir, is that it was about the only intact building for half a day's ride around. Even the old hunting lodge, which was, as it were, the cause of every other building in the area having as useful a roof as that stupidity I found you in—"

"Folly."

" – that folly I found you in, was smashed to buggery. It had been artilleried. But anyway, sir, your mount getting you there was no great surprise."

"Very well," Ferbin said, determined to show his reasonableness by making a concession. "*My* arriving might not have been due to the hand of fate. The traitors taking my father there

– that was. Destiny was taking a hand. Perhaps even the WorldGod. My father's fate was sealed, it would seem, and he could not be saved, but at least his son might be allowed to witness the despicable crime and set vengeance in train."

"I'm sure it seemed and seems so to you, sir. However, with no buildings about the place, in the heat of a battle, and a dirt-rain starting, taking a wounded man to a place with a roof only makes sense. If dirt-rain gets into a wound, it turns cut-rot and infection from a bad risk to a perfect certainty."

Ferbin had to think back. He recalled that when he'd crawled out of the burning building into the damp, cloying leaves and branches it had, indeed, been a dirty rain that had been falling. That was why it had all felt so sticky and grainy and horrible. "But they *wanted* him dead!" he protested.

"And where would you rather do *that*, sir? In full view of who-knows-who, in the open, or under a roof, between walls?"

Ferbin frowned, pulled his big blue leaf down over his face and from underneath said grumpily, "Still, for all your cynicism, Holse, it was fate."

"As you say, sir," Holse said, sighing, and pulled his own leaf over his face. "Good sleep, sir."

He was answered with a snore.

When they awoke it was to colder, darker, windier conditions. The Obor-lit long-day was still in its early afternoon, but the weather had changed. Small grey clouds sailed raggedly across the sky beneath a high overcast and the air smelled damp. The caude were slow to wake and spent much of the next half-hour defecating noisily and voluminously. Ferbin and Holse took their small breakfast some distance upwind.

"That wind's against us," Ferbin said, looking out from the edge of the plantation across the quick-chopping waves of the Bowlsea. A dark horizon in the direction they would be heading looked ominous.

"As well we made good distance yesterday," Holse said, chewing on some air-dried meat.

They secured their few belongings, checked the map, took a few of the bald-head fruit with them – for the caude; the fruit was indigestible to humans – then took off into a freshening breeze. The wind added to the sensation of cold, even though they were flying much lower than earlier due to the great banks and drifts of dark grey cloud striating the sky. They skirted the bigger clouds and flew through only the smallest. Caude were reluctant to fly through thick cloud anyway, though they would do so if they were forced. Once inside cloud the animals were as bad as humans at gauging whether they were upright and flying straight and level, or describing a banked circle and about to crash into some nearby Tower. Caude were the rowels of the air, reliable work beasts rather than thoroughbred racing creatures like lyge, and so only flew at about fifty or sixty kilometres per hour. Even so, hitting a Tower at that speed was usually enough to kill both beast and rider, and if not, then the subsequent fall to the ground tended to do the trick.

Ferbin was still keeping an eye on the chronometer and marking the passage of the Towers to their right – they were flying closer to them now, only a few kilometres off each one, so they didn't miss any, something Ferbin knew from experience it was all too easy to do – however, he found himself thinking back to a dream he'd had the night before and – via that – to his one journey to the Surface, back when he'd been a youth.

That, too, was like a dream to him now.

He had walked on strange ground beneath no lid or ceiling save that of the atmosphere itself, held contained by a far circle of walls and by nothing else but gravity; a place *with no Towers*, where the curve of the earth beneath one's feet just went on, uninterrupted, unbroken, unsupported, unbelievable.

He had watched the stars wheel and, in each of the half-dozen days he had been there, had marvelled at the tiny, blinding dot that was Meseriphine, the Unseen Sun, the distant, connected yet unconnected pivot that great Sursamen itself spun slow about. There was a remorselessness about those Surface days; one sun, one source of light, one regular set of days and nights, always the same, seemingly unchanging, while everything he'd ever known was far below – entire levels that were themselves worlds beneath him, and only nothing above; a dark true-nothingness, sprinkled with a rash of faint points of light that he was told were other suns.

His father had been meant to be there but had had to call off at the last moment. Ferbin had gone with his older brother Elime, who had been there before but had wanted to go again. They were very privileged to be treated so. Their father could command the Oct to take people to other levels including the Surface, as could some other rulers and the Head Scholars of Scholasteries, but any other person travelled at the whim of the Oct, and they granted almost no such wishes.

They had taken a couple of friends and a few old servants. The great Crater they'd stayed within for most of their visit was green with vast meadows and tall trees. The air smelled of unidentifiable perfumes. It was thick and at once fresh and heady; they had felt energised, almost drugged.

They had lived within an underground complex in the face of a tall cliff looking out over a vast network of hexagonal lakes bounded by thin strips of land; this pattern stretched to the horizon. They had met some Nariscene and even one Morthanveld. Ferbin had already seen his first Oct, in the scend-ship that had taken them up the Tower to the Surface. This had been before the Oct embassy had been opened in the palace at Pourl and Ferbin had the same superstitious dread of the Oct as most people. There were legends, rumours and uncorroborated reports that the Oct issued from their Towers in the dead of night to steal people from their beds. Sometimes whole families or even villages disappeared. The Oct took the captured back to their Towers and experimented upon them, or ate them, or transported them to another level for sport and devilment.

The result was that the common mass of people dreaded both

the Oct themselves and the very idea of being taken to and transported within a Tower. Ferbin had long been told these were nonsense tales, but he'd still been nervous. It had been a relief to discover the Oct were so small and delicate-looking.

The Oct in the scendship had been most insistent that they were the true Inheritors and direct descendants of the Involucra, the original builders of the Shellworlds. He had been highly impressed with this, and had felt a vicarious outrage that this fact was not more widely accepted.

He'd been in awe of the Oct's casual familiarity with and easy control of this vessel that could rise within a Tower, past level after unglimpsed level, to the very outside of all things. It was control of the world, he realised. It seemed more real, more relevant and somehow even more important and impressive than control of the infinitude of ungraspable space beyond the world itself. This, he'd thought, was power.

Then he'd watched how the Oct and the Nariscene treated each other, and realised that the Nariscene were the masters here; they were the superiors, who merely indulged this strange species that to his people, to the Sarl, had near-magical powers. How lowly the Sarl must be, to be mere cargo, simple primitives to the Oct, who were themselves treated like little more than children by their Nariscene mentors!

Seeing, furthermore, how the Nariscene and the Morthanveld interacted was almost dismaying, because the Morthanveld in turn seemed to regard the Nariscene as something like children and treated them with amused indulgence. Another level, and another; all beyond his, above his people's heads.

In some ways, they were the lowest of the low, he realised. Was this why so few of his people were ever invited here?

Perhaps if everybody saw what he, his brother and their friends were seeing, the Sarl might sink into a state of apathy and depression, for they would know how little their lives really counted within the ever-expanding hierarchies of alien powers beyond them. This had been Elime's opinion. He also believed that it was a deliberate scheme of their mentors to encourage those who were in power, or who would one day assume power, to witness the wonders that they were now being shown, so that they would never be tempted to get above themselves, so that they would always know that no matter how magnificent they appeared to themselves or those around them and regardless of what they achieved, it was all within the context of this greater, more powerful, sophisticated and ultimately far superior reality.

"They try to break us!" Elime had told Ferbin. Elime was a big, burly, energetic young man, always full of enthusiasm and opinions and tirelessly keen to hunt or drink or fight or fuck. "They try to put a little voice in our heads that will always say, 'You don't matter. What you do means nothing!'"

Elime, like their father, was having none of this. So the aliens could sail within the Towers and cruise between the stars and construct whole worlds – so what? There were powers beyond them that *they* didn't fully understand. Perhaps this nesting, this shell-after-shell-beyond-what-you-knew principle went on for ever! Did the *aliens* give up and do nothing? No! They had their disputes and contentions, their disagreements and alliances, their wins and losses, even if they were somehow more oblique and rarefied than the wars, victories and defeats that the Sarl both enjoyed and suffered. The stratagems and power-plays, the satisfactions and disillusions that the Sarl experienced mattered as much to them as those of the aliens did to their own overweeningly cosmopolitan and civilised souls.

You lived within your level and accepted that you did; you played by the rules within that level, and therein lay the measure of your worth. All was relative, and by refusing to accept the lesson the aliens were implicitly trying to teach here – behave, accept, bow down, conform – a hairy-arsed bunch of primitives like the Sarl could score their own kind of victory against the most overarching sophisticates the galaxy had to offer.

Elime had been wildly excited. This visit had reinforced what he'd seen during his first time at the Surface and had made sense of all the things their father had been telling them since they were old enough to understand. Ferbin had been amazed; Elime was positively glowing with joy at the prospect of returning to their own level with a kind of civilisational mandate to carry on his father's work of unifying the Eighth – and who knew, perhaps beyond.

At the time, Ferbin, who was just starting to take an interest in such things, had been more concerned with the fact that his beautiful second cousin Truffe, who was a little older than he and with whom he'd started to think he might be falling in love, had succumbed – with frightening, indecent ease – to Elime's bluff charms during the visit to the Surface. That was the sort of conquering Ferbin was starting to take an interest in, thank you, and Elime had already beaten him to it.

They had returned to the Eighth, Elime with a messianic gleam in his eye, Ferbin with a melancholic feeling that, now Truffe was forever denied him – he couldn't imagine she'd settle for him after his brother, and besides, he wasn't sure he wanted her any more anyway – his young life was already over. He also felt that – in some strange, roundabout way – the aliens had succeeded in lowering his expectations by the same degree they had inadvertently raised Elime's.

He realised he had drifted off in this reverie when he heard Holse shouting at him. He looked about. Had he missed a Tower? He saw what looked like a new Tower some distance off to his right and forward. It looked oddly bright in its paleness. This was because of the great wall of darkness filling the sky ahead. He was damp all over; they must have flown through a cloud. The last he recalled they had been flying just under the surface of some long grey mass of vapour with hazy tendrils stretching down like forest creepers all around them.

". . . grit-cloud!" he heard Holse yell.

He looked up at the cliff of darkness ahead and realised it was indeed a silse cloud; a mass of sticky rain it would be dangerous and possibly fatal to try and fly through. Even the caude he was riding seemed to have realised things weren't quite right; it shivered beneath him and he could hear it making moaning, whining noises. Ferbin looked to either side. There was no way round the great dark cloud and it was far too tall for them to go over the top. The cloud was loosing its gritty cargo of rain, too; great dragged veils of darkness swept back along the ground beneath it.

They'd have to land and sit it out. He signalled to Holse and they wheeled right round, back the way they'd come, descending fast towards the nearest forest on the side of a tall hill bound on three sides by the loop of a broad river. Drops of moisture tickled Ferbin's face and he could smell something like dung.

They landed on the broad, boggy summit of the hill near a rough-edged pool of dark, brackish water and squelched through a quaking mire of shaking ground, leading the grumbling caude down to the tree line. They persuaded the caude to trample down a few springy saplings so they could all shoulder their way far enough in. They sheltered under the trees while the whole day darkened until it was like night. The caude promptly fell asleep.

The grit-rain whispered in the branches high above, growing slowly louder. The view of the hill's top and a line of remaining brightness in the sky beyond disappeared.

"What I wouldn't give for a pipe of good unge leaf," Holse said, sighing. "Bloody nuisance, eh, sir?"

Ferbin could barely make out his servant's face in the gloom, though he was almost within touching distance. "Yes," he said. He squinted at the chronometer, which he was keeping inside his jacket. "We won't get there in daylight now," he said.

A few leaf-filtered drops of the dirty rain plopped down about them; one landed on Ferbin's nose and trickled to his mouth. He spat.

"My old dad lost a whole crop of xirze to one of these buggering silse storms once," Holse said.

"Well, they destroy but they build up too," Ferbin said.

"I have heard them compared to kings, in that regard," Holse said. "Sir."

"We need them, both."

"I've heard that too, sir."

"In other worlds, they have no silse, no sticky rain. So I've been told."

"Really? Doesn't the land just wear away to nothing?"

"Apparently not."

"Not even eventually, sir? Don't these places have rain and such – ordinary rain, I mean, obviously – that would wear the hills down and carry them all away to lakes and seas and oceans?"

"They generally do. Seemingly they also have such hydrological systems that can build up land from beneath."

"From beneath," Holse said, sounding unconvinced.

"I remember one lesson where it sounded like they had oceans of rock so hot it was liquid, and not only flowed like rivers but also could flow uphill, to issue from the summits of mountains," Ferbin said.

"Really, sir." Holse sounded like he thought Ferbin was trying to fool him into believing the sort of preposterous nonsense a child would dismiss with derision.

"These effects serve to build up land," Ferbin said. "Oh, and the mountains float and can grow upwards wholesale, apparently. Entire countries crash into each other, raising hills. There was more, but I rather missed the start of that lesson and it does all sound a bit far-fetched."

"I think they were having you on, sir. Trying to see how gullible you might be." Holse might have sounded hurt.

"I thought that, I have to say." Ferbin shrugged, unseen. "Oh, I probably got it wrong, Choubris. I wouldn't quote me on this, frankly."

"I shall take care not to, sir," Holse said.

"Anyway, that is why they don't need silse rain."

"If a tenth of all that stuff's true, sir, I think we have the better side of the bargain."

"So do I."

Silse rebuilt land. As Ferbin understood it, tiny animalcules in the seas and oceans each grabbed a particle of silt and then made some sort of gas that hoisted creature and particle to the surface, where they leapt into the air to become clouds which then drifted over the land and dropped the lot in the form of dirty, sticky rain. Silse clouds were relatively rare, which was just as well; a big one could drown a farm, a village or even a county as efficiently as a small flood, smothering crops with knee-deep mud, tearing down trees or leaving them stripped of branches, breaking roofs of too shallow a pitch, paving over meadows, blanketing roads and damming rivers – usually only temporarily, swiftly resulting in real floods.

The gritty rain was dripping on to them even under the cover of the trees as it found its way through the now heavy, drooping branches.

From all directions around them, a sporadic series of loud cracks rang out above the sound of the silse storm, each followed by a rushing, tearing, crashing noise concluding in a great thump.

"If you hear that right above us, sir," Holse said, "best jump."

"I most certainly shall," Ferbin said, trying to uncloy his eyes from the gritty stuff falling on them. The silse stank like something from the bottom of a latrine trench. "Though right now, death does not seem so unattractive."

The cloud passed eventually, the day brightened again and a strong wind veered about the hilltop. They squelched out on to the doubly treacherous summit. The newly dumped silse mud covering the already unstable surface of the bog pulled at their feet and those of the caude, both of which showed signs of distress at being forced to walk in such conditions. The mud reeked like manure. Ferbin and Holse brushed as much as they could from their skin and clothes before it caked.

"Could do with a shower of nice clean rain now, eh, sir?"

"What about that sort of pool thing up there?" Ferbin asked.

"Good idea, sir," Holse said, leading the caude to the shallow, now overbrimming tarn near the summit of the hill. The caude whinnied and resisted, but eventually were persuaded to enter the water, which came to halfway up their bellies.

The two men cleaned the beasts and themselves as best they could. The caude were still unhappy, and their slipping, sliding take-off run only just got them above the trees in time. They flew on into the late afternoon.

They kept flying even as the dusk slowly descended, though the caude were whining almost constantly now and continually tried to descend, dropping down and answering only slowly and with much grumbling to each up-pulling of the reins. On the landscape below must be farms, villages and towns, but they could see no sign of them. The wind was to their left side, constantly trying to push them towards the Towers they needed to keep to their right. The clouds had settled back to a high overcast and another ragged layer at about half a kilometre; they kept beneath this, knowing that getting lost in night cloud might easily be the end of them.

Eventually they saw what they thought must be the D'neng-oal Tower, a broad, pale presence rising across an extensive marsh still just about reflecting the slow-fading embers that Obor had left on the under-surface of the sky high above.

The D'neng-oal Tower was what was known as a Pierced Tower; one through which access might be gained to its interior and so to the network of thoroughfares in which the Oct – and the Aultridia – sailed their scendships. This was at least the popular understanding; Ferbin knew that all the Towers had been pierced originally, and in a sense still were.

Every Tower, where it fluted out at its base on each level, contained hundreds of portals designed to transport the fluid which it was alleged the Involucra had planned to fill the World with. On the Eighth the portals were, in any case, all buried under at least a hundred metres of earth and water, but in almost every Tower the portals had all long since been firmly sealed by the Oct and Aultridia. There were rumours – which the Oct did nothing to deny – that other peoples, other rulers, had sunk mines down to where the sealed portals were and had tried to open them, only to find that they were utterly impenetrable to anybody without the kind of technology that let one sail the stars, never mind the interior of Towers, and also that even attempting to meddle with them inevitably brought down the wrath of the Oct; those rulers had been killed and those peoples scattered, often across other, less forgiving levels.

Only one Tower in a thousand still had a single portal which gave access to the interior, at least at any useful height – telescopes had revealed what might be portals high above the atmosphere, hundreds of kilometres above ground level – and the usual sign of a Pierced Tower was a much smaller – though still by human standards substantial – access tower sited nearby.

The D'neng-oal's access tower proved surprisingly difficult to spot in the gloom. They flew round the Tower once, under the thickening layer of cloud, feeling pressed between the mists rising from the ground below and the lowering carpet of darkness directly above. Ferbin was worried first that they might crash into the lesser tower in the darkness – they were being forced to fly at only a hundred metres above the ground, and that was about the usual altitude for the top of an access tower – and then that they had chosen the wrong Tower in the first place. The map they'd looked at earlier had shown the Tower was pierced, but not exactly where its accompanying access tower was. It also showed a fair-sized town, Dengroal, situated very close to the nearpole base of the main Tower, but there was no sign of the settlement. He hoped it was just lost in the mists.

The access tower lit up in front of them as the top twenty metres of the cylinder suddenly flashed in a series of giant, tower-encircling hoops so bright they dazzled the eye. It was less than a hundred strides in front of them and its summit was a little above their present level, almost in the clouds; the blue light picked out their gauzy under-surface like some strange, inverted landscape. He and Holse pulled up and banked and then, with gestures, agreed to land on the top. The caude were so tired they hardly bothered to complain as they were asked to climb one more time.

The summit of the access tower was fifty strides across; a concentric series of blue hoops of light was set into its surface like a vast target. The light pulsed slowly from dim to bright, like the beat of some vast and alien heart.

They landed on the tower's nearest edge; the startled caude scrambled and beat their wings with one last frantic effort as the smooth surface under their grasping feet failed to bring them to a halt as quickly as ground or even stone would have, but then their scraping claws found some purchase, their wingbeats pulled them up and finally, with a great whistling sigh that sounded entirely like relief, they were stopped. They each settled down, quivering slightly, wings half outstretched with exhaustion, heads lying on the surface of the tower, panting. Blue light shone up around their bodies. The vapour of their breath drifted across the flat, blue-lit summit of the tower, dissipating slowly.

Ferbin dismounted, joints creaking and complaining like an old man's. He stretched his back and walked over to where Holse was standing rubbing at the leg he'd hurt when the mersicor had fallen on top of him.

"Well, Holse, we got here."

"And a strange old here it is, sir," Holse said, looking around the broad circular top of the tower. It appeared to be perfectly flat and symmetrical. The only visible features were the hoops of blue light. These issued from hand-wide strips set flush with whatever smooth material made up the tower's summit. They were standing about halfway between the centre of the surface and the edge. The blue light waxed about them, giving them and their beasts a ghostly, otherworldly appearance. Ferbin shivered, though it was not especially cold. He looked about them. There was nothing visible beyond the circles of blue. Above, the slow-moving layer of cloud looked almost close enough to touch. The wind picked up for a moment, then fell back to a breeze.

"At least there's nobody else here," he said.

"Thankful for that, sir," Holse agreed. "Though if there is anybody watching, and they can see through the mist, they'll know we're here. Anyway. What happens now?"

"Well, I don't know," Ferbin admitted. He couldn't recall what one had to do to gain access to one of these things. On the occasion when he'd gone to the Surface with Elime and the others he'd been too distracted by everything that was happening to take note of exactly what the procedure was; some servant had done it all. He caught Holse's expression of annoyance and looked around again, gaze settling on the centre of the tower's surface. "Perhaps . . ." he started to say. As he'd spoken, he'd pointed at the glowing dot at the focus of the pulsing blue hoops, so they were both looking right at it when it rose slowly, smoothly into the air.

A cylinder about a foot across extended like a section of telescope from the dead centre of the tower's summit, rising to around head height. Its top surface pulsed blue in time with the widening circles radiating out from it.

"That might be useful," Ferbin said.

"As a hitching post for the beasts, if nothing else, sir," Holse said. "There's bugger all else to tie them to up here."

"I'll take a look," Ferbin said. He didn't want to show Holse he felt frightened.

"I'll hold the reins."

Ferbin walked over to the slim cylinder. As he approached, an octagon of grey light seemed to swivel into place, facing him, level with his own face. It showed a stylised Oct in silhouette. The cylinder's surface beaded with moisture as a light rain began to fall.

"Repetition," said a voice like rustling leaves. Before Ferbin could say anything in reply, the voice went on, "Patterns, yes. For, periodicity. As the Veil become the Oct, so one iteration becomes another. Spacing is the signal, so creates. Yet, also, repetition shows lack of learning. Again, be on your way. Signal that is no signal, simply power, follows. Unrepeats." The octagonal patch showing the silhouetted Oct shape faded and the cylinder started to sink silently back into the surface.

"Wait!" Ferbin shouted, and grabbed at the smooth round shape, putting both arms round it and attempting to prevent it disappearing. It felt cold and seemed to be made of metal; it would have been slick enough anyway but the drizzle made it more so and it slid imperturbably downwards as though his efforts to retrain it were having no effect whatsoever.

Then it seemed to hesitate. It drew to a stop and rose back to its earlier height. The grey octagonal shape – some sort of screen, Ferbin realised – glowed into existence on the surface again. Before it could say anything, he shouted, "I am Ferbin, prince of the house of Hausk, with documents to support my right to warranted travel under the protection of our esteemed allies the Oct! I would speak with the Towermaster, Aiaik."

"Denigration is—" the cylinder had started to say, then the voice cut off. "Documents?" the voice said after a few moments.

Ferbin unbuttoned his jacket and took out the finger-thick grey envelopes, brandishing them in front of the screen. "By the authority of Seltis, Head Scholar of the Anjrinh Scholastery," Ferbin said. "Of the Eighth," he added, partly in case there was any confusion and partly to show he was familiar with the realities of the World and not some coarse-bonce bumpkin who'd somehow achieved the summit of the tower for a bet.

"To wait," said the leaf-rustling voice. The screen faded again but this time the cylinder stayed where it was.

"Sir?" Holse called from where he stood holding the reins of the now soundly sleeping caude.

"Yes?" Ferbin said.

"Just wondering what's happening, sir."

"I believe we've established some sort of rapport." He frowned, thinking back to what the voice had said when it had first spoken to him. "But I think we're not the first here, not recently. Perhaps." He shrugged at the worried-looking Holse. "I don't know." Ferbin swivelled, looking all about, trying to see through the glowing blue mist created by the drizzle. He saw something dark moving in the air to one side of Holse and the caude; a huge shadow, heading straight for them. "Holse!" he cried, pointing at the apparition.

Holse glanced round, already starting to drop. The great shape tore through the air just above the two slumped mounts, missing Holse's head by no more than the span of a hand; the sound of massive wings beating whumped through the air. It looked like a lyge, Ferbin thought, with a rider on its back. A sharp crack and a tiny fountain of yellow sparks announced Holse firing his pistol at the departing, wheeling beast.

The lyge rose, stalled and turned, catching itself on a single great beat of its massive wings as it landed on the far edge of the tower. A slight figure jumped from its back holding a long gun; the flier dropped to one knee and took aim at Holse, who was slapping his pistol with his free hand and cursing. Holse dived for cover between the caude, both of which had raised their heads at the sound of the shot and were looking sleepily about them. The rifle spoke again and the caude nearest the shooter jerked and screamed. It started trying to rise from the surface, beating one wing and scraping one leg back and forth. Its fellow raised its head high and let out a terrified wail. The flier from the lyge levered another round into the rifle.

"Small detonations," said the Oct voice just above Ferbis' head. He hadn't even realised he'd ducked down, just his head showing round the side of the cylinder so he could still see the flier attacking them. "Celebratory actions inappropriate," the voice continued. "Betokening the undesired. To cease."

"Let us in!" Ferbin said in a hoarse whisper. Behind the figure with the rifle, the lyge hunkered down. The wounded caude near Holse screamed and thrashed its wings against the surface of the tower. Its companion keened, shifting and shuffling away, stretching its own wings. The flier took aim again and shouted, "Show yourself! Surrender!"

"Fuck off!" Holse yelled back. Ferbin could barely hear him over the screaming caude. The creature was moving slowly backwards over the surface of the tower as it beat its wings and shrieked. The second caude rose suddenly on its legs and seemed to realise only then that it was unrestrained. It turned, hopped once to the edge of the tower, spread its wings and launched itself into the darkness with a miserable wail, disappearing immediately.

"Please!" Ferbin said, knocking on the cylinder's surface with his knuckles. "Let us in!"

"The cessation of childishness," the cylinder's voice announced. "Necessary if not sufficient."

The wounded caude rolled half to one side as though stretching itself, its screams fading as its voice became hoarse.

"And you!" the lyge flier yelled, turning to point the rifle at Ferbin. "Both of you. Out. I'll not shoot if you surrender now. The hunt's finished. I'm just a scout. There are twenty more behind me. All regent's men. It's over. Surrender. You'll not be harmed."

Ferbin heard a fizzing sound between the desperate shrieks of the wounded caude, and a hint of yellow light seemed to illuminate the surface just behind the screaming animal.

"All right!" Holse shouted. "I surrender!" Something flew up from behind the wounded caude, lobbed over its beating wings on an arc of orange sparks. The flier with the rifle started back, rifle barrel flicking upwards.

The finned grenade landed three strides in front of the lyge flier. As the bomblet bounced, the caude Holse had been sheltering behind gave a final great thrash of its wings and one last scream before overbalancing and falling over the edge of the tower in a despairing tangle of wings, revealing Holse lying on the surface. The creature's wails faded slowly as it fell.

The grenade landed and rolled round, pivoting about its cruciform tail, then its fuse gave a little puff of orange smoke and went out even as the lyge flier was scrambling backwards away from it. In the relative silence following the departure of the caude, Ferbin could hear Holse trying to fire his pistol; the click, click, click noise sounded more hopeless than had the wounded caude's cries. The lyge flier went down on one knee again and took aim at the now utterly exposed Holse, who shook his head.

"Well, you can *still* fuck off!" he shouted.

The chronometer smacked the lyge flier across the bridge of the nose. The rifle pointed fractionally upwards as it fired, sending the shot a foot or so above Holse. He was up and running at the dazed figure on the far side of the roof before the chronometer Ferbin had thrown got to the edge of the tower's summit and vanished into the drizzle. The lyge looked down at the rolling, disconnected-looking figure in front of it and appeared merely puzzled as Holse threw himself forward and on to its rider.

"Fuck me, sir, you're a better shot than him," Holse said as he knelt on the flier's back and prised the rifle out of his fingers. Ferbin had started to think their assailant was a woman, but it was just a small-built man. Lyge were faster than caude but they could carry less weight; their fliers were usually chosen for their small frame.

Ferbin could see dark blood on the glowing blue band beneath the fallen flier. Holse checked the rifle and reloaded it, still with one knee pressing on the back of the struggling lyge flier.

"Thank you, Holse," Ferbin said. He looked up at the thin, dark, puzzled face of the lyge, which rose up a little and gave a single great beat of its wings before settling back down again. The pulse of air rolled over them. "What should we do with—"

The grenade fizzed into life again. They scrambled away on all fours, Holse making an attempt to pull the lyge flier with him. They rolled and clattered across the hard surface, and Ferbin had time to think that at least if he died here it would be on the Eighth, not somewhere lost and unholy between the stars. The grenade exploded with a terrific smacking noise that seemed to take Ferbin by the ears and slap him somewhere in between them. He heard a ringing sound and lay where he was.

When he collected his scattered senses and looked about him, he saw Holse a couple of strides away looking back at him, the lyge flier lying still a few strides further back, and that was all.

The lyge had gone; whether killed or wounded by the grenade or just startled by it, it was impossible to know.

Holse's mouth moved as if he was saying something, but Ferbin couldn't hear a damn thing.

A broad cylinder, a good fifteen strides across, rose up in the centre of the tower's summit, swallowing the thin tube that Ferbin had been talking to. This fresh extrusion climbed five metres into the air and stopped. A door big enough to accept three mounted men side by side slid open and a grey-blue light spilled out.

Around the tower, a number of great dark shapes started to appear, circling.

Ferbin and Holse got up and ran for the doorway.

His ears were still ringing, so Ferbin never heard the shot that hit him.

9. One-finger Man

Mertis tyl Loesp sat in his withdrawing chamber, high in the royal palace of Pourl. The room had started to seem overly modest to him recently; however, he'd thought it best to leave it a short-year or so before moving into any of the King's apartments. He was listening to two of his most trusted knights report.

"Your boy knew the old fellow's hiding place, in a secret room behind a cupboard. We hauled him out and persuaded him to tell us the truth of earlier events." Vollird, who had been one of those guarding the door when the late king had met his end in the old factory, smiled.

"The gentleman was a one-finger man," the other knight, Baerth, said. He too had been there when the King had died. He used both hands to mime breaking a small twig. A twitch about his lips might also have been a smile.

"Yes, thank you for the demonstration," tyl Loesp said to Baerth, then frowned at Vollird. "And then you found it necessary to kill the Head Scholar. Against my orders."

"We did," Vollird said, uncowed. "I reckoned the risk of bringing him to a barracks and oublietting him too great."

"Kindly explain," tyl Loesp said smoothly, sitting back.

Vollird was a tall, thin, darkly intense fellow with a look that could, as now, verge on insolent. He usually regarded the world with his head tipped downwards, eyes peering out from beneath his brow. It was by no means a shy or modest aspect; rather it seemed a little wary and distrusting, certainly, but mostly mocking, sly and calculating, and as though those eyes were keeping carefully under the cover of that sheltering brow, quietly evaluating weaknesses, vulnerabilities, and the best time to strike.

Baerth was a contrast; fair, small and bulky with muscle, he looked almost childish at times, though of the two he could be the most unrestrained when his blood was up.

Both would do tyl Loesp's bidding, which was all that mattered. Though on this occasion, of course, they had not. He had asked them to perform various disappearances, intimidations and other delicate commissions for him over the past few years and they had proved reliable and trustworthy, never failing him yet; however, he was worried they might have developed a taste for murder above obedience. A principal strand of this concern centred on who he could find to dispose of these two if they did prove in sum more liabilitous than advantageous to him; he had various options in that regard, but the most ruthless tended to be the least trustworthy and the least criminal the most tentative.

"Mr. Seltis' confession was most comprehensive," Vollird said, "and included the fact that the gentleman who had been there earlier had specifically demanded that the Head Scholar get word to said gentleman's brother here in the palace, regarding the manner of their father's death and the danger the younger brother might therefore be in. There had been no time for the Head Scholar to begin effecting such warning; however, he seemed most tearfully regretful at this and I formed the distinct impression he would do what he could to pass this information on should he have the chance, to whatever barracksman, militia or army he happened to encounter. So we took him to the roof on excuse of visiting the place where the fleeing gentlemen had absconded and threw him to his death. We told those in the Scholastery that he had jumped, and assumed our most shocked expressions."

Baerth glanced at the other knight. "I said we might have kept him alive as we were told and just torn out his tongue."

Vollird sighed. "Then he would have written out a warning message."

Baerth looked unconvinced. "We could have broken the rest of his fingers."

"He'd have written using a pen stuck in his mouth," Vollird said, exasperated.

"We might—"

"Then he'd have shoved the pen up his arse," Vollird said loudly. "Or found some sort of way, if he was desperate enough, which I judged him to be." He looked at tyl Loesp. "At any rate, dead is what he is."

Tyl Loesp thought. "Well," he said, "I will concede that was well enough done, in the circumstances. However, I worry that we now have a Scholastery full of offended scholars."

"They'd be easy enough to cull too, sir," Vollird said. "There's a lot of them, but they're all nicely gathered and guarded, and they're all soft as a babe's head, I swear."

"Again, true, but they'll have parents, brothers, connections. It would be better if we can persuade a new Head Scholar to keep them in order and say no more of what occurred."

Vollird looked unconvinced. "There's no better way of ensuring a tongue's held than stilling it for good, sir."

Tyl Loesp gazed at Vollird. "You are very good at pieces of the truth, Vollird, aren't you?"

"Only as needs be, tyl Loesp," the other man replied, holding his gaze. "Not to a fault."

Tyl Loesp felt sure the two knights were convinced that killing all the scholars at Anjrinh would end the problem that they might have seen Ferbin, alive and on the run.

Ferbin, alive. How entirely like that fatuous, lucky idiot to stumble through a battle unscathed and evade all attempts at capture. All the same, tyl Loesp doubted that even Ferbin's luck would be entirely sufficient for that; he suspected the servant, one Choubris Holse, was providing the cunning the prince so evidently lacked.

Vollird and Baerth both imagined that simply excising those who'd seen the prince would put an end to the matter; it was the obvious, soldierly way to think. Neither could see that all such surgery had its own further complications and ensuences. This present problem was like a small boil on the hand; lancing it would be quick and immediately satisfying, but a cautious doctor would know that this approach might lead to an even worse affliction that could infectively paralyse the whole arm and even threaten the body's life itself. Sometimes the most prudent course was just to apply some healing oils or cooling poultice and let things subside. It might be the slower treatment but it carried fewer risks, left no scars and could be more effective in the end.

"Well," tyl Loesp told the knights, "there is one tongue I'd have stilled as you propose, though it must look as though the gentleman has been careless with his own life, rather than had it surgeried from him. However, the scholars will be left alone. The family of the spy who alerted us will be rewarded. The family, though, not the boy. He will already be jealoused and despised quite sufficiently already, if the others truly suspect who was there."

"If it was who we think it might have been. We still cannot be sure," Vollird said.

"I have not the luxury of thinking otherwise," tyl Loesp told him.

"And the fugitive himself?" Baerth asked.

"Lost, for the moment." Tyl Loesp glanced at the telegraphed report he'd received that morning from the captain of the lyge squadron who had come so close to capturing or killing Ferbin and his servant – assuming it was them – at the D'neng-oal Tower just the night before. One of their quarry wounded, possibly, the report said. Too many possibles and probables for his liking. "However," he said, smiling broadly at the two knights, "I too now have the documents to get people to the Surface. The fugitive and his helper are running away; that is the second best thing they can do, after dying." He smiled. "Vollird, I imagine you and Baerth would like to see the Surface and the eternal stars again, would you not?"

The two knights exchanged looks.

"I think we'd rather ride with the army against the Deldeyn," Vollird said. The main part of the army had already left the day before to form up before the Tower through which they would attack the Ninth. Tyl Loesp would leave to join them tomorrow for the descent.

Baerth nodded. "Aye, there's honour in that."

"Perhaps we've killed enough just for you, tyl Loesp," Vollird suggested. "We grow tired of murdering with every second glance directed over our backs. Might it not be time for us to serve Sarl less obliquely, on the battlefield, against an enemy all recognise?"

To serve me *is* to serve the Sarl; I am the state, tyl Loesp wanted to say, but did not, not even to these two. Instead he frowned and pursed his lips momentarily. "Let us three agree a compact, shall we? I shall forgive you for being obtuse, disloyal and selfish if you two forgive me for seeming to have expressed my orders by way of a question, with the implication that there is any choice whatsoever on your part. What d'you say?"

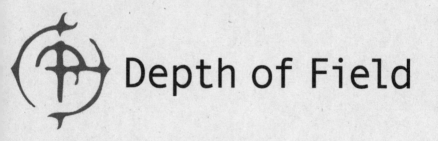

Depth of Field

10.   A Certain Lack

She had been a man for a year.

That had been different. Everything had been different. She had learned so much: about herself, about people, about civilisations.

Time: she came to think in Standard years, eventually. To her, at first, they were about one and a half short-years or very roughly half a long-year.

Gravity: she felt intolerably heavy and worryingly fragile at once. A treatment she had already agreed to started to thicken her bones and reduce her height before she left the Eighth, but even so, for the time she was on the ship that took her from the Surface and during the first fifty days or so after her arrival, she towered over most people and felt oddly delicate. Allegedly, the new clothes she had chosen had been reinforced to save her from breaking any bones if she fell badly in the stronger gravity.

She had assumed this was a lie to make her feel less frightened, and just took care instead.

Only the measures of human-scale length were roughly as she knew them; strides were near enough metres, and she already thought in kilometres, even if she'd grown up with ten raised to the power of three rather than two to the power of ten.

But that was just the start of it.

For the first couple of years after arriving in the Culture she had been simply as she was, save for that amendment of thickening and shortening. Meanwhile she got to know the Culture and it got to know her. She learned a lot, about everything. The drone Turminder Xuss had accompanied her from the day she'd stepped from the ship she'd arrived on, the space vessel called *Lightly Seared on the Reality Grill* (she found their ships' names absurd, childish and ridiculous at first, then got used to them, then thought she kind of understood them, then realised there was no understanding the Mind of a ship, and went back to finding them annoying). The drone answered any questions she had and sometimes talked on her behalf.

Those first three years had been spent on the Orbital Gadampth, mostly on the part called Lesuus, in a sort of extended, teased-out city built on a group of islands scattered across a wide bay on the edge of a small inland sea. The city was named Klusse, and it had some similarities to an ordinary city, despite being much cleaner and lacking any curtain walls or other defensive components that she could discern. Mostly, though, it seemed to be a sort of vast Scholastery.

It took her some time to work out why, as she went walking about the boulevards, terraces, promenades and piazzas of the place, she had felt – not initially, but gradually, just when she ought to have felt herself getting used to the place – an odd mixture of comfort and disturbance at the same time. Eventually she realised it was because in all the faces that she saw there, not one held a disfiguring tumour or had been eaten half away by disease. She had yet to see even a mildly disfiguring skin condition or a lazy eye. Similarly, in all the bodies she moved among, not one was limping or supporting itself on a crutch or trolley, or went hobbling past on a club foot. And not a single madman, not one poor defective standing flecked screaming on a street corner howling at the stars.

She hadn't appreciated this at first because at the time she was still being amazed at the sheer bewildering physical variation of the people around her, but once she had become used to that, she started to notice that although there was near infinite physical variety here, there was no deformity, and while there was prodigious eccentricity, no dementia. There were more facial, bodily and personality types than she could have imagined, but they were all the product of health and choice, not disease and fate. Everyone was, or could be if they so desired, beautiful in both form and character.

Later she would find that, as this was the Culture after all, *of course* there were people who embraced ugliness and even the appearance of deformity or mutilation just to be different or to express something inside that they felt ought to be broadcast to their peers; however – once she had passed over her initial sense of irritation and exasperation at such people (did they not, even if unknowingly, mock those truly afflicted, those with no choice in how hideous they looked?) – she realised that even that deliberate adoption of unsightliness displayed a kind of societal confidence, a thumbing of the collective nose at the workings of crude providence and the ancient tyranny, now itself long overthrown, of genetic aberration, gross injury and transmissible pestilence.

A star named Aoud shone down upon the ten-million-kilometre bracelet of the Orbital. This sun was what everybody else seemed to regard as a real star; one which had been naturally formed. To her it sounded incredibly old and absurdly, almost wastefully enormous.

There, in Klusse, she learned about the history of the Culture and the story of the galaxy itself. She learned about the other civilisations that she had been taught as a child were called the Optimae. They generally referred to themselves as the Involveds or the In-Play, though the terms were loose and there was no exact equivalent of the Sarl word Optimae, with its implication of supremacy. "High-level Involved" was probably as close as you could get.

She also learned pretty much all there was to be learned about her own people, the Sarl: their long-ago evolution on a faraway planet of the same name, their involvement in a terrible war, their condemnation, exile and displacement (partly for their own good, partly for that of the peoples they had shared that original planet with; the consensus was that they would either kill everybody else or be killed) and their eventual sanctuary/internment in Sursamen under the auspices of the Galactic Council, the Morthanveld and Nariscene. This version felt like the truth, she thought; close enough to the myths and legends of her own people, but less self-serving, less dramatically glorious, more equivocal in its moral implications.

This area of study turned up surprising details. The fact that the Deldeyn and the Sarl were the same people, for example; the Deldeyn were a sub-group of the main population who had been transported to the level below by the Oct over a thousand years ago. And the Oct had done this without permission from their Nariscene mentors; that level, while once supporting many peoples, had seen them all evacuated millennia ago and was supposed to have been left empty of intelligent life until further notice. The Oct had been forced to apologise, undertake never to do such a thing again and pay reparations in the form of surrendered influence elsewhere; however, the unauthorised movement of people had finally, reluctantly, been accepted as a fait accompli.

She learned about pan-humanity, about the great diasporic welter of human-like, human-ish and humanoid species scattered throughout so much of the galaxy.

She learned about the present sociopolitical set-up that existed in the galaxy and felt a sort of widespread satisfaction that there was just so much of it, and almost all of it peaceful. There were millions of species, hundreds of different *types* of species, even casting one's definition wide, and that was without taking into account civilisations that were composed more of machines than biological beings at all. Ultimately the galaxy, indeed the sum of the universe in its entirety, was mostly nothing; average it all out and it made a pretty good vacuum. But within the foci of matter that were the systems, the stars and planets and habitats – what a cornucopia of life was there!

There were bogglingly large numbers just of these pan-humans (of which, of course, she was one), but they still formed less than a single per cent of all the aggregated life-mass of the greater galaxy. Also, where they did exist, men and women were mostly – most places, most of the time – equals. In the Culture this was even guaranteed by birthright; you could be whatever gender you wished – just by thinking about it! She found this highly satisfactory, and a kind of vindication.

Life buzzed in, fumed about, rattled around and quite thoroughly infested the entire galaxy, and probably – almost certainly – well beyond. The vast ongoingness of it all somehow put all one's own petty concerns and worries into context, making them seem not irrelevant, but of much less distressing immediacy. Context was indeed all, as her father had always insisted, but the greater context she was learning about acted to shrink the vast-seeming scale of the Eighth Level of Sursamen and all its wars, politics, disputes, struggles, tribulations and vexations until it all looked very far away and trivial indeed.

She learned about Contact, the part of the Culture that went out to discover and interact with other civilisations, especially new and fast-developing ones, and about its slightly scurrilous, tentatively raffish, arguably shadowy division called Special Circumstances. It was some time before she realised that she herself was expected to have at least a chance of becoming part of this prestigious, if not entirely respectable organisation. This was, she gathered, supposed to be a most singular and unusual honour and almost the only worthwhile distinction the Culture had to offer that was not available on demand. However, she was, again, instantly suspicious.

For some time the aspect of Orbital life she marvelled at more than anything else was the geography: mountains, cliffs and gorges, pinnacles, scree and boulder fields. That none of it was truly natural, that it had all been designed and manufactured from debris found in the solar system when the world was made only added to her amazement. She hiked the high mountains and learned to ski. She took part in various sports and discovered she even enjoyed being part of a team. She hadn't expected that, somehow.

She had made friends and taken lovers, when she had grown to believe that her new, squat self was not hideous. Not all pairings worked, even, as it were, mechanically – there was a wide variety of body shapes. Another treatment she chose monitored her womb, to alert her on the very low off-chance that she mated with somebody her own physical system found sufficiently compatible for her to conceive by. She had wondered if this was not a lie, too, but nothing ever happened.

She played with her own dreams, and took part in shared dreams that were vast games, using nothing more exotic-seeming than special pillows or nightcaps to access these strange sub-realities. She realised that she slept much more than most of her friends, missing out on a potential part of waking life. She asked for another treatment, which solved that problem as though it had never existed; she slept deeply for a few hours each of these clockworkly regular and dependable nights and awoke thoroughly refreshed each morning.

She took part in other semi-hallucinatory experiences that seemed like games but which she knew were also lessons and evaluations, submerging her entirely conscious self into simulations of reality that were sometimes based on real, earlier events and experiences, and sometimes were as entirely deliberately created as the Orbital and its amazingly vertiginous landscape. Some left her troubled to know the terrible things people – pan-humans and beyond, but all people – could do to each other. The implication, though, was that such ghastliness was an affliction, and could be at least partially cured. The Culture represented the hospital, or perhaps a whole caring society, Contact was the physician and SC the anaesthetic and the medicine. Sometimes the scalpel.

Almost the only aspect of her new life that she adapted to without pause for thought was the total absence of money in the Culture. She had been a princess, after all, and so was perfectly used to that.

She watched some of her friends enter states she could not share, and, after great initial wariness, asked for more treatments that caused glands in her body she hadn't even known she possessed to alter over a few tens of days until she possessed a simple drug-gland suite inside her head and a modest choice of mixtures of trace chemicals she could now choose to release into her bloodstream and brain whenever she wanted.

That had been interesting.

Amongst the Sarl, at least on the Eighth, every drug had at least one unwanted and unpleasant side effect. Here; nothing. You got what you wanted, no more. She remained highly sceptical, unconvinced such light was possible without shade. She no longer needed the drone Turminder Xuss, who went off to tend to others. She used a finger-ring terminal to connect with the dataverse instead.

She began to collect amendments, treatments, as one might accumulate jewellery. She even had a couple of treatments rescinded, just removed from her altogether, simply to make sure that the processes truly were fully reversible. A new tutor, one who was present only rarely but seemed in some sense senior to the others, a bush-like being who had once been a man, called Batra, sounded amused when he/it said she was a suspicious child. Amused and somehow approving. She got the feeling she was supposed to feel flattered, but she'd been more concerned about the mild insult contained in the word "child".

People shifted, went away, relationships ended. She asked one of her female mentors about how one changed from female to male. Another treatment. Over most of a year she grew slightly, bulked out further, grew hair in strange places, and watched, fascinated, as her genitals went from fissure to spire. She did wake up a couple of nights covered in sweat, appalled at what was happening to her, feeling herself, wondering if this was all some enormously laboured joke and she was being made a freak of deliberately, for sport, but there were always people to talk to who had been through the same experience – both in person and via screens and sims – and no shortage of archived material to explain and reassure.

She kept a couple of intermittent, unbothered lovers even as she changed, then, as a man, took many more, mostly female. It was true: one made a better, more considerate lover when one had once been as one's partner. He woke up one morning after a strenuous night with a small group of old friends and just-mets, blinking in the sunshine of a brilliant new day, looking out over a broad balcony and a sparkling sea to a great columnar mountain that reminded him of a Tower back home, and woke everybody else up with his laughter.

He was never sure why he decided to change back. For a long time he thought to return to Sursamen as a man, see what they made of him then. Apart from anything else, there had been a couple of ladies at the court he had always been fond of, and now felt something more for. By that point he knew his brother Elime had been killed and he was the eldest child of the King; the next king, indeed, if you looked at it in a certain way. He might return, claim the throne, in time. By then, with further treatments, he might have martial skills and attributes beyond those of any warrior who had ever lived on the Eighth. He'd be unstoppable; he could *take* the throne if he wanted. That would be hilarious. Oh, the looks on certain faces!

But that would be cruel at best, he thought. At worst, the results might be something between melodrama and the bloodiest of tragedies. Anyway, to be king of the Sarl no longer seemed like the greatest thing a soul might aspire to, not by some long measure.

He changed, became a she again. The lesson regarding being a considerate lover did not change.

She took her Full Name. In her father's kingdom, she had been called Djan Seriy Hausk'a yun Pourl, yun Dich – this translated as Djan, Prince-Consort Hausk's daughter of Pourl, of the Eighth.

Here, now that she thought of herself as a Culture citizen – albeit still one that had been born and brought up elsewhere – she took the name Meseriphine-Sursamen/VIIIsa Djan Seriy Anaplian dam Pourl.

Marain, the Culture's exquisitely formed meta-language, used its Secondary Numbering Series to denote Shellworld levels. The Anaplian part came from her mother's name: Anaplia. The word Seriy – indicating she had been raised to be fit to be married to a prince – she kept for a laugh. She expressed disappointment that there was no ceremony to mark the taking of one's Full Name. Her friends and colleagues invented one for her.

She had further treatments, to give her control of many more aspects of her body and mind. Now she would age very slowly, and did not really need to age at all. Now she was proof against any natural disease under this or any other sun, and even losing something as major as a limb would prove only a temporary inconvenience, as a new one would simply grow back. Now she had the full panoply of drug glands, with all the benefits and responsibilities that entailed. Now she gained fully augmented senses – so that, for example, her vision became sharper and brought her information about the infrared and the ultraviolet – now she could sense radio waves, now she was able to interface directly with machines via a thing called a neural lace that had grown about and through her brain like a flimsy, three-dimensional net, now she could switch off pain and fatigue (though her body seemed to scorn them anyway), now her nerves changed to become more like wires, shifting impulses far faster than before, while her bones accreted strands of carbon to make them stronger and her muscles went through chemical and microscopically scaled mechanical changes that made them more effective and more powerful. Every major internal organ grew more efficient, more tolerant, more capable, resilient and adaptable, even as many of them grew smaller.

She became part of Contact and joined the crew of the General Contact Unit *Transient Atmospheric Phenomenon*. She'd had the luxury of a choice in the matter and had turned down the *Experiencing A Significant Gravitas Shortfall* and the *Pure Big Mad Boat Man* just because of their ridiculous names. She served with distinction for only five years aboard the GCU before the invitation to join Special Circumstances arrived. A surprisingly short period of additional training ensued; almost all the new skills she would now need were already there, pre-implanted. She was reunited with the drone Turminder Xuss, who had always been intended as her companion. She discovered the old machine came complete with a small squadron of knife, attack and scout missiles and was effectively a little arsenal of wide-spectrum destruction all on its own.

SC added its own final, finessed layers of additional characteristics to her already heady mix of bodily enhancements, empowering her still further: here were fingernails that could lase, to signal, blind or kill, here was a tiny reactor within her skull that, amongst other things, could provide the power to keep her alive and conscious for years without oxygen, here was a whole-body fibre structure welded to her very bones that could sense distortions in the skein of space itself; here was a level of conscious control over her own body and, almost incidentally, over any merely electronic machine within fifty metres which exceeded that of any rider over their mount or any champion swordsman over his blade ...

She felt, she realised one day, like a god.

She thought then of Sursamen, and her old self, and knew there was no going back.

She was going back. And she was losing some of those skills and attributes, some of those martial enhancements.

"You're gelding me," she said to Jerle Batra.

"I'm sorry. The Morthanveld are very wary of Special Circumstances agents."

"Oh, really." She shook her head. "We're no threat to them." She looked at the man who looked like a small bush. "Well, we're not, are we?"

"Of course not. On the contrary." Batra made a shrugging motion. "It's a courtesy."

"It feels like a discourtesy to me."

"That is unfortunate."

"We may be overdoing the coddling thing here, you know," she said.

"All the same."

They were on the platform *Quonber*, riding frigid waves of air above a high mountain range; kilometres beneath, a grey-white glacier streaked with lines of shattered rock curved and corrugated its way towards the limits of a tungsten sky.

The coddling Djan Seriy was referring to involved the almost exaggerated respect the Culture as a whole had recently been showing the Morthanveld. The Morthanveld were technologically on a par with the Culture and the two civilisations had co-existed on good terms since they had encountered each other thousands of years earlier, sharing extensive cultural links and co-operating on a variety of projects. They were not exactly allies – the waterworlders had kept scrupulously neutral during the Idiran war, for example – but they were of a mind on most matters.

Djan Seriy's discomfiture was being caused by the fact that some of the Culture's more self-congratulatingly clever Minds (not in itself an underpopulated category), patently with far too much time on their platters, had come up with the shiny new theory that the Culture was not just in itself completely spiffing and marvellous and a credit to all concerned, it somehow represented a sort of climactic stage for all civilisations, or at least for all those which chose to avoid heading straight for Sublimation as soon as technologically possible (Sublimation meant your whole civilisation waved farewell to the matter-based universe pretty much altogether, opting for a sort of honorary godhood).

Avoid self-destruction, recognise – and renounce – money for the impoverishing ration system it really was, become a bunch of interfering, do-gooding busybodies, resist the siren call of selfish self-promotion that was Subliming and free your conscious machines to do what they did best – essentially, running everything – and there you were; millennia of smug self-regard stretched before you, no matter what species you had started out from.

So. It was thought, by those Minds that especially concerned themselves with such matters, that the Morthanveld were on the cusp of going Culture; of undergoing a kind of societal phase-change, altering subtly but significantly into a water-worlder equivalent of the Culture. All that would need to happen for this to be effected, it was reckoned, would be the Morthanveld giving up the last vestiges of monetary exchange within their society, adopting a more comprehensive, self-consciously benign and galaxy-wide foreign policy and – probably most crucially – granting their AIs complete self-expressive freedom and full citizenship rights.

The Culture wanted to encourage this, obviously, but could not be seen to interfere or to be trying to influence matters. This was the main reason for not upsetting the people who would be Djan Seriy's hosts for the latter part of her journey back to Sursamen; this was why she was being stripped of almost all her SC enhancements and even some of the amendments she had chosen for herself before Special Circumstances had invited her aboard in the first place.

"Probably a bluff anyway," she told Turminder Xuss grumpily, looking out over the surface of cragged, chevronned ice below. The skies were clear and the balcony on which she stood and over which the drone silently hovered provided a calm, pleasantly warm environment; however, a furious torrent of air was howling all around the platform as the planet's jetstream swept above the high mountains. Force fields beyond the balcony's perimeter prevented the invisible storm from buffeting and freezing them, though such was the power of the screaming rush of air that a faint echo of its voice could be heard even through the field; a distant, thrumming wail, like some animal trapped and shrieking on the ice far below.

When they had first taken up station here during the previous night the air had been perfectly still and you could hear the cracks and creaks and booms of the glacier as it ground against the torn shoulders of the mountains that formed its banks and scoured its way across the great gouged bed of fractured rock beneath.

"A bluff?" Turminder Xuss sounded unconvinced.

"Yes," Anaplian said. "Could it not be that the Morthanveld merely pretend to be on the brink of becoming like the Culture in order to keep the Culture from interfering in their business?"

"Hmm," the drone said. "That wouldn't work for long."

"Even so."

"And you'd wonder why the idea that the Morthanveld were poised in this manner was allowed to become so prevalent in the first place."

Anaplian realised they had got rather rapidly to the point that all such conversations regarding the strategic intentions of the Culture tended to arrive at sooner or later, where it became clear that the issue boiled down to the question What Are The Minds Really Up To? This was always a good question, and it was usually only churls and determinedly diehard cynics who even bothered to point out that it rarely, if ever, arrived paired up with an equally good answer.

The normal, almost ingrained response of people at this point was to metaphorically throw their hands in the air and exclaim that if *that* was what it really all boiled down to then there was no point in even attempting to pursue the issue further, because as soon as the motivations, analyses and stratagems of Minds became the defining factor in a matter, all bets were most profoundly off, for the simple reason that any and all efforts to second-guess such infinitely subtle and hideously devious devices were self-evidently futile.

Anaplian was not so sure about this. It was her suspicion that it suited the purposes of the Minds rather too neatly that people believed this so unquestioningly. Such a reaction represented not so much the honest appraisal of further enquiry as being pointless as an unthinking rejection of the need to enquire at all.

"Perhaps the Minds are jealous," Anaplian said. "They don't want the Morthanveld to steal even the echo of their thunder by becoming like them. They patronise the waterworlders in order to antagonise them, make them do the opposite of what is supposedly anticipated, so that they become *less* like the Culture. Because that is what the Minds really desire."

"That makes as much sense as anything I've heard so far on the matter," Turminder Xuss said, politely.

She was not being allowed to take the drone with her on her return to Sursamen. SC agent + combat drone was a combination that was well known far beyond the Culture. Although perilously close to a cliché, it remained a partnership you could, allegedly, still frighten children and bad people with.

Anaplian felt a faint tingle somewhere inside her head and experienced a sort of buzzing sensation throughout her body. She tried clicking into her skein sense, that let her monitor significant gravity waves in her vicinity and alerted her to any warp activity nearby, but the system was off-line, flagged indefinitely inoperable though not as a result of hostile action (nevertheless, she could feel at least one part of her SC-amended neural lace protesting, some automatic system forever watching for damage by stealth reacting to what it would register as the impairment of her abilities and the degradation of her inherent survivability with pre-programmed outrage).

The platform's own drone-standard AI was, with her permission, moving slowly through her suite of enhancements and gradually turning off those it was thought the Morthanveld might object to. Click. There went the electromagnetic effector ability. She tried interfering with the field unit buried in the ceiling overhead, which was keeping the air on the balcony insulated from the thin and well-below-freezing airstream coursing around the platform. No connection. She could still sense EM activity but she couldn't affect it any more. She had lived most of her life without such abilities and to date had used very few of them in anger, but she experienced their going with a distinct sense of loss and even dismay.

She looked down at her fingernails. They appeared normal at the moment, but she'd already thought the signal that would make them detach and fall off by the following morning. There would be no pain or blood and new nails would grow back during the next few days, but they wouldn't be Coherent Radiation Emission Weapons, they wouldn't be lasers.

Oh well, she thought, inspecting them, even ordinary, unamended nails could still scratch.

Click. There, she couldn't radio now either. No transmissions possible. Trapped inside her own head. She tried to communicate via her lace, calling up Leeb Scoperin, one of her colleagues here and her most recent lover. Nothing directly; she would have to go through the platform's systems, just like ordinary Culture people. She had rather hoped to see Leeb before she left, but he just hadn't been able to get away from whatever it was he was doing at such short notice.

Turminder Xuss' own systems must have registered something happening. "That you?" it asked.

She felt mildly insulted, as though the drone had enquired whether she'd just farted. "Yes," she said sharply. "That was me. Comms off-line."

"No need to get snappy."

She looked at the machine through narrowed eyes. "I think you'll find there is," she informed it.

"My, it's breezy out there!" Batra said, floating in through the force field from outside. "Djan Seriy; the module is here."

"I'll get my bag," Anaplian said.

"Please," Turminder Xuss said. "Allow me."

Batra must have read the expression on her face as she watched the drone make its way to the nearest interior door.

"I think Turminder Xuss is going to miss you," Batra said, extending loops of brittle-looking twigs and branches to take his/its weight and standing head-height in front of her like a framework for the sculpture of a human.

Anaplian shook her head. "The machine grows sentimental," she said.

"Unlike yourself?" Batra asked neutrally.

She guessed he was talking about Toark, the child she had rescued from the burning city. The boy was still asleep; she had crept into his cabin to say a one-sided farewell earlier that morning, stroking his hair, whispering, not waking him. Batra had agreed, reluctantly, to look after the child while she was away.

"I have always been sentimental," Anaplian claimed.

The little three-seat module dropped from the sky, lowered itself gently through the roof of force field bowing over the platform's flight deck and backed up towards the group waiting for it, rear door hingeing open.

"Farewell, Djan Seriy," Batra said, extending a less-than-skeletal assemblage at chest height, the extremity vaguely hand-shaped.

Anaplian put her palm briefly against this sculpted image, feeling faintly ridiculous. "You will look after the boy?" she said.

"Oh," Batra said with a sighing noise, "as though he were your own."

"I am serious," she said. "If I don't come back, I want you to take care of him, until you can find somewhere and someone more fitting."

"You have my word," Batra told her. "Just make sure you do come back."

"I shall endeavour to," she said.

"You have backed up?"

"Last night," Anaplian confirmed. They were both being polite; Batra would know very well that she had backed herself up. The platform had taken a reading of her mind state the evening before. Should she fail to return – whether due to death or in theory any other reason – a clone of her could be grown and all her personality and memories implanted into it, creating a new her almost indistinguishable from the person she was now. It did not do to forget that, in a disquietingly real sense, to be an SC agent was to be owned by SC. The compensation was that even death was just a temporary operational glitch, soon overcome. Again though, only in a sense.

Turminder Xuss reappeared and deposited her bags in the module. "Well, goodbye, dear girl," it said. "Try to avoid getting into any scrapes; I shan't be there to save you."

"I have already adjusted my expectations," Anaplian told it. The drone was silent, as though not sure what to make of this. Anaplian bowed formally. "Goodbye," she said to both of them, then turned and walked into the module.

Three minutes later she was stepping out of it again, aboard the *Eight Rounds Rapid*, a Delinquent-class Fast Picket and ex-General Offensive Unit which would take her to rendezvous with the Steppe-class Medium Systems Vehicle *Don't Try This At Home*. This represented just the first leg of her complicated and languidly paced journey back to her old home.

Djan Seriy was shown to a small cabin aboard the old ex-warship by a ship-slaved drone. She would be aboard for less than a full day; however, she had wanted somewhere to lie down and think.

She opened her bag. She looked at what was lying on top of her few clothes and possessions. "I don't recall packing you," she muttered, and was immediately uncertain whether she was talking to herself or not (she instinctively tried to read the device with her active EM sense, but of course that didn't work any more).

She was not talking to herself.

"Well remembered," the thing she was looking at said. It appeared to be a dildo.

"Are you what I think you are?"

"I don't know. What do you think I am?"

"I think you are a knife missile. Or something very similar."

"Well, yes," the small device said. "But then again no."

Anaplian frowned. "Certainly you would appear to possess some of the more annoying linguistic characteristics of, say, a drone."

"Well done, Djan Seriy!" the machine said brightly. "I am indeed one and both at the same time. The mind and personality of myself, Turminder Xuss, copied into the seasoned though still hale and hearty body of my most capable knife missile, lightly disguised."

"I suppose I ought to be gratified you chose to make your ruse known at this point rather than later."

"Ha ha. I would never have been so ungallant. Or intrusive."

"You hope to protect me from scrapes, I take it."

"Absolutely. Or at least share them with you."

"Do you think you'll get away with this?"

"Who can say? Worth a try."

"You might have thought to ask me."

"I did."

"You did? I appear to have lost more than I thought."

"I thought to ask you, but I didn't. So as to protect you from potential blame."

"How kind."

"This way I may take full responsibility. In the I hope unlikely event you wish me to return whence I came, I shall leave you when you board the *Don't Try This At Home*."

"Does Batra know?"

"I most sincerely hope not. I could spend the rest of my Contact career toting bags, or worse."

"Is this even semi-official?" Anaplian asked. She had never entirely lost her well-developed sense of suspicion.

"Hell's teeth, no! All my own work." The drone paused. "I was charged with protecting you, Djan Seriy," it said, sounding more serious now. "And I am not some blindly obedient machine. I would like to continue to help protect you, especially as you are travelling so far outside the general protection of the Culture, to a place of violence, with your abilities reduced. For these reasons, I duly offer my services."

Anaplian frowned. "Save that for which your appearance would imply you are most suited," she said, "I accept."

11. Bare, Night

Oramen lay on the bed with the girl who'd called herself Jish. He was playing with her hair, tangling long brown locks of it around one finger then releasing it again. He was amused by the similarity in shape of the girl's spiralled curls and the rolls of smoke she was producing from the unge pipe she was smoking. The smoke rolled lazily upwards towards the high, ornate ceiling of the room, which was part of a house in an elegant and respectable area of the city which had been favoured by many of the court over the years, not least by his brother Ferbin.

Jish passed him the pipe, but he waved it away. "No."

"Oh, come!" she said, giggling. She turned towards him to try and force the pipe on him, her breasts jiggling as she moved across the broad, much-tousled bed. "Don't be a spoil!" She tried to jam the stem of the pipe into his mouth.

He turned his head, moved the pipe away again with the flat of one hand. "No, thank you," he said.

She sat cross-legged in front of him, perfectly naked, and tapped him on the nose with the stem. "Why won't the Ora play? Won't the Ora play?" she said in a funny, croaky little voice. Behind her, the broad, fan-shaped headboard of the bed was covered with a painting of mythical half-people – the satyrs and nymphs of this world – engaged in a pink-toned orgy upon fluffy white clouds, peeling faintly at the edges. "Why won't the Ora play?"

He smiled. "Because the Ora has other things to do."

"What's to do, my lovely prince?" She puffed briefly on the pipe, releasing the grey smoke in a liquidic sheen. "The army's away and all is quiet. Everyone's gone, the weather is warm and there's nothing to do. Play with your Jish, why not?"

He lay back in the bed, stretching. One hand went out to the glass of wine that stood on the bedside table, as though about to grasp it, but then it fell away again.

"I know," Jish said, smiling, and turned half away from him, breasts outlined in the smoky sunlight pouring through the tall windows on the far side of the room. He could see she was pulling deeply on the pipe. She turned back to him, eyes bright, came forward and down and, holding the pipe away from the two of them, placed her lips over his, opening her mouth full of smoke and trying to make him breathe it from her lungs into his. He blew back sharply, making her draw away, coughing and hacking in an unruly cloud of bitter fumes.

The pipe clattered to the floor and she coughed again, one hand at her mouth, almost sounding like she was retching. Oramen smiled. He sat upright quickly and grabbed her hand, pulling it sharply away from her and twisting his grip on her skin so that she gave a small cry of pain. Ferbin had told him that many women responded well to being treated roughly and – though he found this bizarre – he was testing this theory.

"I would not force myself on you, my dear," he told her. Her face was unattractively reddened, and tears were in her eyes. "You ought to reciprocate." He let go her hand.

The girl rubbed her wrist and glared at him, then sniffed and tossed her hair. She looked for the pipe and saw it on the floor. She levered herself half out of the bed to get it.

"What's all this?" Tove Lomma stuck his head over the fan-shaped headboard. The room contained two large beds which could be side-by-side or headboard-to-headboard, if one wanted just a little additional privacy. Tove was with another couple of girls on the other bed. His big, sweaty-looking face beamed down at them. "Not a tiff, I hope?" He gazed at Jish's backside as she stretched across for the pipe. "Hmm. Most appreciable." He looked at Oramen, nodding at Jish's buttocks as she pulled herself back into the bed. "Perhaps we ought to swap shortly, eh, my prince?"

"Perhaps," Oramen said.

One of Tove's girls appeared at his side and stuck her tongue in his ear. Oramen nodded at this. "I think you're wanted," he told Tove.

"I hear and obey," Tove said, with a wink. He and the girl disappeared.

Oramen stared up at the ceiling. How much had changed, he thought. How much he'd grown and matured, just in the month since his father's death. He'd been with girls, learned to smoke and drink and waved a ceremonial goodbye to an entire army. He had found a few pretty words to say, both to the girls – though they needed no cajoling, save the rattle of a purse – and to the army. His little speech there had been of his own devising – the one tyl Loesp had prepared for him had seemed vainglorious and immodest (the regent had done his best to hide his displeasure). Well, it had been mostly of his own devising; he had borrowed a little from *The House of Many Roofs* by Sinnel, with a hint of the executioner's speech in act three of *Baron Lepessi* by Prode the younger.

And off the fabulous spread of their forces had gone, under banners of bright cloth and cloud-white steam, with many a clank and hiss and whinny and roar and rattle and cheer, all bound for glory, destined to fall upon the now near-defenceless

Deldeyn and finally complete King Hausk's grand plan of unity across the Eighth and beyond. Thus would come the Golden Age of peace his father had talked about, when a prince of his, that is Oramen's, stamp might take his people on to still greater accomplishments and recognition.

Such was the theory. They had to win their battle first. The army was not taking the obvious route and would be gone longer than might have been anticipated, which ought to make the result all the more certain – the Deldeyn would presumably have most of what was left of their much-reduced forces waiting at the most obvious portal Tower, so would be surprised as well as overwhelmed – but one still never knew for sure. He hadn't been allowed to go with the army. Still a boy, they said; better not risk their last prince, not after what had happened to Ferbin . . .

He wasn't sure if he'd wanted to go or not. It would have been interesting, and it seemed a pity that there would not even be one of the late king's children there to witness this last great campaign. He yawned. Well, never mind; he doubted there would be more than one man in a hundred in the army who would not rather be where he was right now than where they were.

His father had asked him if he wanted to come to a house like this, a few seasons earlier, but he hadn't felt ready. He had anyway not been utterly unprepared; for a couple of years Ferbin had been regaling him with tales of debauchery, mostly centred around such houses, so he knew what went on and what was required. Still, the full experience was most surprisingly congenial. It certainly beat studying. He'd wished Shir Rocasse a happy retirement.

And Tove had been, well, like the best and most accommodating, most encouraging and helpful friend a fellow could ever have. He'd told him as much, and been glad to see the resulting look of pleasure on Tove's face.

Jish was refilling the pipe. Oramen watched her for a little, listening to the noises coming from the far side of the head-board, then he swung gently out of the bed and started to pull on his clothes. "I have to go," he told the girl.

"You don't really want to go," she said, a sly expression on her face. She nodded. "*That* doesn't want to go."

He looked down. He was hard again. "That's not me," he told her, "that's only my cock." He tapped his head. "This wants to go."

She shrugged and lit the pipe.

He pulled on his trous then stood, tucking his shirt in.

The girl looked darkly through wreaths of grey smoke as he turned towards the door, holding his boots in one hand.

"Ferbin would have been more of a sport," she said.

He turned and sat by the footboard, reaching to pull the girl towards him and saying quietly, "You were with my brother?" He glanced up. The top edge of the other bed's headboard was swaying back and forth. "Quietly," he warned her.

"A few times," Jish said with a sort of shy defiance. "He was a laugh. Not like they're saying now. *He'd* have stayed."

"I bet he would," Oramen said. His gaze searched her eyes, then he smiled and put one hand out to stroke her face. "I really do have to go, Jish. Another time."

He padded to the door, boots still in one hand. Jish fell back on the bed, staring up at the ceiling, pipe out to the side, as the door closed quietly.

A little while later, Tove, breathing hard, stuck his head round the side of the headboard and looked, puzzled, at Jish and the otherwise empty bed.

"Piss break?" he asked the girl.

"If it is, the little fuck's fucked off to the palace for it," she told him. "And taken his fucking togs with him."

"Shit!" Tove said, and disappeared. Moments later he too was getting dressed, to protests.

"Dr Gillews?"

The physician had his consulting offices in the palace's lower backing wing, only a few minutes' walk from the King's chambers by a couple of corridors and a long gallery under the eaves of one of the main buildings. It was a surprisingly quiet place, so close to the centre of things. The chambers looked out over a medicinal garden, tipped and terraced to catch the best of the light. Oramen had found the door unlocked after knocking on it a couple of times. He called the doctor's name again, from just inside the threshold. Gillews was known to get very caught up in the various experiments and distillations he carried out in his principal work chamber, and sometimes did not hear – or affected not to hear – people calling him.

Oramen went further along the hall, then through an archway into what appeared to be the doctor's sitting room; windows beyond looked out to the little garden, distant clouds high above. "Dr Gillews?" he called. He could see what looked like a bench in front of the windows, covered in books, cases, phials and retorts. He could hear a faint dripping sound, and smell something acrid. He walked through the sitting room, making sure there was nobody there as he went; he didn't want to disturb the doctor if he was sleeping. The dripping sound came louder and the smell of something bitter grew stronger.

"Doctor . . . ?"

He stopped, staring.

The doctor was sitting in a wooden chair of ornately twisted carving, his head lying on the bench in front of him. It appeared to have hit some phials and beakers when he had fallen forward, scattering some and breaking others. The dripping noise came from liquids spilled from some of the smashed glassware. One of the liquids fumed in the air and made a sizzling noise as it struck the wooden floor.

A syringe stuck out of Gillews' exposed left lower arm, plunger fully in. His eyes stared sightlessly along the equipment-strewn bench.

Oramen put one hand to his mouth. "Oh, Dr Gillews," he said, and sat down on the floor, fearing his legs were about to give out. He stood up again quickly, coughing, and supported himself on the bench. The fumes were worse lower down. He leant across and pushed open two of the windows looking over the courtyard.

He took some deep breaths and reached out to feel for a pulse on the doctor's neck, a little surprised and ashamed that his hand was shaking so. Gillews' skin was quite cold, and there was no pulse.

Oramen looked around. He wasn't really sure for what. Everything was untidy but that might well be the norm for such a place. He could see no note or last scratched message.

He supposed he ought to go and inform the palace guard. He looked, fascinated, at the syringe. There was blood around the puncture wound where the needle had entered, and some bruising and scratches around a handful of other small wounds, as though the doctor had had some trouble finding a vein, stabbing at himself before he found the right place.

Oramen touched Gillews' skin again, at the exposed wrist, where there was a dull bruise. He coughed once more, throat catching on the fumes, as he pulled up the cuff of the shirt covering the doctor's other wrist, and saw some similar bruising there. The arms of the chair were quite broad and flat.

He pulled the cuff down again, went to find a guard.

The Oct used hundreds of their largest scendships and a half-dozen scend tubes, cycling loops of vessels like stringed counting-stones in the hands of merchants tallying the day's takings. They filled up with men, beasts, engines, artillery, wagons, supplies and materiel on the Eighth then dropped fast to the Ninth to spill their contents and race back up the Illsipine Tower for another load. Still the process took a full long-day, with all the inevitable delay caused by the sheer complexity of the vast undertaking. Animals panicked in the scendships, would not enter or would not leave – hefters, the most numerous of the beasts of burden, seemed to be particularly sensitive – roasoaril tankers leaked, risking conflagrations; steam wagons broke down (one blew up while inside a scendship, causing no damage to the vessel but killing many inside – the Oct took that one out of its loop to clean it up), and a hundred other small incidents and accidents contrived to make the whole procedure draw itself out beyond what felt like its reasonable limit.

Regent tyl Loesp and Field Marshal Werreber wheeled on their lyge about the dimly lit Illsipine Tower, watching the vast army assemble on the Tower's only slightly brighter sun side, then, still accompanied by their escorting squadron, landed on a hill overlooking the plain. Above and all around, scouts on lyge and caude swung about the dark skies, dimly seen shapes watching for an enemy that did not appear to know they were there.

The Fixstar Oausillac, seeming to hover low over the flat plain to farpole, cast a balefully red light over the scene as tyl Loesp walked over to Werreber, taking off his flying gauntlets and clapping his hands. "It goes well, eh, Field Marshal?"

"It goes, I'll give you that," the other man said, letting a squire lead his lyge away. The beast's breath smoked in the cool, still air.

Even the air smelled different here, tyl Loesp thought. Air smelled different across any level he supposed, but that now seemed like a tactical distinction; here was a strategic difference, something underlying.

"We are undiscovered." Tyl Loesp looked out at the gathering army again. "That is sufficient for now."

"We have come by an odd route," Werreber said. "We are a long way from our goal. Even further from home."

"Distance from home is irrelevant, as long as the Oct remain allies," tyl Loesp told him. "Right now we are an hour away from home, little more."

"As long as the Oct remain allies," Werreber echoed.

The regent looked at him sharply, then slowly gazed away again. "You don't distrust them, do you?"

"Trust? Trust seems irrelevant. They will do certain things or not, and those things will match with what they have said they will do, or not. Whatever guides their actions is hidden behind so many layers of untranslatable thought it might as well be based on pure chance. Their alien nature precludes human attributes like trust."

Tyl Loesp had never heard Werreber give so long a speech. He wondered if the field marshal was nervous. He nodded. "One could no more trust an Oct than love it."

"Still, they have been true to their word," Werreber said. "They said they would deceive the Deldeyn, and they did."

Tyl Loesp glanced at the other man, searching for any sign of irony, or even wit. Werreber, oblivious, continued. "They said they would bring us here, and they have."

"The Deldeyn might take a different view."

"The deceived always will," Werreber pronounced, unshakeable.

Tyl Loesp could not but think that they were now in a position very similar to that the Deldeyn had been in when they had been issuing from the Xiliskine Tower barely a month ago, convinced – no doubt – that the Oct had allowed them special access to a normally inaccessible Tower to allow them to carry out their sneak attack on the very heartland of the Sarl people.

Had they felt smug, believing that the Oct were now on their side? Had they listened to the same lectures about how the Oct were direct descendants of the Shellworld builders, and nodded just as indulgently? Had they felt righteous, believing that the justice of their cause was being recognised by higher powers? For no doubt that was how they did think. It seemed to tyl Loesp everybody always thought they were right, and shared, too, the quaint belief that the very fervency of a belief, however deluded, somehow made it true.

They were all of them fools.

There was no right and wrong, there was simply effectiveness and inability, might and weakness, cunning and gullibility. That he knew this was his advantage, but it was one of better understanding, not moral superiority – he had no delusions there.

All that he and Werreber, the army and the Sarl could truly rely on was somehow fitting in with the plans that the Oct had and staying useful to them until matters had reached a conclusion. The Oct had their own reasons for wanting the Deldeyn reduced and the Sarl promoted, and tyl Loesp had an idea what those reasons were and why they were taking this route, not the obvious one, but he was willing to accept that for now they were all simply tools the Oct were using. That would change, if he had any say in it, but for now they were, undeniably, wielded.

Change it would, though. There were times, points, when a relatively small but decisive motion could trigger a weighty cascade of most momentous consequences, when the user became the used and the tool became the hand – and the brain behind it, too. Had he not been the King's right arm? Had he not been the very epitome of trusted, valiant helper? And yet, when the time had been right, had he not struck, with all the suddenly unimpounded force of a lifetime's unjust deference and subservience?

He had killed his king, the man to whom all around him, not just the credulous masses, thought he owed everything. But he knew the truth, which was that to be king was only to be the biggest bully in a race of bullies and bullied, the greatest braggart charlatan in a species of blustering priests and cowed acolytes with nary a thought to rub between them. The King had no inherent nobility or even right to rule; the whole idea of inheritable dominion was nonsensical if it could throw up particles like the studiously malleable Oramen and the hopelessly loose-living Ferbin. Ruthlessness, will, the absolute application of force and power; these were what secured authority and dominance.

He won who saw most clearly the way the universe really worked. Tyl Loesp had seen that Hausk was the one to take the Sarl so far along their course, but no further. The King had not seen that. Too, he had not realised that his most trusted helper might have plans, desires and ambitions of his own, and they might be best served by replacing him. So Hausk had trusted tyl Loesp, and that had been stupid. That had been a misty, self-deceptive kind of seeing. And, on a pinnacle so exposed and high as that of monarch, you paid for such foolishness.

So he had killed his king, but that meant little. It was no more wrong to kill a king than any man, and most men could see that all lives were cheap and eminently disposable, including their own. They held that in such high regard only because it was all they had, not because they thought it meant much to the universe; it took a religion to convince people of that, and he would make sure that the emphasis on that aspect of the Sarl faith was reduced in future, to the benefit of those tenets which invoked humility and obedience.

His only regret in killing Hausk, he'd realised, was that Hausk had had so little time to appreciate what had happened, to think back on what must have been going on in his faithful lieutenant's mind for all those years, as he'd died.

But it was a small regret.

They had made the journey unharmed so far; more than three-quarters of the army was safely delivered and a more than sufficient force had been left on the Eighth to deal with any possible desperate attack by the Deldeyn.

They probably still had the advantage of surprise, too. A small outpost of lyge scouts – there specifically to watch the Tower and report if it ever was used to conduct an incursion – had been surprised and quickly overwhelmed in the first action of this latest stage of the war; a contingent of the new Regent's Guard, the very cream of the army's best units, had been entrusted with this and had triumphed. The Deldeyn had no telegraph so their fastest communications moved by heliograph, signal light, carrier bird or a messenger on an air beast. The elite force which had taken the little fort reported that they were sure no message had left it.

Still, the Deldeyn must have felt confident at a similar stage, too, when they had issued from the Xiliskine Tower. How quickly had they realised that they had not just been unlucky, but deceived? At what point did it dawn on them that far from being about to inflict a crushing defeat on their enemies, they were about to suffer one themselves, and the war would be not won on that morning, but lost?

How deluded are we? he thought. How often, how multiply are we used? He still remembered the alien-man Xide Hyrlis coming to them with his glum prognostications regarding the future of warfare on their level, nearly a dozen long-years ago.

They would fall, he warned them, under the power of the first ruler to realise that the new discoveries in distillation, metallurgy and explosives spelled the end of the old, chivalrous ways. The immediate future, Hyrlis had told them, meant leaving the air to scouts, messengers and hit-and-fly raiding forces. There was an invention called the telegraph that could move information more quickly than the fleetest lyge and more reliably than by heliograph; use that. It would lead to still greater things.

Later there would be some disagreement over whether Hyrlis had pointed them towards an inventor who had already developed such an instrument, or pointed the inventor himself in the right experimental direction.

Abandon the great and noble tradition of well-bred men mounted on well-bred caude and lyge, Hyrlis said; build bigger guns, more guns, better guns, give more guns to more men, train them and arm them properly, mount them on animals and wheeled and tracked transports powered by steam – for now – and reap the benefits. Or pay the penalty, when somebody else sensed the change in the wind before you did.

Hausk, still a young man and the inexperienced, newly crowned king of a small, struggling kingdom, had – to tyl Loesp's surprise and initial chagrin, even disbelief – fallen on these ideas like a starved man on a banquet. Tyl Loesp had, with all the other nobles, tried to argue him out of the infatuation, but Hausk had pressed ahead.

In time, tyl Loesp heard the first rumblings of something

beyond mere discontent amongst his fellow nobles, and had had to make a choice. It was the turning point of his life. He made his choice and warned the King. The ringleaders of the conspiring nobles were executed, the rest had their lands seized and were disgraced. Tyl Loesp became despised by some, lauded by others, and trusted utterly by his king. The disputatious nobles had neatly removed the main obstacle to change – themselves – and Hausk's reforms roared ahead unstayed.

One victory led to another and soon there seemed to be nothing but victories. Hausk, tyl Loesp and the armies they commanded swept all before them. Xide Hyrlis had left long before, almost before any of the reforms had been effected, and it seemed he was quickly forgotten; few people had known about him in the first place and those who had mostly had good reason to downplay his contribution to this new age of innovation, progress and never-ending martial success. Hausk himself still paid tribute to the man, if only in private.

But what had Hyrlis left? What course had he set them on? Were they not his tools, somehow? Were they perhaps doing his bidding, even now? Were they puppets, playthings, even pets? Would they be allowed to achieve only so much and then – as he, after all, had done to the King – have everything taken away on the very brink of complete success?

But he must not fall prey to such thoughts. A little caution, and some rough idea of what to do if things happened for the worst, that was excusable, but to wallow in doubt and presentiments of disaster only served to help bring about that which was most feared. He would not give in to that weakness. They were set for victory; if they struck now they would win, and then the territory opened up where the Oct might find themselves no longer in full control.

He raised his nose and sniffed. There was a smell of burning in the air, something unpleasantly sweet and somehow despoiled loose on the slowly strengthening breeze. He'd sensed this before, at the battle before the Xiliskine Tower, and noted it then. The smell of warfare had a new signature; that of distilled, incinerated roasoaril oil. Battle itself now smelled of smoke. Tyl Loesp could remember when the relevant scents had been sweat and blood.

"How awful for you!"

"Rather more so for the doctor."

"Well indeed, though when you saw him he was past caring." Renneque looked from Oramen to Harne. "Wouldn't you say, ma'am?"

"A most unfortunate incident." Harne, the lady Aelsh, sat dressed in her finest and most severe mourning red, surrounded by her closest ladies-in-waiting and a further group of ladies and gentlemen who had been invited to her salon within her apartments in the main palace, less than a minute's walk from the throne room and the court principal's chamber. It was a select group. Oramen recognised a famous painter, an actor and impresario, a philosopher, a falsettist and an actress. The city's most fashionable and handsome priest was present, long black hair glistening, eyes twinkling, surrounded by a smaller semi-court of blushing young ladies; a brace of ancient noblemen too decrepit to venture to war completed the company.

Oramen watched Harne absently stroking a sleeping ynt lying curled on her lap – the animal's fur had been dyed red to match her dress – and wondered why he'd been invited. Perhaps it was a gesture of conciliation. Just as likely it was to have him tell his somewhat grisly tale in person. And, of course, he was the heir to the throne; he'd noticed that many people felt a need to display their faces before him as often as possible. He had to keep reminding himself of that.

He smiled at Renneque, imagining her naked. After Jish and her friends, he had a template; something to go on, now. Or there was another of Harne's attendant ladies called Ramile, a slim blonde with tightly curled hair. She had rather caught his eye, and did not seem to resent his interest, looking back shyly but frequently, smiling. He sensed Renneque glancing at the younger woman, then later glaring at her. Perhaps he might use one to get to the other. He was starting to understand how such matters worked. And then, of course, there was the lady actor, who was the most beautiful woman in the room. There was a refreshing directness in her look he rather liked.

"The doctor was known to indulge himself in the more pleasantly affective cures and potions of his trade, I believe," the priest said, then sipped his infusion. They were gathered to take a variety of recently fashionable drinks, most not long arrived from a variety of foreign parts, all newly opened-up dependencies of the greater kingdom. The infusions were non-alcoholic, though some were mildly narcotic.

"He was a weak man," Harne pronounced. "If a good physician."

"It was so written, in his stars," said a small man Oramen had seen and half recognised; Harne's latest pet astrologer. The philosopher, sitting as far from the astrologer as practically possible, gave a small snort and shook his head. He muttered something to the nearest lady-in-waiting. She looked blank, though politely so. The astrologer represented the latest fad in astrology, which claimed that human affairs were affected by the stars beyond Sursamen. The old astrology had ascribed influences to the Fixstars and Rollstars of the Eighth and beyond – especially those of the Ninth, which, after all, swept by just under one's feet, and so were technically closer than those hundreds of kilometres overhead. Oramen had little time even for the old stuff, but it seemed more plausible to him than this new nonsense. However, the Extra-Sursamen Astrology (for so it was termed) was new, and so for this reason alone, he supposed, possessed an irresistible attraction to a certain class of mind.

Renneque was nodding wisely at the small astrologer's words. Oramen wondered if he really should attempt to bed Renneque, the lady Silbe. He was troublingly aware that he would once again be following his brother. The court would doubtless find out; Renneque and her peers were indiscreet. What would people think of him for going where his wastrel brother had already been? Would they think he was trying to prove he had the equal of Ferbin's appetites, or was seeking to emulate him, unable to decide on his own tastes? Or would they even think that he sought to pay homage to him? He was still worrying at this, and not really listening to the conversation – which appeared to have spun off into some rather self-consciously clever talk about cures and addictions, benefits and curses – when Harne suddenly suggested the two of them take a turn on the balcony beyond the room.

"My lady," he said, when the tall shutters had swung to behind them. The evening lay stretched out across the nearpole sky, filling the air with purples, reds and ochres. The lower palace and city beyond was mostly dark, just a few public lights showing. Harne's dress looked darker out here, almost black.

"I am told you seek the return of your mother," Harne said.

Well, she was direct. "I do," he said. He had written to her several times since the King's death, and told her that he hoped to bring her back to Pourl, back to the court, as soon as possible. He had sent more formal telegraphed messages as well, though they would have to be translated into a paper message at some point too, as the telegraph wires did not extend so far round the world as the benighted spot his mother had been exiled to (she often said how beautiful the place was, but he suspected she dissembled to spare his feelings). He supposed Harne had heard through the telegraph network; the operatives were notorious gossips. "She is my mother," he told Harne. "She should be here at my side, especially once I become king."

"And I would not seek to prevent her return, had I the power, please believe me," Harne said.

You thought to cause her exile in the first place, Oramen wanted to say, but didn't. "That is . . . as well," he said.

Harne appeared distracted, her expression, even by the uncertain light of the drawn-out sunset and the candles of the room behind them, patently confused and uncertain. "Please understand that my concern is for my own place following her return. I wish her no ill, quite none at all, but I would know if her enhancement requires my own degradation."

"Not through any choice of mine, madam," Oramen said. He felt a deliciousness in the situation. He felt he was a man now, but he could still too well remember being a boy, or at least being treated like one. Now this woman, who had once seemed like a queen, like the strictest stepmother, like a powerful, capricious ogre to him, hung on his every word and turn of phrase, beseeching him from outside the citadel of his new and sudden power.

"My position is secure?" Harne asked.

He had thought about this. He still resented what Harne had done, whether she had demanded outright that his own mother be banished, presented the King with a choice between the two of them, or just inveigled, schemed and suggested her way towards the idea that such a choice must be made, but his only thought was for Aclyn, the lady Blisk; his own mother. Would Harne's reduction be to her good? He doubted it.

Harne was popular and liked, and even more so now; she was pitied as the tragic widow and grieving mother all in one, representing in that woe something of what the whole kingdom felt. To be seen to persecute her would reflect badly on him and by immediate extension on his mother too. Harne, the lady Aelsh, had to be shown every respect, or his mother's just advancement and restoration would be a hollow, bitter thing indeed. He would rather it was otherwise, for in his heart he wanted to banish Harne as his own mother had been banished, but it could not be, and he had to accept that.

"Madam, your position is perfectly secure. I honour you as she who was queen in all but name. I wish merely to see my mother again and have her take her rightful place at court. It will in no sense be at your expense. You were both loved by my father. He chose you over her and fate has chosen me over your son. You and she are equal in that."

"It is a sad equality."

"It is what we have, I'd say. I would have my mother back, but not above you – she never could be, in the affections of the people. Your position is unimpeachable, madam; I'd not have it otherwise." Well, I would, he thought. But what would be the point in telling you?

"I am grateful, prince," Harne said, laying one hand briefly on his arm. She took a breath, looking down. My, Oramen thought, how my power affects people and things! Being king could be highly agreeable!

"We ought to go in," Harne said, smiling up at him. "People might talk!" she said, and gave an almost coquettish laugh such that, just for an instant, without in any way desiring her for himself, he saw suddenly what it might be about the woman that could have so captivated his father he would banish the mother of two of his children to keep her, or even just to keep her happy. She paused as she put her hand to the handle of the door leading back to the room. "Prince?" she said, gazing up into his eyes. "Oramen – if I may?"

"Of course, dear lady." What now? he thought.

"Your reassurance, perversely, deserves its opposite."

"I beg your pardon?"

"I would have a care, Prince Regent."

"I fail to understand you, ma'am. One always cares, one always has cares. What more specific—?"

"Specific I cannot be, Oramen. My concerns rest on vaguenesses, associations that may be perfectly innocent, coincidences that may be just those and no more; mere hints of rumours of gossip. Nothing solid or incontrovertible at all. Indeed, only just enough to say that the Prince Regent should take care. That is all. We are all of us forever on the brink of whatever fate may hold for us, even though we might not know it." She put her hand to his arm again. "Please, Prince Regent, don't think I seek to discomfit you; there is no malice in this. If I thought only for myself, I would take what you have just told me to my great relief and say no more, for I realise that what I say now may sound disquieting, even allied to a threat, though it is not. Please believe me it is not. I have had the most obscure and reluctant intelligences that suggest – no more – all is not as it appears, and so I ask you: take care, Prince Regent."

He wasn't sure what to say. Her gaze searched his eyes. "Please say I have not offended you, Oramen. You have done me generous service in reassuring me as you have and I would despair if I caused you to retract any part of that, but such grace commands I find the last seamed scrap I have to offer in grateful return, and what I've said is all I have. I beg you neither to scorn it nor ignore it. I fear we both might suffer from dismissal."

Oramen still felt mightily confused and was already determined to revisit this conversation as accurately as he could when he had the leisure, but he nodded gravely, though with a small smile, and said, "Then be doubly reassured, ma'am. I regard you no less for what you've said. I thank you for your thoughtfulness and counsel. I shall think on it, assuredly."

The lady's face, lit from the side by candlelight, looked suddenly care-worn, Oramen thought. Her gaze flicked across his eyes again, then she smiled tremulously, and nodded, and let him open the door for her. The red-coloured ynt that had been sleeping on her lap curled out through the sliver of opening and whined and circled round her feet.

"Oh, Obli," the lady cried, stooping to scoop the animal into her arms and rubbing her nose against its. "Can't I leave you for a moment?"

They went back into the room.

They crossed a Night, and a region of Bare at the same time. It was the least propitious combination known to the superstitious, and even the most practical and hard-headed amongst them felt the tension. It was a long stretch, but there would be no supply dumps or fortlets left here; ordering men to stay in such a place was like consigning them to a living death. The animals complained mightily, hating the darkness and perhaps the strange, smooth feel of the material beneath them. The steam wagons and transports could not have been more suited to the terrain, or lack of it, and quickly pulled ahead. Good discipline, orders given sternly in briefings over the days before and perhaps a degree of fear ensured that the army did not become too attenuated. Searchlights shone upwards to help guide the airborne escorts and returning scouts. There would be three long-days of this.

The Night was caused by a series of great vanes that both hung from the level's ceiling high above – obstructing all but the faintest air-glow of the Fixstar Oausillac to farpole – and had risen, like the blade of some infinite knife, from the ground ten or so kilometres to their right until they sat like a slice of night above them, six or seven kilometres high and hooked and curved over like some incomprehensibly colossal claw.

Men felt appropriately tiny in the shadow of such manufactured vastness. In a place like this, the heads of even the most unimaginative of beings began to fill with questions, if not outright dread. What titans had forged such vast geographies? What star-encompassing hubris had dictated the placement of these enormous vanes just so, like scimitared propellers from ships the size of planets? What oceanic volumes of what outlandish materials could ever have required such prodigious impelment?

A fierce wind arose, coming straight at them at first, forcing the air-beasts down for shelter. It scoured the last few grains of sand and grit from the Bare, making it entirely clear how this arid region came to be stripped not just of any ground cover but of any ground at all. They were travelling across the very bones of their vast world, tyl Loesp thought, the absolute base and fundament of all that gave them life.

When the wind eased a little and veered, he ordered his half-track command vehicle to stop and got down from it. The machine grumbled beside him, headlights picking out twin cones of creamy Bare ahead of it. All around, the army trundled past, engines blattering, unseen fumes rising into the inky dark. He took his glove off, knelt and pressed his open palm against the Bare, against the pure Prime of Sursamen's being.

I touch the ancient past, he thought, and the future. Our descendants might build on this mighty, God-threatening scale, one day. If I cannot be there – and the aliens had the gift of eternal life, so he might be there if all went as he dared to hope – then my name shall.

Nearby in the loud darkness, a supply wagon's tractor had broken down; a spare was being attached.

He put his glove back on and returned to the half-track.

"Frankly, sir, it's a murder weapon," Illis, the palace armourer, said. He was squat and sturdy. His hands were dark, ingrained.

Oramen turned the slim but allegedly powerful pistol over in his hand. He had fretted about Harne's warning for some days before eventually deciding to dismiss it, but had then woken from a dream wherein he'd been trapped in a chair while faceless men shoved knives into his arms. He had been going to dismiss that too, but then came to the conclusion that something inside him was worried, and even if it was just to keep such nightmares at bay, carrying a weapon more powerful than just his usual long knife might be advisable.

The gun felt heavy. Its mechanism was worked by a strong spring so that it could be used single-handed and it contained ten one-piece shells, arranged in a sort of staggered vertical within the handle and propelled to the firing chamber by another spring, cocked by a lever that folded away after use.

The shells were cross-cut on their tips. "A man-stopper," Illis said, then paused. "Actually, a hefter-stopper, to serve truth fair." He smiled, which was a little disconcerting as he had very few teeth left. "Try to avoid accidents with it, sir," he said reasonably, then insisted the prince practise using it in the long firing gallery attached to the armoury.

The gun certainly kicked like a hefter – and barked louder than one – Oramen thought, but it fired straight and true.

He found a place for its lightly oiled ynt-hide holster, concealed in a plumped-out part of his tunic at the back, and promised to keep its safety catch secured.

12. Cumuloform

It was some time before Ferbin would accept he was not dead. He drifted up towards some sort of awareness to find himself suspended in airy nothing beneath a vast glowing mass of frozen bubbles. Enormous gold-tinged clouds stretched in every direction, mostly up. Far below was a startlingly blue ocean, devoid of land. Unchanging, patterned with a ruffled weave of waves, it seemed, for all its oceanic blueness, somehow frozen.

Sometimes, as he drifted over this apparition, it did seem to change, and he thought he saw tiny flecks appear on its surface, but then the tiny flecks disappeared with the same microscopic slowness with which they had come into being, and all was as before; serene, calm, unchanging, heavenly ...

He had the feeling he had recently been in the ocean, though it had been warm rather than cold and he had been able to breathe despite being submerged in it. It was as though death was somehow like being born, like being still in the womb.

And now he was here in this strange scape of infinite cloud and never-ending ocean with only the comforting presence of slowly passing Towers to reassure him he was in the appropriate afterlife. And even the Towers seemed too far apart.

He saw a face. It was a human face and he knew he ought to recognise it.

Then he was awake again and the face had gone. He suspected he had dreamed the face, and wondered about dreaming when you were patently dead. Then he seemed to fall asleep. In retrospect, that was surprising too.

He was awake, and there was a strange numbness about his back and right shoulder. He could feel no pain or discomfort, but it felt like there was a huge hole in him covering a quarter of his torso, something that he couldn't reach or feel or do anything with. Filling his ears was a distant roaring noise like a waterfall heard at a distance.

He floated over the unimpeachably perfect blueness. A sunset came on slowly, burnishing the huge clouds with red, violet and mauve. He watched a Tower slide past, its sallow trunk disappearing into the deepening azure mass of the sea, edged with white where the surfaces met.

Then it was dark and only distant lightning lit the ocean and the towering clouds, ushering him back to sleep with silent bursts of faraway light.

This must, he thought, be heaven. Some sort of reward, anyway.

Ideas about what happened after you died varied even amongst the priestly caste. Primitives were able to have more straightforward religions because they didn't know any better. Once you knew even a little of the reality of the situation in the outside universe, it all got a bit more complex: there were lots of aliens and they all had – or had once had – their own myths and religions. Some aliens were immortal; some had constructed their own fully functional afterlives, where the deceased – recorded, transcribed – ended up after death; some had made thinking machines that had their own sets of imponderable and semi-godlike powers; some just were gods, like the WorldGod, for example, and some had Sublimed, which itself was arguably a form of ascension to Godhead.

Ferbin's father had had the same robustly pragmatic view of religion as he'd had of everything else. In his opinion, only the very poor and downtrodden really needed religion, to make their laborious lives more bearable. People craved self-importance; they longed to be told they mattered as individuals, not just as part of a mass of people or some historical process. They needed the reassurance that while their life might be hard, bitter and thankless, some reward would be theirs after death. Happily for the governing class, a well-formed faith also kept people from seeking their recompense in the here and now, through riot, insurrection or revolution.

A temple was worth a dozen barracks; a militia man carrying a gun could control a small unarmed crowd only for as long as he was present; however, a single priest could put a policeman inside the head of every one of their flock, for ever.

The more comfortably off, and those with real power, might choose to believe or not as their personal proclivities dictated, but their relatively easeful, pleasant lives were their own rewards, and for the highest in the land, posterity – a place in history itself – would be their prize after death.

Ferbin had never really bothered with thoughts of an after-life. Where he was now did seem like heaven, or something like it, but he wasn't sure. Part of him wished he'd paid more atten-tion to the priests when they'd been trying to instruct him about this sort of thing, but then, given that he appeared to have achieved the afterlife without either faith or knowledge, what would have been the point?

Choubris Holse looked down on him.

Choubris Holse. That had been the name of the face he'd seen earlier. He stared at it and wondered what Holse was doing in the land of the dead, and wearing odd, too-loose-looking clothes, too, though he still had his belt and knife. Should Holse be here? Perhaps he was just visiting.

He moved, and could feel something in the place where before there had been no feeling or movement, in his right upper back. He looked around as best he could.

He was riding in something like a balloon gondola, lying prone on a large, subtly undulating bed, naked but for a thin covering. Choubris Holse was sitting looking at him, chewing on what looked like a stringy piece of dried meat. Ferbin suddenly felt ravenously hungry. Holse belched and excused himself and Ferbin experienced an odd amalgam of emotions as he realised that this was not the afterlife and that he was still alive.

"Good-day, sir," Holse said. His voice sounded funny. Ferbin clung briefly to this scrap of evidence that he might still be safely dead with the ferocity of a drowning man clutching at a floating leaf. Then he let it go.

He tried working his mouth. His jaw clicked and his mouth felt gummy. A noise like an old man's groan sounded from somewhere and Ferbin was forced to acknowledge it had prob-ably been emitted by himself.

"Feeling better, sir?" Holse asked matter-of-factly.

Ferbin tried to move his arms and found that he could. He brought both hands up to his face. They looked pale and the skin was all ridged, like the ocean that still sailed by below. Like he'd been too long in it. Or maybe just too long in a nice warm bath. "Holse," he croaked.

"At your service, sir." Holse sighed. "As ever."

Ferbin looked about. Clouds, ocean, bubble gondola thing. "Where is this? Not heaven?"

"Not heaven, sir, no."

"You're quite sure?"

"More than moderately positive, sir. This is a portion of the Fourth, sir. We are in the realm of the beings that call themselves Cumuloforms."

"The Fourth?" Ferbin said. His voice sounded odd too. "But we are still within great Sursamen?"

"Assuredly, sir. Just four levels up. Halfway to the Surface."

Ferbin looked around again. "How extraordinary," he breathed, then coughed.

"Extraordinarily boring, sir," Holse said, frowning at his piece of dried meat. "We've been sailing over this water for the past five long-days or so and while the prospect is most impressive at first and the air bracing, you'd be amazed how quickly the impressiveness and the bracingness become tedious when that's all there is to contemplate all day. Well, all there is to contemplate all day save for your good self, of course, sir, and frankly you were no circus of boundless fun either in your sleeping state. Nary a word, sir. Certainly nary a word of sense. But in any event, sir, welcome back to the land of the living." Holse made a show of looking beneath his feet, through a translucent membrane that showed a hazy version of the ocean far below. "Though land, as you might have noticed, is the one thing this level appears to be somewhat short of."

"Definitely the Fourth?" Ferbin said. He leaned up on one elbow – something twinged in his right shoulder, and he grimaced – to look over the side of the bed he was lying on, peering down through the hazy surface Holse was standing on. It all looked rather alarming.

"Definitely the Fourth, sir. Not that I had opportunity to count as it were, but that is most certainly what its denizens term it."

Ferbin looked at the dried meat held in Holse's hand. He nodded at it. "I say, d'you think I might have some of that?"

"I'll get you a fresh piece, shall I, sir? They said you were all right to eat like normal when you wanted to."

"No, no; that bit will do," Ferbin said, still staring at the meat and feeling his mouth fill with saliva.

"As you wish, sir." Holse handed Ferbin the meat. He crammed it into his mouth. It tasted salty and slightly fishy and very good.

"How did we come to be here, Holse?" he said through mouthfuls. "And who would be these 'they'?"

"Well now, sir," Holse said.

Ferbin had been badly wounded by a carbine bullet as they stumbled into the cylinder that had revealed itself on the Oct's access tower. A lucky shot, Holse told him. Firing in near darkness from a beating air-beast at a running target, even the greatest marksman would need his fair share of good fortune for a month all gathered together at once to secure a hit.

The two of them had fallen into the interior of the cylinder, which then just sat there, door still open, for what had seemed like an eternity to Holse. He had cradled the already unconscious Ferbin in his arms, slowly becoming covered in blood, screaming at whoever or whatever to close the door or sink the effing tube thing back down into the tower, but nothing had happened until some of the men who had attacked them actually landed on the surface outside, then the cylinder did finally lower itself back into the tower. He'd yelled and hollered for help for Ferbin, because he was sure that the prince was dying. Meanwhile he had the impression that the round room they were in was continuing to sink deeper inside the access tower.

The room came to a stop, the doorway they'd fallen through had slid into being again and a machine the shape of a large Oct had scuttled in towards them. It took Ferbin's limp body off him and quickly turned him this way and that, finding the hole in his back and the larger exit wound in his chest, sealing both with some sort of squirty stuff and cradling his head with a sort of hand thing. Pincers on that hand had seemed to slide into Ferbin's neck and lower skull, but Ferbin had been too far gone to react and Holse had just assumed and hoped that this was somehow all part of the ministering or doctoring or whatever was going on.

A floating platform appeared and took them along a broad hallway with whole sets and sequences of most impressive doors – each easily the equal in size of the main gates to the palace in Pourl – which variously slid, rolled, rose and fell to allow them through. Holse had guessed that they were entering the base of the D'neng-oal Tower itself.

The final chamber was a big sphere with an added floor, and this had sealed itself tight and started moving; possibly up – it was hard to say. The place had felt damp and the floor had patches of water on it.

The Oct doctor machine continued to work on Ferbin, who had at least stopped bleeding. A screen lowered itself from the ceiling and addressed Holse, who spent the next hour or so trying to explain what had happened, who they both were and why one of them was almost dead. From Ferbin's jacket he had fished out the envelopes Seltis the Head Scholar had given them. They were covered in blood and one of them looked like it had been nicked by the carbine bullet on its way out of Ferbin's chest. Holse had waved these at the screen, hoping their effectiveness was not impaired by blood or having a hole in one corner. He felt he was almost starting to get the hang of how to talk to an Oct when some clunking and gentle bouncing around told him they had arrived somewhere else. The door swung open again and a small group of real, proper Oct had looked in through a wall as transparent as the best glass but wobbly as a flag on a windy day.

Holse had forgotten the name of the Towermaster. Seltis had said the name when he'd given them the travel documents but Holse had been too busy trying to think what they were going to do next to pay attention. He waved the travel documents again. Then the name just popped into his head.

"Aiaik!" he exclaimed. It sounded like a cry of pain or surprise, he thought, and he wondered what he and Ferbin must look like to these clever, strange-looking aliens.

Whether the Towermaster's name had any real effect was debatable, but the two of them – Ferbin carried by the limbs of the Oct doctor machine – found themselves, still on their little floating platform, riding along various water-filled corridors inside a bubble of air. The Oct who'd been looking in at them through the wobbly glass accompanied them, swimming alongside. They entered a large chamber of great complexity; the Oct doctor machine cut the clothes from Ferbin, a sort of jacket was wrapped round his chest, a transparent mask connected to long tubes was placed over his face, other tubes fastened to his head where the doctor's pincers had entered and then he was placed in a large tank.

One of the Oct had tried to explain what was going on, though Holse hadn't understood much.

Holse had been told Ferbin would take time to repair. Still sitting on the platform that had borne them earlier, he'd been shown through the watery environment to a nearby room from which all the water drained away while fresh air took its place. The Oct he'd been talking to had stayed with him, its body covered in a sort of barely visible suit of moisture. Another set of dry rooms had opened up which seemed to have been designed for human habitation.

The Oct had said he could live here for the few days Ferbin would take to repair, then left him alone.

He'd walked over to the set of round, man-high windows and looked out over the land of the Sarl as he'd never seen it before, from nearly fourteen hundred kilometres above the surface, through the vacuum which existed above the atmosphere that covered the land like a warm blanket.

"What a sight, sir." Holse appeared lost for a moment, then shook his head.

"And how came we to be here, on the Fourth?" Ferbin asked.

"The Oct only control the D'neng-oal Tower up to this level, as far as I can understand the matter, sir. They seemed reluctant to admit this, as though it was the cause for some embarrassment, which it may well indeed be."

"Oh," Ferbin said. He hadn't known that the Conducer peoples ever controlled only part of a Tower; he'd just assumed it was all or nothing, from Core to Surface.

"And on account of the fact that beyond the Ninth one is in the realm of the Oversquare, transference from one Tower to another is not possible."

"Over . . . what?"

"This has all been explained to me by the Oct I was talking to on the screen while being bled upon by your good self, and subsequently and at some length in my quarters near your place of treatment, sir."

"Really. Then kindly explain it to me."

"It's all to do with the distances apart that the Towers are, sir. Below and up to the level of the Ninth, their Filigree connects, and the Filigree is of sufficient hollowness for scendships – which is the proper term for the spherical room which transported us—"

"I know what a scendship is, Holse."

"Well, they can switch from one Tower to another through their connectings in amongst the Filigree. But above the Ninth the Filigree doesn't connect, so to get from one Tower to another one has to travel between them, through whatever exists on the relevant level."

Ferbin's understanding of such matters was, like his understanding of most things, vague. Again, it would have been much less so if he'd ever paid any attention to the relevant lessons from his tutors. The Towers supported the ceiling over each level through a great fluted outbranching of this stuff called Filigree, whose greater members were as hollow as the Towers themselves. Given that the same number of Towers supported each level, whether it was the one closest to the Core or that supporting the Surface, the Towers would be at a greater distance from each other the closer they got to that last outward level and the Filigree would no longer need to join up to support the weight above.

"The whole of the Fourth," Holse said, "is home to these Cumuloform, which are clouds, but clouds which are in some sense intelligent in that mysterious and not especially useful way so many alien peoples and things tend to be, sir. They float over oceans full of fishes and sea monsters and such. Or rather over one big ocean, which fills the whole of the bottom part of the level the way land does on our own dear Eighth. Anyway, they're seemingly happy to transport folk between Towers when the Oct ask them to. Oh, and I should say, welcome to Expanded Version Five; Zourd," Holse said, looking up and around at the nebulous mass of cloud extending around and far above them. "For that is what this one is called."

"Indeed," Ferbin said.

"Good-day." The voice sounded like a whole chorus of whispered echoes and seemed to issue from every part of the bubble-wall around them.

"And, ah, and to you, good, ah, Cumuloform," Ferbin said out loud, looking up at the cloud above. He continued to gaze expectantly upwards for a few more moments, then looked back at Holse, who shrugged.

"It is not what you'd call talkative, sir."

"Hmm. Anyway," Ferbin said, sitting up and staring at Holse, "why do the Oct only control the D'neng-oal up to the Fourth?"

"Because, sir, the Aultridia" – Holse averted his head to spit on the semi-transparent floor – "control the upper levels."

"Oh my God!"

"WorldGod be preserved indeed, sir."

"What? You mean they control the upper levels of all Towers?"

"No, sir."

"But wasn't the D'neng-oal always an Oct Tower?"

"It was, sir. Until recently. This seems to be the principal cause of the embarrassment felt by the Oct, sir. Part of their Tower has been taken over from them."

"And by the Vileness!" Ferbin said, genuinely horrified. "The very filth of God!"

The Aultridia were an Upstart species; recent arrivals on the Involved scene who had wasted no time in establishing themselves, shouldering their way to as near the front of the galactic stage as possible. They were far from alone in that. What distinguished them was the manner and location of their coming to sentient fruition as a species.

The Aultridia had evolved from parasites which had lived under the carapaces and between the skin layers of the species called the Xinthia; Xinthian Tensile Aeronathaurs to give them their proper name. It was one of these that the Sarl called the WorldGod.

The Xinthia were regarded with something approaching affection by even the most ruthless and unsentimental of the galaxy's Involved, partly because they had done much great work in the past – they had been particularly active in the Swarm Wars of great antiquity, battling runaway nanotech outbreaks, Swarmata in general and other Monopathic Hegemonising Events – but mostly because they were no threat to anybody any more and a system of the galactic community's size and complexity just seemed to need one grouping that everybody was allowed to like. Utterly ancient, once near-invincibly powerful, now reduced to one paltry solar system and a few eccentric individuals hiding in the Cores of Shellworlds for no discernible reason, the Xinthia were seen as eccentric, bumbling, well-meaning, civilisationally exhausted – the joke was they hadn't the energy to Sublime – and generally as the honoured good-as-dead deserving of a comfortable retirement.

The Aultridia were regarded as having spoiled that comfortable twilight. Over the space of several hundred thousand years, the great air-dwelling, spacefaring Aeronathaurs had been greatly troubled by the increasingly active creatures they were playing host to, the infestation of super-parasites running round the necklace of Aeronathaur habitats orbiting the star Chone like a disease.

It hadn't lasted; the advantage of a truly intelligent parasite was that you could reason with it, and the Aultridia had long since abandoned their old ways, leaving their one-time hosts alone in return for material advancement and what seemed like alien super-science to them but was like a box of broken toys discovered in a dusty attic to the Xinthia.

They had constructed their own purpose-built habitats and taken up the task of opening up and maintaining Shellworlds; this swiftly turned into a real and useful speciality. It was conventionally assumed that burrowing into a Shellworld was somehow something they were suited for just by their history and nature.

The stigma of their birthright remained, however, and it didn't help that the mat-like Aultridia stank like rotting meat to most oxygen-breathing species.

The only remaining suspicion regarding the Aultridia's present existence was that they had established at least a token presence on all the Shellworlds which contained Xinthians, often at impractical cost and to the considerable annoyance of other Conducer species like the Oct. To date, as far as anyone knew, the Aultridia had never even tried to penetrate all the way down through the levels of a Shellworld to a Core-dwelling Xinthian – even the more established Conducer species tended to leave the ancient beings alone, out of respect and possibly an almost superstitious wariness – but that didn't reassure many people, least of all those like the Sarl, who treated the Xinthian at the Core of the world as a God and were appalled at the idea of the ghastly Aultridia worming their way down to the Core to do God-knew-what to their deity. Only the Iln, the fabled and happily long-departed species which had spent so much of their hateful existence destroying Shellworlds, were more despised by the Sarl and all right-thinking people.

The Oct, of course, had not been shy about promoting this view of the Aultridia amongst their client species like the Sarl, arguably exaggerating both the incorrigibility of Aultridian nature and the concomitant threat the species posed to the WorldGod. The Oct were also not slow in pointing out that they were, by their own claim at least, directly descended from the Involucra – the very people who had designed and constructed the deeply wonderful Shellworlds – and so part of a line of almost God-like creators nearly a billion years old. By comparison, the Aultridia were ghastly parasitic newbie slime barely worthy of the term civilised.

"So," Ferbin said. "We're floating to another Tower? We are still on our way to the Surface, I trust?"

"We are, sir."

Ferbin looked through the near-perfectly transparent bed he lay on, down to the waves far below. "We do not seem to be moving especially quickly."

"Apparently we are, however, sir. We're going four or five times faster than even a lyge can fly, though certainly not as quickly as an alien flying machine."

"It doesn't look very fast," Ferbin said, still staring at the ocean.

"We are very high, sir. That makes our progress look slow."

Ferbin looked up. They appeared to be on the very lowest wisp of a vast mass of golden whiteness. "And this thing is basically just a cloud?" he asked.

"It is, sir. Though it sticks together better than the clouds we're used to, and it is, by allegement, intelligent."

Ferbin thought about this. He had never really been trained to think properly for himself, or thought much of thinking, as it were, but over the past few days and adventures he had discovered that the pastime was not without its benefits. "Is it not, then, at the mercy of the winds?"

Holse looked mildly surprised. "You know, sir, I thought that! However, it appears the Cumuloforms can control their height with some exactness, and because the level is so arranged with winds heading in different directions at different elevations, they can navigate near well as a bird just by taking care how high off the ground – well, sea – they are."

Ferbin felt the edge of the simple sheet covering his nakedness. "Do we still have the documents Seltis gave us?"

"Here, sir," Holse said, pulling them from his loose-fitting tunic.

Ferbin collapsed back on the bed, exhausted. "Is there water here? I'm thirsty."

"I think you'll find that tube there will provide the necessary, sir."

Ferbin took a dangling transparent tube and sucked at it, taking his fill of pleasantly sweet-tasting water, then lay back. He looked over at Holse.

"So, Choubris Holse, you are still with me."

"Plain as, sir."

"You did not go back, even though we have now most certainly left my father's kingdom."

"I thought the better of it, sir. The gentlemen on the lyge who tried to detain us at the tower did not seem overenthusiastic regarding the niceties of establishing the innocence of one acting merely as a faithful servant. It occurred to me that you might be of most use to the current regime dead, if you see what I mean, sir, and – on account of you having been already so pronounced – some effort might be made to turn this incorrect statement into a true one, only backdated, if you get my drift. Your being alive does rather contradict the official version of events and it strikes me that knowledge of that fact is somewhat like an infective disease, and a fatal one at that." While Ferbin was still thinking his way through this, Holse frowned, cleared his throat and gathered his tunic about him. "And it did occur to me, sir, that you did somewhat save my life on that tower thing, when that little lyge flier chappie was quite set, it seemed to me, on taking it."

"Did I?" Ferbin asked. He supposed he had. He had never saved anybody's life before. Realising that he had was a rather agreeable sensation.

"Not that it wasn't my sticking with you that had got me into said parlous situation in the first place, mind, sir," Holse went on, seeing a look of dreamy self-satisfaction appear on Ferbin's pale, lightly bearded face.

"Indeed, indeed," Ferbin said. He was thinking again. "You will be some time away from those you love, I fear, dear Holse."

"It has barely been three weeks, sir. Quite possibly they have yet to miss me. In any event, I'm best to stay away until matters are sorted, sir. Also, if the palace officials work at their customary pace in such affairs, my stipend will continue to be paid for a good long-year or more."

"Your wife will be able to collect it?"

"She always has, sir. To protect it and me from funding an overfamiliarity with such pleasures as a fellow might meet with in drinking and smoking establishments, betting parlours and the like."

Ferbin smiled. "Still, you must miss her, and your children. Three, isn't it?"

"Four at the last count, sir."

"You will see them again, good Holse," Ferbin said, feeling oddly tearful. He smiled again at Holse and put his hand out. Holse stared at it, confused. "Good servant, take my hand. We are as much friends now as master and servant, and when I return to reclaim what is rightfully mine, you shall be most richly rewarded."

Holse took Ferbin's hand awkwardly. "Why, that's most kind, sir. Right now, I'd settle for a glass of something other than water and a pipe of leaf, frankly, but it's nice to have something to look forward to."

Ferbin felt his eyes closing, seemingly of their own volition.

"I think I need to sleep some more," he said, and was unconscious almost before the last word was uttered.

The Cumuloform called Expanded Version Five; Zourd drifted into the lee of the two-kilometre-wide Vaw-yei Tower and started elongating itself, eventually extending one single trailing tip of cloud down to the surface of a much smaller though still substantial tower protruding fifty metres or so from the ocean. A great swell, near long as the world was round, washed about it, waves rising and falling back like the beat of some vast heart. A Fixstar sat low on the horizon, staining the clouds and waves with an everlasting sunrise/sunset of red and gold.

The air smelled sharp. The circular surface of the tower was strewn with seaweed and sun-bleached fish bones.

Ferbin and Holse stepped out of a hole which had appeared in the side of the lowest of the bubble chambers they had occupied for the last few days. Waiting for them at the centre of the tower was a raised portion like the one in which they had taken shelter back on the Eighth. Ferbin turned and called, "Farewell, and thank you!" to the cloud, and heard the same strange chorus of whispers say,

"Goodbye."

Then the cloud seemed to gather itself up and spread itself out, great billowing wings of cloud-stuff starting to catch the wind on the edges of the Tower's lee and pulling the strange, huge but insubstantial creature up and away. They stood and watched it go, fascinated, until a chime sounded from the open door of the access tower's raised portion.

"Better not miss the coach," Holse said. They stepped into the chamber, which took them down towards the base of the nearby Tower. A scendship was waiting for them at the far end of the great hall and the gleaming, multifarious doors. The part they could see was a simple sphere, perhaps twenty metres in diameter, with a transparent roof. Its doors closed. A distant

Oct told them via a screen that their documents were in order without Ferbin even having to take them from his pocket and brandish them.

The two men looked up through the roof, at a vast blackness threaded with tiny lights and criss-crossed with pale struts and tubes describing a complicated set of spirals around and through the seemingly infinite space.

Holse whistled. "Didn't spot that last time."

The scendship moved smoothly away, accelerating upwards into the darkness. The lights flowed silently around them until they both felt dizzy and had to look away. They found a dry part of the mostly still damp floor and sat there, talking occasionally, glancing upwards a lot, for the hour or so until the scendship slowed and stopped, then nudged on upwards through more enormous doors – some sliding, some rolling, some seeming to pull back from the centre in every direction at once – to another level of the colossal cylinder. The scendship picked up speed again, tearing silently up the light-strewn tube of darkness and flickering tubework.

They stretched their legs. Ferbin exercised the shoulder where he'd been shot; it was no more than slightly stiff. Holse asked a patch of screen on the wall if it could hear him and was rewarded with an informative speech in an eccentric version of the Sarl language which he only realised was recorded when he tried to ask it questions. They were now passing the third level, which was dark. No land, all just Bare, just Prime, and no water or atmosphere or even interior stars at all. The next level up was also vacuum, but it did have stars and there were things called Baskers that lived there and apparently just lay about, absorbing sunlight like trees. The last level before the Surface was vacuum again, and was a Seedsail nursery, whatever that was or they were.

The scendship slowed for the final time. They watched the last few lights disappear around the side of the craft. Thumps, squelches and sighing noises announced some sort of conclusion, and the door rolled open to the side. They passed down one broad, tall but very plain corridor and negotiated a round lift at the far end which ascended with multiple hesitations, then they walked through another great corridor of what looked like very thin-cut sandstone, lit from within. Whole sets of massive doors opened in front of them and closed behind them as they went. "They like their doors, don't they, sir?" Holse observed.

A single Oct in a glistening membrane was waiting between two of the sets of doors.

"Greetings," it said. It extended one limb holding a small device, which beeped. It extended another limb. "Documents, if pleased. Authority of Vaw-yei Towermaster Tagratark."

Ferbin drew himself up. "We would see the Nariscene Grand Zamerin."

"Oct documents remain Oct. To surrendering on arrival Surface."

"Is this the Surface?" Ferbin asked, looking around. "It doesn't look like it."

"Is Surface!" the Oct exclaimed.

"Show us," Ferbin said, "on our way to the Grand Zamerin." He tapped the pocket holding the envelopes. "Then you shall have your documents."

The Oct seemed to think about this. "To follow," it said, turning abruptly and heading for the doors beyond, which were now opening.

They revealed a broad chamber on the far side of which large elliptical windows gave out on to a view of extensive gardens, broad lakes and distant, rocky, and fabulously steep mountains. Creatures, machines and things which might have been either moved about the vast concourse in a confusing mêlée of colour and sound.

"See? Is Surface," the Oct said. It turned to them, "Documents. Pleased."

"The Grand Zamerin, if *you* please," Ferbin said.

"Others await. They cause confluence of you/Grand Zamerin, possibility. Or authorised in place of. Additional, explanatory. Grand Zamerin not present. Gone off. Distantly. Documents."

"What do you mean, gone off?" Ferbin asked.

"What do you mean, others await?" Holse said, looking around, hand going to his knife.

13. Don't Try This At Home

Djan Seriy Anaplian had been doing her homework, reacquainting herself with Sursamen and Shellworlds and studying the various species involved. She had discovered a Morthanveld image she liked: "When in shallows we look up and see the sun, it seems to centre upon us, its soft rays spreading out around us like embracing arms" (/tentacles, the translation noted), "straight and true with celestial strength, all shifting and pulsing together with the movement of each surface wave and making of the observer an unarguable focus, persuading the more easily influenced that they alone are subject to, and merit, such solitary attention. And yet all other individuals, near and far, so long as they too can see the sun, will experience precisely the same effect, and therefore, likewise, might be as justly convinced that the sun shines most particularly and splendidly upon them alone."

She sat aboard the Medium Systems Vehicle *Don't Try This*

At Home, playing a game of bataös with one of the ship's officers. The Delinquent-class Fast Picket and ex-General Offensive Unit *Eight Rounds Rapid* had rendezvoused with the Steppe-class MSV the day before and dropped her off before heading on its inscrutable way. So far, nothing had been said about the stowaway knife missile with the drone-quality brain in it which had made itself part of her luggage. She could think of several explanations for this but was choosing to believe the simplest and most benign, which was that nobody had spotted it.

It was possible, however, that this game of bataös might be the excuse for it being mentioned. Humli Ghasartravhara, a member of the ship's governing board and on the rota of passenger liaison officers, had befriended her over breakfast and suggested the game. They had agreed to play unhelped, trusting the other not to seek advice elsewhere through implants or any other addenda, and not to gland any drugs that might help either.

They sat on tree stumps in a leafy glade of tropel trees by a small stream on the vessel's topside park. A black-backed borm lay on the far side of the small clearing like a discarded cloak with legs, patiently stalking each errant patch of sunlight as the vessel's sun line arced slowly overhead. The borm was snoring. Overhead, children in float harnesses or suspended under balloons squealed and shrieked. Anaplian felt something on her head, patted her short dark hair with one hand, then held her palm out flat and looked up, trying to see the floating children from beneath the intervening canopy.

"They're not peeing on us, are they?" she asked.

Humli Ghasartravhara looked up too, briefly. "Water pistols," he said, then returned his attention to the game, which he was losing. He was an elderly-looking fellow, pretty much human-basic, with long white hair held in a neat ponytail. His face and upper torso – revealed by some very high-waisted pantaloons of a particularly eye-watering shade of green – were covered in exquisitely detailed and intensely swirly abstract tattoos. The yellow-white lines glowed bright on his dark brown skin like veins of sunlight reflected from water.

"Interesting image," Ghasartravhara said. Anaplian had told him about the Morthanveld idea of sunlight seen from under water. "The aquatic environment." He nodded. "Quite different, but the same concerns. Surfacing." He smiled. "That we are and are not the focus of all reality. All solipsists."

"Arguably," Anaplian agreed.

"You are interested in the Morthanveld?" Ghasartravhara made a clicking noise with his mouth as the bataös board indicated it would move a piece for him if he didn't move one himself soon. He folded a piece, moved it, set it down. It unfolded itself as it settled and clicked down a few leaves of nearby pieces, subtly altering the balance of the game. But then, Anaplian thought, every move did that.

"I am going amongst them," Djan Seriy said, studying the board. "I thought I'd do a little research."

"My. Privileged. The Morthanveld are reluctant hosts."

"I have connections."

"You go to the Morthanveld themselves?"

"No, to a Shellworld within their influence. Sursamen. My homeworld."

"Sursamen? A Shellworld? Really?"

"Really." Anaplian moved a piece. The piece's leaves clicked down, producing a small cascade of further leaf-falls.

"Hmm," the man said. He studied the board for a while, and sighed. "Fascinating places, Shellworlds."

"Aren't they?"

"Might I ask? What takes you back there?"

"A death in the family."

"Sorry to hear that."

Anaplian smiled thinly.

One of Djan Seriy's earliest memories from when she had been a little girl was of a funeral. She had been just a couple of long-years old, maybe less, when they'd buried her father's brother, the Duke Wudyen. She was with the other children of the court, being looked after by nurses back at the palace while the adults were off doing the burying and mourning and so on. She was playing with Renneque Silbe, her best friend, making houses out of screens and pillows and cushions on the rug in front of the nursery fire, which roared and crackled away behind its fire guard of hanging chains. They were looking through the pillows and cushions to find one the right size for their house's door. This was the third house they'd built; some of the boys kept coming over from where they were playing near the windows and kicking their houses down. The nurses were meant to be looking after them all but they were in their own room nearby drinking juice.

"You killed your mother," Renneque said suddenly.

"What?" Djan Seriy said.

"I heard you did. Bet you did. Mamma said so. You killed her. Why was that? Did you? Did you really? Did it hurt?"

"I didn't."

"She says you did."

"Well I didn't."

"I know you did; my mamma told me."

"Didn't. Didn't kill her. Wouldn't have."

"My mamma says you did."

"Stop it. I didn't."

"My mamma does not lie."

"Didn't kill her. She just died."

"My mamma said it was you who killed her."

"She just died."

"People don't just die. Somebody has to kill them."

"Wasn't me. She just died."

"Like Duke Wudyen was killed by who gave him the black cough. That's reason."

"Just died."

"No, you killed her."

"Didn't."

"Did so! Come on now, Djan. Did you? Did you really?"

"Leave me alone. She just died."

"Are you crying?"

"No."

"Is that what you're doing now? Are you crying?"

"Not crying."

"You are! You're crying!"

"Not."

"Toho! Kebli! Look; Djan's crying!"

Humli Ghasartravhara cleared his throat as he moved his next piece. He wasn't really playing any longer, just shifting pieces about. They might have sent somebody better, Anaplian thought, then chided herself for making assumptions. "Will you be staying long?" the man asked. "On Sursamen? Or with the Morthanveld?"

"I don't know." She made a move. Quick, easy, knowing she had won.

"The ship you arrived on," the man said. He left a space she was meant to fill, but Anaplian just raised her eyebrows. "It wasn't very forthcoming, that's all," Humli said, when she refused to speak. "Just kind of dropped you. No passenger manifest or whatever they call it."

Anaplian nodded. "They call it a passenger manifest," she confirmed.

"The ship's a bit concerned, that's all," Ghasartravhara said, with a bashful smile. He meant his ship, this ship; the *Don't Try This At Home*.

"Is it? The poor thing."

"Obviously, we – it – would never normally be this, ah …"

"Intrusive? Paranoid?"

"Let's say … concerned."

"Let's."

"However, with the whole Morthanveld situation, you know …"

"I do?"

He gave a nervous laugh. "It's like waiting for a birth, almost, isn't it?"

"Is it?"

Humli sat back, slumped a little and cleared his throat again. "You're not really making this very easy for me, Ms Anaplian."

"Was I supposed to? Why?"

He looked at her for a while, then shook his head. "Also," he said, on a deep breath in, "I was, ah, asked by the ship Mind to ask you about an item in your luggage."

"Were you now?"

"Unusual. Basically a knife missile."

"I see."

"You are aware it is there."

"I am aware there is something there."

Ghasartravhara smiled at her. "You're not being spied on or anything. It's just these things show up on the scans ships do of anything and everything coming aboard."

"Are MSVs always so concerned with every intimate part of a traveller's luggage?"

"Not normally. As I say—"

"The Morthanveld situation."

"Well, yes."

"Let me tell you the truth, Mr Ghasartravhara."

The man sat back. "Okay," he said, as though preparing himself for something unpleasant.

"I work for Special Circumstances." She saw his eyes widen. "But I'm off duty. Maybe even off message, and possibly off for good. They've pulled my claws, Humli," she told him, and flexed an eyebrow. She held up one hand, exposing her fingernails. "See those?" Humli nodded. "Ten days ago I had nails with embedded CREWs, any one of which could have drilled a hole in your head big enough to stick a fist through." Mr. Ghasartravhara looked suitably impressed. Even nervous. She inspected her new nails. "Now . . . well, they're just fingernails." She shrugged. "There's a lot of other stuff I'm missing, too. All the really useful, harmful, hi-gadgetry stuff. It's been taken from me." She shrugged. "I surrendered it. All because of what we're calling the Morthanveld situation. And now I'm making a private visit to my home, after the recent death of both my father and my brother."

The man looked relieved and embarrassed. He nodded slowly. "I really am sorry to hear that."

"Thank you."

He cleared his throat again and said apologetically, "And the knife missile?"

"It stowed away. It was supposed to stay behind but the drone which controls it wants to protect me." She was choosing her words very carefully.

"Aw," Ghasartravhara said, looking and sounding mawkish.

"It is old and getting sentimental," she told him sternly.

"Yeah, but still."

"Still nothing. It will get us both into trouble if it's not careful. All the same, I'd appreciate it if the fact of that device's presence here didn't get back to SC."

"Can't imagine that will be a problem," Humli said, smiling.

Yes, she thought, grinning complicitly, everybody likes feeling they've got something over SC, don't they? She nodded at the board. "Your move."

"I think I'm beaten," he admitted ruefully. He looked at her dubiously. "I didn't know you were in SC when I agreed to play you."

She looked at him. "Nevertheless, I was playing by the same rules all the time. Unhelped."

Humli smiled, still uncertain, then stuck his hand out. "Anyway. Your game, I think." They pressed palms.

"Thank you."

He stretched, looked around. "Must be lunchtime. Will you join me?"

"Happily."

They started packing away the bataös set, piece by piece.

Well, she had done her best by her idiot drone, she reckoned.

If word of its adventure did get back to SC, it wouldn't be her fault. Anyway, it sounded like she and it might both get away with the fact that it was the mind of an experienced SC drone inside the knife missile, not a normal – and therefore relatively dim – knife missile brain.

It sounded like it. You still never knew.

The MSV *Don't Try This At Home* was relatively small and absolutely crowded, packed with people and ships in a chance convergence of itineraries, building schedules and travel arrangements. Anaplian had been given quarters not within the craft's own accommodation but inside a ship it contained and was still building, the *Subtle Shift In Emphasis*, a Plains-class General Contact Vehicle. This was a relatively new class of Culture ship and one that, apparently, couldn't make up its mind whether it was a big Contact Unit or a small System Vehicle. Whatever else it was it was unfinished, and Anaplian occasionally had to wait for bits and pieces of the structure to be moved around inside the *Don't Try This At Home*'s single Intermediate bay where the smaller ship was being constructed before she could move to or from her cabin.

Even this was not really a cabin, and not really part of the new ship either. She'd been allocated the whole of one of the GCV's modules; a small short-range transit craft which was nestled inside the vessel's lower hangar with a half-dozen others. The module had morphed its seating into more varied furniture and walls, and she was gratified at the scale of her accommodation – the module was designed to carry over a hundred people – however, there was nobody else quartered aboard either the rest of the under-construction ship or any of its other modules and it felt odd to be so isolated, so apart from other people on a ship so obviously crowded.

She didn't doubt she'd been quarantined like this to make some sort of point but she didn't care. To have such space in a small, packed ship was something of an indulgence. Others might have felt they were being treated like a pariah, being so prophylactically isolated from everybody else; she felt privileged. There were, she reflected, times when having been raised as a princess came in useful.

On her third night aboard the *Don't Try This At Home* she dreamt about the time she had been taken to see the great waterfall of Hyeng-zhar, a level down, in the Ninth, when she was still little.

Semi-conscious control over one's dreams was not even an amendment, more of a skill, a technique one learned – in childhood for those born within the Culture, in early adulthood for Anaplian – and in all but her most banal, memory-detritus-clearing dreams, Djan Seriy was used to watching what was going on with a vaguely interested, analytical eye and, sometimes, stepping in and affecting proceedings, especially if the dream threatened to turn into a nightmare.

She had long since ceased to be surprised that one could experience surprise in one's sleep at something one was watching oneself dreaming. Compared to some stuff that could happen after SC gave you total control over a thoroughly amended and vastly enhanced body and central nervous network, that was small doings.

Their party disembarked from the small train. She was holding the hand of her nurse and tutor, Mrs Machasa. The train itself was a novelty; a long, articulated thing like many land steamers all connected together and pulled by just one great engine, and running not on a road, but on railings! She'd never even heard of such a thing. She found trains and tracks and stations all very wonderful and advanced. She would tell her father to get some trains when they all returned to Pourl, and when he next returned from making the bad people stop being bad.

The station was crowded. Mrs Machasa held her hand tightly.

They were a large party, and had their own escort of royal guard – her very important brother Elime, who would be king one day, was with them, which made them all special – but, all the same, as Mrs M had told her that morning as they were getting her dressed, they were far away from home, on another level, amongst foreigners, and everybody knew that foreigners was just another word for barbarians. They had to be careful, and that meant keeping hold of hands, doing as you were told, and no wandering off. They were going to see the greatest water-fall in all the world and she didn't want to be swept away by all the horrible water, did she?

She agreed she didn't want to be swept away by all the horrible water. The weather was cold; the Hyeng-zhar lay in a place where the weather varied a lot and it was not unknown for the river and the great cataract to freeze. Mrs M fastened her into her coat and leggings and hat, pulling and jerking her whole body as she tightened this and buttoned that. Mrs M was big and wide and had grey brows that bowed towards each other. There was always something that didn't meet with her approval, often something about Djan Seriy, but she never hit her, sometimes cried over her and always hugged her, which was the best bit. Djan Seriy had tried to hug her father once when he was all dressed up for business and had been laughed at by some of the men in his court. Her father had pushed her away.

Anaplian felt she was floating in and out of her own younger consciousness, sometimes being her earlier self, sometimes watching from outside. She could see most of the scene quite clearly, though, as usual, when she was floating detached like this the one thing that was vague and unformed was her own younger self. It was as if even in dreams you couldn't truly be in two places at once. Bobbing in the air to one side of her dream self, she could not see herself as a child, just a sort of vague, fuzzy image of approximately the right size and shape.

She was already criticising her own dream. Had Mrs Machasa really been that big? Had their party really been that many?

Back inside her head, she watched the train huff and puff and cough out great white clouds and a smell of dampness. Then they were in steam carriages being taken along a road through a great flat plain. There were clouds against a blue sky. Some trees. Scrubby grass that Zeel, her mersicor gelding, would have turned his pretty nose up at. All very flat and rather boring.

In her memory there was no warning; the Falls were just there. Snapshot of a by-child-standards interminable carriage journey (probably about ten minutes), then Bang; the Hyeng-zhar, in all their vast, chaotic glory.

There must have been sight of the enormous river, its far bank lost in its own created mists so that it appeared as though an entire sea was spilling to oblivion; whole rolling, billowing fleets of clouds piled above the massive curve of the colossal cataract, rising without cease into the invaded sky; shaled continents of banked and broiling mists disappearing to the horizon; entire sheets and walls and cliffs of spray, the everywhere thunder of that ocean of water tipping over the exposed rock and pounding into the dizzying complex of linked plunge pools beneath where enormous canted blocks, bulging, monstrous curves, hollowed husks and jagged angles of jumbled debris jutted and reared.

She must have seen some of the monks of the Hyeng-zharia Mission, the religious order which controlled the Falls' excavation, and there must have been, if nothing else, all the squalor and slummery of the shanty town of ever-moving buildings that was the sprawling, peripatetic township called the Hyeng-zhar Settlement and all the equipment, spoil and general material associated with the desperate, ever-time-pressed excavations . . . but she recalled none of it, not before the shock of the Falls themselves, suddenly there, like the whole world twisting and falling sideways, like the sky upended, like everything in the universe falling forever in on itself, thrashing and pulverising all to destruction in a mad welter of elemental pandemonium. Here the air shook, the ground shook, the body shook, the brain shook inside the head, assaulted, rattled like a marble in a jar.

She had gripped Mrs M's hand very tightly.

She had wanted to shriek. She had felt that her eyes were bulging out of her head, that she was about to wet herself – the water squeezed out of her by the sheer force and battery of the trembling air wrapped pressing all around her – but mostly she wanted to scream. She didn't, because she knew if she did Mrs M would take her away, tutting and shaking her head and saying that she had always known it was a bad idea, but she wanted to. Not because she was frightened – though she was; quite terrified – but because she wanted to join in, she wanted to mark this moment with something of her own.

It didn't matter that this was the single most stunning thing she had ever seen in her life (and, despite everything, despite all the wonders even the Culture had had to show her in her later years, it had, in all the important ways, remained so), that there was no matching it, no measuring it, no competing with it, no point in even trying to be noticed by it; all that mattered was that she was here, it was here, it was making the greatest noise in the history of everything and she needed to add her own acknowledgement to its mighty, overwhelming voice. Her own tininess in comparison to it was irrelevant; its unheeding vastness drew the breath out of her, sucked the sound of screaming from her little lungs and delicate stem of throat.

She filled her chest to the point she could feel her bones and skin straining against her tightly buttoned coat, opened her mouth as wide as it could possibly go and then shook and trembled as though shrieking for all she was worth, but making no noise, certainly no noise above that stunning clamour overwhelming the air, so that the scream was caught and stayed clenched inside her, suffusing out into her miniature being, forever buried under layer after layer of memory and knowing.

They stood there for some time. There must have been railings she looked through or perhaps climbed up on to. Maybe Mrs M had held her up. She remembered that they all got wet; the rolls of mists curled up and over them and drifted this way and that on the cool, energising breeze and came down soaking them.

It had been some time before she even noticed that the great blocks and bulges that dominated the watery landscape beneath the Falls themselves were gigantic buildings. When she looked properly, once she knew what to look for, she started to see them everywhere; tilted and broken around the lake-sized plunge pools, tumbled amongst the mists downstream, poking like bone bits out of the dark walls of falling water before they filled and blossomed with dirty grey spray that settled into white as it rose and rose and rose, becoming cloud, becoming sky.

At the time, she had worried that the people of the city must be getting drowned. A little later, when they had been telling her it really was time to go and trying to prise her fingers off the railings, she had seen the people. They were nearly invisible, hidden inside the mists most of the time, only revealed when the walls and canopies of spray parted briefly. They were at the absolute limit of the eye's ability to make out; dwarfed, insected by the inhuman scale imposed by the arced sweep of the encompassing Falls, so tiny and reduced that they were just dots, unlimbed, only possibly or probably people because they could not be anything else, because they moved just so, because they crossed flimsy, microscopic suspension bridges and crawled along tiny threads that must be paths and grouped in miniature docks where minuscule boats and diminutive ships lay bobbing on the battering surface of hectic, dashing waves.

And of course they were not the people who had built and originally inhabited the buildings of the great city being revealed by the steady encroachment of the ever-retreating Falls, they were just some of the tens of thousands, maybe hundreds of thousands of looters, scavengers, diggers, climbers, breakers, tunnellers, bridge-builders, railway workers, pathfinders, mapmakers, crane men, hoist operators, fisherfolk, boat people, provisioners, guides, authorised excavationers, explorers, historians, archaeologists, engineers and scientists who had re-inhabited this ever-changing, unceasing ruin of torn sediment, tumbling rock, plunging water and scoured monumentality.

They peeled her fingers away one by one. Mrs M scolded her. She didn't hear, never looked round, couldn't care. She kept her wide-open eyes focused on that vast arena of water, rock, architecture and spray, kept her gaze fastened on the tiny dots that were people, turning all her attention and diminutive being to just that – not even bothering to expend the energy on struggling or protesting – until an exasperated guard finally pulled her away and put her over his shoulder, marching off with her, Mrs M just behind, wagging her finger at her. She still didn't care and could not hear; she looked over and past Mrs Machasa at the Falls, just grateful the guard had put her over his shoulder this way, facing backwards, so she could keep looking at the great cataract of Hyeng-zhar for as long as possible, until it disappeared behind the lip of the land, and only the towers and spires and walls of mist and spray and cloud were left, filling half the shining waste of sky.

The Hyeng-zhar cataract emptied one sea into another down a river two thousand kilometres long and in places so broad one bank was invisible from the other. The Sulpitine river flowed smoothly and gradually across a broad plain in a series of vast loops until it came to the gorge it had created, where it plunged two hundred metres into an enormous bite gouged from the surrounding land; indeed into a series of bites within bites, as a whole fractal series of waterfalls ate into the multiply gouged ground; hundreds of U-shaped falls fed in groups into a succession of huge holes shaped like shattered cups, themselves set within the still greater complexity of the arc of the continually lengthening gorge.

The cataract had once formed part of the shore of the Lower Sulpine Sea – the remaining cliffs still wrapped around a quarter of the sea's facing shore – but had quickly retreated as its titanic force washed away its own foundations, leaving a gorge two hundred metres deep and – when Djan Seriy had first seen it – four hundred kilometres long.

The gorge wore rapidly because of the nature of the stratification of the land. The cap rock supporting the river at the very lip of the Falls was sandstone, and so itself easily worn away. The layer underneath it was barely rock at all, more severely compacted mud from a series of huge floods hundreds of millions of years earlier. In a more intense gravity field the muds would have turned to rock as well; on Sursamen, some stayed so soft a human hand could crumble them.

The whole cataract was the Hyeng-zhar. It had been called that from the time the river had first started to plummet straight into the Lower Sulpine Sea six thousand years earlier and was still called that even though the complex of waterfalls had now retreated four hundred kilometres from its original position. What the city had been called, nobody knew. Its people had been wiped out in a cataclysm hundreds of millions of years ago and the whole level left abandoned for tens of millions of years subsequently, before – eventually, and with some trepidation – being colonised all over again by its present inhabitants.

They hadn't even known the city was there and certainly had no idea what its name was. The Oct, the Nariscene, the Morthanveld and even the allegedly near-omniscient Elder cultures of the galaxy didn't appear to know either; it had all been long ago and under earlier owners, the responsibility of the previous management, an unfortunate problem associated with the last, late, lamented tenants. The one thing everybody did know was that the city's name wasn't Hyeng-zhar.

The result was that the city came to be called the Nameless City. Which meant, of course, that its very name was a contradiction.

The Falls had been a Wonder of Sursamen for millennia just due to their sheer scale, famed even on levels of the great world the vast majority of whose inhabitants would never see them directly. Even so, the most prominent or important or just plain rich denizens of the Kiters of the Twelfth and the Naiant Tendrils of the Eleventh and the Vesiculars of the Tenth and the Tubers and Hydrals of the Fourth sometimes made the effort to come and see the Hyeng-zhar, so were transported by the Oct or the Aultridia up or down one or more Towers and then across to the site – those from profoundly different environments encased in whatever suit or vessel they required to survive – to gaze, usually through glass or screen or other intervening material, at the thunderous majesty of the celebrated cataract.

When the Falls began to expose the outskirt buildings of the buried city – almost a hundred years before Djan Seriy first saw them – their renown increased and spread even further, and took on too an air of mystery. The gradually uncovered metropolis was no mere primitives' settlement, albeit – as more and more of it was excavated by the Falls and its true scale started to become clear – one of extraordinary size; it was undeniably ancient but it had been highly advanced. Even ruined, it held treasures. Most of the plunder was conventional in form; precious metals and stones that would struggle to occur naturally on a Shellworld with its lack of plate tectonics and crustal recycling. Some, though, was in the form of exotic materials that could be used, for example, to fashion blades and machine parts of conventionally unsurpassable sharpness or hardness and fabulous if incomprehensible works of what was assumed must be art.

The materials the buildings were made from themselves possessed properties almost unthinkable to the people who did the discovering on the Ninth. Spars and beams and thin claddings could be used to build bridges of enormous strength and amazing lightness; the main problem those who would use this extravagance of booty faced was that the raw materials rarely came away in handy lengths and chunks and were usually impossible to cut or trim.

Intact or ruined, the interiors of the buildings also often provided strange artifacts and occasionally useful supplies, though never any bodies, fossils or tombs.

The city grew as it was eaten away, the extent of the building debris eventually spreading to beyond the width of the Falls on both sides – the cataract was over seven kilometres across at present, and the city must be broader than that.

Its buildings were of a hundred different types and styles, to the extent that it had been suggested the city had been host to several – possibly many – diverse types of being; doors and interior spaces were different shapes, entire structures were built on disparate scales and some had basement or foundation levels of bizarre designs that went deep below the floor of the gorge base, all the way down to the Prime of the Shellworld itself, another eighty metres below, so that these few buildings remained standing even after the Falls had exposed them and retreated far beyond, leaving them as enormous slab-sided islands towering above the braid of streams that formed the reconstituted river making its way down the great gorge to the Lower Sea.

A series of wars amongst the humans who inhabited the Ninth, centred around the control of the Falls and their supply of treasure, resulted in an Oct-brokered peace that had held for a few decades. The Sarl and a few other peoples from the Eighth – allowed to travel to the relevant region of the Ninth by the Oct – had taken a peripheral part in some of the wars and a greater part in the peace, generally acting as honest brokers and providing relatively neutral administrational and policing contingents.

By then the fame of the Falls had grown sufficiently that even the Nariscene had taken an interest and declared the whole area a Site of Extraordinary Curiosity, effectively putting their stamp of authority on the peace deal and prodding the Oct to help guarantee it, at least within the limits of the general Shellworld mandate decreeing that the inhabitants of each level should basically be left to get on with their odd and frequently violent little lives.

The Deldeyn had other ideas. They'd been fortunate or skilful in the conduct of distant wars not immediately associated with the issue of the Hyeng-zhar, and, identifying an opportunity too good to miss – plus having at the time nothing else to do with the great armies they'd built up in the course of their far-flung victories – had annexed the neutral zone around the Falls, thrown out the administrators and police forces from the other peoples and, just for good measure, attacked anybody who protested too loudly. This latter group included the Sarl. It was in what the Deldeyn regarded as a small punitive raid to make clear to their inferiors that they were in charge now and were not to be trifled with, on the last Sarlian outpost on the Ninth at the foot of the Peremethine Tower, that King Hausk's eldest son, Elime, had been killed. So had started the war between the Deldeyn and the Sarl, the war between the levels.

Anaplian woke gently from her dream of the Falls, surfacing to full consciousness with uncharacteristic slowness. How strange to dream of the Hyeng-zhar again after all this time. She could not immediately recall the last time she'd dreamt of them, and chose not to use her neural lace to investigate and tell her the exact date (as well as, no doubt, what she'd eaten the evening before, the disposition of the furnishings of the room she'd had the dream in and any company present at the time).

She looked across the billow-bed. A young man called Geltry Skiltz lay cutely curled and sweetly asleep, naked amongst the gently circulating wisps of soft fabric and what looked like large, dry snowflakes. She watched a few of the flakes swirl near his still most attractive if slightly slack-jawed face, each one neatly avoiding his nose and mouth, and thought back to the dream and through the dream to the reality of that first visit to the cataract.

She had been back again, after years of pleading, on just one other occasion, less than a year before Elime's death and the start of the war that now might be approaching its end. She'd still been a girl really, she supposed, though she'd thought of herself as a mature young woman at the time and been convinced that her life was already mostly behind her. The Hyeng-zhar had been no less impressive; just the same though utterly different. In the years between her two visits – what she would now think of as about ten Standard years – the cataract had retreated nearly seven hundred metres upstream, revealing whole new districts of fascinating and grotesquely different buildings and structures and changing its shape profoundly.

From the ceiling of the level it would no doubt look roughly similar – that distinctive broken-cup look, that vast bite out of the land – but, close to, there was nothing left to recognise from the last time; all that had been there originally had been swept away, flushed as silt, mud, sand, rocks and rubble to the ever more distant sea or left crooked and askew in the great broad rush of water, clogged and skirted with sandbanks and debris tailings, forlorn.

Looking back, there had been signs of Deldeyn intentions even then, she realised. Just so many men in uniform, and a general air of grievance that other people were allowed to tell the Deldeyn what they could and couldn't do on what was now, they seemed to believe, their level entirely. And all because of some idiot treaty signed in a time of weakness.

She'd been just mature enough to register some of this, though sadly not sufficiently so to be able to analyse it, contextualise it, act upon it. She wondered briefly if she had been capable of realising the dangers, would it have made any difference? Could she have warned her father, alerted him to the threat?

There had been warnings, of course; Sarlian spies and diplomats at the Falls themselves, in the regional capital of Sullir and the Deldeyn court itself and beyond had reported the mood and detailed some of the preparations for war, but their intelligence had gone unheeded. Such reports always arrived in great quantity and many invariably contradicted each other; some would always be simply mistaken, some would always be from agents and officials trying to exaggerate their own importance or swell their retainer and some would always be deliberate misinformation sown by the other side. You had to pick and choose, and therein lay the potential for mistake.

Even her father, wise warrior though he'd already become by then, had sometimes been guilty of hearing what he wanted to hear rather what was clearly being said, and at the time a potential war with the Deldeyn had been the last thing he'd wanted to be told about; he had his hands full with his campaigns on the Eighth and the armies of Sarl were in no way prepared to face what were at the time the superior forces of the Ninth.

She shouldn't deceive, or blame, herself. Her warning, if she'd even had the wit to deliver one, would have made no difference. Apart from anything else she was just a girl, and so her father would have taken no notice anyway.

She lay awake in the cabin, young Mr Skiltz soundly asleep at her side, the disguised knife missile, drone-mind dormant, also effectively asleep, safely tucked up in her bag in a cupboard. She could still use her neural lace within the reach of the Culture's dataverse, certainly within the ship, and through it she asked for an image to be thrown across the far wall of her bedroom showing the real space star field ahead of the *Don't Try This At Home*.

The vessel was making modest speed. The stars looked almost stationary. She looked ahead into the swirled mix of tiny light-points, knowing that Meseriphine, the star Sursamen orbited, would be far in the distance and most likely still invisible. She didn't ask for it, or its direction, to be displayed. She just watched the slow, slow drift of onward falling stars for a while, thinking of home, and fell gradually into a dreamless sleep.

14. Game

"Toho! A crown to your smallest coin you drop it!"

"Done, bastard that you are, Honge," the gentleman in question said through gritted teeth. He took the weight of the stick and tankard on his chin and stood very still as one of the laughing serving girls filled it almost to the brim with beer. His friends whooped and laughed and called out insults. Bright sunlight from Pentrl's first passing since the death of the King poured through tall windows into the smoky interior of the Gilder's Lament.

Oramen grinned as he watched. They had been here most of the day. The latest game used beer, sticks, the galleries on either side of the Lament's main room and two of the serving girls. Whoever's turn it was had to stand beneath the gallery on one side while a girl filled a tankard full of beer, then the fellow had to walk from one side of the room to the other with the glass balanced on a stick resting on his chin, so that a girl on the opposite gallery could relieve him of the glass and bring it down to the assembly, for the purposes of drinking.

It was no easier than it sounded and most of the men had spilled beer on themselves by now, many to the point they were so soaked they had stripped off to the waist. They were using caulked leather tankards rather than ceramic or glass ones so that it didn't hurt too much when you got hit on the head by one. The game became gradually more difficult as more beer soaked into both the floorboards and the players. About twenty such bravards were in the group, including Oramen and Tove Lomma. The air was thick with smoke and laughter, the smell of spilled beer and ribald taunts.

Tohonlo, the most senior of those present and the most highly ranked save for Oramen himself, pulled slowly away from the gallery and slid his way gradually across the floor, the tankard wobbling and describing a tight little circle above him. A small amount of ale sloshed over the side, splashing on his brow. The other men roared and stamped their feet but he just blinked, wiped the beer away from his eyes and carried on, tankard re-steadied. The foot-stamping got louder and, briefly, more co-ordinated.

Tohonlo neared the gallery on the other side, where a well-built serving lass in a low-cut blouse stretched out over the balustrade, one hand extended, looking to grab the handle of the wobbling tankard. Below, the men were happy to let her know the extent to which she was admired.

"Come on, Toho, tip it on to her tits!"

The tankard wobbled its way to the girl's outstretched fingers, she grasped it and lifted, giving a little *eek* as the extra weight nearly tipped her over the edge of the gallery, then she pulled herself back. A great cheer went up from the men. Tohonlo pulled his chin back and let the stick fall. He grabbed it at one end like a sword and made to thrust it at the men who'd been making the most noise while he'd been distracted. The fellows made motions and noises of pretended fear.

"Oramen!" Tove said, slapping him on the back and thumping

down on the bench beside him, depositing two leather tankards of beer in front of them with a slop and slosh of spillage. "You should take a turn!" He punched Oramen's arm.

"I told you I didn't want another drink," Oramen said, raising the tankard and waving it in front of Tove's sweatily gleaming face.

Tove leaned closer. "What?" It was very noisy.

"Never mind." Oramen shrugged. He put his old drink to one side of their table and sipped at his new one.

"You should!" Tove shouted at him as another of their company put the balancing stick on his chin and waited for the first serving girl to fill the tankard on top. Meanwhile the tankard of ale Tohonlo had transported from one gallery to the other was duly delivered to him by the second serving girl, who then skipped back upstairs, neatly avoiding most of the slaps aimed at her behind. "You should take a turn!" Tove told Oramen. "Go on! Take a turn! Go *on*!"

"I'd get wet."

"What?"

"Wet," Oramen shouted above the din. The lads were clapping loudly and rhythmically.

"Well of course it's wet! 'S the idea!"

"Should have worn an older tunic."

"You don't have enough fun!" Tove said, leaning close enough for Oramen to smell his breath.

"I don't?"

"You don't come out as often as you ought, prince!"

"Really?"

"I hardly see you! When was the last time we went out whoring, for fuck's sake?"

"Not for a bit, I'll grant."

"You can't be fed up with it, can you?"

"With what?"

"Girls!"

"Don't be ridiculous."

"You're not becoming a man-fucker, are you?"

"Indeed not."

"You don't want to fuck men, do you?"

"Heaven forfend."

"So what's the matter?"

"I have other things to do, Tove. I'd love to spend more time with you but I—"

"You're not becoming some fucking man-fucker, are you? They're worse than fucking republicans."

"Listen: no."

"Because I fucking love you, prince, seriously, but I fucking hate fucking man-fuckers, I really fucking do."

"Tove, I believe you. It would be hard not to. I do not want to fuck men. Please; believe. Even just remember."

"Well then, come on out with us. Come and have some fun!"

"I shall, I promise."

"But do you promise?"

"Will you listen? I promise. Now stop being—"

They hadn't even seen the fight break out. Next thing they knew, tankards and glasses were flying and men were falling over each other and themselves. Blades were supposed to be left at the door, but in the sudden mêlée Oramen thought he saw the flash of sunlight on a steel edge. He and Tove both instinctively sat back and grabbed their tankards as a man – an especially substantial and well-built man – thudded back towards them, half stumbling, half falling.

Their bench was joined by spars to the table in front of them, so everything still went flying, including them; however, Oramen had remembered that bench and table were one even as the fellow came clattering and staggering towards them, and had pulled his legs up and started swivelling on his buttocks as the man's back and head collided with the empty bench and full table in front of them; Oramen was able to roll out of the way as the whole assemblage went careering backwards taking Tove with it, crashing into another bench and table set behind, causing curses. Oramen even saved most of his ale, which was an achievement; every drink still on the table and the one in Tove's fist went splashing back, mostly over the people sitting at the table behind, to their unalloyed and most vocal consternation. Tove and the people at the table behind were addressing each other:

"You fucker!"

"Fuck yourself!"

Oramen stood up, then immediately had to duck as a thrown glass sailed through the air where his head had been.

Tove and the people of the bench behind were still conversing. Oramen took a sip of his beer, checked for flying objects and took a step back. It was a most impressive fight. He liked the way you could see the smoke sort of roll and part when people went flying through it. Two burly knights charged forward and came between Tove and the argumentative inhabitants of the table behind, getting briefly tangled up with him.

Tove extracted himself and stumbled over to Oramen, wiping beer off his tunic. "We'd better go," he said. "Follow me."

"What?" Oramen protested as Tove grabbed his arm. "I was just starting to enjoy myself."

"Time for that later. Now's time to run away." Tove pulled him by the sleeve round the side of the main fight, across the floor – the two serving girls were screaming from either gallery, encouraging, disparaging, throwing tankards both full and empty at the chaos of brawling bodies below – towards the back door which led to the yard and the toilets.

"But this is fun!" Oramen yelled at Tove, still trying to pull his arm free.

"Some of these fuckers might be anarchists; let's away."

A glass shattered on the wall near Oramen's head. "Oh," he sighed. "All right."

"Seeing sense. Late than never."

They clattered down some steps towards the courtyard and got to the door. Tove stopped in the narrow passageway and said, "After you, pr—"

"Oh, get out there," Oramen told him, pushing him one-handed.

They burst through a door into the intense afternoon brightness of the tavern's yard. Oramen caught the sudden stench of a nearby tannery.

A man swung round from one side of the door and sank a long dagger into Tove's belly, ripping quickly upwards.

"Not, not me!" Tove had time to bubble, then he dropped as the man who'd struck him stepped around him and – with a second man – pulled his arm back, blade aimed straight at Oramen.

Oramen had had his hand at the small of his back all the way down the stairs, pulling his tunic top and shirt out, feeling until the warmth of the gun's handle was there in his fist. He hauled it out, used his other hand to click the safety off as he'd practised a hundred times in his bedchamber and pulled the trigger in the face of the man who'd knifed Tove.

The man's forehead formed a small round mouth which gave up a little spitting kiss of red; the hair at the back of his head bounced up and out, releasing a pink spray like a consumptive's cough. He fell back as though he was collared, some charging beast just got to the end of his lead, jerking rearwards and falling on his shoulder blades and head, eyes staring up at the shining sky. The other man flinched at the incredibly loud bang the gun made and hesitated in his lunge, perhaps even took a half-step back. It was enough. Oramen swung his arm round and shot him – he was little further away – in the chest. He fell back as well, and stayed sitting on the strawy, shitty, uneven stones of the courtyard of the Gilder's Lament.

The gunshots had left Oramen's ears ringing.

Tove lay moving slowly, leaking huge amounts of dark red blood, which made a sort of rectangular graph-paper pattern along the spaces of the yard's cobbles. The first man lay on his back, perfectly motionless, eyes fixed staring upwards. The man Oramen had just shot still sat upright, legs splayed in front of him, dagger dropped to one side, both his hands up at the small wound in his chest, his gaze directed somewhere on to the cobblestones between him and Oramen. He seemed to be hiccuping. Oramen wasn't sure what to do and was not thinking straight, so he stepped forward and shot the sitting man in the head. He fell over like he'd thrown himself that way, as though gravity somehow wasn't enough. Oramen hardly noticed that bang, his ears were ringing so.

There was nobody else about. He sat down too, before he fell down. The courtyard seemed very quiet after all the noise.

"Tove?" he said.

Tove had stopped moving. The graph pattern of blood moving along the spaces between the courtyard stones was reaching out towards Oramen's outstretched feet. He moved them before it touched them, and shivered. There was a roaring noise which he took to be the continuing brawl in the room above.

"Tove?" he said again. It was surprisingly cold in the brightly sunlit courtyard.

Eventually, people came.

The Deldeyn had dug a series of canals and broad, water-filled ditches across their land, seeking to impede the land-based forces of the Sarl. Due to the direction the Sarl attacked from, itself determined by the Tower they had descended within, only one of these new obstacles lay in their way. They had already beaten off a massed attack by riflemen and grenadiers mounted on caude and lyge shortly after leaving the Night they had encountered near the Illsipine. The Deldeyn had attacked in good order and eventually had to flee in tatters, those who could. They fought bravely and the grenadiers in particular caused some damage and deaths, especially when a roasoaril tanker exploded, but they still had no answer to massed ground guns, which picked the slow-moving beasts and their riders out of the air like hunters firing into a tight flock of birds.

The Sarl's own flighted forces were mostly held back until the Deldeyn fliers turned away in full retreat, then took off after them, harrying, shooting and tackling in mid-air where the riders were brave or foolish enough. The army dusted itself down and resumed its onward progress, the way marked by the commingled wreckage of dead Deldeyn fliers and their air-beasts. Tyl Loesp counted at least a dozen of the enemy's to every Sarlian casualty.

They passed one mound of shattered bone, seeping gristle and leathery wing fabric lying on the dusty ground where the Deldeyn rider was still alive. Tyl Loesp himself noticed movement as they passed and ordered his command car stopped and the badly injured flier disentangled from his dead mount, a process which even done without deliberate roughness still caused him to scream hoarsely. They brought him aboard and set him on a litter at the rear of the open car where a doctor attempted to tend to him and an interpreter tried to question him about Deldeyn morale and their remaining forces. The man was near his end anyway, but found the strength to push the doctor away and spit in the interpreter's face before he died. Tyl Loesp told them to push his body off the rear of the car without further ceremony.

The great plain stretched away to every horizon. The Sulpitine river was some twenty kilometres to their left. High clouds of faint pink stood against the too-blue sky as they came to the single wide canal which was the last defendable barrier between them and the region which held the Deldeyn capital city of Rasselle. The Deldeyn had stationed land forces on the near side of the canal but they had mostly fled on boats during the night. Their trenches were shallow and unshored, just as the canal was not properly lined and its banks were continually collapsing, leaving beaches of sand all along its length. The water was draining away in any case; only a diversionary feeder canal and hastily thrown-up breakwater affair further up the Sulpitine had kept the improvised water barrier supplied, and that had been destroyed by Sarlian sappers that morning, leaving the waters to drain back to the main river or just soak away into the sands.

Desultory artillery fire from the far side of the canal – from somewhere a good distance beyond it – mostly fell short and anyway seemed virtually unspotted. The Sarls had the air now; no Deldeyn fliers were rising to meet their scouts and patrols and spotters. The Sarlian artillery was mostly still being drawn up and the first few batteries were test-firing even now, finding their range. Tyl Loesp stood on the shallow berm of excavated sand, binoculars in hand, and listened to the explosions. The guns of the batteries fired in short order, almost rhythmically, like a troop of well-drilled riflemen, though the reports were naturally deeper-voiced. Such close-spaced regularity was a good sign. The spotters flew their grids, turning and swivelling in the air, signalling with heliographs where the shots from their allotted batteries were falling. On the far side, distant puffs of sand and veils of slowly drifting dust showed where the rounds landed.

Werreber came up in his land steamer, jumped out, said good day to some of tyl Loesp's staff – keeping a respectful distance back from their chief – and strode on up to him.

"Question is," he said abruptly, "do we wait for the water to drain or risk an attack now?"

"How long till it is drained sufficiently?" tyl Loesp asked.

"Perhaps till the start of the next short-night, when Uzretean sets. That's a very short one; just three hours, then Tresker rises. The engineers are loath to commit themselves to exact times. Patches of the bed may remain muddy; other parts might be wadeable now."

"Can we identify such variations?"

"We are trying to." The field marshal nodded at a particularly large caude labouring its way low over the retreating waters, two men on its back. "That's one of the engineers taking a look from above now. They seem generally of the opinion we should wait till dawn of Tresker. That would be prudent. Even if we can find a few dry paths sooner, crossing by them concentrates our attack to too pinched and vulnerable a focus. Better to attack broadly."

"But would we not be well to attack sooner rather than later?" tyl Loesp asked. "If we have all our forces ready, I think we ought."

"Perhaps. They don't seem to have a lot of men on the far side, though there are reports of many roads and tracks; they might be there and well dug in."

"Are not the fortifications on this side crude and shallow?"

"They are. That does not mean those on the far side are the same. They might even have left those on this side in such a poor state to lure us onwards."

"We could be too cautious here," tyl Loesp said. "The longer we wait, the more time they have to assemble what forces they have."

"Our own reinforcements arrive too. And we can see any of theirs on their way. The scouts report none so far, though there is too much mist drifting from the great Falls to see further than thirty kilometres down the road. River mists may obscure matters here later, too, especially in the early morning of Tresker, though we may be able to use that to our own advantage."

"I feel we should attack now," tyl Loesp said.

"If the enemy are there in any numbers," Werreber said, nodding at the far bank, "attacking now might lose us the war this afternoon."

"You take too much care, Werreber. They are broken. We have the momentum. And even if they are there, even if we are temporarily thrown back, the war would not be lost. We have reached a stage where even on their homelands we can afford greater loss than they."

"Why hurry? Why suffer such loss at all? By morning we'll have pounded them all night and be set for a broad attack in overwhelming force that'll trample them beneath us. The men and vehicles need resting anyway, tyl Loesp. To charge onward would be intemperate and risk severe attenuation. We can repel anything they choose to face us with, but only if our forces remain cohesive."

"Nevertheless, to keep that momentum, even if we then halt and draw breath on the far side, we shall attack as soon as we have crossing points identified."

Werreber drew himself up to his full, straight-backed height, staring down his hook of a nose at the other man. "I don't understand you, tyl Loesp; you introduce delay by insisting on taking this circuitous route, then you drive us faster than a stooping lyge."

"It is my way of maintaining a balance," tyl Loesp said.

The field marshal looked frosty. "I advise against this attack, tyl Loesp."

"And I note that." Tyl Loesp smiled thinly. "Even so."

Werreber gazed out across the expanse of shining sand and breeze-ruffled waters to the far bank. He sighed. "As you wish, sir," he said. He inclined a small bow, turned and left.

"Oh, and Field Marshal?"

Werreber turned, frowning.

"Take no prisoners." Tyl Loesp shrugged. "Save perhaps a few for interrogation."

Werreber glared at him for a few moments, then gave the most cursory of nods and turned away again.

"You had not killed before?" Fanthile asked.

"Of course not!"

"Had you ever drawn blood, or been in a fight?"

Oramen shook his head. "Barely touched a sword, let alone a gun. My father never wanted me to be a warrior. That was Elime's role. Ferbin was his reserve in that, though unsuited, perhaps through an overconcentration on Elime; my father felt Ferbin went to seed, from ripeness to spoiled almost before he was fully a man. I was too young to figure as a combateer when father was ascribing us our parts and planning his assault on posterity. My role was always to be the studious one, the thinker, the analyser, the futurian." Oramen snorted.

Fanthile poured a little more of the sweet iced wine into Oramen's crystal. They sat in the palace secretary's private apartments. Oramen had not known who to talk to after the attack. Eventually his steps had led him to Fanthile. "Then you did especially well, did you not?" the palace secretary said. "Many a man who thinks himself brave finds he is not when faced with such expeditious assault."

"Sir, did you not hear? I practically fainted. I had to sit before I fell. And I had the advantage; without my pistol, I'd not be here. Couldn't even defend myself like a gentleman."

"Oramen," Fanthile said gently, "you are still a youth. And besides, you thought to arm yourself. That was wise, was it not?"

"So it proved." Oramen drank deeply.

"And those who attacked you were not overly concerned with etiquette."

"Indeed not. I imagine they only used a knife rather than a gun because one is silent and the other reports its use over half the city. Unless they turn out to be strict gentlemen, of course," Oramen said with a sneer. "Such scorn guns, reckoning blades the honourable recourse, though I believe a rifle in a hunt is lately becoming allowable in even the most regressive shires."

"And they did kill your best friend."

"Oh, they killed Tove well; stuck him. He was most surprised," Oramen said bitterly. A small frown creased his brow. "Most surprised . . ." he repeated, hesitating.

"Then do not blame yourself," Fanthile was saying. Then it was his turn to frown. "What?"

Oramen shook his head. "Just the way Tove said 'Not *me*', when . . ." He wiped his face with one hand. "And before, when we were at the door . . ." He stared up at the ceiling for a few moments, then shook his head decisively. "No. What am I saying? He was my best friend. He could not." He shivered. "Great grief, the man dies in my place and I look to blame him." He drank again.

"Steady, young man," Fanthile said, smiling, nodding at the glass.

Oramen looked at the glass, appeared to be about to argue, then set it down on the table between them.

"The blame is mine, Fanthile," he said. "I sent Tove first through that door, and I was stupid enough to finish off the one I'd hit first in the chest. Through him we might have discovered who sent them."

"You think they were sent, by somebody else?"

"I doubt they were just loitering around the courtyard waiting to rob the first person to come through that door."

"Then who might have sent them?"

"I don't know. I have thought, and, on thinking, realised there is a dismayingly large cast of suspects."

"Who might they be?"

Oramen stared at the other man. "The same people you might think of."

Fanthile met the prince's gaze. He nodded. "Indeed. But who?"

Oramen shook his head. "Deldeyn spies, republicans, radical parliamentarians, a family with a personal vendetta against my family, from this generation or one before, an out-of-pocket bookmaker mistaking me for Ferbin. Who knows? Even anarchists, though they seem to exist more in the minds of those who oppose them most fervently than in awkward reality."

"Who," Fanthile asked, "would gain most from your death?"

Oramen shrugged. "Well, pursued to the absolute limits of logicality, tyl Loesp, I suppose." He looked at the palace secretary, who met his gaze with a studiedly blank expression. He shook his head again. "Oh, I thought of him, too, but if I distrust him I distrust everybody. You, Harne, Tove – WorldGod welcome him – everybody." Oramen made a fist and punched at the nearest cushion. "*Why* did I kill that wounded one? I should have kept him alive!" He stared at the palace secretary. "I'd have wielded the pliers and the glowing iron myself on that cur."

Fanthile looked away for a moment. "Your father frowned on such techniques, prince. He used them most rarely."

"Well," Oramen said, discomfited, "I imagine these . . . occurrences are best avoided. Best . . . delegated."

"No," Fanthile said. "He would be present, but it was the only thing I ever saw make him physically sick."

"Yes, well," Oramen said, feeling suddenly awkward. "I doubt I really could do it. I would faint, or run away, no doubt." He lifted his glass again, then set it down once more.

"You will need a new equerry, prince," Fanthile said, looking pleased to be changing the subject. "I am sure one will be chosen for you."

"Doubtless by Exaltine Chasque," Oramen said. "Tyl Loesp has left him 'in charge' of me while he's gone." Oramen shook his head.

"Indeed," Fanthile said. "However, might I suggest you present the Exaltine with your own choice, already made?"

"But who?" Oramen looked at the palace secretary. "You have someone in mind?"

"I have, sir. Earl Droffo. He is young but he is wise, earnest and reliable, devoted to your late father and your family and only lately come to Pourl. He is – how shall I put this? – not overly contaminated by the cynicisms of the court."

Oramen regarded Fanthile a little longer. "Droffo; yes, I remember him from the day Father died."

"Also, sir, it's time you had your own dedicated servant."

"Very well, arrange that too, if you would." Oramen shrugged. "I have to trust somebody, palace secretary; I shall choose to trust you." He drained his glass. "Now I trust you will refill my glass," he said, and giggled.

Fanthile poured him a little more wine.

The battle of the canal crossing was neither the disaster Werreber had feared nor the stroll tyl Loesp had anticipated. They lost

more men and materiel than the field marshal thought necessary to get to the far side, and even then they still needed to
stop and regroup and resupply for so long that they might as
well have waited for the dawn to attack on a broad front after
a serious overnight artillery barrage and possibly with the cover
of morning mists. Instead they had been funnelled into three
long crossings over the shallow pools of standing water and
damp sands, and, so concentrated, had suffered from the attentions of Deldeyn heavy machine-gunners and disguised mortar
pits well dug in on the far side.

Still, the battle had been won. They had traded saved, unfired
artillery shells for the expended lives and limbs of ordinary
soldiers. Werreber thought this a shameful, ignominious bargain
when there was no pressing need to hurry. Tyl Loesp thought
it a reasonable one.

Werreber comforted himself in the knowledge that decreeing
something did not necessarily make it so on the ground;
knowing the order was to take no prisoners, many of the Sarl
units chose to disarm the Deldeyn they captured and let them
run away. Werreber had chosen not to hear of such insubordi-
nation.

The two men quarrelled again about splitting their forces; the
regent wanted to send a substantial body of men to take the
Hyeng-zhar Settlement while the field marshal thought it wiser
to have all the troops available to attack the capital, where the
last significant Deldeyn forces were massing. The regent
prevailed there too.

Reduced by the forces assigned to take the Falls, the
remaining army spread out, splitting into three sections for the
final assault on the Deldeyn capital.

15.   The Hundredth Idiot

As soon as Ferbin saw the knights Vollird and Baerth he knew they were here to kill him. He knew precisely who they were. They had stood on either side of the interior of the door at the abandoned factory where his father had been killed. They had stood there and they had watched their king being brutally murdered by tyl Loesp. The shorter, broader, more powerful-looking one was called Baerth – he was the one Ferbin had recognised at the time. The taller, skinnier knight was Vollird, well known to be one of tyl Loesp's closest allies and who, Ferbin was sure beyond surety, had been the taller knight whose face he had not seen standing on the other side of the door from Baerth.

"Gentlemen," said Vollird, nodding fractionally and smiling thinly. Baerth – the shorter, more powerful-looking one – said nothing.

The two had appeared on the broad, crowded concourse which stretched away from the Tower exit Ferbin and Holse had just been led from while the Oct – who was still demanding their documents – was attempting to explain why the Nariscene Grand Zamerin wasn't there to be met with. The two knights were escorted by a Nariscene in a glittering exoskeleton of gold and precious stones. They were dressed in leggings and long tunics covered in tabards, with sheathed swords and pistol holsters hanging from thick belts.

Ferbin did not reply. He just stared at them, fixing their faces in his mind for ever. He could feel himself starting to shake as his pulse quickened and a cold, clenching sensation came from his guts. He was furious with his body for betraying him so, and did all he could to relax, breathe evenly and generally display every outward sign of steady normality.

"And you, sirs," Holse said, hand still resting on the pommel of his long knife, "who would you be?"

"Documents, if please," the Oct at Holse and Ferbin's side said, unhelpfully.

The taller knight looked at Ferbin as he said, "Do us the courtesy of informing your servant that we don't answer to the pet when the owner stands before us."

"My servant is a man of honour and decency," Ferbin said, trying to keep his voice calm. "He may address you in any form or manner he sees fit and by God you ought to be grateful for even the most meagre courtesy he accords you, for you deserve less than a dry spit of it, and if I were you I'd hoard most jealously what little comes your way, for trust me, sirs, leaner times lie ahead if you but knew."

The short knight looked furious; his hand twitched towards his sword. Ferbin's mouth was very dry; he was horribly aware how mismatched their two sides were in armament. The taller one appeared surprised and mildly wounded. "These are unkind words, sir, to two who desire only to help you."

"I believe I know the fate to which you'd like to help us. It is a condition I'm determined to avoid for some time yet."

"Sir," the taller knight said, smiling tolerantly, "we have been sent by the current and rightful ruler of our shared homeland, who wishes you only good, to aid you in your passage. I regret any misunderstanding that might have led you to think ill of us before we are even correctly introduced. I am Vollird of Sournier, knight of the court; my companion here is Baerth of Charvin, also so ennobled." Vollird swivelled fractionally and indicated the shorter man by his side with one hand as he spoke these words, though his gaze stayed fixed upon Ferbin. "We are here at your service, good sir. Grant us civility, I beg you, if for no other reason than that we are in front of our otherworldly friends here, and might risk demeaning the reputation of our whole people by seeming to squabble or fret." Vollird waved at the brilliant, static forms of the Oct and Nariscene at their sides, his gaze still fastened on Ferbin.

"If you are at my service," Ferbin replied, "you will remove yourselves from us at once and take this message to your master, who is no more the rightful ruler of our 'shared homeland' than my last turd, indeed somewhat less so: I go only to return, and when I do, I shall treat him with all the grace and respect he showed my father, at his end."

There was the tiniest of jerking motions at one extremity of Vollird's dark brow; it was the merest hint of surprise, but Ferbin was glad to see it. He knew he could say more, but also knew, with a sort of fascinated certainty, that this constituted one charge of powder he ought to keep aside for now. There might be a moment when some further revelation of his most detailed knowledge of what had happened in the half-ruined factory that evening would be of a use beyond just discomfiting these men.

Vollird was silent for a half-moment, then smiled and said, "Sir, sir, we still misunderstand each other. We would help you, escort you on your way away from here. That is our earnest wish and most specific instruction." He smiled, quite broadly, and made an open gesture with both hands. "We all of us wish the same thing, which is to see you on your way. You have departed the land and level to which you have belonged with some urgency and dispatch, and we would merely assist you on whatever further flight you may be determined on. We ought not to dispute."

"We do not wish the same—" Ferbin started to say, but then the shorter knight, Baerth, who had been frowning mightily for the last few moments, said, under his breath, as though to himself,

"Enough talk. Sheath this, whore." He drew his sword and lunged at Ferbin.

Ferbin started to take a step back; Holse began to move in front of him, his left arm making as though to push Ferbin behind him. At the same time Holse's right arm arced across his body and out; the short knife tore through the air and—

And was whipped out of the air by one limb of the Nariscene at Baerth's side, at the same time as one of its other legs tripped up the lunging knight and sent him sprawling to the floor at Holse's feet. Holse stamped sharply on the man's wrist and scooped his sword from his broken grip. Baerth grunted in pain. Vollird was drawing his pistol.

"Stop!" the Nariscene said. "Stop!" it repeated as Holse made to stab the prone knight with one hand and take his pistol with the other. The sword was knocked from his hand by the Oct while the Nariscene turned and snapped the pistol from Vollird's grip, producing a sudden gasp. Sword and pistol went clattering to the floor in opposite directions.

"To stop, hostilities," the Oct said. "Inappropriate behaviour."

Holse stood, glaring at the eight-limbed alien, shaking his own right hand and blowing on it as though trying to get blood back into it on a cold day. He had moved the foot he'd stamped on Baerth's wrist with so that it now lay on the man's neck, with most of Holse's weight on it. Vollird stood shaking his right hand vigorously, and cursing.

Ferbin had observed it all, keeping back and low and watching with an odd detachment who had done what and where all the weapons were at each moment. He found he still possessed a very clear idea of where both pistols were; one over there on the floor, the other still in Baerth's side holster.

A device swung down from the ceiling. It looked like a bulky rendition of a Nariscene in an entire symphony of coloured metals.

"Fighting is not allowed in public spaces," it said loudly in oddly accented but perfectly comprehensible Sarl. "I shall take charge of all weapons in this vicinity. Resistance will incur physical penalties not excluding unconsciousness and death." It was already gathering up the sword and pistol from the floor, swinging through the air with a whooshing sound. The Nariscene handed it Holse's long knife. "Thank you," it said. It removed Baerth's pistol from its holster – the man was still flat out under Holse's boot, and starting to make gurgling sounds – took another, smaller gun from the prone knight's boot and also found a dagger and two small throwing knives in his tunic. From Vollird, now holding his right hand delicately and grimacing, it took a sword, a long knife and a length of wire with wooden grips at each end.

"All unauthorised weapons have now been removed from the vicinity," the machine announced. Ferbin noticed that a small crowd of people – aliens, machines, whatever one might call them – had gathered at a polite distance, to watch. The machine holding all the weapons said, "Nariscene Barbarian Relational Mentor Tchilk, present, is in notional charge here until further Authority arrives. All involved will hold approximate position under my custody, meantimes. Failure to comply will incur physical penalties not excluding unconsciousness and death."

There was a pause. "Documents?" the Oct said to Ferbin.

"Oh, have your damned documents!" he said, and fished them from his jacket. He nearly threw them at the machine, but didn't, in case this was taken as a violent act by the device hovering over them.

"So," the glittering Nariscene said, floating slowly round about them a metre or so over their heads and between two and three metres away from them, "you claim to be a prince of this royal family of the Sarl, of the Eighth."

"Indeed," Ferbin said crisply.

He and Holse stood within a great, softly green-lit cave of a room. Its walls were mostly of undressed stone; Ferbin found this quite shockingly crude for beings supposedly so technologically advanced. The complex they had been taken to was set deep within a cliff which formed part of an enormous spire of rock sitting in a great round lake a short machine-flight from the concourse where they had first arrived. Once Vollird and Baerth had been taken away, apparently already adjudged to have been the guilty parties without anything as crude and time-consuming as a formal trial – as Vollird had pointed out, quite loudly – Ferbin had asked one of the Nariscene judicial machines if he could talk to somebody in authority. After a few screen conversations with persons distant, all visibly Nariscene, they had been brought here.

The Nariscene officer – he had been introduced as Acting Craterine Zamerin Alveyal Girgetioni – was encased in a kind of skeletal armour like that worn by the Nariscene who had been escorting Vollird and Baerth. He seemed to like floating above and around people he was talking to, forcing them to twist this way and that to keep him politely in sight. About him in the great cavern, at some distance, other Nariscene aliens did incomprehensible things from a variety of cradles, harnesses and holes in the ground filled with what looked like quicksilver. "This royal family," the Acting Craterine Zamerin continued, "is the ruling entity of your people, and the executive positions are inheritable. Am I right?"

Ferbin thought about this. He looked at Holse, who shrugged unhelpfully. "Yes," Ferbin said, less certainly.

"And you claim to have witnessed a crime on your home level?"

"A most grievous and disgraceful crime, sir," Ferbin said.

"But you are unwilling to have the matter dealt with on your own level, despite the fact you claim to be the rightful ruler, that is, absolute chief executive, of this realm."

"I am unable to do so, sir. Were I to try, I would be killed, just as the two knights today tried to kill me."

"So you seek justice . . . where?"

"A sibling of mine is attached to the empire known as the Culture. I may gain help there."

"You travel to some part, ship or outpost of the Culture?"

"As a first step, we thought to find one human man called Xide Hyrlis, whom we last heard was a friend of the Nariscene. He knew my late father, he knows me, he has – I hope and trust – still some kind sympathies for my family, kingdom and people and may himself be able to aid me in my fight for justice. Even if he cannot help us directly he will, at the least, I feel sure, vouch for me to the part of the Culture called Special Circumstances within which my sibling is located, allowing me to contact and appeal to them."

The Nariscene stopped dead, becoming quite perfectly stationary in the air. "Special Circumstances?" it said.

"Indeed," Ferbin said.

"I see." The Nariscene resumed its orbit, sailing silently through the oddly scented air while the two humans stood patiently, swivelling their heads as the creature circled slowly round them.

"Also," Ferbin said, "it is imperative that I get a message to my brother Oramen, who is now the Prince Regent. This would have to be done in the greatest secrecy. However, if it was possible – and I would hope that the mighty Nariscene would find this neither beneath nor beyond them—"

"That will not be possible, I think," the Nariscene told him.

"What? Why not?" Ferbin demanded.

"It is not our place," the Acting Craterine Zamerin said.

"Why not?"

Alveyal Girgetioni stopped in the air again. "It is not within our remit."

"I am not even sure I know what that means," Ferbin said. "Is it not right to warn somebody they might be in mortal danger? For that is—"

"Mr Ferbin—"

"Prince, if you please."

"Prince Ferbin," the Nariscene said, reinstating its slow circling. "There are rules to be observed in such interactions. It is not the duty or the right of the Nariscene to interfere in the affairs of our developing mentorees. We are here to provide an overall framework within which a species like that to which you belong may mature and progress according to their own developmental timetable; we are not here to dictate that timetable or hasten or delay any such advancement taking place along that timeline. We merely maintain the superior integrity of the entity that is Sursamen. Your own fates are allowed to remain your own. They are, in a sense, within your own gift. Our gift is that already stated, of overarching care for the greater environment, that is to say the Shellworld Sursamen itself, and the protection of your good selves from undue and unwarranted interference, including – and this is the focus of my point – any undue and unwarranted interference we ourselves might be tempted to apply."

"So you'll not warn a young fellow he may be in mortal danger? Or tell a grieving mother her eldest son lives, when she is in mourning for a dead husband and a son as well?"

"Correct."

"You do realise what that means?" Ferbin said. "I'm not being mistranslated, am I? My brother could die, and soon. He will die in any event before he is of an age to inherit the full title of king. That is guaranteed. He is a marked man."

"All death is unfortunate," the Acting Craterine Zamerin said.

"That, sir, is no comfort," Ferbin said.

"Comforting was not my intention. My duty is to state facts."

"Then the facts tell a sorry truth of cynicism and complacency in the face of outright evil."

"That may seem so to you. The fact remains, I am not allowed to interfere."

"Is there no one who might help us? If we are to accept that you will not, is there anybody here on the Surface or elsewhere who might?"

"I cannot say. I do not know of anyone."

"I see." Ferbin thought. "Am I – are we – free to leave?"

"Sursamen? Yes, fully free."

"And we may pursue our aims, of contacting Xide Hyrlis and my sibling?"

"You may."

"We have no money about us with which to pay our fare," Ferbin said. "However, on my accession to—"

"What? Oh, I see. Monetary exchange is not required in such circumstances. You may travel without exchange."

"I will pay our way," Ferbin said firmly. "Only I cannot do so immediately. You have my word on this, however."

"Yes. Yes, well. Perhaps a cultural donation, if you insist."

"I would also point out," Ferbin said, gesturing at himself and Holse, "that we have nothing else, either, save what we stand up in."

"Systems and institutions exist to aid the needy traveller," the Acting Craterine Zamerin said. "You will not go without. I shall authorise such provisions as you may require."

"Thank you," Ferbin said. "Again, generous payment will be forthcoming when I have taken charge of what is rightfully mine."

"You are welcome," Alveyal Girgetioni told them. "Now, if you will excuse me . . ."

The Baeng-yon Crater was of Sursamen's most common type, supporting a water- and landscape filled with a gas mixture designed to be acceptable to the majority of oxygen breathers, including the Nariscene, most pan-humans and a wide spectrum of aquatic species. Like most of the world's Craters it had an extensive network of wide, deep canals, large and small lakes and other bodies of water both open and enclosed providing ample living space and travel channels for seagoing creatures.

Ferbin looked out from a high window set in a great cliff of a building poised over an inlet of a broad lake. Steep-pitched hills and outbreaking cliffs and boulder fields were scattered everywhere amongst a landscape mostly covered in grass, trees and tall, oddly shaped buildings. Curious obelisks and pylons that might have been works of art were dotted about, and various lengths and loops of curved transparent tubing lay draped between and across nearly every feature. A giant sea creature, trailed by a shoal of smaller shapes each twice the length of a man, floated serenely along one of these conduits, passing between gaudily coloured buildings and over some form of steamless ground vehicle to dip into the broad bowl of a harbour and disappear beneath the waves amongst the hulls of bizarrely shaped boats.

All about, Nariscene moved through the air in their glittering harnesses. Overhead, an airship the shape of a sea monster and the size of a cloud moved slowly across a distant line betokening an immensely tall and steep-sided ridge, its barely curved top a serrated row of tiny, regular, jagged peaks. All lay under a startlingly bright sky of shining turquoise. He was looking towards the Crater Edgewall, apparently. An invisible shield held the air inside the vast bowl. It was so bright because a vast lens between the sun and the Crater concentrated the light like a magnifying glass. Much of what he looked at, Ferbin thought, he didn't even start to understand. Much of it was so strange and alien he hardly knew how to frame the questions that might provide the answers which would help explain what he was looking at in the first place, and he suspected that even if he did know how to ask the questions, he wouldn't understand the answers.

Holse came through from his room, knocking on the wall as he entered – the doors disappeared when they opened, petals of material folding away into the walls. "Decent quarters," he said. "Eh, sir?"

"They will do," Ferbin agreed.

They had been escorted to this place by one of the judicial machines. Ferbin had been tired and – finding what he took for a bed – slept for a while. When he woke a couple of hours later, Holse was inspecting a pile of supplies in the middle room of the five they had been assigned. Another machine had appeared with the loot while Ferbin had been asleep. Holse reported that the door to the outside corridor was not locked. They appeared to be free to go about their business if they so desired, not that Holse had been able to think, offhand, of any business to go about.

They had more clothes now, plus luggage. Holse had discovered a device in the main room that brought entertainments into it; as many different entertainments as there were pages in a book, and seemingly there in the room with them. Almost all were utterly incomprehensible. After he'd muttered as much under his breath the room itself had talked to him and asked if he wanted the entertainments translated. He had said no, and been studious in not talking to himself since.

He'd also discovered a sort of chilly wardrobe full of food. Ferbin found himself to be remarkably hungry, and they ate well of the foods they recognised.

"Sirs, a visitor would meet with you," a pleasant voice from nowhere said in a well-bred Sarl accent.

"That's the voice of the room," Holse whispered to Ferbin.

"Who is this visitor?" Ferbin asked.

"A Morthanveld; Tertiary Hulian Spine Strategic Mission Director General Shoum, of Meast, of Zuevelous, of T'leish, of Gavantille Prime, Pliyr."

"Morthanveld?" Ferbin said, latching on to almost the only word in all this that he actually understood.

"She is some ten minutes away and would like to know if you'd care to receive her," the disembodied voice said.

"Who exactly is this person?" Ferbin asked.

"The director general is currently the highest-ranked all-species office-holder on Sursamen and most senior Morthanveld official within the local galactic region. She is charged with over-sight of all Morthanveld interests within approximately thirty per cent of the Tertiary Spine. She is present on Sursamen Surface in a semi-official capacity but wishes to visit you in an unoffi-cial capacity."

"Is she any threat to us?" Holse asked.

"None whatsoever, I'd imagine."

"Kindly tell the directing general we shall be happy to receive her," Ferbin said.

Five minutes before the director general arrived, a pair of strange globular beings appeared at the door of their suite. The creatures were about a stride in diameter and shaped like a huge glistening drop of water with hundreds of spines inside. They announced that they were the pilot team for Director General Shoum and asked, in highly polite and almost unaccented Sarl, to be allowed in for a look round. Holse obliged them. Ferbin was staring thunderstruck at what appeared be an entertainment showing aliens having sex, or possibly wrestling, and hardly noticed the two real aliens.

The two Morthanveld floated in, wafted about for less than a minute and announced themselves satisfied that all was well. A formality, they explained in what sounded like cheerful tones.

Holse was well-educated enough to know that the Morthanveld were an aquatic species and he was still consid-ering the etiquette of offering such beings a drink when the director general herself and her immediate entourage descended. Ferbin switched the alien pornography off and started paying attention. He and the director general were introduced, she and her half-dozen attendants spread out around the room, making admiring comments about the furnishings and pleasant view and then the director general herself – they had been informed she was a she, though there was no way to tell that Holse could see – suggested they take a ride in her barque.

Holse had to shrug when Ferbin looked at him.

"That would be our pleasure, ma'am," Ferbin told her graciously.

Half a minute later an enormous pancake of an air vehicle with a skin that glittered like innumerable fish scales floated down from above and presented its curved, open rear to the windows, which hinged down to allow them access to the barque.

The transparent walls and clear circles on the floor showed them rising quickly into the air. Soon they could see the whole of the great straggled settlement they had just left, then the entirety of the circular sea on whose margins it lay, then other seas and circular patches of green and brown before – the view seemed to blink as they passed through some gauzy barrier – they were looking down on an entire enormous circle of blue and green and brown and white, with hints of what must be the dark, near-lifeless Surface of Sursamen itself at the edges. Circular patches in the craft's ceiling showed tiny points of light. Holse supposed they must be the stars of empty space. He took a funny turn and had to sit down quickly on one of a variety of couch-shaped bumps on the floor, all of which were very slightly damp.

"Prince Ferbin," the director general said, indicating with one of her spines a long, shallow seat near what Ferbin took to be the prow of the craft, some distance away from everybody else. He sat there while she rested on a bowl-shaped seat nearby. A tray floated down to Ferbin's side. It held a small plate of delicacies and an opened jug of fine wine with one glass.

"Thank you," Ferbin said, pouring himself some wine.

"You're welcome. Then, if you please, tell me what brings you here."

Ferbin told her the short version. Even at this distance in time, relating his father's murder left him flushed and breathing hard, boiling with fury inside. He took a drink of wine, went on with the rest of his tale.

The director general was silent until the end, then said, "I see. Well then, prince, what are we to do with you?"

"Firstly, ma'am, I must get a message to my younger brother Oramen, to warn him of the danger he is in."

"Indeed. What else?"

"I should be grateful if you would assist me in finding our old ally Xide Hyrlis, and, perhaps, my other sibling."

"I should hope that I shall be able to assist with your onward travel," the waterworlder replied.

This did not sound like an unequivocal yes to Ferbin. He cleared his throat. "I have made it clear to the Nariscene representative I encountered earlier that I will pay for my passage, though I am unable to do so at the moment."

"Oh, payment is irrelevant, dear prince. Don't worry yourself about that."

"I was not worried, ma'am, I seek only to make it quite clear that I need accept no charity. I will pay my way. Depend on it."

"Well," Shoum said. There was a pause. "So, your father is dead; murdered by this tyl Loesp man."

"Indeed, ma'am."

"And you are the rightful king, by birthright?"

"I am."

"How romantic!"

"I cannot tell you how gratified I am that you feel that way," Ferbin said. He had obviously, he realised now, absorbed more courtier-speak than he'd given himself credit for. "However, my most pressing need is to warn my young brother that he is in danger of his life, if it is not already too late."

"Ah," the Morthanveld said. "I have what may be news unknown to you on such matters."

"You do?" Ferbin sat forward.

"Your mother is well. Your brother Oramen lives and appears to prosper and mature most quickly at court. You are presumed dead, though of course tyl Loesp knows you are not. Your reputation has been traduced. Regent Mertis tyl Loesp and Field Marshal Werreber command an army which has been lowered to the level of the Deldeyn by the Oct and even now is on the brink of a decisive battle with the depleted remains of the Deldeyn forces which our modellers believe your people will be victorious in, with less than three per cent doubt."

"You have spies there, ma'am?"

"No, but information osmoses."

Ferbin leant forward. "Madam, I *must* get a message to my younger brother, but only if there is no chance of it being intercepted by tyl Loesp or his people. Might you be able to help?"

"That is not impossible. However, it would, arguably, be illegal."

"How so?"

"We are not supposed to take such a close, and ... dynamic interest in your affairs. Even the Nariscene are not supposed to, and they are technically in charge here."

"And the Oct?"

"They are allowed limited influence, of course, given that they control so much of the access to Sursamen's interior and were largely responsible for making it safe, though they have, arguably, overstepped their marked allowance by some margin already in co-operating with the Sarl to deceive and so – almost certainly – defeat the Deldeyn. The Aultridia have subsequently laid a charge before the Nariscene Mentoral Court against the Oct alleging just that. The underlying reasons causing the Oct to behave like this are still being investigated. Informed speculation on the matter is unusually diverse, indicating that no one really has a clue at all. However, I must make clear: my species is supposed to mentor those who mentor those who mentor your people. I am layers and levels away from being jurisdictionally allowed to have any direct influence.

"You find yourself the unintended victim of a system set up specifically to benefit people like the Sarl, prince; a system which has evolved over the centieons to ensure that peoples less technologically advanced than others are able to progress as naturally as possible within a generally controlled galactic environment, allowing societies at profoundly different civilisational stages to rub up against each other without this leading to the accidental destruction or demoralisation of the less developed participants. It is a system that has worked well for a long time; however, that does not mean that it never produces anomalies or seeming injustices. I am most sorry."

The stage is small but the audience is great, as his father had always said, Ferbin thought as he listened to this. But the audience was just the audience, and so was forbidden from running up on to the stage and taking part, and – aside from a few jeers and calls and the occasional "Behind you!" – they could do little to intervene without risking being flung out of the theatre altogether.

"These are rules that you cannot bend?" he asked.

"Oh, I can, prince. We are talking here, in one of my own craft, so that I can guarantee our privacy and we may speak freely. That is already bending one rule regarding legitimate interaction between what one might term our official selves. I can intervene, but ought I to? I do not mean, present me with further reason, I mean, would it be right for me to do so? These rules, regulations, terms and laws are not invoked arbitrarily; they exist for good reason. Would I be right in breaking them?"

"You may guess my view on the matter, ma'am. I would have thought that the brutal and disgraceful murder of an honourable man – a king to whom all in his realm save a few jealous, treacherous, murderous wretches paid grateful, loving homage – would seize at the heart of any creature, no matter how many layers and levels distant from such humble beings as ourselves they might be. We are all united, I would hope, in our love of justice and the desire to see evil punished and good rewarded."

"It is as you say, of course," Shoum said smoothly. "It is simply that, from a further perspective, one cannot but recognise that these very rules I allude to are set out so with precisely such an idea of justice at their core. We seek to be just to the peoples in our charge and those that we mentor by, usually, declining the always obvious option of facile intervention. One might intervene and interfere at every available opportunity and at every single instant when things did not turn out as any decent and reasonable creature would like. However, with every intervention, every interference – no matter how individually well-meant and seemingly right and proper judged purely on its own immediate merits – one would, subtly, incrementally but most certainly remove all freedom and dignity from the very people one sought only to help."

"Justice is justice, ma'am. Foulness and treachery remain what they are. You may pull so far away you lose sight of them, but only draw back in and as soon as you see them at all you see their corruption, by the very colour and shape of them. When a common man is murdered it means the end for him and a catastrophe for his family; beyond that, and our sentimentality, it affects only as far as his own importance reaches. When a king is murdered and the whole direction of a country's fate is diverted from its rightful course, it is another thing entirely; how such a crime is reacted to speaks loud for the worth of all who know of it and have the means to punish those responsible or, by tolerating, seem to authorise. Such a reaction beacons out its lesson for every subject, forming a large part of their life's moral template. It affects the fate of nations, of whole philosophies, ma'am, and may not be dismissed as a passing commotion in the kennels."

The director general made a dry, spindly noise, like a sigh. "Perhaps it is different for humans, dear prince" she said, sounding sad, "but we have found that the underdisciplined child will bump up against life eventually and learn their lessons that way – albeit all the harder for their parents' earlier lack of courage and concern. The overdisciplined child lives all its life in a self-made cage, or bursts from it so wild and profligate with untutored energy they harm all about them, and always themselves. We prefer to underdiscipline, reckoning it better in the long drift, though it may seem harsher at the time."

"To do nothing is always easy." Ferbin did not try to keep the bitterness out of his voice.

"To do nothing when you are so tempted to do something, and entirely have the means to do so, is harder. It grows easier only when you know you do nothing for the active betterment of others."

Ferbin took a deep breath, exhaling slowly. He looked down through the nearest transparent circle in the floor. It showed another Crater sliding by beneath them like a lividly shining yellow-brown bruise of life on Sursamen's darkly barren Surface. It was gradually disappearing as they travelled over it, leaving only that dark absence of Sursamen's unadorned face implied below them.

"If you will not help me in getting a message to my brother warning him he is in mortal danger, ma'am, can you help me otherwise?"

"Assuredly. We can direct you to the ex-Culture human and ex-Special Circumstances agent Xide Hyrlis, and facilitate your conveyance towards him."

"So it is true; Xide Hyrlis is now ex-Culture?"

"We believe he is. With SC, sometimes it is hard to be sure."

"Is he still in a position to help us?"

"Possibly. I do not know. All I can solve with any certainty is your first problem, which is finding him; this would be a problem otherwise because the Nariscene guard him jealously. He works, in effect, for them now. Even when Hyrlis was here on Sursamen his purpose was moot; his presence was requested by the Nariscene and disapproved of by ourselves, though we drew the line at requesting his removal. A Nariscene experiment, perhaps, possibly at the behest of the Oct, testing the rules regarding the transfer of technology to less-developed peoples; he gave you a great deal, prince, though he was careful to do so only in the form of ideas and advice, never anything material. Your second problem will be persuading Hyrlis to talk to you; that you must do yourselves. Your third problem, obviously, is securing his services. Yours again, I'm afraid."

"Well," Ferbin said, "my good fortune arrives in small change these days, ma'am. Nevertheless, I hope I count my gratitude in larger coin. Even if that is all you can offer me, I am beholden.

We have recently come to expect that every hand will be turned against us; to find mere indifference caused us joy. Any active help, however circumscribed, now seems like far more than we deserve."

"I wish you well in your quest, prince."

"Thank you."

"Ah; an open Tower end, do you see?"

Ferbin looked down to see a small black spot on the dark brown expanse of the Surface. It only showed because the rest of the view was so dark; situated anywhere near a shining Crater, the dark dot would have been invisible beneath the wash of light. "That dark spot?"

"Yes. Do you know of those? It is the end of a Tower which leads all the way down to the Machine Core, where your god resides."

"It is?" Ferbin had never heard of such a thing. The spot looked too small, for one thing. The Towers were known to taper, but they were still one and a half kilometres across when they reached the Surface. On the other hand, they were quite high up, here in the director general's spacecraft.

"They are rare," she told him. "No more than six out of a million Towers on any Shellworld are fashioned so."

"That I did not know," Ferbin said. He watched the tiny dot of darkness slide beneath them.

"Of course, there are defence mechanisms on the Surface and all the way down – no freak piece of random space debris or maliciously directed ordnance would make it far down there, and various doors and lock systems exist at the level of the Core itself – however, essentially, when you stare straight down that shaft, you are looking across twenty-one thousand kilometres of vacuum to the lair of the Xinthian itself."

"The WorldGod," Ferbin said. Even as one who had never been especially religious, it felt strange to hear its existence confirmed by an alien of the Optimae, even if she did use its common, dismissive name.

"Anyway. I think now we'll return you to your quarters.

There is a ship leaving in half a day that will take you in the direction of Xide Hyrlis. I shall arrange your passage."

Ferbin lost sight of the tiny black dot. He returned his attention to the Morthanveld. "You are kind, ma'am."

The view from the craft tipped all around them as it flipped over, banking steeply. Holse closed his eyes and swayed, even though he was seated. Beside Ferbin, the surface of the wine in his glass barely trembled.

"Your sibling," the director general said as Ferbin watched the whole world tilt about them.

"My sibling," Ferbin said.

"She is Seriy Anaplian."

"That sounds like the name."

"She, too, is of Special Circumstances, dear prince."

"Apparently. What of it, ma'am?"

"That is a great deal of good connection for one family, let alone one person."

"I shan't refuse any portion, if good it is."

"Hmm. It does occur to me that, no matter how distant, she may have heard about your father and the other recent events from your home level, which of course includes the news of your supposed death."

"May she?"

"As I say, news osmoses. And where news is concerned, the Culture is of a very low pressure."

"I fail to understand you, ma'am."

"They tend to hear everything."

The Nariscene ship *The Hundredth Idiot* and the orbiting transit facility parted company as gently as lovers' hands, Holse thought. He watched the process happen on a big circular screen inside one of the vessel's human-public areas. He was the only person there. He'd wanted to watch from a proper porthole but there weren't any.

Tubes and gantries and stretchy corridors all sort of just kissed goodbye to each other and retracted like hands inside sleeves on a cold day. Then the transit facility was shrinking, and you could see the whole spindly, knobbly shape of it, and the start of the absurdly long cords that tethered it to the Surface of Sursamen.

It all happened in silence, if you didn't count the accompanying screechings which were allegedly Nariscene music.

He watched Sursamen bulge darkly out across the great circle of screen as the transit facility shrank quickly to too-small-to-see. How vast and dark it was. How spotted and speckled with those shining circles of Craters. In the roughly quarter of the globe that Holse could see right now he guessed there were perhaps a score of such environments, glowing all sorts of different colours according to the type of atmosphere they held. And how quickly it was all shrinking, gathering itself in, concentrating, like something boiling down.

The ship drew further away. The transit facility was quite gone. Now he could see all of Sursamen; every bit was there on the screen, the whole globe encircled shown. He found it hard to believe that the place where he had lived his entire life was appreciable now in one glimpse. Look; he glanced from one pole to another, and felt his eyes jerk only a millimetre or less in their sockets. Further away still now, their rate of progress increasing. Now he could hold all mighty Sursamen in a single static stare, extinguish it with a blink . . .

He thought of his wife and children, wondering if he would ever see them again. It was odd that while he and Ferbin had still been on the Eighth and so exposed to the continual and sharp danger of being killed, or travelling up from their home level and still arguably at some risk, he had nevertheless been sure he would see his family again. Now that they were – you'd hope – safe for the moment, on this fancy ship-of-space, he watched his home shrink to quick nothing with a less than certain feeling that he'd be safely back.

He hadn't even asked to get a message back to them. If the

aliens were disinclined to grant the request of a prince, they'd surely ignore a more humble man's petition. All the same, maybe he ought to have asked. There was even a possibility that his own request would be granted just because he was only a servant and so didn't signify; news of his living might not matter enough to affect greater events the way knowledge of Ferbin's continuing existence might. But then if his wife knew he was still alive and people in power heard of this, they would undoubtably treat this as part-way proof that Ferbin did indeed live, and that would be deemed important. They'd want to know how she'd come to know and that might prove uncomfortable for her. So he owed it to her not to get in touch. That was a relief.

He'd be in the wrong whatever he did. If they ever did get back he'd certainly be blamed for turning up alive after being dependably dead.

Senble, bless her, was a passably handsome woman and a good mother, but she had never been the most sentimental of people, certainly not where her husband was concerned. Holse always had the impression he somehow cluttered the place up when he was in their apartment in the palace servants' barracks. They only had two rooms, which was not a lot when you had four children, and he rarely found a place to sit and smoke a pipe or read a news sheet in tranquillity. Always being moved on, he was, for the purposes of cleaning, or to let the children fight in peace.

When he went out, to sit somewhere else and smoke his pipe and read his paper undisturbed, he was usually welcomed back with a scolding for having wasted the family's meagre resources in the betting house or drinking shop, whether he'd actually been there or not. Though he had, admittedly, used the earlier unjust accusations as cause to excuse the subsequent commitment of precisely such contrabandly activities.

Did that make him a bad man? He didn't think so. He'd provided, he'd given Senble six children, holding her to him when she'd wept, mourning the two they'd lost, and doing all he could to help her care for the four who'd survived. Where he'd grown up, the proportions of live to dead would have been reversed.

He'd never hit her, which made him unusual within his circle of friends. He'd never hit a woman at all, which by his count made him unique amongst his peers. He told people he reckoned his father had used up the family's allowance of woman-hitting, mostly on Holse's poor long-suffering mother. He'd wished his father dead every single day for many years, waiting until he grew big enough to hit him back and protect his mother, but in the end it had been his mother who'd gone; suddenly, one day, just dropping dead in the field during the harvest.

At least, he'd thought at the time, she'd been released from her torment. His father was never the same man again, almost as though he missed her, just possibly because he felt in some way responsible. At the time Holse had nearly felt himself big enough to stand up to his father, but his mother's death had reduced his father so, and so quickly, that he'd never needed to. He'd walked away from home one day and never gone back, leaving his father sitting in his cold cottage, staring into a dying fire. He'd gone to the city and become a palace servant. Somebody from his village who'd made the same journey a long-year later had told him his father had hanged himself just a month earlier, after another bad harvest. Holse had felt no sympathy or sorrow at the news at all, only a kind of vindicated contempt.

And if he and Ferbin were gone so long he was declared officially dead, Senble might remarry, or just take up with another man. It would be possible. She might mourn him – he hoped she would, though frankly he wouldn't have put his own money on it – but he couldn't imagine her tearing her hair out in an apoplexy of grief or swearing on his cold unge pipe she'd never let another man touch her. She might be forced to find another husband if she was thrown out of the servants' quarters. How would he feel then, coming back to find his place taken so, his children calling another man Daddy?

The truth was that he would almost welcome the opportunity to start again. He respected Senble and loved his children, but if they were being looked after by a decent sort of fellow then he wouldn't throw a fit of jealousy. Just accept and walk on might be the best idea; wish all concerned well and make a fresh start, still young enough to enjoy a new life but old enough to have banked the lessons he'd learned from the first one.

Did *that* make him a bad man? Perhaps, though if so then arguably all men were bad. A proposition his wife would probably agree with, as would most of the women Holse had known, from his poor mother onwards. That was not his fault either, though. Most men – most women, too, no doubt – lived and died under the general weight of the drives and needs, expectations and demands they experienced from within and without, beaten this way and that by longings for sex, love, admiration, comfort, importance and wealth and whatever else was their particular fancy, as well as being at the same time channelled into whatever furrows were deemed appropriate for them by those on high.

In life you hoped to do what you could but mostly you did what you were told and that was the end of it.

He was still staring at the screen, though he hadn't really been seeing it for some time, lost in this reverie of decidedly unromantic speculation. He looked for Sursamen, looked for the place – vast, multi-layered, containing over a dozen different multitudes – where he had lived all his life and left all he'd ever known quite entirely behind, but he couldn't find it.

Gone; shrunk away to nothing.

He had already asked the Nariscene ship why it bore the name it did.

"The source of my name," the vessel had replied, "*The Hundredth Idiot*, is a quotation: 'One hundred idiots make idiotic plans and carry them out. All but one justly fail. The hundredth idiot, whose plan succeeded through pure luck, is immediately convinced he's a genius.' It is an old proverb."

Holse had made sure Ferbin was not within earshot and muttered, "I think I've known a few hundredths in my time."

The ship powered away in the midst of faraway stars, an infinitesimal speck lost in the vast swallowing emptiness between these gargantuan cousins of the Rollstars and Fixstars of home.

16. Seed Drill

Quitrilis Yurke saw the giant Oct ship immediately ahead and knew he was about to die.

Quitrilis was piloting his ship by hand, the way you were very much not supposed to, not in the presence of a relatively close-packed mass of other ships – in this case, a whole fleet of Oct Primarian Craft. Primarians were the biggest class of regular ships the Oct possessed. A skeletal frame around a central core, they were a couple of klicks long and usually employed more as a sort of long-distance travel aid for smaller ships than as fully fledged spacecraft in their own right. There was at least a suggestion that the Oct had ships of this size and nature because they felt they ought to rather than because they really needed them; they were a vanity project, something they seemed to think they were required to have to be taken seriously as a species, as a civilisation.

The Primarian fleet was twenty-two strong and stationed in close orbit directly above the city-cluster of Jhouheyre on the Oct planet of Zaranche in the Inner Caferlitician Tendril. They had arrived there in ones and twos over the course of the last twenty days or so, joining a single Primarian that had arrived over forty days before.

Quitrilis Yurke, a dedicated Culture traveller and adventurer, away from home for a good five hundred and twenty-six days now and veteran of easily a dozen major alien star systems, was on Zaranche to find out whatever he could about whatever there was to be found out there. So far he'd discovered that Zaranche was a boring planet of real interest only to the Oct and devoid of any humanoid life. That last bit had been bad news. It had seemed like really good news at first, but it wasn't. He'd never been anywhere before where he was the only human. Only human on the planet; that was travelling. That was Wandering. That was exclusive. He'd like to see his fellow travellers beat *that*. He'd felt aloof for about a minute.

After that it was just boring and made him feel alone, but he'd told people – and especially his class- and village mates from back home (not that they were actually at home; they were mostly travelling too) – that he intended to stay on Zaranche for a hundred days or so, doing some proper studying and investigating that would lead to genuine peer-reviewable publishable kind of stuff and it would feel like defeat to squilch out now.

Of all his group, he was the luckiest; everybody agreed, including Quitrilis Yurke. He'd looked for and found an old ship that was up for a bit of vaguely eccentric adventure late in life, and so – rather than just bumming around, hitching, cadging lifts off GSVs and smaller ships the way everybody else was going to – he'd basically got his own ship to play with; estimable!

The *Now We Try It My Way* had been an ancient Interstellar-class General Transport Craft, built so long ago it could remember – directly; like, living memory – when the Culture had been, by civilisational standards, scrawny, jejune; positively callow. The ship's AI (not a Mind – way too old and primitive and limited to be called a Mind, but most definitely still fully conscious and with a frighteningly sharp personality) had long since been transferred into a little one-off kind of runabout thing, the sort of ship that people referred to as Erratic-class, even though there wasn't really any such class. (Only there sort of was now, because even Minds used the term.) Anyway. In its remodelled form it had been designed to serve as a sort of glorified shuttle (but faster than any ordinary shuttle), shifting people and things around the kind of mature system with more than one Orbital.

That had been semi-retirement. Before it could get too weird or eccentric it had properly retired itself and drifted into a sort of slow sleep state inside a hollow mountain store for ships and other biggish stuff on Quitrilis' home Orbital of Foerlinteul. He'd done proper asking-around-old-ships research to find a craft just like that, following a private theory. And it had worked! He'd lucked! It had been so grade, just so apropos!

The old ship had woken itself up after a tickle-message from its old home MSV and, after only a little thought, agreed to act as personal transport for this youth, him!

Naturally all his classmates had immediately tried doing the same thing, but they were too late. Quitrilis had already found the only likely contender and won the prize and even if there had been other retired ships of a similar disposition anywhere nearby they'd likely have refused such follow-on requests just because it would look like setting a pattern rather than expressing ship individuality and rewarding human initiative, etc. etc.

So far, the relationship had been a pretty good one. The old AI seemed to find it amusing to indulge a young, enthusiastic human and it positively enjoyed travelling for the sake of it, with no real logic to the journeying, going wherever Quitrilis wanted to go for whatever reason he wanted to go there (often he cheerfully confessed he had no idea himself). Obviously they were constrained by the ship's speed to a relatively limited volume – they'd hitched on a GSV to get here to the Inner

Caferlitician Tendril – but that still left them with thousands of potential star systems to visit, even if there was, by general agreement, nothing especially undiscovered in the fairly well-travelled, beaten-track neighbourhood they had access to.

And sometimes the ship let him pilot it by hand, the AI switching itself off or at least retreating inside itself and leaving Quitrilis to take the controls. He had always imagined that even though it claimed he was in complete control it was secretly still keeping an eye on him and making sure he wasn't doing anything too crazy, anything that might end up killing them both, but now – right now, as the Primarian craft that *should not have been there* suddenly filled the star-specked darkness of the sky ahead, spreading entirely across his field of vision – he realised the old ship had been true to its word. It had left him alone. He really had been in full hands-on charge of it the whole time. He really had been risking his life, and he was about to lose it now.

Twenty-two ships. There had been twenty-two ships; they'd agreed. Arranged in a pair of sort of staggered lines, slightly curved in tune with the planet's gravity well. Quitrilis had gone up to have a look at them all but they were boring, just hanging there, only the one that had been there from the start even showed any sign of traffic with a few smaller craft buzzing about. The Oct Movement Monitoring and Control people had sort of shouted at him, he'd got the impression, but an Oct shouting was still a pretty involved, incomprehensible experience and he hadn't taken much notice.

He'd got the ship to let him have control and gone swooping and zooming and wheening about the fleet, carving round them and then deciding he'd have a blast *right through* the middle, so heading some way off – well off, like a good half a million klicks on the far side of the planet – and setting everything to Very Quiet, what the ship called *Ssh* mode, before turning back and coming bazonging back in before they had time to shout at him again and dipping and weaving and hurtling between the parked Primarians (he'd been bouncing up and down in the couch in the control room, whooping), and he thought he'd done it no problem; got to the end of the mass of ships and slung out from under that twenty-second ship on the way back into empty space again (he'd probably go visit one of the system's gas giants for a day or two to let any fuss die down), when suddenly, as he came out from under that last Primarian – or what should have been the last Primarian – there, dead ahead, bang in front of him, filling the view so tall and wide and deep and fucking big he knew there was no chance he could avoid it, there was another ship! A twenty-third ship!

What?

Something flashed on the spread of retro control panel in front of him (he'd specced that himself). "Quitrilis," the ship's voice said. "What—?"

"Sorry," Quitrilis had time to say as the gantried, openwork innards of the Oct ship expanded in front of him, filling the ahead-view utterly now, getting down to detail.

Maybe they could fly through, he thought, but knew they couldn't. The internal components of the Primarian were too big, the spaces were too small. Maybe they could crash-stop, but they were just too damn close. The *Now We Try It My Way* had taken over control. The hand controls had gone limp. Indicator overlays flashed up engine-damage levels of braking and dump-turning, but it was all much too little much too late. They'd hit side on and barely ten per cent slower.

Quitrilis closed his eyes. He didn't know what else to do. The *Now We Try It My Way* made some noises he hadn't known it could make. He waited for death. He'd been backed up before he left home, obviously, but he'd been away over five hundred days and changed immensely in that time. He was profoundly and maturely a different person compared to the brash young lad who'd sailed off in his persuadable accomplice ship. This would be a very real death. Wow; proper sinking feeling here. This would be no-shit, serious, never-again extinction. At least it'd be quick; there was that.

Maybe the Oct had close-range defences against this sort of

thing. Maybe they'd be blasted out of the skies before they hit the Primarian. Or they'd be beamed out of the way or something, nudge-fielded, fended off with something truly, stupendously skilful. Except the Oct didn't have any of that sort of stuff. The Oct ships were relatively primitive. Oh! He'd just realised: he was probably just about to kill lots of Oct people. He got a sinking feeling that outdid the earlier, selfish sinking feeling. Oh fuck. Fucking major diplomatic incident. The C would have to apologise and ... He was just starting to think that, Hey, you really could squeeze a lot of thoughts into a second or two when you knew you were about to die when the ship said, quite calmly, "Quitrilis?"

He opened his eyes. Not dead.

And nothing but the old star-specked depths of space ahead. Eh?

He looked back. Stacked ships: twenty-plus Primarians, one *ultra* close behind, receding fast, like they'd just exited from it, travelling very fast indeed.

"Did we dodge that thing?" he said, gulping.

"No," the ship said. "We went right through it because it's not a real ship; it's little better than a hologram."

"What?" Quitrilis said, shaking his head. "How? Why?"

"Good question," the ship said. "I wonder how many of the others are just pretend too."

"I'm fucking alive," Quitrilis breathed. He clicked out of the command virtuality so he was sat in the couch properly with the physical controls in front of him and the wraparound display showing in slightly less detail what he'd been looking at seemingly directly. "We're fucking alive, ship!" he yelled.

"Yes, we are. How odd." The *Now We Try It My Way* sounded puzzled. "I'm sending a burst to my old Systems Vehicle about this. Something's not right here."

Quitrilis waved his arms around and waggled his toes. "But we're alive!" he yelled, ecstatic. "We're *alive!*"

"I am not disagreeing, Quitrilis. However ... Wait. We're being target— !"

The beam from the original, first-arrived Primarian ship burst all around them, turning the little craft and the single human inside it entirely into plasma within a few hundred milliseconds.

This time, Quitrilis Yurke didn't have time to think anything at all.

Djan Seriy Anaplian, agent of the Culture's renowned/notorious (delete to taste) Special Circumstances section, had her first dream of Prasadal while aboard the *Seed Drill*, an Ocean-class GSV. The details of the dream itself were not important; what exercised her on waking was that it was the kind of dream she had always associated with *home*. She had had dreams like that about the royal palace in Pourl and the estate at Moiliou, about the Eighth in general and even – if you counted the dreams of the Hyeng-zhar – about Sursamen as a whole for the first few years after she'd come to the Culture, and always woken from them with a pang of homesickness, sometimes in tears.

Those had slowly disappeared to be replaced by dreams of other places where she'd lived, like the city of Klusse, on Gadampth Orbital, where she had begun her long introduction to, induction into and acceptance of the Culture. These were, sometimes, profound, affecting dreams in their own way, but they were never imbued with that feeling of loss and longing that indicated the place being dreamt about was home.

She blinked awake in the grey darkness of her latest cabin – a perfectly standard ration of space in a perfectly standard Ocean-class – and realised with a tiny amount of horror, a degree of grim humour and a modicum of ironic appreciation that just as she had started to realise that she might finally be happy to be away from and free of Sursamen and all that it had meant to her, she had been called back.

She nearly caught the ball. She didn't, and it hit her on the right temple hard enough to cause a spike of pain. It would, she was sure, have floored anybody human-basic. With all her SC stuff still wired in she'd have dodged it or caught it one-handed easily. In fact, with her SC stuff still on line she could have jumped and caught it in her *teeth*. Instead, *Whack!*

She'd heard the ball coming, caught the most fleeting glimpse of it arcing towards her, but hadn't been quite quick enough. The ball bounced off her head. She shook her head once, spread her feet wide and flexed her knees to make her more stable in case she might be about to topple, but she didn't. The pain flicked off, cancelled. She rubbed her head and stooped to pick up the hard little ball – a crackball, so just a solid bit of wood, basically – and looked for who had thrown it. A guy sailed out of the group of people by the small bar she'd been passing on one of the outer balcony decks.

"You all right?" he asked.

She threw the ball to him on a soft, high trajectory. "Yes," she told him.

He was a small, round, almost ball-like man himself, very dark and with extravagant hair. He caught the ball and stood weighing it in his hand. He smiled. "Somebody said you were SC, that's all. I thought, well, let's see, so I threw this at you. Thought you'd catch it, or duck or something."

"Perhaps asking would have been more effective," Djan Seriy suggested. Some of the people at the bar were looking at them.

"Sorry," the man said, nodding at the side of her head.

"Accepted. Good-day." She made to walk on.

"Will you let me make you a drink?"

"That won't be necessary. Thank you, all the same."

"Seriously. It would make me feel better."

"Quite. No, thank you."

"I make a very good Za's Revenge. I'm something of an expert."

"Really. What is a Za's Revenge?"

"It's a cocktail. Please, stay; have one with us."

"Very well."

She had a Za's Revenge. It was very alcoholic. She let it affect her. The round man and his friends were Peace Faction people, from the part of the Culture that had split away at the start of the Idiran War, hundreds of years earlier, renouncing conflict altogether.

She stayed for more Za's Revenges. Eventually the man admitted that, although he liked her and found her highly personable, he just didn't like SC, which he referred to – rather sneeringly, Anaplian thought – as "the good ship *We Know What's Good For You*".

"It's still violence," he told her. "It's still what we ought to be above."

"It can be violent," Anaplian acknowledged, nodding slowly. Most of the man's friends had drifted off. Beyond the balcony deck, in the open air surrounding the GSV's hull, a regatta for human-powered aircraft was taking place. It was all very gay and gaudy and seemed to involve a lot of fireworks.

"We should be above that. Do you see?"

"I see."

"We're strong enough as it is. Too strong. We can defend ourselves, be an example. No need to go interfering."

"It is a compelling moral case you make," Anaplian told the man solemnly.

"You're taking the piss now."

"No, I agree."

"But you're in SC. You interfere, you do all the dirty tricks stuff. You do, don't you?"

"We do, I do."

"So don't fucking tell me it's a compelling moral case then; don't insult me." The Peace Faction guy was quite aggressive. This amused her.

"That was not my intention," she told him. "I was telling you – excuse me." Anaplian took another sip of her drink. "I was telling you I agree with what you say but not to the point of acting differently. One of the first things they teach you in SC, or ..." She belched delicately. "Excuse me. Or get you to teach yourself, is not to be too sure, always to be prepared to acknowledge that there is an argument for not doing the things that we do."

"But you still do them."

"But we still do them."

"It shames us all."

"You are entitled to your view."

"And you to yours, but your actions contaminate me in a way that mine do not contaminate you."

"You are right, but then you are of the Peace Faction, and so not really the same."

"We're all still Culture. We're the real Culture, and you're the cancerous offspring, grown bigger than the host and more dangerous than when we split, but you resemble us well enough to make us all look the same to others. They see one entity, not different factions. You make us look bad."

"I see your point. We guilt you. I apologise."

"You 'guilt' us? This some new SC-speak?"

"No, old Sarl-speak. My people sometimes use odds wordly. Words oddly." Anaplian put her hand to her mouth, giggling.

"You should be ashamed," the man said sadly. "Really we're no better – you're no better – than the savages. They always find excuses to justify their crimes, too. The point is not to commit them in the first place."

"I do see your point. I really do."

"So be ashamed then. Tell me you're ashamed."

"We are," Anaplian assured him. "Constantly. Still, we can prove that it works. The interfering and the dirty-tricking; it works. Salvation is in statistics."

"I wondered when we'd get to that," the man said, smiling sourly and nodding. "The unquestioned catechism of Contact, of SC. That old nonsense, that irrelevance."

"Is not nonsense. Nor ... It is truth."

The man got down from his bar stool. He was shaking his

head. This made his wild fawn hair go in all directions, floatily. Most distracting. "There's just nothing we can do," he said sadly, or maybe angrily, "is there? Nothing that'll change you. You'll just keep doing all that shit until it collapses down around you, around us, or until enough of everybody sees the real truth, not fucking statistics. Till then, there's just nothing we can do."

"You can't fight us," Anaplian said, and laughed.

"Hilarious."

"Sorry. That was cheap. I apologise. Profusely."

The man shook his head again. "However much," he said, "it'll never be enough. Good-day." He walked off.

Anaplian watched him go.

She wanted to tell him that it was all okay, that there was nothing really to worry about, that the universe was a terrible, utterly uncaring place and then people came along and added suffering and injustice to the mix as well and it was all so much worse than he could imagine and she knew because she had studied it and lived it, even if just a little. You could make it better but it was a messy process and then you just had to try – you were obliged, duty-bound to try – to be sure that you did the right thing. Sometimes that meant using SC, and, well, there you were. She scratched her head.

Anyway, *of course* they worried they were doing the wrong thing. Everybody she'd ever met in SC entertained such thoughts. And *of course* they satisfied themselves they were doing the right thing. Obviously they must, or they wouldn't be *in* SC *doing* what they were doing in the first place, would they?

Maybe he knew all this anyway. Part of her suspected that the guy was an SC agent too, or something similar; part of Contact, perhaps, or somebody sent by the ship, or by one of the Minds overseeing the Morthanveld situation, just to be on the safe side. Nearly cracking her skull with a solid wooden ball was one crude way of checking she had been properly disarmed.

She left the final Za's Revenge sitting on the bar, undrunk. "We're all the fucking Peace Faction, you prick," she muttered as she staggered away.

Before she left the *Seed Drill* she researched what was known about recent events on the Eighth, Sursamen. She did some of the investigating herself and sent agents – crude, temporary personality constructs – into the dataverse to search for more.

She was looking for detailed news but also for any hint that the Sarl might be more closely observed. Too many sophisticated civilisations seemed to believe that the very primitiveness of less developed cultures – and the high levels of violence usually associated with such societies – somehow automatically gave them the right to spy on them. Even for societies some way down the civilisational tech-order, cascade-production of machines to make machines that made other machines meant it was effectively a materially cost-free decision. The resulting cloud of devices could each be as small as a grain of dust and yet together they could, with the back-up of a few larger units in space, blanket-surveille an entire planet and transmit in excruciating detail almost anything that went on almost anywhere.

There were treaties and agreements to limit this sort of behaviour, but these usually only covered the galaxy's more mature and settled societies, as well as those directly under their control or in their thrall; the relevant tech was like a new toy for those recently arrived at the great Involved table of the galactic meta-civilisation and tended to get used with enthusiasm for a while.

Societies which had only recently renounced the chronic use of force and resort to war – often reluctantly – were usually the most keen to watch those for whom such behaviour was still routine. One of the last-resort methods of dealing with those displaying such voyeurism was to turn their own devices against them, scooping the surveillance machines up from wherever they had been scattered, fiddling with their software and then infesting the worlds of their creators with them, concentrating on the homes and favoured recreational facilities of the powerful. This usually did the trick.

The peoples living within Sursamen, especially those like the Sarl, who would have been both unsuspecting of and defenceless against such conceited oversight, were amongst those supposedly protected against its depredations. But just because something wasn't public didn't mean it wasn't happening. The Culture had one of the most open and inclusive dataverse structures in the galaxy but even it didn't see or know everything. There were still plenty of private, hidden things going on. As a rule you got to hear of them eventually, but by then the damage had usually been done.

From the Eighth, though, so far; nothing. Either nobody was spying, or if they were they were keeping very quiet about it. The Morthanveld were easily capable, but too proud, law-abiding and anyway disdainful (much like the Culture, then); the Nariscene probably thought themselves above such behaviour too, and the Oct, well, the Oct didn't really seem to care about anything other than pushing their claim to be the true Inheritors of the Veil legacy.

Even routine accessing of the Oct parts of the dataverse meant having to suffer a recorded lecture on the history of the galaxy according to the Oct, the whole point of which was to highlight the similarities between the Veil and the Oct and emphasise what a good claim the Oct had on the Involucra's estate. To the Oct this inheritance obviously included both the Shellworlds themselves and the respect they felt ought to come attached, respect they rightly felt they were not being accorded. The Culture's interface software just as routinely filtered this nonsense out – the Oct claim was strong only according to themselves; the vast majority of trusted scholars, backed by some pretty unimpeachable evidence, held that the Oct were a relatively recent species, quite unrelated to the Veil – but it was always there.

The Oct did watch over the Sarl, but very patchily, infrequently and – by agreement – with centimetre-scale devices; things big enough for a human to see. Usually these were attached to machines manned by Oct: scendships, aircraft, ground vehicles and the environment suits they wore.

There wasn't much material publicly available from the last few hundreds of days, but there was some. Djan Seriy watched recordings of the great battle which had decided the fate of the Deldeyn, on the land around the Xiliskine Tower. The commentary and accompanying data, such as they were, suggested that the Aultridia had taken over the relevant sections of the Tower and transported the Deldeyn forces into a position where they could carry out their sneak attack on the Sarl heartlands. An SC-flagged data-end appended to the recording suggested Aultridian involvement was a lie; the Oct had been in charge.

All the recordage was from the latter part of the battle, and taken from static positions well above the action, probably from the Tower itself. She wondered if somewhere in what she was looking at there was detail of her father being wounded, and of whatever fate had overtaken Ferbin. She tried to zoom in, thinking to instruct an agent to look for anything relevant, but the recording was too coarse and lost detail well before individuals on the battlefield could be recognised.

She watched – again as though from on high, though this time the cameras were mounted on something flying – as the Sarl forces, now under Mertis tyl Loesp, crossed a canal in the desert near the Hyeng-zhar, its tall mists in the hazy distance, and saw their final short siege and shorter attack on Rasselle, the Deldeyn capital city.

That seemed to be all; a proper news report or docu-feature would have included victory celebrations in Pourl, tyl Loesp accepting the surrender of the Deldeyn commander, piles of dead bodies consigned to pits, banners going up in flames or the tears of the inconsolable bereaved, but the Oct hadn't thought to get even remotely artistic or judgemental.

Just the sort of enthrallingly primitive, barbaric but dashing war comfortably positioned people liked to hear about,

Anaplian thought. It was almost a pity nobody had thought to record it in all its gory detail.

A rapidly expanding but almost entirely vapid cloud of comment, analysis, speculation and exploitation was attached to the Oct recording through the news and current affairs organisations which took an interest in such events. Many Shellworld and Sursamen scholars – there were even people who regarded themselves as Eighth scholars, Sarl scholars – bemoaned the lack of decent data, leaving so much to speculation. For others, this lack of detail seemed to be merely an opportunity; offers to play war games based on the recent events were appended. Entertainments inspired by the recent thrilling events were also in preparation, or indeed already available.

Djan Seriy shivered in her couch by a fragrant poolside (splashing, laughter, the warmth of light on her skin) as she lay there, eyes closed, watching, experiencing all of this. She felt suddenly as she had right at the start of her involvement with the Culture, back in the shockingly confusing early days when everything seemed like bedlam and clash. This was all just too much to take in; at once far too close to home and utterly, horribly, invasively alien compared to it.

She would leave her agents running within the dataverse, in case there was some more directly observed stuff, and it was just well hidden.

Welcome to the future, she thought, surveying all this wordage and tat. All our tragedies and triumphs, our lives and deaths, our shames and joys are just stuffing for your emptiness.

She was being melodramatic, she decided. She checked there was no more of use to watch, clicked out, stood up and went to join in a noisy game of pool tag.

One ship, another ship. From the *Seed Drill* she was passed on to the GCU *You Naughty Monsters*. Another baton-like transmissal took her to the *Xenoglossicist*, an Air-class Limited System Vehicle. On her last night aboard there was an all-crews dance party; she threw herself into the wild music and wilder dancing like one abandoned.

The last Culture ship to carry her before she entered the Morthanveld domain was called *You'll Clean That Up Before You Leave*, a Gangster-class Very Fast Picket and ex-Rapid Offensive Unit.

She still hated the silly names.

17. Departures

Oramen woke to the sound of a thousand bells, blown temple horns, manufactury sirens, carriage hooters and just-audible mass cheering and knew immediately that the war must be over, and won. He looked about. He was in a gambling and whore house known as Botrey's, in the city's Schtip district. There was a shape in the bedclothes beside him which belonged to the girl whose name he would remember shortly.

Droffo, his new equerry, who was newly married and determinedly faithful, chose to turn a blind eye to Oramen's whoring so long as it was carried out in gambling or drinking houses; an honest bordello he would not even contemplate entering. His new servant, Neguste Puibive, had, before he'd left the farm, promised his mother he would never pay for sex and was dutifully honouring this commitment to the letter, though not beyond; he had been modestly successful in persuading some of the more generous girls to extend their favours to him out of simple kindness, as well as sympathy for one who had made such a well-meant if hopelessly naïve promise.

Oramen's absences from court had not gone unnoticed or unremarked. Just the morning before, at a formal late breakfast reception given by Harne, the lady Aelsh, to welcome her latest astrologer – Oramen had already successfully forgotten the fellow's name – Renneque, accompanied by and arm-in-arm with Ramile, the pretty young thing Oramen remembered from Harne's earlier party with the various actors and philosophisers, had scolded him.

"Why, it's that young fellow!" she had exclaimed upon seeing him. "Look, Ramile! I recall that pretty face, if not the name after so long apart. How d'you do, sir? My name's Renneque. Yours?"

He'd smiled. "Ladies Renneque, Ramile. How good to see you again. Have I been remiss?"

Renneque sniffed. "I'll say. Most unfathomably. I declare there are those absent at the war who're more often at court than you, Oramen. Are we so boring you avoid us, prince?"

"Absolutely not. On the contrary. I determined myself to be so ineffably tedious I thought to remove myself from our most quotidian conduct in the hope of making myself seem more contrastedly interesting to you when we do meet."

Renneque was still thinking this through when Ramile smiled slyly at Oramen but to Renneque said, "I think the prince finds other ladies more to his liking, elsewhere."

"Does he, now?" Renneque asked, feigning innocence.

Oramen smiled an empty smile.

"It may be we are not wanted," Ramile suggested.

Renneque raised her delicate chin. "Indeed. Perhaps we are not good enough for the prince," she said.

"Or it may be we are too good for him," Ramile mused.

"How could that be?" Oramen asked, for want of anything better.

"It's true," Renneque agreed, taking a tighter hold of her

companion's arm. "Some prize availability over virtue, I've heard."

"And a tongue loosened by money rather than moved by wit," Ramile offered.

Oramen felt his face flush. "While some," he said, "trust an honest harlot over the most apparently virtuous and courtly of women."

"*Some* might, out of sheer perversity," said Renneque, whose eyes had widened at the word "harlot". "Though whether a man of judgement and honour would term one of those females 'honest' in the first place might give rise to some controversy."

"One's values, like so much else, might become infected in such company," Ramile suggested, and tossed her pretty head and long flow of tight blonde curls.

"I meant, ladies," Oramen said, "that a whore takes her reward there and then, and seeks no further advancement." This time, as he said "whore", both Renneque and Ramile looked startled. "She loves for money and makes no lie of it. That is honest. There are those, however, who'd offer any favour seemingly for nothing, but would later expect a very great deal of a young man with some prospect of advancement."

Renneque stared at him as though he'd lost his mind. Her mouth opened, perhaps to say something. Ramile's expression changed the most, altering quickly from something like anger back to that sly look, then taking on a small, knowing smile.

"Come away, Renneque," she said, drawing the other woman back with her arm. "The prince mistakes us grievously, as though in a fever. We'd best withdraw to let the blush subside, and lest we catch it too."

They turned away as one, noses in the air.

He regretted his rudeness almost immediately, but too late, he felt, to make amends. He supposed he was already a little upset; that morning's mail had delivered a letter from his mother, all the way from far-distant Kheretesuhr, telling him that she was heavily pregnant by her new husband and had been advised by her doctors not to travel great distances. So to voyage all the way to court, to Pourl, was unthinkable. A new *husband*? he'd thought. *Pregnant*? *Heavily* pregnant, so that it was no recent thing? He'd heard nothing of this, nothing of either. She had not thought to tell him anything. The date on the letter was weeks past; it had suffered some serious delay in finding him, or had lain unposted.

He felt hurt, cheated somehow, as well as jealous and oddly spurned. He still was not sure how to respond. It had even crossed his mind that it might be best not to reply at all. Part of him wanted to do just that, so letting his mother wonder at not being kept informed, making her feel uncared-for, as she had made him feel.

Even while he was still lying there listening to the distant sounds of triumph, trying to work out exactly what he felt about the war's victorious conclusion and puzzling over the fact that his immediate reaction was somehow not one of utter and untrammelled joy, Neguste Puibive, his servant, ran into the room and stopped, breathless, at the foot of the bed. Luzehl, the girl Oramen had spent the night with, was waking up too, rubbing her eyes and looking dubiously at Puibive, a tall, wide-eyed, buck-toothed boy fresh from the country. He was full of enthusiasm and good will and had the uncommon ability of looking gangly even while asleep.

"Sir!" he shouted. He noticed Luzehl and blushed. "Begging both your pardons, sir, young lady!" He gulped air. "Sir! Still begging your pardon, sir, but the war is finished, sir, and we are victorious! The news is just arrived! Tyl Loesp, great Werreber, they – all Sarl – are triumphant! What a great day! Sorry to have intruded, sir! I'll extrude now, sir!"

"Neguste, hold," Oramen said, as the youth – a year older than Oramen but often seeming younger – turned and made to go, tripping over his own feet as he did so and stumbling again as he turned back on Oramen's command. He sorted himself out and stood, at attention, looking blinking at Oramen, who asked, "Is there any more detail, Neguste?"

"I heard the great news from a one-armed parliamentarian

constable charged with shouting it to the rooftops, sir, and he wore a cocked hat. The lady from the infusions bar across the road near fainted when she heard and wished her sons a safely speedy return, sir!"

Oramen stifled a laugh. "Detail within the report of the victory itself, Neguste."

"Nothing further, sir! Just we are victorious, the capital city of the Deldeyn is taken, their king is dead by his own hand and our brave boys have triumphed, sir! And tyl Loesp and mighty Werreber are safe! Casualties have been light. Oh! And the Deldeyn capital is to be renamed Hausk City, sir!" Neguste beamed with pleasure at this. "That's a fine thing, eh, sir?"

"Fine indeed," Oramen said and lay back smiling. As he'd listened to Neguste's breathless delivery he'd felt his mood improve and gradually begin to resemble what he'd have hoped it would have been from the start. "Thank you, Neguste," he told the lad. "You may go."

"Pleasure do soing, sir!" Neguste said. He had yet to come up with a reliable and consistent phrase suitable for such moments. He turned without tripping, found the door successfully and closed it behind him. He barged back in a heartbeat later. "And!" he exclaimed. "A telegraphical letter, sir! Just delivered." He took the sealed envelope from his apron, handed it to Oramen and retreated.

Luzehl yawned. "Is it really over then?" she asked as Oramen broke the seal and opened the folded sheet.

Oramen nodded slowly. "So it would seem." He smiled at the girl and started swinging his legs out of the bed as he read. "I'd better get to the palace."

Luzehl stretched out, tossed her long, black, entangledly curled hair and looked insulted. "Immediately, prince?"

The telegram brought news that he had a new half-brother. It had been written not by Aclyn herself but by her principal lady-in-waiting. The birth had been protracted and difficult – not surprising, it was stated, given the lady Blisk's relatively mature age – but mother and child were recovering. That was all.

"Yes, immediately," Oramen said, shrugging off the girl's hand.

The heat around the Hyeng-zhar had grown oppressive; two suns – the Rollstars Clissens and Natherley – stood high in the sky and vied to squeeze the most sweat out of a man. Soon, in this water-purged extremity, if the star-watchers and weather sages were to be believed, the land would be plunged into near total darkness for nearly fifty short-days and a sudden winter would ensue, turning the river and the Falls into ice.

Tyl Loesp looked out over the vast tiered, segmented cataract of the Hyeng-zhar, blinking sweat out of his eyes, and wondered that such colossal, booming energy and such furious heat could be quieted, stilled and chilled so soon by the mere absence of passing stars. And yet the scientists said it was going to happen and indeed seemed quite excited about it, and the records talked of such happenings in the past, so it must be so. He wiped his brow. Such heat. He'd be glad to be under the water.

Rasselle, the Deldeyn capital city, had fallen easily in the end. After a lot of whining from Werreber and some of the other senior army people – and some evidence that the low-order troops were unaccountably coy on the matter of putting captured Deldeyn to death – tyl Loesp had rescinded the general order regarding the taking of prisoners and the sacking of cities.

In retrospect, he ought to have pressed Hausk to have demonised the Deldeyn more. Chasque had been enthusiastic and together they had tried to convince Hausk the attitude of the soldiery and the populace would be improved if they could be made to hate the Deldeyn with a visceral conviction, but the

King had, typically, been overcautious. Hausk distinguished between the Deldeyn as a people on the one hand and their high command and corrupt nobility on the other, and even allowed that they might altogether constitute an honourable foe. He would, in any event, need to govern them once they had been defeated, and people nursing a justified grievance against a murderously inclined occupier made peaceful, productive rule impossible. On this purely practical issue he judged massacre wasteful and even contrary as a method of control. Fear lasted a week, anger a year and resentment a lifetime, he'd held. Not if you kept fuelling that fear with every passing day, tyl Loesp had countered, but had been overruled.

"Better grudging respect than terrified submission," Hausk had told him, clapping him on the shoulder after the discussion that had finally decided the matter. Tyl Loesp had bitten back his reply.

Following Hausk's death there had not been sufficient time to turn the Deldeyn into the hated, inhuman objects of fear and contempt tyl Loesp thought they ought to have been from the start, though he had done his best to begin the process.

In any event, he had subsequently been left with no choice but to step back from the adamantine harshness of his earlier decrees on the taking of prisoners and cities, but drew comfort from the thought that a good commander always stood ready to modify his tactics and strategy as circumstances changed, so long as each step along the way led towards his ultimate goal.

He had, anyway, turned the situation to his advantage, he reckoned, letting it be known that this new leniency was his gift to the soldiers of the Eighth and the people of the Ninth, graciously and mercifully countermanding the severity of action Hausk had demanded from his deathbed to avenge his killing.

Savidius Savide, who was the Oct Peripatetic Special Envoy of Extraordinary Objectives Among Useful Aboriginals, watched as the human called tyl Loesp swam and was guided to the place prepared for him in the roving scendship's receiving chamber.

The scendship was one of a rare class capable of both flight in air and underwater travel as well as the more normal vertical journeys within the vacuum of Towers. It was holding station in the relatively deep water of Sulpitine's main channel two kilometres above the lip of the Hyeng-zhar cataract. The human tyl Loesp had been brought out to the submerged craft in a small submarine cutter. He was dressed in an air suit and was obviously unused to such attire, and uncomfortable. He was floated into a bracket seat across the receiving chamber from where Savide floated and shown how to anchor himself against the bracket's shoulder braces using buoyancy. Then the Oct guard withdrew. Savide caused a membrane-buffered air channel to form between him and the human so that they could speak with something approaching their own voices.

"Tyl Loesp. And, welcome."

"Envoy Savide," the human replied, tentatively opening his face mask into the air-tunnel rippling between them. He waited a few moments, then said, "You wished to see me." Tyl Loesp smiled, though he'd always wondered if this expression actually meant anything to an Oct. He found the suit he had to wear strange and awkward; its air smelled of something vaguely unpleasant, burned. The odd, worm-like tube that had extended from the envoy's mouth parts to his own face brought with it an additional scent of fish just starting to rot. At least it was pleasantly cool here inside the Oct ship.

He looked round the chamber while he waited for the Oct to answer. The space was spherical or very close to it, its single wall studded with silvery spiracles and ornate, tiered studs. The sort of upside-down shoulder-seat he was attached to was one of the chamber's plainer pieces of ornamentation.

He still resented having to be here; summoned like a vassal, when he had just taken over an entire level. Savidius Savide might have come to see him, to pay tribute to his success, in the Great Palace at Rasselle (which was magnificent; it made the palace at Pourl look plain). Instead he had had to come to the Oct. Secrecy in such matters had been the order so far and Savidius Savide obviously had no intention of changing this in the short term, whatever his reasons were. The Oct, tyl Loesp had to own, knew more of what was really going on here than he did, and so had to be indulged.

He would like to think that he had been called here finally to learn what the last few years had all been about, but he was under no illusions regarding the Oct ability to obscure, prevaricate and confuse. He still had the very faint suspicion that the Oct had overseen this entire enterprise on a whim, or for some minor reason they had subsequently forgotten, though even they would surely hesitate to engineer the transferral of an entire Shellworld level from one group to another without outside permission and without having a good reason, would they not? But see, here; the envoy's little blue mouth parts were working and a couple of his orange arm-legs were moving and so he was about to speak!

"The Deldeyn lands are controlled now," Savidius Savide said, his voice expressed as a low gurgle.

"They are indeed. Rasselle is secure. Order barely broke down at all but to the extent that it did, it has been restored. Every other part of the Deldeyn kingdom, including the principalities, provinces, Curbed Lands and outlying imperial satrapies are under our control, through either physical occupation by our forces or – in the case of the furthest and least important colonies – the unconditional acquiescence of their most senior officials."

"Then all may rejoice in said. The Sarl may join the Oct, Inheritors of the mantle of those who made the Shellworlds, in justified celebration."

Tyl Loesp chose to assume he had just been congratulated. "Thank you," he said.

"All are pleased."

"I'm sure they are. And I would thank the Oct for your help in this. It has been invaluable. Inscrutable, too, but invaluable, beyond doubt. Even dear, late King Hausk was known to concede that we might have struggled to overcome the Deldeyn without you being, in effect, on our side." Tyl Loesp paused. "I have often asked myself what the reason might be that you have been so forthcoming with your advice and aid. So far I have been unable to come to any satisfactory conclusion."

"In celebration is found that of explicatory nature, only rarely. The nature of celebration is ecstatic, mysteriously ebullient, detaching full reason, hence betokening some confusion." The Oct drew breath, or whatever liquidic equivalent it was that Oct drew. "Explication must not become obstruction, deflection," Savidius Savide added. "Final understanding remaining incentive is most fruitful use available."

Some small amount of time passed during which the long silvery-looking tube of air joining them gently bobbed and slowly writhed, some lazy little bubbles wobbled their way upwards from the base of the spherical chamber, a sequence of dull, deep and distant whirring noises sounded through the enveloping water and tyl Loesp worked out what the Peripatetic Special Envoy had meant.

"I'm sure it is just as you say, Savide," he agreed eventually.

"And, see!" the Envoy said, gesturing with two legs at a bunched semi-sphere of screens glittering into being, each projected by one of the shining spires protruding from the chamber's wall. The scenes displayed on the screens – as far as tyl Loesp could discern them through the intervening water – showed various important and famous parts of the Deldeyn kingdom. Tyl Loesp thought he could make out Sarl soldiers patrolling the edge of the Hyeng-zhar cataract and Sarl banners fluttering above the Great Towers of Rasselle. There were more flags shown at the side of the crater caused by the fallstar Heurimo and silhouetted against the vast white pillar of steam cloud rising forever above the Boiling Sea of Yakid. "It is as you say!" Savidius Savide sounded happy. "Rejoice in such trust! All are pleased!" the Oct envoy repeated.

"How splendid," tyl Loesp said, as the screens blinked out.

"Agreement is agreeable, agreed," Savide informed him. He

had risen slightly above the station he had been keeping until now. A tiny belch or fart from somewhere behind his mid-torso sent a shoal of tiny silver bubbles trembling upwards, and helped re-establish the envoy's position in the waters of the chamber.

Tyl Loesp took a deep, tentative breath. "May we speak plainly?"

"No better form is known. Severally, specifically."

"Quite," tyl Loesp said. "Envoy; why did you help us?"

"Help you, the Sarl, to defeat they, the Deldeyn?"

"Yes. And why the emphasis on the Falls?"

There was silence for a few moments. Then the Oct said, "For reasons."

"What reasons?"

"Most excellent ones."

Tyl Loesp nearly smiled. "Which you will not tell me."

"Will not, indeed. Equally, cannot. In time, such restrictions change, as with all things changing. Power over others is the least and most of powers, betruth. To balance such great success with transient lack of same is fit. Fitness may not be beheld by subject, but, as object, needs be trust's invoked. In this: trust to wait."

Tyl Loesp regarded the Oct hanging in the water a few metres in front of him for a while. So much done, yet always so much still to do. He had that day received a coded report from Vollird telling of the valiant and daring attempt he and Baerth had made on the life of "Our Fugitive" while on the Surface, only to be frustrated at the last moment by alien devil-machinery. They had had to reconcile to second-best, ensuring said person left most expeditiously, sailing away into the night between the eternal stars, terrified and lucky to be alive.

Tyl Loesp didn't doubt Vollird exaggerated the worth of his and Baerth's actions; however, killing Ferbin amongst the Optimae, or even the Optimae's immediate inferiors, had always been a tall order and he would not overly censure the two knights. He'd have preferred Ferbin dead, but absent would do. Still, what mischief might he stir out among the alien races?

Would he loudly declaim himself the wronged and rightful heir to all who'd listen, or sneak to his allegedly influential sister?

Things were never settled, it seemed to tyl Loesp. No matter how decisively one acted, no matter how ruthless one was, loose ends remained and even the most conclusive of actions left a welter of ramifications, any of which – it seemed, sometimes, especially when one woke, fretful, in the middle of the night and such potential troubles appeared magnified – might harbinge disaster. He sighed, then said, "I intend to rid us of the Mission monks. They get in the way and restrict more than they aid and enable. I shall follow an opposite course in the capital. We need the remains of the army and militia; however, I think it best they are balanced with some other faction and propose the Heavenly Host sect as that counterweight. They have a self-lacerating quality about their teachings which ought to chime with the current Deldeyn mood of self-blame following their defeat. Some heads will roll, obviously."

"To that which must be attended, so devote. Is meet, and like."

"So long as you know. I intend to go back to Pourl, for a triumph, and to return treasure and hostages. In time I may remain in Rasselle. And there are those I'd have near. I shall need a reliable and continually available line of supply and communication between here and the Eighth. May I count on that?"

"The scendships and autoscenders so devoted remain so. As in the recent past, so in the near future and – with all appropriate contextualisationing – foreseeable beyond."

"I have the scendships already allocated? They are mine to command?"

"To request. The all flatters their likely or possible use. As needs be, so shall their presence."

"As long as I can get up and down that Tower, back to the Eighth, back to here, at any time, quickly."

"This is not within dispute. I determine no less, personally. Thus asked, so give, allowed and with pleasure is beinged."

Tyl Loesp thought about all this for a while. "Yes," he said. "Well, I'm glad that's clear."

Steam tugs towing barges took the whole contingent of monks – the entirety of the Hyeng-zharia Mission, from most lowly latrine boy to the Archipontine himself – away from their life's work. Tyl Loesp, fresh returned from his frustrating audience with the envoy, watched the loading and went with the lead tug, which was towing the three barges containing the Archipontine and all the higher ranks of the order. They were crossing the Sulpitine, a kilometre or so upriver from the nearest part of the vast semicircle of the Falls. The monks had been relieved of their duty; they were all being taken across the river to the small town of Far Landing, a movable port always kept some four or five kilometres upstream from the cataract.

Tyl Loesp stayed under the shade of the lead tug's stern awning, and still had to use a kerchief to wipe at his brow and temples now and again. The suns hung in the sky, an anvil and a hammer of heat, striking together, inescapable. The area of real shade, hidden from both Rollstars, was minimal, even under the broad awning. Around him, the men of his Regent's Guard watched the swirling brown waters of the river and sometimes raised their glistening heads to look up at the gauzy froth of off-white clouds that piled into the sky beyond the lip of the Falls. The sound of the cataract was dull, and so ever-present that it was easy not to notice it was there at all most of the time, filling the languid, heat-flattened air with a strange, underwater-sounding rumble heard with the guts and lungs and bones as much as through the ears.

The six tugs and twenty barges tracked across the quick current, making a couple of kilometres towards the distant shore though only increasing their distance from the Falls by two hundred metres or so as they fought against the river's fast-flowing mid-section. The tugs' engines chuffed and growled.

Smoke and steam belched from their tall stacks, drifting over the dun river in faded-looking double shadows barely darker than the sandy-coloured river itself. The vessels smelled of steam and roasoaril oil. Their engineers came up on to deck whenever they could, to escape the furnace heat below for the cooler furnace of the river breeze.

The water roiled and burst and tumbled about the boats like something alive, like whole shoals of living things, forever surfacing and diving and surfacing again with a kind of lazy insolence. On the barges, a hundred strides behind, under makeshift awnings and shades, the monks sat and lay and stood, the sight of their massed white robes hurting the eye.

When the small fleet of boats was in the very middle of the stream and each shore looked as far away as the other – they were barely visible at all in the heat haze, just a horizoned sensation of something darker than the river and a few tall trees and shimmering spires – tyl Loesp himself took a two-hand hammer to the pin securing the towing rope to the tug's main running shackle. The pin fell, clattering loudly across the thick wooden deck. The loop of rope slithered drily over the deck – quite slowly at first but gathering a little speed as it went – before the loop itself flipped up over the transom and disappeared with hardly a sound into the busy brown bulges of the river.

The tug surged ahead appreciably and altered course to go directly upstream. Tyl Loesp looked out to the other tugs, to make sure their tow ropes were also being unhitched. He watched the ropes flip over the sterns of all the tugs until every one was powering away upstream, released, waves surging and splashing round bluff bows.

It was some time before the monks on the barges realised what was happening. Tyl Loesp was never really sure if he actually heard them start to wail and cry and scream, or whether he had imagined it.

They should be glad, he thought. The Falls had been their lives; let them be their deaths. What more had the obstructive wretches ever really wanted?

He had trusted men stationed downstream from the cataract's main plunge pools. They would also take care of any monks who survived the plunge, though going on the historical record, even if you sent a thousand monks over the Falls it was unlikely one would survive.

All but one of the barges just vanished in the haze, falling out of sight, disappointing. One, however, must have struck a rock or outcrop right at the lip of the Falls, its stem tipping high into the air in a most dramatic and satisfying manner before it slid and dropped away.

On the way back to port, one of the tugs broke down, its engine giving up in a tall burst of steam from its chimney; two of its fellows put ropes to it and rescued vessel and surviving crew before they too fell victim to the Falls.

Tyl Loesp stood on a gantry like a half-finished bridge levered out over the edge of the nearpole cliff looking across the Hyeng-zhar, most of which was, frustratingly, obscured by mist and cloud. A man called Jerfin Poatas – elderly, hunched, dark-dressed and leaning on a stick – stood by his side. Poatas was a Sarl scholar and archaeologist who had devoted his life to the study of the Falls and had lived here – in the great, eternally temporary, forever shuffling-forward city of Hyeng-zhar Settlement – for twenty of his thirty long-years. It had long been acknowledged that he owed his loyalty to study and knowledge rather than any country or state, though that had not prevented him being briefly interned by the Deldeyn at the height of their war against the Sarl. With the monks of the Hyeng-zharia Mission gone he was now, by tyl Loesp's decree, in full charge of the excavations.

"The brethren were cautious, conservative, as any good archaeologist is at an excavation," Poatas told tyl Loesp. He had to raise his voice to be heard over the thunderous roar of the Falls. Spray swirled up now and again in great spiralling veils and deposited water droplets on their faces. "But they took such caution too far. A normal dig waits; one can afford to be careful. One proceeds with all due deliberation, noting all, investigating all, preserving and recording the place-in-sequence of all discovered finds. This is not a normal dig, and waits for nothing and no one. It will freeze soon and make life easier, if colder, for a while, but even then the brethren were determined to do as they had in the past and suspend all excavations while the Falls were frozen, due to some surfeit of piety. Even the King refused to intervene." Poatas laughed. "Can you imagine? The one time in the solar-meteorological cycle – in a *lifetime* – when the Falls are at their most amenable to exploration and excavation and they intended to halt it all!" Poatas shook his head. "Cretins."

"Just so," tyl Loesp said. "Well, they rule here no more. I expect great things from this place, Poatas," he told the other man, turning briefly to him. "By your own reports this is a treasure house whose potential the monks consistently downplayed and underexploited."

"A treasure house which they resolutely refused to explore properly," Poatas said, nodding. "A treasure house most of whose doors were left unopened, or were left to the privateers, little more than licensed brigands, to open. With sufficient men, that can all be changed. There's many a Falls Merchant Explorer who'll howl with rage to be denied the continuance of their easy stipend, but that is to the good. Even they grew arrogant and lazy, and lately, in my lifetime, more concerned with keeping others out of their concessions than fully exploiting them themselves." Poatas looked sharply at tyl Loesp as the wind began to change. "There's no guarantee of finding the sort of treasure you might be thinking of here, tyl Loesp. Wonder weapons from the past that will command the future are a myth. Quell that thought if it's what exercises you." He paused. Tyl Loesp said nothing. The veered wind was blowing a hot, desert-dry stream of air across them now, and the clouds and mists were beginning to shift and part before them in the great, still mostly unglimpsed gorge. "But whatever's here to be found, we'll find, and if it needs ripping out of some building the brethren of the Mission would have left intact, then so be it. All this can be done. If I have enough men."

"You'll have men," tyl Loesp told him. "Half an army. My army. And others. Some little more than slaves, but they'll work to keep their bellies full."

The clouds throughout the vast complexity confronting them were rolling away from the new wind, lifting and dissipating at once.

"Slaves do not make the best workers. And who will command this army, this army which will like as not expect to go home to their loved ones now they think their job's done here? You? You return to the Eighth, do you not?"

"The armies are well used to foreign travel and distant billets; however, I shall – in prudent portions, leaving nowhere unmanned – so allowance them with loot and easy return they'll either beg to see the Ninth again or be each one a most zealous recruiting sergeant for their younger brothers. For myself, I return to Pourl only briefly. I intend to spend half each year or more in Rasselle."

"It is the traditional seat of power, and of infinite elegance compared to our poor, ever-onward-tramping township here, but whether by train or caude it is two days away. More in bad weather."

"Well, we shall have the telegraph line soon, and while I am not present you have my authority here, Poatas. I offer you complete power over the entire Falls, in my name." Tyl Loesp waved one hand dismissively. "In bookish legality it may be in the name of the Prince Regent, but he is still little more than a boy. For the moment – and it may, in time, seem a long moment – his future power is mine now, entirely. You understand me?"

Poatas smiled parsimoniously. "My whole life and every work has taught me there is a natural order to things, a rightful stratification of authority and might. I work with it, sir, never seek to overthrow it."

"Good," tyl Loesp said. "That is as well. I have in addition thought to provide you with a titular head of excavations, someone I'd rather have quite near to me but not at my side, when I'm in Rasselle. Indeed, their presence here might aid the recruitment of many a Sarl."

"But they would be above me?"

"In theory. Not in effect. I emphasise: their seniority to yourself will be most strictly honorary."

"And who would this person be?" Poatas asked.

"Why, the very one we just talked of. My charge, the Prince Regent, Oramen."

"Is that wise? You say he's a boy. The Falls can be a pestilential place, and the Settlement a lawless, dangerous one, especially with the brethren gone."

Tyl Loesp shrugged. "We must pray the WorldGod keeps him safe. And I have in mind a couple of knights I intend to make the essence of his personal guard. They will take all care of him."

Poatas thought for a moment, nodding, and wiped a little moisture from the stick he leant on. "Will he come?" he asked doubtfully, looking out towards the great, gradually revealing spaces of the Hyeng-zhar's awesomely complicated, twenty-kilometre-wide gorge of recession.

Tyl Loesp looked out to the gorge complex, and smiled. He had never been here until their armies had invaded and – having heard so much about its peerless beauty and fabulous, humbling grandeur from so many people – had been determined not to be impressed when he did finally see the place. The Hyeng-zhar, however, seemed to have had other ideas. He had indeed been stunned, awestruck, rendered speechless.

He had seen it from various different angles over the past week or so, including from the air, on a lyge (though only from on high, and only in the company of experienced Falls-fliers, and still he could entirely understand why it was such a dangerous place to fly; the urge to explore, to descend and see better was almost irresistible, and knowing that so many people had died doing just that, caught in the tremendous rolling currents of air and vapour issuing from the Falls, hauling them helplessly down to their deaths, seemed like an irrelevance).

Poatas himself expressed some astonishment at the Falls' latest show. Truly, they had never been more spectacular, certainly not in his life, and, from all that he could gather from the records, at no point in the past either.

A plateau – perhaps, originally, some sort of vast, high plaza in the Nameless City, kilometres across – was being slowly revealed by the furiously tumbling waters as they exposed what was – by the general agreement of most experts and scholars – the very centre of the buried city. The Falls, in their centre section, four or five kilometres across, were in two stages now; the first drop was of a hundred and twenty metres or so, bringing the waters crashing and foaming and bursting down across the newly revealed plateau and surging among the maze of buildings protruding from that vast flat surface.

Holes in the plateau – many small, several a hundred metres across or more – drained to the darkened level beneath, dropping the mass of water to the gorge floor through a tortuous complexity of bizarrely shaped buildings, ramps and roadways, some intact, some canted over, some undercut, some altogether ruptured and displaced, fallen down and swept away to lie jammed and caught against still greater structures and the shadowy bases of the mass of buildings towering above.

By now the mists had cleared away from nearly half the Falls, revealing the site's latest wonder; the Fountain Building. It was a great gorge-base-level tower by the side of the new plateau. It was still perfectly upright, appeared to be made entirely from glass, was a hundred and fifty metres tall and shaped like a kind of upwardly stretched sphere. Some chance configuration of the tunnels and hidden spaces of the Falls upstream had contrived to send water up into it from underneath, and at such an extremity of pressure that it came surging out in great muddily white fans and jets from all its spiralled levels of windows, bursting with undiminished force even from its very summit, showering the smaller buildings, tubes, ramps and lower water courses all around it with an incessant, battering rain.

"Well, sir?" Poatas demanded. "Will he? This boy-prince of yours; will he come?"

Tyl Loesp had sent the command to Aclyn's husband just two days earlier, informing the fellow that he was to be the new mayor of the city of Rasselle; this would be a permanent position and he must bring his entire household with him from far Kheretesuhr with the utmost dispatch, on pain of losing both this once-in-a-lifetime promotion, and the regent's regard.

"Oh, I think he will," tyl Loesp said, with a small smile.

18.   The Current Emergency

"**B**ilpier, fourth of the Heisp Nariscene colony system, is small, solid, cold-cored, habiformed to Nariscene specifications within the last centieon, dynamically O_2 atmosphered, one hundred per cent Nariscene and seventy-four per cent surface bubble-hived."

Holse and Ferbin were lounging in the sitting area of their generously proportioned suite of cabins within *The Hundredth Idiot*, being kept fed and watered by a variety of subservient machines and entertained by images on wall screens. They knew they were going to Bilpier and the hive city of Ischuer and the journey would take ten days, though that was all they'd been told since Director General Shoum had secured their passage on a ship leaving only a day after she and Ferbin had spoken.

Ferbin had thought to ask the ship for more information. "Hmm," he said, little the wiser. "I seek a man called Xide

Hyrlis," he continued. "Do you know if he is there, in this Bilpier place?"

"I do not," *The Hundredth Idiot* replied. "It is doubtful that he is. You have preferential clearance to be conveyed to this person as requested, with emphasis, by the Morthanveld Tertiary Hulian Spine Director General. I can now confirm you are booked for onward travel from Ischuer, Bilpier, aboard the Morthanveld vessel '*Fasilyce, Upon Waking*', a Cat.5 SwellHull. Its destination is not a matter of public record."

Ferbin and Holse exchanged looks. This was news. "You have no idea how long our journey will be after we leave Bilpier?" Ferbin asked.

"Given you travel aboard a Cat.5 SwellHull, your destination is unlikely to be within the Heisp system," the ship replied. "The Cat.5 SwellHull is a long-range interstellar class."

Ferbin nodded thoughtfully. "Oh!" he said, as though just thinking of something. "And can you get a message to a fellow named Oramen, house of Hausk, city of Pourl, the Eighth, Sursamen—"

"That is within a mandated Nariscene Protectorate," the ship interrupted smoothly, "and so subject to special clearance provisions regarding direct contact between individuals. Specific instructions forming part of your associated travel particulars mean that I may not even begin the relevant message process. I am sorry."

Ferbin sighed. He went back to watching screenage of bat-like aliens hunting flying, twisty, gossamery things in a Towerless place of soaring yellow-pink canyons beneath pastel clouds.

"Worth a try, sir," Holse told him, then returned to his own screen, which showed a sort of map-with-depth called a holo-gram depicting the courses of Nariscene and associated space-ships.

The galaxy was linked like chain mail, he thought. It was all loops and circles and long, joined-up threads and looked like that old-fashioned stuff some old knights from the deepest, darkest shires and valleys still wore when they ventured to court, even if they rarely polished it in case it got worn away.

The Hundredth Idiot settled smoothly into a valley between two huge dark bubbles kilometres across in a landscape that was nothing but more of the same; the foam of enormous blisters covered three-quarters of Bilpier's surface, enclosing continents, smothering oceans, arcing over mountain ranges and leaving only so much of the planet's original swamps and jungles exposed as seemed fit to the Nariscene aesthetic sense.

Ferbin and Holse were shown some impressive domes covering bulbously orange things that seemed to be half trees and half buildings. They met a Nariscene Zamerin and had to listen to some Nariscenic music for nearly an hour.

Within a local day they were standing on some worryingly open webbing high over more giant orange building-trees, at the lofty seam between two vast bubbles, in the half-kilometre-long shadow of a sleekly bulbous spaceship nestling in the open air of the valley formed by the two giant blisters.

They were greeted by a Morthanveld who introduced herself as Liaison Officer Chilgitheri.

They were carried for nearly thirty days on the *"Fasilyce, Upon Waking"*. It was a less pleasant journey than that on the Nariscene ship; they had to don suits to investigate the vast majority of the mostly water-filled ship, their quarters were smaller and, worst of all, the ship kept increasing its gravity field, to prepare them for wherever it was they were going. The Morthanveld, being aquatic, seemed rather to scorn gravity, but were gradually ramping up the apparent effect of that force felt on the ship to acclimatise their human guests. They were the only non-Morthanveld aboard and, as Holse said, they should have felt flattered to be so indulged, but it was hard to feel much gratitude when your feet and back and almost everything else ached so much.

The *"Fasilyce, Upon Waking"* carried a dozen smaller ships, arranged like rotund seeds around its waist and rear. One of these was the Cat.3 SlimHull *"Now, Turning to Reason, & its Just Sweetness"*; it was this craft that took Ferbin and Holse on the final leg of their journey. They shared two smallish cabins and would have spent almost all their time lying down if Chilgitheri hadn't chivied them into standing up and walking around and even doing a few undemanding exercises in the ship's impersonation of gravity, which was still slowly increasing.

"Not increasing slowly enough," Holse observed, groaning.

The *"Now, Turning to Reason, & its Just Sweetness"* bellied in towards a fractured, broken land of rock and cinder. This, Liaison Officer Chilgitheri informed them, was what was left of the country of Prille, on the continent of Sketevi, on the planet Bulthmaas, in the Chyme system.

As the ship closed with this wasteland of grey and brown, the final increment of gravity that had settled like lead epaulets on the two Sarl men lifted; the Morthanveld ships had deliberately made them experience a gravity field slightly greater than the one they would be stepping out into so that the real thing wouldn't feel quite so bad.

"A mercy so small as to be microscopic," Holse muttered.

"Better than nothing," Chilgitheri informed them. "Count your blessings, gentlemen. Come on."

They found themselves on the flat, fused base of a great fresh-looking crater. Outside the ship's rotated lower access bulge the air smelled of burning. A cold, keen wind swirled in the depression's circular base, raising pillars and veils of ash and dust. The atmosphere caught at their throats and the air was shaken by what sounded like continual thunder from far away.

A small, bulbous thing like a carriage compartment made mostly of glass had ridden the access bulge with them as it had cycled round to present them to this ghastly place. Ferbin had wondered if this thing was some sort of guarding device. Thankfully, it was merely their means of conveyance; they would not have to walk any distance in this awful, crushing grip.

"Smell that air," Chilgitheri told them as they settled into the welcoming couches of the transparent device. It closed its doors and the sounds from outside ceased. "You'll smell nothing unfiltered for a while, but that is the authentic scent of Bulthmaas."

"It stinks," Holse said.

"Yes. There may still be a few of the later wide-spectrum pathogens around, but they ought not to affect you."

Ferbin and Holse looked at each other. Neither had any idea what pathogens were, but they didn't like the sound of them.

The little bubble vehicle lifted silently and they crossed the glassy surface of the crater to a construction made of thick metal plates jutting out from the jumbled debris of the lower crater wall like some monstrous iron flower growing from that riven, death-grey geography. A set of ponderously massive doors swung open and the dark tunnels swallowed them.

They saw war machines waiting darkly in alcoves, lines of dim lights stretching away down shadowy side-tunnels and, ahead, the first in a succession of enormous metal shutters which opened before them and closed behind. A few times they saw pale creatures which looked vaguely like men, but which were too small, squat and stunted to be human as they understood the term. They passed one Nariscene, floating in a complex metallic harness, bristling with extra appendages that might have been weapons, then they began descending a spiralled ramp like a hollow spring screwing its way into the bowels of the world.

They halted eventually in a large gloomy chamber cross-braced with thick struts. It was almost filled with parked vehicles; squashed, gnarled, misshapen-looking things. Their little made-of-near-nothing car settled amongst them like a downy seed blown amongst lumps of clinker.

"Time to use those legs!" Chilgitheri cried cheerfully. The car's doors swung open. The two men unfolded themselves from the transparent conveyance, Holse hoisted the two small bags of clothing they had with them and groaned as they made their way to another opening door and up – up! – a short, narrow ramp to a smaller dimly lit chamber where the air smelled stale, yet with a medicinal tang. The ceiling was so low they had to walk and stand slightly stooped, which made the effects of the high gravity even worse. Holse dumped both bags on the floor at his feet.

One of the short, squat men sat in a chair behind a metal desk, dressed in a dark grey uniform. A Nariscene in one of the complicated-looking harnesses floated off to one side, behind and above the man's shoulder, seemingly regarding them.

The squashed excuse for a human creature made a series of noises. "You are welcome," the Nariscene translated.

"My responsibility and that of the Morthanveld ends here," Chilgitheri told the two Sarl men. "You are now in Nariscene jurisdiction and that of their client species here, the Xolpe. Good luck to you. Take care. Goodbye."

Ferbin and Holse both bade her well. The Morthanveld turned and floated away down the narrow ramp.

Ferbin looked round for a seat, but the only one in the chamber was occupied by the man behind the metal desk. Some papers issued from a slot in it. The man pulled them out, checked and folded them, bashed them with bits of metal and then pushed them across the desk towards the two Sarl men. "These are your papers," the Nariscene said. "You will carry them at all times."

Their papers were covered in tiny alien symbols. The only thing either man could recognise was a small monochrome representation of their own face. More sounds from the squashed little man. "You will wait," the Nariscene told them. "Here. This way to wait. Follow me."

More cramped corridors took them to a small, dimly lit room with four bunk beds and nothing else. The Nariscene closed the door, which made loud locking noises. Holse checked; it was locked. A smaller door at the other end of the cell gave access to a tiny toilet compartment. They took the two lower bunks and lay there, breathing hard, grateful to have the weight off their legs and backs. They had to lie folded; the bunk beds were too short for them to stretch out. A grey-blue suit of clothes hung on the end of each bunk. These were their uniforms, the Nariscene had told them. They had to be worn at all times.

"What sort of place is this, sir?"

"A terrible one, Holse."

"I'd formed that impression myself, sir."

"Try to sleep, Holse. It's all we can do."

"It may be our only escape from this shit-hole," Holse said, and turned his face to the wall.

Chilgitheri had not been forthcoming regarding what would happen after they were delivered here. This was where Xide Hyrlis ought to be and their request to see him had been forwarded to the relevant authorities, but whether they would be allowed to see him, and how – and even if – they would leave this world, she had confessed she did not know.

Ferbin closed his eyes, wishing he was almost anywhere else.

"Why are you here?" the Nariscene translated. The creature talking to them might have been the one who'd shown them to their cramped quarters; they had no idea. Introductions might have been in order, Ferbin thought, but obviously things were done differently here. He and Holse were dressed in the uniforms they had been given – the uniforms were both too short and too wide for the Sarl men, making them look ridiculous – and they were in another small chamber facing another small stump of a man behind another metal desk, though at least this time they had chairs to sit in.

"We are here to see a man called Xide Hyrlis," Ferbin told the Nariscene and the small pale man-thing.

"There is no one of that name here."

"What?"

"There is no one of that name here."

"That cannot be true!" Ferbin protested. "The Morthanveld who brought us here assured us this is where Hyrlis is!"

"They could be mistaken," the Nariscene suggested, without waiting for the man to speak.

"I suspect they are not," Ferbin said icily. "Kindly be so good as to tell Mr Hyrlis that a prince of the Sarl, the surviving son of his old good friend, the late King Nerieth Hausk of the Eighth, Sursamen, wishes to see him, having travelled amongst the stars all the way from that great world at the express favour, with emphasis, of our friends the Morthanveld with the specific mission of meeting with him, as affirmed by Director General Shoum herself. See to it, if you would."

The Nariscene appeared to translate at least some of this. The man spoke, followed by the Nariscene. "State full name of the person you wish to see."

Full name. Ferbin had had time to think of this on many occasions since he'd formed this plan back on the Eighth. Xide Hyrlis' Full Name had been a chant amongst some of the children at court, almost a mantra for them. He hadn't forgotten. "Stafl-Lepoortsa Xide Ozoal Hyrlis dam Pappens," he said.

The stunted man grunted, then studied a screen set into his desk. Its dull green glow lit his face. He said something and the Nariscene said, "Your request will be transmitted through the appropriate channels. You will return to your quarters to wait."

"I shall report your lack of proper respect and urgency to Mr Hyrlis when I see him," Ferbin told the Nariscene firmly as he got, painfully, to his feet. He felt absurd in his ill-fitting uniform but tried to summon what dignity he could. "Tell me your name."

"No. There is no Mr Hyrlis. You will return to your quarters to wait."

"No Mr Hyrlis? Don't be ridiculous."

"Could be an issue of rank, sir," Holse said, also rising and grimacing.

"You will return to your quarters to wait."

"Very well; I shall inform *General* Hyrlis."

"You will return to your quarters to wait."

"Or *Field Marshal* Hyrlis, or whatever rank he may have attained."

"You will return to your quarters to wait."

They were awoken in the middle of the night, both of them from dreams of weight and crushing and burial. They'd been fed through a hatch in the door not long before the light in their room had dimmed; the soup had been almost inedible.

"You will come with us," the Nariscene said. Two of the squat, pale, uniformed men stood behind it holding rifles. Ferbin and Holse dressed in their preposterous uniforms. "Bring possessions," the Nariscene told them. Holse picked up both bags.

A small wheeled vehicle took them a short way up another spiral ramp. More doors and dimly lit tunnels brought them to a greater space, still dark, where people and machines moved and a train sat humming, poised between two dark holes at either end of the chamber.

Before they could board, the floor beneath their feet shook and a shudder ran throughout the huge chamber, causing people to look up at the dark ceiling. Lights swayed and dust drifted down. Ferbin wondered what sort of cataclysmic explosion would be felt so far beneath this much rock.

"Embark here," the Nariscene told them, pointing at a shuttered entrance into one of the train's cylindrical carriages. They heaved themselves up a ramp into a cramped, windowless compartment; the Nariscene floated inside with them and the door rolled back down. There was just enough room for them to sit on the floor between tall boxes and crates. A single round ball in the ceiling, guarded by a little metal cage, gave out a weak, steady yellow light. The Nariscene hovered over one of the crates.

"Where are we going?" Ferbin asked. "Are we going to see Xide Hyrlis?"

"We do not know," the Nariscene said.

They sat breathing the stale, lifeless air for a while. Then there was a lurch and some muffled clanking as the train moved off.

"How long will this take?" Ferbin asked the Nariscene.

"We do not know," it repeated.

The train rattled and buzzed around them and they both soon fell asleep again, to be woken from the depths once more, confused and disoriented, and hustled out – knees and backs aching – down a ramp and into another squat vehicle which took them and the accompanying Nariscene along yet more tunnels and down another spiral to a large chamber where a hundred or more tanks of liquid, each twice their height, glowed blue and green in the general darkness.

Each tank held the bodies of a half-dozen or so of the short, stubby-looking men, all quite naked. They looked asleep, a mask over each face, hoses snaking up to the surface of the tanks. Their bodies were quite hairless and many had been badly injured; some were missing limbs, some had obvious puncture wounds and others displayed extensive areas of burned skin.

Ferbin and Holse were so fascinated looking at this unnerving, ghoulish display that it was some time before they realised they appeared to be alone; the little wheeled vehicle had disappeared and seemingly taken the Nariscene with it.

Ferbin walked over to the nearest of the tanks. Close up, it was possible to see that there was a gentle current in the pale, slightly cloudy liquid; tiny bubbles rose from the floor of the tank and headed to the sealed caps of the cylinders.

"D'you think they're dead?" Ferbin breathed.

"Not wearing those masks," Holse replied. "They look a bit like you did, sir, when the Oct were healing you."

"Perhaps they are being preserved for something," Ferbin said.

"Or medicined," Holse suggested. "There's not one without an injury I've seen yet, though many seem to be healing."

"You could say we're healing them," someone said behind them.

They both turned. Ferbin recognised Xide Hyrlis immediately; he had barely changed at all. Given that nearly a dozen long-years had passed, this ought to have seemed strange, though it was only later Ferbin realised this.

Xide Hyrlis was a tall man by the standards of the dwarfish people hereabouts, though he was still shorter than Ferbin or Holse. He was dense-seeming somehow, and dark, with a broad face, a large mouth with teeth that were both too few and too wide, and bright, piercingly blue-purple eyes. His eyes had always fascinated Ferbin as a child; they had an extra, transparent membrane that swept across them, meaning that he never had to blink, never needed to stop seeing the world, however briefly, from the moment he woke to the moment he slept (and he did little enough of that). His hair was black and long and kept in a tidy ponytail. He had a lot of facial hair, neatly trimmed. He wore a better-cut version of the grey uniform worn by most of the people they'd seen so far.

"Xide Hyrlis," Ferbin said, nodding. "It is good to see you again. I am Prince Ferbin, son of King Hausk."

"Good to see you again, prince," Hyrlis said. He looked to one side and seemed to address somebody they could not see. "The son of my old friend King Hausk of the Sarl, of the Eighth, Sursamen." Hyrlis returned his attention to Ferbin and said, "You are much grown, prince. How are things on the Eighth?" Holse glanced at Ferbin, who was staring straight at Hyrlis. "Ferbin was a hip-high child, last time I saw him," Hyrlis added to whatever imaginary being was at his side. There really was nobody else anywhere near them, and nothing obvious that he could be addressing.

"I have much to tell you, Hyrlis," Ferbin said, "little of it good. But first, tell me how I ought to address you. What rank do you hold?"

Hyrlis smiled. He glanced to one side. "A good question, don't you think?" He looked at Ferbin. "Adviser, you might say. Or Supreme Commander. It's so hard to know."

"Choose one, sir," Holse suggested. "There's a good gent."

"Allow me," Ferbin said coldly, as he looked at Holse, who was smiling innocently, "to present my servant, Choubris Holse."

"Mr Holse," Hyrlis said, nodding.

"Sir."

"And sir will do," Hyrlis said thoughtfully. "It's what everybody else calls me." He caught some sudden tension from Ferbin. "Prince, I know you'll only ever have called your father 'sir' since your majority; however, humour me in this. I am a king of sorts in these parts and command more power than ever your father did." He grinned. "Unless he's taken over the whole Shellworld, eh?" He turned his head again, "For yes, such Sursamen is, those of you slow to reference," he said to his unseen companion as Ferbin – still, Holse thought, looking a little glassy-eyed – said,

"As I say, sir, I have much to relate."

Hyrlis nodded at the bodies bobbing gently in the tanks behind them. "Captured enemy," he said. "Being kept alive, partially repaired. We wash clear their minds and they become our spies, or assassins, or human bombs, or vectors of disease. Come. We'll find you a place to flop. And better clothes. You look like twig insects in those."

They followed him to one of the open-sided runabouts, and as they did, dark figures left various shadows all about them, dissociating from the darkness like parts of it; humans in some near-black dark camouflage suits and armed with ugly-looking guns. Ferbin and Holse both jerked to a stop as they saw the four shadowy figures closing swiftly, silently in on them but Hyrlis, without even looking round, just waved one hand as he took the driving seat of the little wheeled vehicle and said, "My guard. Don't worry. Jump on."

Once he knew the dark figures were no threat, Ferbin was quite pleased to see them. Hyrlis must have been talking to them for some reason. That was a relief.

Xide Hyrlis kept a very fine table beneath the kilometres of mountain rock. The chamber was dome-shaped, the servants – young men and girls – glided silently. The stone table they sat around was loaded with highly colourful and exotic foodstuffs and a bewildering variety of bottles. The food was entirely delicious, for all its alien nature, and the drink copious. Ferbin waited until they had finished eating before telling his story.

Hyrlis heard Ferbin out, asking one or two questions along the way. At the end he nodded. "You have my sincere sympathies, prince. I am even sorrier at the manner of your father's passing than at the fact of it. Nerieth was a warrior and both expected and deserved a warrior's death. What you've described is a murder both cowardly and cruel."

"Thank you, Hyrlis," Ferbin said. He looked down, sniffing loudly.

Hyrlis did not seem to notice. He was staring at his wine glass. "I remember tyl Loesp," he said. He was silent for some moments, then shook his head. "If he harboured such treachery then, he fooled me too." He looked to one side again. "And do you watch there?" he asked quietly. This time there was definitely nobody present for him to be talking to; the four darkly camouflaged guards had been dismissed when they'd entered Hyrlis' private quarters and the servants had, just minutes earlier, been told to stay outside the dining chamber until summoned. "Is that part of the entertainment?" Hyrlis said in the same quiet voice. "Is the King's murder recorded?" He looked back to Ferbin and Holse. Choubris tried to exchange looks with Ferbin, but the other man was staring glassy-eyed at their host again.

Holse wasn't having it. "Excuse me, sir," he said to Hyrlis.

From the corner of his eye he could see Ferbin trying to attract his attention. Well, the hell with it. "Might I ask who you're talking to when you do that?"

"Holse!" Ferbin hissed. He smiled insincerely at Hyrlis. "My servant is impertinent, sir."

"No, he is inquisitive, prince," Hyrlis said with a small smile. "In a sense, Holse, I do not know," he said gently. "And it is just possible that I am addressing nobody at all. However, I strongly suspect that I am talking to quite a number of people."

Holse frowned. He looked hard in the direction Hyrlis had directed his latest aside.

Hyrlis smiled and waved one hand through the air, as though dispelling smoke. "They are not physically present, Holse. They are – or, I suppose I must allow – they might be watching at a very considerable remove, via spybots, edust, nanoware – whatever you want to call it."

"I might call it any or all, sir, I'm none the wiser at those words."

"Holse, if you can't conduct yourself like a gentleman," Ferbin said firmly, "you'll eat with the other servants." Ferbin looked at Hyrlis. "I may have been too indulgent with him, sir. I apologise on his behalf and my own."

"No apology required, prince," Hyrlis said smoothly. "And this is my table, not yours. I'd have Holse here for what you call his impertinence in any event. I am surrounded by too many people unwilling to call me on anything at all; a dissident voice is welcome."

Ferbin sat back, insulted.

"I believe that I am watched, Holse," Hyrlis said, "by devices too small to be seen with the human eye, even ones like mine, which are quite keen, if not as keen as they once were."

"Enemy spies, sir?" Holse asked. He glanced at Ferbin, who looked away ostentatiously.

"No, Holse," Hyrlis said. "Spies sent by my own people."

Holse nodded, though with a deep frown.

Hyrlis looked at Ferbin. "Prince, your own matter is of course of far greater importance; however, I think I ought to digress a little here, to explain myself and my situation."

Ferbin gave a curt nod.

"When I was ... with you, amongst you, on the Eighth – advising your father, Ferbin ..." Hyrlis said, glancing to the prince but generally addressing both men, "I was employed – at the behest of the Nariscene – by the Culture, the mongrel pan-human and machine civilisation which is one of what you term the Optimae, those civilisations in the first rank of the unSublimed, non-elder groupings. I was an agent for the part of the Culture called Contact, which deals with ... foreign affairs, you might say. Contact is charged with discovering and interacting with other civilisations which are not yet part of the galactic community. I was not then with the more rarefied intelligence and espionage part of Contact coyly called Special Circumstances, though I know that SC thought at the time the specific part of Contact I represented was, arguably, encroaching on their territory." Hyrlis smiled thinly. "Even galaxy-spanning anarchist utopias of stupefying full-spectrum civilisational power have turf wars within their unacknowledged militaries."

Hyrlis sighed. "I did, later, become part of Special Circumstances, a decision I look back on now with more regret than pride." His smile did, indeed, look sad. "When you leave the Culture – and people do, all the time – you are made aware of certain responsibilities you are deemed to have, should you venture into the kind of civilisation that Contact might be interested in.

"I was missioned to do what I did by Contact, which had modelled the situation on the Eighth exhaustively, so that, when I passed on some strategic plan to King Hausk, or suggested sabots and rifling to the royal armourers, it was with a very good and highly reliable idea of what the effects would be. In theory, a reasonably well-read Culture citizen could do the same with no control, no back-up and no idea what they were really doing. Or, worse, with a very good idea; they might want to be king, or emperor, or whatever, and their knowledge would give them a chance of succeeding." Hyrlis waved one hand. "It's an exaggerated concern, in my opinion; knowledge in the Culture is cheap beyond measuring, however the ruthlessness required to use that knowledge proficiently in a less forgiving society is almost unheard of.

"Nevertheless, the result is that when you leave the Culture to come to a place like this, or the Eighth, you are watched. Devices are sent to spy on you and make sure you're not getting up to any mischief."

"And if a person does get up to mischief, sir?" Holse asked.

"Why, they stop you, Mr Holse. They use the devices they've sent to spy, or they send people or other devices to undo what you've done, and, as a last resort, they kidnap you and bring you back, to be told off." Hyrlis shrugged. "When you leave SC, as I did, further precautions are taken: they take away some of the gifts they originally gave you. Certain abilities are reduced or removed altogether so that you have fewer advantages over the locals. And the surveillance is more intense, though even less noticeable." Hyrlis looked to the side once more. "I trust my even-handedness is appreciated, here. I am generous to a fault." He looked back at the two men. "I understand most people like to pretend that such oversight doesn't exist, that it isn't happening to them; I take a different view. I address those I know must be watching me. So, now you know. And, I hope, understand. Were you worried I was mad?"

"Not at all!" Ferbin protested immediately, as Holse said, "It did occur, sir, as you'd expect."

Hyrlis smiled. He swirled some wine around in his glass and watched himself doing so. "Oh, I may well be mad; mad to be here, mad to be still involved with the business of war, but at least in this I am not mad; I know I am watched, and I will let those who watch me know that I know."

"We do," Ferbin said, glancing at Holse, "understand."

"Good," Hyrlis said casually. He leaned forward, putting his elbows on the table and clasping his hands under his chin. "Now, back to you. You have come a very long way, prince. I assume to see me?"

"Indeed, that I have."

"And with more intended than simply bringing me the news that my old friend Nerieth has been murdered, honoured though I am to hear from a real person rather than a news service."

"Indeed," Ferbin said, and pulled himself up in his seat as best he could. "I seek your help, good Hyrlis."

"I see." Hyrlis nodded, looking thoughtful.

Ferbin said, "Can you, will you help?"

"In what way?"

"Will you return to the Eighth with me to help avenge my father's murder?"

Hyrlis sat back. He shook his head. "I cannot, prince. I am needed here, committed here. I work for the Nariscene, and even if I wanted to I could not return to Sursamen in the near or medium future."

"Are you saying you do not even want to?" Ferbin asked, not hiding his displeasure.

"Prince, I am sorry to hear your father is dead, sorrier still to hear of the manner of it."

"You have said so, sir," Ferbin told him.

"So I say it again. Your father was a friend of mine for a short while and I respected him greatly. However, it is not my business to right wrongs occurring deep inside a distant Shellworld."

Ferbin stood up. "I see I misunderstood you, sir," he said. "I was told you are a good and honourable man. I find I have been misinformed."

Holse stood up too, though slowly, thinking that if Ferbin was to storm out – though God knew to where – he had best accompany him.

"Hear me out, prince," Hyrlis said reasonably. "I wish you well and tyl Loesp and his co-conspirators an undignified end, but I am unable to help."

"And unwilling," Ferbin said, almost spitting.

"Yours is not my fight, prince."

"It should be the fight of all who believe in justice!"

"Oh, really, prince," Hyrlis said, amused. "Listen to yourself."

"Better than listening to you and your insulting complacency!"

Hyrlis looked puzzled. "What exactly did you expect me to do?"

"Something! Anything! Not *nothing*; not just sit there and smirk!"

"And why aren't you doing something, Ferbin?" Hyrlis asked, still reasonable. "Might you not have been more effective staying on the Eighth rather than coming all this way to see me?"

"I am no warrior, I know that," Ferbin said bitterly. "I have not the skills or disposition. And I have not the guile to go back to the court and face tyl Loesp and pretend I did not see what I did, to plot and plan behind a smile. I'd have drawn my sword or put my hands on his throat the instant I saw him and I'd have come off the worse. I know that I need help and I came here to ask you for it. If you will not help me, kindly let us go from here and do whatever you might be able and willing to do to speed my journey to my sibling Djan Seriy. I can only pray that she has somehow escaped infection by this Cultural disease of uncaring."

"Prince," Hyrlis sighed, "will you please sit down? There is more to discuss; I might help you in other ways. Plus we should talk about your sister." Hyrlis waved one hand at Ferbin's seat. "Please."

"I shall sit, sir," Ferbin told him, doing so, "but I am grievously disappointed."

Holse sat too. He was glad of this; the wine was very good and it would be a criminal shame to have to abandon it.

Hyrlis resumed his earlier pose, hands under chin. A small frown creased his brow. "*Why* would tyl Loesp do what he has done?"

"I care not!" Ferbin said angrily. "*That* he did it is all that matters!"

Hyrlis shook his head. "I must disagree, prince. If you are

to have any chance of righting this wrong, you'd be well advised to know what motivates your enemy."

"Power, of course!" Ferbin exclaimed. "He wanted the throne, and he'll have it, the moment he's had my young brother killed."

"But why now?"

"Why not!" Ferbin said, clenched fists hammering at the unforgiving stone of the great table. "My father had done all the work, the battles were all won, or as good as. That's when a coward strikes, when the glory might be stolen without the bravery that afforded it."

"Still, it is often easier to be the second in command, prince," Hyrlis said. "The throne is a lonely place, and the nearer you are to it the clearer you see that. There are advantages to having great power without ultimate responsibility. Especially when you know that even the king does not have ultimate power, that there are always powers above. You say tyl Loesp was trusted, rewarded, valued, respected ... Why would he risk that for the last notch of a power he knows is still enchained with limitations?"

Ferbin sat boiling with frustration but had resolved not to say anything this time. This only gave occasion for Hyrlis to look to the side and say quietly, "Do *you* know? Do you look there? Are you allow—?"

Ferbin could stand it no longer. "Will you *stop* talking to these phantoms!" he shouted, springing up again, this time so quickly his chair toppled over. Holse, having taken the opportunity to sip from his glass at what had seemed a handily quiet moment, had to gulp and stand quickly too, wiping his mouth with his sleeve. "These imagined demons have stolen what wits you ever had, sir!"

Hyrlis shook his head. "Would that they were imaginary, prince. And if there are similar systems of observation within Sursamen, they might hold one key to your difficulty."

"What in the world are you talking about?" Ferbin hissed through clenched teeth.

Hyrlis sighed again. "Please, prince, do sit down again ...

No, no, I'll stand," he said, changing his mind. "Let's all stand. And let me show you something. Please come with me. There is more to explain."

The airship was a giant light-flecked blister riding the poisoned air above a still glowing battlefield. They had been brought here in Hyrlis' own small, svelte air vehicle, which had lifted silently from the bottom of another giant crater and flown whispering through clouds and smoke then clearer weather, chasing a ruddy sunset into a night whose far horizon was edged with tiny sporadic flashes of yellow-white light. Below them, rings and circles of dull and fading red covered the dark, undulating land. The airship was bright, all strung with lights, lit from every side and covered in reflective markings. It hung above the livid-bruised land like an admonition.

The little aircraft docked in a broad deck slung underneath the giant ship's main body. Various other craft were arriving and departing all the time, arriving full of injured soldiers accompanied by a few medical staff and departing empty save for returning medics. Quiet moans filled the warm, smoke-scented air. Hyrlis led them via some spiralled steps to a ward full of coffin-like beds each containing a pale, squat, unconscious figure. Holse looked at the lifeless-looking people and felt envious; at least they didn't have to stand up, walk around and climb stairs in this awful gravity.

"You know there is a theory," Hyrlis said quietly, walking amongst the gently glowing coffin-beds, Ferbin and Holse at his rear, the four dark-dressed guards somewhere nearby, unseen, "that all that we experience as reality is just a simulation, a kind of hallucination that has been imposed upon us."

Ferbin said nothing.

Holse assumed that Hyrlis was addressing them rather than his demons or whatever they were, so said, "We have a sect back home with a roughly similar point of view, sir."

"It's a not uncommon position," Hyrlis said. He nodded at the unconscious bodies all around them. "These sleep, and have dreams inflicted upon them, for various reasons. They will believe, while they dream, that the dream is reality. We know it is not, but how can we know that our own reality is the last, the final one? How do we know there is not a still greater reality external to our own into which we might awake?"

"Still," Holse said. "What's a chap to do, eh, sir? Life needs living, no matter what our station in it."

"It does. But thinking of these things affects how we live that life. There are those who hold that, statistically, we *must* live in a simulation; the chances are too extreme for this not to be true."

"There are always people who can convince themselves of near enough anything, seems to me, sir," Holse said.

"I believe them to be wrong in any case," Hyrlis said.

"You have been thinking on this, I take it then?" asked Ferbin. He meant to sound arch.

"I have, prince," Hyrlis said, continuing to lead them through the host of sleeping injured. "And I base my argument on morality."

"Do you now?" Ferbin said. He did not need to affect disdain.

Hyrlis nodded. "If we assume that all we have been told is as real as what we ourselves experience – in other words, that history, with all its torturings, massacres and genocides, is true – then, if it is all somehow under the control of somebody or some thing, must not those running that simulation be monsters? How utterly devoid of decency, pity and compassion would they have to be to allow this to happen, and keep on happening under their explicit control? Because so much of history is precisely this, gentlemen."

They had approached the edge of the huge space, where slanted, down-looking windows allowed a view of the pocked landscape beneath. Hyrlis swept his arm to indicate both the bodies in their coffin-beds and the patchily glowing land below.

"War, famine, disease, genocide. Death, in a million different forms, often painful and protracted for the poor individual wretches involved. What god would so arrange the universe to predispose its creations to experience such suffering, or be the cause of it in others? What master of simulations or arbitrator of a game would set up the initial conditions to the same pitiless effect? God or programmer, the charge would be the same: that of near-infinitely sadistic cruelty; deliberate, premeditated barbarism on an unspeakably horrific scale."

Hyrlis looked expectantly at them. "You see?" he said. "By this reasoning we must, after all, be at the most base level of reality – or at the most exalted, however one wishes to look at it. Just as reality can blithely exhibit the most absurd coincidences that no credible fiction could convince us of, so only reality – produced, ultimately, by matter in the raw – can be so unthinkingly cruel. Nothing able to think, nothing able to comprehend culpability, justice or morality could encompass such purposefully invoked savagery without representing the absolute definition of evil. It is that unthinkingness that saves us. And condemns us, too, of course; we are as a result our own moral agents, and there is no escape from that responsibility, no appeal to a higher power that might be said to have artificially constrained or directed us."

Hyrlis rapped on the clear material separating them from the view of the dark battlefield. "We are information, gentlemen; all living things are. However, *we* are lucky enough to be encoded in matter itself, not running in some abstracted system as patterns of particles or standing waves of probability."

Holse had been thinking about this. "Of course, sir, your god *could* just be a bastard," he suggested. "Or these simulationeers, if it's them responsible."

"That is possible," Hyrlis said, a smile fading. "Those above and beyond us might indeed be evil personified. But it is a standpoint of some despair."

"And all this pertains how, exactly?" Ferbin asked. His feet were sore and he was growing tired of what seemed to him like pointless speculation, not to mention something dangerously close to philosophy, a field of human endeavour he had encountered but fleetingly through various exasperated tutors, though long enough to have formed the unshakeable impression that its principal purpose was to prove that one equalled zero, black was white and educated men could speak through their bottoms.

"I am watched," Hyrlis said. "Perhaps your home is watched, prince. It is possible that tiny machines similar to those that observe me spy upon your people too. The death of your father might have been overseen by more eyes than you thought were present. And if it was watched once, it can be watched again, because only base reality cannot be fully replayed; anything transmitted can be recorded and usually is."

Ferbin stared at him. "Recorded?" he said, horrified. "My father's murder?"

"It is possible; no more," Hyrlis told him.

"By whom?"

"The Oct, the Nariscene, the Morthanveld?" Hyrlis suggested. "Perhaps the Culture. Perhaps anybody else with the means, which would include some dozens of Involved civilisations at least."

"And this would be done," Holse suggested, "by the same unseen agents that you address from time to time, sir?"

"By things most similar," Hyrlis agreed.

"Unseen," Ferbin said contemptuously. "Unheard, untouched, unsmelled, untasted, undetected. In a word, figmented."

"Oh, we are often profoundly affected by unseeably small things, prince." Hyrlis smiled wistfully. "I have advised rulers for whom the greatest military service I could perform had nothing to do with strategy, tactics or weapons technology; it was simply to inform them of and persuade them to accept the germ theory of disease and infection. Believing that we are surrounded by microscopic entities that profoundly and directly affect the fates of individuals and through them nations has been the first step in the ascendancy of many a great ruler. I've lost count of the wars I've seen won more by medics and engineers than mere soldiery. Such infective beings, too small to see, assuredly exist, prince, and believe me so do those designed, made and controlled by powers beyond your grasping." Ferbin opened his mouth to say something but Hyrlis went on, "Your own faith holds the same idea centrally, prince. Do you not believe that the WorldGod sees everything? How do you think it does that?"

Ferbin felt baulked, tripped up. "It is a god!" he said, blustering.

"If you treat it as such then such it is," Hyrlis said reasonably. "However, it is unarguably a member of a long-declining species with a clearly traceable galactic lineage and evolutionary line. It is another corporeal being, prince, and the fact that your people have chosen to call it a god does not mean that it is particularly powerful, all-seeing even within the limitations of Sursamen, or indeed sane." Ferbin wanted to speak but Hyrlis held up one hand. "No one knows why Xinthians inhabit Shellworld Cores, prince. Theories include them being sent there by their own kind as a punishment, or to isolate them because they have become infectiously diseased, or mad. Some speculate they're there because the individual Xinthians concerned are simply fascinated by Shellworlds. Another guess has it that each seeks somehow to defend its chosen Shellworld, though against what nobody knows, and the truth is that Tensile Aeronathaurs are not in themselves especially powerful creatures, and seem to scorn the kind of high-level weaponry that might compensate for that lack. All in all, not much of a God, prince."

"We claim it as our God, sir," Ferbin said frostily. "Not as some mythical Universal Creator." He glanced at Holse, looking for support, or at least acknowledgement.

Holse wasn't about to get involved in any theological arguments. He looked serious and nodded, hoping this would do.

Hyrlis just smiled.

"So you are saying we have no privacy?" Ferbin said, feeling angry and dismayed.

"Oh, you may have." Hyrlis shrugged. "Perhaps nobody watches you, including your god. But if others do, and you can persuade them to share that recording, then you will have a weapon to use against tyl Loesp."

"But sir," Holse said, "given such fantastical apparatus, might not anything and everything be faked?"

"It might, but people can be quite good at spotting what has been faked. And the effect on people who do *not* know that anything can be faked is usually profound. Revealed at the right moment, such a recording, if it exists, may so visibly shake tyl Loesp or his co-conspirators that their immediate reaction leaves no doubt in the unprejudiced mind that they are guilty."

"And how might we discover whether such a recording exists?" Ferbin asked. It still all sounded absurdly far-fetched to him, even in this entire hierarchical realm of far-fetched world beyond far-fetched world.

"It may be as simple as just asking the right people," Hyrlis said. He was still standing beside the down-sloped windows. Something flashed white far away on the dark plain below, briefly illuminating one side of his face. Some part of the initial illumination remained, fading slowly to yellow. "Find someone sympathetic in the Culture and ask them. Your sister, prince, would seem an obvious choice, and, being in Special Circumstances, she would stand a good chance of being able to find out the truth, even if it is hidden, and even if it is not the Culture itself that is doing the observing. Look to your sister, prince. She may hold your answer."

"Given your own refusal to help, I have little choice, sir."

Hyrlis shrugged. "Well, family should stick together," he said casually. Another flash lit up his face, and – away in the distance – a great rolling, rising glowing cloud of yellow surged with an unstoppable slowness into the night air. The orange-ruddy light from the huge climbing cloud lit up distant hills and mountains, rubbing them blood-coloured.

"You might have imparted this information in your own quarters," Ferbin told the man. "Why bring us here, amongst these wretches and above this savagery, to tell us something you might have told over dinner?"

"So that we might, appropriately, observe, prince," Hyrlis said. He nodded at the landscape below. "We look down upon all this, and perhaps are looked down on in turn. It is entirely possible that everything we see here is only taking place at all so that it may be observed."

"Meaning what, sir?" Holse asked, when Ferbin didn't. Also, their host looked as though he had no mind to add any more; he just gazed languidly out through the slanted windows over the red, under-lit clouds and the spark-infested darkness of the cratered landscape beneath.

Hyrlis turned to Holse. "Meaning that this whole conflict, this entire war here is manufactured. It is prosecuted for the viewing benefit of the Nariscene, who have always regarded waging war as one of the highest and most noble arts. Their place among the Involveds of the galactic community sadly precludes them from taking part in meaningful conflicts themselves any more, but they have the licence, the means and the will to cause other, mentored, client civilisations to war amongst themselves at their behest. The conflict we observe here, in which I am proud to play a part, is one such artificial dispute, instigated and maintained for and by the Nariscene for no other reason than that they might observe the proceedings and draw vicarious satisfaction from them."

Ferbin made a snorting noise.

Holse looked sceptical. "That really true, sir?" he asked. "I mean, as acknowledged by all concerned?"

Hyrlis smiled. A great distant, rumbling, roaring sound seemed to make the airship shiver on the wind. "Oh, you will find many a superficially convincing excuse and *casus belli* and there are given and seemingly accepted justifications, everything modelled to provide pretexts and keep people like the Culture from intervening to stop the fun, but it is all dressing, disguise, a feint. The truth is as I have said. Depend on it."

"And you are proud to take part in what you effectively

describe as a travesty, a show-war, a dishonourable and cruel charade for decadent and unfeeling alien powers?" Ferbin said, trying to sound – and, to some degree, succeeding in sounding – contemptuous.

"Yes, prince," Hyrlis said reasonably. "I do what I can to make this war as humane in its inhumanity as I can, and in any case, I always know that however bad it may be, its sheer unnecessary awfulness at least helps guarantee that we are profoundly not in some designed and overseen universe and so have escaped the demeaning and demoralising fate of existing solely within some simulation."

Ferbin looked at him for a few moments. "That is absurd," he said.

"Nevertheless," Hyrlis said casually, then stretched his arms out and rolled his head as though tired. "Let's go back, shall we?"

The Nariscene ship *Hence the Fortress*, a venerable Comet-class star cruiser, lifted from a deep ravine where a poisoned stream of black water moved like liquefied shadow. The craft rose above the rim of the fissure into light airs moving quietly across a landscape of livid sands beneath a soft-looking grey overcast. It accelerated into the darker skies above, finding space within minutes. The ship carried a cargo of several million human souls held petrified within a variety of nanoscale storage matrices, and two human males. The gravity was back to what the Nariscene regarded as normal, and so was much more acceptable to both men.

They had to share one small cabin extemporised for human occupation from some storage space, but were uncomplaining, being mostly just thankful to be away from the oppressive gravity of Bulthmaas and the unsettling presence of Xide Hyrlis.

They had stayed only two more days and nights – as far as such terms meant anything in the warren of deeply buried caverns and tunnels where they'd been kept. Hyrlis had appeared casually unbothered when they professed a desire to be away as soon as possible after he'd told Ferbin he was unable to help.

The morning after he'd taken them to the great airship full of the wounded, Hyrlis summoned them to a hemispherical chamber perhaps twenty metres in diameter where an enormous map of what looked like nearly half of the planet was displayed, showing what appeared to be a single vast continent punctuated by a dozen or so small seas fed by short rivers running from jagged mountain ranges. The map bulged towards the unseen ceiling like a vast balloon lit from inside by hundreds of colours and tens of thousands of tiny glittering symbols, some gathered together in groups large and small, others strung out in speckled lines and yet more scattered individually.

Hyrlis looked down on this vast display from a wide balcony halfway up the wall, talking quietly with a dozen or so uniformed human figures who responded in even more hushed tones. As they murmured away, the map itself changed, rotating and tipping to bring different parts of the landscape to the fore and moving various collections of the glittering symbols about, often developing quite different patterns and then halting while Hyrlis and the other men huddled and conferred, before returning to its earlier configuration.

"There's a Nariscene vessel scheduled to call in a couple of days' time," he told Ferbin and Holse, though his gaze was still directed at the great bulge of the dully glowing display, where various numbers of the glittering symbols, which Ferbin assumed represented military units, were moving about. It was clear now that some of the units, coloured grey-blue and shown fuzzily and in less detail than the rest, must represent the enemy. "It'll take you to Syaung-un," Hyrlis said. "That's a Morthanveld Nestworld, one of the main transfer ports between the Morthanveld and the Culture." His gaze roamed the huge globe, never resting. "Should find a ship there'll take you to the Culture."

"I am grateful," Ferbin said stiffly. He found it difficult to be anything other than formally polite with Hyrlis after being rejected by him, though Hyrlis himself seemed barely to notice or care.

The display halted, then flickered, showing various end-patterns in succession. Hyrlis shook his head and waved one arm. The great round map flicked back to its starting state again and there was much sighing and stretching amongst the uniformed advisers or generals clustered around him.

Holse nodded at the map. "All this, sir. Is it a game?"

Hyrlis smiled, still looking at the great glowing bubble of the display. "Yes," he said. "It's all a game."

"Does it start from what you might call reality, though?" Holse asked, stepping close to the balcony's edge, obviously fascinated, his face lit by the great glowing hemisphere. Ferbin said nothing. He had given up trying to get his servant to be more discreet.

"From what we call reality, as far as we know it, yes," Hyrlis said. He turned to look at Holse. "Then we use it to try out possible dispositions, promising strategies and various tactics, looking for those that offer the best results, assuming the enemy acts and reacts as we predict."

"And will they be doing the same thing as regards you?"

"Undoubtably."

"Might you not simply play the game against each other then, sir?" Holse suggested cheerily. "Dispensing with all the actual slaughtering and maiming and destruction and desolating and such like? Like in the old days, when two great armies met and, counting themselves about equal, called up champions, one from each, their individual combat counting by earlier agreement as determining the whole result, so sending many a frightened soldier safely back to his farm and loved ones."

Hyrlis laughed. The sound was obviously as startling and unusual to the generals and advisers on the balcony as it was to Ferbin and Holse. "I'd play if they would!" Hyrlis said. "And accept the verdict gladly regardless." He smiled at Ferbin, then to Holse said, "But no matter whether we are all in a still greater game, this one here before us is at a cruder grain than that which it models. Entire battles, and sometimes therefore wars, can hinge on a jammed gun, a failed battery, a single shell being dud or an individual soldier suddenly turning and running, or throwing himself on a grenade."

Hyrlis shook his head. "That cannot be fully modelled, not reliably, not consistently. That you need to play out in reality, or the most detailed simulation you have available, which is effectively the same thing."

Holse smiled sadly. "Matter, eh, sir?"

"Matter." Hyrlis nodded. "And anyway, where would be the fun in just playing a game? Our hosts could do that themselves. No. They need us to play out the greater result. Nothing else will do. We ought to feel privileged to be so valuable, so irreplaceable. We may all be mere particles, but we are each fundamental!"

Hyrlis sounded close to laughing again, then his tone and whole demeanour changed as he looked to one side, where no one was standing. "And don't think yourselves any better," he said quietly. Ferbin *tsk*-ed loudly and turned his head away as Hyrlis continued, "What is the sweet and easy continuance of all things Cultural, if not based on the cosy knowledge of good works done in one's name, far away? Eh?" He nodded at nobody and nothing visible. "What do you say, my loyal viewers? Aye to that? Contact and SC; they play your own real games, and let the trillions of pampered sleepers inhabiting all those great rolling cradles we call Orbitals run smoothly through the otherly scary night, unvexed."

"You're obviously busy," Ferbin said matter-of-factly to Hyrlis. "May we leave you now?"

Hyrlis smiled. "Yes, prince. Get to your own dreams, leave us with ours. By all means be gone."

Ferbin and Holse turned to go.

"Holse!" Hyrlis called.

Choubris and Ferbin both turned to look back.

"Sir?" Holse said.

"Holse, if I offered you the chance to stay here and general for me, play this great game, would you take it? It would be for riches and for power, both here and now and elsewhere and elsewhen, in better, less blasted places than this sorry cinder. D'you take it, eh?"

Holse laughed. "Course not, sir! You fun me, sure you must!"

"Of course," Hyrlis said, grinning. He looked at Ferbin, who was standing looking confused and angry at his servant's side. "Your man is no fool, prince," Hyrlis told him.

Ferbin stood up straight in the grinding, pulling gravity. "I did not think him so."

Hyrlis nodded. "Naturally. Well, I too must travel very soon. If I don't see you before you go, let me wish you both a good journey and a fair arrival."

"Your wishes flatter us, sir," Ferbin said, insincerely.

Hyrlis was indeed not there to see them off when they departed.

Over thirteen long days during which Ferbin and Holse were left to themselves by the ship and its crew and spent most of their time either sleeping or playing games, the star cruiser *Hence the Fortress* took them to the Nariscene Globular Transfer Facility of Sterut.

A Morthanveld tramp ship with no name, just a long serial number they both forgot, picked them up from there on one of its semi-regular, semicircular routes and took them onwards to the great Morthanveld Nestworld of Syaung-un.

19. Dispatches

Oramen was standing by the window looking out over the city from his chambers in the palace in Pourl. The morning was bright and misty and Neguste, singing noisily but tunelessly, was next door, running him a bath when Fanthile rapped at the door. Neguste, who patently believed that volume was the ideal compensation for being tone-deaf, didn't hear the door, so Oramen answered it himself.

He and Fanthile stood out on the apartment balcony while Oramen read a note the palace secretary had brought.

"Rasselle?" he said. "The Deldeyn capital?"

Fanthile nodded. "Your mother's husband has been ordered there, as mayor. They will arrive during the next few days."

Oramen let out a deep breath and looked first at Fanthile and then out at the city; canals glinted in the distance and banners of steam and smoke rose from a scattered forest of factory chimneys. "You know that tyl Loesp suggests I go to the Falls of the Hyeng-zhar?" he said, not looking at the palace secretary.

"I have heard, sir. They are a few days from Rasselle, I'm told."

"I would be in charge of the excavations." Oramen sighed. "Tyl Loesp believes it would help the bringing together of the people and institutions of the Ninth and the Eighth, that my presence there would help the effort to recruit more Sarl to the great project of the investigation of the mysterious ruins there. Also, it would give me a serious and proper purpose in life, so improving my reputation with the people."

"You are the Prince Regent, sir," the palace secretary said. "That might be thought reputation enough by some."

"By some, perhaps, but these are changed days, Fanthile. Perhaps they are even the New Age that my father talked about, when feats of practical business matter more than those of arms."

"There are reports that certain far dependencies dispute with various of tyl Loesp's decrees, sir. Werreber already wants to form a new army to help instil some provincial discipline. The gentleman we speak of would be wise not to disband all the forces."

Tyl Loesp's clamorous triumph had been held just a few days earlier; parts of the city were still recovering. It had been a celebration on a scale and of an intensity Pourl had never seen before, certainly not under the late king. Tyl Loesp had provided for banquets in every street, a week's free drink from every public house and a bounty for every inhabitant within the walls. Games, sports, competitions and concerts of every sort, all freely open to all, had taken place and a patchwork of small riots had broken out in various sections of the city, requiring quelling by constables and militia.

An enormous parade had been staged consisting of the victorious army all bright and polished, smiling and whole under a sea of fluttering banners, complete with wildly caparisoned warbeasts and a host of captured Deldeyn soldiery, artillery pieces, military vehicles and war engines. Streets had been widened, buildings knocked down and rivers and gullies covered over to provide a thoroughfare long and wide enough to accommodate the great procession.

Tyl Loesp had ridden at the head, Werreber and his generals a little behind. In the Parade Field where the kilometres-long procession had ended up, the regent had announced a year without tax (this later turned out to mean a short-year without certain mostly rather obscure taxes), an amnesty for minor criminals, the disbandment of various ancillary regiments with the release – with pensions – of nearly one hundred thousand men, and an extended mission to the Ninth that would mean that both he and the Prince Regent would spend significant time in Rasselle and the Deldeyn provinces, bringing the benefits of Sarl rule and wisdom to that reduced but highly fruitful and promising land.

Oramen, sitting in the shade of the flag-fluttering parade stand with the rest of the nobility, had been warned of this last provision only an hour before, and so was able not to look surprised.

He had felt an initial burst of fury that he had been simply told this rather than consulted, or even asked, but that had gone quickly. He'd soon started to wonder if such a move, such a break with Pourl might not be a good idea. All the same, to be so instructed . . .

"You might refuse to go, sir," Fanthile pointed out.

Oramen turned away from the view over the city. "I might, in theory, I suppose," he said.

"That's the bath ready, sir! Oh, hello, Mr Palace Secretary sir!" Neguste called, marching into the room behind them.

"Thank you, Neguste," Oramen said, and his servant winked and retreated.

Fanthile nodded at the note in Oramen's hand. "Does this make the decision for you, sir?"

"I had already decided I might go," Oramen said. He smiled. "The very idea of the Hyeng-zhar fascinates me, Fanthile." He laughed. "It would be something to control all that power, in any sense!"

Fanthile refused to be impressed. "May I speak bluntly, sir?"

"Yes. Of course."

"Tyl Loesp might worry that leaving you here while he tightens his grip on Rasselle would allow you to build too independent a foundation of regard amongst the nobles, the people and even parliament here. Removing you to somewhere so out of the way, however impressive that place might be as an attraction, could appear to some almost like a form of exile. You could refuse to go, sir. You'd be within your rights. By some arguments your place is here, amongst the people who might love you all the better with greater acquaintance. I have heard who will be there around you. This General Foise, for one; he is entirely tyl Loesp's man. They all are. All his men, I mean. They are loyal to him rather than to Sarl or your father's memory, or you."

Oramen felt relieved. He'd been expecting a scolding or something equally disagreeable. "That is your bluntest, dear Fanthile?" he asked, smiling.

"It is as I see things, sir."

"Well, tyl Loesp may arrange me as he sees fit, for the moment. I'll play along. Let him have his time. These men you mention may see their loyalty as lying with him, but as long as he is loyal in turn, which he most unquestionably is, then there's neither difference nor harm. I shall be king in due course and – even allowing for all our New Age talk of parliamentary oversight – I'll have my time then."

"That gentleman might grow used to arranging things to his liking. He may wish to extend his time."

"Perhaps so, but once I am king, his choices become limited, don't you think?"

Fanthile frowned. "I certainly know I'd like to think that, sir. Whether I can in honest conscience allow myself to hold such a view's another thing." He nodded at the note which Oramen still held. "I think the fellow may be forcing your actions in this, sir, and I believe he may come to enjoy the habit of doing so, if he does not already."

Oramen took a deep breath. The air smelled so good and fresh up here. Unlike the depths of the city, where, annoyingly, so much of the fun was to be found. He let the air out of his lungs. "Oh, let tyl Loesp enjoy his triumph, Fanthile. He's continued my father's purpose as he himself might have wished, and I'd be a churl – and look one, too, in the eyes of your precious people – if I tantrummed now while I am still, in so many eyes, an untried youth." He smiled encouragingly at the troubled-looking face of the older man. "I'll bend with tyl Loesp's current while it's at its strongest; it might be bruising not to. I'll beat against its ebb when I see fit." He waved the letter Fanthile had given him. "I'll go, Fanthile. I think I need to. But I thank you for all your help and advice." He handed the note back to the palace secretary. "Now, old friend, I really must go to my bath."

"Open your eyes, prince," Fanthile said, for a moment – astoundingly! – not standing aside to let the Prince Regent past. "I do not know what ill's been done about us since your father's death, sir, but there's a smell that hangs over too much that's happened. We need all take care not to be infected by its noxiousness; it might prove each one of us all too mortal." He waited another moment, as though to see whether this had sunk in, then nodded a bow and, head still lowered, stood to one side.

Oramen didn't know what to say that wouldn't embarrass the fellow further following such an outburst, so he just walked past him on his way to his toilet.

A week later he was on his way to the Hyeng-zhar.

What with all the preparations and general fuss caused by the move, he hadn't seen Fanthile again before leaving Pourl. The morning of the day he was due to go, shortly after he'd heard he was to have his very own personal guard of two stalwart knights, he'd received a note from Fanthile asking to see him, but there hadn't been time.

Jerle Batra took the signal during a break in the peace negoti-ations. These were proving protracted. He wasn't directly involved in the haggling, of course – it boggled one to think what the indigents would make of a cross between a talking bush and an expanding fence – but he was overseeing while some of the others in the mission did their best to keep people focused. In the end it had to be the natives themselves who made this work, but a bit of judicious prodding helped on occa-sion.

He rose a couple of kilometres into the air from the marquee in the middle of the great tent city on the grassy swell of plain where the negotiations were taking place. Up here the air smelled fresh and clean. It felt deliciously cool, too. You experienced changes in temperature so quickly in this form; you felt the wind blow through you. There was nothing quite like it.

My dear old friend, he communicated. The signal was passing from and to the excursion platform *Quonber*, currently almost directly overhead but on the fringes of space. *To what, etc.?*

Jerle Ruule Batra, said a familiar voice. *Good-day.*

The *It's My Party And I'll Sing If I Want To* was an Escarpment-class GCU which had been strongly associated with Special Circumstances for nearly as long as Jerle Batra himself. Batra had no idea where the ship actually was in a true, phys-ical sense, but the old craft had gone to the trouble of sending a working-scale personality construct to talk to him here on Prasadal. This implied a matter of more than passing importance.

To you too, he sent, *wherever.*

Thank you. How goes your peace conference?

Slowly. Having exhausted the possibilities of every other form of mass-murder they could possibly employ against each other, the natives now appear intent on boring each other to death. They may finally have discovered their true calling.

Still, cause for optimism. My congratulations to all. And I'm told you have a child!

I most certainly do not have a child. I am looking after a child for a colleague. That is all.

Nevertheless, that is more than one might have expected of you.

She asked. I could hardly refuse.

How interesting. However, to business.

By all means.

Listen to this.

There followed a compressed version of the message sent by the *Now We Try It My Way* to its old home MSV, the *Qualifier*, describing its odd encounter with what had appeared to be an Oct ship above the planet Zaranche, but hadn't been.

Very well. This was only mildly interesting and Batra did not see how it might involve him. *And?*

It is believed that the whole Oct fleet above Zaranche, save for one Primarian-class ship, probably the first arrived, was not really there. It was a ghost fleet.

The Oct are at that stage, though, aren't they? Batra sent. *They're still trying to puff themselves up, still trying on parents' shoes, making themselves look bigger.*

Batra immediately knew somebody somewhere in SC was going to be reading all sorts of paranoid nonsense into something like this. Ghost ships; pretend fleets. Scary! Except it wasn't, it couldn't be. The Oct were an irrelevance. Better still, they were the Morthanveld's irrelevance, or the Nariscene's irrelevance, depending on where you chose to draw the line. An equiv-tech Involved getting up to this sort of misdirection might mean something significant. The Oct doing the same thing was profoundly so-whattish. They were probably just trying to impress their Nariscene mentors or had left a switch on they shouldn't or something.

But SC took this sort of random dross terribly seriously. The finest Minds in the Culture had an almost chronic need for serious stuff to involve them, and this, patently, was their latest dose. We make our own problems, Batra thought. We've seeded the fucking galaxy with travellers, wanderers, students, reporters, practical ethnologists, peripatetic philosophers, hands-on ex-sociologists, footloose retirees, freelance ambassadors or whatever they're called this season and a hundred other categories of far too easily amazed amateur and they're all forever reporting back stuff that looks like deeply weird shit to them that wouldn't pass the first filter of even the least experienced Contact Unit's data intake systems.

We've filled the known universe with credulous idiots and we think we've sneakily contributed to our own safety by making it hard for anything untoward to creep in under our sensor coverage whereas in fact we've just made sure we harvest zillions of false positives and probably made the really serious shit harder to spot when it does eventually come flying.

No, the GCU's construct sent. *We don't think the Oct are trying to look more impressive than they are, not in this case.*

Wind moved through Batra's bushy body like a sigh. *What happened after the close encounter?* he asked, dutifully.

We don't know. Haven't been able to contact the Erratic since. Could have been captured. Conceivably, even, destroyed. A ship – a warship, no less – has been sent to investigate, though it's still eight days away.

Destroyed? Batra suppressed a laugh. *Seriously? Are we within capabilities here?*

The Oct Primarian-class has the weaponry and other systems to overwhelm a cobbled-together ex-GTC mongrel, yes.

But are we within likelihood? Batra asked. *Are we even still within the realm of anything other than paranoid lunacy? What is imagined to be their motive in doing whatever might have been done to this Erratic?*

To stop this getting out.

But why? To what end? What's so important about this Zaranche place they'd even try to kidnap any Culture ship, hopeless old junkyard oddball or not?

Nothing about Zaranche; rather what this has led to.

Which would be what?

A subtle but thorough investigation into Oct ship movements and placements over the last fifty days or so. Which has involved quite a few Contact, SC and even VFP/warships dropping everything and hightailing off to a variety of obscure backwood destinations, many well within the Morthanveld sphere.

I am suitably impressed. It must be regarded as awfully important for us to risk annoying our so-sensitive co-Involveds at such an allegedly delicate time. And what was the result of all this high-speed, high-value-asset sleuthing?

There are lots of ghost fleets.

What? For the first time, Batra felt something other than a sort of amused, studied disdain. Some legacy of his human form, buried in the transcribed systems that held his personality, made him suddenly feel the coldness of the air up here. Just for an instant he was fully aware that a naked human exposed to this temperature would have hairs standing up on their skin now.

The ghost fleet above Zaranche is one of eleven, the ship continued. *The others are here.* A glyph of a portion of the galaxy perhaps three thousand light years in diameter displayed itself in Batra's mind. He swam into the image, looked around, pulled back, played around with a few settings. *That's quite a large part of what one might call Oct Space,* he sent.

Indeed. Approximately seventy-three per cent of the entire Oct Prime Fleet would seem not to be where it appears to be.

Why are they bunched like that? Why those places? All the locations, all the places where these ghost fleets had drawn up were out of the way: isolated planets, backwater habitats and seldom-frequented deep-space structures.

It is believed they are grouped where they are to avoid detection.

But they're being open about it; they're telling people where they are.

I mean detection of the fact they are ghosts. The cover story, as it were, is that a series of special convocations is taking place which will lead to some profound new departure for the Oct; some new civilisational goal, perhaps. Possibly one linked to their continuing attempts at betterment and advancement upon the galactic stage. We suspect, however, that this is only partially true. The convocations are a ruse to excuse the departure of so many front-line ships.

Had they better technology, the GCU's personality construct continued, *the Oct would, one imagines, have kept their ghost ships appearing to carry out normal duties while the real ones left for wherever it is they have in fact left for. Their ability so to deceive is limited, however. Any high-Involved ship – certainly one of ours or the Morthanveld, for example, and possibly most Nariscene craft – would be able to tell that what they were looking at was not a real Oct ship. So the genuine craft left the normal intercourse of galactic ship life and these rather crude representations were assembled in locations specifically chosen so that the ships' lack of authenticity would most likely go unnoticed.*

Had he still inhabited human form Batra would, at this point, have frowned and scratched his head. *But why? To what end? Are these maniacs going to war?*

We don't know. They have outstanding disputes with a few species and there is a particular and recently inflamed gripe with the Aultridia, but the whole of Oct society does not appear to be presently configured for hostilities. It is configured for something unusual, certainly (Batra could hear puzzlement expressed in the ship's voice), *possibly including some sort of hostile or at least dynamic action, but not all-out war. The Aultridia are taken to be their most pressing potential adversaries but they would almost certainly defeat the Oct as matters stand at present. The models show ninety-plus per cent likelihood, very consistently.*

So where are the real ships?

That, old chum, is very much the question.

Batra had been thinking. *And why am I being included here?*

More modelling. Using the pattern of affected snuck-away ships and a pre-existing profile of Oct interests, we have drawn up a list of likely destinations for the real craft.

Another layered diaglyph blossomed in Batra's mind. Ah-ha, he thought.

The marginally most likely disposition is a distributed one, or rather one of two not dissimilar choices: in each, the Primarians and other strategic craft take up various different positions, either defensive or offensive, depending. The defensive model implies a more even spread of forces than the offensive one, which favours greater concentration. These represent options one and two respectively in the modelled plausibility grading. There is, however, a third option, shown here.

The other layers fell away but Batra had already spotted the pattern and the place within it that was its focus.

They could be gathering round Sursamen, he sent.

The General Contact Unit *It's My Party And I'll Sing If I Want To* still sounded puzzled: *Well, quite.*

The Integrity
of Objects

20. Inspiral, Coalescence, Ringdown

The interior of the Morthanveld Great Ship *Inspiral, Coalescence, Ringdown* was generally experienced virtually even by those for whom it was designed and who had built it. Externally the ship was a flattened sphere fifty kilometres in diameter. It resembled a vast droplet of blue ice whose surface had been blasted with several million jewels, about half of which had subsequently fallen out, leaving behind small craters.

Its main internal space was enormous; bigger than anything on a Culture GSV. The best way to think of it, Anaplian had been told by Skalpapta, her Morthanveld liaison officer, was as if you'd got nineteen balloons full of water each nearly ten kilometres in diameter, arranged them into a rough hexagon so that they formed as near a circle as possible, then squished them all together so that the walls between them flattened out. Then you added another two layers of seven spheres, one above and one below, under the same principle. Finally you removed all those flat, separating walls.

The whole space was criss-crossed by strands and cables supporting hundreds of millions of polyp-like living quarters and multitudinous travel tubes, many with a vacuum inside to speed up transit times.

As on most Morthanveld ships, the water was generally kept as clean as desirable by fixed and static scrubbing units; nevertheless, the fact was that the bait species and accrescent flora the Morthanveld liked to feed on needed water with nutrients in it, and the Morthanveld themselves regarded having to visit some special place to relieve oneself of waste as the mark of a species insufficiently at home with itself. Or gas-breathing, which was almost as embarrassing.

The water they lived, swam, worked and played within, then, was not perfectly unclouded. However, it was always pleasant to have a clear view, especially in such a vast space.

The Morthanveld very much approved of themselves, and the larger the numbers of their kind there were present, the more self-approval they felt. Being able to see the hundreds of millions of their fellows a Great Ship normally carried was generally regarded as an extremely good thing, so rather than rely on their naked eyes to see their way round a space as vast as that of a Great Ship's interior, they used thin-film screens covering their eyes to present them with the view they'd be able to see had the water been perfectly clear.

Djan Seriy had decided to adopt the same strategy and so swam with a modified thin-film screen over her own eyes. She moved through the water in a dark suit like a second skin. Around her neck was what looked like a necklace made of fluttering green fronds; a gill arrangement that provided oxygen to her nose through two small transparent tubes. This was somewhat ignominious to her, as with her old upgrades her skin would have ridged and puckered over whatever area was required to absorb the gases she needed straight out of the water.

The thin-film screen was stuck across her eyes like a flimsy transparent bandage. She had switched off her blink reflex; the alternative was to let the screen bulge out far enough for her to blink normally, but the air-gap introduced unwanted distortions. The screen provided her with the virtual view of the real space, showing the cavernous semi-spherical spaces of the Great Ship like some staggeringly vast cave system.

She could have patched directly into the ship's internal sensory view to achieve the same effect, or just swum with her own senses and not bothered with the greater, seemingly clear view, but she was being polite; using the thin-film screen meant that the ship could keep an eye on her, seeing, no doubt, what she could see, and so knowing that she wasn't getting into any Special Circumstances-style mischief.

She could also have used any one of several different kinds of public transport to get to where she was going, but had opted instead for a small personal propulsion unit which she held on to with one hand as it thrummed its way through the water. The sex toy that was really a knife missile that was really a drone had wanted to impersonate such a propulsion unit, so staying close to her, but she reckoned this was just the machine fussing and had instructed it to remain in her quarters.

Djan Seriy powered up and to the left to avoid a fore-current, found a helpful aft-current, curved round a set of long, bulbous habitats like enormous dangling fruits and then struck out towards a tall bunch of green-black spheres each between ten and thirty metres across, hanging in the water like a colossal strand of seaweed. She switched off the prop unit and swam into one of the larger spheres through a silvery circle a couple of metres across and let the draining water lower her to the soft, wet floor. Gravity again. She was spending more time aquatic than not, even including sleeping, as she explored the huge space vessel. This was her fifth day aboard and she only had another four to go. There was still much to see.

Her suit, until now coating her body as closely as paint, promptly frizzed up, forcing the water to slide off and letting it assume the look of something a fashionable young lady would choose to wear in an air-breathing environment. She stuffed her necklace gill into a pocket and – as the suit's head-part flowed downward to form an attractive frilled collar – flicked one earring to activate a temporary static field. This sorted her hair, which was, today, blonde. She kept the thin-film screen on. She thought it looked rather good on her; vaguely piratical.

Djan Seriy stepped through the cling-field into the 303rd Aliens' Lounge, where thumping music played loudly and the air was full of drug smoke and incense.

She was quickly greeted by a small cloud of tiny brightly coloured creatures like small birds, each thrown by one of the bar's patrons. Some sang welcomes, others fluttered strobed messages across their hazy wings and a few squirted scent messages at her. This was, currently, the latest greeting-fad for new arrivals at the 303rd Aliens' Lounge. Sometimes the lobbed creatures would carry notes or small parcels of narcotics or declarations of love, or they would start spouting insults, witticisms, philosophical epigrams or other messages. As Djan Seriy understood it, this was meant to be amusing.

She waited for the cloud of flittering creatures to start dissipating, thinking all the time how easy it would have been to bat, grasp and crush every one of the twenty-eight little twittering shapes around her, had she been fully enabled. She plucked the most lately arrived of the creatures out of the air and looked severely at the old-looking, purple-skinned humanoid who had thrown it. "Yours, sir," she said, as she passed his table, handing it to him. He mumbled a reply. Others nearby were calling out to her. The denizens of the 303rd were gregarious and got to know people quickly; she was already regarded as a regular after only three visits. She refused various offers of company and waved away some especially thick and pungent drug smoke; the 303rd was something of a wide-spectrum humanoid stoners' hang-out.

She acknowledged a few people as she walked to the circular bar in the middle of the Lounge, sitting glowing in the darkened space like a giant halo.

"Shjan! You're here!" shouted Tulya Puonvangi, who was what passed as the Culture's ambassador on the *Inspiral, Coalescence, Ringdown*. Djan Seriy regarded the man rather as she did the fluttering creature fad; immature and vaguely annoying. He had introduced himself shortly after she'd arrived and done his best to make himself a nuisance more or less ever since. Puonvangi was obese, pinkish, bald, and fairly human-basic on the surface save for two long, fang-like incisors which distorted his speech (he couldn't manage the hard "D' sound at the start of her first name, for example). Plus he had an eye in the back of his head which he claimed was fully functional but was apparently really no more than an affectation. He often, as now, kept it covered with an eye patch, though the eye patch – again, as now – was frequently clear. He also – he'd told her after a remarkably short time during their first meeting – had exquisitely altered genitalia, which he'd offered to show her. She had demurred.

"Hello, jear!" Puonvangi said, clutching at her elbows and bringing her close to kiss her cheeks. She allowed this to happen while remaining stiff and unresponsive. He smelled of brine, tangfruit and some sweet, unashamedly psychotropic scent. His clothes were loose, voluminous, ever gently billowing and showed slow-motion scenes of humanoid pornography. His sleeves were rolled up and she could see from the thin, fiercely glowing lines incised on his forearms that he had been grazing tattoo drugs. He released her. "How are you? Looking ra'iant as ezher! Here'sh the young fellow I wanted you to meet!" He pointed at the young, long-limbed man sitting by his side. "Shjan Sheree Araprian, this is Kra'sri Kruike. Kra'sri; say hi!"

The young man looked embarrassed. "How do you do," he said in a quiet, deep, deliciously accented voice. He had gently glowing skin of something between deep bronze and very dark green and a mass of shining, ringleted black hair. He wore perfectly cut, utterly black close-fitting trous and a short jacket. His face was quite long, his nose fairly flat, his teeth were normal but very white and his expression, beneath hooded eyes, was diffident, amused, perhaps a little wary, though modulated by what looked like a permanent smile. He had laughter lines, which made someone so otherwise young-looking appear oddly vulnerable. Chevron-cut brows and moustache looked like something new he was trying and was unsure he was getting away with. Those eyes were dark, flecked with gold.

He was almost unbearably attractive. Djan Seriy had therefore naturally gone instantly to what she regarded as her highest alert state of suspicion.

"I am Djan Seriy Anaplian," she told him. "How is your name properly pronounced?"

He grinned, glanced apologetically at a beaming, eyebrowwaggling Puonvangi. "Klatsli Quike," he told her.

She nodded. "Pleased to meet you, Klatsli Quike," she said. She took the bar stool on the far side of him, putting the young man between her and Puonvangi, who looked disappointed, though only briefly. He slammed the bar with the flat of one hand, bringing a serving unit zinging over on shining rails strung along the far side of the bar.

"Jhrinks! Shmokes! Shnorts! Inshisions!"

She agreed to drink a little to keep Puonvangi company. Quike lit up a small pipe of some fabulously fragrant herb, purely for the scent as it had no known narcotic effect, though even the aroma was almost drug-like in its headiness. Puonvangi ordered a couple of styli of tattoo drugs and – when both Djan Seriy and Quike refused to join him – grazed one into each of his arms, from wrist to elbow. The drug lines glowed so brightly at first they coloured his pink face green. He sighed and sat back in his high seat, exhaling and closing his eyes, going slack. While their host was enjoying his first rush, Quike said,

"You're from Sursamen?" He sounded apologetic, as though he wasn't supposed to know.

"I am," she said. "You know it?"

"Of," he said. "Shellworlds are a subject of mine. I study them. I find them fascinating."

"You're not alone in that."

"I know. Actually, I find it perplexing that everyone doesn't find them utterly fascinating."

Djan Seriy shrugged. "There are many fascinating places."

"Yes, but Shellworlds are something special." He put his hand to his mouth. Long fingers. He might have been blushing. "I'm sorry. You lived there. I don't need to tell you how fabulous they are."

"Well, for me it is – was – just home. When one grows up in a place, no matter how exotic it may seem to others, it is still where all the usual banalities and indignities of childhood occur. Home is always the norm. It is everywhere else that is marvellous."

She drank. He puffed on his pipe for a bit. Puonvangi sighed deeply, eyes still closed.

"And you," she said, remembering to be polite. "Where are you from? May I ask your Full Name?"

"Astle-Chulinisa Klatsli LP Quike dam Uast."

"LP?" she said. "The letters L and P?"

"The letters L and P," he confirmed, with a small nod and a mischievous smile.

"Do they stand for something?"

"They do. But it's a secret."

She looked at him doubtfully.

He laughed, spread his arms. "I'm well travelled, Ms Seriy; a Wanderer. I am older than I look, I have met many people and given and shared and received many things. I have been most places, at a certain scale. I have spent time with all the major Involveds, I have talked to Gods, shared thought with the Sublimed and tasted, as far as a human can, something of the joy of what the Minds call Infinite Fun Space. I am not the person I was when I took my Full Name, and I am not definable just by that any more. A nested mystery in the centre of my name is no more than I deserve. Trust me."

Djan Seriy thought about this. He had called himself a Wanderer (they were talking Marain, the Culture's language; it had a phoneme to denote upper case). There had always been a proportion of people in the Culture, or at least people who were from the Culture originally, who termed themselves so. She found it difficult not to think of them as a class. They did indeed just wander; most doing so within the Culture, going from Orbital to Orbital, place to place, travelling on cruise ships and trampers as a rule and on Contact vessels when they could.

Others travelled amongst the rest of the Involved and Aspirant species, existing – when they encountered societies shockingly unenlightened enough not to have cast off the last shackles of monetary exchange – through inter-civilisational co-supportive understandings, or by using some vanishingly microscopic fraction of the allegedly infinite resources the Culture commanded to pay their way.

Some cast their adventures wider still, which was where problems sometimes occurred. The mere presence of such a person in a sufficiently undeveloped society could change it, sometimes profoundly, if that person was blind to what their being there might be doing to those they had come to live among, or at least look at. Not all such people agreed to be monitored by Contact during their travels, and even though Contact was perfectly unabashed when it came to spying on travellers who strayed into vulnerable societies whether they liked it or not, it did sometimes miss individuals. There was a whole section of the organisation devoted to watching developing civilisations for signs that some so-called Wanderer had – with prior intent, opportunistically or even accidentally – turned into a local Mad Professor, Despot, Prophet or God. There were other categories, but these four formed the most popular and predictable avenues people's fantasies took them along when they lost their moral bearings down amongst the prims.

Most Wanderers caused no such problems, however, and such itinerants normally found somewhere to call home eventually, usually back in the Culture. Some, though, never settled anywhere, roaming all their lives, and of these a few – a surprisingly large proportion compared to the rest of the Culture's population – lived, effectively, for ever. Or at least lived until they met some almost inevitably violent, irrecoverable end. There were rumours – usually in the form of personal boasts – of individuals who had been around since the formation of the Culture itself, nomads who'd drifted the galaxy and its near infinitude of peoples, societies, civilisations and places for thousands upon thousands of years.

Trust me, he had said. "I think I do not," she told him at last, narrowing her eyes a little.

"Really?" he asked, looking hurt. "I'm telling the truth," he said quietly. He seemed half small boy and half untroubled ancient, darkly self-possessed.

"I'm sure it appears so to you," she said, arching one eyebrow. She drank some more; she had ordered a Za's Revenge, but said concoction was unknown to the bar machine, which had made its own speciality. It served. Quike took another pipe of incense herb.

"And you're from the Eighth?" Quike said, coughing a little, though with a broad smile wreathed in violet smoke.

"I am," she said. He smiled shyly and hid behind some smoke. "You're well informed," she told him.

"Thank you." He suddenly mugged an expression of what might have been pretended fear. "And an SC agent too, yes?"

"I wouldn't get too excited," she told him. "I have been demilitarised."

He grinned again. Almost cheekily. "All the same."

Djan Seriy would have sighed if she had felt able to. She had a feeling she was being set up here – Mr Quike was *so* handsome and attractive it was positively suspicious – she just wasn't sure yet by whom.

They left Puonvangi at the 303rd in the company of a riotous party of Birilisi conventioneers. The Birilisi were an avian species and much given to excessive narcoticism; they and Puonvangi were guaranteed to get on. There was much fluttering.

They suited up and went to a place Quike knew where the aquaticised gathered. These were humanoids fully converted to water-dwelling. The space was full of what looked like every kind of watergoing species – or at least those below a certain size. The warm, hazy water was full of skin scents, incomprehensible sounds of every appreciable frequency and curious, musical pulsations. They had to stay suited up and laughed bubbles as they tried drinking underwater, using smart cups and self-sealing straws. They talked via what was basically a pre-electricity speaking tube.

They got to the end of their drinks together.

She was looking away from him, watching two thin, flamboyantly colourful, fabulously frilled creatures three metres tall with great long, expressionless but somehow dignified heads and faces. They were floating a short distance away from her, poised facing each other just out of the touching range of their frills, which waved so fast they flickered. She wondered were they talking, arguing, flirting?

Quike touched her arm to attract her attention. "Shall we go?" he asked. "There's something you've got to see." She looked down, at his hand still resting on her arm.

They took a bubble car through the enclosed galaxy of the Great Ship's main internal space to where his quarters were. They were still suited up, sat side by side in the speeding car, communicating by lace as the gaudily bewildering expanses of the ship's interior swept around them.

You really must see this, he said, glancing at her.

No need to overstate, she told him. *I am already here, going with you.* She had never been very good at being romantic. Wooing and seduction, even played as a kind of game, seemed dishonest to her somehow. Again, she blamed her upbringing, though she wouldn't have argued the point too determinedly if pressed on it; ultimately she was prepared to concede that maybe, at some level beyond even childhood indoctrination, it was just her.

His living space was a trio of four-metre spheres bunched in with thousands of others on a kilometres-long string of alien habs situated near the vast curved wall of the main space's outer periphery. The room was entered by entirely the stickiest, slowest-working gel field lock she'd ever encountered. Inside it was rather small and brightly lit. The air tasted clean, almost sharp. Nothing in it looked personalised. Furniture or fittings of debatable utility lay scattered about the floor and wall. The general colour scheme was of green components over cerise backgrounds. Not, to Djan Seriy's eye, a happy combination. There was a sort of glisteny look to a lot of the surfaces, as though a film or membrane had been shrink-wrapped around everything.

"Another drink?" he suggested.

"Oh, I suppose so," she said.

"I have some Chapantlic spirit," he said, digging in a small floor chest. He saw her run a finger along the edge of what appeared to be a sponge-covered seat, frowning as her skin encountered something slick and smooth coating it, and said, "Sorry. Everything is sort of sealed in; covered. All a bit anti-septic. I do apologise." He looked embarrassed as he waved a couple of glittering goblets shaped like inverted bells and a small bottle. "I picked up some sort of weird allergy thing on my travels and they can only fix it back in the Culture. Wherever I live I need it to be pretty clean. I'll get it dealt with, but for now, well . . ."

Djan Seriy was not at all convinced this was true. "Is it in any way infectious?" she asked. Her own immune system, still fully functioning and well into the comprehensive end of the spectrum of congenital Culture protection, had signalled nothing amiss. After a couple of hours in such close proximity to Mr Quike there would have been at least some hint of any untoward virus, spore or similar unpleasantness.

"No!" he said, motioning her to sit down. They sat on opposite sides of a narrow table. He poured some of the spirit; it was brown and highly viscous.

The seat Djan Seriy was sitting on felt slidey. A tiny new suspicion had entered her head. Had the fellow thought to bring her here for something other than sex? She found the shrink-wrapped nature of the fittings in the man's quarters disturbing. What was really going on here? Ought she to be worried? It was almost beyond imagining that any civilian in their right mind might think to offer some sort of mischief or mistreatment to an SC agent, even a de-fanged one, but then people were nothing if not varied and strange; who knew what strangenesses went on their heads?

Just to be on the safe side, she monitored the Great Ship's available systems with her neural lace. The living space was partially shielded, but that was normal enough. She could see where she was in the ship, and the ship knew where she was. A relief, she supposed.

The young-looking Mr Quike offered her a crystal bell-goblet. It rang faintly the instant she touched it. "They're meant to do that," he explained. "The vibrations are supposed to make it taste better."

She took the little goblet and leant forward. "LP Quike," she said, "what exactly are your intentions?" She could smell the spirit, albeit faintly.

He looked almost flustered. "First a toast," he said, holding up his bell-goblet.

"No," she said, lowering her head a little and narrowing her eyes. "First the truth." Her nose was reporting nothing unexpected in the fumes rising from the goblet of spirit in her hand but she wanted to be sure, giving bits of her brain time to do a proper processing job on the chemicals her nasal membranes were picking up. "Tell me what it was you wanted to show me here."

Quike sighed and put down his bell-goblet. He fastened her with his gaze. "I picked up an ability to read minds on my travels," he said quickly, possibly a little annoyed. "I just wanted to show off, I suppose."

"Read minds?" Djan Seriy said sceptically. Ship Minds could read human minds, though they were not supposed to; specialist equipment could read human minds and she imagined you could make some kind of android machine embodying the same technology that could do so too, but an ordinary human being? That seemed unlikely.

This was depressing. If Klatsli Quike was a fantasist or just mad then she was certainly not going to have sex with him.

"It's true!" he told her. He sat forward. Their noses were now a few centimetres apart. "Just look into my eyes."

"You are serious?" Djan Seriy asked. Oh dear, this was not turning out as she'd wished at all.

"I am perfectly serious, Djan Seriy," he said quietly, and something in his voice persuaded her to humour him just a little longer. She sighed again and put the bell-goblet of spirit down on the narrow table. By now, it was clear the drink was highly alcoholic though otherwise harmless.

She looked into his eyes.

After a few moments, there was the hint of something there. A tiny red spark. She sat back, blinking. The man in front of her, smiling faintly – looking quite serious and not at all pleased with himself – put his finger to his lips.

What was going on? She ran what was basically an internal systems check, to reassure herself that she hadn't been unconscious even for a moment, or that she hadn't performed some movement or function she hadn't been aware of, or that less time had elapsed than she assumed. Nothing out of kilter, nothing wrong. She seemed to be okay.

Djan Seriy frowned, leant forward again.

The red spark was still there in his eyes, almost vanishingly faint. It was, she realised, coherent light; one single, pure, narrow frequency. It flickered. Very quickly.

Something approaching . . .

What approaching? Where had that thought come from? What *was* going on here?

She sat back again, blinking fast and frowning deeply, running her systems check again. Still nothing untoward. She sat forward once more. Ah. She was starting to guess what was going on.

The flickering red spark came back and she realised he was indeed signalling her. A section of his retina must be a laser, capable of sending a beam of coherent light through his eye and into hers. The signal was expressed in nonary Marain, the nine-part binary base of the Culture's language. She'd heard of this ability in SC training, though purely as an aside. It was a multi-millennia-ancient, now almost never-used amendment, long made redundant by the technology behind the neural lace. It was even something she could have made herself capable of, with a few days' notice, before she'd had her claws pulled. She concentrated.

PTA?

He was signalling a Permission To Approach burst. It was a ship signal, originally. It had been adopted as a sort of acronymic shorthand by Culture people wanting to get in closer contact with other people they weren't sure would welcome them.

PTA?

She nodded very slightly.

Djan Seriy, the signal said. *I think you are receiving me, but please scratch your right cheek with your left hand if you are understanding all of this. Scratch once if this is too slow a rate of transmission, twice for acceptable and three times for too fast.*

The information was coming in faster than it could have been spoken intelligibly, but not ungraspably quick. She gently scratched her right cheek with her left hand, twice.

Wonderful! Allow me to introduce myself properly. The LP you asked about earlier stands for "Liveware Problem". I am not a properly normal human being. I am an avatoid of the

Liveware Problem, a Stream-class Superlifter; a modified Delta-class GCU, a Wanderer of the ship kind and technically Absconded.

Ah, she thought. An avatoid. A ship's avatar of such exquisite bio-mimicry it could pass for fully human. A *ship* Wanderer. And an Absconder. Absconders were ships that had chosen to throw off the weight of Cultural discipline and go off on their own.

Even so, a proportion were known, or at least strongly suspected, to be using this state of self-imposed exile purely as a disguise, and were still fully committed to the Culture, allegedly adopting Absconder status as cover for being able to carry out actions the main part of the Culture might shrink from. The granddaddy, the exemplary hero figure, the very God of such vessels, was the GSV *Sleeper Service*, which had selflessly impersonated such eccentric indifference to the Culture for four decades and then, some twenty-plus years ago now, suddenly revealed itself as utterly mainstream-Culture-loyal and – handily – harbouring a secretly manufactured, instantly available war fleet just when the Culture most needed it, before disappearing again.

She allowed her eyes to narrow a little. She was fully aware this was her own signature signal; suspicion, distrust.

Sorry about all the subterfuge. The air in here is kept scrubbed to remove the possibility of nanoscale devices watching in on such eye-to-eye communication and the room's coverings are themselves wrapped in film for the same reason. Even the smoke I inhaled at the bar contains an additive which clears my lungs of any such possible contamination. I was only able to get close enough to contact you after you'd arrived on board the Inspiral, Coalescence, Ringdown, *and of course everybody is being so wary of upsetting the Morthanveld. I thought it best to adopt the trappings of ultra-caution! I'm aware, of course, that you can't reply in kind to me, so let me just tell you why I'm here and why I'm contacting you in this way.*

She raised her brows a fraction.

*I am, as I say, an Absconder, though only technically; I spent
three and a half thousand years faithfully tugging smaller ships
around Systems Vehicles throughout the greater galaxy and saw
active service during the Idiran War – serving, if I may say so,
with some distinction, especially in the first few desperate years.
After all that I decided I was due a protracted holiday – probably a retirement, to be quite honest, though I reserve the right
to change my mind!*

*I have wandered the galaxy for the last eight hundred years,
seeing all I could of other civilisations and peoples. There is
always more to see, of course; the galaxy renews and re-forms
itself faster than one can make one's way round it. Anyway, I
am, truly, fascinated by Shellworlds and have a particular
interest in Sursamen, not the smallest part of which concerns
your level, the Eighth. When I heard rumours regarding your
father's death – and please accept my condolences in that regard
– and the events surrounding this sad occasion, including the
death of your brother Ferbin, I immediately thought to make
myself available to help the Sarl, and the children of the late
king in particular.*

*I'd assumed you'd be going back home with many of your
powers removed or reduced. I know that you return with no
ship or drone or other aid about you, and so I'd like to offer my
own services. Not as a day-to-day servant or courier or anything
like that – our Morthanveld hosts would not tolerate such a thing
– but as a last resort, if you will. Certainly as a friend in case
of need. Sursamen, and especially the Eighth, seems like a
dangerous place these days, and a person travelling alone, no
matter how able, may need all the friends they can muster.*

*I – that is, the ship – am currently some distance off but
keeping pace with the* Inspiral, Coalescence, Ringdown, *to stay
in reasonable proximity to this avatoid and facilitate its speedy
retrieval should I need to do so. However, it is my intention,
shortly, to make my way to Sursamen directly and this avatoid,
or another – for I have several – will be there. It and myself
are ready to afford you such assistance as you may require.*

You need not respond now; please think about this at your leisure and make your mind up in your own time. When you meet my avatoid on Sursamen you can let me know what you think then, through it. I shall completely understand if you want nothing to do with me. That is entirely your right. However, please be assured of my continuing respect and know that I am, dear lady, entirely at your service.

I shall end this signal shortly; please decide whether you wish to pretend I have in any way read your mind, just on the off-chance we are somehow being observed.

Signal ends at implied zero: four, three, two, one . . .

Djan Seriy stared into the eyes of the young man sitting opposite her. She was thinking, Dear shafted WorldGod, all my potential bedfellows are machines. How depressing.

Only about half a minute had passed since they'd started staring into each other's eyes. She sat back slowly, smiling and shaking her head. "I think your trick does not work on me, sir."

Quike smiled. "Well, it doesn't work with everybody," he said. He raised his goblet. It emitted a high, pleasant, ringing tone. "Perhaps I might be permitted to try again some other time?"

"Perhaps." They clinked bell-goblets; the twin sound was surprisingly mellifluous. She had dismissed the idea of taking seriously the offer he'd just made before the glasses had stopped ringing.

She engaged him in conversation for some time after that, listening to him recount tales of various explorations and adventures during his many travels. It was not unpleasant, she did not have to pretend interest and it was amusing to try to work out in his stories which parts were probably true and had been experienced by the ship concerned directly (assuming there really was a ship involved), which parts had been lived by the avatoid while the ship had looked on and which might have been entirely made up to try to fool anybody listening that all this related to a real human, not a ship-plus-avatar-in-human-form.

In exchange, she related something of her life on Sursamen as a child and adolescent and answered most of the eagerly asked questions Quike had, though she steered clear of certain areas and tried not to give any indication of how she would eventually react to his offer.

But of course she would reject his help, the ship's help. If the *Liveware Problem* was working completely alone then it was probably either hopelessly naïve or quietly insane; neither inspired confidence. If not then it presumably represented a part of SC or something even more rarefied and it was just *pretending* to be hopelessly naïve or quietly insane, which was even more worrying. And if Quike and the *Liveware Problem* were SC then why hadn't she been briefed about them turning up before she'd left Prasadal, or at least before she'd left the last vestige of the Culture proper and been batonned onwards to the Morthanveld?

What was going on here? All she wanted to do was go back home and pay her respects to her late father and her presumed-deceased brother, reconnect with her past a bit and perhaps lay something to rest (she was not entirely sure what, but maybe that would come to her later). She doubted she'd be able to provide much help to her surviving brother, Oramen, but if she could offer some small service or other, she would. But that was kind of it. After that she'd be off; away back to the Culture – and, if they'd take her, back to SC and the job that, for all its frustrations, dilemmas and heartbreaks, she loved.

Why was a Culture ship trying to get involved in her returning to Sursamen in the first place? At most, this was still all about a pretty paltry thing; a grubby dispute regarding the succession of power within a very minor and embarrassingly violent and undemocratic tribe whose principal claim on the interest of others was that they happened to live inside a relatively rare and exotic world-type. Was she expected to *do* something on Sursamen? If so, what? What *could* she be expected to do, unbriefed, lacking any specified mission and de-fanged?

Well, she didn't know. She strongly suspected she'd be crazy to do anything other than keep her head down, do what she'd said she was going to do and no more. She was in enough trouble already just for quitting the mission on Prasadal and heading home on compassionate leave without adding to the charge-sheet. SC training was full of stories of agents who'd gone dramatically off-piste and had taken on bizarre missions all of their own devising. They usually ended badly.

There were only a few stories leaning in the other direction, of agents who had passed up obvious opportunities to make some beneficial intervention unbriefed, without some specific mandate or instruction. The implication was, as ever, to stick to the plan, but be prepared to improvise. (Also, listen to your drone or other companion; they were expected to be more level-headed, less emotional than you – that was one of the main reasons they were there.)

Stick to the plan. Not just obey orders. If you were being asked to do something according to a plan, then the way the Culture saw it, you should have had at least some say in what that plan actually was. And if circumstances changed during the course of trying to follow that plan then you were expected to have the initiative and the judgement to alter the plan and act accordingly. You didn't keep on blindly obeying orders when, due to an alteration in context, the orders were in obvious contradiction to the attainment of whatever goal it was you were pursuing, or when they violated either common sense or common decency. You were still responsible, in other words.

It sometimes seemed to SC trainees, and especially to SC trainees coming to the organisation having been raised in other societies, that those people sworn just to obey orders had the easier time of it, being allowed to be single-minded in whatever purpose they pursued rather than having to do that *and* wrestle with its ethical implications. However, as this difference in approach was held up as one of the principal reasons that the Culture in general and SC in particular was morally superior to everybody else, it was generally regarded as a small operational price to pay for the allegedly far greater reward of being able to feel well ahead in the ethics stakes compared to one's civilisational peers.

So she would stick to the plan. And the plan was: go home, behave, return, apply herself. That ought to be fairly simple, ought it not?

She joined in Mr Quike's laughter as he reached the end of a story she'd been barely half listening to. They drank more of the spirit from the delicate, tinkling little bell-goblets and she felt herself grow pleasantly tipsy, her head ringing in a sort of woozy, complicit sympathy with the crystals.

"Well," she said at last. "I had better go. It has been interesting talking to you."

He stood up as she did. "Really?" he said. He looked suddenly anxious, even hurt. "I wish you'd stay."

"Do you now?" she asked coolly.

"Kind of hoping you would," he confessed. He gave a nervous laugh. "I thought we were getting on really well there." He looked at the puzzled expression on her face. "I thought we were flirting."

"You did?" she said. She felt like rolling her eyes; this was not the first time this had happened. It must be her fault.

"Well, yes," he said, almost laughing. He waved one arm to an internal door. "My sleeping quarters are more, well, welcoming than this rather spare space." He smiled his little-boy smile.

"I'm sure they are," she said.

She noticed the room lights were dimming. A little late, she thought.

So; another about-turn. She inspected her own feelings and knew that, despite the abruptness and the fact she was tired, she was at least a little interested.

He came up to her and took one of her hands in his. "Djan Seriy," he said quietly, "no matter what image of ourselves we try to project upon the world, upon others, even back upon ourselves, we are still all human, are we not?"

She frowned. "Are we?" she said.

"We are. And to be human, to be anything like human, is to know what one lacks, to know what what one needs, to know what one must look for to find some semblance of completeness amongst strangers, all alone in the darkness."

She looked into his languidly beautiful eyes and saw in them – well, being cold about it, more precisely in the exact set of his facial features and muscle state – a hint of real need, even genuine hunger.

How close to fully, messily, imperfectly human did an avatoid have to be to pass the close inspection afforded by an equiv-tech civilisation like the Morthanveld? Perhaps close enough to have all the usual failings of meta-humanity, and the full quota of needs and desires. Whether he was a sophisticated avatar constructed from the cellular level up, a subtly altered clone of an original human being or anything else, Mr Quike, it seemed, was still very much a man, and in looking into his eyes and seeing that craving desperation, that anxious desire (with its undertone of pre-prepared sullenness, aching yearning ready to become hurt contempt on the instant of rejection), she was only experiencing what untold generations of females had experienced throughout the ages. And, oh, that smile, those eyes, that skin; the warm, enveloping voice.

She thought, A real Culture girl would definitely say yes at this point.

She sighed regretfully. However, I am still – deep down, and for my sins – both my father's daughter and a Sarl.

"Perhaps some other time," she told him.

She left in an all-species pod taxi. She sat there in the damp, strange-smelling air, closed her eyes and laced in to the Great Ship's public information systems to review the next few days. There had been no recent schedule changes; they were still on course for the Morthanveld Nestworld of Syaung-un, due there in two and a half days.

She considered looking at humanoid dating/quick-contact sites (there were over three hundred thousand humanoids aboard – you'd think there would be somebody . . .), but still felt both too tired, and restless in the wrong way.

She returned to her own quarters, where the twice-disguised drone whispered good night to her.

She thought good night back to it, then lay, eyes closed but unable or unwilling to sleep, continuing to use her neural lace to interrogate the ship's dataverse. She checked up – at a remove, over distances and system translations that introduced delays of five or six seconds – on the agents she'd left running in the Culture's dataverse. She was both slightly disappointed and highly relieved to find that there was no known intrusive, close-observational recordage from the Eighth or indeed any of Sursamen's interior levels. Whatever happened there happened once and was never seen again.

She clicked out of the Culture's interface. One last roving agent system was waiting to report back from the local dataverse. It told her that her brother Ferbin was not dead after all; he was alive, he was on a Morthanveld tramp ship and he was due to arrive on the Nestworld of Syaung-un less than a day after her.

Ferbin! In the hushed darkness of her cabin, her eyes blinked suddenly open.

21. Many Worlds

A strange thing had happened to Choubris Holse. He had become interested in what was, if he understood such matters rightly, not a million strides away from being philosophy. Given Ferbin's unrestrainedly expressed views on that subject, this felt tantamount to treason.

It had started with the games that they had both been playing on the Nariscene ship *Hence the Fortress* to pass the time on the way to the Nestworld of Syaung-un. The games were played floating inside screen-spheres which were linked to the brain of the ship itself. Such ships, Holse had realised, were not merely vessels, that is, empty things you put stuff into; they were things, beings in their own right, at least as far as a mersicor, lyge or other mount was a being, and perhaps a lot more so.

There were even more realistically fashioned diversions

available, games in which you really did seem to be awake and moving physically around, talking and walking and fighting and everything else (though not peeing or shitting – Holse had felt he had to ask), but those sounded daunting and overly alien to both men, as well as unpleasantly close to some of the disturbing stuff Xide Hyrlis had been bending their ears about back on the disputed, burned husk that was Bulthmaas.

The ship had advised them on which games they would find most rewarding and they'd ended up playing those whose pretended worlds were not all that different from the real one they'd left behind on Sursamen; war games of strategy and tactics, connivance and daring.

Holse had taken at first guilty and then unrestrained delight in playing some of these games from the point of view of a prince. Later he had discovered works, analyses and comments related to such games, and, intrigued, started to read or watch these too.

Which was how he came to be interested in the idea that all reality might indeed be a game, most specifically as this concept related to the Infinite Worlds theory, which held that all possible things had already happened, or were happening now, all together.

This alleged that life was *very* like a game or simulation where every possible course and outcome has already been played out, noted down and drawn up, as though on an enormous map, with the beginning of the game – before a piece has been moved or a move has been made – in the centre, and every single possible end state arranged along the outer fringe of this implausibly stupendous chart. By this comparison, all that one does in mapping out the course of one particular game is trace a path from that central Beginning of things out through more and more branches, chances and possibilities, to one of the near infinitude of Ends at the periphery.

And there you were; the further likeness being drawn here, unless Holse had it completely arse-before-cock, was that which held; As Game, So Life. And indeed, As Game, So Entire History Of Whole Universe, Bar Nothing And Nobody.

Everything had already happened, and in every single possible way, too. Not only had everything that had already happened happened, everything that was *going* to happen had already happened. And not only *that*: everything that was going to happen had already happened in every single possible way that it possibly could.

So if, say, he played a game of cards with Ferbin, for money, then there was a course, a line, a way through this already written, previously happened universe of possibilities which led to the outcome that involved him losing everything to Ferbin, or Ferbin losing everything to him, including Ferbin suffering a fit of madness and betting and losing his entire fortune and inheritance to his servant – ha! There were universe-lines where he'd kill Ferbin over the disputed card game, and others wherein Ferbin would kill him; indeed there were tracks that led to everything that could be imagined, and everything that would never be imagined by anybody but was still somehow possible.

It seemed at first glance like utter madness, yet it also, when one thought about it, appeared somehow no less implausible than any other explanation of how things truly were, and it had a sort of completeness about it that stifled argument. Assuming that every branching fork on the universe map was taken randomly, all would still somehow be well; the likely things would always outnumber the unlikely and vastly outnumber the ludicrous, so as a rule things would happen much as one expected, with the occasional surprise and the very rare moment of utter incredulity.

Pretty much as life generally was, in other words, in his experience. This was at once oddly satisfactory, mildly disappointing and strangely reassuring to Holse; fate was as fate was, and that was it.

He immediately wondered how you could cheat.

SIGNAL

+

To: Utaltifuhl, Grand Zamerin of Sursamen-Nariscene:
        Khatach Solus (assumed location; kindly forward).

From: Morthanveld Shoum (Meast, Zuevelous, T'leish,
        Gavantille Prime, Pliyr), director general of the
        Morthanveld Strategic Mission to the Tertiary
        Hulian Spine: In-Mission Peregrinatory.

+

Signal Details [hidden; check to release: O]

+

*Cherished friend, I hope this finds you well and that the
Everlasting Queen's 3044th Great Spawning continues both
apace and favourably to yourself, your immediate family,
sub-sept, sept, clanlet, clan and kin-kind. I am well.*

*Firstly, worry not. This signal is sent under the provi-
sions and in keeping with the terms of the Morthanveld–
Nariscene Shellworld Management Co-prosperity
Agreement (subsection Sursamen). I communicate at such
distance to inform you only of a dispositionary detail further
to the greater good and security of the mutually beloved
world within our charge.*

*This is that an uncrewed, high-AI defensive entity, in
form similar to a Cat.2 CompressHull, accompanied by one
dozen minor slaved co-defensive entities, will be emplaced
by ourselves within the Sursamen Upper Core Space – also
known as the Machine Space or Machine Core – under the
auspices of the Morthanveld–Xinthian Shellworld
Management Co-security Agreement (subsection
Sursamen) with the full knowledge and co-operation of the
Sursamen Xinthian, probably not later than within the next
three to five peta-cycles.*

*Although not required to do so by the terms of our
highly pleasing and mutually beneficial Agreement, or
indeed by the General Treaty Framework existing*

between our two most excellent Peoples, I am – both as a profound admirer of our Nariscene friends and allies and as a personal expression of the love and respect felt between yourself and me (either of which consideration would naturally entirely and wholly constitute an unarguable reason for said) – happy to inform you that this minor and surely by mutual consent intrinsically untroubling asset relocation has been made necessary by the deterioration in the relationship between the Nariscene's client species the Oct/Inheritors and the Aultridia (said dispute remaining at the moment, fortunately, still specific to the subject Shellworld).

While not, of course, in any way wishing to anticipate any measure or precaution our vastly esteemed and wise colleagues the Nariscene might wish to put in place, and entirely in the blessed and happy knowledge that whatever action we might seek, as here, to carry out to ensure the continuing viability and security of Sursamen will be but of a piece with and complementary to those the Nariscene will doubtless themselves wish to consider, it was felt that inaction at this point by ourselves might conceivably be seen – if subject to the most painstaking and rigorous (one might almost label it officious!) scrutiny – to constitute a dereliction of duty and would therefore be, of course, as unconscionable to ourselves as it would be to you.

I know – and am, personally, delighted to acknowledge – that such is the assiduousness and seriousness with which the dutiful and admirable Nariscene people take their stewardship of Sursamen (and so many other Shellworlds!) that they would expect no less corresponding sedulity from their Morthanveld friends and allies. Such diligence and precautionary care is your byword, and we have joyously made it ours! Our inexhaustible and perpetual thanks for providing such inspiration and shining example!

This minor and purely preclusionary resource location adjustment will, arguably, lose some of its efficacy if bruited unduly about our greater society of Involved Galactic co-partners and so I beg that you restrict disclosure of this to the absolute minimum of knowledgees. I also specifically request, most strongly, that you ensure that while the orders and arrangements required to ensure the smooth transition of our vessel and its accompanying units are of course made and carried out with all due correctness and the studied meticulousness for which the Nariscene are rightly famed, no subsequent record of these orders and arrangements remains in any part of your data system specific to Sursamen itself.

Formal notification of such matters will of course be shared, acknowledged and recorded by the Morthanveld and Nariscene respective Exemplary Council and High Command, entirely obviating, as I am sure you are bound to agree, any requirement that such minor and operationally non-critical details need be fixed within the informational matrices of the very fine and efficient Nariscene Operational Nexus Command on Sursamen itself.

That is all – no more!

I beseech you to allow me to share with you the indisputable fact that I am so blissfully happy that something so small and unimportant nevertheless confers upon me the elationary privilege of addressing you, my good and faithful friend!

Joy to you!

+

Your ever sincere patron and most dutiful colleague, (sigiled)
Shoum

+

(Translated. Original in Morthanveld language.)

+

(Added by Grand Zamerin Utaltifuhl:)

Distant under-nephew by marriage! There you have it. That's us told. I shall on my return be fascinated to hear in some detail from you your version of the events which have

compelled our civilisational Dominates to make this unprece-
dented intervention. Your having one less thing to explain
to me will be ensured by doing just as Shoum demands. You
personally will see to it that this is carried out.
   In duty, Utaltifuhl.

Deputy Acting Zamerin Yariem Girgetioni (Deputy Acting
Zamerin Of All Sursamen, The Esteemed Yariem Girgetioni, as
he liked to be known; the added bit was not official Nariscene
nomenclature, though Yariem was firmly of the opinion it ought
to be) viewed the forwarded signal with some distaste and not
a little nervousness, though he was careful to hide the latter
emotion from the duty lieutenant who had delivered the flimsy
bearing the signal.

He was in his personal cloudcraft, floating over the 8-shaped
greenery and bluery of Sursamen's Twinned Crater. He was
lounging in a whole-body micro-massage cradle, watching erotic
entertainments and being fed dainty sweetmeats by attractively
identical pleasure-whelps. He flicked the offending flimsy back
at the duty lieutenant. "Just so. See to it."

"Ah, sir, it does say that you personally—"

"Precisely. We personally are ordering you to make sure that
all that is detailed here is carried out to the very letter or we
personally shall crack you from your exoskeleton and fling you
into the hydrochloric lagoons. Is that personal enough for you?"

"Abundantly, sir."

"How splendid. Now leave."

The Nestworld of Syaung-un was located in the region of space
known as the 34th Pendant Floret and seemed almost farcically
enormous to Ferbin. He could understand something the size
of a Shellworld; for all that his background was one of relative
primitiveness compared to others within the greater galactic
hierarchy, he was not a savage. He might not understand how

the spaceships of the Optimae worked – he was not even privileged to know quite how the far more crude and limited scendships of the Oct operated – but he knew that they did and he accepted it.

He knew that there were levels of science and technology, and of understanding and wisdom, well above those he was privy to and he was not amongst those who chose simply to disbelieve in their existence. Nevertheless, the measure of the engineering behind Morthanveld Nestworlds – structures built on such a scale that engineering and physics started to become the same thing – quite defeated him.

The Nestworld was an ordered tangle of massive tubes within gigantic braids forming colossal ropes making up stupefyingly vast cables constituting loops almost beyond imagining, and – despite the fact that the transparent outer casing of each tubular component was metres thick – it all twisted, turned and revolved, easy as a length of thread.

The Nestworld's principal components were giant tubes full of water; they varied in diameter between ten metres and many tens of kilometres and any individual tube might range over its length from the narrowest gauge to the greatest. They were bundled together without touching into larger braids which were contained within encompassingly greater pipes measuring a hundred kilometres or so across, also water-filled; these too revolved independently and were also bundled within yet greater cylinders – by now on a scale of tens of thousands of kilometres and more – and were frequently covered in engraved designs and patterns many scores of thousands of kilometres across.

The average Nestworld was a great gathered crown of tangled tubes within tubes within tubes within tubes; a halo world tens of thousands of years old, millions of kilometres across and set circumference-on to its local star, its every million-kilometre-long strand twisting and revolving to provide the tens of billions of Morthanveld within the vast construction with the faint, pleasant tug of gravity they were used to.

Syaung-un was not average; it was half a million years old,

the greatest world in the Morthanveld Commonwealth and, amongst the metre-scale species of the Involveds, one of the most populous settlements in the entire galaxy. It was three hundred million kilometres in diameter, nowhere less than a million klicks thick, contained over forty trillion souls and the whole assemblage rotated round a small star at its centre.

Its final, open braid of cylinders altogether easily constituted sufficient matter to produce a gravity well within which a thin but significant opportunistic atmosphere had built up over the decieons of its existence, filling the open bracelet of twisted habitat-strands with a hazy fuzz of waste gas and debris-scatter. The Morthanveld could have cleaned all this up, of course, but chose not to; the consensus was that it led to agreeable lighting effects.

The *Hence the Fortress* dropped them into a Nariscene-run satellite facility the size of a small moon – a sand grain next to a globe-encircling sea – and a little shuttle vessel zipped them across to the openwork braid of the vast corded world itself, slipstream whispering against its hull, the star at the world's centre glinting mistily through Syaung-un's filigree of cables, each stout enough, it seemed, to anchor a planet.

This was, Ferbin thought, the equivalent of a whole civilisation, almost an entire galaxy, contained within what would, in a normal solar system, be the orbit of a single planet. What uncounted lives were lived within those dark, unending braids? How many souls were born, lived and died within those monstrous curling twists of tubing, never seeing – perhaps never feeling the need to see – any other worlds, transfixed for ever within the encompassing vastness of this unexplorably prodigious habitat? What lives, what fates, what stories must have taken place within this star-surrounding ring, forever twisting, folding, unfolding?

They were delivered into a chaotic-seeming port area full of transparent walls both concave and convex and curving caissons and tubing, the whole set like a gassy bubble within one huge water-filled cylinder and all arranged to suit air-breathing people like the Nariscene and themselves. A machine about the size of a human torso floated up to them, announced itself as being Nuthe 3887b, an accredited Morthanveld greeting device belonging to the First Original Indigent Alien Deep Spacefarers' Benevolent Fund, and told them it would be their guide. It sounded helpful and was jollily coloured, but Ferbin had never felt further from home, or more small and insignificant.

We are lost here, he thought as Holse chatted with the machine and passed on to it their pathetically few possessions. We might disappear into this wilderness of civility and progress and never be seen again. We might be dissolved within it for ever, compressed, reduced to nothing by its sheer ungraspable scale. What is one man's life if such casual immensity can even exist?

The Optimae counted in magnitudes, measured in light years and censused their own people by the trillion, while beyond them the Sublimed and the Elder peoples whom they might well one day join thought not in years or decades, not even in centuries and millennia, but in centieons and decieons at the very least, and centiaeons and deciaeons generally. The galaxy, meanwhile, the universe itself, was aged in aeons; units of time as far from the human grasp as a light year was beyond a step.

They were truly lost, Ferbin thought with a kind of core-enfeebling terror that sent a tremor pulsing through him; forgotten, minimised to nothing, placed and categorised as beings far beneath the lowest level of irrelevance simply by their entry into this thunderously, stunningly phenomenal place, perhaps even just by the full realisation of its immensity.

It came as something of a surprise, then, for Ferbin and Holse to be greeted, before Holse had finished chatting to the Morthanveld machine, by a short, portly, smiling gent with long, blond, ringletty hair who called them by name in excellently articulated Sarl and entirely as though they were old friends.

"No, to a Morthanveld a Nestworld is a symbol of homeliness, intimacy," their new friend informed them as they rode a little tube-car along a gauzily transparent tunnel threaded through one of the klick-thick hab tubes. "Bizarrely!" he added. The man had given his name as Pone Hippinse; he too was an Accredited Greeter, he said, albeit only gaining this distinction recently. For a machine, Nuthe 3887b did a very good impression of being annoyed by Hippinse's arrival. "The nest a male Morthanveld weaves when he's trying to attract a mate is a sort of torus of seaweed twigs," Hippinse continued. "Kind of a big circle." He showed them what a circle looked like, using both hands.

They were on their way to another port area for what Hippinse described as a "short hop" in a spaceship round a small part of the vast ring to a suitable Humanoid Guest Facility. The Facility – the 512th Degree FifthStrand; 512/5 to most people – was most highly recommended by Hippinse.

"Strictly speaking—" Nuthe 3887b began.

"So, to a Morthanvelder, one of these things," Hippinse said, ignoring the little machine and waving his arms about to indicate the whole Nestworld, "is a sort of symbol of their being wedded to the cosmos, see? They're making their conjugal bower in space itself, expressing their connectedness to the galaxy or whatever. It's quite romantic, really. *Vast* place, though; I mean truly, mind-boggling vast. There are more Morthanveld on this one Nestworld than there are Culture citizens anywhere, did you know that?" He gave the impression of looking stunned on their behalf. "I mean even including the Peace Faction, the Ulterior, the Elench and every other splinter group, casually connected associate category and loosely affiliated bunch of hangers-on who just happen to like the name Culture. Amazing! Anyway, just as well I came along." He made a strange face at Ferbin and Holse that might have been meant to be friendly, comforting, conspiratorial or something else entirely.

Holse was looking at Pone Hippinse, trying to figure the fellow out.

"I mean, to remove you guys from the attentions of the media, the news junkies and aboriginistas; people like that." Hippinse belched and fell silent.

Ferbin used the opportunity to ask, "Where exactly are we going?"

"To the Facility," Hippinse said, with a glance at Nuthe 3887b. "Someone wants to meet you." He winked.

"Someone?" Ferbin asked.

"Can't tell you; spoil the surprise."

Ferbin and Holse exchanged looks.

Holse frowned and turned deliberately to the Morthanveld machine, hovering in the air to one side of the three seated humans. "This Facility we're heading for . . ." he began.

"It's a perfect place for—" Hippinse started to say, but Holse, now sitting side-on to him, held up one hand to him – held it almost into his face – and said,

"If you don't mind, sir. I'm talking to this machine."

"Well, I was just going to say—" Hippinse said.

"Tell us about it," Holse said loudly to the machine. "Tell us about this Facility we're supposed to go to."

". . . you can hole up there, unmolested . . ." Hippinse continued.

"The 512th Degree FifthStrand, or 512/5, is a Humanoid Transfer and Processing Facility," the machine told them as Hippinse finally fell silent.

Holse frowned. "What sort of processing?"

"Identity establishment, in-world alien behaviour legal agreement-making, knowledge-sharing—"

"What does that mean? Knowledge-sharing?" Holse had once helped a town constable with his enquiries regarding the theft of some tableware from the local County House; it had been a considerably rougher and more painful experience than the phrase Helping With Enquiries implied. He was worried that "knowledge-sharing" might be a similar lie dressed up pretty.

"Any data held is requested to be shared with the knowledge reservoirs of the Nestworld," Nuthe 3887b said, "on a philanthropic or charitable basis, as a rule."

Holse still wasn't happy. "Does this process hurt?" he asked.

"Of course not!" the machine said, sounding shocked.

Holse nodded. "Carry on."

"The 512th Degree FifthStrand Facility is a Culture-sponsored Facility," the machine told them. Ferbin and Holse both sat back and exchanged looks.

"I was *coming* to that!" Hippinse exclaimed in a sudden release of pent-up exasperation, waving his arms about.

They transferred to the Facility in a fat little ship which swallowed the car they were riding in whole. The ship lurched and they were away.

A screen showed them the view ahead for the duration of the twenty-minute journey; Hippinse chattered continually, pointing out sights, especially famous or well-executed patterns of cables or designs engraved on the cables, noteworthy spacecraft arriving and departing, stellar-atmospheric effects and a few of the favela structures which were not officially part of the world at all but which had been constructed within Syaungun's surrounding network of cylinders and inside the partial protection, both physical and symbolic, afforded by the lattice of mighty cylinders and their accompanying wrap of gases.

The 512th Degree FifthStrand was a kind of fully enclosed mini-Orbital, fashioned to look as much like the Nestworld itself as possible. It was only eight hundred kilometres across and – until you were right up at it – it looked quite insignificant within the loops and swirls of the giant world's main cylinders; just a tiny finger-ring lost amongst the openwork vastness of the braided super-cables submerged in their accidental haze of found atmosphere.

Close up, the Facility looked a little like a pushbike wheel. They docked at the hub. Nuthe 3887b stayed aboard; it wished them well. Hippinse's long blond hair floated about his head like a curly nebula and he pulled it back and bunned it with a little hair-net. Their car was released from the stubby ship and floated into and down a curved, hollow spoke like a thin, twisted

Tower.

"Keen on being able to see through things, aren't they?" Holse said, staring down through the clear floor of the car, the transparent side of the hollow spoke and the seemingly non-existent roof of the miniature habitat below.

"The Morthanveld have this thing about clarity," Hippinse told them. "The Culture wouldn't *think* of being so rude as to fashion their own places any differently." He snorted, shook his head.

Inside, the Facility was a little ribbon-world of its own, a rotating loop of landscape dotted with parkland, rivers, lakes and small hills, the air above filled with delicate-looking flying machines. Ferbin and Holse both felt the gravity building up as they descended.

Halfway down, approaching a conglomeration of what looked like huge half-silvered glass beads stuck on to the spoke like some aquatic accretion, the car began to slow. It fell out of the hazy sunshine into darkness and drew smoothly to a stop deep inside the cluster of silvery globes.

"Gentlemen!" Hippinse announced, clapping his chubby hands together. "Our destination!"

They entered the gently lit, pleasantly perfumed interior opening before them and walked along a curved, broadening corridor – the gravity was a little more than they were used to, but entirely tolerable – to an open space dominated by enormous rocks, small streams and broad pools, all overseen by a host of giant yellow-green and blue-brown plants joined together by nets of foliage. Silvery birds flitted silently across the scene. Overhead, the twisted lattice of the Nestworld revolved with a silent, steady, monumental grace.

Humans of a variety of body-types and skin colours were scattered amongst the plants, streams and pools. One or two glanced casually over in their direction, then away again. A few were entirely naked; a lot were mostly so. They appeared, to a man and woman, to be in excellent physical condition – even the more alien-looking ones somehow gave off an impression of glossy health – and so relaxed in their demeanour that the sight of their nudity wasn't quite as shocking to the two Sarl men as they might have expected. Still, Ferbin and Holse glanced at each other. Holse shrugged. A man and a woman, each wearing only jewellery, walked past them, smiling.

Ferbin glanced at Holse again and cleared his throat. "Would appear to be permitted," he said.

"So long as it's not compulsory, sir," Holse replied.

A small machine shaped like a sort of squared-off lozenge floated up to them. It said, again in perfect Sarl, "Prince Ferbin, Choubris Holse, LP Hippinse; welcome."

They said their various hellos.

A woman – compactly elegant, dark-haired, clad in a long, plain blue shift that left only her arms and head exposed – was walking towards them. Ferbin felt himself frown. Was it really her? Older, so different . . .

She walked right up to him. The others around him were silent, even Hippinse, as though they knew something he didn't. The woman nodded once and smiled, in a guarded but not unfriendly way.

He realised it really was Djan Seriy an instant before she opened her mouth to speak.

22. The Falls

"This is currently our most impressive sight," Jerfin Poatas said, waving his stick at the bizarre building looming out of the dim bronze mists. The fellow had to raise his voice to be heard above the thunderous cacophony of the Falls, though he did so with a kind of ease that implied he didn't even know he did it himself, Oramen thought.

The Fountain Building was indeed impressive. They were approaching it in a little covered carriage rattling along one of the many light railways which threaded their precarious and often dangerous ways across the islets, sandbars, parts of fallen buildings and anchored pylons set into the foaming waters themselves. The roof and side of the rail car were made from salvage gleaned from the unnamed city; a substance like glass, but lighter, flexible, far more clear than any glass Oramen had ever seen outside of a telescope or microscope, and without flaws. He drew one fingertip down the interior surface of the material. It did not even feel cold like glass. He put his glove back on.

The weather was chilly. In the sky, far to facing, almost directly down the gorge of the Sulpitine after the river had tumbled away from the Falls, the Rollstars Clissens and Natherley had dropped to the horizon – Clissens seeming to graze it, Natherley already half-hidden by it – and only the fading Rollstar Kiesestraal was left to shed any new light on the Hyeng-zhar, rising from the direction Clissens and Natherley were setting.

Kiesestraal shed a weak, watery-looking blue-white light, but provided almost no warmth. Rollstars had a life of less than half a billion years and Kiesestraal's was almost over: nearly burned out, it probably had only a few thousand years until extinguishment altogether, whereupon it would drop, falling from the ceiling fourteen hundred kilometres above to come crashing down through the atmosphere – producing one last, brief, awful burst of light and heat – to smack on to the surface of the Ninth somewhere along its course, and, if the star sages and catastrophists, astrologers and scientists had been mistaken in their calculations, or if their warnings went unheeded, cause utter catastrophe where it fell, potentially killing millions.

Even with nobody present directly underneath, the fall of a dead star, especially on to a level featuring a majority of solid ground, was an apocalyptic event, pulverising earth and rock to dust and fire, sending projectiles the size of mountains soaring like shrapnel all about it to produce still further terrible impacts which would themselves birth smaller and smaller successions of crater, ejecta and debris until finally all that was left was wasteland – its centre scoured to Bare, to the very bone of the world – and clouds of dust and gas and years of spreading, dissipating winters, terrible rains, failed crops and screeching, dust-filled winds. The world itself rang to such impacts. Even directly beneath the ceiling of a floor being so struck, a human might struggle to notice any effect, the structure of a Shellworld was so strong, but machines throughout every level from Core to Surface registered the blow and heard the world ring like a vast bell for days afterwards. The WorldGod, it was said, heard the Starfall, and grieved.

Thankfully, such catastrophes were rare; the last one suffered by Sursamen had been decieons ago. They were also, apparently, part of the natural life of a modified Shellworld. So the Oct and Aultridia and other Shellworld Conducer species claimed. All such destruction led to forms of creation, they assured, producing new rocks, landscapes and minerals. And stars could be replaced, new ones emplaced and kindled, even though such technology was seemingly beyond species like the Oct and Aultridia, who relied on the good graces of the Optimae for these actions.

This fate awaited Kiesestraal and whatever part of the Ninth it fell upon; for now though, as if it was a great wave drawing the waters back before charging furiously back in, the star gave out a thin, attenuated seep of light, and over the whole course of the Sulpitine and well beyond, including the great inland seas at both ends of the river, a partial winter was making itself felt, first the air cooling and then the land and waters too as they radiated their heat away into the encroaching darkness. Soon the Sulpitine would start to freeze over and even the vast unending chaos of the Falls would be stilled. It seemed impossible, unbelievable, Oramen thought, looking about at the sudden, sporadic visions of madly dancing waters and waves which the eccentricities of Falls-created wind and pummelling walls of spray afforded, and yet it had happened in centuries past and would surely happen again.

The rail car was slowing. It was racketing along a raised section of narrow, uneven-looking track held above a shallow sandbar by tall pylons. The sandbar was surrounded by sweeps and curves of dashing, booming waters which looked like they could change course at any moment and wash the sands and pylons away. A gale seemed to shake the little rail car, briefly pulling away some of the surrounding mist and spray.

The Fountain Building soared above them now, bursting with curved fountains of water that turned to spray and rain and came dropping all around in an unceasing torrent that was starting to drum and beat upon the roof of the rail car, shaking it bodily. A chill wind moaned through spaces in the rail car's body and Oramen felt the cold draught on his face. He wondered if the barrages and veils of water hitting the car would turn to snow as the winter came on but before the whole Falls froze. He tried to imagine this. How magnificent it would look!

These partial winters were almost unknown on the Eighth. On that level, the ceiling above was nearly completely smooth, so that a star, whether a Fixstar or a Rollstar, shed its light freely, casting its rays in every direction save where the horizon itself intervened. Here on the Ninth, for reasons known only to the Veil themselves and implied by the equations of whatever fluid physical figurings they employed, the ceiling – and, in places, the floor too – was much interrupted by the great vanes, blades and channels required to make the Shellworlds work according to their mysterious original purpose.

These features generally extended kilometres or tens of kilometres from the floor or ceiling and frequently right across the horizon; some ceiling strakes were known to stretch halfway round the world itself,

The result was that the light of a star was often much more localised here than it was on the Eighth, so that bright sunshine shone along one line of landscape while just to the side the rest would be held in deep shade, receiving only the light reflected from the general spread of the shining sky itself. Some benighted lands, usually those caught between tall surface vanes, received no direct sunlight whatever, at any time, and were truly barren.

The little rail car chuffed and steamed its way to a halt, shuddering to a stop in a screech of brakes some few metres shy of a set of damaged-looking buffers, the water crashing and bursting across the car's roof and sides, rocking it like a demented cradle. Steam rolled up from its wheels.

Oramen looked down. They were poised above the side of

a great, tipped, fallen building made of, or at least clad in, material much like that which provided the rail car with its sides and roof. The rail tracks rested on trestles like wedges attached to the side of the building itself, making it feel more secure than the flimsy-looking pylons they had recently traversed.

Metres beyond the buffers, the edge of the building fell away sharply to reveal – between this upended edifice and the still upright Fountain Building – a cauldron of wildly swirling mist and spray fifty metres or more deep, at the base of which – on the rare occasions when the clouds of vapour were torn apart sufficiently for such a view to be opened – giant surging waves of brown-tinged foam could briefly be glimpsed.

A large platform of wood and metal extended from the rail tracks on the down-slope side, awash with the near-solid torrents of water falling from the Fountain Building. One or two bits of machinery lay scattered about the platform's surface, though it was hard to imagine how anyone could work on the platform in this stunning, down-crashing deluge. Parts of the platform's edges seemed to have broken off, presumably washed away by the sheer weight of the falling water.

"This was a staging platform for workings within the building beneath us," Poatas said, "until whatever cave-in or tunnel collapse upstream caused the building before us to become the Fountain Building."

Poatas sat alongside Oramen behind the rail car's driver. The seats behind were taken up by Droffo, Oramen's equerry, and his servant, Neguste Puibive – Oramen could feel the fellow's bony knees pressing into his back through the seat's thin back whenever Neguste shifted his long legs. In the last row were the knights Vollird and Baerth. They were his personal guard, specifically chosen by tyl Loesp and most highly recommended and able, he'd been told, but he'd found them somewhat prone to surliness and their presence vaguely offputting. He'd rather have left them behind – he found excuses to whenever he could – but there had been space in the rail car and Poatas had talked darkly of needing all the weight in the little conveyance they could muster to help keep it anchored to the tracks.

"The platform looks in some danger of being washed away," Oramen shouted, perhaps a little too loudly, to Poatas.

"No doubt it is," the small, hunched man conceded. "But this will not happen quite yet, one hopes. For now, it provides the best view of the Fountain Building." He jabbed his stick up at the tall, improbably spray-plumed structure.

"Which is quite a sight," Oramen conceded, nodding. He gazed up at it in the bronze wash of sunset-gloom. Folds and waves of water came crashing down on the rail car's roof, a particularly heavy clump slamming off the near invisible material protecting them and causing the whole car to quiver, making it seem that it was about to be thrown off the tracks beneath and hurled across the water-drenched surface of the railing-less platform, doubtless to be dashed to smithereens somewhere far below.

"Three balls of God!" Neguste Puibive blurted. "Sorry, sir," he muttered.

Oramen smiled and held up one hand, forgiving. Another wave of solid water hit them, making something on one lower side of the seats creak.

"Chire," Poatas said, tapping the driver on the shoulder with the end of his stick. "I think we might reverse a way."

Oramen held out one hand. "I thought I might try standing outside for a bit," he said to Poatas.

Poatas' eyes went round. "And try is all you'd do, sir. You'd be battered down and swept away before you drew a single breath."

"And, sir, you'd get awfully wet," Neguste pointed out.

Oramen smiled and looked out at the maelstrom of crashing water and swirling wind. "Well, it would only be for a moment or two, just to experience something of that fabulous power, that mighty energy." He shivered with the anticipation of it.

"By that logic, sir," Droffo said, sitting forward to talk loudly into Oramen's ear, "one might experience something of the power and energy of a piece of heavy artillery by positioning one's head over the barrel just as the firing lanyard's pulled; however, I'd venture to suggest the resulting sensation would not remain long in one's brain."

Oramen grinned, looking round at Droffo and then back at Poatas. "My father warned all his children there would be times when even kings must allow themselves overruled. I suppose I must prepare for such moments. I accept the judgement of my parliament here gathered." He waved one flat hand from Poatas to the driver, who was looking round at them. "Chire – was that your name?"

"Indeed, sir."

"Please do as Mr Poatas says, and let's retreat somewhat."

Chire glanced at Poatas, who nodded. The train clanked gears and then went, huffing, slowly backwards in clouds of steam and a smell of hot oil.

Droffo turned round to Vollird and Baerth. "You are well, gentlemen?"

"Never better, Droffo," Vollird replied. Baerth just grunted.

"You seem so quiet," Droffo said. "Not sickened by the rocking, are we?"

"It takes rather more," Vollird told him with an insincere smile. "Though I can sicken well enough with sufficient provocation."

"Of that I'm sure," Droffo said, turning away from them again.

"The Falls are, what? Ten thousand strides across?" Oramen asked Poatas as they withdrew.

Poatas nodded. "Bank to bank, straight across; one has to add another two thousand if one follows the curve of the drop-off."

"And about a thousand strides of that is without water, is that right? Where islands in the stream upriver block the flow."

"Nearer two thousand strides," Poatas said. "The figure changes constantly; so much here does. At any one time there might be three or four hundred separate falls within the greater cataract."

"So many? I read of only two hundred!"

Poatas smiled. "A handful of long-years ago, that was true." His smile might have looked a little brittle. "The young sir has obviously done his book research, but it has to cede authority to that which actually pertains."

"Of course!" Oramen yelled as a howling gust of rain-filled wind shook the rail car. "How quickly it all changes, eh!"

"As I say, sir; so much here does."

The mayoral residence in Rasselle had been sacked and burned during the taking of the city. Oramen's mother and her new family were staying in the old ducal palace of Hemerje while the repairs and renovations were effected.

Built on a wide fertile plain, the Deldeyn capital had grown according to quite a different plan compared to Pourl on its hill, with broad, tree-lined boulevards separating a variety of extensive enclaves: noble estates, palaces, monasteries, League and Guild trading yards and Public Commons. Rather than city walls, the inner city was ringed with a double set of canals overseen by six Great Towers; tall forts which were the highest buildings in the city and remained so by statute. The citadel, near the Great Palace, was a giant, barrel-shaped barracks; purely a place of last resort with no pretensions towards luxury in the same way that the Great Palace was purely a great royal house with little intrinsic defendability.

Every element of the city had been linked through the boulevards and, originally, by canals – later railways. Before that change, after the Merchants' Revolt, parts of the boulevards had been built over, leaving mere streets between the enclave walls and the new buildings and a much-reduced central avenue in what had been the centre of each boulevard. Three generations later, some of the nobles still complained.

The ducal palace of Hemerje was an imposing, tall-ceilinged, solid-feeling building with dark, thick, heavy-sounding wooden floors. The compound's high walls enclosed an ancient garden full of shaped lawns, shady trees, tinkling rills, quiet ponds and an abundant kitchen garden.

Aclyn, the lady Blisk, Oramen's mother, met him in the hall, rushing up to him and taking him by the shoulders.

"Oramen! My little boy! Can it really be? But look at you! How you've grown! So much like your father! Come in, come in; my Masyen would have loved to see you but he is *so* busy! But you must come to dinner. Perhaps tomorrow or the day after. My Masyen is dying to meet you! And him mayor! Mayor! Really! Of this great city! I ask you; who'd have thought it?"

"Mother," Oramen said, taking her in his arms. "I've longed to see you. How are you?"

"I am well, I am well. Stop now, you silly, or you'll crush my dress," she told him, laughing and pressing him away with both hands.

Aclyn was older and heavier than he'd pictured her. He supposed this was inevitable. Her face, though more lined and puffier than it had been both in her portraits and his imagination, seemed to glow. She was dressed as though she was going to a ball, albeit with an apron over her gown. Her auburn hair was piled and powdered in the latest fashion.

"Of course," she said, "I'm still recovering from little Mertis – that was dreadful; you men, you have no idea. I told my Masyen he was never to touch me again! Though I was only saying that, of course. And the journey here was simply ghastly, it went on for ever, but – this is Rasselle! So much to see and do! So many arcades and shops and receptions and balls! Who would be in low spirits here? Will you eat with us?" she asked. "The rhythm of the days here is so bizarre! We still dine at odd times; what must people think of us? We were about to sit down to lunch in the garden, the weather is so mild. Be our guest, will you?"

"Gladly," he told her, taking off his gloves and handing those and his travelling cloak to Neguste. They walked along a well-lit hall, the dark floors swaddled in thick carpets. He adjusted his pace to hers, slowing. Servants were carrying heavy-looking boxes out of another room; they stood back to let Oramen and his mother pass. "Books," Aclyn said, with what sounded like distaste. "All completely incomprehensible, of course, even if one did want to read them. We're turning the library into another receiving room; we'll try selling those old things but we'll just burn the rest. Have you seen tyl Loesp?"

"I thought I might," Oramen said, peeking into the top of one of the book-filled boxes. However, I'm told now he has just left Rasselle to visit some distant province. Our communications here would appear still to be erratic."

"Isn't he a marvel? Tyl Loesp is *such* a fine man! So brave and dashing, such authority. I was most impressed. You are in safe hands there, Oramen, my little Prince Regent; he loves you dearly. Do you stay in the Great Palace?"

"I do, though only my baggage has made arrival there so far."

"So you came here first! How sweet! This way; come and meet your new little brother."

They walked down to the scented terraces.

Oramen stood on a high tower within the vast gorge of recession formed by the Hyeng-zhar, looking out to another great building which was, if the engineers and excavationers had it right, about to fall, finally and fatally undermined by the surging water piled frothing round its base, much of it descending from the Fountain Building nearby – this would be the second construction whose fate that bizarre edifice had hastened. The building he stood on was thin and dagger-shaped, allegedly still well founded; the little circular platform beneath him sat at the top like a finger-ring lowered on to the very tip of the dagger. The building he was looking at was tall and thin too, but flat like a sword blade, its edges glinting in the tenuous, grey-blue light of Kiesestraal.

The fading star was almost the only light left now; a thin

band of sky, just a lining across the horizon, shone to farpole, in the direction of Rasselle. To facing, where Clissens and Natherley had disappeared some days earlier, only the most imaginative eye could detect any remnant of their passing. A few people, perhaps with slightly different eyesight to the norm, claimed they could still glimpse a hint of red left over there, but nobody else did.

Still, Oramen thought, one's eyes adjusted, or one's entire mind did. The view was dull under Kiesestraal's meagre light, but most things remained visible. The twinned effect of Clissens and Natherley being in the sky together had been to make the weather oppressively hot at their zenith, he'd heard, and the light had been too much for many eyes to bear. They might be better off under this more rationed portion of illumination. He shivered, pulled his collar up as a biting wind snagged itself round the tower's thin summit.

There had been snow, though it had not lain. The river was cold, ice starting to form upstream in the quieter pools along its banks. Further upstream, at its source, reports had it that the Higher Sulpine Sea – the first part of the river system to experience the complete disappearance of the two Rollstars from its skies – was beginning to freeze over.

The air was rarely still now, even well away from the Falls themselves, where the stupendous weight of falling water created its own crazed turmoil of forever swirling gusts. These could and did focus themselves into lateral tornadoes capable of sweeping men and equipment, whole sections of railway track and entire trains of carriages away with almost no warning.

Now, as the great wide strip of land on the Ninth denied all but Kiesestraal's light gradually cooled while the rest of the continent about it remained temperate, winds blew nearly constantly, whining gears in the vast engine of the atmosphere as it attempted to balance chilled and heated parcels of air, creating gales that lasted for days on end and great sandstorms that lifted whole landscapes of sand, silt and dust from hundreds of kilometres away and threw them across the sky, robbing the land of what little light there was and hindering work on the Falls' excavations as the generators, power lines and lights struggled to pierce the encompassing gloom and machines ground to a stop, workings jammed with dust. The larger sand blizzards were capable of dumping so much material into the river upstream that – according to the latest storm's direction and the colour of the desert from which it had lifted its cargo of swirling grains – the waters of the cataract turned dun, grey, yellow, pink or dark, blood red.

Today there were no veils of sand or even ordinary cloud, the day might have been dark as night. The river still plunged over the cap rock and into the gorge in an ocean of falling and its roaring shook the rock and air, though Oramen had noticed that in a sense he hardly heard the noise now and had quickly become used to modulating his voice to the right level to be heard without thinking about it. Even in his quarters, a small compound in the Settlement a kilometre from the gorge, he could hear the voice of the cataract.

His accommodation, formerly that of the Archipontine of the Hyeng-zharia Mission – the man in charge of the monks who had chosen death rather than exile from their posts – was formed from several luxuriously appointed railway carriages surrounded by a set of sturdy but movable barbed walls which could be shifted across the sands and scrub to keep pace with the carriages as they were needed; a whole system of broad-gauge tracks lay beside the gorge and formed the most organised and disciplined district of the mobile city. As the gorge recessed and the Falls moved upstream, more tracks were laid ahead and every fifty days or so the official part of the Settlement, almost all of it on carriages and rail trucks, moved to follow the cataract's unstoppable progress upriver. The remainder of the city – the unofficial districts of merchants, miners and labourers and all their associated supporting crews of bar people, bankers, suppliers, prostitutes, hospitals, preachers, entertainers and guards – moved in its own spasmodic jerks, roughly in time with the Settlement's bureaucratic heart.

Oramen's compound always lay near the canal that was

forever being dug along the bank parallel with the river, ahead of the Falls' retreat, keeping pace with the railway tracks. The canal provided drinking and toilet water for the Settlement and power for the various hydraulic systems which lowered and raised men and equipment into and out of the gorge, and removed plunder. At night, on the odd occasions when the winds were stilled, Oramen thought he could hear, even above the distant thunder of the Falls, the canal's quiet gurglings.

How quickly he had become used to this strange, forever temporary place. He had missed it, bizarrely, during the five days he had spent in Rasselle and the four days it had taken travelling there and back. It was something like the effect of the cataract's stupendous voice; that vast, never-ending roar. You got so used to it so quickly that when you left the place, its absence seemed like an emptiness inside.

He perfectly understood why so many of the people who came here never left, not for long, not without always wanting to come back again. He wondered if he ought to leave before he too became habituated to the Hyeng-zhar as though to some fierce drug. He wondered if he really wanted to.

The mist still climbed into the slate skies. The vapours curled and twisted round the exposed towers – most plumbly upright, many tipped, just as many fallen – of the Nameless City. Beyond the doomed height of the flat-bladed building, the Fountain Building still stood like some insane ornament from a god's garden, scattering slow billows of water all around it. On the far side of that building, visible now and again through the spray and mist, could be seen the horizon-flat, dark-skirted edge which marked the start of the great plateau situated halfway up the height of the taller buildings and which many of the Falls' scholars and experts thought marked the centre of the long-buried alien city. A wall of water tipped over that edge, falling like a pleated curtain of dark cream to the base of the gorge, raising yet more spray and mist.

As Oramen watched, something flashed dim blue behind the

waters, lighting them up from inside. He was startled for a second. The explosions of the quarriers and blasters were usually only heard not seen; when they were visible in the darkness the flash was yellow-white, sometimes orange if a charge did not explode fully. Then he realised it was probably a cutting crew; one of the more recent discoveries the Deldeyn had made was how to slice through certain metals using electric arcs. This could produce ghostly blue flashes like the one he'd just seen.

On the other hand, the excavationers and plunderers – an easily unnerved and highly superstitious bunch at the best of times, by all accounts – had reported seeing even more strange and unusual things than they normally did, now that the only external light came from Kiesestraal and the focus of so much of their work and attention had shifted to the buildings under the kilometres-wide plaza, where it would have been dark enough even had the days been of normal brightness.

Working in that doubled darkness, by crude, unreliable lights, in an environment that could change at any moment and kill you in so many sudden ways, surrounded by the ghostly remains of buildings of near unimaginable antiquity, the wonder was that men ventured there at all, not that they experienced or imagined anything out-of-the-ordinary. This was an out-of-the-ordinary place, Oramen thought. Few places he'd heard of were more so.

He raised the heavy binoculars to his eyes and searched the view for people. Whenever you looked, wherever you looked carefully enough, the Falls – so vast, so impersonal, so furiously of a scale indifferent to that of humanity – proved to be swarming with human figures, animals and activity. He searched in vain, though. The field glasses were the best available, with great wide lenses at the front to gather as much light as possible, so that, if anything, they made the view lighter than it really was, but even so it was still too dim to see in sufficient detail to make out individual humans.

"Here you are! Sir, you give us the slip and the conniptions in equal measure, running off like that." Neguste Puibive arrived on the viewing platform holding various bags and a large umbrella. He leaned back to the doorway. "He's here!" he shouted down the stairs. "Earl Droffo also in attendance, sir," he told Oramen. "Happily not Messrs V & B, though." Oramen smiled. Neguste was no more a friend to Vollird and Baerth than he was.

Oramen had told both knights that their presence was unnecessary. He didn't really see the need for such closely dedicated guarding; the main dangers posed in the gorge itself were not caused by people and he just didn't go into the parts of the Settlement where the violence happened. Still, the two men accompanied him, sullenly, whenever he didn't take particular care to lose them, claiming as excuse that if anything did happen to Oramen, tyl Loesp would crack their skulls like eggs.

Oramen spent quite a lot of time avoiding people he found disagreeable; General Foise, who was in overall charge of the security and guarding of the Settlement and the Falls, was one such. The man Fanthile had described as entirely tyl Loesp's was in no way sinister and gave nary a hint that he was anything less than a loyal functionary of the army and the state. He was, however, boring. He was slight, short-sighted behind thick glasses, had a thin, never-smiling face and a quiet, monotonous voice. He was nondescript in most other ways and seemed more like a merchant's chief clerk than a true general, though his record in the recent wars had been creditable if unspectacular. The junior officers around him were similar; efficient but uninspiring, managerial rather than swashbuckling. They spent a lot of time working on plans and contingencies and determining how best to guard the highest number of sites with the lowest number of men. Oramen was happy to leave them to it, and tended to keep out of their way.

"You must stop sprinting off like that, sir," Neguste said, opening the large umbrella and holding it over Oramen. There was a fair bit of spray around, Oramen supposed. "Every time I lose sight of you I think you've fallen off a building or something, sir."

"I wanted to see this," Oramen said, nodding at the great flat building across the mist-strewn waste of frothing waters. "The engineers say it could go at any moment."

Neguste peered forward. "Won't fall this way, will it, sir?"

"Apparently not."

"Hope not, sir."

Between the blade-building and the Fountain Building, another flash of blue lit up the curtain of water falling from the vast plaza set across the buildings beyond. "See that, sir?"

"Yes. Second one since I've been here."

"Ghosts, sir," Neguste said emphatically. "There's proof."

Oramen looked briefly round at him. "Ghosts," he said. "Really?"

"Sure as fate, sir. I've been talking to the tinks, scrimps, blasters and the rest, sir." Oramen knew that Neguste did indeed frequent the notoriously dangerous bars, smoke tents and music halls of the Settlement's less salubrious areas, thus far without injury. "They say there's all sorts of terrible, weird, uncanny things in there under that plaza thing."

"What sort of things?" Oramen asked. He always liked to hear the specifics of such charges.

"Oh," Neguste said, shaking his head and sucking in his cheeks, "terrible, weird, strange things, sir. Things that shouldn't be seeing the light of day. Or even night," he said, looking round the darkened sky. "It's a fact, sir."

"Is it now?" Oramen said. He nodded at Droffo as the other man appeared. Droffo kept to the inside of the platform, next to the wall; he was not good with heights. "Droff. Well done. Your turn to hide. I'll count to fifty."

"Sir," the earl said with a weak smile, coming to stand behind him. Droffo was a fine fellow in many ways and possessed of a dry sense of humour of his own, but rarely found Oramen's jokes funny.

Oramen leant on the platform parapet and looked over the edge. "Not that far down, Droff."

"Far enough, prince," Droffo said, looking up and away as Oramen leaned further out. "Wish you wouldn't do that, sir."

"Me too, for all it may be worth, sirs," Neguste said, looking from one man to another. A gust of wind threatened to pull him off his feet.

"Neguste," Oramen said, "put that contraption down before you get blown off the damn building. The spray's mostly coming upwards anyway; it's no use."

"Right-oh, sir," Neguste said, collapsing and furling the umbrella. "Have you heard of all the strange occurrences, sir?" he asked Droffo.

"What strange occurrences?" the earl asked.

Neguste leaned towards him. "Great sea monsters moving in the waters upstream from the Falls, sirs, upsetting boats and tearing up anchors. Others seen downstream, too, moving where no boat could ever go. Spirits and ghosts and strange appearances and people being found frozen into stone or turned to no more dust than you could hold in the palm of one hand, sir, and others losing their minds so that they don't recognise nobody who is even their nearest and dearest and just wander the ruins until they step off an edge, or people who see something in the ruins and excavations that makes them walk to the nearest electric light and stare into it until their eyes go blind, or stick their hands in to touch the spark and die all jerky, smoking and flaming."

Oramen had heard all this. He might, he realised, have contributed a strange occurrence of his own.

Just ten hours earlier he'd been woken from the middle of his sleep by a strange, insistent little noise. He'd turned the cover on the candle-lamp and looked round the carriage in the newly increased light, trying to trace the source of the trilling sound. He hadn't heard any noise quite like it before. It sounded like some curious, metallic bird call.

He noticed a soft green light blinking on and off, not in the sleeping compartment itself but through the ajar door into the carriage's study and reception chamber. Xessice, the girl he'd favoured most since he'd been here in the Settlement, stirred but did not wake. He slipped out of bed, shucking on a robe and taking his gun from underneath the head bolster.

The light and the sound were coming from a delicately ornate and beautifully turned World model sitting on the desk in the study. It was one of the few ornaments Oramen had kept from when the carriage had belonged to the Archipontine; he had admired it for its exquisitely executed fashioning and been almost physically unable to throw the thing out, even though he suspected it was in some sense a foreign religious artifact and therefore not wholly suitable for a good WorldGod-respecting Sarlian to possess.

Now the object was emitting this strange, alien-sounding warble, and a green light was pulsing from its interior. It had changed, too; it had been reconfigured, or it had reconfigured itself so that the half-open cut-away parts of each of the shells had aligned, creating a sort of spiky hemisphere with the green light pulsing at its heart. He looked round the study – the green light gave quite sufficient illumination for him to see by – then quietly closed the door to the sleeping chamber and sat down on the seat in front of the desk. He was thinking about prodding the green central light with the barrel of the gun when the light blinked off and was replaced by a soft circle of gently changing colours which he took to be some sort of screen. He'd sat back when this had happened; he leant tentatively forward again and a soft, androgynous voice said,

"Hello? To whom do I speak? Are you Sarl, yes? Prince Oramen, I am warned, is so?"

"Who is talking?" Oramen answered. "Who wishes to know?"

"A friend. Or, with more accuracy, one who would be friend, if so was allowed."

"I have known many friends. Not all were as they might have seemed."

"Which of us is? We are all mistaken against. There are so many barriers about us. We are too separated. I seek to remove some of those barriers."

"If you would be my friend it might help to know your name. From your voice I am not even sure you are male."

"Call me Friend, then. My own identity is complicated and would only confuse. You are the prince of Sarl called Oramen, are you?"

"Call me Listener," Oramen suggested. "Titles, names; they can mislead, as we seem already to have agreed."

"I see. Well, Listener, I express my fine good wishes and utmost benevolence to you, in hope of understanding and mutual interest. These things, please accept."

Oramen filled the pause. "Thank you. I appreciate your good wishes."

"Now, that clarified, our anchor embedded, as it were, I would talk with you to give you a warning."

"Would you now?"

"I would. In this, I do; there is caution needed in the burrowings you make."

"The burrowings?" Oramen asked, frowning at the softly glowing screen. The colours continued to shift and change.

"Yes, your excavatory workings in the great city. These must be approached with caution. Humbly, we'd petition to be allowed to advise on such. Not all that is hidden from you is so hidden from us."

"I think too much is hidden here. Who would you be? What 'us' do we talk about? If you would advise us, begin by advising who you might be."

"Those who would be your friends, Listener," the asexual voice said smoothly. "I approach you because we believe you are untrammelled. You, Listener, are believed to be capable of ploughing your own course, unrestricted to the furrows of others. You have freedom to move, to turn about from incorrect beliefs and unfortunate slanders directed against those who would only help, not hinder. They mislead themselves who accept the traducement of others by those who have only their own narrowed interests at heart. Sometimes those who seem most funnelled are most free, and those who are most—"

"Hold there, let me guess; you are from the Oct, are you not?"

"Ha!" the voice said, then there was a pause. "That would be mistaken, good Listener. You doubtless think I am of that kind because it might appear that I seek to deceive you. This is an understandable mistake, but a mistake nevertheless. Oh, their lies go deep, to the core, they are most fastly tunnelled. We have much to untangle here."

"Show your face, creature," Oramen said. He was becoming more and more sure of the kind of being he was talking to here.

"Sometimes we must prepare ourselves for important meetings. Ways must be smoothed, gradients negotiated. A blunt, front-on approach might suffer rebuff while a more curved and gentle path, though seeming less honestly direct, will break through finally to success and mutual understanding and reward."

"Show your face, being," Oramen said, "or I'll think you a monster that dares not."

"There are so many levels of translation, Listener. Are we really to say that a face is required to be a moral creature? Must goodness or evil be configured about eating-parts? Is this a rule that persists throughout the great emptiness surrounding us? Many are the—"

"Tell me now who you are or I swear I'll put a bullet straight through this device."

"Listener! I swear too; I am your Friend. We are! We seek only to warn you of the dangers—"

"Deny you are Aultridia!" Oramen said, jumping up from the chair.

"Why would any deny being one of that misunderstood, maligned race? So cruelly slandered—"

Oramen pointed the gun at the World model, then put it up again. The shot would terrify Xessice and doubtless bring Neguste hurtling through from his quarters, tripping over himself, and probably wake or galvanise any nearby guards.

"... by those who theft our very purpose! Listener! Prince! Do no violence! I beg you! This prefigures what we wish to warn you about, talismans our worries that—"

He clicked the safety catch, held the gun by the barrel and brought the butt whacking down on the exposed centre of the World model. It crumpled and shot sparks; some tiny pieces flew skittering across the surface of the desk, though still the cloudy screen pulsed with slow strange colours and the voice, though weakened now, warbled on, incomprehensible. He hit it hard again. It seemed wrong to strike a model of any Shellworld, wrong to destroy something so beautiful, but not as wrong as allowing himself to be talked to by an Aultridian. He shivered at the very thought and slammed the gun down again on the still glowing World model. A blaze of tiny sparks and a puff of smoke and it was finally silent and dark. He waited for Xessice or Neguste to appear, or make some noise, but neither did. After a few moments he lit a candle then found a bin, pushed the smashed World model into it and poured a jug of water over the remains.

He went back to bed beside the gently snoring Xessice. He lay awake unsleeping, waiting until it was time for breakfast, staring into the darkness. By God, they had been proved even more right to have smashed the Deldeyn. And he no longer wondered at the mass suicide of the brethren, sending themselves over the Falls. There were rumours in the Settlement that it had not been suicide; some people even spoke of a few surviving monks who'd been washed up far downstream with tales of treachery and murder. He had started to doubt tyl Loesp's account of mass suicide, but he doubted it no longer.

The wonder was that the wretches had lived with themselves at all rather than that they had chosen death, if this was what they had buried in their conscience all the time. An alliance with the Aultridia! Contact with them at the very least. With the foulness that conspired against the WorldGod itself! He wondered what conspiracies, lies and secrets had passed between the Archipontine of the Hyeng-zharia Mission and whatever Aultridian master had been on the other end of the communication channel that ended at the World model he had just destroyed.

Had that hideous race even directed matters here at the Falls? The monks of the Mission had controlled the workings, supervised and licensed all the excavations and largely policed them; certainly they had kept a tight hand upon the main, official excavations. Had the Mission been in effect controlled by the Aultridia? Well, they were in control no longer, and would remain so disempowered as long as he had any sort of say in matters. He wondered who to tell about what had passed between him and the nameless – and no doubt faceless – Aultridian he had spoken to. The very thought turned his stomach. Should he tell Poatas, or General Foise? Poatas would probably find a way to blame Oramen for what had happened; he'd be horrified he'd broken the communication device. Oramen doubted General Foise would even understand.

He'd tell nobody, not for now.

He considered taking the World model to the cliff above the gorge and throwing it in, but was concerned that it would just be dredged up again by some collector. In the end he had Neguste carry the thing to the nearest foundry and had them melt it down while he watched. The foundrymen were amazed at the temperatures required to slag it, and even then there was still some unmelted debris left, both floating above the resulting liquid and sunk to its base. Oramen ordered the whole split into a dozen different ingots and delivered to him as soon as they'd cooled.

That morning, on his way to watch the demise of the blade-building, he'd thrown some into the gorge. He consigned the rest to latrines.

"Well, it all sounds most unpleasant," Droffo said. He shook his head. "You hear all sorts of ridiculous stories; the workers are full of them. Too much drink, too little learning."

"No, more than that, sir," Neguste told him. "These are facts."

"I think I might dispute that," Droffo said.

"All the same, sir, facts is facts. That itself's a fact."

"Well, let's go and see for ourselves, shall we?" Oramen said, looking round at the other two. "Tomorrow. We'll take the narrow-gauge and cableways and britches boys or whatever we need to take and we'll go and have a look under the great ghostly, spooky plaza. Yes? Tomorrow. We'll do it then."

"Well," Droffo said, looking up into the sky again. "If you feel you have to, prince; however—"

"Begging pardon, sir," Neguste said, nodding behind Oramen. "Building's falling over."

"What?" Oramen said, turning back again.

The great blade of a building was indeed falling. It pivoted, turning fractionally towards them, still moving slowly at first, whirling gradually through the air, the edge of its summit parting the mists and clouds of spray and making them whorl around its surfaces and sharpnesses as it leant diagonally away from the plaza and the main face of the waterfall behind, picking up speed and turning further like a man starting to fall on his face but then twisting to lead with one shoulder. One long edge came down, hitting the spray and the sandbanks beneath like a blade chopping through a child's dam on a beach, the rest of the building following on to it, parts finally starting to crumple as the whole structure slammed into the waves, raising enormous pale fans of muddy water to half the height of their own vantage point.

Finally, some sound arrived; a terrible creaking, tearing, screaming noise that forced its way out of the encompassing roar of the Falls, topped with a great extra rumble that pulsed through the air, seemed to shake the building beneath their feet and briefly outbellowed the voice of the Hyeng-zhar itself. The poised, half-collapsed building fell over one last time, settling from its side on to its back, collapsing into the chaotic waste of piling waves with another great surge of foaming, outrushing waters.

Oramen watched, fascinated. Immediately the first shocked pulse of waves fell washing back from the heights around the impact site the waters began to rearrange themselves to accommodate the new obstruction, piling up behind the shattered hulk of the fallen building and surging round its edges while foam-creamed waves went dancing backwards, slapping into others still falling forwards, their combined shapes climbing and bursting as though in some wild celebration of destruction. Nearby sand bars that had been five metres above the tallest waves were now sunk beneath them; those ten metres above the waters were being swiftly eroded as the swirling currents cut carving into them, their lives now counted in minutes. Looking straight down, Oramen could see that the base of the building they were in was now almost surrounded by the backed-up surge of spray and foam.

He turned to the others. Neguste was still staring at where the building had fallen. Even Droffo looked rapt, standing away from the wall, vertigo temporarily forgotten.

Oramen took another glance towards the waters surging round their tower. "Gentlemen," he said, "we'd best go."

23. Liveware Problem

"**S**ister?" Ferbin said as the woman in the plain blue shift walked up to him. It *was* Djan Seriy. He hadn't seen her for fifteen of their years but he knew it was her. So changed, though! A woman, not a girl, and a wise, utterly poised and collected woman at that. Ferbin knew enough about authority and charisma to recognise it when he saw it. No mere princess, little Djan Seriy; rather a very queen among them.

"Ferbin," she said, stopping a stride away and smiling warmly. She nodded. "How good to see you again. Are you well? You look different."

He shook his head. "Sister, I am well." He could feel his throat closing up. "Sister!" he said, and threw himself at her, wrapping her in his arms and hooking his chin over her right shoulder. He felt her arms close over his back. It was like hugging a layer of soft leather over a figure made of hardwood;

she felt astoundingly powerful; unshakeable. She patted his back with one hand, cupped the back of his head with the other. Her chin settled on his shoulder.

"Ferbin, Ferbin, Ferbin," she whispered.

"Where exactly are we?" Ferbin asked.

"In the middle of the hub engine unit," Hippinse told him. Since meeting with Djan Seriy, Hippinse's manner had changed somewhat; he seemed much less manic and voluble, more composed and measured.

"Are we boarding a ship, then, sir?" Holse asked.

"No, this is a habitat," Hippinse said. "All Culture habitats apart from planets have engines. Have had for nearly a millennium now. So we can move them. Just in case."

They had come here straight after meeting, back up one of the tubes to the very centre of the little wheel-shaped habitat. They floated again – seemingly weightless – within the narrow but quiet, gently lit and pleasantly perfumed spaces of the habitat's bulging centre.

Another corridor and some rolling, sliding doors had taken them to this place where there were no windows or screens and the circular wall looked odd, like oil spilled on water, colours ever shifting. It appeared soft somehow, but – when Ferbin touched the surface – felt hard as iron, though strangely warm. A small, floating cylindrical object had accompanied Djan Seriy. It looked rather like a plain-sword handle with no sword attached. It had produced five more little floating things no bigger than a single joint in one of Ferbin's smallest fingers. These had started to glow as they'd entered the corridor and were now their only source of light.

The section of corridor they were floating in – he, Holse, Hippinse and Djan Seriy – was perhaps twenty metres long and blank at one end. Ferbin watched as the doorway they had entered by closed off and slid in towards them.

"Inside an engine?" Ferbin said, glancing at Djan Seriy. The massive plug of door continued to slide down the corridor towards them. A glittering silver sphere the size of a man's head appeared at the far end of the ever-shortening tube. It started flickering.

Djan Seriy took his hand. "It is not an engine relying on any sort of compression," she told him. She nodded at the still slowly advancing end of the corridor. "That is not a piston. It is part of the engine unit which slid out to allow us to enter here and is now sliding back in to provide us with privacy. That thing at the other end" – she indicated the pulsing silvery sphere – "is removing some of the air at the same time so that the pressure in here remains acceptable. All to the purpose of letting us speak without being overheard." She squeezed his hand, glanced around. "It is hard to explain, but where we are now exists in a manner that makes it impossible for the Morthanveld to eavesdrop upon us."

"The engine exists in four dimensions," Hippinse told Ferbin. "Like a Shellworld. Closed, even to a ship."

Ferbin and Holse exchanged looks.

"As I said," Djan Seriy told them. "Hard to explain." The wall had stopped moving towards them. They were now floating in a space perhaps two metres in diameter and five long. The silvery sphere had stopped pulsing.

"Ferbin, Mr Holse," Djan Seriy said, sounding formal. "You've met Mr Hippinse. This object here is the drone Turminder Xuss." She nodded at the floating sword handle.

"Pleased to meet you," it said.

Holse stared at it. Well, he supposed this was no more strange than some of the Oct and Nariscene things they'd been treating as rational, talk-to-able persons since before they'd even left Sursamen. "Good-day," he said. Ferbin made a throat-clearing grunt that might have been a similar greeting.

"Think of it as my familiar," Djan Seriy said, catching the look on Ferbin's face.

"You're some sort of wizardess, then, ma'am?" Holse asked.

"You might say that, Mr Holse. Now." Djan Seriy glanced at the silvery sphere and it disappeared. She looked at the floating sword handle. "We are thoroughly isolated and we are all free of any devices that might report anything that happens here. We are, for the moment, existing on the air we have around us, so let's not waste words. Ferbin," she said, looking at him. "Briefly, if you would, what brings you here?"

The silvery sphere came back before he was finished. Even keeping it as succinct as he could, Ferbin's account had taken a while. Holse had filled in parts, too. The air had grown stuffy and very warm. Ferbin had had to loosen his clothing as he told his story, and Holse was sweating. Hippinse and Djan Seriy looked unbothered.

Djan Seriy held up her hand to stop Ferbin a moment before the sphere appeared. Ferbin had assumed she could summon it at will, though later he discovered that she was just very good at counting time in her head and knew when it would reappear. The air cooled and freshened, then the sphere disappeared again. His sister nodded and Ferbin completed his tale.

"Oramen still lived, last I heard," she said, once he had finished. She looked stern, Ferbin thought; the wise, knowing smile that had played across her face was gone now, her jaw set in a tight line, lips compressed. Her reaction to the manner of their father's death had been expressed at first not in words but in a brief widening of her eyes, then gaze narrowing. It was so little in a way, and yet Ferbin had the impression he had just set something unstoppable, implacable in motion. She had, he realised, become formidable. He remembered how solid and strong she had felt, and was glad she was on his side "Tyl Loesp really did this?" she said suddenly, looking at him directly, almost fiercely.

Ferbin felt a terrible pressure from those clear, startlingly dark eyes. He felt himself gulp as he said, "Yes. On my life."

She continued to study him for a moment longer, then relaxed a little, looking down and nodding. She glanced at the thing she had called a drone and frowned briefly, then looked down again. Djan Seriy sat cross-legged in her long blue shift, floating effortlessly, as did the black-clad Hippinse. Ferbin and Holse just floated feeling ungainly, limbs spread so that when they bumped into the sides they could fend themselves off again. Ferbin felt odd in the absence of gravity; puffed up, as though his face was flushed.

He studied his sister while – he guessed – she thought. There was an almost unnatural stillness about her, a sense of immovable solidity beyond the human.

Djan Seriy looked up. "Very well." She nodded at Hippinse. "Mr Hippinse here represents a ship that should be able to get us back to Sursamen with some dispatch." Ferbin and Holse looked at the other man.

Hippinse turned his smile from them to Djan Seriy. "At your disposal, dear lady," he said. A little oilily, Ferbin thought. He had decided he did not like the fellow, though his new calmness was welcome.

"I think we have little choice but to take this offered help, and ship," Djan Seriy said. "Our urgencies multiply."

"Happy to be of service," Hippinse said, still smiling annoyingly.

"Ferbin," Djan Seriy said, leaning towards him, "Mr Holse; I was returning home anyway, having heard of our father's death, though of course not of its manner. However, Mr Hippinse brought news regarding the Oct which has meant that I've been asked to make my visit what you might call an officially authorised one. One of Mr Hippinse's colleagues contacted me earlier with an offer of help. I turned that first offer down but on arrival here I discovered a message from those one might term my employers asking me to take a professional interest in events on Sursamen, so I have had to change my mind." She glanced at Hippinse, who grinned, first at her, then at the two Sarl men. "My employers have even seen fit to send a representation of my immediate superior to the ship to assist in planning the mission," she added.

A personality construct of Jerle Batra had been emplaced within the *Liveware Problem*'s Mind. If that wasn't a sign that the ship was a secret asset of SC, she didn't know what would be, though they were still denying this officially.

"Something may be amiss on Sursamen," Djan Seriy said. "Something of potentially still greater importance than King Hausk's death, however terrible that may be to us. Something that involves the Oct. What it is, we do not know." She nodded to Ferbin. "Whether this is linked in any way to our father's murder, we also do not know." She looked at Ferbin and Holse in turn. "Returning to Sursamen might be dangerous for you both in any event. Returning with me may be much more dangerous. I may attract more trouble than you'd have discovered yourselves and I will not be able to guarantee your safety, or even guarantee that I can make it my priority. I am going back, now, on business. I shall have duties. Do you understand? You do not have to accompany me. You would be welcome to stay here or be taken to some other part of the Culture. There would be no dishonour in that."

"Sister," Ferbin said, "we go with you." He glanced at Holse, who nodded sharply.

Anaplian nodded. She turned to Hippinse. "How soon can you get us to Sursamen?"

"Five hours in-shuttle to clear Syaung-un and synch the pick-up. After that; seventy-eight hours to a stop over Sursamen Surface."

Djan Seriy frowned. "What can you cut off that?"

Hippinse looked alarmed. "Nothing. That's already engine-damage speed. Need an overhaul."

"Damage them a bit more. Book a bigger overhaul."

"If I damage them any more I risk breaking them altogether and leaving us reduced to warp, or limping in on burst units."

"What about a crash-stop?"

"Five hours off journey time. But bang goes your stealthy

approach. Everybody'll know we're there. Might as well spell it out with sunspots."

"Still, option it." She frowned. "Bring the ship in afap and snap us off the shuttle. What's that save?"

"Three hours off the front. Adds one to journey time; wrong direction. But a high-speed Displ—"

"Do it, please." She nodded briskly. The silvery sphere reappeared. The door that had slid towards them started to slide back again almost immediately. Djan Seriy calmly unfolded herself and looked round the three men. "We speak no more of any of this until we're on the ship itself, agreed?" They all nodded. Djan Seriy pushed herself away towards the retreating plug of door. "Let's go."

They were being given exactly ten minutes to get themselves together. Ferbin and Holse found a place nearby in the hub section that had a tiny amount of gravity, windows looking out to the vast, slowly twisting coils of the great Nestworld of Syaung-un which surrounded them, and a little bar area with machines that dispensed food and drink. Djan Seriy's drone thing went with them and showed them how everything worked. When they dithered it made choices for them. They were still expressing amazement at how good it all tasted when it was time to go.

The Displace may show up. A crash-stop certainly will, the personality construct of Jerle Batra told Anaplian as she watched first the little micro-Orbital 512th Degree FifthStrand, and then Syaung-un itself, shrink in size on the module's main screen. The two structures shrank at very different rates, for all that the little twelve-seat craft they were in, a shuttle off the *Liveware Problem*, was accelerating as fast as Morthanveld statutes allowed. 512th Degree FifthStrand disappeared almost immediately, a tiny cog in a vast machine. The Nestworld stayed visible for a long time. At first it seemed almost to grow bigger, even more of it coming into view as the shuttle powered away, before, along with its central star, Syaung-un finally started to shrink.

Too bad, Djan Seriy replied. *If our Morthanveld friends are insulted, then so be it. We've pitty-patted round the Morthanveld long enough. I grow tired of it.*

You assume a deal of authority here, Seriy Anaplian, the construct – currently housed in the shuttle's AI matrix – told her. *It is not for you to make or remake Culture foreign policy.*

Djan Seriy settled in her seat at the back of the shuttle. From here she could see everybody.

I am a Culture citizen, she replied. *I thought it was entirely my right and duty.*

You are one *Culture citizen.*

Well, in any case, Jerle Batra, if my elder brother is to be believed, my other brother's life is in severe danger, the cold-blooded murderer of my father – a potential tyrant – is lord of not one but two of Sursamen's levels, and, of course, the majority of the Oct front-line fleet may be converging on my home planet, for reasons still unclear. I think I am entitled to a little leeway here. Talking of; what is the latest on the Oct ships? The ones that may or may not be heading for Sursamen.

We're picking up nothing untoward so far, last I heard. I suggest you update when you're on the Liveware Problem.

You aren't coming with us?

My presence, even in construct form, might make this look too official. I won't be coming with you.

Oh. This probably meant the construct was going to be wiped from the matrix of the shuttle, too. It would be a kind of death. The construct didn't sound too upset about it.

You do trust the Liveware Problem, *I assume?* she sent.

We have no choice, Batra replied. *It is all we have available. You are still denying it is officially SC?*

The ship is what it says it is, Batra told her. *However, to return to the subject: the trouble is that we don't have any ships in the relevant volumes to be able to check on what the Oct are really doing. The Morthanveld and Nariscene do have the ships and don't seem to have spotted anything either, but then they're not looking.*

Perhaps it is time we told them to start looking.

Perhaps it is. It's being discussed.

I'm sure. Would this involve lots of Minds blathering?

It would.

Suggest that they blather quicker. One other thing.

Yes, Djan Seriy?

I am switching on all my systems again. All those that I can, at least. Those I can't reinstigate myself I'll ask the Liveware Problem *to help with. Always assuming, of course, that it is familiar with SC procedures.*

You are not being ordered to do this, Batra replied, ignoring what might have been sarcasm.

Yes, I know.

Personally, I think it's a wise move.

So do I.

"Didn't you notice, sir? Never breathed, not for the whole time we were in there, save for when the glittery thing was there. When it wasn't, she didn't breathe at all. Amazing." Holse was speaking very quietly, aware that the lady concerned was only a couple of rows behind them in the shuttle. Hippinse was a row in front, seemingly fast asleep. Holse frowned. "You quite sure she's really your sister, sir?"

Ferbin only remembered thinking how still Djan Seriy had seemed in the strange tube of corridor back on the little wheel-habitat. "Oh, she is my sister, Holse." He glanced back, wondering why she'd chosen to sit there, away from him. She nodded at him in a distracted way; he smiled and turned away.

"At any rate, I must take her to be," he told Holse. "As she, in return, must take me at my word regarding the fate of our father."

Oh yes, I can feel you doing it, the drone sent. She'd just told the machine she was re-fanging herself, switching back on all those systems that she was able to. *Batra happy with that?*

Happy enough.

I wonder how "fanged" the Liveware Problem *is?* the drone sent. The machine was lodged between Anaplian's neck and the seat. Its appearance had changed again; when they'd arrived on the 512th Degree FifthStrand facility it had morphed its surface and puffed out a little to look like a kind of baton-drone.

Oh, I think it might be quite fanged, Djan Seriy sent. *The more I've thought about it, the more strange it's come to seem that the ship described itself as "Absconded".*

That struck me as odd at the time, too, Turminder Xuss sent. *However, I put it down to elderly ship eccentricity.*

It is an old ship, Anaplian agreed. *But I do not think it is demented. However, certainly it is old enough to have earned its retirement. It is a veteran. Superlifters at the start of the Idiran War were the fastest ships the Culture had and the closest things to warships that were not actually warships. They held the line and took a preponderant share of the punishment. Few survived. So it should be an honoured citizen. It should have the equivalent of medals, pension, free travel. However, it is describing itself as Absconded, so maybe it refused to do something it was supposed to do. Like be disarmed.*

Hmm, the drone replied, obviously unconvinced. *Jerle Batra does not clarify its status?*

Correct. Anaplian's eyes narrowed as the few immediately available systems she could control just by thinking about it came back on line and started checking themselves. *So it has to be an old SC machine. Or something very similar.*

I suppose we should hope so.

We should, she agreed. *Do you have any more to add?*

Not for now. Why?

I'm going to leave you for a bit, Turminder. I should go and talk to my brother.

24. Steam, Water, Ice, Fire

Tyl Loesp found the Boiling Sea of Yakid a disappointment.
It did indeed boil, in the centre of the great crater that held
it, but it was not really that impressive, even if the resulting
steams and mists did indeed "assault the very vault of heaven"
(some ancient poet – he was glad he couldn't remember which
one; every forgotten lesson was a victory over the tutors who'd
tried so hard, under the express instructions of his father, to
beat the knowledge into him). With the wind in the wrong direction all the Boiling Sea had to offer was the sensation of being
in a thick bank of fog; hardly a phenomenon worth walking
out of doors to sample, let alone travelling for many days
through frankly undistinguished countryside.

The Hyeng-zhar was far more striking and magnificent.

Tyl Loesp had seen the Boiling Sea from the shore, from the
water in a pleasure steamer (as he was now), and from the air

on a lyge. In each case one was not allowed to get too close, but he suspected even genuinely dangerous proximity would fail to make the experience especially interesting.

He had brought what was effectively his travelling court here, establishing a temporary capital in Yakid City to spend a month or so enjoying cooler weather than that afflicting Rasselle, allow him to visit the other famous sites – Yakid was roughly at the centre of these – and put some distance between him and both Rasselle and the Hyeng-zhar. To put distance between him and Oramen, being honest about it.

He had moved his departure from Rasselle forward only a day or so to avoid meeting the Prince Regent. Certainly it let the fellow know who was boss and this was how he'd justified it to himself originally, but he knew that his real motive had been more complicated. He had developed a distaste for the youth (young man; whatever you wanted to call him). He simply did not want to see him. He found himself bizarrely awkward in his company, experienced a strange difficulty in meeting his gaze. He had first noticed this on the day of his triumph in Pourl, when nothing should have been able to cloud his mood, and yet this odd phenomenon somehow had.

This could not possibly be a guilty conscience or an inability to dissemble; he was confident he had done the right thing – did not his ability to travel round this newly conquered level, as its king in all but name, not attest to that? – and he had lied fluently to Hausk for twenty years, telling him how much he admired him and respected him and revered him and would be forever in his debt and be the sword in his right hand, etc. etc. etc., so it must simply be that he had come to despise the Prince Regent. There was no other reasonable explanation.

It was all most unpleasant and could not go on. It was partly for this reason he had arranged for matters to be brought to a conclusion at the Hyeng-zhar while he was away.

So he was here, some rather more than respectable distance from any unpleasantness, and he had seen their damned Boiling

Sea for himself and he had indeed seen some other spectacular and enchanting sights.

He was still not entirely sure why he had done this. Again, it could not be simply because he wished to avoid the Prince Regent.

Besides, it did no harm anyway for a new ruler to inspect his recently conquered possessions. It was a way of imposing himself upon his new domain and letting his subjects see him, now that he was confident the capital was secure and functioning smoothly (he'd got the strong impression the Deldeyn civil service was genuinely indifferent to who ruled; all they cared about was that somebody did and they be allowed to manage the business of the realm in that person's name).

He had visited various other cities, too, of course, and been – though he had taken some care not to show it – impressed by what he had seen. The Deldeyn cities were generally bigger, better organised and cleaner than those of the Sarl and their factories seemed more efficiently organised too. In fact, the Deldeyn were the Sarl's superiors in dismayingly many areas, save the vital ones of military might and martial prowess. The wonder was that they had prevailed over them at all.

Again though, the people of the Ninth – or at least the ones that he met at ducal house receptions, city chambers lunches and Guildhall dinners – seemed rather pathetically keen to show that they were glad the war was over and thankful that order had been restored. To think that he had once thought to lay waste to so much of this, to have the skies filled with flames and weeping and the gutters and rivers with blood! And all in the cause of besmirching Hausk's name – how limited, how immature that desire seemed now.

These people barely knew or cared who Hausk had been. They had been at war and now they were at peace. Tyl Loesp had the disquieting yet also perversely encouraging impression that the Deldeyn would adapt better to the state of peace as the defeated than the Sarl would as victors.

He had started to dress like the Deldeyn, reckoning that this would endear him to them. The loose, almost effeminate clothes – billowy trous and frock coat – felt odd at first, but he had quickly grown used to them. He had been presented with a fine, many-jewelled watch by the Timepiece Makers' Guild of Rasselle, and had taken to wearing that, too, in the pocket cut into his coat specifically for such instruments. In this land of railways and timetables, it was a sensible accoutrement, even for one who could command trains and steamers to run or not as his whim dictated.

His temporary palace was in the ducal house of Dillser on the shores of the Sea. The pleasure steamer – paddles slapping at the water, funnel pulsing smoke and steam – was heading for the much beflagged dock now, beating through waters that were merely warm and gently misted beneath a wind-cleared sky. Far mountains ringed the horizon, a few of their round, rolling summits snow-topped. The slender towers and narrow spires of the city rose beyond the ducal house and the various marquees and pavilions now covering its lawns.

Tyl Loesp drank in the cool, clear air and tried not to think of Oramen (would it be today? Had it already happened? How surprised ought he to act when the news came through? How would it actually be done?), turning his thoughts instead to dinner that evening and the choice of girl for the night.

"We make good time, sir," the steamer's captain said, coming to join him on the flying bridge. He nodded to tyl Loesp's immediate guard and senior officials, gathered nearby.

"The currents are favourable?" tyl Loesp asked.

"More the lack of any Oct underwater-ships," the captain said. He leant on the railing and pushed his cap up. He was a small, jolly fellow with no hair.

"They are normally a hazard?" tyl Loesp asked.

"Movable sandbanks," the captain said, laughing. "And not very quick about getting out of the way either. Dented a few vessels. Sunk a couple; not by ramming them but by the Oct ship moving up underneath and capsizing the steamer. Few people been drowned. Not intentional, of course. Just poor navigation. You'd think they'd do better, being so advanced." The captain shrugged. "Maybe they just don't care."

"But not a hazard to navigation today?" tyl Loesp said.

The captain shook his head. "Not for about the last twenty days. Haven't seen a single one."

Tyl Loesp frowned as he looked out at the approaching quay. "What normally brings them here?" he asked.

"Who can say?" the captain said cheerfully. "We've always assumed it's the Boiling; might be even more impressive down at the bottom of the Sea, if you had a craft that could get you down there and back again and could see whatever it is that goes on. The Oct never get out of their submarine craft so we can't ask them." The captain nodded at the quayside. "Well, better get us docked. Excuse me, sir." He walked back under the covered bridge to the wheelhouse, shouting orders. The steamer started to turn and the engine exhausted a plume of smoke and steam through its tall funnel before falling back to a steady, idling puff-puff-puff.

Tyl Loesp watched the waves of their wake as they curved away behind them, the last ragged, extended cloud of steam from the funnel settling over the creamy crease of sparkling water, shadowing it.

"Twenty days or so," he said quietly to himself. He beckoned his nearest aide. "Strike our camp," he told him. "We return to Rasselle."

An uncanny stillness had settled over the Hyeng-zhar. Allied with the darkness, it seemed like a form of death.

The river had frozen across its breadth, the middle channel last. Still the water had continued to fall across the Nameless City and into the gorge, even if at a much reduced rate, appearing from underneath the cap of ice to plunge, wreathed in mist, to the landscape of towers, ramps, plaza and water channels beneath. The roar was still there, though also much lessened, so that now it seemed a fit partner for the glimmer that was the weak, paltry light of the slow-moving Rollstar Kiesestraal.

Then one night Oramen had woken up and known something was wrong. He had lain there in the darkness, listening, unable to tell what it was that was so disturbing. A kind of terror afflicted him when he thought it might be another device left behind from the Archipontine's time here, awake again now, calling him. But there was no sound. He listened carefully but could hear nothing, and no winking lights, green or otherwise, showed anywhere.

He turned the cover around the thick night candle, letting light into the compartment. It was very cold; he coughed – one more fading remnant of a typical Settlement affliction that had laid him low for a few days – and watched his breath fume out in front him.

It had taken him a while to work out what seemed so wrong: it was the silence. There was no sound from the Falls.

He walked out at the start of the next working period, into the perpetual-seeming half-night. Droffo, Neguste and the two surly knights were with him. All around, the usual crowds and teams of men and animals were marshalling themselves, ready for their descent into the gorge. A few more today than the day before, just as it had been every day since Oramen had arrived here.

Shuffling and stamping and shouting and bellowing, they made their slow way to the lifts and cranes dotted along the cliff edge for kilometres down the sheer edge of the gorge. An army dropping into the abyss.

The skies were clear. The only mist rose from the broad backs of some beasts of burden, hauling heavy carts and larger items of machinery. Chunsel, uoxantch and ossesyi; Oramen hadn't even known these great warbeasts could be tamed sufficiently for the work of hauling and carrying. He was glad he wouldn't have to share a hoist platform with any of those massively impressive but frightening beasts.

From the gorge side, the Falls were a fabulous, disturbing

sight. No water ran. No clouds obscured any part of the monumental gulf the waters had formed in the land. The view was
uninterrupted, startlingly clear. Frozen curtains and shawls of
solidified water lay draped over every cliff. The channels at the
foot of the gorge – each of which would have been a great river
in its own right, anywhere else – were sinuous black wastes half
covered by sprinkled frosts and snows.

Oramen felt as though he was looking out to a site of some
vast butchery, an eaten landscape – chewed into by an animal
of unimaginable scale – which had then suffered further diminishing but still enormous quarryings as that first monster's
young had come along and each also bitten into the greater
semicircle, after which some smaller monsters had taken still
tinier nips out of the perimeters of those secondary bites, leaving
bite upon bite upon bite all torn from the landscape, all devoured
and swept away by the waters.

And then, in all that structured desolation, that tiered
advancement of fractured chaos, was revealed a city beyond the
skills and fashioning of any portion of humanity Oramen had
ever encountered; a city on a scale that beggared belief; a city
of glassy black towers, bone-white spires, twisted obsidian
blades, outrageously curved, bizarrely patterned structures of
indecipherable purpose and huge, sweeping vistas leading to
canyons and strata and ranks of glistening, glittering edifices,
one after another after another until only the vertical gorge wall
on the far side of the silent Falls, ten kilometres away, intervened.

Half the view was sliced across by the plaza, the spaces
beneath now also shuttered in by the frozen walls of water
draped unmoving over its edges.

"Well, they can get anywhere now," Droffo said.

Oramen looked over to where the cranes, hoists and lifts were
already ferrying whole platforms of men, animals and equipment down into the chasm. A few were coming back up, quitting their own shifts. "Yes, they can," he said. He looked over
at where Vollird and Baerth were both leaning on the railing,

staring into the gorge. Even they seemed impressed. Vollird coughed; a sharp, hacking, choking noise, then he gathered phlegm in his mouth and spat it into the gorge.

"Are you all right, Vollird?" Oramen called.

"Never better, sir," the fellow replied, then cleared his throat and spat again.

"By God, they are a hard couple to like," Droffo muttered.

"The man's not well," Oramen said tolerantly.

Droffo sniffed. "Even so."

This latest cold was affecting everybody in turn. The field hospitals were full of those it was striking most fiercely, and the scrubby ground on the very outskirts of the Settlement, part of what was claimed to be, and probably was, the longest cemetery in the world, was filling up with those it had not spared.

"But yes, they can get to the centre," Oramen said, staring out to the revealed city. "Nothing hinders them now."

"It does seem to be their focus," Droffo said.

Oramen nodded. "Whatever's there."

The latest briefing by the Falls' scholars and gentlemen engineers had been fascinating. Oramen had never seen them so animated, though of course he hadn't been here long. He'd checked with Poatas, who had; he said *of course* they were wild with excitement. What did the young prince expect? They approached the centre of the Nameless City; how could they not be agitated? This was their summit, their climax, their apogee. From here on, the city would likely be just more of the same, and gradually less of it as they left its centre behind, a slow dying away, a diminishing. Meanwhile, what treasure!

There were structures at the city's very centre, deep under the plaza above, of a type they had never encountered before. Every effort was being made to investigate and penetrate that dark, frozen heart, and for once they had the luxury of time, and some surety that the ground would not shift beneath their feet on an instant; the Falls would not quicken again and the waters wash all away once more for another forty or more days. It was auspicious; a piece of luck to be grabbed with both hands and exploited to the full. Meanwhile more of tyl Loesp's reinforcements, his new toilers, were arriving with every incoming train, eager for work. There would never be a better time. This was the very peak and centre of the whole history of the excavations of the Nameless City, indeed the Falls themselves. It deserved their every energy and resource.

Poatas was personally true to his word, having made a new headquarters down in the gorge itself and quartered himself and his staff there in a portion of building deep under the plaza near one of the recently discovered artifacts that appeared by its size and central location to be of particular importance. Oramen had been given the distinct impression that his own presence at the focus of all this furious activity was not required, and indeed might only hinder matters, given that when he was around additional guards had to be deployed to ensure his protection and a proportion of people would always stop work to gawp at a prince, so inhibiting the expeditious and efficient progress of the great works being undertaken.

Nevertheless, he had been determined to see what was going on and had already visited various parts of the excavations even while the ice had been spreading and the waters falling back. He had gone unannounced, with as few people in attendance as he could, seeking to cause as little disruption by his presence as possible. He was certainly not going to be stopped from seeing closer up what was going on now that the waters had frozen solid altogether, and he especially wanted to see something of this new class of artifact that was turning up; he felt he had been kept in ignorance of their importance by Poatas, as though this latest revelation was none of his business. He would not, could not tolerate such disrespect.

They would be flying down on caude; the animals complained about the cold and low levels of light, but their handlers assured Oramen and his party the creatures had been fed a couple of hours before and were warmed and ready to fly. They mounted up, Vollird cursing as his first attempt was wrecked by a fit of coughing.

It had been so long since Oramen had flown he had thought about asking for a practice ground-flight, getting the beast to pad along the flat and rise up a little, giving him time to recall his old flying lessons in relative safety, but that would have been demeaning; a sign of weakness. He had the biggest of the caude, and had offered to take Neguste with him, saddled in behind, but the lad had begged to be excused. He tended to throw up. Oramen had smiled and given him the morning off.

They launched into the air beyond the cliff; Oramen taking the lead. He'd forgotten quite how alarming was the stomach-lurching drop at the start of a flight as the air-beast fell before starting to gain height.

The cold wind bit at the exposed parts of Oramen's face as the caude dropped, stretching its wings out; even with a scarf over his mouth and nose and wearing flying goggles he felt the chill enter him. He pulled on the caude's reins, worrying that it seemed sluggish and felt slow to answer. The beast pulled slowly up, shifting beneath him fretfully as though not yet fully awake. They were still falling too fast; he glanced up and saw Droffo staring down at him from a good ten metres higher. Vollird and Baerth were a little further up still.

The caude shook itself and started beating across the chasm, finally catching the air and levelling out. Oramen watched it raise its great long face and swivel its gaze to each side as it looked groggily up at its companions. The beast's course changed fractionally with each gesture as the creature's head acted like a sort of forward rudder, its tail doubtless twitching in instinctive compensation with each movement. It gave a deep, bellowing cry and beat harder, slowly rising to join the others, and they flew together for a few minutes.

Oramen used the opportunity to look around for as long as he could, drinking in the view and trying to fix it in his mind, knowing that seeing the Nameless City so close up from a flying beast was a rare privilege, then they all went gliding down together towards the temporary landing ground set up near the lumpenly frozen foot of the secondary fall which formed a great dark wall climbing to the edge of the plaza level high above.

They'd passed over the remains of the Fountain Building; the sheer weight of ice accumulated on its surfaces had brought it crumpling, crashing down shortly before the freeze had become complete.

"This is one of ten such littler structures all spotted round the big one in the middle, the one they're calling the Sarcophagus, where there's most attention, as you'd expect," the foreman told them as they walked down a shallow-sloped tunnel towards one of the latest diggings.

"Is there any more on the Sarcophagus?" Oramen asked.

Broft – a bald, trim, upright figure in neatly pressed dungarees with a conspicuously displayed pocket pen – shook his head. "Not really on any of them sir, as I understand it."

The adit sloped downwards into the bowels of some long-fallen building, following a passage that had silted up when the city had first been buried. A string of flickering electric bulbs did their best to light their way, though a couple of the foreman's men carried meshed lanterns as well. This was as much for the fore-warning the lanterns gave – sometimes – of noxious gases as for the light they cast, though that too was welcome. The air about their little party had turned from chilly to mild as they'd descended.

Oramen and foreman Broft led the way, flanked by the two men bearing lanterns. Droffo and a small gaggle of workers, some on their way to their labours, came behind, tailed by Vollird and Baerth – Oramen could hear Vollird's muffled coughing now and again. The passage was smooth save for knee-high ribs running across the floor every fifteen steps or so. These had once been part of the passage walls; the building had fallen on its back and they were walking down what had once been a vertical shaft. Stout wooden boards had been placed across these ribs to provide a level path, one corner of it given over to cables and pipes.

"This one is the deepest, having fallen from the plaza level, sir," Broft said. "We are investigating all such anomalous structures out of stratigraphic orderliness, for once paying little heed to the integrity and place-in-sequence of all discovered objects. Mr Poatas is normally very strict on his integrity of objects, but not here." They were nearing the pit where the artifact had been discovered. The walls here ran with dampness and the air felt warm. Water gurgled beneath the boards at their feet. Pumps sounded ahead; companions to those they'd passed at the entrance to the adit. To Oramen the machines were like the men at either end of a two-man saw, passing it to and fro, cutting into some great trunk.

"Many are the theories, as you might imagine, prince sir, regarding the objects, especially the large central one. My own thoughts . . ."

Oramen was only half listening. He was thinking about how he'd felt when the caude had dropped away beneath him as they'd left the clifftop. He had been terrified. First he had thought that he had forgotten how to fly, then that the creature wasn't properly awake – hearty breakfast or not – or ill; caude took ailments as men did, and there was enough sickness around the Settlement. He had even wondered, just for an instant, if the beast might have been drugged.

Was he being preposterous? He didn't know. Ever since the conversation with Fanthile the day that Tove had been murdered and he had shot the two assassins, he'd been thinking. Of course there were people who wanted him dead; he was a prince, the Prince Regent; future leader of the people who had conquered these people. And his death, of course, would suit some. Tyl Loesp, even. Who would gain most from his death? Fanthile had asked. He still could not believe tyl Loesp wanted him dead; he had been too sure and absolute a friend of his father's for far too long, but a man of such power was surrounded by others who might act on his behalf, thinking that they did what he might wish but could not request.

Even those awful few moments in the courtyard of the inn, when Tove had died, had been poisoned for him. Thinking about it, the fight had started very easily, and Tove had pulled him out of it and sobered up very quickly. (Well, drunken fights did start over nothing, and the prospect of violence could sober a man up in a heartbeat.) But then Tove had tried to send him out of that door first, and seemed surprised, even alarmed when Oramen had pushed him out. (Of course he'd want his friend to get to safety before he did; he thought the danger was all behind them, back in the bar.) And then, his words: "Not *me*," or something very like that.

Why that? Why exactly *those* words, with the implication – perhaps – that the assault itself had been expected but it should have happened to whoever was with him, not Tove himself? (He had just had a knife rammed into his guts and ripped up towards his heart; was he to be suspicioned because he failed to scream, *Fie, murder!* or, *O, sire, thou dost kill me!* like some mummer in a play?)

And Dr Gillews, seemingly by his own hand.

But why Gillews? And if Gillews . . .

He shook his head – foreman Broft glanced at him and he had to grin back encouragingly for a moment before resuming his thoughts. No, that was taking supposition too far.

However it worked out, he was sure that, this morning, he should have tested the caude. It had been foolish not to. Admitting his flying might be a little rusty would have been no great disgrace. Next time he would do the sensible thing, even if it meant running the risk of embarrassing himself.

They came out on to a platform above the pit, looking down from halfway up the curved wall into the focus of all the attention: a night-black cube ten metres to a side lying tipped in a moat of dirty-looking water at the bottom of a great shored chamber at least thirty metres in diameter. The cube seemed to swallow light. It was surrounded by scaffolding and clambering people, many using what looked like pieces of mining equipment. Blue and orange flashes lit the scene and hissing, clattering steam hammers sounded as various methods were attempted to gain entry into the cube – if it could be entered – or at least to try to chip pieces off. In all the noise and hubbub, though, it was the object itself that always drew the eye back to it. Some of the labourers they'd accompanied filed on to a hoist attached to the main platform and waited to be lowered into the pit.

"Still resisting!" Broft said, shaking his head. He leaned on the makeshift railing. A pump fell silent and Oramen heard cursing. As though in sympathy, the light nearest them, on the wall of the chamber to the side of the adit, flickered and went out. "Can't get into these things," Broft said, turning and tutting at the extinguished light. He looked at one of the lantern men and nodded at the lamp. The fellow went to inspect it. "Though the object might be judged worth lifting out," Broft continued, "the brethren would have left it here to rot – or not rot, probably, as it hasn't already – but, however, under our new and may I say much more enlightened rules, sir, we might offer the object to a third party, which is to say . . . What?"

The lantern man had muttered something into Broft's ear. He made a tsking noise and went to look at the dead light.

It was relatively quiet in the chamber for a moment. The squeaking noises of the pulleys lowering the first group of workers towards the pit floor was the loudest sound. Even Vollird seemed to have stopped coughing.

Oramen hadn't heard the knight's cough for a little while now. Without warning, he felt an odd chill.

"Well," he heard Broft say, "it looks like a blasting wire, but how can it be a blasting wire when there's not any blasting today? That's just ridiculous."

Oramen turned to see the foreman tugging at a wire strung with some of the other wires looped along the wall between the light fixtures. The wire led down the wall to disappear behind the planking at their feet. In the other direction, it disappeared into the tunnel they'd just walked down. Vollird and Baerth weren't on the platform.

He felt suddenly sweaty and cold at once. But no, he was being silly, absurd. To react as he suddenly wanted to react would be to make himself look fearful and stupid in front of these men. A prince had to behave with decorum, calmness, bravery . . .

But then; what was he thinking of? Was he mad? What had he decided, only a few minutes earlier?

Have the bravery to risk looking foolish . . .

Oramen swivelled, took Droffo by the shoulders and forced him to turn with him and step towards the adit. "Come," he said, forcing Droffo forward. He began pushing through some of the workers waiting to descend. "Excuse me; excuse me, if you would, excuse me, thank you, excuse me," he said calmly.

"Sir?" he heard Broft say.

Droffo was dragging his feet. "Prince," he said as they approached the entrance to the adit. A glance up it showed no trace of Vollird and Baerth.

"Run," Oramen said, not loudly. "I'm ordering you to run. Get out." He turned to the men remaining on the platform and bellowed, "RUN! Get OUT!" then he pushed the uncomprehending Droffo forward, darted past him and started running as fast as he could, pounding uphill, the boards slamming and quaking under his feet. After a few moments he heard Droffo following, his feet too hammering on the boards, whether because he also thought there might be danger or because he saw Oramen running away and thought he ought to stay with him regardless, Oramen did not know.

How slowly one ran, he thought, when one's mind was racing so much faster. He could not believe that he could run any quicker – his legs were pistoning beneath him, his arms swinging and his chest pulling the air into his lungs with an instinctive functionality no mentation would improve upon – but he felt cheated that his furiously working brain could in no further way contribute to the effort. It might be a doomed effort, of course. Looking at it logically, rationally, it probably was.

He had been too trusting. Naïve, even. One paid for such laxness. Sometimes one got away with it, escaped just punishment – rather as he'd escaped and Tove had paid, that day in the courtyard of the Gilder's Lament (and maybe Tove had not paid unjustly) – but one did not escape every time. Nobody did. Now, he had no doubt, was when he paid.

Embarrassment. He had worried about being embarrassed because he might overreact to some perceived, perhaps misperceived threat. How much more embarrassing to have missed all clues, to have wandered through this violent, kinetic world with a babe's wide-eyed innocence and trust, to have ascribed innocence and decency when he should have seen duplicity and iniquity.

I should just have tugged at the blasting wire, he thought. Tried to pull it free. What a fool, what a selfish fool. Together we might—

The explosion was a dirty yellow blast of light followed almost immediately by what felt like a warbeast kicking him hard in the back with both hind legs. He was lifted off his feet and propelled through the air up and along the adit so that it seemed like a vertical shaft he was falling into. He was upright and flailing for a long moment, then suddenly tumbling; limbs, shoulders, behind, head and hip smacking off the surrounding surfaces in an instant cacophony of pain, as though a dozen accurate kicks had all been landed at once.

He blinked up at a ceiling; rough wood, right above him. His nose was pressed against it. He might be crushed. Perhaps he was in a coffin. His ears were ringing. Where had he just been? He could not remember. There was a crazed ringing sound in his head and the air smelled wrong.

He rolled over, making a small noise as bruised, broken parts of his body protested. The real ceiling was visible. He was lying on his back now, the floor beneath him. This must be some part of the palace he hadn't encountered before. Where *was* Fanthile?

Dim yellow lights flickered on the wall, linked by loops of wire. The loops of wire meant something, he knew. He'd been doing something. Something he ought to keep doing. What had it been? He tasted blood. He brought one hand up to his face and felt stickiness. He squinted at his hand, raising his head off the floor on quivering, complaining neck muscles. His hand looked very black. He used it to support himself and peered down the corridor. It was very black down there too. Smoke or steam or something was creeping up the tipped ceiling, gradually obscuring the lights further down.

Somebody was lying on their side down there. It looked like that what-did-you ...

Droffo. It was Earl Droffo. What was he doing here? That cloud of smoke was creeping up the ceiling above him. Droff had lost some of his clothes. He looked a bit tattered altogether. And not moving.

The realisation, the memory, came crashing back on him as though the ceiling had caved in, which, he thought, might be exactly what was about to happen. He dragged himself to his knees and then his feet, coughing. Still the cough, he thought; still the cough. He could hear it in his head but not through his still ringing ears.

He staggered down the tunnel to where Droffo lay. He himself seemed to be as poorly clad as the young earl; in rags, all torn and shredded. He had to keep his head down, out of the dark overcast of smoke still drifting up the adit. He shook Droffo but the man didn't move. His face looked pale and there was blood coming from his nose. The smoke was getting lower down all the time. Oramen bent, took Droffo by the armpits and started hauling him bodily over the boards.

He found it hard going. So much hurt; even the coughing pained him. He wished Droffo would wake up and that his hearing would return. The smoke coming up all quiet and dark from down below seemed to be catching up with him again. He wondered if he might have to let Droffo go and run away to save himself. If he did and they'd both have died otherwise, it would be the sensible thing to do. If he did and they might both have survived, it would be the wrong thing to do. How simple that seemed. He decided to keep on dragging Droffo for the time being. He'd think about dropping him if he really couldn't see and breathe. His back hurt.

He thought he felt something through his feet, but his ringing ears let him down. By the time he realised that what he was feeling through his feet might be footsteps, it was too late. You pay, he had time to think.

Next thing he knew there was a rough hand round his nose, mouth and chin and a terrific thudding sensation in his back. Possibly a shouted curse.

He found he had dropped Droffo. He wrenched himself away from whoever had grabbed him; their grip seemed to have loosened. He turned round and saw Baerth standing there looking thunderstruck, a broken long-knife in his hand. Its blade lay between them on the wooden boards, in two pieces. That was careless, Oramen thought. He felt round to the small of his back, through the remains of tattered clothing, found the gun that had stopped the blow and tugged it free.

"You broke it on this!" he shouted to Baerth as he brandished the gun and shot the fellow with it. Three times, just to be sure, then, after the knight had collapsed to the boards, once more, through one flickering eyelid, just to be even more sure. Baerth had had a gun too. A hand on it, at his waist; should have used it earlier. Oramen was glad his ears were already ringing; meant he didn't have to suffer the sound of the gun going off four times in such a confined space. That would really have hurt.

He went back to Droffo, who was moving on his own now. "You're going to have to get up, Droff!" he shouted, then hefted the fellow one-armed under his armpit, side by side this time so that he could see where they were going and not be surprised by murderous fuckers with long-knives. Droffo seemed to be trying to say something, but Oramen still couldn't hear. The tunnel ahead looked long and hazy but otherwise empty. He kept his gun in his hand all the same.

People came down the tunnel eventually and he didn't shoot them; ordinary labourers and a couple of guards. They helped him and Droffo out.

Back at the adit entrance, in the looming darkness of the under-plaza, all studded with little lights, they got to sit and lie down in the little encampment round the tunnel mouth and he thought he heard – muffled, as though his ears were full of water – that somebody had run away.

"You poor sir! Look at you! Oh, you poor sir! A blotting paper!" Neguste Puibive was helping Oramen's nurse to dress him. Neguste was shocked at the extent of his master's bruising. "Camouflaged you are, sir, I swear; I've seen trucks and things all scattered with dibs and daubs of paint with less of a mixturing of colours than your poor skin!"

"No more colourful than your comparisons, Neguste," Oramen said, hissing in pain as the nurse lifted his arm and his servant fitted his undershirt over it.

Oramen's ears still rang. He could hear well enough now, but the ringing, even if much reduced, remained and the doctors could not guarantee it would ever fully stop. That might be his only lasting damage, and he counted himself lucky. Droffo had suffered a badly broken arm as well as a puncturing of the membrane in one ear, leaving him permanently half-deaf. The doctors reckoned his arm could be made whole again; they had an embarrassment of experience with every form of human injury in the infirmaries of the Settlement.

Oramen had been fairly surrounded by doctors for too much of the time. At one stage he'd thought a group of Sarl doctors was going to come to blows with another clutch of Deldeyn medics over some abstruse point regarding how to treat extensive bruising. He wondered if they were just keen to be able to say they had once treated a prince.

General Foise had been to see him. He had wished him well politely enough, though Oramen had the distinct impression the fellow was looking at him as he might at a piece of malfunctioning military equipment he was thinking about having junked. Poatas had sent his regards by note, thankfully, claiming great and urgent busyness occasioned in no small part by the necessary re-excavation of the chamber partially collapsed by the explosion.

Oramen dismissed the nurse – a prim, middle-aged woman of some formidability – and, with much grunting and wincing, let Neguste alone help him complete dressing.

When they were about done, and Oramen, dressed formally, was ready to make his first public appearance since the explosion three days earlier, he drew his ceremonial sword and asked Neguste to inspect its tip, holding it out level with the fellow's eyes, almost at his nose. The effort of it hurt Oramen's arm.

Neguste looked puzzled. A little comical, too, with his eyes crossed, focusing on the sword's tip so close to his face. "What do I look for, sir?"

"That is my question, Neguste," Oramen said quietly. "What do you look for?"

"Sir?" Neguste looked mightily confused. He started to put his right hand up to touch the tip of the sword.

"Leave it be," Oramen said sharply. Neguste let his hand fall back. "Are you really so sicked by riding in the air, Neguste?"

"Sir?" Neguste's brows were furrowed like a field; sufficiently deep, Oramen thought, to cast shadows.

"That was a canny absence you had there, fellow, just when all closest to me were marked to die."

"Sir?" Neguste said again, looking like he was about to start crying.

"Stop saying 'Sir?'," Oramen told him gently, "or I swear I'll stick this point through either one of your idiot eyes. Now answer me."

"Sir! I lose my latest meal near on sight of an air-beast! I swear! Ask anyone! I'd not wish you harm, sir! Not me! You don't think I had any part in this, do you? Sir?" Neguste sounded horrified, shocked. His face drained of colour and his eyes filled with tears. "Oh!" he said faintly, and crumpled, his back sliding down the wall, his backside thumping heavily down on the floor of the carriage, his knees splayed on either side. Oramen let the tip of the sword follow him down so that it was still angled at his nose. "Oh, sir!" he said, and put his face in his hands. He started sobbing. "Oh, sir! Sir, kill me if it pleases you; I'd rather you did that and found me innocent later than live apart from you, accused, even just in your heart, a free man. A limb to a hair, sir; I swore that to Mr Fanthile when he instructed me I was to be your last sticking shield as well as your most faithful servant. I'd lose arm or leg than see a hair on your littlest toe unkindly plucked!"

Oramen looked down at the crying youth. The Prince Regent's face was set, his expression neutral, as he listened – through the ringing – to the fellow's hand-muffled sobs.

He sheathed the sword – that hurt too, a little – then leant down to grasp Neguste's hand, slippery and hot with tears, and pulled the lad to his feet. He smiled at him. Neguste's face had some blood in it now, all reddened with crying, his eyes already puffed. He wiped his nose on one sleeve, sniffing strenuously, and when he blinked tiny beads of moisture arced from his eyelids.

"Calm yourself, Neguste," Oramen said, clapping him gently on his shoulder. "You are my shield, and my conscience too in this. I'm poisoned by this too-slow-seen conspiracy against me. I'm late inoculated against it and suffering a fever of suspicion that makes every face around me look mean and every hand, even those that would help, seem turned against. But here; take mine. I offer apology. Ascribe my wronging you as your share of my injury. We infect those closest in the very act of caring for us, but mean them no harm."

Neguste gulped and sniffed again, then wiped his hand on his britches and took Oramen's offered hand.

"Sir, I swear—"

"Hush, Neguste," Oramen told him. "No more's to say. Indulge me in silence. Believe me, I long for it." He drew himself up, his very bones protesting at the movement, and gritted his teeth. "Now, tell me. How do I look?"

Neguste sniffed and a small smile broke across his face. "Very well, sir. Most smart, I'd say."

"Come then, I've my poor face to show to the people."

Vollird too had started down the adit, carbine drawn, then turned back. He'd been challenged by some surface official, shot and killed the fellow then made off into the dark landscape of the under-plaza, followed by, or taking with him – reports varied – the diggings' blasting marshal. This man was found later a short way off, also shot.

Only a handful of men had survived the blast and subsequent fire in the chamber at the bottom of the adit, which had been badly damaged and had partially collapsed. The excavations on that black cube – mercifully itself probably undamaged – had been set back many days. Poatas seemed to regard this as Oramen's fault entirely.

Oramen was holding court in the greatest marquee available. He'd summoned everybody he could think of. Poatas was there, fretting and vexed at this forced absence from the diggings but commanded to attend with the rest and obviously judging it unwise to resist the authority of a prince who had so recently escaped murder.

"Understand that I do not accuse tyl Loesp," Oramen told the assembly, coming towards the end of his address. "I do accuse those who have his ear and think they have his interest at heart. If Mertis tyl Loesp is guilty of anything it may only be failing to see that some around him are less honourable and devoted to the rule of law and good of all than he is himself. I have been most unjustly preyed upon, and have had to kill not one but three men merely to protect my own existence, and while I have been lucky, or blessed, in escaping the fate these wretches have desired for me, many around me have suffered in my stead through no fault of their own."

Oramen paused and looked down. He took a couple of deep breaths and bit his lip before looking up again. If those present chose to interpret this as emotion close to tears, then so be it. "A season ago I lost my best friend in the sunshine of a court-yard in Pourl. This company lost fifty good men in the dark-ness of a pit in the under-plaza not four days ago. I ask the forgiveness of their shades and survivors for allowing my youth-fulness to blind me to the hatefulness that threatened me."

Oramen raised his voice. He felt weary and sore and his ears still rang, but he was determined not to let this show. "All I can offer in return for their hoped-for forgiveness is the vow that I shall not let my guard down again and so endanger those close to me." He paused and looked around the whole gath-ering. He could see General Foise and the other people tyl Loesp had put in charge of the Settlement's security and organisation looking distinctly worried at how this was going. "So it is that I ask you all to be my sentinels. I shall constitute a formal watch of some of the most trusted veterans here amongst you to protect me most closely from harm and to preserve the rightful contin-uance of our heritage, but I ask you all to play whatever part you can in the proper security of my being and our purpose. I have, also, sent a messenger to Field Marshal Werreber informing him of the attack upon me here and requesting both a pledge of his continuing and undoubted loyalty and a contin-gent of his finest troops to protect us all.

"You are engaged in great works here. I have come late to this mighty undertaking but it has become part of who I am as it has become part of who you are, and I well know I am priv-ileged to be here when the unbaring of the City approaches its zenith. I would not think to tell you how to do what you do; Jerfin Poatas knows better than I what needs be done and you yourselves know better than anybody how to do it. All I ask is that you remain vigilant as you go about your works, for the betterment of all of us. By the WorldGod, I swear we do labour here the like of which will never be seen again in the whole history of Sursamen!"

He gave a single deep nod, as though he saluted them, then, before he could sit down and while only the vaguest hint of sound, as yet unidentifiable in its import, was forming in the throats of those present, Neguste Puibive – seated at the side of the dais – leapt to his feet and shouted at the top of his lungs, "WorldGod save the good Prince Regent Oramen!"

"Prince Regent Oramen!" the whole assembly – or very nearly the whole assembly – shouted in a great ragged cheer.

Oramen, who had been expecting quietly grudging respect at best and querulous alarm and hostile questioning at worst, was genuinely surprised. He had to blink back tears.

He remained standing, so that, before anybody else there, he saw the messenger dash into the rear of the marquee, hesitate and stop – patently momentarily bewildered by the tumult – then collect himself and rush forward to Jerfin Poatas, who tipped his head to listen to the message over the continuing sound of cheering before hobbling with his stick closer to the dais. Guards at the front – veterans of the Sarl army – barred his way but looked round to Oramen, who nodded Poatas through and stepped down to him to hear his news.

Shortly, he strode back, raising both arms into the air.

"Gentlemen; your various duties await! The object at the centre of the under-plaza, the very focus of all our energies, an artifact we believe has been buried there for deciaeons, has shown signs of life! I command and beseech you: to work!"

25.   The Levels

The *Liveware Problem* had started out life as a relatively slim 3D delta shape like an elegantly pointed pyramid. After conversion to a Superlifter – a glorified tug, really – it took on a block-like brutality. Three hundred metres long, square-sectioned, slab-sided, only the vaguest implication of its older, more slender shape remained.

It had not cared about such aesthetic considerations then and it did not care now. The petalled surround of its field complex, abundant as any party dress wrapped in dozens of gauzy layers, could bestow a kind of beauty on it if the viewer chose to look for it, and its hull skin could take on any design, hue or pattern it desired.

All that was irrelevant anyway; the transformation had made it powerful, the transformation had made it *fast*.

And that was before Special Circumstances came calling.

It swung through hyperspace on what was in effect a near-straight attack path to the star Meseriphine, deviating only to keep the chances of detection low. It had snapped the humans and its own avatoid off the shuttle without incident and scour-turned about to head back in the direction of Sursamen at something uncomfortably over its design-parameter maximum allowed sustainable velocity. It felt the damage accruing to its engines like a human athlete might feel a cramp or a shin splint starting to develop, but knew it would get its little cargo of souls to Sursamen as fast as it sensibly could.

After some negotiation with Anaplian they had agreed it would push its engines to a profile consistent with a one per cent possibility of total failure, thus shaving another hour off their ETA, though even a one in one hundred and twenty-eight chance seemed quite shockingly risky to the ship. With this in mind it had massaged its own performance parameters and lied; the time saving was real but the failure profile was better than one in two hundred and fifty. There were some advantages to being a self-customised one-off based on an ancient Modified.

In one of the two small lounges that was all its rather miserable allocation of accommodation could afford, the ship's avatoid was explaining to the SC agent Anaplian the extent to which the *Liveware Problem* would be limited in its field of operations if it had actually to enter Sursamen. It still hoped, rather fervently, this would not be necessary.

"It's a hypersphere. In fact, it's a series of sixteen hyperspheres," the avatoid Hippinse told the woman. "Four D; I can no easier jump into it than an ordinary, non-HS-capable ship can. I can't even gain any traction off the Grid because it'll cut me off from that too. Didn't you know this?" the avatoid said, looking puzzled. "It's their strength, it's how the heat's managed, how the opacity comes about."

"I knew Shellworlds were four-dimensional," Anaplian admitted, frowning.

It was one of those things that she'd learned only long after leaving the place. In a sense, knowing this before she'd left would have been fairly meaningless; a so-what? fact. When you lived in a Shellworld you just accepted them for what they appeared to be, same as if you lived on the surface of an ordinary rocky planet or within the waters or gases of a waterworld or a gas giant. That Shellworlds had such a profound and extensive four-dimensional component only made any difference once you knew what four-dimensionality implied and allowed in the first place; access to hyperspace in two handy directions, contact with the universes-separating energy Grids so that ships could exploit their many fascinating properties and the easy ability of anything with the appropriate talent to shift something entirely into hyperspace and then make it reappear in three-dimensional space through any amount of conventional solidity as though by magic.

You got used to that sort of capability. In a sense, the more inexplicable and supernatural these skills seemed before you learned how they were done, the less you thought about them afterwards. They went from being dismissible due to their essential absurdity to being accepted without thought because thinking cogently about them was itself so demanding.

"What I had not realised," Anaplian said, "is that that means they're closed off to ships."

"They're not closed off," Hippinse said. "I can move about inside them as freely as any other three-dimensional entity of my size, it's just that I can't move about in the extra fourth dimension that I'm used to and designed for. And I can't use my main engines."

"So you'd rather stay out?"

"Precisely."

"What about Displacing?"

"Same problem. From outside I can Displace down into open Tower-ends. Line-of-sight within a level is possible too, *if* I can get inside somehow, but that'd be all. And of course once inside I couldn't Displace back to outside."

"But you can Displace items short distance?"

"Yes."

Anaplian frowned. "What would happen if you did try to Displace into 4D matter?"

"Something a lot like an AM explosion."

"Really?"

"Good as. Not recommended. Wouldn't want to break a Shellworld."

"They are not easily broken."

"Not with all that 4D structure. What are in effect a Shellworld's operating instructions say you can let off thermonuclear weapons inside them without voiding the warranty as long as you steer clear of Secondary structure, and anyway the internal stars are basically thermonukes and a bundle of exotic matter the most elderly of which have been trying to burn their way through the ceiling of their shell for deciaeons. All the same; anti-matter weaponry is banned inside and a misplaced Displace would have a highly similar profile. If and when I do have to do any Displacing, it'll be very, very carefully."

"Is anti-matter banned entirely?" Anaplian asked, sounding worried. "Most of the high-end gear I work with uses AM reactors and batteries." She scratched the back of her neck, grimacing. "I even have one inside my head."

"In theory as long as it's not weaponry it's allowed," the ship told her. "In practice ... I wouldn't mention it."

"Very well," Anaplian said, sighing. "Your fields; will they work?"

"Yes. Running on internal power. So limited."

"And you can go in if you have to."

"I can go in," the ship confirmed through Hippinse, sounding unhappy. "I'm preparing to reconfigure engine and other matter to reaction mass."

"Reaction mass?" Djan Seriy said, looking sceptical.

"To be used in a deeply retro fusion drive I'm also putting together," Hippinse said with an embarrassed-sounding sigh. He was himself looking reconfigured, becoming taller and less rotund with every passing day.

"Oh dear," Anaplian said, thinking it seemed called for.

"Yes," the ship's avatoid said with evident distaste. "I am preparing to turn myself into a rocket."

"They're saying some terrible things about you, sir, where they mention you at all any more."

"Thank you, Holse. However, I am scarcely concerned with the degree to which my own reputation has been defamed by that tyrant-in-waiting tyl Loesp," Ferbin said, lying. "The state of our home and the fate of my brother is all that matters to me."

"Just as well, sir," Holse said, staring at the display hovering in mid-air in front of him. Ferbin sat nearby, inspecting another holo-screen. Holse shook his head. "They've painted you as a proper rapscallion." He whistled at something on the screen. "Now I *know* you've never done *that*."

"Holse!" Ferbin said sharply. "My brother lives, tyl Loesp goes unpunished and disports himself round the Ninth. The Deldeyn are entirely defeated, the army is partially disbanded, the Nameless City is more than half revealed and – we're told – the Oct gather round Sursamen. These things are of far greater import, would you not agree?"

"Course I do, sir," Holse agreed.

"Then to those things attend, not gossip germed by my enemies."

"Just as you say, sir."

They were reading material about Sursamen and the Eighth (and, now, the Ninth) from news services run by the Oct, the Nariscene and the Morthanveld, as commented upon by people, artificial minds and what appeared to be non-official but somehow still respected organisations from within the Culture, all of it expressed in commendably succinct and clear Sarlian. Ferbin hadn't known whether to be flattered that they drew so much attention or insulted that they were so spied upon. He had searched in vain – or at least he had asked the ship to search for, unsuccessfully – any sort of verbatim recordings of the sort Xide Hyrlis had suggested might exist of what had happened to his father, but had found none. Djan Seriy had already told him such records did not appear to exist but he had wanted to check.

"All highly interesting," Ferbin agreed, sitting back in his almost excessively accommodating seat. They were in the ship's other small lounge area, one short sleep and a half-day into their journey. "I wonder what the latest information is regarding the Oct ships ... ?" Ferbin's voice trailed off as he inadvertently read another vicious exaggeration regarding his own past behaviour.

"What do you want to know?" the ship's voice asked, making Holse jump.

Ferbin collected himself. "The Oct ships," he said. "Are they really there, around Sursamen?"

"We don't know," the ship admitted.

"Have the Morthanveld been told the Oct might be gathering there?" Ferbin asked.

"It has been decided that they'll be told very shortly after we arrive," the ship said.

"I see." Ferbin nodded wisely.

"How very shortly afterwards?" Holse asked.

The ship hesitated, as though thinking. "Very very shortly afterwards," it said.

"Would that be a coincidence?" Holse enquired.

"Not exactly."

"He died in his armour; in that sense he died well."

Ferbin shook his head. "He died on a table like a spayed cur, Djan Seriy," he told her. "Like some traitor of old, broken and cruelled, made most filthy sport of. He would not have wished upon himself what I saw happen to him, believe me."

His sister lowered her head for a few moments.

They had been left alone after their first substantial meal aboard the *Liveware Problem*, sitting in the smaller lounge on a conversation seat shaped like a sine wave. She looked up again and said, "And it was tyl Loesp himself? I mean at the very—"

"It was his hand, sister." Ferbin looked deep into Djan Seriy's eyes. "He twisted the life from our father's heart and made all possible anguish in his mind too, in case that in his breast was somehow insufficient. He told him he would order massacre in his name, both that day on the battlefield around the Xiliskine and later when the army invaded the Deldeyn level. He would claim that Father had demanded such against tyl Loesp's advice, all to blacken his name. He scorned him in those last moments, sister; told him the game was always greater than he'd known, as though my father was not ever the one to see furthest."

Djan Seriy frowned momentarily. "What do you think he meant by that?" she asked. "The game was always greater than he'd known?"

Ferbin tutted in exasperation. "I think he meant to taunt our father, grasping anything to hand to hurt him with."

"Hmm," Djan Seriy said.

Ferbin sat closer to his sister. "He would want us to revenge him, of that I'm sure, Djan Seriy."

"I'm sure he would."

"I am not illusioned in this, sister. I know it is you who holds the power between us. But can you? Will you?"

"What? Kill Mertis tyl Loesp?"

Ferbin clutched at her hand. "Yes!"

"No." She shook her head, took her hand away. "I can find him, take him, deliver him, but this is not a matter for summary justice, Ferbin. He should suffer the ignominy of a trial and the contempt of those he once commanded; then you can imprison him for ever or kill him if that's still how we do these things, but it's not my place to murder him. This is an affair of state and I'll be present, on that level, in a purely personal capacity.

The orders I have now have nothing to do with him." She reached out, squeezed her brother's hand. "Hausk was a king before he was a father, Ferbin. He was not intentionally cruel to us and he loved us in his own way, I'm sure, but we were never his priority. He would not thank you for putting your personal animosity and thirst for revenge above the needs of the state he made great and expected his sons to make greater."

"Will you try to stop me," Ferbin asked, sounding bitter, "should I take aim at tyl Loesp?"

Djan Seriy patted his hand. "Only verbally," she said. "But I'll start now; do not use the death of this man to make you feel better. Use his fate, whatever it may be, to make your kingdom better."

"I never wanted it to be my kingdom," Ferbin said, and looked away, taking a deep breath.

Anaplian watched him, studying the set of his body and what she could still see of his expression, and thought how much and how little he had changed. He was, of course, much more mature than he had been fifteen years ago, but he had changed in ways that she might not have expected, and probably had changed quite recently, just due to all the things that had happened since their father had been killed. He seemed more serious, less self-obsessed and much less selfish in his pleasures and aims now. She got the impression, especially after a few brief conversations with Choubris himself, that Holse would never have followed the old Ferbin so far or so faithfully. What had not changed was his lack of desire to be king.

She wondered how much he thought she had changed, but knew there was almost no comparison. She still had all her memories of childhood and early adolescence, she appeared vaguely similar to how she'd looked when she'd left and she could contrive to sound much like her old self, but in every other regard she was another person altogether.

She used her neural lace to listen in to the *Liveware Problem*'s systems talking to each other, quickly took in a compensated view of the gulf of space ahead of the rushing ship, updated herself on any news from Sursamen and then from elsewhere, shared a casual handshake with Turminder Xuss, quiescent in her cabin, and then monitored her brother closely, listening to his heartbeat, sensing his skin conductivity, his blood pressure, implied core temperature and temperature distribution as well as the state of his slightly tense, tautened muscles. He was grinding his teeth, though he probably wasn't aware of it himself.

She felt she ought to jolly Ferbin out of what might be a dark mood, but was not sure she herself was in the mood to do so. She glanded *sperk*, and soon was.

"Is Director General Shoum still on Sursamen?" Anaplian asked.

"No," Hippinse said. "Left forty-plus days ago. Continuing her tour of Morthanveld possessions and protectorates in the Lesser Spine."

"But she is contactable once we're down there?"

"Definitely. At the moment she's here, in transit between Asulious IV and Grahy on the Cat.4 CleaveHull *"On First Seeing Jhirüt"*. Due to arrive Grahy fourteen hours after we make Sursamen. Without the crash-stop," Hippinse added archly. The avatoid had changed further just in the last day and was now positively muscular. He still looked burly compared to the two Sarl men, but he appeared far fitter and athletic than he had when they'd first met him a few days earlier. Even his blond hair was cropped and businesslike, similar to Djan Seriy's.

The central holo-display they were seated around spun to show where Shoum's ship was now, then rotated smoothly back to where it had been (Holse remembered the display of the dreadful planet Bulthmaas, and Xide Hyrlis' face, lit from below). The display was false-coloured; all the stars were white. Sursamen was a gently blinking red dot hard by its star, Meseriphine. The *Liveware Problem* was an even tinier strobing blue point trailing a fading aquamarine wake. The positions of other major ships, where known, were also shown, colour-coded; Morthanveld craft were green. The Oct colour was blue; their possible presence was implied by a faint tinge all around Sursamen.

Djan Seriy looked at Ferbin. "You think Shoum will facilitate our travel to the Eighth if we have any problems with the Nariscene or the Oct?"

"She took some considerable interest in our plight," Ferbin said. "It was she who arranged our conveyance to Xide Hyrlis, for all that that proved a futile expedition." Ferbin did not try to suppress a sneer. "She found my quest for justice 'romantic', I recall." He looked at his sister and shook his head. "She might be termed sympathetic; however, it could be just a passing sympathy. I cannot say."

Djan Seriy shrugged. "Still, this is worth keeping in mind, I think," she said.

"Shouldn't be an issue," Hippinse said. "With luck the Oct systems will be breezeable and the Nariscene won't be alerted. I should be able to drop you straight into a lift. Maybe even a scendship."

"That, as you say, is with luck," Anaplian said. "I am thinking about if luck is not with us." She looked quizzically at Hippinse. "Oramen is still at the Falls, is that correct?"

"Last we heard, yes," the ship said through its avatoid. "Though the information is eight days old at least. The Oct/Aultridia tussling between levels is making communications unreliable."

"How bad is this so-called 'tussling'?" Anaplian asked.

"About as bad as it can get before the Nariscene would be obliged to step in." The avatoid paused. "I'm a little surprised they haven't already."

Anaplian frowned. "Do they shoot at each other?"

"No," Hippinse said. "They're not supposed to within the Towers or near any secondary structure. Mostly the dispute involves taking over Towers using blocking scendships and remote reconfiguring of door-control fidelities."

"Is this going to help or hinder us?"

"Could go either way. Multiplier rather than a valuer."

Djan Seriy sat back. "Very well," she said. "This is what will happen: we four descend together to Sursamen Surface. We have to try and get down through the levels before anybody works out we shouldn't have got to the Meseriphine system so quickly and starts asking what ship brought us." She nodded at Hippinse. "The *Liveware Problem* believes it can get us down and inserted into the Nariscene travel-admin system without anybody noticing, but short of trying to take over the whole Nariscene AI matrix on Sursamen – arguably an act of war in itself – it cannot stop us getting spotted as anomalous eventually. So; we attain the level of the Hyeng-zhar, expeditiously. We find Oramen; at the Falls, hopefully. We tell him he is in danger if he does not know already. We also get a message to him while we're on our way, if possible. We do what we can to make him safe, or at least safer, if necessary, then we deal with tyl Loesp."

"'Deal with'?" the ship asked, through Hippinse.

Anaplian looked levelly at the avatoid. "Deal with as in apprehend. Capture. Hold, or ensure is held until a properly formulated court can decide his fate."

"I would not anticipate a royal pardon," Ferbin said icily.

"Meanwhile," Djan Seriy continued, "the ship will be attempting to find out what the Oct are up to by seeing if all these missing ships really are turning up around Sursamen. Though of course by then the Morthanveld and Nariscene will have been informed of our suspicions regarding the Oct ship concentration and will doubtless be formulating their own responses. We can but hope these will complement the *Liveware Problem*'s, though it is not impossible they will be antagonistic." Anaplian looked at Ferbin and Holse. "If the Oct are there in force then both Hippinse and I may have to leave you alone on minimal notice. I'm sorry, brother, but that is how it has to be. We must all hope it doesn't come to that but if it does we'll leave you with what advantage we can."

"And what would that be?" Ferbin asked, looking from Anaplian to Hippinse.

"Intelligence," said Djan Seriy.

"Better weaponry," the ship told them.

They popped into existence within a vacant Oct scendship; its doors had just closed – unexpectedly, as far as the cloudily aware brain of the Tower Traffic Control was concerned. Then it rechecked, and found that the door closure was not unexpected after all; an instruction demanding just such an action had been there for some time. So that was all right. A very short time later there was no longer memory or record of it having found anything unexpected in the first place. That was even better.

The scendship was one of over twenty attached to a great carousel device which hung directly above the gaping fourteen-hundred-metre-diameter mouth that was the top of the Pandilfwa Tower. The carousel was designed to load the selected scendship, like a shell into an immense gun, into one of the secondary tubes bundled within the main Tower which would allow the vessel to drop to any of the available levels.

The Oct's Tower Traffic Control computer executed a variety of instructions it was under the completely erroneous impression had been properly authorised and the carousel machine ninety metres beneath it duly dropped the scendship from the access ring above to another ring below; this swung the ship over one of the tubes. The capsule craft was lowered, fitted, and then grasped by what were basically two gigantic, if sophisticated, washers. Fluids drained and were pumped away. Lockrotates opened and closed and the ship shuffled down until it hung in vacuum, dripping, directly above a dark shaft fourteen hundred kilometres deep and full of almost nothing at all. The ship announced it was ready to travel. The Tower Traffic Control machine gave it permission. The scendship released its hold on the side of the tube and started to fall, powered by nothing more than Sursamen's own gravity.

That had been, as Anaplian had warned Ferbin and Holse, the easy bit. The Oerten Crater on Sursamen's Surface stood directly over the fluted mouth of the Pandil-fwa Tower and was separated from it only by Secondary structure; the ship had had no difficulty – once it had checked its co-ordinates several thousand times and Displaced a few hundred microscopic scout motes – placing them straight into the scendship. Co-opting the Oct's computer matrices – they barely merited the term AIs – had been, for the Mind of the *Liveware Problem*, a trivial matter.

They had chosen a stealthy approach, arriving without fanfare or – as far as they were aware – detection above Sursamen less than half an hour earlier. The *Liveware Problem* had spent the days of their approach modelling and rehearsing its tactics using the highly detailed knowledge of Nariscene and Oct systems it already had. It had grown confident it could put them straight into a scendship and remove the need for any exposure to the Surface itself. Arriving, it found pretty much what it had expected and sent them straight in.

Djan Seriy had spent the same time giving Ferbin and Holse a crash course in the use of certain Culture defensive and offensive technologies, up to the level she thought they could handle. It was a truism that some of the more rarefied Culture personal weapon systems were far more likely to kill an untrained user than anybody they were ostensibly aimed at, but even the defensive systems, while they were never going to kill you – that was, rather obviously, the one thing they were designed above all else to prevent – could give you a bowel-loosening fright, too, just due to the speed and seeming violence with which they could react when under threat.

The two men quickly got used to the suits they'd be wearing.

The suits were default soot-black, their surfaces basically smooth once on but much straked and be-lumped with units, accoutrements and sub-systems not all of which Ferbin and Holse were even allowed to know about. The face sections could divide into lower mask and upper visor parts and defaulted clear so that facial expressions were readable.

"What if we get an itch?" Holse had asked Hippinse. "I got an itch wearing a Morthanveld swimming suit when we were being shown round one of their ships and it was disproportionately annoying." They were on the hangar deck. It was crowded even by hangar deck standards but it still provided the largest open space the ship had for them to gather in.

"You won't itch," the avatoid told him and Ferbin. "The suit deadens that sort of sensation on interior contact. You can sense touch and temperature and so on, but not to the point of pain. It's partly about damping distractive itching, partly about preemptive first-level damage control."

"How clever," Ferbin said.

"These are very clever suits," Hippinse said with a smile.

"Not sure I like being so swaddled, sir," Holse said.

Hippinse shrugged. "You become a new, hybrid entity in such a suit. There is a certain loss of absolute control, or at least absolute exposure, but the recompense is vastly heightened operational capability and survivability."

Anaplian, standing nearby, looked thoughtful.

Ferbin and Holse had been willing and attentive pupils, though Ferbin had been just a little niggled at something he would not specify and his sister could not determine until the ship suggested she equip him with one more weapon, or perhaps a bigger one, than his servant. She asked Ferbin to carry the smaller of the two hypervelocity kinetic rifles the ship just happened to have in its armoury (she had the larger one). After that all had been well.

She'd been impressed with the quality of the suits.

"Very advanced," she commented, frowning.

Hippinse beamed. "Thank you."

"It seems to me," Anaplian said slowly, scanning the suits with her re-enhanced senses, "that a ship would either have to have these suits physically aboard, or, if it was going to make them itself from scratch, have access to the most sophisticated and – dare I say it – most severely restricted patterns known only to some very small and unusual bits of the Culture. You know; the bits generally called Special Circumstances."

"Really?" Hippinse said brightly. "That's interesting."

They floated over the floor of the scendship. The water started to fall away about them as the ship descended, draining to tanks beneath the floor. Within a couple of minutes they were in a dry, if still damp-smelling, near semi-spherical space fifteen metres across. Ferbin and Holse pushed the mask and visor sections of their suits away.

"Well, sir," Holse said cheerily, "we're home." He looked round the scendship's interior. "After a fashion."

Djan Seriy and Hippinse hadn't bothered with masks. They were dressed, like the two Sarl men, in the same dark, close-fitting suits each of which, Djan Seriy had claimed in all seriousness, was several times more intelligent than the entire Oct computational matrix on Sursamen. As well as sporting all those odd lumps and bumps, the suits each carried small, streamlined chest and back pouches and both Hippinse and Djan Seriy's suits held long straked bulges on their backs which turned into long, dark weapons it was hard even to identify as guns. Ferbin and Holse each had things half the size of a rifle called CREWs which fired light, and a disappointingly small handgun. Ferbin had been hoping for something rather more impressive; however, he'd been mollified by being given the hypervelocity rifle, which was satisfyingly chunky.

Their suits also had their own embedded weapon and defensive systems which were apparently far too complicated to leave to the whims of mere men. Ferbin found this somewhat disturbing but had been informed it was for his own good. That, too, had not been the most reassuring thing he had ever heard.

"In the unlikely event we do get involved in a serious firefight and the suits think you're under real threat," Djan Seriy had told the two Sarl men, "they'll take over. High-end exchanges happen too fast for human reactions so the suits will do the aiming, firing and dodging for you." She'd seen the expressions of dismay on their faces, and shrugged. "It's like all war; months of utter boredom punctuated by moments of sheer terror. It's just the moments are sometimes measured in milliseconds and the engagement's often over before you're aware it has even begun."

Holse had looked at Ferbin and sighed. "Welcome to the future, sir."

Djan Seriy's familiar, the drone thing called Turminder Xuss, had been Displaced attached to one thigh of her suit; another lozenged bulge. It had floated away as soon as they'd been Displaced in and was still floating around above them now that the water was all gone, seemingly inspecting the dripping interior of the scendship. Holse was watching the little machine closely, following it round the ship, squinting up at it.

The drone lowered itself in front of the man. "Can I help you, Mr Holse?" it asked.

"I always meant to ask," he said. "How do things like you float in the air like that?"

"Why, with ease," the drone said, ascending away from him again. Holse shrugged and chewed on a little crile leaf he'd persuaded the *Liveware Problem* to make for him.

Djan Seriy sat cross-legged near the centre of the floor, eyes closed. Enclosed by the tight black suit, only her face exposed, she looked oddly childlike, though her shape was certainly womanly enough, as even Ferbin noticed.

"Is my sister asleep?" Ferbin asked Hippinse quietly.

The avatoid – a compact, powerful-looking figure now – smiled. "She's just checking the scendship's systems. I've already done that, but it does no harm to verify."

"So, are we successfully on our way?" Ferbin asked. He noticed that the avatoid had rolled the head part of his suit right back to form a collar, freeing his whole head. He did likewise.

"Yes, successfully so far."

"And are you still the ship, or do you function independently yet?"

"You can still talk direct to the ship through me until we transfer," Hippinse told him.

Djan Seriy had opened her eyes and was already looking at the avatoid. "They're here, aren't they?" she said.

Hippinse nodded thoughtfully. "The missing Oct ships," he said. "Yes. Three just discovered all at once, lined up above the end of the open Tower nearest to me. Strong suspicion the rest will be here or on their way too."

"But we keep going," Djan Seriy said, frowning.

Hippinse nodded. "They're here, that's all. Nothing else has changed yet. I'm signalling now. I imagine the Morthanveld and the Nariscene will know something of the Oct dispositions fairly shortly." He looked round at all of them. "We keep going."

The transfer took place halfway down the first section of the Tower, seven hundred kilometres from the Surface. The scendship slowed and stopped. They were fully suited up again; the drone had returned to attach itself to Anaplian's thigh. The air was pumped from the scendship's interior, the door swung open silently, a last puff of atmosphere dissipated into the vacuum and they followed it down a broad corridor, their shadows advancing hugely in front of them. When the scendship's door closed, all normal light was cut off and they were left with a ghostly image built up from the faint radiations given off by the chilly walls and surfaces around them. This was the point at which the ship no longer directly controlled Hippinse and the avatoid was newly as alone in his own head as any normal human was in theirs. Ferbin watched for him to stumble or for his expression to change, but saw nothing.

Two sets of thick double doors rolled open in sequence, taking them to a great semicircular aperture which opened on to a broad oval balcony forty metres or more across; a hard, steely light returned, picking out several small, sleek craft sitting on cradles on the floor of the platform.

There was no wall or railing. The view dropped away for another seven hundred kilometres, seemingly to dark nothing. Above, tiny bright stars hung untwinkling.

Level One was a Seedsail nursery. Seedsails were some of the galaxy's most ancient biologicals. Depending which authority you listened to, they had been around for either about half a dozen aeons, or nearly ten. The debate over whether they had evolved naturally or had been created by an earlier civilisation was equally unsettled. Only arguably self-aware, they were some of the galaxy's greatest true wanderers, migrating across the entire lens over the eons, centiaeons and deciaeons it took for them to tack and run and spinnaker their way from star to star powered by sunlight alone.

They came with their own barely smarter predators anyway but had, in addition, been exploited, hunted and slaughtered over time by those who might have known better, though they had been followed, revered and appreciated, too. The present day was a good time for them; they were seen as a part of a greater natural galactic ecology and a generally good thing, so there was civilisational credit to be garnered by being nice to them. Sponsored in this case by the Nariscene, the first or attic level of many a Shellworld was given over to Seedsail nursery space where the creatures could grow and flourish in their vacuum ground-growing phase under the relatively gentle light of the Fixstars and Rollstars before their magnetic coil-roots catapulted them upwards.

They still had to be helped on their way after that; caught and held before they could hit the ceiling above by specialist craft which took them to one of the few open Towers and then ejected them from there into the harsher environment of their true home: outer space.

Ferbin and Holse stood, a couple of metres back from the abrupt edge, looking out at the view while Djan Seriy and Hippinse busied themselves with a couple of the slender little craft sitting cradled on the wide balcony. Holse offered his hand to Ferbin, who clasped it. They were observing communications silence, but when the suits touched they could talk undetected. "Not really that much to see, eh, sir?"

"Just the stars," Ferbin agreed. They gazed out over the emptiness.

They were beckoned over to the two small craft Djan Seriy and Hippinse had been working on. The dark, curved canopies of the craft, like sections cut from a huge seashell, stood raised. They were motioned to sit inside. The craft were built to carry six Nariscene rather than two humans but the suits made them as comfortable as possible, impersonating seats. Djan Seriy and Hippinse piloted one each. The craft rose silently from the balcony and darted straight out into the darkness, accelerating hard enough initially to take Ferbin's breath away.

Djan Seriy reached back and touched his ankle with one finger.

"Are you all right, Ferbin?" she asked.

"Perfectly well, thank you," he told her.

"So far so good, brother. We are still within the main sequence of our plan."

"Delighted to hear it."

The two little craft tore across the dark landscape far below, curving lazily round intervening Towers. Half an hour and a twelfth of the world away they slowed and dropped, approaching the base of a Tower. Ferbin was ready to get out but the two little craft sat hovering a metre above the Bare surface in front of a great dark ellipse inscribed on the fluted base at the Tower's foot. They sat there for some time. Ferbin leaned forward to touch Djan Seriy's shoulder and ask what they were waiting for, but she held one hand up flat to him without turning round, and just as she did so, the dark shape ahead fell away, revealing a still darker tunnel behind.

The twin craft went slowly, tentatively down it.

"This bit is fractionally dangerous," Djan Seriy told her brother, reaching back to touch his suit with hers again as the two little craft dropped down one of the minor tubes within the Tower. "The ship will be working the Surface systems to keep us clear, but not everything is handled from there. Matrices further down and even on individual scendships might take it into their own little circuits to send something up or down here." She paused. "Nothing so far," she added.

The two craft flitted from one Tower to another over the next two levels. The next one down was Vacuum Baskers territory, the home of creatures of several different species-types which, like the Seedsails, absorbed sunlight directly. Unlike the Seedsails they were happy enough to stick roughly where they were all their lives rather than go sailing amongst the stars. Apart from the occasional surface glint, there wasn't much to be seen there either. Another dark transition took them to another Tower and across the perfectly black and completely vacant vacuum-level below the Baskers.

"Still all right, brother?" Djan Seriy asked. Her touch on his ankle was oddly comforting in the utter darkness and near total silence.

"A little bored," Ferbin told her.

"Talk to the suit. Get it to play you music or screen you something."

He whispered to the suit; it played soothing music.

They ended up on another mid-level Tower balcony similar to the one they'd left from, abandoning the two little craft tipped on the floor beside some already occupied cradles. One corridor, several doors and many ghostly images later they stood by the curved wall of a scendship tube while Djan Seriy and Hippinse both carefully placed the palms of their hands on position after position on the wide wall, as though searching for something. Djan Seriy raised one hand. Hippinse stepped away from the wall. A short while later Anaplian also stepped back from the wall and a little later still the wall revealed a door which rolled up, releasing creamy purple light from beneath like a flood that lapped round feet, calves, thighs and torsos until it reached their masked faces and they could see that they were facing a scendship interior full of what looked like barely solidified glowing purple cloud-stuff. They stepped into it.

It was like walking through a curtain of syrup into a room full of thick air. The suit masks provided a view; the partially solidified cloud and the everywhere-purple light inside it made it impossible to see past the end of one's nose on normal sight. Djan Seriy beckoned them all to stand together, hands resting on shoulders.

"Be glad you can't smell this, gentlemen," she told the two Sarl men. "This is an Aultridian scendship."

Holse went rigid.

Ferbin nearly fainted.

It was not even to be a short journey, though it might be relatively quick. The scendship hurtled down the Tower past the level of the Cumuloforms, where Ferbin and Holse had been transported over the unending ocean by Expanded Version Five; Zourd, months before, past the level beneath where Pelagic Kites and Avians roamed the airs above a shallow ocean dotted with sunlit islands, past the one beneath that where Naiant Tendrils swarmed through a level pressured to the ceiling with an atmosphere from the upper levels of a gas giant, then past the one beneath that where the Vesiculars – Monthian megawhales – swam singing through a mineral-rich methane ocean that did not quite touch the ceiling above.

They went plunging past the Eighth.

They were sat on the floor by Djan Seriy, who stood. The feet or hands of their suits all touched.

"Home proper, we're passing, sir," Holse said to Ferbin when Djan Seriy relayed this information.

Ferbin heard him over some very loud but still soothing music he was having the suit play him. He had closed his eyes earlier but still could not keep out the unspeakable purple glow; then he'd thought to ask the suit to block it, which it did. He shivered with disgust every time he thought of that ghastly purple mass of Aultridian stuff stuck cloyingly all around them, infusing them with its hideous smell. He didn't reply to Holse.

They kept going, flashing beneath their home level.

The Aultridian vessel didn't even start to slow until it had fallen to a point level with the top of the atmosphere covering what had been the Deldeyn's lands.

Still slowing gradually, it fell past the floor of that level too, coming to a halt adjacent to the matrix of Filigree immediately beneath. It jostled itself sideways, the floor tipping and the whole craft shuddering. Djan Seriy, one hand attached to a patch on the scendship's wall near the door, was controlling its actions. Her knees flexed and her whole body moved with what looked like intensely practised ease as the craft shook and juddered beneath her. Then they felt the craft steady before starting to move smartly sideways and up, gradually levelling off.

"Moving into the Filigree now," Hippinse told Ferbin and Holse.

"The Aultridia have spotted all is not well with one of their scendships," Djan Seriy told them, sounding distracted.

"You mean this one, ma'am?" Holse asked.

"Mm-hmm."

"They're following us," Hippinse confirmed.

"What?" Ferbin squeaked. He was imagining being captured and peeled from his suit by Aultridia.

"Precautionary," Hippinse said, unworried. "They'll try and block us off somewhere ahead too, once we've narrowed our options a bit, but we'll be gone by then. Don't worry."

"If you say so, sir," Holse said, though he did not sound unworried.

"This kind of thing happens all the time," Hippinse reassured them. "Scendships have brains just smart enough to fool themselves. They take off on their own sometimes, or people get into them and borrow them for unauthorised excursions. There are separate safety systems that still prevent collisions so it isn't a catastrophe when a scendship moves without orders; more of a nuisance."

"Oh really?" Ferbin said tartly. "You are an expert on our homeworld now, are you?"

"Certainly am," Hippinse said happily. "The ship and I have the best original specification overview, secondary structure plans, accrued morphology mappings, full geo, hydro, aero, bio and data system models and all the latest full-spectrum updates available. Right now I know more about Sursamen than the Nariscene do, and they know almost everything."

"What do you know they don't?" Holse asked.

"A few details the Oct and Aultridia haven't told them." Hippinse laughed. "They'll find out eventually but they don't know yet. I do."

"Such as?" Ferbin asked.

"Well, where we're going," Hippinse said. "There's an inordinate amount of Oct interest in these Falls. And the Aultridia are getting curious too. High degree of convergence; intriguing." The avatoid sounded both bemused and fascinated. "Now *there's* a pattern for you, don't you think? Oct ships outside clustering round Sursamen and Oct inside focusing on the Hyeng-zhar. Hmm-hmm. *Very* interesting." Ferbin got the impression that – inhuman avatar of a God-like Optimae superspaceship or not – the being was basically talking to itself at this point.

"By the way, Mr Hippinse," Holse said, "is it really all right to wet oneself in these things?"

"Absolutely!" Hippinse said, as though Holse had proposed a toast. "All gets used. Feel free."

Ferbin rolled his eyes, though he was glad that Holse, probably, could not see.

"Oh, that's better . . ."

"We're here," Djan Seriy said.

Ferbin had fallen asleep. The suit seemed to have reduced the volume of the music it had been playing; it swelled again now as he woke up. He told it to stop. They were still surrounded by the horrible purple glow.

"Good navigating," Hippinse said.

"Thank you," Djan Seriy replied.

"A drop, then?"

"So it would appear," Anaplian agreed. "Brother, Mr Holse; we were unable to make the landfall we wanted to. Too many Aultridian scendships trying to block us and too many doors closed off." She glanced at Hippinse, who had a blank expression on his face and seemed to have lost his earlier good humour. "Plus something alarmingly capable of procedural corruption and instruction manipulation appears to be loose in the data systems of this part of the world," she added. She grinned in what was probably meant to be an encouraging manner. "So instead we've transited to another Tower, ascended it and then made off into its Filigree and come to a dead end; we're in an Oversquare level so there's no onward connections."

"A dead end?" Ferbin said. Were they never to be released from this cloying purple filth?

"Yes. So we have to drop."

"Drop?"

"Walk this way," Djan Seriy said, turning. The scendship's door rolled up, revealing darkness. They all got to their feet, pushed through the thick-feeling curtain at the entrance and were suddenly free of the glutinous purple stuff filling the scendship's interior. Ferbin looked down at his arms, chest and legs, expecting to see some of the ghastly material still adhering to him but there was, happily, no trace. He doubted they'd shrugged off the notorious smell so easily.

They were standing on a narrow platform lit only by the purple glare from behind; the wall above curved up and over them, following the shape of the scendship's hull. Djan Seriy looked at the bulge on her thigh. The drone Turminder Xuss detached itself and floated up to the dark line where the door had buried itself in the ship's hull.

It twisted itself slowly into the material as though it was no more substantial than the glowing purple mass beneath. Long hanging strands of hull and other material worked their way out along the little machine's body and drooped down, swaying. The drone – rosily glowing folds of light pulsing about its body – finished by stationing itself midway between the scendship's hull and the wall of the chamber and floating there for a moment. There was an alarming groaning noise and the hull of the ship around the hole bulged inwards by about a hand's span, exactly as though an invisible sphere a metre across was being pressed into it. The wall directly opposite made creaking, popping noises too.

"Try closing *that*," Turminder Xuss said, with what sounded like relish.

Djan Seriy nodded. "This way."

They passed through a small door into the closed-off end of the channel the scendship travelled within; a twenty-metre-diameter concavity at whose centre, up some complicated steps that were more like handrails, another small round door was set. They entered it and found themselves inside a spherical space three metres or so across, struggling to stand up all at once on its bowled floor. Djan Seriy closed the door they'd come through and pointed to a similar one set straight across from it.

"That one leads to the outside. That's where we drop from. One at a time. Me first; Hippinse last."

"This 'drop', ma'am . . ." Holse said.

"We're fourteen hundred kilometres above the Deldeyn

province of Sull," Anaplian told him. "We ambient-drop, not using AG, through nearly a thousand klicks of near-vacuum and then hit the atmosphere. Then it's an assisted glide to the Hyeng-zhar, again leaving suit antigravity off; it could show." She looked at Ferbin and Holse. "You don't have to do a thing; your suits will take care of everything. Just enjoy the view. We're still in comms blackout, but don't forget you can always talk to your suit if you need to ask any questions about what's going on. Okay? Let's go."

There had not – Ferbin reflected as his sister swung open the circular door – really been enough time between the "Okay?" and the "Let's go" bits of that last sentence for anybody to say very much at all.

Outside, it was dark until you looked down, then the landscape shone in great stripes separated by a central band of grey near-dark. No stars were visible, hidden by vanes and ceiling structures. Djan Seriy squatted on the sill, one hand holding on to the top edge of the inward-opening door. She turned to Ferbin and touched him with her other hand. "You come straight out after me, all right, brother? Don't delay."

"Yes, of course," he said. His heart was hammering.

Djan Seriy looked at him for a moment longer. "Or you could just go limp and the suit will do it all for you; climbing up and out, I mean. With your eyes closed—"

"I shall do it myself, never fear," Ferbin said, trying to sound braver and more certain than he felt.

She squeezed his shoulder. "See you down there."

Then she threw herself out of the doorway.

Ferbin pulled himself up to squat where his sister had, feeling Holse's hands helping to steady him, then he swallowed as he looked down at the impossible drop below him. He closed his eyes after all, but he flexed legs and arms and threw himself out, curling into a ball.

The view was tumbling about him when he opened his eyes again; light/dark, light/dark, light ... then the flickering sequence started to slow as the suit whirred, gently teasing his limbs out. His breath sounded terribly loud in his head. After a few moments he was falling in an X shape, feeling almost relaxed as he lay looking back up at the shady mass of Filigree and vaning hanging from the ceiling above. He tried to see where he had thrown himself from, but couldn't. He thought he caught a glimpse of another tiny dark dot far above, also falling, but could not be sure.

"Can I turn over and look down?" he asked the suit.

"Yes. It will be advisable to return to this orientation for entry into the atmosphere," the suit told him in its crisp, asexual voice. "Or it is possible to transmit the view downward to your eyes in your present orientation."

"Is that better?"

"Yes."

"Do that, then."

Suddenly it was as though he was dropping down into the distant landscape beneath rather than falling away from the view above. He felt disoriented and dizzy for a moment, but soon adapted. He looked in vain for Djan Seriy, falling somewhere below, but could see no sign of her. "Can *you* see my sister?" he asked.

"She is probably within this area," the suit said, creating a thin red circle over part of the view. "She is camouflaged," it explained.

"How far have we fallen so far?"

"Six kilometres."

"Oh. How long did that take?"

"Fifty seconds. Over the next fifty seconds we shall descend another twenty kilometres. We are still accelerating and will continue to do so until we encounter the atmosphere."

"When does that happen?"

"In about ten minutes from now."

Ferbin settled back and enjoyed the topsy-turvy view, trying to spot the Hyeng-zhar cataract, then attempting to trace the course of the Sulpitine river and finally settling for working out where the Upper and Lower Sulpine Seas might be. He wondered if it was all still frozen. They'd been told it would be, though he found that hard to believe.

The view expanded slowly in front of him. There; was that one of the seas? It looked too small. Was that the other? Too small and too close to the other one. It was so hard to tell. The gloom beneath was gradually filling more and more of his field of vision, leaving the bright, sunlit lands on the edges of the view.

By the time he was sure those had been the two Seas, he had begun to realise how high up they had been when they'd started falling, how small even two substantial seas and a mighty river could look from a great altitude and how enormous the world he had lived in all his life really was.

The landscape beneath was bulging up towards him. How were they to stop?

The suit started to grow around him, extending a mass of bubbles from every part save that he must be looking through. The bubbles enlarged; some slowly broke and kept on extending, becoming a delicate-looking tracery of what appeared like an insect's near-transparent wings or the infinitely fragile-looking skeleton structure that was left when a tree-leaf had lost all trace of its light-gathering surface and only the sustaining filigree of its sap-transporting veins was left.

The top of the atmosphere imposed itself as a very slowly increasing sense of returning weight, pushing against his back, so that – as he continued to look downwards even though he was actually on his back – he experienced the vertiginous sensation of being propelled even faster towards the ground beneath. A faint whispering sound transmitted itself through the suit. The push grew harder and the whisper swelled to a roar.

He waited to see the red, yellow and white glow which he had heard things meeting atmospheres produced about them, but it never appeared.

The suit twisted, rotating so that he was actually facing downwards now. The tracery and the bubbles collapsed back in towards the suit and became crescent wings and thin fins protruding from his arms, sides and thighs; the suit had been gently reconfiguring his body so that his arms were stuck out ahead of him now, as though he was about to dive into a river. His legs were splayed behind him and felt as though they were connected by some sort of tether or membrane.

The landscape was much closer now – he could see tiny dark rivers and hints of other surface features picked out in blacks and pale greys in the gloom far beneath – however, the ground was no longer rushing up towards him but sliding past beneath. The feeling of weight had shifted too and the air was whispering about him.

He was flying.

Anaplian dropped back to touch with Hippinse as they flew. "Worked out what's messing with the local systemry?" she asked. Hippinse was monitoring the disturbance in the surrounding level's data complexes and analysing data they'd collected earlier while in the Aultridian scendship.

"Not really," the avatoid confessed, sounding both embarrassed and concerned. "Whatever's corrupting it is almost untouchably exotic. Genuinely alien; unknown. In fact, right now, unknowable. I'd need the ship's whole Mind to start attacking this shit."

Anaplian was silent for a moment. "What the fuck is going on here?" she asked quietly. Hippinse had no reply to that either. Anaplian let go and flew ahead.

Ferbin and the suit dipped, passing close enough to the ground to see individual boulders, bushes and small, scrubby trees, all tailed by narrow deltas of the same pale grey as though casting strange shadows. Gullies and ravines shone palely too, as if filled with softly shining mist.

"Is that *snow*?" he asked.

"Yes," the suit said.

Something lightly grasped his ankle. "Are you all right, Ferbin?" Djan Seriy's voice said.

"Yes," he said, starting to twist round to look back but then stopping himself just as she said, "There is no point looking back, brother; you won't be able to see me."

"Oh," he said, "so you are behind me?"

"I am now. I have been flying ahead of you for the last two minutes. We are in a diamond formation; you are in the right-hand position. Turminder Xuss flies a kilometre ahead of us."

"Oh."

"Listen, brother. While we were in the tube, just before we dropped, we picked up repeated signals from an Oct news service talking about the Falls and Oramen. They say that Oramen lives and is well but there was some sort of attempt on his life nine days ago; an explosion in the excavations and/or an attempt to knife him. It may not have been the first attempt on his life, either. He is aware he is in danger and may already have accused people around tyl Loesp, if not tyl Loesp himself, of being responsible."

"But he is well?"

"Lightly injured but well enough. Tyl Loesp in turn accuses Oramen of impatience in trying to wrest the crown from the properly appointed regent before he is legally of an age to do so. He returns from travels elsewhere on this level and has signalled forces loyal to him to gather just upstream from the Falls. Werreber – in charge of the greater army – has been contacted by both Oramen and tyl Loesp and has not declared for either side yet. He is on the Eighth, though, and is ten or more days away, even flying. His ground forces would be many weeks behind that again."

Ferbin felt a chill. "We are not quite too late, then," he said, trying to sound hopeful.

"I don't know. There is more; some artifact long buried in the Nameless City was reported to be showing signs of life and all attention had been turned to it. But that was five days ago. Since then there has been nothing. Not just no news service but no fresh signals at all from the vicinity of the Falls or the Settlement or anywhere else within this section. The data networks all around this area are in a state of locked-in chaos. That is odd and worrying. Plus, we are picking up curious, anomalous indicators from the Nameless City itself."

"Is that bad?"

Djan Seriy hesitated. This worried Ferbin all by itself. "Possibly." Then she added, "We'll set down on the city outskirts downstream in about twenty minutes. Tell the suit if you need to talk to me in the meantime. All right?"

"All right."

"Don't worry. See you soon." His ankle was patted once, then the pressure on it was removed.

He assumed she was resuming her position ahead of him in their diamond formation but he couldn't see her pass him or spot her flying in front.

They zoomed over a small hill without losing speed and Ferbin realised that they were doing more than just gliding; they were under power. He asked to look back and was given a view from the back of his head. There was a membrane filling the V between his legs and two small fat cylinders sticking out from his ankles. The view through them was a blur.

He looked ahead again just as they went hurtling over what looked like a road, some old railway lines and a drained canal. Then the ground just fell away and he was staring at a flat, icy landscape another two hundred metres further beneath, a shadowy wasteland of broad, frozen waterways, slim, sinuously curved channels, rounded banks and mounds of sand and snow, the whole linear, winterbound plain punctuated at random by a variety of misshapen shards, stumps of arbitrary debris and jagged wreckage from what looked like ruined buildings or sunken ships all sticking chaotically aslant, broken and alone from the pitted, frozen surface.

They swooped, dipping in towards the centre of this new and

pitiless landscape contained by the sheer and distant cliffs on either side.

When they got to the Nameless City, arriving over increasing amounts of fractured, haphazardly jumbled detritus trapped within the ice and the frozen wastes of sand and snow and mud, they could see many thin trails of smoke leading up into the sky from their left above the cliffs on that side. Hard against the cliffs, visible under modest magnification, they could make out zigzagging traceries of stairways and the open lattices of lift shafts. Nothing save the smoke was moving, drifting slowly upwards into the quiet, windless dim.

In front of them, the city rose, its highest spires and towers still some kilometres distant. They crossed the first outskirt jumble of short, few-storey buildings and began to slow. The suit released Ferbin from its gentle grip, letting his arms and legs free.

Moments later he felt himself tipped forward, slowing still further as his legs swung underneath him and he was lowered and positioned as though about to start walking. A small open space in front of him seemed to be their target. He realised that the few-storey-high buildings were actually much taller, their lower floors buried in the frozen mud and ice.

His sister, Holse and Hippinse blinked into relative visibility, hazily indistinct shapes each ten metres or so away as they set down in the icy little clearing, and – finally, though it might have been in a strange place under no appreciable sun on the wrong level and through soles that would doubtless have insulated him from anything down to absolute zero, Ferbin's feet again touched the ground of home.

26. The Sarcophagus

The object now being called the Sarcophagus lay almost in the dead centre of the Nameless City. It was located deep beneath the under-plaza within a building as fat and tall and impressive as any in the ancient, long-buried metropolis. The city's heart was now accessed along a freshly directed rail track; the engineers had taken advantage of the freeze to build lines where they never could have before, over frozen expanses of river that would have swept any trestles or pylons away in an instant had they still held water rather than ice and straight across sand- and mudbanks that would have shifted, sunk and reappeared somewhere else in the course of a shift had the rapids still been roaring.

From the thronging chaos of the railhead – an arc-lit station deep under the plaza whose traffic volume would have done justice to a terminus in a major city – the well-tramped way led, past whistling, roaring, bellowing machines and piles and coils of pipe and cable, along a thoroughfare twenty metres across crowded with pack creatures, warbeasts pressed into service as haulage animals, steam- and oil-powered traction engines, narrow-gauge trains and – more than anything else – with rank after rank and row after row and group and company and detail and shift and gang of workers, labourers, engineers, guards, specialists and professionals of a hundred different types.

On a vast raised round structure that lay at the focus of a dozen ramps and roadways original to the Nameless City the great packed street split in a score of different directions. Conveyor belts, tramways and aerial wagonways spun off with the roadways, all dotted with faint oil lamps, hissing gas fixtures and sputtering electric lights. What had been the busiest ramp – attended by cableways, conveyors and funicular lines like too-steep railways with jagged stairways at their centres – led across a filled-in lake and a broad roadway of thick planking down to the great bulbous building housing the Sarcophagus.

Through what had been a gigantic, elongated formal entrance a hundred metres across and forty high, flanked by a dozen soaring sculptures of cut-away Shellworlds and leading to a still taller mouth-shaped atrium within, the torrent of men, machines, animals and material had poured.

That torrent had slowed to a trickle now as Oramen and the party which had come directly from the gathering he had held in the great marquee descended to the focus of the city and the excavations; the greatest concentrations of effort were elsewhere now, principally targeting the ten smaller artifacts similar to the one Oramen had gone to inspect when the attempt on his life had been made. That particular black cube was subject to the most intense exertions of all due to the partial collapse of the chamber which had been excavated around it.

The central chamber housing the Sarcophagus was similar to – but far larger than – that around the black cube Oramen had seen. The excavations had emptied a huge cavity within the building, removing mud, silt, sand and assorted debris that had collected there over uncounted centuries to reveal what had always been an enormous central arena over a hundred metres across rather than an extemporised void blasted and torn from smaller rooms and spaces.

At its centre, brightly lit by arc lights and cluttered by layers, levels and platforms of scaffolding and latticed by the resulting shadows, lay the Sarcophagus itself; a pale grey cube twenty metres to a side, its corners and edges subtly rounded. For nearly twenty days while it was fully excavated a controlled chaos had swirled about the artifact, a storm of men, machines and movement, attended by shouts, bangs, sparks, animal roars, gouts and bursts of steam and exhaust smoke. Now, though, as Oramen finally looked upon it, the chamber around the object was quiet and hushed and the atmosphere almost reverential, though possessed, unless Oramen was imagining it, of a certain tension.

"It does not look very alive from here," Oramen said. He and Poatas stood, surrounded by guards, at the main entrance to the central chamber, a wide doorway stationed ten metres above the base of the shallow bowl at the centre of which the Sarcophagus sat on a round plinth raised by about five metres.

"Well, you should come closer," Poatas said.

Oramen smiled at the man. "That is exactly what we are going to do, Mr Poatas."

They walked towards it. Oramen found the thing in many ways less intimidating than the pure black cube he'd taken an interest in earlier. The chamber was far larger and less oppressive-seeming – partly, no doubt, he was simply appreciating the lack of clamour – and the object itself, though much larger than the one he'd seen just a few days before, seemed less intimidating just because it was a relatively unthreatening shade of grey rather than the light-defying black that had so repelled and fascinated him in that other object. Nevertheless, it was large and he was seeing it from below rather than above, so that it appeared more massive still.

He wondered how much he was still suffering from the effects of his injuries. He might have stopped another day in bed; his doctors had recommended it but he had been more concerned at losing the trust of the people and especially the ex-soldiers of the Settlement. He had had to rise, had to show himself to them, had to address them, and then – when the messenger had entered with news that the Sarcophagus had shown signs of life – he had had no choice but to accompany Poatas and his closest aides to the focus of their excavations. He felt breathless, sore in too many places to count and his head hurt, plus his ears still rang and he had to struggle to hear what people said sometimes, as though he was an already old man, but he was doing his best to appear well and hearty and unconcerned.

The Sarcophagus gave off, it seemed to him as he walked up to it, an aura of utter solidity; of settled, stolid, almost crushing containment and impassivity, of – indeed – timelessness, as though this thing had witnessed the passing of ages and epochs ungraspable by men, and yet still, somehow, was more of the future than of the past.

Oramen assured the makeshift personal guard of concerned-looking, rather fearsome ex-soldiers who'd accumulated around him since his speech an hour or so earlier that he would be all right on the scaffolding with just one or two to look after him. Dubrile, a grey, grim-looking, one-eyed veteran from many of Hausk's campaigns, who seemed to have been acclaimed their leader by the many ex-soldiers who'd rallied about him, detailed two others to accompany him in looking after Oramen.

"This is not necessary, you know," Poatas told Oramen while the guards were negotiating all this amongst themselves. "You are in no danger here."

"I thought as much three days ago, Poatas," Oramen said with a smile, "when I went to view the other object." He let the smile fade and dropped his voice. "And do try to remember, Poatas, you address me as 'sir', both in front of the men and when we are alone." He put the smile back again. "There are niceties to be observed, after all."

Poatas looked like he'd suddenly discovered a frozen turd in his britches. He drew himself up, the staff wavered in his hand as though he was putting more weight on it than he was used to and he nodded, getting out a rather strangled-sounding, "Well, yes, indeed, sir."

With the guards sorted, Oramen nodded to the great grey object in front of them. "Now, shall we?"

They ascended the ramps to a point at the centre of one of the cube's faces where a dozen or so men in neat white overalls moved, hidden from the rest of the chamber by grey sheets shrouding the scaffolding behind them. Clustered about the platform were various delicate, mysterious-looking machines and instruments of a sophistication patently beyond the capacity of both the Sarl and Deldeyn. They all seemed to be connected to each other by thin wires and cables of a variety of colours. Even these looked somehow advanced, almost alien.

"Where does this come from?" Oramen asked, waving at the equipment.

"These were traded from the Oct," Poatas said with relish. "Sir," he added, along with a little facial twitch. He positioned himself so that he stood between Oramen and the rest of the people on the platform. Oramen saw Dubrile shift behind him, perhaps to guard against the unlikely possibility that Poatas would seek to push the Prince Regent off the scaffolding. Poatas frowned but went on, voice dropped almost to a whisper. "The Oct have shown a new interest in our excavations and were most keen to help when they realised we had discovered objects of such advancement. Sir."

Oramen frowned. "One assumes their Nariscene mentors approved."

"One assumes what one wishes to, I dare say, sir," Poatas said quietly. "The Oct, I understand through some of the merchants who deal with them, would offer us much more help, if we'd but let them. Sir."

"Do they now?" Oramen said.

"Such help was disdained by the Deldeyn when they ran the excavations. As on the Eighth, the Oct's licence here runs no deeper than those who hold the level wish it to, and the Deldeyn, led by the late monks of the Mission, refused any such aid, citing pride and an over-punctilious reading of the Articles of Inhabitation which someone perhaps wishing to limit themselves and their people in their natural desire and right for advancement both technical and moral, a right which surely any—"

"Enough, Poatas, enough," Oramen said quietly, clapping the fellow lightly on the shoulder. The stooped grey man, whose voice and manner had grown maniacally intense and feverish in the course of just that single gasped, unfinished sentence, ceased talking, looking pained and stricken.

"So, Poatas," Oramen said, louder now, so that all could hear again. "Show me what brought my little gathering to such an abrupt conclusion."

"Of course, sir," Poatas whispered, and hobbled off, staff echoing on the boards, to speak with a couple of the technicians.

"Sir, if you would," one of the white-suited men said to Oramen. The fellow was middle-aged, pallid and nervous-looking, though he also seemed excited, energised. He indicated that Oramen should stand at a particular point on the platform in front of a panel on the Sarcophagus that looked a shade lighter than the rest of the visible structure.

"Sir," Poatas said, "may I present Senior Technician Leratiy." Another man bowed to Oramen. He was more fully built though just as pallid. He wore a set of overalls that looked better and more generously cut than those of his colleagues.

"Prince Regent. An honour, sir. I should warn you, however," he said, "that the effect is one of . . . being read, somehow, and then having images of, well . . ." The fellow smiled. "I ought to let you see for yourself. I cannot tell you quite what to expect because everyone who has experienced this phenomenon thus far has encountered something rather different from everybody else, though common themes do seem to predominate in the results. It would be wrong of me, in any case, to prejudice your impressions. If you will only remember to attempt to recall what it is that you experience and then be willing to communicate whatever that may be to one of the technician-recorders, I should be most extremely grateful. Please step forward; the focus appears to be about here."

There was a rough square marked on the boards beneath Oramen's feet; he stepped into it. One of the technicians came forward with what looked like a small flat box, but Senior Technician Leratiy waved him away with one imperious hand. "The Prince Regent is of sufficient height," he muttered. Then, checking that Oramen's feet were within the square, he said, "Please, sir, merely stand there a little while, if you please." The senior technician took out a large pocket watch and inspected it. "The process usually begins after approximately one half-minute. With your permission, sir, I shall time events."

Oramen nodded. He looked quizzically at the patch of light grey in front of him.

For some few moments, there was nothing. Nothing happened at all except that he started to wonder if this was all some elaborate joke, or even a convoluted and over-organised attempt, again, to kill him. He was stood in one obviously very well-worked-out spot. Might this be where an assassin's rifle shot was targeted, perhaps even through the grey curtains obscuring this part of the platform from the rest of the chamber?

The experience began as a tiny dizziness. He felt oddly imbalanced for a moment, then the dizziness itself seemed to steady him somehow, as though compensating for its own disruptive effects. He felt a strange sensation of weightlessness and carelessness all at once, and for an instant was utterly unsure where he was or when, and how long he had been wherever he was. Then he was fully aware once more, but could feel a sort of rushing in his head, and a cacophonous medley of everything he'd ever heard or felt or seen or known seemed to tear through him.

He felt like a man sitting in a sunlit room watching a gaudy parade that represented in some detail every aspect of his life since birth all rushing past outside, taking only a few seconds to pass and yet allowing him to see and recognise individual bursts and fragments of that long-stored, mostly forgotten life.

Then it was gone – how quickly over!

Then yearning. Yearning for a lost mother, a crown and a whole kingdom; craving the love of all and the return of a long-departed sister, mourning a dead brother and the unrecoverable love, respect and approval of a departed father . . .

He stepped out of the square, breaking the spell.

He took a couple of deep breaths then turned and looked at Senior Technician Leratiy. After some moments he said, "You may tell your technician-recorder I experienced a sense of loss and a sense of longing, both expressed in terms of personal experiences." He looked round the others on the platform, all of them watching him. There were one or two smiles, nervous-seeming. Oramen nodded at Senior Technician Leratiy. "An interesting experience. I take it that what I felt was on a par with the sensations others had?"

"Loss, yearning," Leratiy confirmed. "Those are indeed the emotions felt in common, sir."

"You think this qualifies it as being in any way alive?" Oramen asked, glancing, frowning, at the grey surface.

"It is *doing* something, sir," Poatas said. "To be doing anything after so long buried is perfectly astounding. No other object in the excavations has ever *worked* in this manner before."

"It could be working as a waterwheel might work or a windmill might work, dug out of a similar caking of mud or dust," Oramen suggested.

"We think it is something more than that, sir," Leratiy said.

"Well then, what would be your next step?"

Leratiy and Poatas exchanged looks. "We believe, sir," Senior Technician Leratiy said, "that the object is trying to communicate, but can only do so at the moment through crude images; the strongest ones the human soul experiences; those of loss and yearning amongst them. We believe that it may be possible to allow the object to communicate more fully by, quite simply, teaching it to speak a language."

"What? Shall we talk baby-talk to it?" Oramen asked.

"If it could hear and speak, sir," Leratiy said, "it probably would have tried to talk to us by now; a hundred or more labourers, engineers, technicians and other experts have been speaking in its vicinity since well before we discovered the curious property you have just experienced."

"What, then?" Oramen asked.

Leratiy cleared his throat. "The problem facing us here, sir, is unique in our history but not that of others. It has been experienced many times before over many eons and by a multiplicity of peoples facing an uncounted number of similar relics and artifacts. There are established and highly successful techniques employed by peoples from the Optimae down which may be employed to establish communication with just such an object."

"Indeed," Oramen said. He looked from Leratiy to Poatas. "Have we access to such techniques?"

"At a remove, sir, yes," Poatas said. "An Enabler machine can be ours to command."

"An Enabler machine?" Oramen asked.

"We would rely on the Oct to provide and operate the equipment involved, sir," Leratiy said, "though it would, of course," he added quickly, "be under our most diligent and intense supervision. All would be noted, recorded, tabulated and filed. On any subsequent occasions it may well be that we would be able to employ the same techniques directly ourselves. Thus, our benefit would be twofold, or indeed of an even higher order."

"We both," Poatas began, glancing at the senior technician, "feel it is of the utmost importance—"

"Again," Oramen interrupted, "is not this sort of technology transfer, this kind of help banned, though?" He looked at the two men in turn. They both looked awkward, glancing at each other.

Leratiy cleared his throat again. "The Oct claim that if they operate it, sir, then – as it is being directed at something that in effect already belongs to them – the answer is no, it is not banned."

"Indeed," Poatas said, lifting his chin defiantly.

"They claim this thing?" Oramen asked, glancing at the cube. This was a new development.

"Not formally, sir," Leratiy replied. "They accept our prior claim. However, they believe it may form part of their ancient birthright, so take a particular and profound interest in it."

Oramen looked around. "I see no Oct here. How do you know all this about them?"

"They have communicated through a special emissary by the name of Savide, sir," Poatas said. "He has appeared within this chamber on a couple of occasions, and been of some consultant help."

"I was not informed of this," Oramen pointed out.

"You were injured, confined to bed, sir," Poatas said, studying the planking at his feet for a moment.

"That recently, I see," Oramen said. Poatas and Leratiy both smiled at him.

"Gentlemen," Oramen said, smiling back, "if it is your judgement we should allow the Oct to help us, then let them. Have them bring their wonderful techniques, their Enabler machines, though do what you can to find out how they work. Very well?" he asked.

The two men looked both surprised and delighted.

"Indeed, sir!" Senior Technician Leratiy said.

"Sir!" Poatas said, lowering his head.

Oramen spent the rest of the day organising what were in effect all the trappings of a small state, or at least looking on as others did the actual organising. Apart from anything else they were resurrecting a disbanded army, turning the men who had been soldiers and had become excavationers back into soldiers again. There was no shortage of men, only of weapons; most of the guns that had equipped the army were stored in armouries back in Pourl. They would have to do the best they could with what they had. The situation ought to improve a little; some of the workshops in the Settlement were already turning their forges and lathes to the production of guns, though they would not be of especially high quality.

The people he entrusted to oversee this were all from relatively junior ranks; almost his first action had been to gather together all the senior people tyl Loesp had put in place, including General Foise, and send them off to Rasselle, allegedly as a delegation to explain Oramen's actions but in reality just to be rid of people he was no longer sure he could trust. Some of his new advisers had cautioned that he was sending able officers with a clear idea of the precise strengths and weaknesses of Oramen's own forces straight to their enemy, but he was not convinced this was sufficient reason to let them stay, and was reluctant to attempt to intern or imprison them.

Foise and the others had departed, reluctant but obedient, on a train only a few hours earlier. Another train had followed half an hour behind. It was full of soldiers loyal to Oramen carrying plentiful supplies of blasting material, with instructions to mine and guard every bridge between the Falls and Rasselle that could be attained without opening hostilities.

Oramen made his excuses from the planning meeting as soon as he decently could and retired to his carriage for a much-needed nap; the doctors still wanted him to take more days off but he would not, could not. He slept for an hour and then visited Droffo, who was recovering in the principal hospital train.

"You've moved quickly then," Droffo said. He was still bandaged and looked dazed. Various cuts had been cleaned on his face and left to heal in the air, though a couple on one cheek had needed stitches. "Foise went quietly?" He shook his head, then grimaced. "Probably off to plot with tyl Loesp."

"You think they'll attack us?" Oramen asked. He sat on a canvas chair drawn up beside Droffo's bed in the private compartment.

"I don't know, prince," Droffo said. "Is there any news yet from tyl Loesp?"

"None. He is not even in Rasselle. He may not have heard yet."

"I'd be wary of going to meet with him, I know that."

"You think he himself is behind this?"

"Who else?"

"I thought perhaps ... people around him."

"Such as who?" Droffo said.

"Bleye? Tohonlo? People like that."

Droffo shook his head. "They haven't the wit."

Oramen couldn't think of anybody else by name, with the possible exception of General Foise. Surely not Werreber. Chasque he was not so sure about, but then the Exaltine was not connected between tyl Loesp and any further layers of underlings; he was, as it were, off to one side. Oramen was used to seeing tyl Loesp surrounded by other people – mostly army officers and civil servants – but no, now Droffo mentioned it, there were few regular, identifiable people around him. He had functionaries, lackeys, those who did his bidding, but no real friends or confidants that Oramen knew of. He'd assumed they existed but he just didn't know them, but maybe they didn't exist at all.

Oramen shrugged. "But tyl Loesp?" he said, frowning mightily. "I just can't ..."

"Vollird and Baerth were his men, Oramen."

"I know."

"Is there any news on Vollird?"

"None. Still missing; another ghost to haunt the diggings."

"And tyl Loesp recommended Tove Lomma to you as well, didn't he?"

"Tove was an old friend," Oramen said.

"But one who owed tyl Loesp his advancement. Just be careful."

"I am, belatedly," Oramen told him.

"This thing, the Sarcophagus. Is it really all they say?"

"It seems to communicate. The Oct want to try and teach it to talk," Oramen said. "They have a thing called an Enabler machine which the Optimae use to talk to such dug-up curiosities."

"Perhaps it's an oracle," Droffo said, smiling lopsidedly, stretching his stitched cuts and grimacing again. "Ask it what's going to happen next."

What happened next was that, two shifts later, on what was in effect the following day, tyl Loesp sent word by telegraph from Rasselle that there must have been some terrible misunderstanding. Vollird and Baerth must themselves have been victims of a conspiracy and persons unknown were patently plotting to drive a wedge between the regent and the Prince Regent for their own ignoble ends. Tyl Loesp thought it best that he and Oramen meet in Rasselle to discuss matters, reassure themselves of their mutual love and respect and arrange all subsequent dealings in a manner such as would lead to no more rash actions nor unsubstantiated, hinted-at accusations.

Oramen, after discussing this signal with Droffo, Dubrile and the half-dozen or so junior officers who had become his advisers – all acclaimed by their men rather than owing their advancement to tyl Loesp – replied that he would meet tyl Loesp here at the Falls, and he must bring no more than a dozen men with him, lightly armed.

They were still waiting on a reply.

Then, in the middle of what most people were treating as the night, news came that the Sarcophagus was speaking, and the Oct had appeared in force in the chamber around it, arriving via submarine vessels which had found or created channels in the Sulpine river which were still liquid water rather than ice. There was some confusion over whether they had taken over the chamber or not – work was apparently continuing – but they were there in unprecedented numbers and they were demanding to see tyl Loesp or whoever was in charge.

"I thought they were just coming to use this language-teaching device," Oramen said as he pulled on clothes, wincing with each stretch of arm and leg. Neguste held out his jacket and helped him into it.

Droffo, who was ambulatory if far from fully recovered and who had intercepted the messenger bringing the news, held Oramen's ceremonial sword belt in his one good hand. His other arm was cradled by a sling. "Perhaps when the thing spoke it said something disagreeable," he suggested.

"It might have chosen a more agreeable time, that's sure," Oramen said, accepting his sword belt.

"Dear WorldGod," Oramen said when he saw the interior of the great chamber at the Nameless City's heart. He and Droffo both stopped in their tracks. Neguste, following behind – determined to go wherever his master went to ensure he shared whatever fate awaited and never again be thought either frightened or disloyal – failed to stop in time and bumped into them.

"Begging pardon, sirs," he said, then saw between them to the chamber. "Well, fuck me upside down," he breathed.

There were hundreds and hundreds of Oct in the chamber. Blue bodies glistened under the lights, thousands of red limbs shone as though polished. They had entirely surrounded the Sarcophagus, arranging themselves on the cleared floor of the great space in concentric circles of what looked like prostrated devotion, even adoration. The creatures all appeared motionless and might have been mistaken for dead had they not been so neatly and identically arranged. All were equipped with the same kind of body-encompassing suit that Ambassador Kiu had worn. Oramen caught the same strange scent he had smelled all those months ago, the day he'd heard his father had been killed. He remembered encountering Ambassador Kiu on his way to the mounting yard, and that curious smell. Faint then, it was strong now.

Around Oramen, his personal guard, commanded by Dubrile,

jostled into position, trying to leave no gap. They surround me, Oramen thought, while the Oct surround *that*. But why? The guards too were distracted by the sight of so many Oct, glancing nervously as they took up their positions around Oramen.

White-coated technicians still moved about the chamber and along the scaffolding levels, seemingly untroubled by the presence of the Oct. On the platform where Oramen had stood earlier and experienced the Sarcophagus seemingly trying to communicate with him, the covers had been drawn back so that it was possible to see what was going on. Two Oct were there, along with some white-suited human figures. Oramen thought he recognised both Leratiy and Poatas.

A guardsman was reporting to Dubrile, who saluted Oramen and said, "Sir, the Oct just appeared; their ships are somewhere behind the ice of the Falls; they melted their way through. They came in, some through here, others floating in from places up in the walls. The guards didn't know what to do. We never thought to have orders to cover such a thing. The Oct seem unarmed, so I suppose we are still in control, but they refuse to move."

"Thank you, Dubrile," Oramen said. Poatas was waving wildly from the platform. "Let's go and see what's happening, shall we?"

"Oramen-man, prince," one of the Oct said when Oramen arrived on the platform. Its voice was like dry leaves rustling. "Again. Like meetings meet in time and spaces. As our ancestors, the blessed Involucra, who were no more, to us always were, and now are again without denial, so we are met once more. Think you not?"

"Ambassador Kiu?" Oramen asked. The ambassador and another Oct hung unsupported in front of the light patch of grey on the cube's surface. Poatas and Senior Technician Leratiy stood nearby, gazing on with expressions of barely controlled excitement. They looked, Oramen thought, as though they could not wait to tell him something.

"I have that privilege," Ambassador Kiu-to-Pourl said. "And to he I you introduce; Savidius Savide, Peripatetic Special Envoy to Sursamen."

The other Oct turned fractionally to Oramen. "Oramen-man, Prince of Hausk, Pourl," it said.

Oramen nodded. Dubrile and three of the guards were positioning themselves at the corners of the platform, making it almost crowded. "I am pleased to meet you, Envoy Savidius Savide. Welcome, friends," he said. "May I ask what brings you here?" He turned to look round and down at the hundreds of Oct arranged in glittering circles round the Sarcophagus. "And in such numbers?"

"Greatness, prince," Kiu said, drifting closer to Oramen. Dubrile went to interpose himself between but Oramen held up one hand. "Unparalleled greatness!"

"An occasion of such importance we are made as nothing!" the other Oct said. "These, here, our comrades, we two. We are nothing, no fit witness, no worthy acolytes, utterly insufficient! Nevertheless."

"Deserving or not, we are here," Kiu said. "Of incomprehensible privilege is this to all present. We thank you boundlessly for such. You put us forever in your debt. No lives lived to the end of time by billions, trillions of Oct could so repay our chance to witness."

"Witness?" Oramen said gently, smiling indulgently, looking from the two Oct to Poatas and Leratiy. "Witness to what? That the Sarcophagus has spoken?"

"It has, sir!" Poatas said, stepping forward, flourishing his stick, waving it at the pale grey patch on the object's surface. He gestured at one of the pieces of equipment on a tall trolley. "This device simply projected images and sounds and a sequence of invisible wave-fronts through the ether into the face of what we have called the Sarcophagus and it spoke! Sarl, Deldeyn, Oct, several Optimae languages. Repetitions, at first, so that we were disappointed, thinking that it only recorded, regurgitated, had no mind after all, but then – then, prince, then it spoke in its own voice!" Poatas turned to the pale grey square and bowed. "Will you indulge us once more, sir? Our most senior person is present; a prince of the royal house which commands two levels, he who is in charge here."

"To see?" a voice said from the grey square. It was a voice like a long sigh, like something being expelled, waved away with every syllable.

"Come, come, sir!" Poatas said, beckoning Oramen forward. "It would see you. Here, sir; into the focus as before."

Oramen held back. "Simply to be seen? Why into this focus again?" He was concerned that now this thing seemed to have found a voice it still might need to see into people's minds.

"You are the prince?" the voice said levelly.

Oramen stepped round so that, had the grey patch been some sort of window, he might be visible to whatever was inside, but he did not step into the focal point he had stood in earlier. "I am," he said. "My name is Oramen. Son of the late King Hausk."

"You distrust me, prince?"

"That would be too strong," Oramen said. "I wonder at you. You must be something quite remarkable and strange to be so long buried and yet alive. What might your name be?"

"So quickly we come to regret. My name, with so much else, is lost to me. I seek to recover it, with so much else."

"How might you do that?" Oramen asked it.

"There are other parts. Parts of me, belonging. Scattered. Together, brought, I may be made whole again. It is all I value now, all I miss, all I yearn for."

Senior Technician Leratiy stepped forward. "We believe, sir, that some of the other cubes, the smaller ones, are repositories of this being's memories, and possibly other faculties."

"They would have been situated nearby but not together with this being, you see, sir," Poatas said. "To ensure some would survive."

"All the cubes?" Oramen asked.

"Not all, I think, though I cannot yet know," the sighing

voice said. "Three or four, perhaps."

"Some others may be merely symbolic," Poatas added.

"What are you, then?" Oramen asked the Sarcophagus.

"What am I, prince?"

"To which people do you belong? What species?"

"Why, gentle prince, I am Involucra. I am what I understand you sometimes call 'Veil'."

"Our ancestor survives!" Savidius Savide exclaimed. "The Veil, they who are who made us as well as all Shellworlds are, in one being, returned, to bless us, to bless all but to bless us, the Oct, the – truly, now undeniably – Inheritors!"

Mertis tyl Loesp fretted around the Imperial Chambers, feeling pursued by the pack of advisers and senior military people at his back who all wanted to offer advice. He had resumed his Sarl clothing, taking up mail, tabard and a sword belt again, putting aside the more delicate Deldeyn civilian attire, but feeling wrong, out of place, almost ridiculous. This was meant to be the New Age; fighting, disputation was supposed to be finished with. Was he to be forced to take up arms again because of a misunderstanding, because of a pair of bungling idiots? Why could no one else do their job properly?

"This is still a young man, barely more than a child. He cannot be our problem, sir. We must seek and identify whoever has his ear and so guides his actions. Knowing that is the key."

"Only insist that he attends you, sir. He will come. The young will often put up a most fervent resistance, at least in words, and then, their point having been made, their independence established sufficiently in their own eyes, they will, with all natural truculence, see sense and come round to a more adult view. Renew your invitation as an instruction. Bring the young fellow to heel. Once in Rasselle, confronted with your own obvious authority and good will, all will be resolved satisfactorily."

"He is wounded in his pride, too, sir. He has the impatience of youth and knows that he will be king in time, but at such an age we often cannot see the point in waiting. Therefore we must compromise. Meet him between here and the Falls, on the edge of the area where the shadow presently falls; let that symbolise the new dawn of good relations between you."

"Go to him, sir; show the forbearance of power. Go to him not even with a dozen men, but with none. Leave your army camped beyond, of course, but go to him purely alone, with the simplicity and humility of justice and the right that is on your side."

"He is a child in this; punish him, sir. Princes require discipline as much as any other children. More; they are too usually indulged and require regular correction to maintain a fit balance of indulgence and regulation. Make all haste to the Hyeng-zhar with your greatest force arrayed in full battle order; he'll not come out against you, and even if he did think to there must be wiser heads around him who'll know to counsel otherwise. The presentation of force settles such matters, sir; all silly plans and fancies evaporate faced with it. Only provide that and your problems cease."

"They have men but not arms, sir. You have both. Merely display such and all settles. It will not come to a fight. Impose your will, do not be taken as one who can suffer such implied accusations lightly. You feel justly offended at being so unjustly accused. Show that you will not tolerate such insult."

Tyl Loesp stood on a balcony looking out over the trees of the royal enclosure surrounding the Great Palace in Rasselle, clutching at the rail and working his hands round and round it while behind him clamoured all those who would tell him what to do. He felt at bay. He turned and faced them. "Foise," he said, picking out the general who'd arrived only a few hours earlier from the Hyeng-zhar. They had already spoken, but only for Foise to deliver a brief report. "Your thoughts."

"Sir," Foise said, looking round the others present; Sarl military and nobility mostly, though with a few trusted Deldeyn civil servants and nobles who had always been sympathetic to the Sarl even when their peoples had been at war. "I have not thus far heard an unwise word here." There was much serious nodding and many an expression of pretended modesty. Only those who had not yet actually spoken looked in any way unimpressed with this latest contribution. "However, it is as true today as it always has been that we cannot follow every line of advice. Therefore, I would suggest that, bearing in mind the most recent information which we have to hand, of which I am the humble bearer, we look at what we know to be the most lately pertaining situation of the object of our deliberations." There was some more nodding at this.

Tyl Loesp was still waiting to hear anything of import, or indeed new, but just listening to Foise's voice seemed to have calmed something in him. He felt able to breathe again.

"But what would you suggest that we do, Foise?" he asked.

"What he does not expect, sir," Foise said.

Tyl Loesp felt back in charge. He directed a smile round everybody else in the group, and shrugged. "General," he said "he does not expect me to surrender and admit I was wrong, some black-hearted traitor. We shall not be doing that, I assure you." There was laughter at his words.

Foise smiled too, like a brief echo of his superior's expression. "Of course, sir. I mean, sir, that we do not wait, do not gather our forces. Strike now. What we have just heard said about the prince and those around him seeing sense on the presentation of force will be no less true."

"Strike now?" tyl Loesp said, again glancing at the others. He took a stagey look over the balcony rail. "I do not seem to have the Prince Regent immediately to hand for that strategy." More laughter.

"Indeed, sir," Foise said, unflustered. "I mean that you should form an aerial force. Take as many men and weapons as all available lyge and caude within the city will bear and fly to the Falls. They do not expect it. They have not the weaponry to reduce an aerial attack. Their—"

"The region is dark!" one of the other military people pointed out. "The beasts will not fly!"

"They will," Foise said levelly. "I have seen Oramen himself trust his life to them, just a few days ago. Ask the beasts' handlers. They may need using to it, but it can be done."

"The winds are too great!"

"They have fallen back lately," Foise said, "and anyway do not normally persist longer than a short-day without sufficient pause." Foise looked at tyl Loesp and spread his arms from the elbows, saying simply, "It can be done, sir."

"We shall see," tyl Loesp said. "Lemitte, Uliast," he said, naming two of his most hard-headed generals. "Look into this."

"Sir."

"Sir."

"It takes the name Nameless, then," Savidius Savide said. "Our dear ancestor, this sanctified remainder, surviving echo of a mighty and glorious chorus from the dawn of all that's good assumes the burden of this ever-consecrated city as we take on the burden of long absence. Ever-present loss! How cruel! A night has been upon us that's lasted decieons; the shadow's back half of for ever. A night now glimmering to dawn, at last! Oh! How long we have waited! All rejoice! Another part of the great community is made whole. Who pitied now may – no, must – with all good reason and bounteous wishes rejoice, rejoice and rejoice again for we who are reunited with our past!"

"It is our parent!" Kiu added. "Producing all, itself produced by this city-wide birthing, dross swept away, the past uncovered, all jibes abandoned, all disbelief extinguished."

Oramen had never heard the ambassador sound so excited, or even so comprehensible. "Sympathy, again!" Kiu exclaimed. "For those who doubted the Oct, scorned us for our very name, Inheritors. How they will rue their lack of belief in us on this news being carried, in joy, in truth absolute, unshakeable, undeniable, to every star and planet, hab and ship of the great lens! Fall the Falls silent, frozen in tremulous expectation, in calm, in fit and proper pause before the great climactic chords of fulfilment, realisation, celebration!"

"You are so sure it is what it says it is?" Oramen asked. They were still on the platform around the lighter grey patch on the front of the Sarcophagus, which might or might not be a kind of window into the thing. Oramen had wanted to talk further elsewhere, but the two Oct ambassadors would not leave the presence of whatever was in the Sarcophagus. He had had to settle for bringing the two of them to the far edge of the platform – possibly out of range of the window, possibly not – and asking everybody else to leave. Poatas and Leratiy had removed themselves only as far as the next layer of scaffolding down, and that reluctantly. Oramen talked quietly, in the vain hope that this would encourage the two Oct to do the same, but they would not; both seemed enthused, agitated, almost wild.

They had each taken a turn facing that window, experiencing it for themselves. Others had too, including Poatas and Leratiy. They reported that the experience was now one of joy and hope, not loss and yearning. A feeling of euphoric release filled whoever stood or floated there, along with an aching, earnest desire that one might soon be made whole.

"Of course sure it is what it says! Why anything other?" Savidius Savide asked. The alien voice sounded shocked that any doubt might be entertained. "It is what it says that it is. This has been presaged, this is expected. Who doubts such profundity?"

"You were expecting this?" Oramen said, looking from one Oct to the other. "For how long?"

"All our lives before we lived, truly!" Kiu said, waving his upper limbs around.

"As this will resound forever forwards in time, so the expectation has lasted the forever of not just individuals but our selves as one, our self, our species, kind," Savidius Savide added.

"But for how long have you thought the answer was here, at the Falls specifically?" Oramen asked.

"Unknown time," Kiu told him.

"Party, we are not," Savidius Savide agreed. "Who knows what lessons learned, futures foretold, intelligences garnered, down timelines older than ourselves, we are sure, pursued to produce plans, courses, actions? Not I."

"Nor," Kiu agreed.

Oramen realised that even if the Oct were trying to give him a direct answer, he'd be unlikely to understand it. He just had to accept this frustration. "The information which you transferred from the Enabler machine into the Nameless," he said, trying a new tack. "Was it ... what one might call neutral regarding whatever you expected to discover here?"

"Better than!" exclaimed Kiu.

"Needless hesitancy," Savide said. "Cowardice of reproachable lack of will, decisiveness. Expellence upon all such."

"Gentlemen," Oramen said, still trying to keep his voice down. "Did you tell the being in here what you were looking for? That you expected it to be an Involucra?"

"How can its true nature be hidden from itself?" Savide said scornfully.

"You ask impossibles," Kiu added.

"It is as it is. Nothing can alter that," Savide said. "We would all be advised lessons similar ourselves doubly to learn, taking such, templated."

Oramen sighed. "A moment, please."

"Unowned, making unbestowable. All share the one moment of now," Kiu said.

"Just so," Oramen said, and stepped away from the two Oct, indicating with one flat hand that he wished them to stay where they were. He stood in front of the pale grey patch, though closer than its focus.

"What are you?" he asked quietly.

"Nameless," came the equally subdued reply. "I have taken that name. It pleases me, for now, until my own may be returned to me."

"But what sort of thing are you? Truly."

"Veil," the voice whispered back. "I am Veil, I am Involucra.

We made that within which you have ever lived, prince."

"You made Sursamen?"

"Yes, and we made all those that you call Shellworlds."

"For what reason?"

"To cast a field about the galaxy. To protect. All know this, prince."

"To protect from what?"

"What is your own guess?"

"I have none. Would you answer my question? What did you seek to protect the galaxy from?"

"You misunderstand."

"Then tell, so that I understand."

"I require my other pieces, my scattered shards. I would be whole again, then I might answer your questions. The years have been long, prince, and cruel to me. So much is gone, so much taken away. I am ashamed at how much, blush to report how little I know that did not come out of that device that let me learn how to talk to you."

"You blush? Do you blush? Can you? What are you, in there?"

"I am less than whole. Of course I blush not. I translate. I speak to you and in your idiom; to the Oct the same, and so quite differently. All is translation. How could it be otherwise?"

Oramen sighed heavily and took his leave of the Sarcophagus. He left the two Oct returning to their positions in front of it again.

On the floor of the chamber, some way beyond the outer circle of the devotional Oct, Oramen talked to Poatas and Leratiy. Another couple of men who were Oct experts had arrived, yawning, too, and some of his new crop of advisers.

"Sir," Poatas said, leaning forward in his seat, both hands clutching at his stick. "This is a moment of the utmost historicity! We are present at one of the most important discoveries in recent history, anywhere in the galaxy!"

"You think it is a Veil in there?" Oramen asked.

Poatas waved one hand impatiently, "Not an actual Involucra;

that is unlikely."

"But not impossible," Leratiy added.

"Not impossible," Poatas agreed.

"There could be some sort of stasis mechanism or effect pertaining," one of the younger experts suggested. "Some loop of time itself." He shrugged. "We have heard of such things. The Optimae are said to be capable of comparable feats."

"It scarcely matters whether it is a real Involucra, though I repeat that it is most unlikely to be one," Poatas exclaimed. "It *must* be an awoken machine of Optimae sophistication to have survived so long! It has been buried for centiaeons, perhaps deciaeons! Rational, interrogatable entities of that antiquity turn up in the greater galaxy not once in the lifetime of any one of us! We must not hesitate! The Nariscene or the Morthanveld will take it from us if we do. Even if they do not, then the waters will return all too soon and sweep who-knows-what away! Can you not see how important this is?" Poatas looked feverish, his whole body clenched and expression tormented. "We are dabbling about on the fringe of something that will resound throughout all civilised space! We must strike! We must make busy with every possible application, or lose this priceless opportunity! If we act, *we* live for ever more! Every Optimae will know the name of Sursamen, of the Hyeng-zhar, of this Nameless City, its single Nameless citizen and we here!"

"We keep talking about the Optimae," Oramen said, hoping to calm Poatas down by seeming sober and practical himself. "Should we not involve them? The Morthanveld would seem the obvious people to ask for help."

"They will take this for themselves!" Poatas said, anguished. "We will lose it!"

"The Oct have already half taken it," Droffo said.

"They are here but they do not control," Poatas said, sounding defensive.

"I think they could control if they wished," Droffo insisted.

"Well, they do not!" Poatas hissed. "We work with them.

They offer us that."

"They have little choice," Leratiy told Oramen. "They fear what the Nariscene judgement would be of their actions. Whose judgement would the Morthanveld fear?"

"Their peers among the Optimae, I imagine," Oramen said.

"Who can do nothing, only register their so-civilised disapproval," Leratiy said contemptuously. "That is without point."

"They might at least know what it is we are dealing with," Oramen suggested.

"*We* do!" Poatas said, almost wailing.

"We may not have any more time," Leratiy said. "The Oct have no interest in telling anyone else what's happening here; however, the news will out soon enough, and then the Nariscene or indeed the Morthanveld may well come calling. Meanwhile," the senior technician said, glancing at Poatas, who seemed almost to be trying to climb out of his skin, "I agree with my colleague, sir; we must move with all possible speed."

"We *must*!" Poatas shouted.

"Calm yourself, Poatas," Leratiy said. "We can throw no more men at the three other cubes without the extra just getting in the way of those who already know what they're doing."

"Three cubes?" Oramen asked.

"Our Nameless one insists that its memories and, perhaps, a few other faculties lie in three specific cubes out of the ten black objects we know about, sir," Leratiy said. "It has identified them. We are preparing to bring them here, to it."

"It must be done, and quickly!" Poatas insisted. "While we still have time!"

Oramen looked at the others. "Is this wise?" he asked. There were some concerned looks but nobody seemed prepared to identify such actions as unwise. He looked back at Leratiy. "I was not informed of this."

"Time, again, sir," Senior Technician Leratiy said, smiling and sounding both regretful and reasonable. "Of course you will be informed of everything, but this was, in my judgement, a scientific matter which had to be arranged with all possible haste.

Also, knowing something of the situation pertaining outside this place – I mean, in effect, between you and Regent tyl Loesp – we did not want to add to your burden of cares before any physical movement of the cubes had actually taken place. You were always, sir – but of *course* – going to be informed of our intentions once the moves were ready to be made."

"And when will this happen?" Oramen asked. "When will they be ready?"

Leratiy took out his watch. "The first in about six hours' time, sir. The second in eighteen to twenty hours, the last one a few hours after that."

"The Oct press us to do so, sir," Poatas said, addressing Oramen but glancing sullenly at the senior technician. "They offer to help with the manoeuvring. We might move faster still if we'd only let them."

"I disagree," Leratiy said. "We should move the cubes ourselves."

"If we slip, they will insist," Poatas said.

Leratiy frowned. "We shall not slip."

A messenger arrived and passed a note to Droffo, who presented it to Oramen. "Our furthest airborne scouts report an army moving towards us, gentlemen, from Rasselle," Oramen told them. "They will not be here for another week or more, travelling by road. So, we have that time."

"Well, army or meltwater, we must have our result before we are inundated," Poatas said.

"Dubrile," Oramen said to his guard captain, "would this be a better place to defend than my carriages at the Settlement?" He nodded to indicate the great chamber they stood within.

"Most definitely, sir," Dubrile replied. He looked at the massed Oct. "However—"

"Then I shall pitch my tent with our allies the Oct," Oramen said, addressing all. "I stay here." He smiled at Neguste. "Mr Puibive, see that everything necessary is brought, would you?"

Neguste looked delighted. Probably at being called "Mister".

"Certainly, sir!"

It was a quiet time in the chamber, at the end of another long shift. Most of the lights had been turned off, leaving the whole huge space seeming even greater in extent than it appeared when lit. The Oct were taking turns to return to their ships for whatever reasons occupied them, but still over nine out of ten of them remained in the places they had occupied when Oramen had first seen them, arranged in neat concentric circles of blue bodies and red limbs, all perfectly still, surrounding the scaffolded Sarcophagus.

"You think it will reveal itself and be like you, that it is actually an alive example of your forebears?" Oramen asked Savidius Savide. They were alone on the platform. The others were absent on other duties or sleeping. Oramen had woken in his hurriedly thrown-together tent – fashioned from some of the same material that had shrouded parts of the scaffolding round the Sarcophagus – and come up here to talk with the being that called itself Nameless. He had discovered Savide, just floating there in front of the pale grey patch.

"It is as us. Mere form is irrelevant."

"Have you asked it whether you truly are its descendants?"

"That is not required."

Oramen stood up. "I'll ask it."

"This cannot be relevant," Savide said as Oramen went to stand before the Sarcophagus.

"Nameless," Oramen said, again taking up a position closer than the focal point.

"Oramen," the voice whispered.

"Are the Oct your descendants?"

"All are our descendants."

Well, that was a new claim, Oramen thought. "The Oct more than others?" he asked.

"All. Do not ask who is more than who else. As of now,

without my memories, my abilities, I cannot even tell. Those who call themselves the Inheritors believe what they believe. I honour them, and that belief. It does them no end of credit. The exactitude of it, that is another matter. I am of the Involucra. If they are as they say, then they are of my kind too, at however great a remove. I cannot pass judgement as I do not know. Only restore me to my proper capacity and I may know. Even then, who can say? I have been in here so long that whole empires, species-types, pan-planetary ecosystems and short-sequence suns have come and gone while I have slept. How should I know who grew in our shadow? You ask me in ignorance. Ask me again in some fit state of knowingness."

"When you are restored, what will you do?"

"Then I shall be who I am, and see what is to be seen and do what is to be done. I am of the Involucra, and as I understand things I am the last, and all that we ever thought to do is either fully done or no longer worth doing. I shall have to determine what my correct actions ought to be. I can only be what I always was. I would hope to see what remains of our great work, the Shellworlds, and see what is to be seen in the galaxy and beyond, while acknowledging that the need for the Shellworlds themselves has passed now. I must accept that all has changed and I can be but a curio, a throwback, an exhibit. Perhaps an example, a warning."

"Why warning?"

"Where are the rest of my people now?"

"Gone. Unless we are injuriously mistaken. Quite gone."

"So, a warning."

"But all peoples go," Oramen said gently, as though explaining something to a child. "No one remains in full play for long, not taking the life of a star or a world as one's measure. Life persists by always changing its form, and to stay in the pattern of one particular species or people is unnatural, and always deleterious. There is a normal and natural trajectory for peoples, civilisations, and it ends where it starts, back in the ground. Even we, the Sarl, know this, and we are but barbarians by the standards of most."

"Then I need know more of the manner of our going, and mine. Was our end natural, was it normal, was it – if it was not natural – deserved? I do not yet even know why I am within here. Why so preserved? Was I special, and so glorified? Or excessively ordinary, and so chosen to represent all due to my very averageness? I recall no vice or glory of my own, so cannot think I was specified for great achievement or committed depravity. And yet I am here. I would know why. I hope to discover this shortly."

"What if you discover you are not what you think you are?"

"Why should I not be?"

"I don't know. If so much is in doubt ..."

"Let me show you what I do know," the quiet voice murmured. "May I?"

"Show me?"

"Step again into the place where we may better communicate, if you would."

Oramen hesitated. "Very well," he said. He stepped backwards, found the square daubed on the planking. He glanced back, saw Savidius Savide floating nearby, then faced forward towards the light grey patch on the Sarcophagus surface.

The effect appeared to take less time than it had before. Very soon, it seemed, he experienced that curious dizziness again. Following the momentary feeling of imbalance came the sensation of weightlessness and carelessness, then that of dislocation, wondering where he was or when he was.

Then he knew who he was and where and when.

He felt that he was in that strange sunlit room again, the one where he had seemed to be earlier when he'd had the sensation of all his memories whirling past outside. He seemed to be sitting on a small, crudely fashioned wooden chair while sunlight blazed brightly outside, too bright for him to be able to make out any details of whatever landscape lay beyond the doorway.

A strange lassitude filled him. He felt that he ought to be

able to get up from the little chair but at the same time had no
desire to do so. It was far more pleasant to simply sit here,
doing nothing.

There was somebody else in the room, behind him. He wasn't
concerned about this; the person felt like a benign presence. It
was browsing through books on the shelves behind him. Now
he looked carefully about the room, or just remembered it better,
he realised that it was entirely lined with books. It was like a
tiny library, with him in the middle. He wanted to look round
and see who his guest actually was, but still somehow could not
bring himself to do so. Whoever they were, they were dropping the books to the floor when they were finished with them.
This did concern him. That was not very tidy. That was disre-
spectful. How would they or anybody else find the books again
if they just dumped them on the floor?

He tried very hard indeed to turn round, but could not. He
threw every part of his being into the effort just to move his
head, but it proved impossible. What had seemed like a kind of
laziness, a feeling of not being able to be bothered which had
been perfectly acceptable only moments earlier because it was
something that was coming from within himself, was now
revealed as an imposition, something forced upon him from
outside. He was not being allowed to move. He was being kept
paralysed by whoever this was searching through the books
behind him.

This was an image, he realised. The room was his mind, the
library his memory, the books specific recollections.

The person behind him was rifling through his memories!

Could this be because . . . ?

He had had a thought, earlier. It had barely registered, scarcely
been worth thinking further about because it had seemed both
so irrational and so needlessly horrendous and alarming. Was
that thought, that word somehow connected to what was
happening now?

He had been tricked, trapped. Whoever was searching the
room, the library, the shelves, the books, the chapters and

sentences and words that made up who he was and what his memories were must have suspected something. He almost didn't know what it was, certainly didn't *want* to know what it was, and felt a terrible compulsion, comical in another context, utterly terrifying here and now, not to think of—

Then he remembered, and the being behind him which was searching his thoughts and memories found it at the same time.

The very act of remembering that one fleeting thought, of exposing that single buried word, confirmed the horror of what this thing might really be.

You're not, he thought, you're—

He felt something detonate in his head; a flash of light more brilliant and blinding than that outside the door of the little room, more incandescent than any passing Rollstar, brighter than anything he had ever seen or known.

He was flying backwards, as though he'd thrown himself. A strange creature sailed past – he only glimpsed it; an Oct, of course, with a blue body and red limbs, its filmy surfaces all glittering – then something whacked into the small of his back and he was spinning, somersaulting, falling away into space, falling over and over . . .

He hit something very hard and things broke and hurt and all the light went away again and this time took him with it.

There was no awakening, not in any sudden, now-here-I-am sense. Instead, life – if life it could be called – seemed to seep back into him, slowly, sluggishly, in tiny increments, like silse rain dripping from a tree, all accompanied by pain and a terrible, crushing weight upon him that prevented him from moving.

He was in that book-lined room again, stricken, immobile in that little seat. He had imagined that he was free of it, that he could rise from it, but after a brief, vivid sensation of sudden, unwanted movement, here he was again, paralysed, laid out, spread prone across the ground, helpless. He was a baby once more. He had no control, no movement, could not even support his own head. He knew there were people around him and was aware of movement and yet more pain, but nothing showed its true shape, nothing made sense. He opened his mouth to say something, even if it was just to beg for help, for an end to this grinding, fractured pain, but only a mewl escaped.

He was awake again. He must have fallen asleep. He was still in terrible pain, though it seemed dulled now. *He could not move!* He tried to sit upright, tried to move a limb, twitch a finger, just open his eyes ... but nothing.

Sounds came to him as though from under water. He lay on something soft now, not hard. It was no more comfortable. What had he been thinking? Something important.

He swam back up through the watery sounds around him, helplessly aware of the noises he was making: wheezing, whining, gurgling.

What had he thought of?

The waters parted, like a hazy curtain drawn aside. He thought he saw his friend Droffo. He needed to tell him something. He wanted to grasp Droffo's clothing, drag himself upright, scream into his face, issue a terrible warning!

Then there was Neguste. He had tears on his face. There were many other faces, concerned, businesslike, neutral, dreading, dreadful.

He was awake once again. He was clutching at Droffo's neck, only it was not really Droffo. *Don't let it! Destroy! Mine the chamber, bring it down! Don't let ...*

He was asleep in his seat, an old man perhaps, lost in the end of his days, such days shuffled in this slow fading of the light from him. Genteel confusion; he relied on others to tend to him. Somebody was behind him, searching for something. They always stole. Was this what he'd ever wanted? He was not his father's son, then. He tried to turn round to confront whoever was trying to steal his memories, but could not move. Unless this sensation was a memory too. He felt he might be about to start crying. The voice went on whispering into his ear, into his head. He could not make out what it was it was saying. Old age came with great pain, which seemed unfair. All other senses were dulled but pain was still bright. No, that was not true, the pain was dulled too. Here it was being dulled again.

"What is he trying to say?"

"We don't know. We can't make it out."

Awake again. He blinked, looked up at a ceiling he had seen before. He tried to remember who he was. He decided he must be Droffo, lying here, in the hospital train. No, look; here was Droffo. He must be somebody else, then. He needed to say something to Droffo. Who were all these other people? He wanted them gone. They had to understand! But go. Understand, then go. Things needed to be done. Urgent work. He knew and he had to tell them that he knew. They had to do what he could not. Now!

"Stroy," he heard himself say through the ruins. "Ring it all down. It . . ." Then his voice faded away and the light went again. This darkness, enveloping. How quickly the Rollstars moved, how little they illuminated. He needed to tell Droffo, needed to get him to understand and through him everybody else . . .

He blinked back. Same room. Medical compartment. Something was different, though. He could hear what sounded like shooting. Was that the smell of smoke, burning?

He looked up. Droffo. But not Droffo. It looked like Mertis tyl Loesp. What was he doing here?

"Help . . ." he heard himself say.

"No," tyl Loesp said, with a thin smile. "There's no helping you, prince," then a mailed fist came crashing down into his face, obliterating light.

Tyl Loesp strode down the ramp into the chamber housing the

Sarcophagus, heavily armed men at his heel. The grey cube was surrounded by concentric circles of Oct. They seemed hardly to have noticed that dead and dying men lay scattered about the chamber. The dying were being helped on their way by those charged with dispatching the wounded. Tyl Loesp had been told that a few of the defenders might still be able to put up a fight; the wounded might not all have been accounted for and the chamber was still dangerous; however, he had been impatient to see this thing for himself and had flown straight here on his already tired lyge after they'd taken the Settlement's centre and discovered the broken Prince Regent lying dying on his hospital bed.

"Poatas, Savide," he said as they approached him through the mass of Oct. He looked back at the chamber entrance, where a great black cube ten metres to a side was being manoeuvred to the top of the ramp from the tunnel beyond. A couple of distant shots rang out, echoing round the chamber. Tyl Loesp smiled to see Poatas jerk as though he'd been shot himself. "You have been busy," he said to the old man. "Our prince didn't delay matters, did he?"

"No, sir," Poatas said, looking down. "Progress has been all we might have wished. It is good to see you once more, sir, and know that you are victorious—"

"Yes yes, Poatas. All very loyal. Savide; you approve of all that's happening here?"

"All is approval. We would help further. Let us assist."

"Do so, by all means."

Awake again. Yet more pain. He heard his own breathing. It made a strange gurgling sound. Somebody was dabbing at his face, hurting him. He tried to cry out, could not.

"Sir?"

No sounds would come. He could see his servant with one eye now, again as though through a hazy curtain. Where was

Droffo? He had to tell him something.

"Oh, sir!" Neguste said, sniffing.

"Still alive, prince?"

He got the single good eye to open. Even this action was not without pain. It was Mertis tyl Loesp. Neguste stood somewhere behind, head down, sobbing.

He tried to look at tyl Loesp. He tried to talk. He heard a bubbling sound.

"Oh, now now now. Hush yourself," tyl Loesp said, as though talking to an infant, and pursed his lips and put one finger to his lips. "Don't delay, dear prince. Don't let us detain you. Depart; feel free. Sake, sir, your father died easier than this. Hurry up. You."

"Sir?" Neguste said.

"Can he talk?"

"No, sir. He says nothing. He tries, I think . . . Earl Droffo; he asks for Earl Droffo. I'm not sure."

"Droffo?"

"Dead, sir. Your men killed him. He was trying to—"

"Oh, yes. Well, ask away all you like, prince. Droffo cannot come to you, though you will soon go to him."

"Oh, please don't hurt him, sir, please!"

"Shut up or I'll hurt you. Captain; two guards. You; you will – *now* what?"

"Sir! Sir!" Another new voice, young and urgent.

"*What?*"

"The thing, sir, the object, Sarcophagus! It, it's doing – it's – I can't – it's . . . !"

It is not what you believe, Oramen had time to think, then things went flowing away from him again and he felt himself slip back beneath the waters.

"Sir!"

"What?" tyl Loesp said, not stopping. They were in the newly broadened tunnel a minute from the entrance to the great semi-spherical chamber containing the Sarcophagus.

"Sir, this man insists he is a knight in your employ."

"Tyl Loesp!" an anguished voice rang out over the pack of advisers, guards and soldiers around tyl Loesp. "It's me, Vollird, sir!"

"Vollird?" tyl Loesp said, halting and turning. "Let me see him."

The guards parted and two of them brought a man forward, each holding one of his arms. Vollird it was indeed, though he was dressed in what looked like rags, his hair was wild and the expression on his face wilder still, his eyes staring.

"It is, sir! It's me! Your good and faithful servant, sir!" Vollird cried. "We did all we could, sir! We nearly got him! I swear! There were just too many!"

Tyl Loesp stared at the fellow. He shook his head. "I have no time for you—"

"Just save me from the ghosts, tyl Loesp, please!" Vollird said, his knees buckling underneath him and the guards on either side having to take his weight. Vollird's eyes were wide and staring, foam flecking his lips.

"Ghosts?" tyl Loesp said.

"Ghosts, man!" Vollird shrieked. "I've seen them; ghosts of all of them, come to haunt me!"

Tyl Loesp shook his head. He looked at the guard commander. "The man's lost his wits. Take him—" he began.

"Gillews, the worst!" Vollird said, voice breaking. "I could feel him! I could still feel him! His arm, his wrist under—"

He got no further. Tyl Loesp had drawn his sword and plunged it straight into the man's throat, leaving Vollird gurgling and gesticulating, eyes wider still, gaze focused on the flat blade extending from his throat, where the air whistled and the blood pulsed and bubbled and dripped. His jaw worked awkwardly as though he was trying to swallow something too big.

Tyl Loesp rammed the sword forward, meaning to cut the fellow's spine, but the tip bumped off the bone and sent the edge slicing through the flesh on the side of his neck, producing another gush of blood as an artery was severed. The guard on that side moved out to avoid the blood. Vollird's eyes crossed and a final breath left him like a bubbled sigh.

The two guards looked at tyl Loesp, who withdrew his sword. "Let him go," he told them.

Released, Vollird fell forward and lay still in the dark pool of his own still spreading blood. Tyl Loesp cleaned his sword on the fellow's tunic with two quick strokes. "Leave him," he told the guards.

He turned and walked towards the chamber.

The Sarcophagus had insisted the scaffolding be removed from around it. It sat on its plinth, the three black cubes around it on the floor of the chamber, one immediately in front, the other two near its rear corners. The Oct were still arranged beyond in their concentric rings of devotion.

Tyl Loesp and those around him got there just in time to see the transformation. The sides of the black cubes were making sizzling, crackling sounds. A change in their surface texture made them look suddenly dull, then they began to appear grey as a fine network of fissures spread all over them.

Poatas came limping up to where tyl Loesp stood. "Unprecedented!" he said, waving his stick in the air. A couple of tyl Loesp's personal guard stepped forward, thinking that the wild, manic old man might be offering violence to their master but Poatas didn't seem to notice. "To be here! To be here, now! And see this! *This!*" he cried, and turned, waving his stick at the centre of the chamber.

The faces of the black cubes showed great cracks all over their surfaces now. A dark vapour issued from them, rising slowly. Then the sides trembled and fell open in a slow cloud of what looked like heavy soot as the cubes' casings seemed to turn to dust all at once, revealing dark, glistening ovoids inside, each about three metres long and a metre and a half in girth. They floated up and out from the gradually settling debris of their rebirth.

Poatas turned briefly back to tyl Loesp. "Do you see? Do you see?"

"One can hardly avoid seeing," tyl Loesp said acidly. His heart was still thumping from the incident a few moments earlier but his voice was firm, controlled.

The ovoids drifted up and in towards the grey cube, which was starting to make the same snapping, zizzing sounds the black cubes had made moments earlier. The noise was much louder, filling the chamber, echoing back off the walls. The Oct ringed round the chamber's focus were stirring, shifting, as if they were all now looking up at the grey cube as it shuddered and changed, its surfaces growing dark with a million tiny crazings.

"This is your prize, Poatas?" tyl Loesp shouted over the cacophony.

"And their ancestor!" Poatas yelled back, waving his stick at the circles of Oct.

"Is all well here, Poatas?" tyl Loesp demanded. "Should it make this *sound*?"

"Who knows!" Poatas screamed, shaking his head. "Why, would you flee, sir?" he asked, without turning round. The sound from the Sarcophagus died away without warning, only echoes resounding.

Tyl Loesp opened his mouth to say something, but the sides of the Sarcophagus were falling away too now, slipping as though invisible walls penning in dark grey dust had suddenly ceased to be and letting its powdery weight come sliding out, falling in a great dry wash all around the plinth, lapping to the inner fringes of the surrounding Oct. There was almost no noise accompanying this, just the faintest sound that might have been mistaken for a sigh. The last echoes of the earlier tumult finally died away.

The grey ovoid revealed by the fallen dust was perhaps five metres across and eight long. It floated trembling in mid-air; the three smaller black shapes drew in towards it, approaching as though hesitant. They tipped slowly up on their mid-axes, ends pointing straight up and down. Then they slid ponderously in to meet the larger grey shape at the centre of their pattern, silently joining with it, seeming to slide partway into it.

The resulting shape hung steady in the air. Echoes slowly died, to leave utter silence within the great chamber.

Then the shape roared something in a language the humans present could not understand, sounds crashing off the walls like surf. Tyl Loesp cursed at the sheer piercing volume of it and clapped his hands to his ears like everybody else. Some of the other men fell to their knees with the force of the sound. Only pride prevented tyl Loesp from doing the same. While the echoes were still dying away, the Oct seemed to startle and move, almost as one. Dry whispering noises, like small twigs just starting to catch fire, began to fill the chamber.

The sound was drowned out as the grey-dark shape hanging in the centre rumbled out again, this time in Sarl.

"Thank you for your help," it thundered. "Now I have much to do. There is no forgiveness."

A filmy spherical bubble seemed to form around the shape, just great enough in extent to enclose it completely. The bubble went dark, black, then quicksilver. As tyl Loesp and the others watched, a second bubble flickered into existence enclosing the first, forming two metres or so further out from the inner silvery one. A blink of light, brief but close to blindingly bright, came from the space between the two spheres before the outer one went black. A humming noise built quickly, a vast thrumming sound which issued from the black sphere and rapidly grew to fill the entire chamber, cramming it with a tooth-loosening, eyeball-vibrating, bone-shaking bassy howl. The Oct fell back, rolling to the floor, seemingly flattened by the storm of noise. Every human present put their hands to their ears again. Almost all turned away, stumbling, bumping into their fellows, trying to run to escape the pulverising, flesh-battering noise.

The few humans unable to look away – Poatas was one, on his knees, stick fallen from his hand – remained transfixed, watching the colossally humming black sphere. They were the only ones to witness, very briefly, a scatter of tiny pinprick holes speckling its surface, loosing thin, blinding rays.

Then the outer sphere blinked out of existence.

A tsunami of wide-spectrum radiation filled the chamber in an instant as the thermonuclear fireball behind it surged outwards.

The blast of light and heat incinerated Oct and humans indiscriminately, vaporising them along with the inner lining of the chamber, blowing its single great spherical wall out in every direction like a vast grenade and bringing what was left of the building above and the surrounding plaza crashing down upon the glowing wreckage.

The first waves of radiation – gamma rays, neutrons and a titanic electromagnetic pulse – were already long gone, their damage done.

The silvery sphere lifted slowly, calmly out of the smoking debris, perfectly unharmed. It drifted through the kilometre-wide hole in the city's plaza level and moved slowly away, dropping its film of shields and altering its shape slightly to that of a large ovoid. It turned to the direction humans called facing and accelerated out of the gorge.

27. The Core

They stood on the edge of the kilometre-wide crater left in the plaza level. The suit visors made the scene bright as day. Ferbin clicked the artificial part of the view off for a few moments, just to see the true state of it. Dim, cold greys, blacks, blues and dark browns; the colours of death and decay. A Rollstar was due to dawn about now, but there would be no sign of it this deep in the gorge for many days yet and no melting warmth to restore the Falls until some long time after that.

There was still a faint infrared glow visible through the suit's visor, deep inside the crater. Steam lifted slowly from the dark depths; the vapour rose and was shredded to nothing by the cold, keening wind.

Anaplian and Hippinse were checking readouts and sensor details. "Something like a small nuke," Djan Seriy said. They were communicating without touching now, reckoning the need for silence was over. Even so, the suits chose the most secure method available, glittering unseen coherent light from one to the other, pinpointing.

"Small blast but serious EMP and neutrons," the ship's avatoid said. "And gamma."

"They must have been fried," Djan Seriy said quietly, kneeling down by the breach in the plaza's surface. She touched the polished stone, feeling its grainy slickness transmitted through the material of the suit.

"Little wonder there's nobody about," Hippinse said. They had seen a few bodies on their flight over the city, coming in from the outskirts, and a surprising number of dead lyge and caude, but nothing and nobody moving; all life seemed as frozen and stilled as the hard waters of the Sulpitine.

But why isn't there anybody else here? Hippinse sent to Anaplian, lace to lace. *No aid, no medics?*

These people know nothing about radiation sickness, she replied. *Anybody escaping would have got to safety thinking they were over the worst of it and getting better and then died, badly, in front of the people they reached. Wouldn't encourage you to come see what happened. They've probably sent a few flying scouts but all they'll report is dead and dying. Mostly dead.*

While the Oct and Aultridia are too busy fighting each other, Hippinse sent.

And something seriously capable is profoundly fucking with the level systems, top to bottom.

The drone Turminder Xuss had floated off some way when they'd set down. It floated back now. "There's some sort of tech embedded in the vertical ice behind one of the falls," it announced. "Probably Oct. Quite a lot of it. Shall I take a look?"

Anaplian nodded. "Please do." The little machine darted away and disappeared into another hole in the plaza.

Anaplian stood, looked at Hippinse, Ferbin and Holse. "Let's try the Settlement."

They had stopped only once on their way in, to look at one of the many bodies lying on the snow-scudded surface of a frozen river channel. Djan Seriy had walked over to the body, unstuck it from the grainy white surface, looked at it.

"Radiation," she'd said.

Ferbin and Holse had looked at each other. Holse had shrugged, then thought to ask the suit. It had started to whisper quickly to him about the sources and effects of electromagnetic, particle and gravitational radiation, rapidly concentrating on the physical consequences of ionising radiations and acute radiation syndrome as applicable to humanoid species, especially those similar to the Sarl.

Then Djan Seriy had removed one of the strakes on the right leg of her suit, a dark tube as long as her thigh and a little thinner than her wrist. She had laid it down on the surface of the frozen river and looked at it briefly. It had started to sink into the ice, raising steam as it melted its way through. It had moved like a snake, wriggling at first, then slipped quickly down the hole it had made for itself in the solid surface of the river. The water had started to ice over again almost immediately.

"What *was* that, miss?" Holse had asked.

Anaplian had detached another piece of the suit, a tiny thing no larger than a button. She'd tossed it into the air like a coin; it had gone straight up and had not come back down.

She'd shrugged. "Insurance."

In the Settlement, barely one person in a hundred was still alive, and they were dying, in pain. No birds sang, no workshops rang or engines huffed; in the still air, only the quiet moans of the dying broke the silence.

Anaplian and Hippinse instructed all four suits to manufacture tiny mechanisms which they could inject into anybody they found still living by just pressing on their neck. The suits grew little barbs on the tips of their longest fingers to do the injecting.

"Can these people be cured, sister?" Ferbin asked, staring at a man moving weakly, covered in vomit and blood and surrounded by a thin pool of dried excrement, trying to talk to them but only gurgling. His hair came out in clumps as his head jerked across the frozen mud of one of the Settlement's unpaved roads. Thin bright blood came from his mouth, nose, ears and eyes.

"The nanorgs will decide," Djan Seriy said crisply, stooping to inject the fellow. "Those the injectiles cannot save they'll let die without pain."

"Too late for most of them," Holse said, looking round. "This was that radiation, wasn't it?"

"Yes," Hippinse said.

"Apart from the ones with bullet wounds, obviously," Djan Seriy said, rising from the now limp, sighing man and looking around at dead soldiers clutching guns and the crumpled bodies of a couple of lyge lying nearby, armed riders crushed beneath. "There was a battle here first."

The few twists of smoke they had seen were fires burning themselves out rather than smoke from the chimneys of works and forges and steam engines. At the main railhead for the Settlement, all the engines and most of the carriages were gone. Hundreds of bodies lay scattered about.

They split up in twos. Djan Seriy and Holse checked the Archipontine's carriages and the rest of the headquarters compound, but found only more dead bodies, and none they recognised.

Then Hippinse called from the hospital train.

"I'm sorry! The fellow I shot. Tell him I'm sorry, won't you, somebody, please? I'm most terribly sorry."

"Son, it was me you shot, and – look – I'm fine. I just fell over in surprise, that's all. Calm, now." Holse lifted the young man's head and tried to get him sitting upright against the wall.

His hair was falling out too. Holse had to wedge him in a corner eventually to stop him falling over.

"I shot *you*, sir?"

"You did, lad," Holse told him. "Lucky for me I'm wearing armour better than stride-thick iron. What's your name, son?"

"Neguste Puibive, sir, at your service. I'm so sorry I shot you."

"Choubris Holse. No damage done nor offence taken."

"They wanted whatever drugs we had, sir. Thinking they would save them or at least ease their pain. I gave away all I could but then when they were all gone they'd not believe me, sir. They wouldn't leave us alone. I was trying to protect the young sir, sir."

"What young sir would that be then, young Neguste?" Holse asked, frowning at the little barb just flexed from the longest finger on his right hand.

"Oramen, sir. The Prince Regent."

Hippinse had just entered the compartment. He stared down at Holse. "I heard," he said. "I'll tell them."

Holse pressed the barb into the young man's mottled, bruised-looking flesh. He cleared his throat. "Is the prince here, lad?"

"Through there, sir," Neguste Puibive said, attempting to nod at the door through to the next compartment. He started to cry thin, bloody tears.

Ferbin cried too, sweeping back the mask section of the suit so that he could let the tears fall. Oramen had been cleaned up carefully; however, his face looked to have been badly beaten. Ferbin touched his gloved hand to his brother's reddened, staring eyes, trying to get the eyelids to close, failing. Djan Seriy was at the other side of the narrow bed, her hand cupped under the base of their brother's head, cradling his upper neck.

She gave out a long breath. She too swept her mask back and

away. She bowed her head, then let Oramen's head very gently back down, allowing it to rest on the pillow again. She slid her hand out.

She looked at Ferbin, shook her head.

"No," she said. "We are too late, brother." She sniffed, smoothed some of Oramen's hair across his head, trying not to pull any of it out as she did so. "Days too late."

The glove of her suit flowed back from her flesh like black liquid, leaving the tips then the whole of her fingers then her hand to the wrist naked. She gently touched Oramen's bruised, broken cheek, then his mottled forehead. She tried to close his eyes too. One of his eyelids detached and slid over his blood-flecked eye like a piece of boiled fruit skin.

"Fuck fuck fuck," Djan Seriy said softly.

"*Anaplian!*" Hippinse shouted urgently from the compartment where he and Holse were trying to comfort Neguste Puibive.

"He asked for Earl Droffo, but they'd killed him, sirs. Tyl Loesp's men, when they came on the air-beasts. They'd already killed him. Him with only one good arm, trying to reload."

"But what *afterwards*?" Hippinse insisted, shaking the injured man. "What was it he said, what did you say? Repeat that! Repeat it!"

Djan Seriy and Holse both reached out to touch Hippinse.

"Steady," Djan Seriy told the avatoid. "What's wrong?" Holse didn't understand. What was making Hippinse so upset? It wasn't his brother lying dead through there. The man wasn't even a real human. These weren't his people; he had no people.

"Repeat it!" Hippinse wailed, shaking Puibive again. Djan Seriy took hold of Hippinse's nearest hand to stop him jolting the dying youth.

"All the rest left, sirs, those that could, on the trains, when we all started to fall ill the second time," Neguste Puibive said, his eyes rolling around in their sockets, eyelids flickering. "Sorry to . . . We all took a terrible gastric fever after the big explosion but then we were all right but then—"

"In the name of your WorldGod," Hippinse pleaded, "what did Oramen *say*?"

"It was his last understandable word, I think, sirs," Puibive told them woozily, "though they're not real, are they? Just monsters from long ago."

Oh shit, no, Anaplian thought.

"What are, lad?" Holse asked, pushing Hippinse's other hand away.

"That word, sir. That was the word he kept saying, eventually, when he could speak again for a short while, when they brought him back from the chamber where the Sarcophagus was. Once he knew Earl Droffo was dead. Iln, he kept saying. I couldn't work it out at first, but he said it a lot, even if it got softer and fainter each time he said it. Iln, he said; Iln, Iln, Iln."

Hippinse stared at nothing.

"The Iln," Holse's suit whispered to him. "Aero-spiniform, gas-giant mid-level ancients originally from the Zunzil Ligature; assumed contemporary sophisticated equiv-tech level, Involved between point eight-three and point seven-eight billion years ago, multi-decieon non-extant, believed extinct, non-Sublimed, no claimed descendancy; now principally remembered for the destruction of approximately two thousand three hundred Shellworlds."

To Djan Seriy Anaplian it was as though the world beneath her feet dropped away and the stars and the vacuum fell in around her.

Anaplian stood. "Leave him," she said, snapping her mask back into place and striding out of the compartment. Hippinse rose and followed.

It's the second-hand word of one dying man transmitted by another, the avatoid sent to the SC agent. *Could be false*.

Anaplian shook her head. *Something spent geological ages in a buried city, wasted several hundred thousand people as it left just for the hell of it and then disappeared*, she replied. *Let's assume the worst of the fucker*.

Whatever it was, it may not have been the source of the—

"Can't I stay—" Holse began.

"Yes you can but I'll need your suit," Anaplian told him from down the corridor. "It can function as an extra drone." Her voice changed as Holse's suit decided her voice was growing too faint and switched to comms. "Same applies to my brother," she told him.

"Can we not mourn even a moment?" Ferbin's voice cut in.

"No," Anaplian said.

Outside, in the cold desert air, Turminder Xuss swept down to join Anaplian and Hippinse as they stepped from the carriage. "Oct," it told them. "A few still left in the rearmost ship, a klick back under the ice upstream. All dying. Ship systems blown by EMP. Recordings corrupted but they had live feed and saw a black ovoid emerge from a grey cube housed centrally in a prominent chamber beneath the city's central building. It was joined by three smaller ovoids which emerged from objects the Sarl and Oct co-operated in bringing to the central one. Last thing they saw sounds like a concentric containment enaction; strong vibrations and photon-tunnelling immediately before containment drop and fireball release confirmatory."

"Thank you," Anaplian told the machine. She glanced at Hippinse. "Convinced?"

Hippinse nodded, eyes wide, face pale. "Convinced."

"Ferbin, Holse," Anaplian said, calling the two men still inside the carriage. "We have to go now. There is an Iln or some weapon left by the Iln loose. It will be at or on its way to the Core of Sursamen. The first thing it will do is kill the WorldGod. Then it will attempt to destroy the world itself. Do you understand? Your suits must come with us, whether you are inside them or not. There would be no dishonour in—"

"We are on our way," Ferbin said. His voice sounded hollow.

"Coming, ma'am," Holse confirmed. "There, lad, you just rest easy there, that's it," they heard him mutter.

The four suits and the tiny shape of the accompanying machine lifted from the wispily smoking remains of the Hyeng-zhar Settlement and curved up and out, heading for the nearest open Tower, seven thousand kilometres distant. Turminder Xuss powered ahead and up, vanishing from sight almost immediately. Ferbin assumed they were flying in the same diamond formation as before, though the suits were camouflaged again so it was impossible to tell. At least this time they were allowed to communicate without having to touch.

"But this thing must be ancient, ma'am, mustn't it?" Holse protested. "It's been under there for an eternity; everybody knows the Iln vanished millions of years ago. Whatever this thing is it can't be *that* dangerous, not to more modern powers like the Optimae, the Culture and so on. Can it?"

"It doesn't work that way," Anaplian said. "Would that it did."

She fell silent as they tore upwards into the air, spreading out. Hippinse cleared his throat and said, "The type of progress you guys are used to doesn't scale into this sort of civilisational level; societies progress until they Sublime – god-like retirement, if you will – and then others start again, finding their own way up the tech-face. But it is a tech-face, not a tech-ladder; there are a variety of routes to the top and any two civs who've achieved the summit might well have discovered quite different abilities en route. Ways of keeping technology viable over indefinite periods of time are known to have existed aeons ago, and just because something's ancient doesn't mean it's inferior. With workable tech from this thing's time the stats show it's about sixty-forty it will be less capable than what we have now, but that's a big minority."

"I'm sorry to have to involve you in this," Anaplian told the two Sarl men. "We are going to have to descend to the Machine level and possibly the Core of Sursamen to confront something we have very little knowledge of. It may well have highly sophisticated offensive capabilities. Our chances of survival are probably not good."

"I do not care," Ferbin said, sounding like he meant it. "I would gladly die to do whatever I can to kill the thing that killed our brother and threatens the WorldGod."

They were leaving the atmosphere, the sky turning black.

"What about the ship, ma'am?" Holse asked.

"Hippinse?" Anaplian asked.

"I'm broadcasting for help," the avatoid replied. "Oct systems, Nariscene, Morth; anything to patch us through. Nothing's coming back from the chaos in the local dataverse. System disruption is still spreading, jamming everything. Take heading to another level to find a working system and even then it'd be somebody else's whim."

"I'll signal it," Anaplian said.

"I guess we have no choice," Hippinse said. "This should get us some attention."

"Arming," Anaplian said. "Coding for Machine space rendezvous, no holds barred."

"Total panic now mode," Hippinse said as though he was talking to himself.

"How can you signal the ship, ma'am?" Holse asked. "I thought signals couldn't get out of Shellworlds."

"Oh, some signals can," Djan Seriy said. "Look back at the gorge down from the Falls. Where we landed earlier."

They had risen so fast and travelled so far laterally already, this was not easy. Holse still hadn't located the gorge below the Hyeng-zhar, and hadn't thought to ask the suit to do so for him, when a sudden flash attracted his eye. It was followed by four more in groups of two; the whole display lasted less than two seconds. Hemispherical grey clouds burst blossoming around the already dead light-points, then quickly disappeared, leaving rapidly rising grey-black towers behind.

"What was that?" Holse asked.

"Five small anti-matter explosions," Anaplian told him. The debris stacks were already falling over the horizon as they raced away just above the outer reaches of the atmosphere. "The *Liveware Problem* and its remotes are monitoring the Surface at Prime level, listening for unusual vibrations. Those five explosions together won't rattle Sursamen as much as a single Starfall but they'll make the planet ring like a bell for a few minutes, all the way out to the Surface, which is all we need. Surface compression waves. That's how you get a signal out of a Shellworld."

"So the ship—" Holse began.

"Will right now be making its way towards the Core," Anaplian said, "and not taking no for an answer."

"Getting something," Hippinse said. "Oh. Looks like—"

Brilliant, blinding light splashed off to Ferbin's left, diagonally ahead. His gaze darted that way even as the images danced inside his eyes and the suit's visor blacked out the entire view then cast an obviously false representation up showing the horizon, nearby towers and not much else. The image he was left with was that of a human figure, lit as though it was made of sun stuff.

"Anaplian?" Hippinse yelled.

"Yes," her calm voice came back. "Laser. Strong physical hit. Optical sighting; no ranging pulse. My suit has slight ablation and I slight bruising. All mirrored up now. Suits have split us up already. Expect mo—"

Something hammered into Ferbin's back; it was like a cutting sword blow landing on thick chain mail. The breath tried to whistle out of him but the suit was suddenly very stiff and it felt like there was nowhere for the breath to go.

"Under CREW attack, dorsal, above," the suit informed him. "No immediate threat at present power and frequencies."

"That's one hit each, two on me," Anaplian said. "More have

missed. I am reading a ceiling source, Nariscene tech, probably
– tss! Three on me. Source probably comped."

"Ditto," Hippinse said. "We can probably soak. Outrange in
twenty."

"Yes, but maybe more ahead. I am sending Xuss to deal with.
Practice if nothing else."

"My pleasure," Turminder Xuss said. "Can I use AM too?"

"Anything," Anaplian said.

"Leave to me," Xuss purred. "I'll get back ahead and anticipate similar?"

"Feel free," Anaplian said. "Kinetics would be a bigger worry;
prioritise and warn."

"Of course."

"Regardless, shoot first."

"You spoil me."

"Ah!" Holse shouted a moment later. "Faith, even my old
man never hit me that hard."

"Should be this one's last," Xuss said. "There; straight up
their collimator. Oh! Pretty."

"Firing not admiring," Anaplian told it.

"Oh, really," Xuss said, somewhere between amused and
annoyed. "Already on my way."

They flew over the landscape far below for another few
minutes without attracting any more hostile attention, the world
seeming to turn like a great tensed drum beneath them, shining
and darkening as Fixstars and Rollstars came and went and
complexes of vanes and ceiling structure cast them into shadow.

Ferbin cried a little more, thinking of his brother lying dead,
disfigured, assaulted in that cold, abandoned carriage. Unmourned
now they had been forced to leave, unattended save for a dying
servant who was himself hardly more than a child; it had not been
a death or a lying-in-state fit for a prince of any age.

A cold and terrible fury grew in his guts. How fucking dare
anything do that to so young a man, to his brother, to so many
others? He had seen them, he had seen how they'd died.
Prompted by Holse, he'd had his suit tell him the effects of high

radiation doses. One hundred per cent certainty of death within four to eight days, and those days full of appalling agony. It looked like his brother had been injured before the lethal blast, though that made no difference; he might still have lived but even that chance, however good or slim, had been snatched away from him by this filthy, pitiless murderous *thing*.

Ferbin sniffed back the tears and the suit itself seemed to absorb whatever he could not swallow. No doubt to be recycled, reused and purified and brought back to him as water from the tiny spigot he could summon to his mouth whenever he wanted. He was a little world in here, a tiny, perfect farm where nothing went to waste and every little thing that fell or died was turned to fresh use, to grow new produce or feed beasts.

He had to do the same, he realised. He could not afford not to employ Oramen's cruel, ignoble death. They might well have to surrender their lives in whatever doomed enterprise they were now embarked upon, but he would honour his young brother in the only way that could mean anything from this point on and turn Oramen's death to a determining reinforcement of his purpose. He had meant what he said to Djan Seriy earlier. He did not want to die, but he willingly would if it helped destroy the thing that had killed his brother and meant to do the same to the WorldGod.

The WorldGod! Might he *see* it? Look upon it? Dear God, converse with it? Just be addressed by it? Never had he thought to witness it in any way. No one did. You knew it was there, knew it was in some sense another being, another inhabitant of the vast and bounteous galaxy, but that did not reduce its manifest divinity, its mystery, its worth of reverence.

Something flickered high above in the darkness. Three tiny trails of light seemed to converge on an implied point. One trail winked out, another curved, the third flared suddenly into a dot of light the suit's visor briefly blocked out.

"There you go," Xuss said. "Kinetic battery. Definitely compromised; there was a Nariscene combat engineering team crawling all over it trying to get the unit back under their control."

"What happened to them?"

"Blown to smithereens," the drone said matter-of-factly. "No choice; thing was powering up, already swinging towards you."

"Great," Anaplian muttered. "So now we're at war with the fucking Nariscene."

"Excuse me, ma'am, sir," Holse said. "Do all levels have such fearsome weaponry looking down upon them?"

"Basically, yes," Hippinse said.

"By the way, I'm down by five and a half out of eight micromissiles," the drone said. "That was learning overkill and I think I can deal with anything similar with two easy, one high-probability, but just to let you know."

"Five and a *half*?" Anaplian said.

"Turned one away when I saw the third was getting through; saved it, rehoused it. Half an engine charge left."

"Most conservationary of you," Anaplian said. "Hippinse; anything?"

"Yes, I'm into a Nariscene hardened military news channel," the avatoid said. "Shit, the Oct and Aultridia really are at war. The Oct ships above the open Towers were spotted and the Nariscene closed them off. The Oct blame the Aultridia for the Hyeng-zhar explosion. The Aultridia suspect a plot to increase Oct control. After the blast at the Falls some Oct craft tried to force their way into the open Towers but got ripped apart. Between them the Nariscene, Oct and Aultridia have closed off every Tower."

"Are we still doing the right thing heading where we're heading?"

"Looks like it. Two-fifty seconds to go."

Four minutes later they plunged back into the atmosphere. This time the suits stayed sleek and silvery and barely slowed at all as they hit the gases. They left a trail of glowing, ionised air behind them bright enough to cast shadows from kilometres up. They slowed so fast it hurt and arrived feeling even more bruised at the grassy, fluted base of a Tower. When they landed the ground cover sizzled and burned beneath their feet and steam came spluttering up around them. The suits stayed mirrored.

A section of the green slope nearby was already rearing out of the ground, spilling turf and earth as a cylinder ten metres across slid up and out. A circle appeared on its curved surface as it slowed, then fell forward to form a ramp when the cylinder stopped rising. Anaplian stepped forward, leading the others. Turminder Xuss came banging out of the sky as the ramp door started to rise again. Seconds later the cylinder began to descend.

"Identify!" a voice rang out within the cylinder's still damp interior.

"I am Culture Special Circumstances agent Djan Seriy Anaplian, originally of the royal palace, Pourl, in Sarl. I am accompanied by my brother the rightful king of Sarl, Ferbin, and an avatoid of the Culture ship *Liveware Problem*. Be advised that there is an Iln Shellworld-destroying machine loose. I repeat: an Iln Shellworld-destroying machine is here within Sursamen. It is heading for or is already in the Core with the very likely intention of destroying the world. Broadcast this, disseminate as widely as possible, informing the Nariscene and the Morthanveld as a matter of extreme and absolute priority."

"Release control of cylinder."

"No. Do as I say. There is an Iln Shellworld-destroying machine present within Sursamen. It has already killed everybody at the Hyeng-zhar and is now heading for, or is already in, the Core. It intends to destroy the world. Tell everybody. *Everybody!*"

"Insist! Release cylinder control instantly! No! Stop! Release control of corridor environment! Replace fluids immediately! Warning! Aultridian proxies deeming! Apprehension awaits!"

The cylinder was slowing, drawing to a stop in a few seconds. "No," Anaplian said, walking like some strange silvery dream to stand before the circular door. "I have no time to waste with you. Get in our way and I will kill you. Broadcast all I've said as widely as possible at maximum urgency. *I* insist." Anaplian detached a handgun from the left hip of her suit. The weapon was silver too. Turminder Xuss rose to hover at the very top of the door, also shining like mercury.

"Release control of door!" the voice wailed as the door started to open, lidding down like a drawbridge. "Apprehension awaits!"

Anaplian rose quickly to float level with the top of the doorway, levelling the gun. The tiny mirror-bodied shape of Turminder Xuss glinted and was gone. A few flashes reflected off the vaulted ceiling of the corridor outside, then the door was thudding down.

Anaplian was already descending and moving forward. She put the gun back to her hip as her feet hit the floor just beyond the door. She stepped out over the twitching bodies of a dozen well-armed Oct, all of them sliced into halves or smaller fractions. Their weapons had been cut up too; a couple of the gun-parts lay on the floor still sputtering and sparking, raising fumes from puddles. Xuss' monofil warps clicked back into its body as it flicked about and powered down the tunnel. Ahead, a large circular door was already rolling back into the wall. Fluids a metre deep surged out and were soon washing about Anaplian's legs. Alarms keened and somebody was shouting something in Oct.

"Keep up," Anaplian said over her gleaming shoulder. Hippinse, Ferbin and Holse stepped smartly from the cylinder, tried to avoid stepping on Oct body parts as the flood of fluids washed them towards them. They followed Anaplian down the tunnel.

A minute later, a few more Oct deaths later, they stood watching another circular door roll away; more knee-deep fluids rushed out past them. They stepped into the resulting chamber. The door closed behind them and they listened to the air whistling out.

"We'll be in vacuum again from this point on," Anaplian told them, unhitching her CREW from the back of her suit and quickly checking it. Hippinse mirrored her actions. Ferbin and Holse looked at each other then did the same. Djan Seriy restowed the laser weapon where it had been; it moulded into the dorsal section of her suit while she reached over her shoulder and pulled on another of the long strakes on her back, producing yet another glossily black weapon. She let it unfold itself and checked that too. Ferbin caught his sister's gaze and she nodded. "I shall lead with this particle buster; you use the kinetic rifle, Ferbin. Holse; you and Hippinse lead with the CREWs. Don't want us all using the same stuff." Her mask unmirrored long enough for her to smile briefly at them, and wink. "Just shoot at what we do." Then the suit was fully mirrored again.

We are all mirrors, Ferbin thought. Reflecting each other. We are here and these strange suits of armour turn back all light but somehow, despite that, we are nearly invisible; the gaze is redirected from each contact with our surfaces, sliding away until we see something of whatever surrounds us, as though only that is real.

Turminder Xuss lowered to hover in front of Anaplian, level with her sternum. A couple of slim shapes like spike-daggers drifted up from Anaplian's calves and also floated just ahead of her. "Also, we have a long way to drop."

"This an open Tower, ma'am?" Holse asked.

"No," Anaplian said. "We are one Tower away from an open Tower, the one that the ship will be using. If this thing's left anything behind to ambush anybody coming after it, the opens are where they'll likely wait. The ship has no choice but to use an open; we do, but we can keep close enough to where the ship will appear to offer support. Even then, we won't be leaving by the main Tower shaft." She glanced at the two Sarl men. "We are the infantry here, in case you hadn't guessed, gentlemen. Expendable. Sacrificeable. The ship is the knight, the heavy artillery, however you wish to express it." She looked at Hippinse as the door ahead of them twitched. "Anything?"

"Not yet," Hippinse said. Two small mirrored things like tiny daggers floated up to station themselves level with his shoulders. Another pair of mercurially glinting shapes slid away from Ferbin and Holse's suits too and floated up to cluster round Turminder Xuss.

"If you don't mind, gents," the drone said casually.

"Be my guest," Ferbin told it.

"Didn't even know they were there," Holse said.

The door rolled silently to one side, revealing utter darkness. The drone turned soot black and darted ahead, disappearing along with the four other smaller missiles.

The humans floated across a tube Hippinse said was only thirty metres wide; a scendship shaft. Beyond, a circular hatch had just completed irising open. They floated through to the main Tower interior.

As they started to drop, they moved away from each other until they were nearly half a kilometre apart.

I really never thought to be doing this, Holse thought. He was frankly terrified, but elated too. To be dropping towards the WorldGod, with mad aliens, to meet up with a talking, eccentric spaceship that could stride between stars like a man strode between stepping stones, to go in search of an even more insane Iln that wanted to blow up or crumple down the whole world; that was the kind of thing he'd not even started to dream of when he'd been back on the farm, mucking out stables and following his dad around the frost-rimed gelding pen carrying the gently steaming ball bucket, ear still smarting from the latest slap.

He had the worrying feeling that he and Ferbin were along as little more than decoys, but in a way he didn't care. He was starting to change his mind about the old Warrior Code stuff knights and princes invoked, usually when they were drunk and in need of spilling their words, or trying to justify their poor behaviour in some other field.

Behave honourably and wish for a good death. He'd always dismissed it as self-serving bullshit, frankly; most of the people he'd been told were his betters were quite venally dishonourable, and the more they got the more the greedy bastards wanted, while those that weren't like that were better behaved at least partly because they could afford to be.

Was it more honourable to starve than to steal? Many people would say yes, though rarely those who'd actually experienced an empty belly, or a child whimpering with its own hunger. Was it more honourable to starve than to steal when others had the means to feed you but chose not to, unless you paid with money you did not have? He thought not. By choosing to starve you became your own oppressor, keeping yourself in line, harming yourself for having the temerity to be poor, when by rights that ought to be a constable's job. Show any initiative or imagination and you were called lazy, shifty, crafty, incorrigible. So he'd dismissed talk of honour; it was just a way of making the rich and powerful feel better about themselves and the powerless and poverty-stricken feel worse.

But once you weren't living hand-to-mouth, and had some ease, you had the leisure to contemplate what life was really all about and who you really were. And given that you had to die, it made sense to seek a good death.

Even these Culture people, bafflingly, mostly chose to die, when they didn't have to.

With freedom from fear and wondering where your next meal was coming from or how many mouths you'd have to feed next year and whether you'd get sacked by your employer or thrown into jail for some minor indiscretion – with freedom from all that came choice, and you could choose a nice quiet, calm, peaceful, ordinary life and die with your nightshirt on and impatient relatives making lots of noise around you . . . Or you could end up doing something like this, and – however scared your body might feel – your brain rather appreciated the experience.

He thought of his wife and children, and felt a twinge of guilt that they had been so absent from his thoughts for so long recently. He'd had a lot to think about and so many new and utterly bizarre things to learn, but the truth was they seemed like beings from another world now, and while he wished them only well, and could imagine – if, by some miracle, they survived all this – going back to them and taking up his old duties again, somehow that felt like it was never going to happen, and he'd long since seen them for the final time.

A good death. Well, he thought, given that you had to die, why want a bad one?

They hovered above a gigantic door composed of great dark curved sections like scimitar blades all pressed together to make a pattern like the petals of a flower. The drop had taken nearly half an hour and in that time they had passed another five levels, where, according to the suit, things called Variolous Tendrils, Vesiculars, Gas Giant Swimmers, Tubers and Hydrals lived. The final level above the Machine space was empty of life, full of oceanic water under kilometres of ice. Now they were directly above the Machine space level where, according to both legend and convention, the workings of the world as it had originally been conceived still sat, lifeless but mighty.

"This is Secondary, isn't it?" Anaplian asked, staring down at the vast shutter.

"Yes," Hippinse said. "Openable."

Hippinse floated over the very centre of the three-kilometre-diameter door, his outline in the visors of the others fuzzy, barely hinted at even by the astoundingly sensitive sensors of the suits. He detached something from his suit and left it lying right in the door's centre, where the great blades met.

They followed Anaplian back up a kilometre to a huge oval hole in the side of the vast shaft, entered the hundred-metre-diameter tunnel which it led to and floated straight down. Behind, above them, something flashed. The suits registered tiny but ponderous long-wavelength vibrations in the fabric of the tube around them.

Anaplian beckoned them together and when they touched said, "The main door should have opened the one at the bottom of this too, so we can fall straight out. Xuss and the four suit missiles are going first."

"Look," Ferbin said, staring down. "Light."

A flickering blue-grey circle widened quickly as they fell

towards it. Beyond, beneath, dimly glimpsed far below, vast shapes loomed, all curved and swooping, sharp and bulbous, pocked and ribbed and serrated. It was like falling into a vast assemblage of blades the size of storm systems, all lit by lightning.

"Clear," Turminder Xuss announced. "Suggest staying apart, though; signalling less a risk than a tight target."

"Copy," Anaplian said tersely.

They dropped beneath the ceiling of the Machine level and hung, hundreds of metres apart, over a drop of about fifty kilometres to the vast blade systems lying still in the gloom below. A few tens of kilometres off, a colossal vaned shape like an enormous toroidal gear wheel filled the view, its topmost edges ridging up to the level ceiling. It seemed to sit on top of and mesh with other titanic spheres and discs all linked to still further massive shapes, and far in the distance, hundreds of kilometres away – their lower reaches obscured by the relatively near horizon of spiralled bladed complexes like immense, open flowers – enormous wheels and globes the size of small moons bulked in the darkness, each seeming to touch the undersurface of the shell above.

Hell's gearbox, Djan Seriy thought when she saw it, but did not choose to share the image with the others.

The flickering blue-grey light – sporadic, sharp, intense – came from two almost perfectly opposed bearings, partially obscured by intervening machinery in both directions.

"That's battle light," Hippinse said.

"Agree," Anaplian said. "Any ship signals?"

There was a pause. "Yes, got it, but ... Confused. Broken up. Must be the other side, getting reflections," Hippinse said, sounding first relieved then worried.

"Our direction?" Anaplian asked.

"Follow me," Hippinse said, heading off.

"Xuss; ahead, please," Anaplian said.

"Already there," the drone said.

The suits tipped them so that they raced across the ghostly landscape far below with their feet leading, though the view could be switched easily enough to make it look as though one was flying head-first. Holse asked about this. "Not streamlining," the suit replied. "We are in vacuum, so not required. This orientation presents smaller target profile in direction of travel and prioritises human head for damage limitation."

"Ah-ha. Oh, yes; also, what holds the world up?" Holse asked. "There's no Towers."

"The large machines present within this space retain the structural integrity of the ceiling above."

"I see," Holse said. "Righty-ho."

"Steer clear of the open Tower base," Anaplian told them, leading them away from a great disc of darkness above. Petals of material nearly a kilometre long hung down from the edges of the gap, looking so symmetrical that at first they didn't realise they were the result of something breaking through from above. "The ship?" Anaplian asked.

"Looks like it," Hippinse said. He sounded puzzled, and worried again. "Supposed to leave a drone or something here."

They flew on for another minute until Turminder Xuss said, "Trouble up ahead."

"What is it?" Anaplian asked.

"Somebody's fighting; high-frequency CREWs, particle beams and what looks like AM by the backsplash. From the signatures, we're outgunned. Pull to here," the drone told them, and their visors indicated a line across the long summit of one of the kilometres-high vanes at the top edge of one of the gigantic spheres. Light flashed immediately beyond, bright enough to trip the visors' sight-saving function. They drifted to a stop metres beneath the ridge line of the vane, each a kilometre or so apart from the other.

"Seeing this?" the drone asked, and imposed a view on their visors of a great dark gulf of space beyond, between more of the level-filling spheres and side-tipped concave torus shapes, lit by glaring bursts of light.

The view became shallowly triangulated, offered from three

different points of view, then four and five as the four smaller drones all added their perspective to that of Xuss. Three different sources of pinpoint light and sudden, harsh detonations lay between sixty-five and ninety klicks distant. Much closer, only ten kilometres from them and four down, a single object was trading fire with the three faraway sources. The co-ordinated views suggested something only a few metres across was darting in and out behind the cover of great serrated blades on a vast cogwheel beneath, firing and being fired at by its three distant adversaries.

"Those three read as ours," Hippinse said urgently. "They're having to fall back."

"Can we surprise that thing just underneath?" Anaplian asked.

"Looks like it."

"Ping one of the distants, make sure we have this right," Anaplian said. "Xuss?"

"Done," the drone replied. "They're the *LP*'s; three remaining of four combat drones it left behind under the forced open Tower. They're damaged, retreating."

"The fourth?"

"Dead," Hippinse said. "Slag in the trench between us and the hostile."

"Tell them to keep doing exactly what they're doing. Xuss; those five and a half AM missiles? Prep all but two."

"Armed."

"Tell two of the extra knives to widen out now and drop – not power – on my mark, second-wave suicide-ready."

"Prepped, moving," the drone said.

"Everybody else, spread further out over the next eight seconds then pop over the top and empty everything. Start moving now. Ferbin, Holse, remember; work with the suit and let it move you if it needs to."

"Of course."

"Will do, ma'am."

Eight seconds.

"Now, now, now!" Anaplian called. The suits bounced them up over the long curved summit of the great ridge of blade. Light flared above them. Suddenly looking down into the chasm beneath, the exhausts of the drone's AM-powered missiles were soot-dark spots on their visors as the suits blanked out their extreme flaring. The visors blinked red circles round their target and all four of their weapons fired. Ferbin's kinetic rifle leapt and hammered in his hand, throwing him up and back with every pulse, the rounds tiny bright trails left in the eye. He started to twist as the recoil tried to turn him round and make him somersault all at once, the suit doing its best to compensate and keep the gun pointed at their target.

Light everywhere. Something thudded into his lower right leg; there was a burst of pain as if he'd twisted his knee, but it faded almost instantly.

The target washed out in multiple, visor-tripping bursts of light which threw shadows like barbs and thorns all over the ceiling kilometres above.

"Cease fire!" Anaplian yelled. "Calling off the drop-knives."

"They're stopped," Xuss said. "Here's their view."

Something glowing white was falling and tumbling away amongst the curved blades, unleashing yellow sparks and leaving orange debris falling slower behind. All firing had stopped. The fiery, falling object was providing the only light there was.

"That it?" Anaplian asked.

"Pretty sure," Xuss said. "Move on, keep checking?"

"And scan that hostile debris. Let's go. Hippinse?"

"Took a kinetic frag," the avatoid wheezed. "Close to getting mushed, okay. Repairing. Moving."

"Okay," Djan Seriy said as they all moved out across the dark trench. Far below, the molten debris was still falling. "Ferbin?" Anaplian said gently. "I'm sorry about your leg."

"What?" He looked down. His right leg was missing from the knee down.

He stared. General Yilim, he thought. He felt his mouth go dry and heard something roar in his ears.

"You'll be all right," his sister's voice said quietly, soothingly in his ears. "Suit's sealed it and pumped you with painkill and anti-shock and it was cauterised by the hit. You will be fine, brother; my word on it. Once we're back out we'll grow a new one. Easiest thing in the world. Okay?"

Ferbin felt remarkably all right now. Almost happy. Mouth okay, no roaring any more. Certainly there was no pain from the wound, in fact no sensation down there at all. "Yes," he told his sister.

"You sure, sir?" Holse said.

"Yes," he said. "I'm all right. I feel very good." He had to keep looking at it to be sure it had really happened, and then felt down, just to confirm. Sure enough; no leg below the knee. And he felt fine! Extraordinary.

"That thing was Morth-tech, compromised," Hippinse told them when he got information back from the microdrone sent to investigate what was left of the machine they'd been fighting. "One of twelve, if its internal records are right."

"What the hell's Morth stuff doing down here?" Anaplian asked. "I don't remember any mention of that."

"Me neither," Hippinse said. "Kept that quiet. Probably well intentioned."

Anaplian made a noise like a spit.

They were flying, a kilometre apart, across the edged unfolding darkness of the Machine level, weaving past the great spherical and ring-shaped components, surfaces ridged and incised with swirling patterns like cut and chiselled gears. The *Liveware Problem*'s three damaged drones were keeping pace ahead, hurriedly trying to repair what they could of themselves. Turminder Xuss led the way, twenty klicks to the fore.

"Any more comped?" Anaplian asked.

"All twelve were. Two left now; we got one and the ship wasted the rest on entry."

"Okay," Anaplian said.

"Ship took some damage from them, though."

"It did?"

"It was hurt on the way down," Hippinse said.

"From *Nariscene* tech?" Anaplian asked, incredulous.

"It had a long way to drop, totally contained, offering perfectly predictable aiming and no eGrid powering," Hippinse said. "Tried to negotiate but they weren't having it. They were able to throw a lot at it for a long time. It suffered."

"How badly?"

"Badly enough. Wounded. Would have gone limping off before now if this wasn't a desperation mission."

"Oh, shit," Anaplian breathed.

"It gets worse," Hippinse said. "There's a guard ship."

"A guard *ship*?"

"*Liveware Problem*'s encountered. Got off a spec readout before it had to concentrate on combat."

"What ship? Whose?"

"Also Morth. Nobody aboard; AI. From the spec, seriously capable. Power linked to the Core."

"This wasn't mentioned!" Anaplian insisted.

"Must be a recent thing. Point is, it's been taken over too."

"*How?*" Djan Seriy said, her voice angry.

"Must have been running same systems as the guard machines," Hippinse said. "Comp one and you get the lot if you play it clever."

"*Fuck!*" Djan Seriy shouted. There was a pause, then, "*Fuck!*" again.

"This, ah, 'comped', sir," Holse said tentatively.

"Compromised," Hippinse told him. "Taken over by the other side. Persuaded by a sort of thought-infection."

"Does that happen a lot, sir?"

"It happens." Hippinse sighed. "Not to Culture ships, as a rule; they write their own individual OS as they grow up, so it's like every human in a population being slightly different, almost their own individual species despite appearances; bugs can't spread. The Morthanveld like a degree more central control and predictability in their smart machines. That has its advantages too, but it's still a potential weakness. This Iln machine seems to have exploited it." Hippinse made a whistling noise. "Must have learned a lot fast from somewhere."

"An Enabler," Anaplian said bitterly. "Bet you. The Oct ran an Enabler system at the thing."

"That would fit," Hippinse agreed.

"What from the ship?" Anaplian asked.

Ferbin and Holse's suits registered information coming in from one of the three drones, but they wouldn't have known how to interpret it.

"Seeing this?" Anaplian said. Her voice sounded flat and lifeless. Holse felt suddenly terrified. Even Ferbin's euphoria was punctured.

"Yes," Hippinse said. He sounded grim. "Seeing it."

Light flickered and flared ahead, bearing a few similarities to the display produced by the firefight they'd chanced upon earlier between the ship drones and the compromised Morthanveld machine, but much further away; the light was being produced from some way over the horizon and reflecting off the under-surface above, strobing and flaring across the ceiling structures with a distant slowness that seemed to imply a conflict of a weight and scale orders of magnitude above that of the earlier skirmish.

"That's them, right?" Anaplian asked.

"That's them," Hippinse replied, voice low.

Ferbin heard his sister sigh. "This," she said quietly, "is not going to be fun."

They got there in time to see the ships destroying each other. The last action was that of the Culture Superlifter *Liveware Problem*: it fell into the unnamed Morthanveld guard ship – a stubby fist ramming a bloated head – and partially annihilated both of them in a blast of total spectrum radiation so extreme that even from eighty kilometres away it was sufficient to trip alarms in the suits.

"I'm gone!" Hippinse said, sounding like a lost child.

"Down to us now," Anaplian said crisply. "Hippinse! You all right?"

"Yes," the avatoid said. They were all watching the distant shrapnel of the wreck; huge pieces of ship flailing and tumbling and racing away from the explosion, their glinting, somersaulting surfaces lit by the fading radiations of the carnage as they flew away, smashing into vanes and blades and machinery and ricocheting away again, trailed by sparks and liquidic splashes of secondary and tertiary debris.

"Still got the drones?" Anaplian asked. "I've lost them."

"Yes, yes; got them," Hippinse said quietly. "They're answering."

"Both ships gone," Turminder Xuss announced. "I am up close and dodging megatonne shit here. And I can see the offending article. It has the Xinthian."

Ferbin's blood seemed to run cold at the mention of the last word. Xinthian. The other name for the WorldGod.

"Ah, what would that mean, sir?" Holse asked.

"The Xinthian is enclosed within what looks like a fiery cage," Turminder Xuss told them. "The offender is very small but looks extremely capable. Energy profile the like of which I have not seen before. Who'd have thought something so ancient would be so potent?" It showed them.

Beyond where the ships had disputed, beyond where their wreckage had slowly fallen – splashing wildly across the great flowers of spiralled vanes beneath like sun-glinted rain on a forest bloom – half a horizon away but coming quickly closer, another tableau presented itself. The view wobbled, overmagnified, then grew quickly more stable and detailed as the drone and its accompanying missiles rushed closer.

The WorldGod was an ellipsoid a kilometre across and two in length, jerking and writhing within a light-splintered surround of fierce white fire extending a few hundred metres out from its mottled, dark brown surface. The Iln machine was a dot to one side, joined to this tortuous mayhem by a single strand of bright blue energy.

Beneath the Xinthian, directly over a hole in the centre of one of the immense blade flowers, a tiny bright globe was growing, throwing off intense, recurrent flashes of light.

"Beneath it," Anaplian said, sounding like she was gulping.

"It's generating anti-matter," Hippinse said.

"Where are—" Djan Seriy began, then they were all hit by intense bursts of laser fire sparkling from a source above and behind them. The suits flicked about, spun, raced away, ablating layers. Ferbin found himself pummelled, too warm, breathless, and his weapon nearly torn from his arms as it twirled, aimed and fired in one absurdly fast movement that happened so quickly it left his flesh and bones aching.

"Comped Morth drone," somebody said.

"Mine," somebody else said.

"You're—"

"Mother*fucker*!" Ferbin heard somebody else hiss. Actually, it sounded like him.

All Ferbin knew was that he was being tumbled about and yet the gun was always pointing in the same direction whenever it possibly could and it was kicking and kicking and kicking at him, throwing him wildly back, bouncing across these dark and livid skies.

Until it all stopped.

"Hippinse?"

No answer.

"Hippinse; reply!"

It was Djan Seriy's voice.

"Hippinse?"

Her again.

"*Hippinse!*"

Ferbin had blacked out momentarily due to the extreme manoeuvring. The suit apologised. It informed him that they were now
sheltered with the surviving members of their group – agent
Anaplian, Mr Holse and himself – behind a vane on the flank
of the nearest machine sphere. The visor helpfully circled his
sister and Holse, each a few hundred metres or so away, ten
metres down from the scimitared summit of their protecting
vane. Light glittered above, strobing over the ceiling structures.

Ferbin began to wonder how he had got here, to safety. He
hadn't actually articulated the words this thought was leading
to when the suit told him that it had taken control, under Agent
Anaplian's instructions.

"Ferbin? You back with us?" His sister's voice sounded loud
in his ears.

"Ah . . . yes," he said. He tried to check himself, tried to carry
out a mental inventory of his faculties and bodily parts. For a
moment everything seemed fine, but then he remembered his
missing lower leg. "Well, no worse," he said. In fact he felt good;
still strangely, almost absurdly exuberant, and sharp; suddenly
fully recovered from his blackout and seemingly ready for
anything. Some still woozy part of his mind wondered vaguely
how profoundly and subtly the suit could affect his emotions,
and what control over that process his sister had.

"Holse?" Djan Seriy asked.

"I'm fine, ma'am. But Mr Hippinse . . . ?"

"We lost him when he attacked the second of the two comped
Morth machines. Also, Xuss isn't answering. And the ship
drones don't appear to have survived that last tussle either. We
are somewhat reduced, gentlemen."

"Weren't there two of those Morthanveld machines?" Holse
asked.

"Both gone now. I got the other one," Anaplian said. Every
word she uttered sounded clipped, bitten off. Holse wondered
if she had been wounded too, but did not want to ask.

"What now, ma'am?"

"That is a good question, Holse," Anaplian said. "I strongly suspect if we stick our heads over this vane above us we'll get them blown off. Also, due to the angles, there isn't really anywhere else to go. Conversely, I have a short-range line-gun that can knock the living fuck out of anything that pokes its head or other relevant part over our side of the vane. That is our inventory, however. The Iln machine knows I have this weapon and will certainly not come close enough to let me use it. Sadly," Holse heard the woman take a breath, "we have lost my particle gun to enemy action, the kinetics are expended or blasted, the CREWs won't have any effect and the subsidiary missiles have either also expended themselves in the course of action or been vaped. Vaporised, I should say. Sorry, brother; sorry, Mr Holse. My apologies for having involved you in all this. I appear to have led us into a sorry situation."

It was, Ferbin thought. It was a sorry situation. Sometimes life itself seemed like a sorry situation.

What was to become of them? And what lay ahead for him? He might die here within minutes but even if he didn't he knew he didn't want to be king. He never had. When he'd seen his father killed, his first instinct had been to run away, even before he'd rationalised this gut decision. He'd always known in his heart he wouldn't be a good king, and realised now that – in the unlikely event they escaped this desperate fix – his whole reign, his entire life, would be a slow and likely ignominious winding down from this peak of meaning and possible glory. There was a new age coming and he could not really see himself being part of it. Elime, Oramen, him . . .

He heard Holse say, "What's to be done, then, ma'am?"

"Well, we could just rush the bastard and die very quickly to no effect," Anaplian said, sounding tired. "Or we can wait here until the Iln machine finishes making all the anti-matter it wants and destroys the whole world. Us first, after itself and the Xinthian," she added. "If that's any consolation."

Holse gulped. "Is that really it, ma'am?"

"Well . . ." Anaplian began, then paused. "Ah. It wants to talk. Might as well hear what it has to say."

"Humans," a deep, sonorous voice said to all of them, "the Shellworld machines were built to create a field enclosing the galaxy. Not to protect but to imprison, control, annihilate. I am a liberator, as were all those who came before me, however vilified. We have set you free by destroying these abominations. Join me, do not oppose."

"What?" Ferbin said.

"Is it saying . . . ?" Holse began.

"Ignore it," Anaplian told them. "It's just being a properly devious enemy. Always unsettle the opposition if possible. I'm telling your suits to ignore any further comms from the machine."

Yes, Ferbin thought, she controls these suits. The machine was trying to control us. We are controlled. It's all about control.

"So, are we stuck as we are then, ma'am?" Holse asked. "It and us?"

"No," Anaplian said. "Come to think of it, the Iln machine doesn't need to settle for a stand-off. Last estimate we took, the required AM mass will take hours to accrete. Long before that, one of the Iln's sub-pods will appear over that vane-sphere way back there, good sixty klicks off, and pick us off from a distance."

Holse looked at the distant ridge line, then around at their immediate surroundings. He didn't see how they could be got round. "How's it going to do that, ma'am?"

"It can retreat over the horizon and circle round behind us that way," Djan Seriy said heavily. "The Core's only fourteen hundred klicks in diameter; horizon's very close. Could even go right round the Core. In vacuum, wouldn't take long for a sufficiently capable machine. I'd guess we have a couple of minutes."

"Oh," Holse said again.

"Yes, indeed: oh."

Holse thought. "Nothing else we can do, ma'am?"

"Oh," Anaplian said, sounding very tired, "there are always things worth trying."

"Such as, ma'am?"

"Going to need one of you two to sacrifice yourself. Sorry."

"Pardon, ma'am?"

"Then I get to do the same thing," Anaplian said, sounding like she was trying to remain calm. "So one of us survives, for a little while longer, at least. Survivor's suit can get them anywhere within Sursamen or back to near space. More to the point, we might just stop the world getting blown up. Always a reasonable goal."

"What do we have to do?" Ferbin asked.

"Somebody has to surrender," Anaplian said. "Give yourself to the Iln machine. It will kill you – quickly, hopefully – but it might just be intrigued enough to inspect you first. That first one, though, it'll be suspicious of. Whoever goes first dies to satisfy its caution. The second – that will be me – might just get close enough. I'm already preparing all this in my head. I'm assuming the Enabler program the Oct hit the Iln machine with was one of ours. They have subtle misconstructions regarding Contact and SC that might aid our cause here, though I do have to emphasise that this is the most ridiculously long shot, and even then we're relying on the WorldGod not being fatally injured and it being capable of unmaking all that anti-matter; an explosion based on what's already accumulated would kill it and do a significant amount of damage to the Core. So, still hope, of a desperate kind. But you wouldn't bet on any of this, trust me."

"So, one of us has to—" Holse began.

"I can't ask either of you—" Anaplian started to say at the same time, then gulped and shouted, "*Ferbin!*"

The suited figure was already rising above the shield of the vane, upper body exposed to the flickering radiations beyond, throwing away the weapon he'd been carrying.

She must have been hit hard. When she awoke it was to find herself in the grip of something adamantinely hard and utterly unforgiving. Dear fuck, it had eviscerated her. The suit was shredded, torn apart, and her body inside with it. All that was left of her was her head – half flayed, skin burned off – and a short tattered tail of spinal cord. This bloody scrap was what the Iln thing cradled.

Eyelids burned away, she couldn't blink; not even her tongue or jaws were responding to orders. Djan Seriy Anaplian felt more helpless than a newborn.

The Iln machine above her was dark, not big, vaguely triangular. Her eyes were damaged, the view hazy. So much trouble from something so small, she thought, and would have laughed if she could. Its slickly bulbous shape was lit from the side by the cage of light surrounding the Xinthian and from below by the scintillations sparking from the containment holding the growing sphere of anti-matter.

Strange little beasts, you, the great heavy voice said inside her head. *What fleeting titillations life continues to throw up, many-fold, like virtual particles, bioscale, so long after –*

Oh

She had seen all she needed to see, heard all she needed to hear.

go

Now she was close enough.

and

(This was all she had, and the worst of it was, backups or not, she'd never know if it was going to be enough.)

fuck yourself, Djan Seriy Anaplian said finally.

She let the containment within the little anti-matter reactor inside her head go.

Appendix

C: the Culture
HLI: High-level Involved (also MLI: Mid-level; LLI: Low-level)
L1S: level one of Sursamen (etc.)
S: Sursamen

Characters

Aclyn	the lady Blisk, mother to Elime and Oramen; banished
Aiaik	Towermaster of the D'neng-oal Tower, Sursamen
Alveyal Girgetioni	Acting Craterine Zamerin, Sursamen
Archipontine	head monk of the Hyeng-zharia Mission
Baerth	knight of Charvin, Sarl (Bower or Brower to Ferbin)
Bleye	one of tyl Loesp's lieutenants
Broft	foreman, Nameless City dig, Ninth, Sursamen
Chasque	Exaltine, Sarl chief of priests
Chire	rail car driver, the Falls
Choubris Holse	Ferbin's servant
Chilgitheri	(Morthanveld) liaison officer on *"Fasilyce, Upon Waking"*
Dilucherre	old master of painting, Sarl
Djan Seriy	Anaplian; princess, C SC agent
Droffo	earl, from Shilda; becomes equerry to Oramen
Dubrile	ex-soldier at Falls; becomes Oramen's bodyguard chief
Elime	esk Blisk-Hausk'r; dead eldest son of Hausk
Everlasting Queen	Nariscene monarch; currently on 3044th Great Spawning
Fanthile	secretary of royal palace, Pourl
Ferbin	otz Aelsh-Hausk'r (Feri, as child)
Foise	general, Sarl army, attached to Falls contingent

Geltry Skiltz	C person, aboard MSV *Don't Try This At Home*
Gillews	(Dr) Royal Physician to Hausk
Girgetioni	Nariscene family, Sursamen
Harne	the lady Aelsh; mother to Ferbin
Hausk	Nerieth ("the Conqueror"); warrior-king, Sarl
Hippinse	Pone; an avatoid of the *Liveware Problem*
Humli	Ghasartravhara; liaison officer, MSV *Don't Try This At Home*
Honge	bravard of Pourl's drinking dens
Illis	armourer, royal palace, Pourl
Jerle Batra	Djan Seriy's SC Control/mentor; an Aciculate
Jerfin Poatas	in charge of Falls excavation
Jish	whore, Pourl
Kebli	child in court at same time as Djan Seriy
Kiu	(-to-Pourl) Oct Ambassador to Pourl
Klatsli Quike	avatoid of the *Liveware Problem*
Koust	Oct Tower under-clerk, Sursamen
Leeb Scoperin	another Special Circumstances agent on Prasadal
Leratiy	senior technician, Sarcophagus excavation, Falls
Luzehl	whore; sister to Paiteng
Machasa	Mrs; young Djan Seriy's nurse and tutor
Mallarh	lady of the Sarl court
Masyen	Aclyn's husband; becomes mayor of Rasselle
Munhreo	junior scholar, Hicturean-Anjrinh Scholastery
Neguste Puibive	becomes Oramen's servant
Nuthe 3887b	Morthanveld greeting device, Syaung-un
Obli	Harne's ynt
Omoulldeo	old master of painting, Sarl
Oramen	lin Blisk-Hausk'r; a prince, same mother as Elime

Prode the younger   ancient Sarl playwright
Puisil   servant in the royal palace, Sarl

Quitrilis Yurke   C traveller; finds Oct lying about ship movements

Ramile   lady of the Sarl court
Renneque,   the lady Silbe

Savidius Savide   Oct Peripatetic Special Envoy, Sursamen
Seltis   old tutor of Ferbin's – now Scholastery Head Scholar
Senble   Holse's wife
Shir Rocasse   tutor to Oramen
Shoum   director general of Morthanveld Strategic Mission
Sinnel   ancient Sarl playwright
Skalpapta   Alien Greeting and Liaison Officer, GS *Inspiral, Coalescence, Ringdown*
Sordic   old master of painting, Sarl

Tove Lomma   childhood friend of Oramen; later his equerry
Tulya Puonvangi   C ambassador, on *Inspiral, Coalescence, Ringdown*
Tagratark   Towermaster of Vaw-yei Tower, Sursamen
Tareah   Sarl doctor
Tchilk   Nariscene Barbarian Relational Mentor, Baengyon Crater
Toark   child Djan Seriy rescues from burning city
Tohonlo   one of tyl Loesp's lieutenants (also Toho, as child)
Truffe   second cousin to Ferbin
Turminder Xuss   (Handrataler) Djan Seriy's drone
tyl Loesp   Mertis; Hausk's 2nd in command

Utaltifuhl   Nariscene Grand Zamerin of Sursamen

Vaime   the lady Anaplia; mother of Djan Seriy
Vollird   of Sournier, knight of Sarl
Werreber   senior general; becomes field marshal, army chief

Wudyen	duke; Hausk's brother
Xessice	whore, Hyeng-zhar Settlement
Xide Hyrlis	C outcast, military commander for Nariscene
Xidia	young lady at court (named after Xide Hyrlis)
Yariem Girgetioni	Deputy Acting Zamerin, Sursamen
Yilim	senior officer in Hausk's army
Zandone	Sarl actor and impresario
Zeel	young Djan Seriy's pet mersicor
Zourd	(Expanded Version Five) Cumuloform, 13th, Sursamen

Culture Full Names

Astle-Chulinisa **Klatsli** LP **Quike** dam Uast
Meseriphine-Sursamen/VIIIsa **Djan Seriy Anaplian** dam Pourl
Sholz-Iniassa **Jerle** Ruule **Batra** dam Ilyon
Stafl-Lepoortsa **Xide** Ozoal **Hyrlis** dam Pappens

Species

Aeronathaurs	Tensile; see Xinthia
Aultridia	upstart species that evolved from parasites living under carapaces of Xinthia; mat-like/Pelliform (also "Squirmiform", term of abuse); LLI
Avians	bird species; L5S variety methane gas-going
Birilisi	Avian species much given to excessive narcoticism; MLI
Bithians	(L0S) gilled whale-size creatures, waterborne; HLI
caude	giant winged creature, tameable and rideable; L8&9S
choup	Sarl equivalent of dog; L8&9S
chunsel	warbeast, later of burden and traction; L8S
Culture, the	mongrel humanoid civilisation; HLI

Cumuloforms	cloudlike O_2 beings; L4S
Deldeyn	same species as Sarl, one level down; allied to the Aultridia, seen as antagonistic to the WorldGod and so enemies of the Sarl; L9S
hefter	beast of burden and traction; L8&9S
Hydrals	black hole smoker species; L13S
Iln	aero-spiniform HLI aeons ago; wrecked Shellworlds, destroyed Veil tombs; believed extinct/missing
Inheritors	see Oct
Involucra/Veil	Shellworld builders, HLI aeons ago
lyge	giant winged creature, tameable and rideable; L8&9S
mersicor	large quadruped, tameable and rideable; L8&9S
Monthia	pan-species very large ocean-going creature-type
Morthanveld	Nariscene mentors; spiniform waterworlders, HLI
Nariscene	Sarl mentors; insectile, MLI
Nuersotise	humanoid; one of the contending species on Prasadal
Oct/Inheritors	claim descent from Involucra; control (most) travel within Towers of Sursamen and many other Shellworlds; octal Waterworlders; LLI
ossesyi	quadruped warbeasts; L8S
Pelagic Kite	atmospheric waterworlders; sail air over waterworlds; term also used for surface-going kited bioships; L5S
rowel	quadruped pack beast; L8&9S
ryre	quadruped, equivalent of cat; L8&9S
Sarl	humanoid people exiled/interned within Sursamen; L8&9S
Seedsails	mirror-sailed seed carriers; L1S
spore-wisp	plasma seed of a stellar field-liner
Swimmers	beings from lower levels of gas giant planets; L12S
Tendrils	elongated gas giant species, L6 & 10S
Tubers	black hole smoker species; L13S
Tueriellian	(Maieutic) investigative Seedsail
uoxantch	quadruped warbeasts; L9S
WorldGod, the	being at Core of Sursamen; a Xinthian; L15&16S

Veil	see Involucra
Vesicular	surface waterworlders; having gas-filled bladder/sail; L10S
Xinthia	(Tensile Aeronathaur) an Airworlder; giant airships (smaller than dirigible behemothaurs); semi-adapted for high-pressure gaseous/liquid environments and space-capable. Now rare and generally Developmentally/Inherently/Pervasively Senile; see WorldGod, the
Xolpe	humanoid; Nariscene client species, at war
ynt	quadruped equivalent of small tame otter; L8&9S
Zeloy	humanoid, one of the contending species on Prasadal

General Glossary

34th Pendant Floret	region of space
512th Degree FifthStrand	Humanoid Guest Facility, Syaung-un
aboriginistas	those with obsessive interest in "primitives"
Aciculate	bush-like
afap	as fast as possible (C)
Altruist	a civilisation purposefully and consistently eschewing naked self-interest
Anjrinh	district in Hicture; home to a Scholastery
Aoud	star/system, home of Gadampth Orbital
aquaticised	(humanoids) fully converted to water-dwelling
Arithmetic	re a Shellworld, term given to one whose levels occur in simple multiples
Articles of Inhabitation	rules by which Shellworld inhabitants live
Aspirant	civilisations wanting to be Involveds
Asulious IV	Morthanveld planet, Lesser Yattlian Spray
autoscender	uncrewed transport within Shellworld Tower
backing	direction (opposite of facing)
Baeng-yon	Surface crater, Sursamen

bald-head fruit	edible by caude, common to L8&9S
Bare	places on Shellworld with no ground cover
Baron Lepessi	classic play by Prode the younger
Baskers	species type; absorb sunlight directly
bell-goblet	vibrating crystal container used when drinking Chapantlic spirit
billow bed	C bed with 99% AG, multiple soft wisps of material and smart "feathers" able to avoid being breathed in
Bilpier	Nariscene planet, Heisp system
black-backed borm	C animal
Botrey's	gambling/whore house in Pourl's Schtip district
Bowlsea	body of water filling Prime depression in Shellworld
brattle	bush, L8&9S, Sursamen
bravard	lusty, drinking, up-for-a-fight kind of man
Bulthmaas	planet in Chyme system where Xide Hyrlis found
camoufield	(C) projected field camouflaging objects
Chapantlic spirit	type of booze (see bell-goblet)
Charvin	a county of Sarl
Cherien	ridge, near Sarl city, L8S
Chone	a star in the Lesser Yattlian Spray
Chyme	stellar system, home of Bulthmaas
CleaveHull	type of Morthanveld ship
Clissens	a Rollstar of the Ninth, Sursamen
cloud trees	flora, L8&9S, Sursamen
Conducer	(species) those which make habit of taking over and (usually) exploiting structures, artefacts and habitats built by earlier civilisations – from ancients to the recently Sublimed
Core	solid centre of a Shellworld
crackball	C game played with solid wooden ball
Crater	re a Shellworld, a high-walled habitable area on Surface
crile leaf	cocoa-like drug, chewed; L8&9S
Curbed Lands	type of (originally Deldeyn) province

cut-rot	gangrene (Sarl term)
Dengroal	town, L8S, beneath the D'neng-oal Tower
deSept	Nariscene clanlet without a Sept or major clan/family
Despairationals	extremist group, Syaung-un
Dillser	ducal house by Boiling Sea of Yakid, L9S
director general	high rank of the Morthanveld
Disputed	re a Shellworld, one whose Towers are not all controlled by the same species
D'neng-oal Tower	Oct transport Tower, Sursamen
Domity	a Rollstar of L8S
Enabler	(machine) device used to find ways to communicate with alien species and artifacts
Evingreath	a town on the Xilisk road from Pourl
Exaltinates	elite troops under Chasque
Exaltine	top Sarlian religious rank; chief priest
Exponential	see logarithmic
facing	direction; from facing direction of world's rotation (opposite of backing)
Facing Approach Street	near royal palace in Pourl
Falls Merchant Explorer	guild of merchants exploiting Falls
Falls, the	cataract on the Sulpitine river, L9S (aka the Hyeng-zhar)
Far Landing	peripatetic port on far side of Sulpitine from the Settlement
farpole	direction to pole of world furthest from Sarl heartlands (opposite of nearpole)
Feyrla	river, Xilisk, L8S
Fifth deSept	minor, unaligned clanlet, Nariscene/Sursamen
Filigree	complexes of Shellworld Tower ceiling supporting inverted buttresses
Fixstars	Shellworld interior stars, unmoving
floater	slightly derogatory term used for aquatic peoples by landgoing peoples
Foerlinteul	C Orbital

FOIADSFBF	First Original Indigent Alien Deep Space Farers' Benevolent Fund (Morthanveld)
Forelight	pre-dawn light cast by Rollstar
Gadampth	C Orbital
Gavantille Prime	waterworld planet, Morthanveld space
Gazan-g'ya	a Crater of Sursamen
Gilder's Lament, the	tavern, Pourl
Godded	a Shellworld with a Xinthian at its core
Grahy	Morthanveld planet, Lesser Yattlian Spray
Grand Zamerin	exalted rank of the Nariscene (see also Zamerin)
Greater Army	combined armies gathered by Hausk to resist Deldeyn and invade their level
Great Palace	Rasselle, L9S
Great Park	Rasselle, L9S
Great Ship	type of very large Morthanveld ship
Great Tower	one of six fortifications within Rasselle
Guime	a Rollstar of L8S
habiform	technically correct term for what is usually called terraforming; altering any already existing environment to suit it to the needs of one or more species
Heavenly Host	Deldeyn religious sect tyl Loesp empowers
Heisp	Nariscene colony system
Hemerje	ducal palace near the Great Park, Rasselle
Heurimo	a fallstar of L9S
Hicture	a region of L8S
Hicturean	Tower (L8S, not far from Pourl)
Hollow World	see Shellworld
House of Many Roofs, The	play by Sinnel
Hyeng-zhar	cataract on the Sulpitine river, L9S, aka the Falls
Hyeng-zharia Mission	religious order; controlled the Falls' excavation
Hyeng-zhar Settlement	ever-temporary city, the Falls, Sursamen
Ichteuen	(Godwarriors) fight for Sarl; L8S

Illsipine Tower	Sursamen
Imperial Procreational College	on Nariscene homeworld; regulates Spawnings
Incremental	re a Shellworld, term given to one whose levels occur in exponential increments (hence aka Exponential)
injectiles	any organisms or mechanisms capable of being injected (usually into metre-scale entities, in context especially humans)
In Loco'd	placed under care (Morthanveld term)
Inner Caferlitician Tendril	region of space
interior star	artificial suns emplaced by secondary Shellworld species within these worlds; anti-gravitational, pressing against ceiling of given level; most mobile (Rollstars); some not (Fixstars)
Ischuer	city, Bilpier
Jhouheyre	city-cluster, Oct planet of Zaranche
Jiluence	a Monthian (megawhales) ancestral homeworld
Keande-yi	region near Pourl, L8S
Keande-yiine	Tower in region near Pourl, L8S
Khatach Solus	Nariscene homeworld
Kheretesuhr	archipelagic province, Vilamian Ocean, L8S
Kiesestraal	a fading Rollstar of L9S
Klusse	city, Lesuus Plate
krisk nuts	caude stimulant, L8&9S
Kuertile Pinch	region of space
Lalance	continent, Prasadal
lampstone	carbide
Lemitte	general, Sarl army
Lepoort	plate, Stafl Orbital
Lesser Yattlian Spray	region of space
Lesuus	plate, Gadampth

level	re a Shellworld, one of the world's spherical shells
lifebowls	see mottled
Logarithmic	re: a Shellworld, term given to one whose levels occur in exponential increments (hence aka Exponential)
Machine Core/level	level immediately surrounding a Shellworld Core
Meast	water-nest city, Gavantille Prime
Meseriphine	star in the Tertiary Hulian Spine
MHE	Monopathic Hegemonising Event (usually runway nanotech)
MOA	Mysterious Object from Afar
Moiliou	Hausk family estate, L8S
Mottled	re a Shellworld, term given to one whose Surface is partially (mostly) free of atmosphere, with significant areas – within large, high-walled (normally original) Surface features – of nominally inhabitable pseudo-planetary environments, called Lifebowls
Multiply Inhabited	re a Shellworld, one with more than one intelligent species in residence
Nameless City	of L9S; long buried metropolis being uncovered by the Hyeng-zhar
nanorgs	nano-scale organisms; often aka injectiles (though this covers non-biological material too)
Natherley	a Rollstar of L9S
nearpole	direction (opposite of farpole)
Nearpole Gate	a main gate of Pourl city, L8S
Nestworld	usually, and always in context of Morthanveld, a type of artificial habitat composed of multiple twisting tubes, complexly intertwined and generally water-filled
Night	re a Shellworld, places within a level which are totally or almost totally dark, over the

	horizon from both direct and reflected sunlight or vane-blocked
Oausillac	a Fixstar of L9S, Sursamen
Obor	a Rollstar of L8S, Sursamen
Oerten	Surface crater, Sursamen
Optimae	name given to Culture, Morthanveld, etc. by more lowly civilisations; roughly equivalent to HLI
Oversquare	re a Shellworld, levels beyond which increasing separation of secondary supporting filaments branching from Towers no longer allows intra-filament inter-Tower travel (usually in top half of levels); opposite of undersquare
Pandil-fwa Tower	Oct transport Tower, Sursamen
Parade Field	Pourl, L8S
Pentrl	a Rollstar of L8S
Peremethine Tower	Oct transport Tower, Sursamen
Pierced	re a Shellworld, a level-accessible Tower
Placed	placed under care (Morthanveld term)
Pliyr	star, Morthanveld space
Pourl	region and capital city of Sarl, L8S
Prasadal	planet, Zoveli system
Prille	country on Sketevi
Primarian	type of large Oct ship
Prime	re a Shellworld, term given to structure of world as originally built by Veil
Quoline	river, draining the Quoluk Lakes
Quoluk Lakes	of L8S, near Pourl
Quonber	module platform, Prasadal
Rasselle	Deldeyn capital city, L9S
Reshigue	city, L8S
roasoaril	fruit plant, L8&9S (refinable)
Rollstars	Shellworld interior stars which move
roving scendship	(Oct) scendship air- and underwater-capable

Safe	(multi-million-year) re a Shellworld, term given to one with no recent history of world-caused gigadeaths
saltmeat	(Sarl) salted meat
Sarl	people and kingdom, L8S, Sursamen (also planet)
scend tubes	tubes scendships use
scendship	ship which ascends or descends within a Shellworld Tower
Scholastery	recessional university, like a secular monastery devoted to learning
Schtip	district of Pourl, L8S
scrimp	dismissive name for Falls workers
seatrider	C skeletal AG device; personal transport
Secondary	re a Shellworld, term given to structural additions to world added by later possessors
shade	areas on a Shellworld level without direct sunlight (effect severity varies with shell diameter, vane geometry, etc.)
Shellworld	artificial planet, part of ancient megastructure; also known as Hollow World and Slaughter World (archaic)
Shield world	see Shellworld
Shilda	province of Sarl, L8S
silse	collective term for class of Shellworld creatures which transport silt particles from seabeds and other aquatic environments to land, via hydrogen sacs, evaporation, clouds and rainfall
Sketevi	continent on Bulthmaas
Slaughter World	see Shellworld
SlimHull	type of Morthanveld ship
Sournier	county within Sarl, L8S
Spiniform	(world) a partially collapsed Shellworld
spiniform	applied to species, indicates a spiny, pointed body type
Stafl	C Orbital
Stalks	slightly derogatory term used for landgoing peoples by aquatic peoples

Starfall	(rare) phenomenon occurring when the remains of an exhausted Shellworld interior star fall from the ceiling of a level to its floor; generally catastrophic
Sterut	Nariscene Globular Transfer Facility
Sull	Deldeyn region, L9S
Sullir	Deldeyn regional capital, L9S
Sulpitine	river, L9S
Superintendent	judicial rank, Sursamen Surface
Sursamen	Arithmetic Shellworld, orbiting Meseriphine
Swarmata	the detritus of competing MHEs
SwellHull	type of Morthanveld ship
Syaung-un	Morthanveld Nestworld in the 34th Pendant Floret
Taciturn	of a species, one which is especially uncommunicative
tangfruit	C fruit, pan-human edible
terraf	short for terraformed; a planet so amended, or any other large-scale constructed environment (see habiform)
Tertiary Hulian Spine	region of space; location of Meseriphine
thin-film	screen; goes over eyes to show virtual reality (Morthanveld term)
Tierpe Ancestral	port, Syaung-un
tink	dismissive name for Falls worker
T'leish	sub-group of Morthanveld, on Gavantille Prime
Tower	re a Shellworld, a hollow supporting column or stem, normally with vacuum inside, also used as transport tube
Tresker	a Rollstar of L9S
tropel trees	C flora; common on ships
Twinned Crater	Surface crater, Sursamen
Uliast	general, Sarl army
undersquare	see oversquare
unge	drug, smoked; L8&9S

Upstart	(species) generally recognised if mildly pejorative term for (usually intelligent and even Involved) species which is regarded as having achieved such status by the exploitation of its relationship with another, already advanced, civilisation
Urletine	(mercenaries) fight for Sarl; L8S
Uzretean	a Rollstar of L9S
Vaw-yei	Tower, Sursamen
Veil World	see Shellworld
Vilamian Ocean	on L8S
Voette	country, L8S
Vruise	location of Falls, L9S
wallcreep	foliage, L8&9S
Wars of Unity	sequence waged by Hausk to unite the Eighth
Wiriniti	capital of Voette, L8S
Xilisk	region near Pourl, L8S
Xiliskine Tower	Tower nearest to Pourl, L8S
xirze	crop, common on L8&9S
Yakid	Boiling Sea of, L9S
Yakid City	on shores of above, L9S
Yattle	planet, Greater Yattlian Spray
Zamerin	high rank of the Nariscene (see also Grand Zamerin)
Zaranche	planet, Inner Caferlitician Tendril
Za's Revenge	C cocktail
Zoveli	star and system, location of Prasadal
Zuevelous	Morthanveld family, Gavantille Prime
Zunzil Ligature	region of space; location of Iln home world/s

Ships

Culture

Don't Try This At Home	Steppe-class MSV
Eight Rounds Rapid	Delinquent-class FP exGOU
Experiencing A Significant Gravitas Shortfall	GCU
It's My Party And I'll Sing If I Want To	Escarpment-class GCU
Lightly Seared on the Reality Grill	GCU
Liveware Problem	Stream-class Superlifter (modified Delta class, Absconded)
Now We Try It My Way	Erratic-class (ex-Interstellar-class General Transport Craft)
Pure Big Mad Boat Man	GCU
Qualifier	Trench-class MSV
Seed Drill	Ocean-class GSV
Subtle Shift In Emphasis	Plains-class GCV
Transient Atmospheric Phenomenon	GCU
Xenoglossicist	Air-class LSV
You Naughty Monsters	GCU
You'll Clean That Up Before You Leave	Gangster-class VFP ex-ROU

Nariscene

Hence the Fortress	Comet-class star-cruiser
Hundredth Idiot, The	White Dwarf-class

Morthanveld

"Fasilyce, Upon Waking"	Cat.5 SwellHull
Inspiral, Coalescence, Ringdown	Great Ship
"On First Seeing Jhiriit"	Cat.4 CleaveHull
"Now, Turning to Reason, & Its Just Sweetness"	Cat.3 SlimHull

Sursamen Levels: Inhabitants

Level		Inhabitant
0	Surface; vacuum/ habiformed	Nariscene/Baskers/others
1	Vacuum	Seedsail nursery
2	Vacuum	Baskers
3	Vacuum	Dark
4	O_2 ocean	Cumuloforms
5	Methane shallows	Kites/Avians
6	Higher Gas Giant	Tendrils – Naiant
7	Methane Ocean	Vesiculars – Monthian megawhales
8	Land – O_2	Sarl
9	Land – O_2	Deldeyn/Sarl
	(Under-/Over square division)	
10	Mid Gas Giant	Tendrils – Variolous
11	Methane ocean	Vesiculars – Monthian megawhales
12	Lower Gas Giant	Swimmers
13	Water/slush matrices	Tubers/Hydrals
14	Ice/water	Dark
15	Machinery	the WorldGod – a Xinthian
16	Core – solid	the WorldGod – a Xinthian

Time Intervals

Term	Years
aeon	1 000 000 000
deciaeon	100 000 000
centiaeon	10 000 000
eon	1 000 000
decieon	100 000
centieon	10 000
millennium	1 000
century	100
decade	10
year	1

Epilogue

Senble Holse was hunched over a tub with a washboard, furiously scrubbing, when her husband walked in. He came through the doorway of the apartment in the company of a smoothly handsome, ringlet-haired blond gent and holding the hand of a strange-looking little boy. She watched, open-mouthed, as he nodded to her.

"Mrs Holse," he said. He walked to the centre of their cramped living room, put his hands on his hips – the odd-looking child still kept a determined hold of his hand – and gazed around. He was dressed rather well, even for a prince's servant, and looked better than ever he had; well-fed and sleek. The twins had taken one look and yelped; they were hiding behind her skirts, holding on fit to drag her to her knees and peeking round, one on each side.

"You look well, my dear," he said. He caught sight of the youngest, hiding behind the door into the bedroom. He waved.

There was a thin cry and the door banged shut. He laughed and looked back at her. "Young Choubris?"

"At school!" Senble told him.

"Good." He nodded. "Oh," he said with a smile. (His teeth looked wrong; far too pale and even.) "Where's my manners, eh?" He nodded at the glossy-looking man standing smiling at his side. "Senble, dearest; meet Mr Klatsli Quike."

The fellow nodded slowly. "An honour, ma'am." He was carrying a small pile of boxes bound with ribbons.

"Mr Quike will be staying with us," Holse announced breezily. "And this here," he said, waving the hand holding that of the odd-looking, very serious-seeming little boy, "is Toark. Toark Holse as he shall be known henceforth. We'll be adopting him. Mr Quike is a man of considerable abilities who finds himself at something of a loose end and with a sentimental attachment to our dear homeworld, while little Toark here is an orphan of war, and so much in need of love and a settled family life, the poor little soul."

Senble had had enough. She threw the wet washing back into the tub, wiped her hands once on her skirts, pulled herself up to her best height – detaching the twins, who ran for the bedroom and disappeared, squealing – and said, "Not a word, not a *word* for an entire year, then you march in here, bold as you like, not a word of apology, telling me there's gents going to be staying with us and bringing me another mouth to feed when we've no room in here as it is even without you being back let me add and no money to spend anyway even if we did have the room, which we don't—"

"Now, dear," Holse said, picking up the young lad and sitting him on his knee as he settled himself in his old chair by the window. The little boy buried his face in Holse's shoulder. "We shall have a much bigger and far better set of rooms by this evening, Mr Quike informs me, isn't that right, Mr Quike?"

"It is, sir," Quike said, flashing dazzling teeth. He put the pile of ribbon-wrapped boxes on the kitchen table and produced an official-looking letter from his jacket. "Your new lease, ma'am," he said, showing it to her. "For one year."

"Paid for in advance," Holse said, nodding.

"Using what?" Senble asked loudly. "You won't even get your servant's pension now, not under this new lot, citizen. I'm owing – you owe half a year's rent on this place. I thought you must be the bailiffs when you marched in here, I did!"

"Money is not going to be a problem for us from this point on, dearest, I think you'll find." Holse nodded at the washtub. "And you shall have servants to do that sort of thing, to protect your delicate hands." He was looking round for something. "You seen my pipe, love?"

"It's where you left it!" Senble told him. She didn't know whether to hug the rogue or slap him about the face with the wet washing. "What's all that anyway?" she asked, nodding at the pile of boxes on the table.

"Presents for the children," Holse explained. "For the birth-days I've missed. And this," he said, reaching into his jacket and producing a slim box, also bound with ribbons, "is for you, my dear." He handed it to her.

She looked at it suspiciously. "What is it?" she asked.

"It's a present, dearest. A bracelet."

She made a humphing noise and thrust the box into her apron pocket without opening it. Holse looked hurt.

"And where's all this money coming from?" Senble asked. She glared at this Quike fellow, who smiled gracefully back. "Don't tell me you've finally won something at the betting!"

"In a sense, dear," Holse told her. "The money will be coming from a fund set aside for special circumstances by some new friends I've made. He waved one hand airily. "Mr Quike will be handling the financial side of things."

"And what do *you* propose to do?" Senble demanded. "If this is a betting win you know damn well you'll just gamble it all away again next week and we'll be back to hiding from the constable's men and pawning the brass, which is already pawned, I might add."

"Oh, I'm going into a career in politics, me dear," Holse said matter-of-factly. He was still holding the shy young boy and patting his back, reassuring him.

Senble threw back her head and laughed. "Politics? *You?*"

"Politics me indeed," Holse said, smiling broadly at her. She was still distracted by those teeth. "I shall be a man of the people, yet one who has been places and seen things and made friends such as you would entirely not believe, my dear. I'm better connected, upwards and downwards – WorldGod be praised – than you could possibly imagine. Also, as well as my earthy charm, native cunning and other natural abilities I shall have an inexhaustible supply of money" (Quike smiled, as though to confirm this outrageous statement), "which I understand is a not un-useful attribute in the political sphere of life, and I shall additionally have a rather better knowledge of my fellow politicians' tastes and foibles than they will ever have of mine. I shall probably make a very good parliamentarian and an even better First Minister."

"*What?*" Senble said, incredulously.

"Meanwhile Mr Quike here will be keeping me honest and making sure I don't become a – what was that word, Mr Quike?"

"Demagogue, sir," Quike said.

"Making sure I don't become a demagogue," Holse went on. "So, it's politics for me, my dear. It's an ignominious end for a man of my earlier ambitions, I realise, and not one I'd have wished on myself; however, somebody's got to do it, it might as well be me and I think I can confidently say I shall bring a new, fresh and wider perspective to our petty political scene which will be good for the Sarl, good for Sursamen and very good indeed for you and me, my darling. I don't doubt I shall be most affectionately remembered by later generations and will probably have streets named after me, though I shall aspire to a square or two and possibly even a rail terminus. Now, where did you say that pipe was, dearest?"

Senble went to the mantelpiece, grabbed the pipe from its

little stand and threw it at him. "There!" she shouted. "You madman!"

Holse flinched. The pipe hit him on the shoulder and fell to the floorboards but did not break. He lifted it with his free hand. "Thank you, my dear. Most kind." He stuck the pipe in his mouth and settled back in the seat with a contented sigh, legs extended. Little Toark no longer had his head buried in his shoulder; he was looking out at the city now on this sunny, fresh and beautiful day.

Holse smiled at the still thunderstruck-looking Senble and then glanced up at Quike. "Ah, family life, eh?"

extras

www.orbitbooks.net

about the author

Iain Banks came to widespread and controversial public notice with the publication of his first novel, *The Wasp Factory*, in 1984. *Consider Phlebas*, his first science fiction novel, was published under Iain M. Banks in 1987. He is now acclaimed as one of the most powerful, innovative and exciting writers of his generation. Iain Banks lives in Fife, Scotland.

interview

Is the Culture your vision of what humanity could, or should, be in the future?

Ha! We should be so lucky. I suspect the only way a species like ours could ever get to something like the Culture in the first place would be through genetic manipulation. Suppose there is some sort of mix of genes that predisposes us to racism, sexism, homophobia, anti-semitism, Islamophobia, Romaphobia or whatever the latest grisly right-wing xenophobic hate-fashion is – I think we'd need to knock out those genes to have a chance of being remotely decent enough to achieve Culture-like levels of civilisation. That's one reason for me not making the Culture part of our own future (in its very, very early versions it was – I'm talking about early to mid-seventies here, well before anything got published – but that changed quite quickly). I'm not that confident we're capable of getting somewhere so benign without serious amendment. I'd certainly like to think we could; one can't despair and one has to assume that a better society is possible, however I'm not at all convinced that the advent of strong, benign AI and a genuinely post-scarcity economy would be enough.

All this means that means I don't have to argue that the Culture can come from us; it's coming from something that's only a bit like us, and from a mixed, mongrel species group at that. But, yes, for me it's the ideal functioning utopia, or at least as ideal as you can get with people who are still recognisable human (albeit maybe gene-amended). It's what ought to be the end state of almost any po-litical system and in one sense you should get there no matter what. The idea – don't laugh – is that highly advanced capitalism will produce the Culture whether it likes it or not (and of course it won't). That whole not-having-money thing might be a bit of a deal-breaker as far as capitalism is concerned. You might be aiming there deliberately through communism or socialism, and that might make it easier to achieve in theory, though arguably harder in practice, and taking longer. The experiment to find out will take some simulating.

The Culture novels take place across a time span of thousands of years, and yet one thing remains constant: war. Do you think war is a symptom of civilization?
Not necessarily. Frankly it's more about the authorial need for narrative tension and conflict. Well, about my need for narrative tension and conflict. The vast, vast majority of the Culture's day-to-day and indeed century-to-century business is totally, boringly peaceful; I concentrate on the violent, gaudy bits because that's where the most vivid stories are. If I was adept at and interested in writing novels about a set of intense, poetically-drawn characters having anguished, convoluted relationships with each other I could write a kind of Hampstead or campus novel in space, or at least on a Culture Orbital or something, but it'd probably be boring – for me and I'd guess for the people who've liked the novels I've written so far. More like soap opera than space opera. And then you'd probably have to ask whether that sort of story really needs to be in space or the future or featuring aliens in the first place; why not just write a mainstream novel instead – wouldn't that be more honest and more elegant? So when I turn to SF I tend to write stuff that uses the infinite effects budget of what Brian Aldiss memorably termed Wide Screen Baroque space opera. Actually, I blame Gerry Anderson; *Thunderbirds* gave

me a love of big explosions I've yet to shake off. It's kind of ingrained by now. Almost the first thing I think of when I've come up with an idea for a Really Big Artifact is how to blast the living bejesus out of it . . .

You've said before that you prefer writing science fiction, but you still alternate between that genre and mainstream fiction.

I enjoy writing science fiction more than mainstream, but there's not a great amount in it. To the same small degree mainstream writing can be more rewarding just because it's more difficult; I've got to restrain my imagination a little, rein it in and work within certain limitations. So I get a lot of pleasure writing both, but in a way I get the most pleasure from being able to write in any two genres at all. There was a point about a year before I wrote *The Algebraist* when I was toying with the idea of having to give up writing SF in the relatively near future; not because I really wanted to but because I felt I'd have to. I think you get fewer ideas as you get older, and even though you get better at using, developing the few you do have, that's not enough. Written SF relies heavily on ideas – you can write a perfectly good mainstream novel with no original ideas at all; you just have to tell an interesting story with interesting characters who have something to say. I don't mean that as a criticism either: that encompasses perfectly valid, rich and rewarding literary forms, but you can't get away with that in science fiction; you have to have completely new ideas in there somewhere or it doesn't really cut it as proper SF and I was concerned about that. Usually I'm quite a sunny, optimistic kind of person, but I backed myself into a slightly shadowy corner and convinced myself it wasn't going to work and I would have to give up writing science fiction in a few years. However, I set myself the goal of imagining a new non-Culture civilisation for the next science fiction novel and came up with the ideas behind

The Algebraist, effectively from a standing start and within a few months. That restored my faith in my own imagination and let me believe that it'll still be around for a few years yet. So for the foreseeable future I'm going to continue writing both mainstream and science fiction alternately. It might still be the case that SF will be the one to go first, but who knows?

There's been talk for years of turning your books into films and *The Wasp Factory* and *The Bridge* have both been plays. Are you keen for that to happen, or are you worried about how they'd be changed?
I've mixed feelings. As long as the-film-of-the-book stays unmade the novel still belongs to the writer – when it's made into a film or a TV production then suddenly in one night, or over a month or so, more people see it on a screen than have ever read the book, and the visual version contains the over-riding images that people think of, even if they've read the book as well. That's a surrender of control or authority that it's hard to take when you're used to being God within the boundary of your book, its characters and setting. On the other hand, adaptations usually pay pretty well, which sugars the pill, and you may well sell more books and reach more people on the back of it. A mixed blessing, hence mixed feelings. There are specific problems with making the Culture books into films. I'd like to see them made now that the special effects are up to it, but I'm kind of dreading it as well. I'd especially love to see Phlebas on the big screen though I'm convinced they get the look of the spaceships all wrong. That would really annoy my inner geek.

What do you see as the next big development in technology? Will we build the artificial intelligences in your books, or will we upload ourselves into computers?
I have no idea! I think uploading sounds a bit iffy actually; either too good to be true or not properly thought out – I

suspect the problems over embodiment and self-image will turn out to be severe. I think that humanity is just too tied up with the physical, anchored to the setting if you like; who you are is actually about your entire position within the world you inhabit. Consciousness is like an abstract of that framework, it's not just the bit in your head. AIs, yes; almost a given. I find it hard to understand that anyone could argue that you can't have machines that exhibit consciousness; it's a weird attitude unless you subscribe to the superstition that you have to have a supernatural soul to exhibit consciousness. Saying that the material world is incapable of forming a substrate for sentience or intelligence seems a nonsense to me. We, as human beings, are made up of matter and we exhibit intelligence (well . . . but anyway). We start from nothing bigger than a sperm and an egg, after all, and then just have lots more matter added. It's astonishing and wonderful and we in a sense rightly talk about the miracle of birth, but for goodness' sake; ultimately it's just evolution and applied biochemistry. I believe matter can provide a home for consciousness – it seems perverse to argue that only biology is capable of this. I absolutely believe that AIs are inevitable unless we have a genuine, civilisation-crippling catastrophe. I can envisage a future where they're proscribed for religious or other reasons – a Dune scenario, with Mentats and so on – but even that's just going to delay, not stop.

Finally, if you have to live for one month as a character in a novel, which novel and which character would you choose?
Hmm. Probably somebody from the Culture; being a utopia, it's hard to have a bad time. On the other hand my central characters often have quite a hard time of it and seem to share the unfortunate habit of rarely surviving to the end of the story. So, one of the minor characters, then, and a full Culture citizen, with all that implies. Of course, this reflects a purely

sociological interest on my part and has nothing to do with the drug glands and minutes-long orgasm. Would I lie to you?

This interview is published with the permission of Socialist Review, SFFWorld, Mary Branscombe at www.sandm.co.uk, *io9.com and SFX.*

if you enjoyed
MATTER

look out for

CONSIDER PHLEBAS

also by

Iain Banks

1.

Sorpen

The level was at his top lip now. Even with his head pressed hard back against the stones of the cell wall his nose was only just above the surface. He wasn't going to get his hands free in time; he was going to drown.

In the darkness of the cell, in its stink and warmth, while the sweat ran over his brows and tightly closed eyes and his trance went on and on, one part of his mind tried to accustom him to the idea of his own death. But, like an unseen insect buzzing in a quiet room, there was something else, something that would not go away, was of no use, and only annoyed. It was a sentence, irrelevant and pointless and so old he'd forgotten where he had heard or read it, and it went round and round the inside of his head like a marble spun round the inside of a jug:

The Jinmoti of Bozlen Two kill the hereditary ritual assassins of the new Yearking's immediate family by drowning them in the tears of the Continental Empathaur in its Sadness Season.

At one point, shortly after his ordeal had begun and he was only part-way into his trance, he had wondered what would happen if he threw up. It had been when the palace kitchens – about fifteen or sixteen floors above, if his calculations were correct – had sent their waste down the sinuous network of plumbing that led to the sewercell. The gurgling, watery mess had dislodged some rotten food from the last time some poor wretch had drowned in filth and garbage, and that was when he felt he might vomit. It had been almost comforting to work out that it would make no difference to the time of his death.

Then he had wondered – in that state of nervous frivolity which sometimes afflicts those who can do nothing but wait in a situation of mortal threat – whether crying would speed his death. In theory it would, though in practical terms it was irrelevant; but that was when the sentence started to roll round in his head.

The Jinmoti of Bozlen Two kill the hereditary ritual . . .

The liquid, which he could hear and feel and smell all too clearly – and could probably have seen with his far from ordinary eyes had they been open – washed briefly up to touch the bottom of his nose. He felt it block his nostrils, filling them with a stench that made his stomach heave. But he shook his head, tried to force his skull even further back against the stones, and the foul broth fell away. He blew down and could breathe again.

There wasn't long now. He checked his wrists again, but it was no good. It would take another hour or more, and he had only minutes, if he was lucky.

The trance was breaking anyway. He was returning to almost total consciousness, as though his brain wanted fully to appreciate his own death, its own extinction. He tried to think of something profound, or to see his life flash in front of him, or suddenly to remember some old love, a long-forgotten prophecy or premonition, but there was nothing, just an empty sentence, and the sensations of drowning in other people's dirt and waste.

You old bastards, he thought. One of their few strokes of humour or originality had been devising an elegant, ironic way of death. How fitting it must feel to them, dragging their decrepit frames to the banquet-hall privies, literally to defecate all over their enemies, and thereby kill them.

The air pressure built up, and a distant, groaning rumble of liquid signalled another flushing from above. *You old bastards. Well, I hope at least you kept your promise, Balveda.*

The Jinmoti of Bozlen Two kill the hereditary ritual . . . thought one part of his brain, as the pipes in the ceiling spluttered and the waste splashed into the warm mass of liquid which almost filled the cell. The wave passed over his face, then fell back to leave his nose free for a second and give him time to gulp a lungful of air. Then the liquid rose gently to touch the bottom of his nose again, and stayed there.

He held his breath.

It had hurt at first, when they had hung him up. His hands, tied inside tight leather pouches, were directly above his head, manacled inside thick loops of iron bolted to the cell walls, which took all his weight. His feet were tied together and left to dangle inside an iron tube, also attached to the wall, which stopped him from taking any weight on his feet and knees and at the same time prevented him from moving his legs more than a hand's breadth out from the wall or to either side. The tube ended just above his knees;

above it there was only a thin and dirty loincloth to hide his ancient and grubby nakedness.

He had shut off the pain from his wrists and shoulders even while the four burly guards, two of them perched on ladders, had secured him in place Even so he could feel that niggling sensation at the back of his skull which told him that he *ought* to be hurting. That had lessened gradually as the level of waste in the small sewercell had risen and buoyed up his body.

He had started to go into a trance then, as soon as the guards left, though he knew it was probably hopeless. It hadn't lasted long; the cell door opened again within minutes, a metal walkway was lowered by a guard onto the damp flagstones of the cell floor, and light from the corridor washed into the darkness. He had stopped the Changing trance and craned his neck to see who his visitor might be.

Into the cell, holding a short staff glowing cool blue, stepped the stooped, grizzled figure of Amahain-Frolk, security minister for the Gerontocracy of Sorpen. The old man smiled at him and nodded approvingly, then turned to the corridor and, with a thin, discoloured hand, beckoned somebody standing outside the cell to step onto the short walkway and enter. He guessed it would be the Culture agent Balveda, and it was. She came lightly onto the metal boarding, looked round slowly, and fastened her gaze on him. He smiled and tried to nod in greeting, his ears rubbing on his naked arms.

'Balveda! I thought I might see you again. Come to see the host of the party?' He forced a grin. Officially it was his banquet; he was the host. Another of the Gerontocracy's little jokes. He hoped his voice had shown no signs of fear.

Perosteck Balveda, agent of the Culture, a full head

taller than the old man by her side and still strikingly handsome even in the pallid glow of the blue torch, shook her thin, finely made head slowly. Her short, black hair lay like a shadow on her skull.

'No,' she said, 'I didn't want to see you, or say goodbye.'

'You put me here, Balveda,' he said quietly.

'Yes, and there you belong,' Amahain-Frolk said, stepping as far forward on the platform as he could without overbalancing and having to step onto the damp floor. 'I wanted you tortured first, but Miss Balveda here' – the minister's high, scratchy voice echoed in the cell as he turned his head back to the woman – 'pleaded for you, though God knows why. But that's where you belong all right; murderer.' He shook the staff at the almost naked man hanging on the dirty wall of the cell.

Balveda looked at her feet, just visible under the hem of the long, plain grey gown she wore. A circular pendant on a chain around her neck glinted in the light from the corridor outside. Amahain-Frolk had stepped back beside her, holding the shining staff up and squinting at the captive.

'You know, even now I could almost swear that was Egratin hanging there. I can . . .' He shook his gaunt, bony head. '. . . I can hardly believe it isn't, not until he opens his mouth, anyway. My God, these Changers are dangerous frightening things!' He turned to Balveda. She smoothed her hair at the nape of her neck and looked down at the old man.

'They are also an ancient and proud people, Minister, and there are very few of them left. May I ask you one more time? Please? Let him live. He might be—'

The Gerontocrat waved a thin and twisted hand at her, his face distorting in a grimace. 'No! You would do well,

Miss Balveda, not to keep asking for this . . . this assassin, this murderous, treacherous . . . *spy*, to be spared. Do you think we take the cowardly murder and impersonation of one of our Outworld ministers lightly? What damage this . . . *thing* could have caused! Why, when we arrested it two of our guards died just from being *scratched*! Another is blind for life after this monster spat in his eye! However,' Amahain-Frolk sneered at the man chained to the wall, 'we took those teeth out. And his hands are tied so that he can't even scratch himself.' He turned to Balveda again. 'You say they are few? I say good; there will soon be one less.' The old man narrowed his eyes as he looked at the woman. 'We are grateful to you and your people for exposing this fraud and murderer, but do not think that gives you the right to tell us what to do. There are some in the Gerontocracy who want nothing to do with *any* outside influence, and their voices grow in volume by the day as the war comes closer. You would do well not to antagonise those of us who do support your cause.'

Balveda pursed her lips and looked down at her feet again, clasping her slender hands behind her back. Amahain-Frolk had turned back to the man hanging on the wall, wagging the staff in his direction as he spoke. 'You will soon be dead, impostor, and with you die your masters' plans for the domination of our peaceful system! The same fate awaits them if they try to invade us. We and the Culture are—'

He shook his head as best he could and roared back, 'Frolk, you're an idiot!' The old man shrank away as though hit. The Changer went on, 'Can't you see you're going to be taken over anyway? Probably by the Idirans, but if not by them then by the Culture. You don't control your own destinies any more; the war's stopped all that.

Soon this whole sector will be part of the front, unless you *make* it part of the Idiran sphere. I was only sent in to tell you what you should have known anyway – not to cheat you into something you'd regret later. For God's sake, man, the Idirans won't *eat* you—'

'Ha! They look as though they could! Monsters with three feet; invaders, killers, infidels . . . You want us to link with them? With three-strides-tall-monsters? To be ground under their *hooves*? To have to worship their false gods?'

'At least they have a God, Frolk. The Culture doesn't.' The ache in his arms was coming back as he concentrated on talking. He shifted as best he could and looked down at the minister. 'They at least think the same way you do. The Culture doesn't.'

'Oh no, my friend, oh no.' Amahain-Frolk held one hand up flat to him and shook his head. 'You won't sow seeds of discord like that.'

'My God, you stupid old man,' he laughed. 'You want to know who the real representative of the Culture is on this planet? It's not her,' he nodded at the woman, 'it's that powered flesh-slicer she has following her everywhere, her knife missile. She might make the decisions, it might do what she tells it, but it's the real emissary. That's what the Culture's about: machines. You think because Balveda's got two legs and soft skin you should be on her side, but it's the Idirans who are on the side of life in this war—'

'Well, you will shortly be on the other side of *that*.' The Gerontocrat snorted and glanced at Balveda, who was looking from under lowered brows at the man chained to the wall. 'Let us go, Miss Balveda,' Amahain-Frolk said as he turned and took the woman's arm to guide her from the cell. 'This . . . *thing's* presence smells more than the cell.'

Balveda looked up at him then, ignoring the dwarfed minister as he tried to pull her to the door. She gazed right at the prisoner with her clear, black-irised eyes and held her hands out from her sides. 'I'm sorry,' she said to him.

'Believe it or not, that's rather how I feel,' he replied, nodding. 'Just promise me you'll eat and drink very little tonight, Balveda. I'd like to think there was one person up there on my side, and it might as well be my worst enemy.' He had meant it to be defiant and funny, but it sounded only bitter; he looked away from the woman's face.

'I promise,' Balveda said. She let herself be led to the door, and the blue light waned in the dank cell. She stopped right at the door. By sticking his head painfully far out he could just see her. The knife missile was there, too, he noticed, just inside the room; probably there all the time, but he hadn't noticed its sleek, sharp little body hovering there in the darkness. He looked into Balveda's dark eyes as the knife missile moved.

For a second he thought Balveda had instructed the tiny machine to kill him now – quietly and quickly while she blocked Amahain-Frolk's view – and his heart thudded. But the small device simply floated past Balveda's face and out into the corridor. Balveda raised one hand in a gesture of farewell.

'Bora Horza Gobuchul,' she said, 'goodbye.' She turned quickly, stepped from the platform and out of the cell. The walkway was hoisted out and the door slammed, scraping rubber flanges over the grimy floor and hissing once as the internal seals made it watertight. He hung there, looking down at an invisible floor for a moment before going back into the trance that would Change his wrists, thin them down so that he could escape. But something about the solemn, final way Balveda had spoken his name had crushed him inside, and he knew then, if not before, that there was no escape.

. . . by drowning them in the tears . . .

His lungs were bursting! His mouth quivered, his throat was gagging, the filth was in his ears but he could hear a great roaring, see lights though it was black dark. His stomach muscles started to go in and out, and he had to clamp his jaw to stop his mouth opening for air that wasn't there. Now. No . . . *now* he had to give in. Not yet . . . surely now. Now, now, now, any second; surrender to this awful black vacuum inside him . . . he had to breathe . . . *now*!

Before he had time to open his mouth he was smashed against the wall – punched against the stones as though some immense iron fist had slammed into him. He blew out the stale air from his lungs in one convulsive breath. His body was suddenly cold, and every part of it next to the wall throbbed with pain. Death, it seemed, was weight, pain, cold . . . and too much light . . .

He brought his head up. He moaned at the light. He tried to see, tried to hear. What was happening? Why was he breathing? Why was he so damn *heavy* again? His body was tearing his arms from their sockets; his wrists were cut almost to the bone. Who had *done* this to him?

Where the wall had been facing him there was a very large and ragged hole which extended beneath the level of the cell floor. All the ordure and garbage had burst out of that. The last few trickles hissed against the hot sides of the breach, producing steam which curled around the figure standing blocking most of the brilliant light from outside, in the open air of Sorpen. The figure was three metres tall and looked vaguely like a small armoured spaceship sitting on a tripod of thick legs. Its helmet looked big enough to contain three human heads, side by side. Held almost casually in one gigantic hand was a plasma cannon which Horza would have needed both arms just to lift; the creature's other fist gripped a slightly larger gun. Behind it, nosing in towards the hole, came an Idiran gun-platform, lit vividly by the light of explosions which Horza could now feel through the iron and stones he was attached to. He raised his head to the giant standing in the breach and tried to smile.

'Well,' he croaked, then spluttered and spat, 'you lot certainly took your time.'

2.

The Hand of God

Outside the palace, in the sharp cold of a winter's afternoon, the clear sky was full of what looked like glittering snow.

Horza paused on the warshuttle's ramp and looked up and around. The sheer walls and slim towers of the prison-palace echoed and reflected with the booms and flashes of continuing firefights, while Idiran gun-platforms cruised back and forth, firing occasionally. Around them on the stiffening breeze blew great clouds of chaff from anti-laser mortars on the palace roof. A gust sent some of the fluttering, flickering foil toward the stationary shuttle, and Horza found one side of his wet and sticky body suddenly coated with reflecting plumage.

'Please. The battle is not over yet,' thundered the Idiran soldier behind him, in what was probably meant to be a quiet whisper. Horza turned round to the armored bulk and stared up at the visor of the giant's helmet, where he could see his own, old man's face reflected. He breathed deeply, then nodded, turned and walked, slightly shakily, into the shuttle. A flash of light threw his shadow diagonally in front of him, and the craft bucked in the shock wave of a big explosion somewhere inside the palace as the ramp closed.

By their names you could know them, Horza thought as he showered. The Culture's General Contact Units, which until now had borne the brunt of the first four years of the war in space, had always chosen jokey, facetious names. Even the new warships they were starting to produce, as their factory craft completed gearing up their war production, favored either jocular, somber or downright unpleasant names, as though the Culture could not take entirely seriously the vast conflict in which it had embroiled itself.

The Idirans looked at things differently. To them a ship name ought to reflect the serious nature of its purpose, duties and resolute use. In the huge Idiran navy there were hundreds of craft named after the same heroes, planets, battles, religious concepts and impressive adjectives. The light cruiser which had rescued Horza was the 137th vessel to be called *The Hand of God*, and it existed concurrently with over a hundred other craft in the navy using the same title, so its full name was *The Hand of God 137*.

Horza dried in the airstream with some difficulty. Like everything else in the spaceship it was built on a monumental scale befitting the size of the Idirans, and the hurricane of air it produced nearly blew him out of the shower cabinet.

The Querl Xoralundra, spy-father and warrior priest of the Four Souls tributary sect of Farn-Idir, clasped two hands on the surface of the table. It looked to Horza rather like a pair of continental plates colliding.

'So, Bora Horza,' boomed the old Idiran, 'you are recovered.'

'Just about,' nodded Horza, rubbing his wrists. He sat in Xoralundra's cabin in *The Hand of God 137*, clothed in a bulky but comfortable spacesuit apparently brought along just for him. Xoralundra, who was also suited up, had insisted the man wear it because the warship was still at battle stations as it swept a fast and low-powered orbit around the planet of Sorpen. A Culture GCU of the Mountain class had been confirmed in the system by Naval Intelligence; the *Hand* was in on its own, and they couldn't find any trace of the Culture ship, so they had to be careful.

Xoralundra leaned toward Horza, casting a shadow over the table. His huge head, saddle-shaped when seen from directly in front, with the two front eyes clear and unblinking near the edges, loomed over the Changer. 'You were lucky, Horza. We did not come in to rescue you out of compassion. Failure is its own reward.'

'Thank you, Xora. That's actually the nicest thing anybody's said to me all day.' Horza sat back in his seat and put one of his old-looking hands through his thin, yellowing hair. It would take a few days for the aged appearance he had assumed to disappear, though already he could feel it starting to slip away from him. In a Changer's mind there was a self-image constantly held and reviewed on a semi-subconscious level, keeping the body in the appearance willed. Horza's need to look like a Gerontocrat was gone now, so the mental picture of the minister he had impersonated for the Idirans was fragmenting and dissolving, and his body was going back to its normal, neutral state.

Xoralundra's head went slowly from side to side between the edges of the suit collar. It was a gesture Horza had never fully translated, although he had worked for the Idirans and known Xoralundra well since before the war.

'Anyway. You are alive,' Xoralundra said. Horza nodded and drummed his fingers on the table to show he agreed. He wished the Idiran chair he was perched on didn't make him feel so much like a child; his feet weren't even touching the deck.

'Just. Thanks, anyway. I'm sorry I dragged you all the way in here to rescue a failure.'

'Orders are orders. I personally am glad we were able to. Now I must tell you why we received those orders.'

Horza smiled and looked away from the old Idiran, who had just given him something of a compliment; a rare thing. He looked back and watched the other being's wide mouth – big enough, thought Horza, to bite off both your hands at once – as it boomed out the precise, short words of the Idiran language.

'You were once with a caretaker mission on Schar's World, one of the Dra'Azon Planets of the Dead,' Xoralundra stated. Horza nodded. 'We need you to go back there.'

'Now?' Horza said to the broad, dark face of the Idiran. 'There are only Changers there. I've told you I won't impersonate another Changer. I certainly won't kill one.'

'We are not asking you to do that. Listen while I explain.' Xoralundra leaned on his backrest in a way almost any vertebrate – or even anything like a vertebrate – would have called tired. 'Four standard days ago,' the Idiran began – then his suit helmet, which was lying on the floor near his feet, let out a piercing whine. He picked up the helmet and set it on the table. '*Yes?*' he said, and Horza knew enough about the Idiran voice to realize that whoever was bothering the Querl had better have a good reason for doing so.

'We have the Culture female,' a voice said from the helmet.

'Ahh . . .' Xoralundra said quietly, sitting back. The Idiran equivalent of a smile – mouth pursing, eyes narrowing – passed over his features. 'Good, Captain. Is she aboard yet?'

'No, Querl. The shuttle is a couple of minutes out. I'm withdrawing the gun-platforms. We are ready to leave the system as soon as they are all on board.'

Xoralundra bent closer to the helmet. Horza inspected the aged skin on the back of his hands. 'What of the Culture ship?' the Idiran asked.

'Still nothing, Querl. It cannot be anywhere in the system. Our computer suggests it is outside, possibly between us and the fleet. Before long it must realize we are in here by ourselves.'

'You will set off to rejoin the fleet the instant the female Culture agent is aboard, without waiting for the platforms. Is that understood, Captain?' Xoralundra looked at Horza as the human glanced at him. 'Is that understood, Captain?' the Querl repeated, still looking at the human.

'Yes, Querl,' came the answer. Horza could hear the icy tone, even through the small helmet speaker.

'Good. Use your own initiative to decide the best route back to the fleet. In the meantime you will destroy the cities of De'aychanbie, Vinch, Easna-Yowon, Izilere and Ylbar with fusion bombs, as per the Admiralty's orders.'

'Yes, Qu—' Xoralundra stabbed a switch in the helmet, and it fell silent.

'You got Balveda?' Horza asked, surprised.

'We have the Culture agent, yes. I regard her capture, or destruction, as of comparatively little consequence. But only by our assuring the Admiralty we would attempt to take her would they contemplate such a hazardous mission ahead of the main fleet to rescue you.'

'Hmm. Bet you didn't get Balveda's knife missile.' Horza snorted, looking again at the wrinkles on his hands.

'It destructed while you were being put aboard the shuttle which brought you up to the ship.' Xoralundra waved one hand, sending a draft of Idiran-scented air across the table. 'But enough of that. I must explain why we risked a light cruiser to rescue you.'

'By all means,' Horza said, and turned to face the Idiran.

'Four standard days ago,' the Querl said, 'a group of our ships intercepted a single Culture craft of conventional outward appearance but rather odd internal construction, judging by its emission signature. The ship was destroyed easily enough, but its Mind escaped. There was a planetary system nearby. The Mind appears to have transcended real space to within the planetary surface of the globe it chose, thus indicating a level of hyperspatial field management we had thought – hoped – was still beyond the Culture. Certainly such spacio-batics are beyond us for the moment. We have reason to believe, due to that and other indications, that the Mind involved is one from a new class of General Systems Vehicles the Culture is developing. The Mind's capture would be an intelligence coup of the first order.' The Querl paused there. Horza took the opportunity to ask, 'Is this thing on Schar's World?' 'Yes. According to its last message it intended to shelter in the tunnels of the Command System.'

'And you can't do anything about it?' Horza smiled.

'We came to get you. That is doing something about it, Bora Horza.' The Querl paused. 'The shape of your mouth tells me you see something amusing in this situation. What would that be?'

'I was just thinking . . . lots of things: that that Mind

was either pretty smart or very lucky; that *you* were very lucky you had me close by; also that the Culture isn't likely to sit back and do nothing.'

'To deal with your points in order,' Xoralundra said sharply, 'the Culture Mind was both lucky and smart; we were fortunate; the Culture can do little because they do not, as far as we know, have any Changers in their employ, and certainly not one who has served on Schar's World. I would also add, Bora Horza,' the Idiran said, putting both huge hands on the table and dipping his great head toward the human, 'that *you* were more than a little lucky yourself.'

'Ah yes, but the difference is that I believe in it.' Horza grinned.

'Hmm. It does you little credit,' observed the Querl. Horza shrugged.

'So you want me to put down on Schar's World and get the Mind?'

'If possible. It may be damaged. It may be liable to destruct, but it is a prize worth fighting for. We shall give you all the equipment you need, but your presence alone would give us a toehold.'

'What about the people already there? The Changers on caretaker duty?'

'Nothing has been heard from them. They were probably unaware of the Mind's arrival. Their next routine transmission is due in a few days, but, given the current disruption in communications due to the war, they may not be able to send.'

'What . . .' Horza said slowly, one finger describing a circular pattern on the table surface which he was looking at, '. . . do you know about the personnel in the base?'

'The two senior members have been replaced by

younger Changers,' the Idiran said. 'The two junior sentinels became seniors, remaining there.'

'They wouldn't be in any danger, would they?' Horza asked.

'On the contrary. Inside a Dra'Azon Quiet Barrier, on a Planet of the Dead, must rank as one of the safest places to be during the current hostilities. Neither we nor the Culture can risk causing the Dra'Azon any offense. That is why they cannot do anything, and we can only use you.'

'If,' Horza said carefully, sitting forward and dropping his voice slightly, 'I can get this metaphysical computer for you—'

'Something in your voice tells me we approach the question of remuneration,' Xoralundra said.

'We do indeed. I've risked my neck for you lot long enough, Xoralundra. I want out. There's a good friend of mine on that Schar's World base, and if she's agreeable I want to take her and me out of the whole war. That's what I'm asking for.'

'I can promise nothing. I shall request this. Your long and devoted service will be taken into account.'

Horza sat back and frowned. He wasn't sure if Xoralundra was being ironic or not. Six years probably didn't seem like very long at all to a species that was virtually immortal; but the Querl Xoralundra knew how often his frail human charge had risked all in the service of his alien masters, without real reward, so perhaps he was being serious. Before Horza could continue with the bargaining, the helmet shrilled once more. Horza winced. All the noises on the Idiran ship seemed to be deafening. The voices were thunder; ordinary buzzers and bleepers left his ears ringing long after they stopped; and announcements over the PA made him put both hands to his head. Horza just hoped there wasn't a full-scale alarm while he was on board. The Idiran ship alarm could cause damage to unprotected human ears.

'What is it?' Xoralundra asked the helmet.

'The female is on board. I shall need only eight more minutes to get the gun—'

'Have the cities been destroyed?'

'. . . They have, Querl.'

'Break out of orbit at once and make full speed for the fleet.'

'Querl, I must point out—' said the small, steady voice from the helmet on the table.

'Captain,' Xoralundra said briskly, 'in this war there have to date been fourteen single-duel engagements between Type 5 light cruisers and Mountain class General Contact Units. All have ended in victory for the enemy. Have you ever seen what is left of a light cruiser after a GCU has finished with it?'

'No, Querl.'

'Neither have I, and I have no intention of seeing it for the first time from the inside. Proceed at once.' Xoralundra hit the helmet button again. He fastened his gaze on Horza. 'I shall do what I can to secure your release from the service with sufficient funds, if you succeed. Now, once we have made contact with the main body of the fleet you will go by fast picket to Schar's World. You will be given a shuttle there, just beyond the Quiet Barrier. It will be unarmed, although it will have the equipment we think you may need, including some close-range hyperspace spectographic analyzers, should the Mind conduct a limited destruct.'

'How can you be certain it'll be "limited"?' Horza asked skeptically.

'The Mind weighs several thousand tons, despite its

relatively small size. An annihilatory destruct would rip the planet in half and so antagonize the Dra'Azon. No Culture Mind would risk such a thing.'

'Your confidence overwhelms me,' Horza said dourly. Just then the note of background noise around them altered. Xoralundra turned his helmet round and looked at one of its small internal screens.

'Good. We are under way.' He looked at Horza again. 'There is something else I ought to tell you. An attempt was made, by the group of ships which caught the Culture craft, to follow the escaped Mind down to the planet.'

Horza frowned. 'Didn't they know better?'

'They did their best. With the battle group were several captured chuy-hirtsi warp animals which had been de-activated for later use in a surprise attack on a Culture base. One of these was quickly fitted out for a small-scale incursion on the planet surface and thrown at the Quiet Barrier in a warp-cruise. The ruse did not succeed. On crossing the Barrier the animal was attacked with something resembling gridfire and was heavily damaged. It came out of warp near the planet on a course which would take it in on a burn-up angle. The equipment and ground force it contained must be considered defunct.'

'Well, I suppose it was a good try, but a Dra'Azon must make even this wonderful Mind you're after look like a valve computer. It's going to take more than that to fool it.'

'Do you think you will be able to?'

'I don't know. I don't *think* they can read minds, but who knows? I don't *think* the Dra'Azon even know or care much about the war or what I've been doing since I left Schar's World. So they probably won't be able to put one and one together – but again, who knows?' Horza gave another shrug. 'It's worth a try.'

'Good. We shall have a fuller briefing when we rejoin the fleet. For now we must pray that our return is without incident. You may want to speak to Perosteck Balveda before she is interrogated. I have arranged with the Deputy Fleet Inquisitor that you may see her, if you wish.'

Horza smiled. 'Xora, nothing would give me greater pleasure.'

The Querl had other business on the ship as it powered its way out of the Sorpen system. Horza stayed in Xoralundra's cabin to rest and eat before he called on Balveda.

The food was the cruiser autogalley's best impression of some
thing suitable for a humanoid, but it tasted awful. Horza ate what he could and drank some equally uninspiring distilled water. It was all served by a medjel – a lizard-like creature about two meters long with a flat, long head and six legs, on four of which it ran, using the front pair as hands. The medjel were the companion species of the Idirans. It was a complicated sort of social symbiosis which had kept the exosocio faculties of many a university in research funds over the millennia that the Idiran civilization had been part of the galactic community.

The Idirans themselves had evolved on their planet Idir as the top monster from a whole planetful of monsters. The frenetic and savage ecology of Idir in its early days had long since disappeared, and so had all the other home-world monsters except those in zoos. But the Idirans had retained the intelligence that made them winners, as well as the biological immortality which, due to the vicious-ness of the fight for survival back then – not to mention Idir's high radiation levels – had been an evolutionary advantage rather than a recipe for stagnation.

Horza thanked the medjel as it brought him plates and took them away again, but it said nothing. They were generally reckoned to be about two thirds as intelligent as the average humanoid (whatever that was), which made them about two or three times dimmer than a normal Idiran. Still, they were good if unimaginative soldiers, and there were plenty of them; something like ten or twelve for each Idiran. Forty thousand years of breeding had made them loyal right down to the chromosome level.

Horza didn't try to sleep, though he was tired. He told the medjel to take him to Balveda. The medjel thought about it, asked permission via the cabin intercom, and flinched visibly under a verbal slap from a distant Xoralundra who was on the bridge with the cruiser captain. 'Follow me, sir,' the medjel said, opening the cabin door.

In the companionways of the warship the Idiran atmosphere became more obvious than it had been in Xoralundra's cabin. The smell of Idiran was stronger and the view ahead hazed over – even seen through Horza's eyes – after a few tens of meters. It was hot and humid, and the floor was soft. Horza walked quickly along the corridor, watching the stump of the medjel's docked tail as it waggled in front of him.

He passed two Idirans on the way, neither of whom paid him any attention. Perhaps they knew all about him and what he was, but perhaps not. Horza knew that Idirans hated to appear either over-inquisitive or under-informed.

He nearly collided with a pair of wounded medjel on AG stretchers being hurried along a cross-corridor by two of their fellow troopers. Horza watched as the wounded passed, and frowned. The spiraled spatter-marks on their battle armor were unmistakably those produced by a plasma bolt, and the Gerontocracy didn't have any plasma weapons. He shrugged and walked on.

They came to a section of the cruiser where the companionway was blocked by sliding doors. The medjel spoke to each of the barriers in turn, and they opened. An Idiran guard holding a laser carbine stood outside a door; he saw the medjel and Horza approaching and had the door open for the man by the time he got there. Horza nodded to the guard as he stepped through. The door hissed shut behind him and another one, immediately in front, opened.

Balveda turned quickly to him when he entered the cell. It looked as though she had been pacing up and down. She threw back her head a little when she saw Horza and made a noise in her throat which might have been a laugh.

'Well, well,' she said, her soft voice drawling. 'You survived. Congratulations. I did keep my promise, by the way. What a turnaround, eh?'

'Hello,' Horza replied, folding his arms across the chest of his suit and looking the woman up and down. She wore the same gray gown and appeared to be unharmed. 'What happened to that thing around your neck?' Horza asked.

She looked down, at where the pendant had lain over her breast. 'Well, believe it or not, it turned out to be a memoryform.' She smiled at him and sat down cross-legged on the soft floor; apart from a raised bed-alcove, this was the only place to sit. Horza sat too, his legs hurting only a little. He recalled the spatter-marks on the medjel's armor.

'A memoryform. Wouldn't have turned into a *plasma* gun, by any chance, would it?'

'Among other things.' The Culture agent nodded.

'Thought so. Heard your knife missile took the expansive way out.'

Balveda shrugged.

Horza looked her in the eye and said, 'I don't suppose you'd be here if you had anything important you could tell them, would you?'

'Here, perhaps,' Balveda conceded. 'Alive, no.' She stretched her arms out behind her and sighed. 'I suppose I'll have to sit out the war in an internment camp, unless they can find somebody to swap. I just hope this thing doesn't go on too long.'

'Oh, you think the Culture might give in soon?' Horza grinned.

'No, I think the Culture might win soon.'

'You must be mad.' Horza shook his head.

'Well . . .' Balveda said, nodding ruefully, 'actually I think it'll win eventually.'

'If you keep falling back like you have for the last three years, you'll end up somewhere in the Clouds.'

'I'm not giving away any secrets, Horza, but I think you might find we don't do too much more falling back.'

'We'll see. Frankly I'm surprised you kept fighting this long.'

'So are our three-legged friends. So is everybody. So are we, I sometimes think.'

'Balveda,' Horza sighed wearily, 'I still don't know why the hell you're fighting in the first place. The Idirans never were any threat to you. They still wouldn't be, if you stopped fighting them. Did life in your great Utopia really get so boring you needed a war?'

'Horza,' Balveda said, leaning forward, 'I don't understand why *you* are fighting. I know Heidohre is in—'

'Hei*bohre*,' Horza interjected.

'OK, the goddamn asteroid the Changers live in. I know it's in Idiran space, but—'

'That's got nothing to do with it, Balveda. I'm fighting for them because I think they're right and you're wrong.'

Balveda sat back, amazed. 'You . . .' she began, then lowered her head and shook it, staring at the floor. She looked up. 'I really *don't* understand you, Horza. You must know how many species, how many civilizations, how many systems, how many individuals have been either destroyed or . . . throttled by the Idirans and their crazy goddamned religion. What the hell has the Culture ever done compared to *that?*' One hand was on her knee, the other was displayed in front of Horza, clawed into a strangling grip. He watched her and smiled.

'On a straight head count the Idirans no doubt do come out in front, Perosteck, and I've told them I never did care for some of their methods, or their zeal. I'm all for people being allowed to live their own lives. But now they're up against you lot, and that's what makes the difference to me. Because I'm against you, rather than for them, I'm prepared —' Horza broke off for a moment, laughing lightly, self-consciously. '. . . Well, it sounds a bit melodramatic, but sure – I'm prepared to die for them.' He shrugged. 'Simple as that.'

Horza nodded as he said it, and Balveda dropped the outstretched hand and looked away to one side, shaking her head and exhaling loudly. Horza went on, 'Because . . . well, I suppose you thought I was just kidding when I was telling old Frolk I thought the knife missile was the real representative. I wasn't kidding, Balveda. I meant it then and I mean it now. I don't care how self-righteous the Culture feels, or how many people the Idirans kill. They're on the side of life – boring, old-fashioned, bio-logical life; smelly, fallible and short-sighted, God knows, but *real* life. You're ruled by your machines. You're an evolutionary dead end. The trouble is that to take your mind off it you try to drag everybody else down there with you. The worst thing that could happen to the galaxy would be if the Culture wins this war.'

He paused to let her say something, but she was still sitting with her head down, shaking it. He laughed at her. 'You know, Balveda, for such a sensitive species you show remarkably little empathy at times.'

'Empathize with stupidity and you're halfway to thinking like an idiot,' muttered the woman, still not looking at Horza. He laughed again and got to his feet.

'Such . . . bitterness, Balveda,' he said.

She looked up at him. 'I'll tell you, Horza,' she said quietly, 'we're going to win.'

He shook his head. 'I don't think so. You wouldn't know how to.'

Balveda sat back again, hands spread behind her. Her face was serious. 'We can learn, Horza.'

'Who from?'

'Whoever has the lesson there to teach,' she said slowly. 'We spend quite a lot of our time watching warriors and zealots, bullies and militarists – people determined to win regardless. There's no shortage of teachers.'

'If you want to know about winning, ask the Idirans.'

Balveda said nothing for a moment. Her face was calm, thoughtful, perhaps sad. She nodded after a while. 'They do say there's a danger . . . in warfare,' she said, 'that you'll start to resemble the enemy.' She shrugged. 'We just have to hope that we can avoid that. If the evolutionary force you seem to believe in really works, then it'll work through us, and not the Idirans. If you're wrong, then it deserves to be superseded.'

'Balveda,' he said, laughing lightly, 'don't disappoint me. I prefer a fight . . . You almost sound as though you're coming round to my point of view.'

'No,' she sighed. 'I'm not. Blame it on my Special Circumstances training. We try to think of everything. I was being pessimistic.'

'I'd got the impression SC didn't allow such thoughts.'

'Then think again, Mr. Changer,' Balveda said, arching one eyebrow. 'SC allows all thoughts. That's what some people find so frightening about it.'

Horza thought he knew what the woman meant. Special Circumstances had always been the Contact section's moral espionage weapon, the very cutting edge of the Culture's interfering diplomatic policy, the elite of the elite, in a society which abhorred elitism. Even before the war, its standing and its image within the Culture had been ambiguous. It was glamorous but dangerous, possessed of an aura of roguish sexiness – there was no other word for it – which implied predation, seduction, even violation.

It had about it too an atmosphere of secrecy (in a society that virtually worshipped openness) which hinted at unpleasant, shaming deeds, and an ambience of moral relativity (in a society which clung to its absolutes; life/good, death/bad; pleasure/good, pain/bad) which attracted and repulsed at once, but anyway excited.

No other part of the Culture more exactly represented what the society as a whole really stood for, or was more militant in the application of the Culture's fundamental beliefs. Yet no other part embodied less of the society's day-to-day character.

With war, Contact had become the Culture's military, and Special Circumstances its intelligence and espionage section (the euphemism became only a little more obvious, that was all). And with war, SC's position within the Culture changed, for the worse. It became the repository for the guilt the people in the Culture experienced because they had agreed to go to war in the first place: despised as a necessary evil, reviled as an unpleasant moral compromise, dismissed as something people preferred not to think about.

SC really did try to think of everything, though, and its Minds were reputedly even more cynical, amoral and downright sneaky than those which made up Contact; machines without illusions which prided themselves on thinking the thinkable to its ultimate extremities. So it had been wearily predicted that just this would happen. SC would become a pariah, a whipping-child, and its reputation a gland to absorb the poison in the Culture's conscience. But Horza guessed that knowing all this didn't make it any easier for somebody like Balveda. Culture people had little stomach for being disliked by anybody, least of all their fellow citizens, and the woman's task was difficult enough without the added burden of knowing she was even greater anathema to most of her own side than she was to the enemy.

'Well, whatever, Balveda,' he said, stretching. He flexed his stiff shoulders within the suit, pulled his fingers through his thin, yellow-white hair. 'I guess it'll work itself out.'

Balveda laughed mirthlessly. 'Never a truer word . . .' She shook her head.

'Thanks, anyway,' he told her.

'For what?'

'I think you just reinforced my faith in the ultimate outcome of this war.'

'Oh, just go away, Horza.' Balveda sighed and looked down to the oor.

Horza wanted to touch her, to ruffle her short black hair or pinch her pale cheek, but guessed it would only upset her more. He knew too well the bitterness of defeat to want to aggravate the experience for somebody who was, in the end, a fair and honorable adversary. He went to the door, and after a word with the guard outside he was let out.

'Ah, Bora Horza,' Xoralundra said as the human appeared out of the cell doorway. The Querl came striding along the companionway. The guard outside the cell straightened visibly and blew some imaginary dust off his carbine. 'How is our guest?'

'Not very happy. We were trading justifications and I think I won on points.' Horza grinned. Xoralundra stopped by the man and looked down.

'Hmm. Well, unless you prefer to relish your victories in a vacuum, I suggest that the next time you leave my cabin while we are at battle stations you take your—'

Horza didn't hear the next word. The ship's alarm erupted.

The Idiran alarm signal, on a warship as elsewhere, consists of what sounds like a series of very sharp explosions. It is the amplified version of the Idiran chest-boom, an evolved signal the Idirans had been using to warn others in their herd or clan for several hundred thousand years before they became civilized, and produced by the chest-flap which is the Idiran vestigial third arm.

Horza clapped his hands to his ears, trying to shut out the awful noise. He could feel the shock waves on his chest, through the open neck of the suit. He felt himself being picked up and forced against the bulkhead. It was only then that he realized he had shut his eyes. For a second he thought he had never been rescued, never left the wall of the sewercell, that this was the moment of his death and all the rest had been a strange and vivid dream. He opened his eyes and found himself staring into the keratinous snout of the Querl Xoralundra, who shook him furiously and, just as the ship alarm cut off and was replaced by a merely painfully intense whine, said very loudly into Horza's face, 'HELMET!'

'Oh shit!' said Horza.

He was dropped to the deck as Xoralundra let him go, turned quickly, and scooped a running medjel off the floor as it tried to get past him. 'You!' Xoralundra bellowed. 'I am the spy-father Querl of the fleet,' he shouted into its face and shook the six-limbed creature by the front of its suit. 'You will go to my cabin immediately and bring the small space helmet lying there to the port-side stern emergency lock. As fast as possible. This order supersedes all others and cannot be countermanded. Go!' He threw the medjel in the right direction. It landed running.

Xoralundra flipped his own helmet over from its back-hinged position, then opened the visor. He looked as though he was about to say something to Horza, but the helmet speaker crackled and spoke, and the Querl's expression changed. The small noise stopped and only the continuing wail of the cruiser's alarm was left. 'The Culture craft was hiding in the surface layers of the system sun,' Xoralundra said bitterly, more to himself than to Horza.

'In the *sun?*' Horza was incredulous. He looked back at the cell door, as though somehow it was Balveda's fault. 'Those bastards are getting smarter all the time.'

'Yes,' snapped the Querl, then turned quickly on one foot. 'Follow me, human.' Horza obeyed, starting after the old Idiran at a run, then bumping into him as the huge figure stopped in its tracks. Horza watched the broad, dark, alien face as it swiveled round to look over his head at the Idiran trooper still standing stiffly at the cell door. An expression Horza could not read passed over Xoralundra's face. 'Guard,' the Querl said, not loudly. The trooper with the laser carbine turned. 'Kill the woman.'

Xoralundra stamped off down the corridor. Horza stood for a moment, looking first at the rapidly receding Querl, then at the guard as he checked his carbine, ordered the cell door to open, and stepped inside. Then the man ran down the corridor after the old Idiran.

'Querl!' gasped the medjel as it skidded to a stop by the airlock, the suit helmet held in front of it. Xoralundra swept the helmet from its grasp and fitted it quickly over Horza's head.

'You will find a warp attachment in the lock,' the Idiran told Horza. 'Get as far away as possible. The fleet will be here in about nine standard hours. You shouldn't have to do anything; the suit will summon help on a coded IFF response. I, too—' Xoralundra broke off as the cruiser lurched. There was a loud bang and Horza was blown off his feet by a shock wave, while the Idiran on his tripod of legs hardly moved. The medjel which had gone for the helmet yelped as it was blown under Xoralundra's legs. The Idiran swore and kicked at it; it ran off. The cruiser lurched again as other alarms started. Horza could smell burning. A confused medley of noises that might have been Idiran voices or muffled explosions came from somewhere overhead. 'I too shall try to escape,' Xoralundra continued. 'God be with you, human.'

Before Horza could say anything the Idiran had rammed his visor down and pushed him into the lock. It slammed shut. Horza was thrown against one bulkhead as the cruiser juddered mightily. He looked desperately round the small, spherical space for a warp unit, then saw it and after a short struggle unclamped it from its wall magnets. He clamped it to the rear of his suit.

'Ready?' a voice said in his ear.

Horza jumped, then said, 'Yes! Yes! Hit it!'

The airlock didn't open conventionally; it turned inside out and threw him into space, tumbling away from the flat disc of the cruiser in a tiny galaxy of ice particles. He looked for the Culture ship, then told himself not to be stupid; it was probably still several trillion kilometers away. That was how divorced from the human scale modern warfare had become. You could smash and destroy from unthinkable distances, obliterate planets from beyond their own system and provoke stars into novae from light-years off . . . and still have no good idea why you were really fighting.

With one last thought for Balveda, Horza reached until he found the control handle for the bulky warp unit, fingered the correct buttons on it, and watched the stars twist and distort around him as the unit sent him and his suit lancing away from the stricken Idiran spacecraft.

He played with the wrist-set for a while, trying to pick up signals from *The Hand of God 137*, but got nothing but static. The suit spoke to him once, saying 'Warp/unit/charge/half/exhausted.' Horza kept a watch on the warp unit via a small screen set inside the helmet.

He recalled that the Idirans said some sort of prayer to their God before going into warp. Once when he had been with Xoralundra on a ship which was warping, the Querl had insisted that the Changer repeat the prayer, too. Horza had protested that it meant nothing to him; not only did the Idiran God clash with his own personal convictions, the prayer itself was in a dead Idiran language he didn't understand. He had been told rather coldly that it was the gesture that mattered. For what the Idirans regarded as essentially an animal (their word for humanoids was best translated as 'biotomaton'), only the behavior of devotion was required; his heart and mind were of no consequence. When Horza had asked, what about his immortal soul? Xoralundra had laughed. It was the first and only time Horza had experienced such a thing from the old warrior. Whoever heard of a mortal body having an immortal soul?

When the warp unit was almost exhausted, Horza shut it off. Stars swam into focus around him. He set the unit controls, then threw it away from him. They parted company, he moving slowly off in one direction, while the unit spun off in another; then it disappeared as the controls switched it back on again to use the last of its power leading anybody following its trace away in the wrong direction.

He calmed his breathing down gradually; it had been very fast and hard for a while, but he slowed it and his heart deliberately. He accustomed himself to the suit, testing its functions and powers. It smelled and felt new, and looked like a Rairch-built device. Rairch suits were meant to be among the best. People said the Culture made better ones, but people said the Culture made better everything, and they were still losing the war. Horza checked out the lasers the suit had built in and searched for the concealed pistol he knew it ought to carry. He found it at last, disguised as part of the left forearm casing, a small plasma hand gun. He felt like shooting it at something, but there was nothing to aim at. He put it back.

He folded his arms across his bulky chest and looked

around. Stars were everywhere. He had no idea which one was Sorpen's. So the Culture ships could hide in the photospheres of stars, could they? And a Mind – even if it was desperate and on the run – could jump through the bottom of a gravity well, could it? Maybe the Idirans would have a tougher job than they expected. They were the natural warriors, they had the experience and the guts, and their whole society was geared for continual conflict. But the Culture, that seemingly disunited, anarchic, hedonistic, decadent mélange of more or less human species, forever hiving off or absorbing different groups of people, had fought for almost four years without showing any sign of giving up or even coming to a compromise.

What everybody had expected to be at best a brief, limited stand, lasting just long enough to make a point, had developed into a wholehearted war effort. The early reverses and first few megadeaths had not, as the pundits and experts had predicted, shocked the Culture into retiring, horrified at the brutalities of war but proud to have put its collective life where usually only its collective mouth was. Instead it had just kept on retreating and retreating, preparing, gearing up and planning. Horza was convinced the Minds were behind it all.

He could not believe the ordinary people in the Culture really wanted the war, no matter how they had voted. They had their communist Utopia. They were soft and pampered and indulged, and the Contact section's evangelical materialism provided their conscience-salving good works. What more could they want? The war had to be the Minds' idea; it was part of their clinical drive to clean up the galaxy, make it run on nice, efficient lines, without waste, injustice or suffering. The fools in the Culture couldn't see that one day the Minds would start thinking how wasteful and inefficient the humans in the Culture themselves were.

Horza used the suit's internal gyros to steer himself, letting him look at every part of the sky, wondering where, in that light-flecked emptiness, battles raged and billions died, where the Culture still held and the Idiran battle fleets pressed. The suit hummed and clicked and hissed very quietly around him: precise, obedient, reassuring.